Groomed and marketed to women as a follow-up to Elvis Presley, Pete Riddle had to pull down the shades for some real loving.
—*Gabfest*

No doubt about it, the character of Pete Riddle is the sexiest, best-hung man on the planet. Even his sons thought so.
—*Queer Biz*

Rosacoke Carson, the leading, long-suffering female character of *Rhinestone Country,* gives new meaning to the phrase, "Stand by Your Man."
—*La Noche*

Heady, nostalgic, and delectable, this novel will get a rise out of you. Beautifully executed, it sweeps with power and tenderness across the racial, social, and sexual landscapes of America's Deep South.
—*Nat og Dag*

This is hardly bedtime reading. I didn't get any sleep at all. Neither did my lover.
---*Between the Covers*

Let's play the guessing game: Which legend in country music was the inspiration for the character of Pete Riddle? A mouthwatering speculation.
—*Island News*

A beautifully written and tantalizing look at a facet of the entertainment world that appears on the surface to be homophobic—that is, until the lights go out in Dixie.
—*De Sade Online*

An avalanche of a novel packed with incident and alive with sex, drama, and tragedy.
—*Evert Elliott*

This vastly entertaining novel creates new pleasures on every page. Like good sex, it's both rough and tender—filled with power and charm as the author pokes deep into the sexual closets of its cast.
—*Kathryn Cobb*

# RHINESTONE COUNTRY

A novel about closeted lives south of the Mason-Dixon line.

Photography by
SylvesterQ.com

by
## Darwin Porter

# Also by Darwin Porter

*Butterflies in Heat*
*Marika*
*Venus*
*Razzle-Dazzle*
*Blood Moon*
*Midnight in Savannah*
*Hollywood's Silent Closet*
and some of *The Frommer Guides*

## The Georgia Literary Association

PO Box 140544, Staten Island, NY 10314-0544
Georgialit@aol.com

Photography by SylvesterQ.com NYC
Graphic Design & Production by Jennings Studio NYC

**The Georgia Literary Association** was established in Wilkes County, Georgia, in 1997, and relocated to New York City several years later. Aware of the distinguished literary history of Georgia, it's dedicated to the promotion of worthwhile reading that might not be endorsed by larger, more conservative publishing companies. In patterns already established through the publication of titles that have included *Midnight in Savannah, Hollywood's Silent Closet, Butterflies in Heat,* and *Blood Moon,* we'll continue to showcase the fine, diverse, and sometimes controversial entertainment coming out of the Deep South.

*"Good reading for folks like us."*

## For Danforth Prince

**About the Author:**

Darwin Porter, one of the most prolific writers in publishing today, was born in Wilkes County, North Carolina, where much of this novel takes place. This world traveler is the author, with his partner, Danforth Prince, of more than 600 Frommer Travel Guides to destinations around the globe. When not traveling (which is rare), he lives in New York City and Key West, Florida.

One reviewer found that Porter's literary niche is "set midway between pure one-handed eroticism and the literary canons of D.H.Lawrence and E.M. Forster." He specializes in artfully brutal sagas, often with overtones of psychosis, sexual obsession, money, power, personal transformation, religion, and love.

His writing is not for the faint-hearted. The morality in his books is a bit untidy, and that's one reason why we love him and his novels. Darwin's work is bold, daring, and ballsy, and we get as many letters denouncing him--especially from the far right--as we get in praise of his sagas. In this tale of the Deep South, he presents a side of Nashville and its music industry in ways that have never been seen before, but which we believe are entirely valid and meritorious.

Darwin's previous works have included *Hollywood's Silent Closet*. Based on interviews with eyewitnesses during the final years of their lives, it presents a vivid but raunchy portrait, set between 1919 and 1926, of the decadent, homosexual, and gossipy world of pre-Talkie Hollywood, which had a lot to be silent about, and where all the sins weren't depicted on the screen.

**The Georgia Literary Association**

# Prologue

Shunning the sprawling mass of Miami airport, Pete Riddle asked his pilot, Junior Grayson, to land his private plane, the Wabash Cannonball, in the northern part of Dade County. "It's closer to the farmers," Pete said, "if there are still any farmers left down there."

He leaned back in his seat and closed his eyes for a moment, as the powerful rays of the Florida sun flooded the plane. "I gotta go where my people are. We'll get a bigger crowd that way. They'll show up in their broken-down pickup trucks with their hound dogs and their kids, but they'll be there. They can't pass up the chance to get a look at Pete Riddle."

Rosacoke wasn't sure. The Coast Guard Airport at Opa-Locka stood for failure in her mind. Opa-Locka itself had been one of those real-estate dreams that had gone bust during the Florida land boom of the 20s. Some land developer had wanted to evoke Morocco or Tunisia, with names like Ali-Baba Boulevard. She wondered if Pete's comeback would be as ill-fated as that scheme.

Nervously she reached into her purse for a mirror, wanting to look for reassurance. None of Nudie's rhinestone-covered clothes today. She didn't want to look too flashy. Pete had hired a consultant from New York to dress not only her, but himself as well. She considered his charcoal-gray pinstripe suit a major concession. He usually associated suits like that with Wall Street bankers.

On the seat beside her, he looked her up and down, the way he did that first night long ago when he came courting. He hadn't checked her out like that, with a glint in his eyes, in many a month.

"Sweetheart, when those cameramen move in on us, I want them to know Jackie Kennedy isn't the only one who knows how to dress. My own baby will show that bitch."

"Now don't you go putting me in her league or calling her names. I'm sure she's nice."

"You're more important than she is. I don't care what some folks say. You're still a big star. Gal Jackie is out of a job. That's what happens to a pussy when her husband gets shot."

The cabin attendant handed Pete another bourbon, and it made her heartsick when he took it, as he'd already downed three. Declining anything to drink, she settled back into a well-upholstered red seat. In a simply

tailored pink business suit with a white blouse designed to conceal her ample breasts, she felt uncomfortable.

The stewardess came back to tell them to fasten their seat belts, as the private plane would land at Opa-Locka in about ten minutes.

Rosacoke reached for his hand, knowing he could sense her fear.

"Now stop thinking about it." His words came out like a sharp command. *"Everything is gonna be okay."*

How could he always read her mind? Her whisper was barely audible. "The press is sure gonna give us the once-over."

"We've always been hot copy," he said. "Ever since we were hillbilly kid singers."

She gripped his hand once again for support. When you had as many secrets to hide as they did, you were never happy to take questions from the press.

No one had probed too deep so far. Maybe her luck would still hold.

\*\*\*

At the door before disembarking, she had one more chance to appraise her husband. He was forty-four, but she would swear that if she met him for the first time, he was no more than twenty-eight.

With a broad and bony face as wide open as the plains, a disarming smile, and those thoroughly vulnerable big blue eyes, he was country handsome--a man of genuine animal magnetism, known for "destroying" the women in his audience.

A finely honed man, aggressive and extroverted, his sunburned face and pink forehead were flushed with color. He was slimmer than he'd been in years. "Elvis and I both have the kind of bod that can put on a lot of weight," he was fond of saying when his weight shot up. She was happy to see him thin again. He called it "lean and mean."

As they headed down the stairs leading from the plane to the tarmac, the crash helmets and magnums at crotch level on the Florida state troopers made her suspect that an assassin might be lurking out there. Did any famous man or woman ever get used to such fear?

About eighty newspeople and plenty of TV cameras hovered about to greet them. Instamatics clicked, a sound she'd grown used to every time she appeared on stage. It was the unfamiliar bang that her ears were cocked to. Once a prankster had popped a paper bag at one of her concerts during one of her lovely, languid ballads. She'd immediately hit the floor.

Ignoring security, Pete brushed past the troopers and headed into the crowd to press the flesh. Everybody from blue-haired insurance widows to halter-topped teenagers were here to welcome him, screaming out their ever-loving lungs. Hoots and whistles, cowpunch style, split the air.

With a quick flick of his head, he signaled her to join him, his lips silently forming the words, "Haul ass." Always leery of crowds, she sucked in the hot September air for courage and moved toward their jostling fans who came on to her like the Hallelujah Chorus. One woman, her cheeks melting into her neck, tugged her hair. "Is that a wig, sweetie, or is all that really yours?" A security guard kept her nosy attacker at bay. But a young man in an undersize Beatles T-shirt broke through, kissing her right on the mouth, his tongue flicking at the closed doorway of her glistening white teeth. An odor of Tequila lingered on his breath.

The men in their polyester suits, the women clad in everything from bathing suits to granny dresses, had come to Opa-Locka from all over The South, many in camper vans from Alabama, others in decaying junk-heaps from the panhandle of Texas. The smell of hairspray on beehive hairdos and after-shave lotion cut through the muggy air. They'd come to Miami for Pete Riddle Day, his first professional appearance in years.

These familiar fans were the same country folk who bought her old records, in which she sang about her Brushy Mountain home and of lost love and unfaithful husbands. They were all here—the blue-collar mechanics with the flattops, farmers with calluses like barnacles on their hands, and aging waitresses in pink smocks wearing starched white handkerchiefs like corsages.

To them, Pete epitomized the American dream. He was the heartthrob of every woman, the envy of every man. He was also one of them, living proof of the myth that *every po' country boy can rise to fame and wealth.* State troopers cut a trail for them to a waiting white Cadillac, part of a six-car caravan that would take them to Miami Beach on the comeback trail.

A few feet from the car door, a farmer with a beet-colored complexion supported his little girl on his broad shoulders. "Look, Betty Sue, there he goes."

Pete slid into the car first. His thin-faced head honcho, Claude Billings, guided her in next.

"See that pretty woman in the pink dress?" the farmer asked Betty Sue. "That's Rosacoke Carson. That gal with her banjo sold three million copies of 'Mountain Momma.'"

***

No one had ever accused her of having good taste. But this Spanish-style villa on a private island in the bay of Miami Beach was a monument to opulent vulgarity. It was owned by a male friend of Pete's, who sometimes—and sometimes with Pete—went here for escapist weekends. But until today she'd never been invited inside.

Their soundproof suite on the top floor was like a Victorian brothel,

with imitation velvet wallpaper, badly molded Greek statues, and a garish-looking lamp rising out of a cornucopia of gilded fruit. White satin covered everything from the kingsize bedcover to heavy draperies which kept out all light. Mae West would feel at home here.

"I'm peeling down to the bone and letting this air conditioning cool off my big balls," Pete said.

"When you're hot you're hot." She said. "I'm gonna go soak myself in a cold tub."

He sat up in bed, a look of apprehension on his face. "They said she'd be here in just half an hour. I told Claude to let her come up. That'll give me at least twenty minutes to rest before putting on my pants and facing her."

"What do you think she wants?"

"I don't know," he said. "She's not a blackmailer. But that little heifer's after something. And when somebody's got you by the *cojones* like she's got us, you'd better grant them an audience. I want it real private like. Up here in the suite. So no one will hear us."

"Do I have to be here?"

"You'd better be," he said. "That pussy's coming up here on some sort of shopping expedition, and I want you to see what goodies she takes from our grocery shelves."

"Let me get into that tub," Rosacoke said. "I want to be cool as a cucumber before facing that one. It's been a long time."

He closed his eyes, and, as she undressed, he drifted into quick sleep. After years on the road, he'd learned to grab shuteye whenever he could, even if he had only fifteen minutes before going on stage. With her butterfly stomach, Rosacoke could never do that.

She delayed heading for the bathroom, her eyes lingering on his beautifully nude body, which on many a night her skilled pink tongue had explored from his big toes to his ears. She turned off the Art Nouveau lamp and, even though blurred by darkness, she could still make out the outlines of his well-muscled body. He seemed to shine like phosphorescence.

An eerie sensation came over her. She felt she was seeing him alive for the last time. Shivering, she shook off the feeling as quickly as it had run up her spine.

Turning from the sight of him in his troubled sleep, she carefully made her way through the maze of unfamiliar furniture, into a bathroom as big as the shanty where she used to live with four people.

Switching on the light, she shut a padded vinyl door behind her, catching the sash of her raw silk robe in the latch. As she rattled the brass knob, she found it stuck. Not wanting to wake Pete with any noise during his short nap, she left the door jammed and slipped out of her robe, leaving it in the trap.

In a full-length mirror, Rosacoke checked her eyes, her own barometer which she used to measure how she felt on any given day. They were clear but also sad. The color was hazel green--at least that's what most folks called them. But her mama used to say that her eyes reflected all the colors of all the sadness that ever was.

A delicate nose and full pink lips gave her the aura of a little girl. But below her neck, there was nothing pubescent about her.

Her exquisitely formed neck flowed into straight shoulders. Considering their enormity, her breasts were unusually firm. Bronzed and smooth, she had a tiny waist, and well-rounded hips tapered to long legs, slender and stunning. If it weren't for the size of those breasts, she'd have the face and body of a goddess. That tow-colored fluff between her legs proved she was a real blonde, too.

Turning on the gilded dolphin taps of the pink marble tub, she watched the water run for a while before taking a seat on its edge. She looped her bright hair into a coil on the crown of her head. That was her real hair. No wig. Who did that no-neck woman at the airport think she was, anyway?

When the water was just below the brim, she glided inside, playing like a child, sliding back and forth. On a glass ledge rested an array of exotic soaps, perfumes, and oils. Not knowing one from the other, she reached for a pink plastic bottle with a red-ribboned top. Unscrewing it, she smelled the perfumed solution before pouring half of it into the tub.

"You've come a long way, baby," she said a little louder than intended. She remembered bathing in a zinc-plated tub on the back porch on Saturday night with water heated on the kitchen stove, fueled by fire wood she'd gathered in the forest only that afternoon.

Now, fragrances filled the room. She was ten years old before she'd ever smelled sweet water, and that was an imitation violet-scented cologne at the five-and-dime. She wondered if the sweet-smelling stuff in the tub would wash off, or if she'd face the press tonight on Miami Beach giving off odor like a two-bit whore. To drown that image she quickly ducked under the water, not minding if she got her hair wet. After all, a hairdresser would come over later.

When she'd surfaced, she still kept her eyes half-closed, enjoying this languid state, letting the warm water do its soothing job on her frayed nerves. She stroked between her legs with a fluffy sponge, wishing Pete would come in and join her in this bath. The tub was so big it made her lonely.

Her delicate fingers slid across her skin where the soap had made the smooth surface slippery. She cupped her breasts, and they felt like heavy melons. Squeezing them, she toyed with the rosy buds of her nipples, causing them to blossom and harden. Quickly she let her hands drop back into the sudsy water. She was turning herself on, and if she didn't exert some self-control, she was going to barge right into that bedroom and at-

tack Pete. Considering what that man had been through and what awaited him tonight, he needed all the rest he could get.

Emerging from the tub, she headed for the adjoining shower stall. Behind its frosted glass doors, she turned on the water, holding her face up to its spray, letting it cleanse her body of the perfumed soap.

As she turned off the tap, she heard angry voices coming from the bedroom. Had their unwanted guest arrived already, even before they had a chance to get dressed? It was just like her. Always wanting to rush things.

Hardly audible at first, just a low murmur, Pete's voice rose to a shout. "Put that down. *Get the fuck out of here!*"

As water still dripped from Rosacoke's body, she froze with fright.

*"No! NO!"*

That was Pete's voice. She'd never heard such a sound of terror from him before.

A shot went off. Then another.

Silence.

Grabbing a big pink towel, she threw it around her body and raced toward the door, her wet feet nearly slipping on the marble floor. The padded door was still jammed.

"Pete!" she screamed.

No sound.

With a rush of strength, she forced the door open, running into the dark bedroom, where the only light came from the door that was now open to the hallway. Someone had left it open, even though she distinctly remembered Pete locking it when they came in.

If the assassin were still there, she would be shot, too. Right now that didn't matter. Finding out if Pete was okay meant everything.

She managed to locate that lamp on the dresser and yanked the chain, flooding the bedroom with light. Her eyes frantically searched every corner, looking for an intruder.

Nothing had changed. Was her mind playing tricks? She had to put a clamp on her nerves. Had she imagined those shots?

No, they were too real. The ruffled bed was empty, the white satin bedcover pulled off to the far side of the bed.

Where was Pete?

With trepidation, she approached the doorway, fearing the assassin might be lurking just outside. Had Pete already run for his life?

There was no sign of anybody in the hallway. If the gun had gone off in the soundproof room, and the door had been shut, Claude from down below might not have heard the shots.

But she'd heard them.

An impulse rose to the surface of her mind, the way you get a sudden

hunch when nothing at first seems clear.

Back in the bedroom, her wet feet soaked into the thick carpet, as she made her way slowly around the padded bedstead to its far side.

This part of the room lay in shadows. A sharp pain stabbed at her heart.

Her pulse racing dangerously, she yanked back the white satin cover.

The scream that came from her throat was like that of a wild animal trapped in a forest by a wolf-pack.

# Chapter 1 (The Forties: Roots)

Sometimes in early autumn, the sun would break through heavy layers of gray clouds after days of rain which turned the Carolina red clay into mud. A soft cool wind, blowing down from the Blue Ridge mountains, would send zephyrs across the dying corn fields, now scattered with pumpkins. These breezes would cause the leaves to flutter on the persimmon trees, whose branches jutted out like hands against the sky. Frost had already put a bite on the orange-red fruit.

On one such day, Rosacoke sat at the bare-planked kitchen table in their shanty made of rough timber, from which much of the chinking had given way to the wind that blew through the holler. Wavering flames from fat pine chunks danced in the hearth.

Every now and then she'd get up to look at all the hammering and sawing going on out back. There big, brawny Sultan, his head shaded by a frayed straw hat, stood in a litter of chips, making a wooden box in which to bury his mother, Clotilda. He wasn't much of a carpenter, and the coffin looked so pathetic she was ashamed to put it in the wagon and haul it to Cub Creek church that afternoon for the funeral.

She went back and sat down at the table. Her eyes, big and excited, closed for a moment of prayer for the soul of Aunt Clotilda. The poor woman wasn't her real aunt, but she'd always seemed to appreciate it when Rosacoke called her that. Sister Clotilda, as she was known by most of the people in the holler, had believed in Jesus all her life, and Rosacoke didn't have any doubts about where the woman's departed soul had gone.

After all that hammering, Sultan would be hungry, and she was supposed to get some supper on the table, but she wasn't in a cooking mood. There was some corn on the cob, already dried out a lot, and some cold turnip greens left over from last night's supper. Maybe she'd fry him some fatback, as he always liked that. Try though she may, she just couldn't put her mind to fixing anything.

All that occupied her was the thought of Aunt Clotilda lying in there all spread out under a patchwork quilt in the front room, its long window covered by a croaker sack. Narcissa was upstairs in the sleeping loft she shared with Rosacoke, with its soiled mattress spewing its straw onto the rough boards. She was working on the black dress Aunt Clotilda was to be buried in. Clotilda owned only one decent piece of clothing, her Sunday go-

to-meetin' dress, and even that needed some emergency repair.

Rosacoke dreaded the funeral. Losing Aunt Clotilda was bad enough, but having to face all those Negro women in the congregation filled her with added fear. Her long blonde hair just stood out, and somehow it had never looked brighter and more glistening than it did today. Only last Sunday a deacon had come over to her and told her he thought it would be better for all concerned if she went to worship at a church of her own kind. After all, she attended the white school.

Trouble was, she didn't have any of her own kind. White people didn't want her any more than the blacks. She was an outcast in the county. "You have only your poor dead mama to blame for that," Aunt Clotilda had once told her. "When Sultan dragged that starving creature here, and you tagging along with your snotty nose, I said it would bring the wrath of the Lord down on my house. And I was right. The Devil took back the mortgage on her soul. Sultan's already the daddy of that yalla gal, Narcissa. You'd think that would be enough sin for us to live with. But that buck's just bustin' his breeches every time he sees a white woman. Lust like that will lead to the death of that nigger."

In spite of her talk, Aunt Clotilda always treated Rosacoke like one of her own. After the first night, the subject of Rosacoke's skin color never came up again.

Sultan had never been like family to Rosacoke. With Aunt Clotilda gone, she was afraid to be alone with him. He had a violent temper, and Aunt Clotilda was the only person in the world who could contain him. She'd pick up a stick of stove wood and chase him out of the house every time he flared up.

Another thing, Rosacoke never liked the way he stared at her. It wasn't a very family-like look. More like a leer, really. He also gaped at Narcissa, his own daughter, in the same way, but Narcissa didn't seem to mind. She was a regular little flirt anyway. She'd even flirt with white boys, especially the four Adams brothers. John, the smallest, was a bit young, but the other three—Hank, Karl, and Tracy, were considered the handsomest boys in the county, even if they were nothing but white trash.

"One day," Narcissa told her, "I'm gonna get me one of them white boys. They look good enough to eat." She made a funny sound from deep within her throat that evoked the growl of a tigress.

"Now you stop talk like that!" Rosacoke warned her. "Besides, those Adams boys are crazy in the head, a real wild bunch."

"I'm just as good as any of you, bitch," Narcissa said. "Why should I have to go to school with the colored? I'm white, too."

"The school board don't think so."

"My mama was just as white as yours. And Sultan's not a real nigger. Not at all. He's part A-rab. Grandma got mixed up with some man, and

she don't know what race he was."

Rosacoke was sure Narcissa was right. Sultan didn't have any of the features of the Negro men in the county. A rich copper color, he had high cheekbones and full, but not thick, lips. He stared back at you through large brown eyes, velvety soft, his strong cleft chin jutting in the air in proud defiance. A big boned man, with a broad chest, he attracted attention wherever he went. "That's one good-looking nigger," Aunt Clotilda always said. "God gave him the looks. Too bad he didn't give him some common sense to go with it."

Narcissa herself was even lighter in complexion than her father. She stayed out of the sun if she could help it, preferring to do housework and letting Rosacoke work outdoors. Narcissa claimed that one day she was going to run away up north. "In Chicago they'll take me for Puerto Rican."

Getting up from the table, Rosacoke took a sip of water from a gourd resting by a bucket on the counter. Like Narcissa, she'd often thought of running away. Now that Aunt Clotilda had died, it was on her mind a lot. Only she didn't know where to go. She'd never been outside the county, and the very idea of crossing a state line was like the end of the earth to her.

She was also afraid of starving to death, and she could just see herself at night, raiding someone's cabbage patch and potato shed for food. The way it was was bad enough. She'd never had enough to fill up her belly. Any money Sultan got, and that was precious little, he spent on bootleg liquor. She couldn't recall the last time he'd ever worked a full day.

The dirty dishes in the sink reminded her of last night's sad funeral supper. She'd have to go to the well and draw some water to wash them.

If anybody came back from the church with them after the funeral, she reckoned it was proper to have something ready to eat. She really should kill one of those big hens cackling outside, but they were such good layers she couldn't bring herself to do it. Selling eggs was the only way she had of raising money to buy a little sugar and flour for them, sometimes a piece of cloth to patch a garment. Shrugging off the thought, she doubted if anyone from the congregation would come home with them anyway.

Aunt Clotilda was a beloved and respected figure in the county, and people seemed to forgive her for raising a son like Sultan. With her gone, Rosacoke suspected that forgiveness was over. They would be shunned, their shanty of mixed blood off-limits to everybody, black or white.

Tiptoeing toward the front room, she sneaked a peek at Aunt Clotilda lying so peacefully there, as flies buzzed about. She was as dead as the catfish in the iron skillet last night. A lip-biting frown was reflected on her fleshy face, as if she'd departed this world none too happy at the condition she'd left her makeshift family in. Rosacoke burst into tears, as she gazed at the elderly woman with her stiff gray hair and walnut-brown complexion. The old woman had treated her like she was her own granddaughter, show-

ing no favoritism. She was as hard on Narcissa as she was on Rosacoke.

She remembered the darkling, whispering twilight when her tall, skinny mama had first brought her to live here. That must have been at least two years ago when she was only fourteen. It was during a dog-day August, and her mama had led her up a winding dusty road. Banks of red clay rose on each side of them, and her mama had steered her clear of a bunch of poison ivy. From the lowlands came the sound of a hound barking, and some crickets chirped nearby.

The moon still hadn't come up. A whippoorwill in the black pines beyond signaled the beginning of night.

Since her daddy had been killed by a logging truck running wild, Rosacoke had been shifted around like this, and she'd gotten used to living in strange new places, as much as one ever gets used to such things.

A sharp crunching sound came from a bush, frightening her. A possum shot out, darting across the field. She held even tighter to her mama's hands, as they cut from the main path and headed across a deserted field of ragweed.

"Christ, child, you're squeezing my hand so tight you'll cut off the blood," her mama had said. "You're like a new-born calf hanging onto its mama's teat."

"I'm hungry."

Her mama stopped in her tracks, her eyes fastening on Rosacoke. The slap stung her face. "Now you hush up. You quit thinking about your gut. Especially at a time like this."

Rosacoke was too stunned to cry. Except for a recent whipping, her mama rarely hit her, so things must be bad. Her mama's face seemed to gleam with a radiance of determination she'd never seen there before.

Instead of holding hands, Rosacoke trailed along. She didn't own a pair of shoes, and the rocks of the field hurt her feet. They were going toward Shakerag, the holler where the colored folk lived, and Rosacoke couldn't figure that one out. No white girl ever went down to Shakerag, except Emma Lou Hayes, and Christian people rarely spoke about her any more. She wanted to ask why her mama was taking her down there, but she figured she'd aggravated her enough for one day.

Her mama had just been fired from her job. It wasn't a real job. In exchange for a room in a dark basement and scraps from the table, Mrs. Deal had let them live under her roof. Bed-ridden most of the time and invariably crotchety, Mrs. Deal was a stern old woman with as many demands as her years.

Rosacoke's mama had been sickly as of late, and she couldn't keep up with all the chores Mrs. Deal demanded of her. Rosacoke helped out, but Mrs. Deal always found fault with her work. When she'd ruined Mrs. Deal's best silk nightgown in the lye-soap wash, that had ended their stay

there. Rosacoke got a whipping from her mama, and although Mrs. Deal looked on in excited approval as the switch cut across her naked buttocks, it wasn't enough to pacify the old woman's anger. She told them she'd hired a new girl, one who was young and strong and who would do what she was told.

Packing to leave wasn't much of a problem. Like her mama, Rosacoke owned only the dress on her back. Except for a few possessions, tied up in a bundle, her mama didn't have much to lug across the field toward a shanty that stood out in the clearing. Oblong with frame sidewalls, and made of rough boards and tarpaper, it was built shotgun-style, with a peaked roof and a tiny lean-to porch, covered in shingles. It stood on stumpy legs made of unmortared concrete block.

When Rosacoke first laid eyes on Sultan, she couldn't believe her mama was taking her to live with him. Leaning a shoulder up against the house, Sultan stared down at her, filling her with fright.

"Mama, he's not my new daddy, is he? Mama, he's …"

"Hush! You're lucky I was able to find a roof over our heads after you got us kicked out. You can either come in this house with me or else run out there in the woods and let the spooks grab hold of you. That old bogey man would just love to get hold of a pretty thing like you."

Sultan had very little to say to her mama and nothing at all for Rosacoke. In the front room she met Clotilda who loudly voiced her objections, before Sultan convinced her to fetch up some molasses on pone, along with some yellow-looking clabber milk for their supper.

When Narcissa had come into the kitchen, before Rosacoke even had a chance to get a good look at her, the girl picked up the pitcher of milk and dumped it over Rosacoke's head.

Completely humiliated, her pride wounded something awful, Rosacoke wanted to burst into tears. But then another, stronger feeling came over her. She was determined not to give Narcissa the satisfaction of knowing how she'd hurt her. "I hear tell milk's good for the hair. Anybody got a towel?

As Aunt Clotilda fetched a towel from the sink, Sultan moved menacingly toward Narcissa who backed off. She looked like she was going to make a break for it, but he was too fast for her. His slap sent her reeling back against the wall. She cried out in pain. "Unless you're cravin' me to do that again, you'll fetch the mop and clean up your mess, you jealous little hussy."

Her mama helped Rosacoke dry her soaked hair. "Don't pay no attention to that one," Clotilda cautioned Rosacoke, as if Narcissa were no longer in the room. "She's a wild thing, just like her white mama was. One day she's gonna cause a lot of men a lot of grief."

Hitching the borrowed mule to the wagon, Sultan lifted the reins, sitting tall on his wooden seat. He was dressed in a brown suit and a white shirt. His red tie was totally wrong for a funeral, and Rosacoke had never seen him in a suit before. She wondered where he got it, fearing he might have stolen it. It was impossible to imagine anyone lending Sultan a decent suit of clothes.

He'd only gotten the wagon and mule because Aunt Clotilda used to do sewing for the white Riddle family down the road. After hearing of her death, the Riddles had driven up to Sultan's shack in their Ford pickup truck, with their teenage son, Pete, in the front seat, and had asked if they could be of any help. Afraid to come out to meet them, Rosacoke hid in the front room, peering out the window until they'd gone, but she'd overheard Sultan ask to borrow the mule and wagon.

In back of the wagon, she sat with some autumn foliage she'd gathered, banking it around Aunt Clotilda's pine box. On top of the flat coffin, she'd placed a wilted rose. "A sad little thing," she said ostensibly to Narcissa, but she might as well be talking to herself. Narcissa paid her no mind. "The last rose of summer." In a wood chair she'd borrowed from the kitchen, she'd seated herself across from Narcissa.

Narcissa had never looked prettier, and Rosacoke was a little envious, yet relieved in a funny kind of way. If Narcissa looked so good, maybe not too many people would pay much attention to her, until she got up to sing which she'd dreaded but Sultan had insisted upon.

"You've got the best voice in the church choir," Sultan had said as he'd emerged from his bedroom in his new suit. "My mama deserves to be sent off to heaven with the best hymn and finest voice we've got to offer."

His selection of Rosacoke as a singer had made Narcissa angry, and Rosacoke had suggested that maybe they could do a duet. Sultan had been adamant. She'd often sung with Narcissa before, but unlike her own voice, Narcissa sounded lowdown and dirty whenever she sang. She somehow made a simple bluegrass number very suggestive, with the slight purr she had in her voice. A gospel song would become a Holy Ghost boogie. In Rosacoke's view, Narcissa's sound was more appropriate in a honky-tonk than a church.

Narcissa was all decked out in a pink chiffon dress, with tiny white ribbons on its neck and sleeves and little flowers sewn all over it. There was no question about it: Narcissa was an exotic-looking thing, with her finely featured and delicately profiled Indian face, her long, lustrous jet black hair, and her big black wide-set eyes, all packaged in a creamy bronze skin with the texture of a magnolia petal. Rosacoke had never seen such beau-

tiful skin on any girl, white or black. Through small nostrils, Narcissa breathed in short gasps, which tended to make her statements more meaningful. At least it attracted your attention. Her prominently curved, sensuous lips carried an enigmatic smile.

"That pink dress looks a little too festive for a funeral," Rosacoke said.

"It's too harmless to wear anywhere else," Narcissa said. "Besides, you're just jealous 'cause you don't have a pretty dress. I'm hummin' and beeboppin' my own tune, so don't give me no sass. The way you look, I'm ashamed to sit next to you in church."

Rosacoke did feel ashamed of her feedsack dress, but it was all she had. At least it was clean. A girl usually had time to prepare for a wedding, but funerals caught you off guard.

"Kee-RICE! You're some sight anyway," Narcissa said. "Going to a Negro funeral. I mean, Grandma wasn't your own kin."

"She was like it to me. Blood don't count for everything."

As the wagon wheels rolled along the bumpy road, across a cotton field, Sultan reached the main highway, and headed down a hill toward the church, past a red clay bank of dogwood and hickory.

To take her mind off the bouncing ride, she thought of her own mama dying. There was no funeral then. The people at the all-white Roaring River Baptist Church didn't want the body. The pastor there, the Rev. L.T. Younger, told Rosacoke, "We don't bury no white woman here who's lived in sin with a nigger. My congregation won't stand for it. Those are respectable people buried out there in the graveyard. We've got to protect their dignity. Didn't your mama die giving birth to Sultan's bastard? God has already shown what he thinks about such acts by striking down the Jezebel and her bastard."

In tears Rosacoke had run from the church.

Even with a child in her belly, Sultan had thrashed Rosacoke's mother one morning in the kitchen when she was seven months pregnant. He didn't like the watery flour gravy she'd made to go with the biscuits. "I want some God damn milk in my gravy, woman, even it if has to come from your own tit." He'd struck her several times before Aunt Clotilda had picked up a stick of fire wood and threatened to bash in his mean skull if he didn't quit hitting her.

In panic, Rosacoke had screamed as Sultan's blows had rained down on her mama.

Narcissa had sat right proud at the table, ignoring the fight and pushing the watery gravy aside, as she'd poured the last of the molasses onto her biscuits.

After her mama had died in childbirth a week later, her infant a stillborn boy, Sultan had built a pinebox coffin for the two of them and had buried them on top of a hill, their grave marked by a big rock. Rosacoke had

wandered through the briars and broomstraw to gather wild flowers to place on the site. After everybody had gone, she'd stood there for hours, tears streaming down, looking at the mound of red dirt, praying that her mama and little baby brother, whom she didn't get a chance to know, wouldn't go to hell.

Such thoughts aside, her attention was jarred back to the present when the wagon rolled past two of the Adams boys, who'd just emerged from the woods in the clearing, carrying two possums they'd caught. Their hounds raced around the legs of the mule, barking furiously. Narcissa smiled at the boys, especially the better-looking one, Hank, who was about twenty-two. Hank winked at Narcissa and grabbed himself obscenely.

When they were out of earshot of the boys, Rosacoke leaned over to speak to Narcissa, keeping her voice down so Sultan couldn't hear. "Gal, have you no self-respect? I saw the way you looked at that no-good Hank Adams. What a way to behave on the road to your own Grandma's funeral. It's a wonder Aunt Clotilda don't turn over in this pinewood box."

Narcissa's face assumed a mask of defiance, her muscles twitching under the velvet skin. "I can't help it if white boys lay eyes on me and find me the best thing since whiskey. The little green bug has bit you, just 'cause no boy finds you pretty. I saw the way you hid out in the front room so you could put a secret eye on that mothahfuggah, Pete Riddle."

"That's a lie."

"She-it! Let's face it. I don't blame you. He's the best-looking stud in the county. But you'd better forget him. He can have any gal he wants, and from what I hear that pole of his stands up for quite a few."

"Some talk to have over Aunt Clotilda's coffin. It's a wonder God don't strike you dead right now."

The rest of the jouncing ride was in silence.

In the shade of a towering oak tree which had been struck twice by lightning, Cub Creek Church came into view, a little unpainted clapboard bandbox. Rosacoke was the first to get down off the wagon. Heading across the bare front yard, she climbed the wooden steps. Opening the creaky door, she found the place empty.

At the front of the church stood the choir, the pulpit, and a wood-burning iron stove where Haydon Eller was supposed to have a roaring fire going. She looked everywhere for Haydon.

Down by the choir pew, where the immediate family of Clotilda's was supposed to sit, she found him sprawled out in his sleep, his paregoric-tainted breath stinking up the place. A gravedigger, he was charged with looking after the church. She shook him until he woke up. "Get up from that bench. There's people coming for a funeral."

His eyes opened wide, and at first he didn't seem to know where he was. "Who passed on to heaven?"

"Sister Clotilda. I bet you ain't dug the grave yet."

"Yes'm, I have. That's why I'm so tired I passed out."

"You'd better get on home to Ida Red and get her to fix you some breakfast and sober you up. You ain't fit to attend no funeral."

"I guess I ain't. You take care of it yourself." He got up and staggered toward the back door.

Some old friends of Clotilda's had slipped in in the meanwhile, filling up the hard back benches.

Four black men in mud-stained boots carried the pinebox coffin into the church, laying it on sawhorses up front for the occasion. It was hard for her to believe that Aunt Clotilda was in that box. She reckoned that when the soul departed, there wasn't much left behind.

Suddenly, Rosacoke burst into tears, grabbing a red handkerchief she'd taken from Sultan and muffling her sobbing into it. With Aunt Clotilda gone, she felt loneliness jagging her heart.

The funeral went by before her like a motion-picture show. She hardly paid attention to it. Muscles taut, she was lost somewhere in her own private grief. Not even the preacher's tongue of cloven flame, as it rumbled and shook, could bring her back to the present, although a phrase now and then would register.

"A good soul."

"Amen."

"A kind woman."

"Amen, amen!"

"She's heaven-bound."

"*Hallelujah, brother!*"

Frost had killed the flowers in the county, and no one could afford to buy any from a shop, so the church looked strangely denuded. What was a funeral without flowers? At least somebody should have provided a wreath.

Narcissa nudged her, and she realized the time had come for her to get up and sing. Although she'd sung in the choir since she was a little girl, she'd never sung alone before, and she was scared. Shaking, she rose on wobbly legs and went to stand at the pulpit, wishing that she had some music to accompany her. But the church couldn't afford a piano. Before launching into "I'll Fly Away," she looked down at Aunt Clotilda, her body covered in a purple veil borrowed from the pastor's wife. The wagon ride had jostled her, and no one had seen fit to rearrange her body.

Summoning all the courage she had in her, Rosacoke managed to get the first words out, and once she hit the right notes, she knew she'd be okay from then on. By the time she'd reached the line, "To a home on God's celestial shore," her spiritually powerful, appealing voice filled the small church. With a high, forceful, lilting quaver in her voice, she got all the words out before breaking down in tears.

At the muddy site, she looked around her, eying the graveyard that used to be an old Indian burial ground. Most people couldn't afford tombstones. Some markers had long ago been stolen, and other smaller rock ones had sunk into the marshy earth. White people selected their graveyard sites on high ground, beyond the reach of the raging flood waters that often swept over these parts. She'd heard stories that these wicked waters were powerful enough to wrench coffins from their burial mounds, sending them tumbling into muddy torrents. Once, so she'd been told, one coffin had been ripped open, exposing its body to onlookers the next day who discovered that a young girl's hair had grown five feet under the ground.

Rosacoke joined Narcissa and Sultan, peering down into the big hole Haydon had so recently dug. Already it was filling up with water. To the doleful sound of "Shall We Gather at the River," she listened respectfully to the pastor's last words, "Ashes to ashes, dust to dust."

Then Narcissa did a strange thing. She dropped something into the grave.

"What's that?" Rosacoke whispered.

"The ninth bone of the tail of a black cat. It's for luck in the world beyond."

It didn't seem right fitting to Rosacoke to do something like that. And where did Narcissa get a black cat's tail? She was a peculiar girl, and Rosacoke wondered if she really believed in Jesus, or else secretly when she was alone practiced voodoo.

As the men shoveled dirt over Aunt Clotilda's coffin, Rosacoke in tears turned away and headed back toward the wagon. The bulky sweater she'd worn over her feedsack dress didn't offer enough protection from the damp Carolina autumn.

The sun disappeared, and the sky had turned a mule gray now. Rolling clouds appeared on the horizon, making winter seem a little nearer.

\*\*\*

She'd been right in her guessing. No one came anywhere near to wanting to come home with them for supper after Aunt Clotilda's funeral. When the beloved old woman was laid to rest, her friends scattered in all directions, not even having the decency to come up to Sultan or Narcissa to pay their respects. Rosacoke was glad she didn't kill any of those chickens, even though she couldn't earn much money selling eggs, because most families kept their own hens.

That reminded her that with Aunt Clotilda gone, there'd be almost no money coming in. Somehow Aunt Clotilda always managed to scrape together a few pennies for the necessities. If it were summer, Rosacoke could hire herself out to work in the fields, a job Narcissa shunned because

of the sun. Rosacoke didn't have breath to waste in asking Sultan to find a job.

The next morning she fixed Sultan a breakfast the way he liked it. She'd even gotten some milk for his gravy, remembering how he'd thrashed her mama. If Sultan got violent, as was his nature, Aunt Clotilda wouldn't be around any more to protect her from his outbursts.

After he finished his eggs, he leaned back in his chair and eyed her. "I'm gonna hitch that mule to the wagon. Take it back to the Riddles. I want you to tag along."

"Why on God's green earth would I want to go see the Riddles? I got no business over there."

"Before mama got too old, she used to do work for those white folks. Not just sewing. Some cooking, washing, canning—you know, a woman's work. You're a big gal. I'm gonna ask 'em if they could use a young heifer around the place to help out. I happen to know they've lost their other gal."

"I'd rather die than ask a good family like that to take me on. I'd be so shame-faced I couldn't even look at 'em."

With his strong arm, he reached out and grabbed her wrist, twisting it, his temper flaring again. She could see the rage bubbling in his eyes. No use calling for Narcissa. That Miss Priss would just love to see her get a beating.

"You don't know what time it is, bitch! I'm boss man around here now. Mama's gone and now you'll do what I say. And don't give me no lip. Just 'cause you're white, don't think that entitles you to no extra goodies."

After he'd released his grip, she massaged her wrist, stumbling to the sink to wash up the breakfast dishes.

"Get yourself ready," Sultan commanded. "Put on your good dress, the one you wore to the funeral. And tie that blonde hair back in a bun, the way mama used to wear hers. It's so bunched up all curly-like all over your head it makes you look like a cheap whore."

Back in the wagon again, she rode in silence up in the front seat with Sultan. The mule was stubborn this morning, probably because it hadn't been fed.

"We ain't got nothing to stuff its gut with," Sultan said. "It can eat when it gets home. The Riddles ain't got a lot of money to throw around, but that's one well-fed bunch of white folks. Take a look at Pete. That stud's shooting up so fast he's gonna overtake me."

Set back from the road, the Riddle family home was surrounded by big oak trees on three sides, a wide sweeping gingerbread-trimmed verandah built on its front. Unlike Sultan's shanty, the antebellum house was painted white, the shutters trimmed in a moss green.

Swaying back and forth on the porch swing, Pete was playing a harmonica. That Narcissa was right about one thing: he was the best-looking

thing in pants that Rosacoke had ever laid eyes on. Long and rangy, he carried himself in such a cocky manner Rosacoke knew at once he was very aware of just how handsome he was. You could tell it in the way he slouched down in that swing, his legs spread-eagled like the whole world wanted to come and worship between them at his fully packed crotch. No bumbling little boy, he was the most self-assured young man she'd seen in the county, even though he couldn't be more than seventeen years old, not much older than her. She knew he'd finished high school only last June, a year ahead of her.

Sultan got down from the wagon and went around to find Mrs. Riddle at the back door, the way colored people were supposed to do. Rosacoke was thankful he didn't ask her to come with him.

When he'd gone, Pete slowly got up from his swing, and, harmonica in hand, sauntered over to the edge of the porch, where he looked at her in a funny way, like he was sizing her up or something. A shock of dark brown hair fell over his forehead, partially obscuring his left eye. Most boys didn't wear their hair that long; in fact, he was the only one she knew who did in the whole county. "You're Rosacoke Carson, aren't you?"

At first she was taken back, noting that he said "aren't" instead of "ain't," the way you're taught in school. She knew better herself but got careless around the house. "Last time I checked." No sooner than the words finally came out of her mouth, than she'd regretted sounding bitchy like Narcissa.

He didn't seem to pay it any mind. "Sorry to hear about your Grandma." He paused in bewilderment, as if he'd realized that Sister Clotilda couldn't possibly have been her kin. "I hope you don't take offense. But I always wanted to know something. Is Sultan your daddy?"

"No," she blurted out, a little too defensively. "My daddy's dead. Mama, too. I'm by myself. Aunt Clotilda took me and my mama in when we didn't have no place else to go."

"So, that's the story. I never could figure it out, and, you know me, I never pay much attention to gossip, especially talk spread about me. I mean, it's clear as your face. You're white. No question about that."

Before she could thank him for conceding that obvious point, Sultan came around the corner of the house, followed by Mrs. Riddle.

"Get down from there," he called out. "Mrs. Riddle wants to talk to you about that job."

"'Cuse me," Rosacoke said to Pete. She felt embarrassed to have him learn why she was here, asking for a job as household help. But if she were going to work for the Riddles, she couldn't keep it from him, now could she?

She jumped down from the wagon, straightened her brown dress, patted the mule, took one final look at Pete, and went over to talk to her future employer.

Mrs. Riddle, though stern, seemed like a real nice woman, and she really did want to work for her. The only thing Rosacoke couldn't understand was why Pete's mama was so old. She must have given birth to Pete when she was in her late forties. She was more like a grandma now, with her yellowing gray hair tied back in a bun. She was clad in a simple black dress with a gingham apron that didn't look too clean.

"You didn't tell a fib, Sultan," said Mrs. Riddle. "This looks like a good strong gal, and I could sure use a little extra help around here ever since that Emma Lou Hayes ran off and hasn't shown her no good hide around these parts in three weeks. If she comes around again, I'm gonna fire her."

Rosacoke was shocked to hear that Emma Lou worked for the Riddles. She was that white gal who often came down to Shakerag. Once she'd heard her mama fighting with Sultan, claiming that he was keeping company with Emma Lou. Now it was clear to Rosacoke why Sultan knew that the Riddles might be looking for another gal.

Sultan went to take the mule back to the barn, and Mrs. Riddle led her inside the dark kitchen to explain some of the duties of the job. "Course, I didn't like a bitch in heat like that Hayes gal hanging out at my house around Pete. A gal like that can put a lot of ideas into a young boy's head."

"I bet."

"But you don't look like that sort yourself. Spite of your living down there in the holler with the niggers, I hear tell you're a respectable Christian gal."

"I am, ma'am."

Mrs. Riddle observed her closely, a stern look on her wrinkled brow. "I think you are, too. Course this job don't pay much. A buck fifty a day. Six days a week unless I cook up a big Sunday dinner for the pastor. Then you'll have to come over at six that morning and stay until the plates are scraped clean and washed. How's the pay sound?"

"Mighty good. I've never had more than two dollars a week coming in, and sometimes not even that."

"Good. Then I'll test you out for a week or so. Mind you, I ain't promising nothing. It's just a try-out."

"I'm mighty grateful for the chance."

Pete came into the kitchen. "Mama, I'm hungry."

Mrs. Riddle went over to the stove to get him a cold biscuit with a slice of country ham. "Son, Rosacoke's gonna be working here a bit for us. Taking Emma Lou's job."

"Isn't she coming back?" He looked disappointed, leading Rosacoke to believe there had been something going on between Emma Lou and Pete. She didn't really know why, but she felt jealous.

"Son, I'm sure you know more about Emma Lou's whereabouts than I would." Mrs. Riddle's usually well-modulated voice took on a sharp, biting

sound, and Rosacoke sensed some problem between Pete and her. Brushing such a thought aside, Rosacoke figured it wasn't her business to go prying into the affairs of other people.

"Child," Mrs. Riddle called to her. "Fetch this big growing boy a tall glass of cold milk." As she placed the ham-stuffed biscuit down in front of him, the softness had come back into the tone of her voice. By the way she caressed the back of his neck as she put the plate down, it was clear to Rosacoke how dog-faced devoted she was to her son.

When she'd gone, Rosacoke filled up a glass with milk and carried it over to the table. As he reached up for it, his hand caressed hers.

She quickly withdrew it.

"I'll miss ole Emma Lou," he said. "But I guess you'll be a mighty fine replacement once you find out just exactly what the job entails. Sorta learn the ropes."

"Reckon so, providing there ain't no knots in that rope to tie me up with." She'd heard a lot about Pete's reputation. His eyes seemed riveted to her breasts, and she stepped back, drawing her sweater around her as if chilled. "I'll do my best, Mr. Pete."

"Just call me Pete. Mr. Pete always sounds like nigger talk to me. You're white, aren't you? You gotta learn to talk like white folks. I learned the proper way to speak. I'm not some dumb piece of white trash, you know. I know more than my teachers at school. In a few years, I'm gonna be a lawyer."

"That's nice." She headed for the kitchen sink to wash the dishes, the way she did at Sultan's shanty. "I heard you playing the harmonica as we came up the road. You sound real good on it."

"I'm very good at music. I sing, too. Wait till you hear me sing. I play the guitar. The banjo. Music's just a hobby with me."

In no time at all, Pete finished his sandwich and came up behind her at the sink, real close like, and his presence sent a tingling sensation up her spine. "I'm gonna go up to my room to study a bit."

"But you're not in school no more."

"I told you, I want to be a lawyer. I learn more up in my room than I ever learned at school. I'm going to college. Anyway, bring me some coffee later. Lots of cream and sugar."

"I sure will."

At the door leading to the upstairs, he paused, a look of real concern on his face. "Listen, I'm glad you're gonna help mama out. She and dad aren't as sprightly as they used to be. I'm sorta considering joining the Navy before college, especially if Roosevelt gets us into a war, the way a lot of people are talking. I'd hate to leave Mama and Dad here all alone. It might be good if they had someone they could depend on while I'm gone."

"I'm right thankful for the job, Mr. ...I mean, Pete."

"I'm sure the two of us are gonna get along mighty fine." He had that same funny look on his face, as he glanced at her once more, before turning and heading up the creaky wooden stairs to his bedroom.

She felt out of place here, but she vowed to try real hard to fit in and make everybody like her, especially that Pete. He downright scared her. She didn't know what it was, but he was the type of boy who seemed to get whatever he asked for, the way he'd demanded food and his mama had rushed to fetch it for him. She'd have to watch her step around that one, as she had no intention of replacing Emma Lou, except in doing household chores.

***

Alone in his upstairs bedroom, Pete opened a window, hoping to catch a breeze blowing up from the holler. No such luck. The air of the early evening was as still as if the dog days of August were lingering on into the late summer. He couldn't wait for the first frost, so he could escape the intense heat of the summer, one of the hottest ever known in these parts.

He walked over to stand in front of a tall vanity mirror that he'd rescued from the attic above his bedroom. It had belonged to a woman who'd been raped and shot by Yankee soldiers in 1865 even though she was seventy-two years old. He'd heard his mama tell the story many times.

He looked at his figure in the mirror and appraised himself carefully. "You're too fucking good looking," he said out loud but in a softly modulated voice. He reached to unbutton his shirt. As he did, he let his fingers travel along the lines of his well-developed chest.

His pectoral muscles were sculpted, his skin smooth and flawless. There was a nice curve from his pecs to the long flatness of his perfect abdomen. When he pinched his nipples, they jerked up and stood at attention. He knew girls liked to have men suck their nipples and even bite them. He wanted someone to kiss and bite his own nipples and even suck on them like a baby draining its mama's life-giving milk.

He pulled off his shirt and tossed it on the bed before kicking off his shoes and pulling off his socks. Straightening up, he appraised his body in the mirror again. He'd filled out this summer by working on his parents' farm like a fucking hired hand. Hot, sweaty labor driving a tractor across dusty fields.

He flexed his muscles and was proud of them. He might be a teenager, but he had a man's body. Wherever he went in the county, men always talked about the beautiful bodies of women—their big tits, their shapely asses, their pussies. He was sick and tired of that talk.

Wasn't there anybody in the county who realized that men too had beautiful bodies that needed to be licked, kissed, loved, and sucked? He

couldn't even bring himself to say fucked. He'd heard about cornholing and everything but the concept was a bit much for him to think about. One day he planned to go off into the woods to find some lonely but scenic spot, and he was going to sit there and give that forbidden subject some serious consideration.

The moment had come. It was a ritual with him and his biggest thrill of the day. He reached to unbuckle his pants, enjoying the feel of the large silver buckle on the leather belt his papa had given him for Christmas last year. "You're getting to be a real man, son," his daddy had told him. "A real man needs a real belt to hold up his pants."

As the buckle unfastened, Pete reached to slowly and provocatively unbutton his pants. This was the part he liked most of all. When he'd reached the final button, he slowly let his fly open wider and wider, revealing a nest of brown pubic hair. He didn't wear underwear and had no intention of ever doing so. He liked the feel of the denim against his cock and balls, even though he was constantly getting hard-ons.

As he pulled the pants down, the base of his cock came into view. Like a stripper, he slowly and tantalizingly exposed it inch by inch. It was a big one.

He'd never seen a man with a hard-on before, but he'd seen a lot of naked boys and men, and he had all of them beat. Even soft, his cock was thick and long—at least six and a half inches. He'd heard from Hank Adams that some men's cocks weren't even six and a half inches long when erect.

When Pete was hard he was a truly impressive sight. He wasn't sure just how many inches he had, but he was going to get a ruler and do some measuring. Hell! A man should know his own dick size, shouldn't he?

In front of the mirror, he pulled back his foreskin and exposed the vermilion fleshy knob. It looked big and delicious, something tastier than any lollipop he was sure. His cock hardened in his hand. As he jerked it, amazed at how firm, thick, and long it had grown, he felt he was wasting a lot of good stuff jerking himself off. That good stuff should be deposited in some other human being who'd really enjoy it.

He'd thought "human being" but actually in the back of his brain he had a more specific sex in mind. He could have any woman he wanted in the county. All the girls came on to him. Even Rosacoke was attracted to him. He could see it in her eyes. It'd be only a matter of days or weeks before he was fucking her. He was hardly anticipating that thrill. He fucked women for relief and because it was expected of him. They were there. They were available, and when he'd shoot his gun they provided some momentary relief.

But there had to be more to love-making than that. What about passion? What about having a kind of sex that got you so hot and bothered that

you actually felt fulfilled when you crawled out of a stranger's bed?

As he fucked his fist harder, images flashed through his mind. Those Adams boys, especially that Hank with his blond hair and rippling muscles, battered him with visions of their working in the fields without their shirts on. Even John, the youngest of the four, was developing muscles. Karl was seventeen, and looked like some marine recruiting poster fantasy, and Tracy was nineteen and firecracker hot.

Pete's sap rising, he reached quickly for a towel, exploding into it. He couldn't stop cumming, it seemed. It was hard to admit to himself what had triggered that massive explosion.

The vision of a nude Sultan fully erect had flashed through his brain at the last moment.

Thinking about the Adams boys nude was hardly acceptable even to himself. But thinking about Sultan nude was sick, and he knew that, but couldn't help himself. It was as if his brain was determined to send out signals without his being able to control his own mind.

Sick or not, he was tired of not getting the kind of sexual satisfaction he craved. Starting tomorrow morning, he was going to devise schemes to get hold of a dick and suck it dry. That's what he wanted. Why should he deny himself the one thing in life he wanted more than anything else?

He dropped the soiled towel and stared at himself in the mirror, as his large cock slowly deflated.

"Pete Riddle," he said his name out loud but still in a whisper. "The stud hoss of Wilkes County." He frowned as he looked up at his beautiful face. "Or so they say." He looked long and hard at his image in that stained mirror.

The time had come to face the truth.

He couldn't bear to say the words out loud, so he silently mouthed them: "Pete Riddle, stud hoss of Wilkes County, is a fucking queer!"

# Chapter 2

After the second day of work at the Riddle household, Rosacoke learned why Pete, at seventeen, had old parents. He'd been adopted. His real parents had died in a car accident one night as they headed for Richmond, Virginia, in a snowstorm. A small baby at the time, Pete had been in the car with them, but, miraculously, had been spared with only minor injuries.

Pete's good looks came from his real parents, certainly not his adopted ones. Mrs. Riddle was not only unattractive, but she didn't keep herself well-groomed. She dipped Blue Mule snuff, and a brown blop of it always accumulated under her lower chin.

Mr. Riddle was a recluse, always complaining of a weak stomach and spending most of his time in a battered old iron bedstead. When he did show up in his bib overalls, he said little. He'd sit at the supper table each night, slurping his black-eyed peas in their soupy gravy, his favorite food. Behind a white beard, he peered out at his limited world over the rim of his glasses.

To Rosacoke, his beard was funny, making him look as if he were grinning all the time. Snowy white hair grew in whorls under his ruddy-colored cheekbones, looking like crinkled white tissue paper. After dinner he'd sit in his favorite rocking chair, with a spittoon on the side to collect the spittings of the tobacco he chewed.

About one thing, Mrs. Riddle was adamant. Every member of the family had to attend church regularly. Soon Rosacoke quit going to her own Baptist church and started to attend services with the Riddle family at the First Assembly of God Church. She still remembered how the Reverend Younger had refused to let her bury her mama in his precious graveyard, and was only too glad to switch her allegiance to another church.

Founded in Hot Springs, Arkansas, in 1914, the Riddle family church was a Pentecostal sect that preached against the movies, dance halls, bootleg liquor, cigarettes, even going swimming or taking out life insurance. "It's old-time religion like I like it," Mrs. Riddle told her. "It don't allow no foolishness."

It was important for Rosacoke to learn about Jesus. She knew that. But her real reason for going to the Riddle church was to listen to Pete's voice ringing clearly and more distinctively than anybody else's in the small choir. He could sing hymns with a gusto unmatched by other members of

the down-home congregation, and sometimes he'd do a solo of "Amazing Grace." His emotionally sincere voice was piercing and gutsy, reflecting how he idolized Roy Acuff and his Smoky Mountain Boys.

Music meant a lot to the Riddles. As a child, Mr. Riddle had made a cornstalk fiddle by cleaning out the pulp, leaving only the stringy fibers which he then played with a stick. As a player, he rated himself "a stomp down good un!"

"We were raised on good country music," Mrs. Riddle told Rosacoke. Much of it had come from their Anglo-Saxon forefathers, who lived in Appalachian hollers and passed down from one generation to the next songs that had once been Irish jigs and Elizabethan folk ballads. Some of the songs rambled on to a dozen verses or more. Over the years many of these excruciatingly sad hymns had picked up the laments of the blacks in the cotton fields.

Not just at church, but at the Riddle home, old-time music prevailed, and often neighbors would drop in for a late summer night's entertainment. Later Rosacoke would serve the guests pumpkin pie she'd baked herself, and they'd sit around the fire cracking hickory and hazelnuts they'd gathered.

Mrs. Riddle played a used Starck upright piano and was also a mean guitar picker. Mr. Riddle, emerging from one of his long spells in his bed-room, was known as the best country fiddler in these parts.

Rosacoke always wanted to join in the impromptu fests, feeling she could sing better than anybody else except Pete, but she was never invited, as she was relegated to the role of servant girl.

Sometimes the family would listen to the records of Fiddlin' John Carson and his Skillet Lickers on their Victrola. Often Pete would work out some of the tunes by ear on his harmonica or play the dickens out of his guitar. His $8.95 mail-order guitar didn't have but three strings on it. With great vocal endurance, he seemed to sing from the pit of his stomach, and at most sessions he'd end up carrying on lustily after everybody else had dropped out.

Rosacoke's own chance to sing finally came not at the Riddles, but at school. One day the principal, Ernest Scrivener, heard her singing in the schoolyard and told her, "With a voice like that, you really should be in the glee club."

"Reckon I don't have time for such things. After school, I have to get over to the Riddles. I help out there."

"Tell you what, then," Scrivener said. "Tomorrow morning, I want you to lead the singing in the chapel."

"I'd be scared to death. I ain't got no place up there making a fool out of myself."

The next morning found her trotting up front and facing twenty two of her classmates. Filled with fright, but urged on by some feeling within her

gut, she sang in a thin, vibrato voice. The other pupils seemed to like her voice which propelled a haunting and melodic sound through the chapel, as she did her rendition of an old mountain song. As she warmed to the number, she gave it a pounding beat no one had ever heard before.

At the end of her song, she couldn't believe the acceptance. A warm glow filled her body as she later spoke to Scrivener. "They really liked me." Disbelief filled her voice. "They really liked me. *Me.*"

Her big chance came when she performed in the class play as a minstrel. Tracy, one of those menacingly sexy Adams brothers, said, "You gonna come out on that stage in black face, bitch?" She ignored him, or at least pretended to, holding back her tears until she could run to the girls' room.

Later that afternoon when she told Mrs. Riddle what had happened, the old woman said, "don't let them get your goat." Rosacoke didn't plan to give anyone the satisfaction of that and was determined to carry on in spite of the talk about her.

One day as she busied herself washing dishes at the Riddles, she sang her favorite tune, "Down in the Valley." Although she'd always liked it, it somehow struck her as the work of a sentimental fool. She just knew she could write something better than that to express the way she felt, and on some bright morning she was going to get around to it.

The way she felt had a lot to do with Pete. Her mind dwelled on him more than it did on music. He was the kind of boy she'd dreamed of marrying. She felt she could really love him, give him anything he wanted.

Unlike some of the other girls in her class, she didn't paint herself with lipstick. Narcissa always did that. She'd quit school and had gotten a job selling tickets at the picture show. That one laid out at all hours of the night. The picture show closed down at ten o'clock every night, but Narcissa never came home until around three or four in the morning. Involved in his own affairs, Sultan never protested. He looked upon a sixteen-year-old girl as a mature woman, fully capable of leading an adult life.

Whereas Narcissa did everything she could to call attention to her glamorous self, Rosacoke tried to conceal many of her obvious charms. In the drab feedsack dress she'd sewed herself and with her tied-up blonde hair, usually hidden under a scarf, she never attracted much attention. She felt she'd become a woman too soon, and the thought frightened her. She especially didn't want boys to notice her large breasts, which Aunt Clotilda had warned her "are much too big for a girl of your years."

Sometimes Pete would wander down by the railroad tracks, and once he invited Rosacoke to go there with him. She wished he'd take her to the moving picture show, as she wanted to see Narcissa's jealous eyes when she showed up there with him to see a Lana Turner movie. But he never did. Once, down by the railroad tracks, he showed her how he'd learned to

imitate locomotive whistles, and he was good at it. But she still would have liked an invitation to the local movie theater, which was playing *The Trail of the Lonesome Pine* with Henry Fonda, her favorite actor.

One day Mrs. Riddle asked her to take some food up to Pete who'd been in his bedroom all day. He hadn't come down for either breakfast or the midday dinner. She knocked on his bedroom door, but he didn't answer. Peering in to see if something bad had happened to him, she found him lying on the floor, his head underneath the dusty bed, sobbing like a child. "I'm a wreck," he said when he reared up, looking embarrassed at having her find him in such a position. "I'll never learn anything. I cram my noodle with facts, and the next morning they just go out my ears. I never retain anything."

"Don't go saying that. You're gonna be the smartest lawyer in these parts."

Often quiet and moody, he would sometimes confide in her. He possessed some vague liberal feelings and seemed to want a purpose in life other than to drive his daddy's coupe all over the county and play hillbilly music. "I feel I can help people. Do some good. God didn't give a lot of people much up in the head. Some of us who've got more sense have to help out our brothers. Right now there are crippled children down in the holler lying on the cold floor screaming in pain."

"What can you do about it?"

"A lawyer—now a lawyer can really help people, instead of just taking their money. That would be a useful career for me, if only I was smart enough to learn what's in those books. I've got to raise money to put myself through college, so I don't end up some dumb tater-raiser."

"No one I know goes to college."

"I'll go," he said. "I mean, if I made enough money after college to have a pot on the stove and a roof over my head, I'd be doing just fine. I wouldn't charge much money for my services either. I'd hit up those who had it and let those off who didn't."

"That's real fine sounding."

She figured Pete got his idea of being a lawyer from Mr. Riddle. The old man had always wanted to be a lawyer himself, and once he'd worked as the assistant to a county judge. Pete, she'd learned, used to attend courtroom cases with Mr. Riddle, and once he got to sit in on a murder trial. Pete got so wrapped up in the innocence of a young Negro man accused of knifing a white boy that he cried when the prisoner was convicted and sentenced to death.

Pete had no racial prejudice. Mr. and Mrs. Riddle were well-respected in the community, and Pete could associate with any family he chose. However, Rosacoke noticed he often preferred the company of poor white trash on the other side of the mountain, and he admired Negroes, especially their

music.

Once he brought two old Negro minstrels, Moss and Fry, to join in one of the Riddle's country hoedowns. Rosacoke knew them and had heard them play many times, as both men were famous throughout the county. Fry was nearly bald and wore a slouchy hat, the kind of headgear often put on a country mule on an August day. She'd never seen him without that hat, but in the presence of Mrs. Riddle he removed it. As he did, his glistening copper-colored pate shone in the light of the parlor. Moss was silvery haired and had plenty of it.

Often in the company of a harmonica player and a washtub bass-player, Moss and Fry would show up at country fairs and square dances. Sometimes when the pickings were slim, the team would go from door to door, serenading the occupants, hoping to pick up a few coins or perhaps an invitation to dinner.

Under the influence of Moss and Fry, the hoedown that night had more jive than Rosacoke had ever seen. To her, Pete—inspired by the team of black men—had never been better. Mr. and Mrs. Riddle were politely restrained, not giving the music their usual gusto.

Later, Rosacoke overheard Mr. Riddle tell Pete, "It ain't proper, son, to bring nigras into your mama's house. I've got nothing against darkies personally, but it goes against the teachings of the Bible to socialize with them." He spoke with the certainty of the Apostle Paul. "It upsets your mama, though she'll never complain, and you know her health ain't been too good lately."

Pete never answered his papa, but Rosacoke could tell he resented what had been said to him. Retreating to his room that night, he never again brought the minstrels around.

Pete spent most of his time every day with his books. Mrs. Riddle told Rosacoke, "I fear that boy is going to rot his brain right in his head, trying to stuff in so much learning. It ain't natural. Growing taters is natural work for a young man. A family can eat taters. A family can't eat book learnin'."

A lot of the boys from down in the holler agreed with that verdict, and Pete often had to prove his manhood. A cocky boy given to sudden temper fits, he occasionally got into fights, although he never seemed to pick one. When cornered, he had a reputation for attacking his opponent with a vengeance, and he seldom, if ever, lost. Once a boy picked a fight with Pete and ended up with a fractured nose and cheekbone. After that, most of the boys in the county had a grudging respect for Pete.

The only thing Rosacoke could never figure out was where Pete went at night. Sometimes she'd work late, lingering around pretending to do chores after Mr. and Mrs. Riddle had turned in early. Secretly she hoped that Pete would ask her out on a date. Instead he'd tell her good night and head for his Ford, spinning the wheels as he hit the open road.

Alone, Rosacoke would cut across the field using a flashlight, making her way back to Sultan's shanty, where things seemed to have grown worse since Aunt Clotilda died. To buy bootleg whiskey, Sultan had sold her chickens. With the eggs gone, their diet had been meager, consisting mainly of salted sowbelly, polk salat, hoecake, molasses, and beans. Sultan owned a rifle and when he didn't have moonshine under his belt he would go hunting, often returning with a squirrel or possum. Once he turned up with a turtle.

Sultan wasn't around much these days, as his attention seemed to have become completely occupied by Emma Lou Hayes. He always complained of having no money. "What kind of job could I get?" he asked Rosacoke one day. "Working a scrawny holler field?"

One night Rosacoke returned to find the house empty, not an unusual occurrence. After cleaning the shanty, she'd gone to bed, but had a troubled sleep. Just as the morning sky brightened into day, she'd awakened, stretched out on the hard cotton mattress. She scanned the dim rafters overhead. A spider web gleamed in a sunbeam, and motes of dust danced into her little loft like diamonds. She looked over to notice that Narcissa's mat hadn't been turned down.

Still half asleep, Rosacoke was suddenly alerted to the sound of a car in the distance. She recognized the familiar noise. From the little upstairs window, she spotted Pete's '34 Ford coupe. Narcissa was getting out of it to sneak across the field where dew lay like silver.

Rosacoke's face twisted into a pitiful grimace, and her hazelnut eyes welled and shimmered with tears. She buried her head in the pillow to muffle the sound of her weeping. When she heard Narcissa climbing the ladder to their loft, she feigned sleep.

Her mind raced on. She'd always prided herself on her virtue, yet if that were driving Pete from her into Narcissa's arms, was it worth it?

No boy had ever asked her out on a date. The white boys shunned her because she lived with Narcissa and Sultan. No Negro boy, she reckoned, would dare ask her out, not that she would accept anyway. Besides, there was no decent place in the county she could go with a black man.

If Narcissa could get dates, especially with Pete, Rosacoke figured her roommate must know what she was doing and was doing it pretty well. Beginning that very day, Rosacoke made up her mind to copy some of Narcissa's slutty ways.

If looking like a cheap Saturday night whore had its rewards, and that prize included Pete Riddle, Rosacoke felt she'd better change her image, and not waste too much more time being a good gal.

\*\*\*

For the third day in a row, his mama had urged Pete to mow the hay to

feed the three cows they kept down in their small stable. The weather stayed unseasonably warm, but there had been no rain. The fields were brown and thirsty, having lost their summer green.

"My back is out," Pete told his mama. Actually there was nothing wrong with his back. He'd been laying out late last night and didn't want to work some dumb country field.

At the kitchen sink, Rosacoke turned to face them. "Sultan don't have no work," she said. "He's often hired to mow hay for white people like yourselves."

"That's a great idea," Pete said, his eyes brightening.

"I don't know," Mrs. Riddle said. "Why should we be paying out hard-earned dollars to hire a nigra man when I've got this strapping young son?"

"I told you," Pete said, growing impatient with his mama. "My back is out." He turned to Rosacoke. "I'm gonna go over and see Sultan right now and hire him for the job. Is he at his shanty?"

"It's a hot day, and when it gets this hot, there's only one place to find Sultan, and that's over at the Blowing Rock Falls. That man loves those falls. He spent practically every afternoon there this past summer."

"I'll go over there and hire that buck right on the spot," Pete said, rushing out the door before Mrs. Riddle could object again.

In his Ford coupe, Pete felt a tingling excitement racing through his body. Instead of autumn approaching, he felt it was a spring day. His sap was rising. His heart was beating faster and faster as he drove to the falls. Those urges he'd been feeling were growing strong and stronger in him as each day passed. He was going to start acting on some of his secret impulses the first chance he got.

He braked his car at the edge of the dusty dirt road and jumped out. He pulled his shirttails from the confines of his pants. He didn't remove his shirt but unbuttoned it completely, exposing his sculpted chest to the early autumn day. He headed down a steep rock-strewn path toward the falls which were hidden in the dark forest. No girls ever went down here, because it was known as a place where boys went skinny-dipping.

Pete had gone once or twice but was too embarrassed to go again. When five trashy white boys from down in the holler had come to the falls at the same time, and had chucked off their overalls, the sight of their male bodies fully nude had given Pete an instant hard-on. He had a hard time willing his erection to go down so he could get out of the water himself and go home.

Through the brush he could hear the sound of the falls, and he knew he was almost there. He was breathing heavily at what he was about to see. He figured that Sultan was not the type of man to go swimming in the falls with a bathing suit. If there was a God in heaven, he knew he was going to get to see that buck stark naked with his dick and balls on display before

Pete's ravenous eyes.

He'd heard tales about Sultan. He was said to visit the beds of some white women when their husbands had to leave the county on business. The rumor was that once a white woman went to bed with Sultan she was ruined for life. After getting fucked by this stallion, no woman could ever be satisfied by any puny white man again. Sultan was said to have the equipment to reach depths inside a woman where no man had ever gone before.

The roar of the falls grew louder and louder. Pete remained protected by the brush. The sound of the falls would drown out his footsteps.

As he peered down into the falls, he thanked Rosacoke in his heart for telling him where to find Sultan. Taking advantage of the unexpected good weather, Sultan had indeed gone to the falls. He was splashing around right under the cascading water, the rippling muscles of his perfectly sculpted body clearly visible. Pete could see Sultan's body just from the waist up. He wanted to see everything.

God granted his wish. Sultan emerged from behind the cascading falls and moved out of the water with the grace of an athlete. He maneuvered himself up on the largest rock at the falls and stood tall and straight, his face turned to the sun, his body nude like an Olympic statue. He stretched his powerful arms into the air.

Pete gasped for breath. He'd seen a lot of pasty white boys swimming nude at the local YMCA, but he'd never taken in such a glorious sight of such perfect male beauty. He wanted to devour all of Sultan's body, absorbing every inch of it and imprinting it on his brain forever, but his eyes focused on only one part of this sculpted man. His groin.

His *café-au-lait* skin was silky smooth as it glistened in the mid-afternoon sun. His biceps and neck and shoulder musculature looked more like they'd been created in a sculptor's studio than down in some darkie's shanty. His huge hairless chest was a riot of hard muscle, his pecs like chiseled teak. As he stretched his arms again, muscle rippled across muscle down his lats and stomach.

Even though soft, his cock was thick and meaty. It was uncut dream meat, a rich, nutty brown in color. It hung down at least eight inches from his body. Up to now, Pete didn't know any man had eight inches soft. Sultan's ballbag also hung low and heavy, full of promise that spoke of creamy riches waiting to spew forth.

Sultan lay down on the rocks, letting the sun bathe his body as he'd let the falls bathe it before. He ran his fingers across his rippling muscles, fondling and squeezing his nipples. Gradually the long fingers on his beautiful hands traveled lower to his brown nest of pubic hair. He tugged real hard on that hair. Pete had never done that before. Even when playing with himself.

Without touching his dick, Sultan's dick thickened and started to rise. Biting his lip in a kind of sexual desperation and tension, Pete was mesmerized by this endless dick, which was up like a pole, reaching its final length. Ever since he was fourteen Pete always felt he had a big dick but nothing to match Sultan's. His piece of man flesh must be a foot long. It was a sight to behold. Pete fantasized what it would taste like.

Finally Sultan's fingers wrapped around his cock as he pulled the skin back. To Pete's surprise, the large full knob was not a nutty brown like Sultan's foreskin but a bright pink head. Gently but with increasing pressure, Sultan began to move his fingers up and down his cock. He was jacking himself off in the sun.

Propelled by a desire that overcame him like none other before, Pete could not hide in the bushes any more. He tried to will himself to stand still but broke through the brushes anyway. He wanted this man even though he had little idea what to do with him. The branches of a rhododendron slapped his face and he propelled himself out of hiding and into the clear light of day.

Sultan immediately stopped jacking off and reared up to look at him. "What have we here?" Sultan asked, not at all embarrassed by his nudity. He didn't seem angry to have caught Pete spying on him. If anything it amused him, and he smiled, flashing Chiclet white teeth.

"I'm sorry," Pete mumbled. "I was looking for you. Wanted to offer you a job."

Sultan stood up from on the rock, then slid off it with panther-like grace, making his way across the shallow water to the bank of the falls. Pete couldn't help noticing that his full erection had not diminished an inch. If anything, it looked bigger and more ominous than before.

As Sultan moved closer to him, crystals of water still clung to his skin. Pete stepped back, stumbling over a tangled vine and falling down on the sand.

Sultan stood over him, a towering giant. "What kind of job did you want me to do for you?"

Pete looked up but all he could see was a massive pole stretching out from Sultan's body. It was a fearsome sight. He suspected such equipment was intended more to be admired than dealt with. Maybe women were built to accommodate the equipment Sultan possessed but Pete feared no man could handle it.

Sultan bent down and grabbed a handful of Pete's hair in his powerful hands. At first Pete feared Sultan was going to smash his fist into his face. Instead Sultan raised him up from the ground and removed his unbuttoned shirt, tossing it aside.

He then lifted Pete's left foot into the air and took off his shoe and sock. He did the same for the right one. Pete lay almost motionless on the ground

as he felt Sultan's fingers unfastening his large silver belt buckle. Sultan unbuttoned Pete's pants. When he'd done that, he reached behind and cupped Pete's ass and pulled the pants down, across his legs. Since Pete didn't wear underwear, he was exposed. Just as nude as Sultan was in the afternoon sun.

"Hot damn," Sultan said, appraising his body.

Under Sultan's eyes, Pete's erection bloomed to its fullest. He'd already started to get hard when he'd first felt Sultan's hand grip his hair.

"Except for me and the Adams brothers, I thought all the other men in this county had small dicks," Sultan said. "Now I see you're entitled to join our exclusive club."

"Don't hurt me," Pete pleaded with Sultan, although hating himself for making such a remark.

"Sultan doesn't hurt. Sultan makes white boys feel good." He gently lowered himself over Pete and with his bright brown eyes, he smiled into Pete's own baby blues. Sultan's lips were full and sensuous. The feel of Sultan's naked body over his own skin made Pete nervous but incredibly excited at the same time. Sultan's thick hard cock ground into Pete's groin, as he reached out and embraced Sultan into his arms, running his fingers up and down the muscled back.

Sultan held his mouth only an inch from Pete's lips. Saliva from Sultan's mouth dripped onto Pete. Sultan was already drooling at the prospect of tasting Pete's mouth. Involuntarily Pete opened his mouth to receive his attacker. Sultan's long, probing tongue descended into Pete's mouth. Without ever having known a tongue in his mouth before, he immediately started to suck on Sultan's tongue. That tongue probed deeper as if invading the back of Pete's throat.

The two men continued for at least five minutes to rub their dicks together as they slurped each other's saliva. At this point Pete was aflame and ready for anything, which wasn't long in coming.

Sultan raised his body from Pete's own flesh and in a swift move turned himself around. Pete looked up in amazement, no longer facing Sultan's face but his massive dick. He wasn't sure how to proceed. He seemed fascinated by the single vein that pulsed the length of Sultan's long cock. Tentatively his fingers reached for that cock whose soft skin he found had the texture of brown velvet. A spectacular fleshy fringe encircled the huge cum-slit. Sultan's ballbag banged against Pete's chin. "Suck that motherfucker," Sultan ordered from below as he buried those sensuous lips in Pete's own groin, kissing and nibbling.

Pete grasped the cock firmly, skinning it back as the tangy taste of man musk filled his nostrils. With his other hand, he weighed Sultan's heavy balls in his hand before fondling them and gently massaging them. He started slowly with a flick of his tongue, liking the taste. With the tip of his

tongue he licked the head of Sultan's cock, his tongue darting out to slip inside the fringe of foreskin.

Gradually but with inexorable force, Sultan was gliding his long dick deeper and deeper into Pete's mouth. Every tastebud in Pete's mouth seemed assaulted with the most delicious flavor. Up to that moment, he had never known that anything in God's world could taste that good. It sure beat his mama's apple pie.

As his mouth was raped, he greedily sucked on the invasion, working his lips around this man flesh as it neared the back of his throat. Only then did Pete gag and back away. Sultan pulled back too as if to grant Pete a little air before relentlessly invading again. Pete willed himself not to gag.

Mind-shattering explosions of sensation shot through his brain as he worked that cock. He heard Sultan moaning with pleasure and Pete knew he'd reached some supersensitive tissues. Sultan's hips began a randy ramming rhythm as he worked his cock in and out of Pete's mouth, invading then pulling back, but never letting the bulbous head go beyond Pete's lips. The thickness made Pete fear that his jaw might become unhinged. He'd worry about that tomorrow.

When Sultan seemed secure that his own cock was being properly serviced by this inexperienced but eager young white man, he called up to Pete. "I always eat what I'm about to fuck."

At first Pete thought Sultan was going to take his cock in his mouth and suck it. But he had other plans.

He licked below Pete's dick as his long thick tongue swallowed one of Pete's balls, bathing it thoroughly before he released it to wash the other one. If his mouth weren't stuffed, Pete would have screamed in ecstasy. Sultan then grabbed each of Pete's buttocks in his strong, firm hands after he planted tiny little kisses and bites on each of the mounds. He seemed to be pulling Pete's asshole apart, stretching it to the limits. Sultan started blowing hot blasts of his breath into Pete's sensitive crack, causing Pete to squirm in pleasure.

Without warning, Sultan's tongue darted inside Pete's hole. Pete stopped sucking and reared up from the ground. He'd never known such a tingling sensation in his life. Until that moment he didn't even know that anybody ever ate anybody's else's asshole, certainly not that it was the greatest sexual sensation he'd ever experienced.

Sultan continued his invasion and Pete thought he was going to cum if Sultan kept this up. He kept that licking, darting tongue moving firmly against Pete's sphincter, and Pete opened for him the way a Saturday night whore would open for her john. Sultan's face pressed hard against Pete's quivering bottom for the assault. Sultan was now roaming freely inside Pete's rectum, tasting the delight of this raunchy white boy. At one point Pete clenched his ass muscles as if capturing Sultan's tongue and wanting to hold

it there forever.

Sultan seemed to sense that Pete was rapidly approaching orgasm, and he obviously was not going to allow that. Before Pete could protest, Sultan's tongue plunged deeper and deeper as Pete squirmed more and more. It was like Pete was getting fucked and in a way he was. Pete ground his ass harder and harder into Sultan's lapping face, his rectum vibrating with pleasure. Pete was rapidly approaching orgasm but Sultan once again had other plans.

When he had Pete completely in bondage to his own sensations, Sultan glided out of Pete's mouth and withdrew his tongue from Pete's ass, leaving Pete moaning and unsatisfied. Pete cried out for relief as he lay there in the hot sun. In a sudden move, Sultan lifted Pete's ankles into the air, resting them on his shoulders. He looked down at Pete with a savage, slavering grin as if signaling that he had the boy totally within his power.

At that moment Pete was ready for anything, although he wasn't exactly sure what was about to happen. Pete's ass was still sloppy wet as Sultan entered him. He felt like some giant oak log was ramming the gates of his ass. At first there was a sharp pain that knifed him. When he started to cry out, Sultan descended lower onto Pete's face, biting his lips. Before his final plunge into Pete, he bit harshly into Pete's shoulder. The pain from that assault caused Pete to momentarily forget about the attack on his ass. He loosened up and allowed his invader to take the final plunge. Pete screamed out into the afternoon air but only birds flying overhead heard him.

Pete struggled at first but Sultan had him totally impaled. He was giving Pete time to adjust to the invasion before beginning his assault. Pete felt his whole body consumed in flames. Every nerve seemed on fire, sending all sorts of mixed signals to his brain. Sultan continued to chew and gnaw on Pete's shoulder. Low animal grunts of satisfaction escaped from Sultan's throat. Pete let out a loud moan and threw back his head, his fingers digging into Sultan's back.

"Fuck me, you bastard," he shouted up at Sultan's face. "Fuck me with that big, nigger dick and fuck hard."

This time Sultan followed his command. As he pounded into Pete, the younger man felt he was going to die, a victim of his own ecstasy. His love-tunnel was on fire and that huge throbbing cock was filling every cranny. Sultan would withdraw except for the huge head, then plunge deeply into Pete again. Every time he did it, Pete imagined his guts being sucked out with Sultan.

Pete wrenched his neck around so that he came into contact with one of Sultan's tits, which he devoured voraciously.

Every one of Sultan's strokes grew more savage than the next. Sultan was working himself into a powerful sweat. His fuckthrusts grew harder

and harder as Sultan worked more brutally, going faster and faster. He was fucking the cum right out of Pete, and Sultan hadn't even touched Pete's hard dick. Trapped into this lusty assault, Pete felt he was having an out-of-body experience. The time and the place meant nothing any more. He wanted to remain in the throes of this heavenly hell forever with the ceaseless assault on his butthole lasting into eternity.

A scream of some wild bird in the forest momentarily distracted Pete but other than that he concentrated fully on his approaching orgasm. He cried out as jets of hot, thick cream blasted out of him and onto Sultan's belly. As if to time himself, Sultan blasted inside him, and Pete's arms reached up to pull Sultan's head closer where he licked and sucked his lips, as blast after blast came from his own body and from the body of that plunging stallion who hovered over him. Animal grunts and growls escaped from Sultan's throat.

His mouth only an inch from Pete's, he said, 'Cuse me while I lap up some of that white boy cream while it's still good and hot. I'm going to make you think you've died and gone to faggot heaven."

A bolt of lightning flashed through the sky, marking the debut of a storm. Pete didn't care how hard it rained. Let the raindrops fall. All he cared about was this man in his arms, draining his saliva and slurping and licking all over his body.

***

Why shouldn't she dress up pretty like some of the other girls and go out and meet her Prince Charming? For years, she'd identified with Cinderella, and, like that fairytale heroine, she, too, was a servant, both at Sultan's shack and at the Riddle household.

Narcissa wore all the fancy clothes, but it was Rosacoke who was blonde and beautiful. Although Narcissa knew how to make herself sexy to attract men, she wasn't really beautiful. A mighty good-looker, but not beautiful in the way Rosacoke was. Certainly not sweet and innocent, in the style of Cinderella alias Rosacoke.

Like Cinderella, Rosacoke hid her beauty, a deliberate act of camouflage. A lot of that was done out of fear. The taunts of the boys at school about the size of her breasts were one thing, Sultan yet another. She'd catch him spying on her when he didn't think she was looking, and she didn't like the leer in his eyes. She always slipped in and took her bath in the kitchen tub when he was off with the lowdown Emma Lou, and Rosacoke always made sure that she was fully dressed when she was around him.

Without telling a soul, she was saving up her money to buy a pretty dress so she could be as resplendent as Cinderella in the picture book. In her finery, she planned to head straight for the school dance Saturday night.

No boy had asked her out, and in spite of some snickers she expected to hear, she'd go alone if it had to be.

She'd spotted the dress at Belk's Department Store and had asked the know-it-all clerk, Mary Hemphill, if she'd hold it for her on the lay-away plan. With a sneer, the old maid had reluctantly agreed after calling the store's manager, cigar-puffing W. G. Gabriel, who had the same name of the angel but apparently shared no other similar qualities.

Nevertheless, W. G. agreed to let her lay the dress away if she'd put two dollars down and pay that much every week. Days before the dance she still hadn't paid for it, but W. G., over Miss Hemphill's objections, had allowed her to take the dress to a cramped little sewing room at the back of the store to be altered.

Here a friendly, gray-haired woman known to everybody as "Mama Grace" greeted her with mischievous eyes and a sparkling wit. Mama Grace had deft fingers and just instinctively knew the alterations that were needed to make the pink and red dress fit perfectly. A little too perfectly in some places, Rosacoke feared.

"You're a right pretty gal," Mama Grace assured her. "Probably the prettiest thing likely to show up at that dance. You're not the only girl who's been in here for a fitting. You're a sure-fire winner when it comes to breasts, though."

Rosacoke blushed in embarrassment.

"Better behave yourself at that dance," Mama Grace warned, as Rosacoke left the sewing room with dress in hand. "You could get in a heap of trouble running out with the wrong kind."

She assured Mama Grace that she'd take plenty good care of herself. W. G. let her carry the dress out of the store, because she'd been faithful up to now in making her payments. She was to continue to pay two dollars a week until the account was marked closed. Afraid that Narcissa would see it, perhaps even wear it, she hid the dress in the attic of the Riddle house.

That night she stole a tube of Narcissa's lipstick and spent an hour or two practicing applying makeup in the mirror, freely using Narcissa's generous supply of powder and rouge. Over the past few weeks she'd carefully watched as Narcissa had made up her own face, and Rosacoke was determined to copy her style.

Sultan had run off and had been gone for three days, probably laying out with that Emma Lou. Rosacoke had come to pay his disappearances no mind. She and Narcissa often lived alone, and this feeling of isolation in such a deserted place threatened her.

It didn't seem to bother Narcissa at all. Only last summer she used to take off all her clothes before an open window, with the kerosene lamp on. Even though their shanty was at least a mile from the nearest road, Rosacoke always slipped off her dress in the dark. You never knew who might be

standing out there in that lonely field looking in.

Before she was scheduled to report to work at the ticket window at the picture show, Narcissa came home early. She'd been tired a lot lately because Rosacoke knew she went every night after work to the Blue Note Café. The joint catered mainly to Negroes, but an occasional white boy wanting to meet up with some black gal also went there.

After Aunt Clotilda died, Rosacoke hadn't had much to do with Narcissa. Tonight, even though she looked tired, Narcissa seemed downright friendly. She usually came at Rosacoke like a pit bull.

"I think me and you should bury the hatchet," Narcissa announced. This struck Rosacoke like a bolt from the blue, and she immediately suspected Narcissa's motive. Narcissa wasn't known for extending a helping hand, unless someone filled up that empty palm.

"I've got no gripe against you," Rosacoke said, feeling a little uneasy.

"Good." Narcissa reached for a Lucky Strike from her pack on the window sill, lit it, and turned to look at Rosacoke. "We're not little girls no more. We've grown up. I'm already big enough to quit school, go out with men, and earn my own way. Just like you."

"I earn my own way, too, but I'm not quitting school until I get my high-school diploma. As for those men you're talking about, no one's asked me out."

"You don't go about it in the right way." She seemed jittery, nervous, as if wanting to say something, but reluctant to come right out with it. "Yeah, coming over here today, I made up my mind I don't need to fight with you. You've got nothing I want, and I'm sure I've got nothing you want."

"Except Pete!" Rosacoke's words rolled so fast off her tongue she shocked herself.

Narcissa, however, didn't seem in the least bit surprised. She laughed in that funny, feline way she had of doing. "I've had Pete. Put another way, he's had me. Don't tell me you have a crush on that buck."

"It should come as no big news to you that I like him a lot. He don't pay me no mind."

"Pete goes out with a lot of girls—not just me. He's only a boy. A fill-in when I don't have a real man like Hank Adams."

"That Hank Adams must be nearly ten years older than you," Rosacoke said.

"And he has an extra inch for every one of those extra years."

Rosacoke didn't know what that meant. She was still flabbergasted at Narcissa's choice of a man. "Why, he's the meanest snake in the county."

"He's got a mean snake all right. Remember on the way to grandma's funeral when he grabbed himself?"

"I sure do. I thought it was disgraceful."

"Whatever. The other night I ran into Hank at the Blue Note Café. He

teased me again, and I stood right up to him. I'm afraid of no man. He grabbed himself again, and I bet him he didn't have all that much to hold onto. That's when he invited me to climb the mountain. I did and I've been scaling that peak ever since."

"Just the other night I spotted you getting out of Pete's car."

"So what? Pete matches Hank in the basket department, but there's a big difference. Hank knows how to use his equipment. With Pete, I just feel he's going through the motions. You get real passion from that sexy Hank."

"Hush, gal. That's no way to talk."

"I'm crazy about that big hunk of mountain man, Hank. He's getting a job up in Chicago, and he's taking me there. He's even promised to tell people up there I'm Spanish. Puerto Rican, maybe."

"You gonna run away?"

"You bet your right knocker." Narcissa crushed out her cigarette and stood up, walking across the wooden plank floor to confront Rosacoke. "There's where you come in. I'm calling a truce. I figured you might find out what I'm up to, and you've got to promise me you won't let Sultan hear of it."

"I won't tell. But I figure you're plenty young to run away and all. With a grown-up man to boot."

"Honey, I want to break into show business up there in Chicago. Learn to sing and dance. Strut my money-maker a bit. I can't do it on my own, but with Hank's help I can."

"I sure do wish you luck, but I'm not exactly sure how Hank is going to help you break into show business."

She made a face, rolled her eyes and yelled, "This is Lady Luck herself you're talking to. Miss Narcissa Cash is gonna see her name up in lights."

"I hope you know what you're doing. Sounds crazy to me."

"So what do you know? The way you're going, you'll end up salesgirling it in some five-and-dime."

"I'm sticking around at least till I finish school."

A look of distress crossed Narcissa's face. "When I go, I want you to get the Riddles to take you in. Me and Hank have talked about it. He don't trust Sultan one minute alone with you, and I don't neither. I hate to say that about my own daddy, but he looks at me the same way he looks at you. One night he'll come home drunk and I won't be here to look after you the way grandma did. I can stand up to him, but you're too jellybelly."

"I guess you're right." A sense of awful dread came over her.

"Hell, yes, I'm right. Now that I've finished with him, go after that Pete. He almost measures up to Hank. Better serve up the cherry to Pete *before* letting Sultan get his gooey lips on it."

"I told you to hush talk like that! You've got the filthiest tongue I've

heard. I don't think such thoughts."

"You'd better start. To begin with, if you want to get Pete, quit fixing yourself up to look like some church mouse. What boy is gonna go for you when you mope around looking like you do? Call attention to yourself. Boys like gals with flash. Wear some tight sweaters. Flaunt those knockers."

"I don't feel right showing myself off like some Jezebel."

"You'll get used to it."

A guilt troubled Rosacoke, and she wanted to confess. "I've been into your makeup. I stole a tube of lipstick and made up myself like a brazen hussy. I got a dress, too. Red and pink. From Belk's Department Store. It ain't paid for yet. I want to go to the dance Saturday."

"Why not? And don't worry about the lipstick. I got plenty more where that came from. 'Bout time you wore lipstick. Tell you what, I'll make you up and help you get all sexy looking for the dance. Sorta get your motor running. And if you keep quiet about my running away with Hank, I'll do you one even better. I'll ask Pete to take you to that damn white folks' dance. He'll be your date."

"Don't do that. I'd die. I'd just die."

"That Pete owes me a favor. And how!"

"But he don't...doesn't think I'm pretty."

"Listen, sweetcheeks, when we get through with you, that white boy is gonna flip out of his ever-lovin' mind. You'll be fighting him off before the first rooster crows."

\*\*\*

After his encounter with Sultan, Pete went to bed early without his supper. In spite of the urging of his mama, he couldn't even think about food. He was hungry—not for 'taters and steak—but man-cream.

Alone in his room with the lights out, he stripped naked and lay on his bed as the Carolina moon bathed him. He planned to remember every enticing detail of that afternoon at Blowing Rock and experience the thrill all over again.

He couldn't believe he'd told Sultan that he loved him. When Pete drove Sultan back to his shanty, Sultan had laughed off that revelation of love. "We call that pillow talk," Sultan said, "but you weren't resting your head on any pillow. More like a rock. I've heard a lot of white women tell me they love me while they're licking my big balls. But the next day they might see me coming down the street and cross over to the other side to avoid running into me. That's how far the love of white folk goes."

As he pulled his coupe to a stop up the road from Sultan's shanty, Pete wanted to thank the stallion for what had happened at Blowing Rock. But

how in the hell did one man thank another man for that? He blurted out his offer of the mowing job.

"How much does it pay?" Sultan asked.

"Ten dollars," Pete asked.

"That's a lot of money." Sultan thought for a minute. "You got that much money on you now."

"Yeah."

"Give it to me," Sultan said.

"You mean, all of it?" Pete asked. "Right now. Before you do the work."

"Honey child, I done did the work back there at the falls. You don't think I go through all that shit we did just for the fun of it? The only people I fuck for free are young white gals. When I go with men of any age, or with women over thirty-five, especially fat white women, I charge ten bucks apiece."

"You're a ..." Pete hesitated, not certain exactly what the word was.

"A male whore. Is that what you're trying to say?"

Pete looked at Sultan in astonishment. "I've heard of women whores, though I've never seen one, but I've never even heard of a male whore."

"You don't see me out working none too much in the fields, now do you? And Sultan always knows how to get his whiskey. I fuck a lot of people in this town. I got five steady men clients. Of course, they're all fat and over fifty and have an ugly wife at home and five or six youngin's. Believe it or not, there are quite a few queers in this county. Pudgy white men who like to suck big nigger dick. Take W. G. Gabriel at Belks Department Store. I feed him the pork at least once a week."

"Gabriel is a queer?" Pete asked in astonishment. "But he's married. How can you be a queer and married too?"

"It's called keeping up appearances," Sultan said. "Queers in this county can't let the word get out that they are what they are. So they get married, have children, go to church on Sunday. Shit like that. But behind the barnyard they're sucking the cock of the first hired hand they can get."

"You are certainly giving me an education," Pete said, "One I can't get from any book learning."

"Hank Adams does the same thing I do," Sultan said, smiling that perfect smile with those Chiclet whites again. He seemed to be amused at shocking Pete with his revelations.

"He's a male whore too?"

"Just like me," Sultan said. "Me and ol' Hank service the same men. Sometimes guys like Gabriel hire us both at the same time. He likes me to fuck him while he sucks off Hank."

"I never heard of such tell. I mean Hank is known as the stud of the county."

"One of the studs," Sultan said. "Narcissa says that the women get together in the crapper and talk about us men. She says that the general opinion is that there are only a handful of young men in this county worth messing up your mouth with. Of course, there's Hank Adams. All of the Adams boys, in fact. Tracy and Karl are growing fast, and are gonna give Hank some competition. And then there's Pete Riddle. No one knows you're queer except me. I'm just some nigger you enjoy sucking off in some hayloft. But Pete Riddle is the one guy in the county that all the white girls dream about marrying. That's what Narcissa says."

"There are some other nice-looking guys in the county," Pete said, thinking for a minute. No image came to mind. "Well, maybe not that many."

"Me and you are it, baby. And ol' Hank. He's got a dick on him like you do. As for the rest of the pasty-ass whites in this county, I don't think one of them has more than four inches to stuff into his wife."

Pete hastily reached into his wallet in his left hip pocket and removed a crisp ten-dollar bill he'd just withdrawn from the bank. Since he was smart in book learning, his mama let him do all the banking for the family.

Sultan held up the money to the light as if inspecting it to see if it were real. "I earned this money and I really showed you a good time. I really got into it. With most white men, I just close my eyes and think of some pussy while I'm plowing into them." Sultan stuffed the money in his pocket and got out of the car.

"When am I gonna see you again?" Pete asked.

Sultan smiled at him. "As soon as you get another one of those crisp ten-dollar bills." He reached for Pete's shirt and pulled him toward him from behind the wheel of his Ford. "I gotta go," Sultan said, pulling Pete's face toward his. "Let me give you a little nigger-lip to remember me by."

After about two minutes of the most delectable kissing, tongue sucking, and mouth slurping, Sultan released him and turned immediately on his heels and headed across the barren field to his broken down shanty.

In bed that night, Pete vowed he was going to go to the bank first thing in the morning and withdraw ten ten-dollar bills. He wanted to have them ready for whenever he got those special urges again.

As the hours went by and sleep didn't come, Pete dreamed on and on. He must have relived the scene with Sultan at the falls a hundred times in his mind. It was like seeing a movie over and over again. It'd been his first time with a man, and it was a special experience that would be etched in his brain forever.

As midnight came and the moon rose high over the holler, his mind, with a will of its own, drifted from Sultan to Hank Adams. If there was a white boy in the county that matched Pete in good looks and sexiness, it was Hank Adams. Both of them dated Narcissa.

Until Sultan's revelation of secrets that afternoon, Pete had never real-

ized that Hank would have sex with a man. He was surely the most masculine-looking young man in the county. There was nothing sissy about him. Any man who ever picked a fight with Hank, if he were that foolish, never did so again—that is, if they lived to tell about it.

Pete tried to picture what Hank looked like without his clothes. All sorts of images flashed through his brain but none was satisfying. After that experience with Sultan, he wanted the real thing. He wanted to taste, lick, suck, and slurp. He closed his eyes tight and imagined that sexy Hank pounding deep into him like Sultan had just done only hours before.

Pete recalled Sultan talking about how queer men had to keep up appearances. Pete planned to do a lot of that too. He'd continue to pursue women even though his heart just wasn't in it. He was a natural born actor and could put on a good show for the gals.

He wasn't exactly sure how to go about it, but beginning tomorrow morning he was going to chase Hank Adams in deadly pursuit. If that good-looking fucker was a male whore like Sultan had said, Pete wanted to sample what Hank had to offer.

Just thinking about what Hank would do to him caused Pete to experience a throbbing hard-on that just wouldn't go down.

\*\*\*

Narcissa kept her promise. From a drab-looking country girl, Rosacoke was transformed into a glamorous young woman. Of course, Narcissa had a lot of raw material to work with in Rosacoke—confident eyes, a challenging smile, and an impudent chin. A fine forehead and slender neck, as well as a nose, straight and classic, had been gifts of nature, but Narcissa always believed in improving on natural God-given assets. Gilt paint on the lily held no terror for her.

Rosacoke was born with full, perfectly developed lips. Ignoring that, Narcissa painted above and below Rosacoke's natural lip line, the way she'd seen Joan Crawford do in an old movie.

Makeup brought a metamorphosis to Rosacoke's face, and the transformation shocked her. No longer looking like a scullery maid, she felt cheap and vulgar in her reincarnation, like the low-down Emma Lou, yet she knew it was a look men responded to. Rosacoke's straggly eyebrows were plucked into a distinctive arch, and her honey-blonde hair was lightened to an ash white with peroxide.

"Sugar, I know enough about hair to work in a beauty parlor," Narcissa claimed. "I struggle to make my own head of steel wool gorgeous. But your hair is soft and naturally pretty."

Under Narcissa's ratting comb, squiggly bangs and tight curls twisted over Rosacoke's ears, giving way to a mass of spit curls crowning the top

of her head. Tiny poufs formed over her ears, and wispy curls adorned her temples. Like an overly decorated birthday cake, her mass of blonde hair became a confectionary dream.

When the last touches were applied, Rosacoke admitted to herself that her own look was stunning. She'd not completely outgrown her clumsy, awkward adolescence, but she would have fooled anybody. Like white jade, her skin was intensely pale, as her summer tan from working the fields had long ago faded. Before the mirror she held up graceful hands, not daring to touch her own face, as if she would destroy the illusion. Imitating Narcissa, she pretended to be alluring, with an enticingly slow, sulky smile.

"*La-dee-dah* and *Kee-RICE!*," Narcissa said, holding up the pink and red dress from Belk's. "This would be just great if you want to go as a Shirley Temple Valentine. I got something hotter and sexier. I bought it for myself to wear to the Blue Note."

She went to her closet and took out a silk jersey dress in panels of white and navy wrapped with a white cummerbund. This was an expensive-looking dress, and Rosacoke knew at once Narcissa didn't earn that kind of money selling tickets at the picture show.

"Okay, okay," Narcissa snapped. "Hank sometimes runs bootleg liquor for Herb Hester. Hank bought the dress for me when he was in Richmond. With that bootleg money, we're heading for Chicago."

Rosacoke held the dress up in front of her body before a broken, oval-shaped floor mirror that had belonged to Aunt Clotilda's sister. "I couldn't wear this. I mean, it's the prettiest, softest dress I've ever seen in my whole life, and I'm right grateful and all. But it shows the flesh right between my breasts. I'd feel naked as a jaybird!"

"That's the whole idea. Men dream about getting hold of some plump, firm melons like you've got. Better make that cantaloupes. Put on the damn dress. If the boys at the dance feel they're getting just a little tiny peek-a-boo at those boobs of yours, they'll be moist all evening."

"Such talk, I do declare." In spite of her uneasiness, she slipped on the dress which held her breasts in prominent positions without a brassiere. She stood for a long moment, looking at herself in the dusty, smeared mirror. The image that greeted her resembled a Hollywood movie star.

Mesmerized by her own vision of herself, Rosacoke asked, "Do you think I really could go to the dance like this?" Already she was intrigued with the idea. "Do I dare? I mean, no gal in the county wears clothes like this. This is something Carole Lombard would wear, and she's got Clark Gable."

"You'd be out of your mind if you didn't show up in that dress. *Gee-zuz!* You'll have Pete coming at you like a wild-ass pig in heat. Can you handle it?"

"I don't know."

"I wish my clothes did that much for me. She-it! If they did, I'd stand Chicago on its ear when I get there."

"Hell with it, I'm gonna do it."

"That's good. 'Cause Pete Riddle's old Ford is just now coming across the field."

***

From the moment his eyes locked onto hers, their relationship underwent a dramatic change. His appreciation of her new look seemed to cover her body like a hot, sudsy bath, one you could drown yourself in.

"Cutie-pie, I don't think me and you have been properly introduced," Pete said. "Whoopie! There's gonna be a hot time in the old town tonight." He stood there in a shiny new brown suit with a peppermint-striped shirt.

"Pleased to make your acquaintance, sir." She smiled as she pretended a mock curtsy.

"Rhett Butler has met his Scarlett." Reluctantly taking his eyes off Rosacoke, he nodded to a cold, disdainful Narcissa. She suddenly seemed to resent her own transformation of Rosacoke, perhaps fearing it took attention away from her.

Pete had never been inside their shanty before, and it was obvious he disapproved of the way they lived. "My god! You might be Scarlett, but this isn't Tara." He took in the bare plank floor, with its huge cracks. "You people live close to the ground, don't you?"

To Narcissa, that remark was like throwing water into a bubbling, crackling iron skillet of bacon fat. "Goddamn it, you're not above comin' down here to our little ole cottinpatch to knock yourself off a piece of ass."

"Narcissa!" Rosacoke blushed in embarrassment, avoiding Pete's eyes.

"Now don't you go getting upset, honey," Pete said, hoping to calm Narcissa. "All I meant was that both you pretty gals should live in mansions. You deserve it."

"*Shee-it!*" Narcissa barged toward the kitchen.

"See you later," Pete called after her.

"Not if I see you first, you white mothahfuggah."

All jittery and nervous, Rosacoke headed toward the door. "Come on. When she gets real mad like this, it takes a long time for her to cool off."

In the car moving up the dirt road, she didn't know what to say to him. Her eyes took in drying cornstalks, cut and bundled for feed, and she dreaded another long, cold winter. At least the car was warm. A coontail dangled from his rear-view mirror, and his guitar rested right below the back window.

A storm seemed to be brewing. A farmer in clay-crusted brogans

stood silently in the fading yellow light. Lightning slashed across the sky.

Head tilted back, Pete stared glassy eyed at the road through half-closed lids. She thought she smelled beer on his breath.

He turned to her and smiled, taking his eyes off the open road for a dangerously long time. "You've been hiding yourself from me up to now. I didn't know you looked like you do."

"What on earth do you mean?" She knew perfectly well what he meant, but wanted to hear him say it anyway.

"Take that hair. That's the blondest hair I ever saw except once on an albino baby. You're like some sweet angel who's never tasted anything but sugarcane all her whole life."

She giggled nervously, a hand over her mouth. "You do have a way of sweet talking a gal, Pete Riddle. I heard tell that about you."

Clouds piled like dark pillows in the twilight sky, split every few minutes by flashes of lightning. He drove along for a little while, saying nothing, and then abruptly shot his brown- and white-shoed foot onto the brake pedal. His coupe squalled off the road to a sliding halt at a picnic ground, deserted since last summer.

He kept the headlights on, as he stared deeply into her eyes. "You look like the kind of gal who could meet every human need a man could ever have. If a man had you, he wouldn't want for anything else. Not ever. Not in his whole life."

A sense of panic overcame her. She'd expected him to be aggressive at some point later in the evening, and she was hardly prepared to deal with that. So soon after leaving the shanty, she was taken by complete surprise at his forward approach. Did he have no respect for her, taking her to be just like that Emma Lou or, about as bad, like Narcissa? She tried to find her voice, and when her vocal cords could formulate sounds, the words came out weak and broken. "Settling down with just one girl isn't exactly the reputation you have. From what I hear."

"Fuck what you hear!"

She had angered him, and this made her all the more nervous. He'd never said a curse word in her presence before. The only man she'd ever heard use such language around her was Sultan.

"What you've heard about is the way I used to be. You could make a new man out of me. A reformed one."

"Wouldn't that miraculous stunt be like parting the Red Sea? How would I go about it?"

"By saying right now—this very minute—that you're going to be my own little sweet angel."

He gazed at her with what appeared to be a serene honesty and a childlike absence of guile. The look, however, was hungry, revealing his need, and it was so powerful she felt she wouldn't be able to resist it if she

didn't turn her eyes away from him right this minute. "I'm not going to go giving myself away so easily and so fast to the first boy who comes along with a good line. Let me out of this here car if that's all you've got on your one-track mind."

He slipped closer to her, as she adjusted her dress, her stockinged knees tight together.

"I'm just made of flesh," he said. "I can't help what's going on in my mind. What's in my heart. All I know is that you're like a sweet juicy peach bursting before my very eyes. You're like something that would step out of a chocolate box on Valentine's Day."

She felt he knew how to press the right buttons, and say just the right thing to a woman. "I sure do appreciate all these compliments, I sure do. On the other hand, if we don't get this car pointed in the right direction, we're gonna be late for the dance."

Breathing a deep sigh that sounded like regret or perhaps defeat, he slammed the car into gear and headed up the road to a dilapidated roller rink that had been converted into a makeshift dance hall for the evening. He flipped off the radio which had been playing "Down the Road a Piece," the boogie-woogie hit record of the past year.

He glanced at her with a lopsided leer. That leer might have distorted some man's face, but it gave his a raffish charm. When she felt he wasn't looking at her, she stole glances at him. She'd be right proud to walk into that roller rink with him on her arm.

His forehead was high and intelligent, and his prominent cheekbones were also high, his cheeks slightly concave planes. His full, sensual mouth opened occasionally to reveal white shining teeth. These, combined with a small cleft in the heart of his chin, made him almost too handsome. His tousled and wavy light brown hair gleamed with coppery lights, and, unlike the other boys in the county, with their closely cropped hair, he wore side-burns. She'd heard that some boys, tough redneck skinheads, had once tried to hold him down and cut his hair, only to have him slug his way out of that and bash in a few teeth. After that, people still made fun of the way he wore his hair behind his back, but no one wanted to challenge him any more to his face.

"You know, that dress you're wearing is the kind of dress a city girl would wear. There won't be one country girl there tonight dressed like you. Does that scare you a bit?"

"It does. A whole lot."

"Just promise me one thing before we get there."

"What's that?"

"Stick right by my side for the whole evening. If another boy comes up and tries to dance with you, I'll tell him where to go."

"Thanks, Pete. And thanks also for taking me out."

"I'm the lucky one. I'll have to fight them off when they take one look at you tonight."

If Pete's prediction were accurate, it would be the fulfillment of a long-ago dream. One day she planned to emerge from her cocoon and show the world she was really a butterfly. The metamorphosis had come sooner than she'd expected.

To all the people who'd made fun of her, putting down her clothes and her look, this was her night to show them.

\*\*\*

It was past dusk when Pete's coupe pulled into the parking lot of the roller skating rink. The thunderstorm had been brief. A gray wash of light still lay over the sand-bottomed parking lot, and lights burned in all the big windows, drawing at least 300 people to the country music of homespun Sleepy Eyed John and his Brushy Mountain Boys.

On the way there, Pete had driven her past empty storefronts which had been closed during the early years of the Depression. No one had been able to reopen them, although she listened on the radio almost nightly about the nation's recovery.

The roller rink stood in a hillside field beside a country road about a mile outside of town. Mud-splattered pickups and battered cars, including a lot of Model Ts, filled the lot.

Even before she climbed the steps to go inside the roller rink, Rosacoke realized Narcissa's style of dress didn't belong on her, at least not here. Rosacoke was still a country girl, and Narcissa, in spite of her coppery color, wanted to be another sultry imitation of Lana Turner. Without Pete at her side, Rosacoke would never have dared to parade into that dance hall.

One woman at the door sold roasted peanuts in little brown paper sacks, and Pete bought her a nickel bag. She didn't want to be seen eating peanuts, feeling that wasn't a very glamorous image, and left the bag on an empty chair.

Inside, the place was bleak and stark, the illumination provided by glaring exposed bulbs overhead. No one could afford decorations that year. Folding chairs were lined up beside plain long tables. The dance was supposed to be chaperoned by Herb Hester, the bootlegger, but Rosacoke couldn't spot him.

She surveyed the crowd of people in front of her, as the amplified sounds of the Brushy Mountain Boys filled the rink. Not one pair of overalls was to be seen, not one flannel shirt. The girls wore mostly cotton dresses, and the boys were dressed in their Sunday-go-to-meetin' clothes. These sons of dirt farmers tossed their dates, often sharecroppers' daughters, into the air in a wild jitterbug.

Without asking her, Pete gently pushed Rosacoke onto the dance floor, and as he twirled her through the air she overcame her self-consciousness. With all that blood rushing to her head, she didn't have time to get embarrassed. Pete was such a fantastic dancer, it was all she could do to keep up with him.

After the dance, Pete led her toward the wide open verandah that flanked one edge of the hall. Along the way, Rosacoke encountered the daughter of the local sheriff, Claude Billings. On her boyfriend's arm, Wanda Mae looked her up and down. "I never seen you so dressed up before. That's a real fancy outfit you've got on there."

"Thanks," Rosacoke said, resenting the way Wanda Mae's boyfriend was staring directly at her breasts.

"Don't thank me," Wanda Mae said. "I didn't say I liked it—I said it's real fancy. Looks like something Narcissa Cash would wear to the Blue Note."

"Get lost!" Pete said, brushing past them and directing her onto the verandah where the night air made her shiver.

"It's cold out here after the rain," she said. "Can't we go back inside?"

"Hold your horses. I've got something to warm you up." He reached inside his coat and pulled out a Mason jar wrapped in a paper bag. Rosacoke noticed several couples on the verandah swilling moonshine.

"Honey, I believe in letting 'er rip on Saturday night," he said. "A good pint or so of corn under my belt, and I become a new man." He looked at the other girls drinking the corn whiskey of their boyfriends. Fearing she'd lose him if she didn't join him, she reached for the pint.

Bracing her mouth and throat for the liquid assault, she downed her first drink of liquor, cut with Seven-Up. "*Whooooeee!*" she shouted. "That's the most powerful stuff I ever drank. But I showed you, didn't I? I didn't choke, not one bit. I willed myself not to cough." She was right proud of herself, and Pete was, too, rewarding her with a quick kiss on the lips. It was just a brush of his mouth against hers, but the sensation was enticing enough to make her shiver. She had a few more drinks before bowing out.

Back in the dance hall, she noticed that many of the young men on the prowl hadn't brought dates. Some of these same boys who'd ignored her at school now asked her to dance, but Pete stood his ground, guarding her as if she was his personal property. She liked that feeling of belonging to somebody. In all her life she'd never felt as if she belonged to anybody, including her mama. After having been ignored by the boys for so long, she enjoyed the attention her new look received, even if she felt her sudden popularity was for the wrong reason.

"That whiskey burns in my gut," she whispered to Pete.

"Herb Hester, our missing chaperone, calls it trachea torching bootleg stuff."

The dance hall spun dizzily around her, like a ride on a merry-go-round. Giddy with pleasure, she felt almost weightless, or at least twenty pounds lighter.

From the makeshift stage, Sleepy Eyed John called out the steps to a square dance, and Rosacoke joined Pete on the floor. "It's gonna be a whole night of hoedown music," Pete promised.

After an hour of intense dancing, she grew tired and excused herself to go to the girls' room. After checking her makeup in a lone broken-glassed Coca Cola mirror, and trying to ignore the disdainful glances of two of her classmates, she went back onto the floor, waiting for Pete.

He was nowhere to be seen.

***

Pete was heading for the men's outhouse down by the river. He'd had a bit to drink and that white lightning and the ginger ale caused him to want to piss real bad.

In the foul-smelling toilet, he was glad for the chance to relieve himself but a bit disappointed as well. The place was empty. Usually at such square dances he'd seen some good sights at the urinal as he'd pissed the night away with some of the young men of the county. His heart always beat faster when he stood next to a man as he unbuttoned his pants and whipped it out. Pete liked taking advantage of these free shows.

Tonight he stood all alone. He stayed an extra long time in the toilet hoping some guy would come in to take a piss. All the other men had been drinking just like he had, and Pete knew they must need relief in the same way. He figured the other guys were pissing in the dark woods, not even bothering to make it all the way to the crapper.

As he made his way back to the dance barn, he was blinded when a flashlight was abruptly shone into his eyes. "Stop right in your tracks." The power behind the flashlight shut it off, and when Pete's eyes adjusted to the moonlit forest he spotted what looked like the sheriff, Claude Billings, standing tall in his uniform.

Pete had always had a crush on Claude. He sure didn't look like any caricature of a pot-bellied southern sheriff. Tall and lanky, the handsome, lean-faced Claude always reminded him of Gary Cooper. Pete attended every Gary Cooper movie showing at the local cinema. He had a crush on Gary Cooper too.

Cooper was just an image up on the silver screen, but Claude Billings was alive, here and now, a real presence.

"I got a bone to pick with you, boy," Claude said. "I just talked to my daughter, Wanda Mae. She claimed you threatened her."

"I just told her to get lost after she made some crack to Rosacoke—

that's all," Pete stammered.

"That's not the way Wanda Mae told it," the sheriff said. "And my daughter is a good Christian gal. I've never known her to lie." He grabbed hold of Pete's shirt and yanked it real hard. "You wouldn't call my daughter a liar, now would you?"

"No, sir, I didn't mean nothing by that."

"Wanda Mae told me something else too," Claude said. "She said you're carrying white lightning on you. Illegal hooch. Not only that, but you're forcing a minor, Rosacoke Carson, to drink the stuff. And she is a minor, even though she's all dolled up to look like a Hollywood whore. It looks like I got quite a few charges to file against you."

"Please, Mr. Billings," Pete pleaded. "I won't do it again. I'll apologize to Wanda Mae. I won't buy any more white lightning. I just did it to keep up with all the other boys who bring it to the dance. I don't even like the stuff."

"Come with me, boy," he said. "Let's go down to my squad car. A night in jail might sober you up."

Claude pushed Pete into the passenger's side of the front seat and slammed the door, getting in on the other side and taking hold of the wheel. The sheriff did not start the car at once but looked over at Pete. "Like I don't have enough charges to book you on, I got one more."

Pete looked at Claude with total fear. The sheriff had him under his power. "What do you mean?"

"Sodomy," Claude said. "There are sodomy laws in this state."

"I haven't broken any laws."

"Bullshit!" The sheriff slapped Pete's face real hard. "Don't lie to me, you little queer. I was fucking Emma Lou Hayes up near Blowing Rock Falls. Whenever I pick up that whore, I haul her up there, even though I make her walk back after I've fucked her. As I was going back to my car, I spotted some guys on the bank of the falls. It turned out to be a man and a boy. Name of Sultan and Pete Riddle. In all my born days I've never seen a man suck off another man. Much less a white boy eat a nigger dick. I stayed around for the whole show. I even saw you get fucked by a big nigger dick. And you sure seemed to be enjoying it."

Pete sank into the car seat as his whole world seemed to dissolve into mud around him. He didn't say anything. Tears welled in his eyes.

Claude looked over at him. "There is a way out of all this. That is, if you're willing to go along with it."

"I'll do anything, mister." Pete said, his voice jerky as his throat was drying up. "Anything. This could ruin me. I'd be driven out of the county."

The sheriff leaned back into his seat and slowly and sensually ran his long fingers along his own crotch, feeling, weighing, and fondling. "All my life I've wanted someone to go down on me and eat me like you were

slurping away at that nigger. I've always wanted to feel a human mouth on my dick. I've never got no one to do that to me before, not even a nigger whore. I might forget all charges against you if you were up to doing that for me. Really pleasure me like I need pleasuring."

Pete couldn't believe his ears. There was a way out of all of this. He could not only get the sheriff to drop the charges, but he could fulfill a fantasy he'd always had about Claude, and that was to taste what he had resting between his legs. Pete couldn't actually face the sheriff. He was far too embarrassed to do that. In a voice hardly audible, he said. "I'll do that for you."

"What are you waiting for? Reach over and take it."

With trembling hands, Pete reached for the sheriff's fly and slowly unbuttoned his pants, the sheriff rearing his hips up to give Pete greater access.

Pete fished into Claude's pants and felt his dick, reaching below to fondle his balls. The dick was nowhere near the size of Sultan's nor even Pete's own prick. It felt a bit small really, but Pete liked the silky feel of it.

In semi-darkness, Pete pulled out the sheriff's cock, skinned back the head and gently lowered his lips over it. He felt it harden at once. With one hand, he reached inside the sheriff's fly to fondle his balls as his mouth engulfed Claude's prick.

By the time Pete had swallowed all of the sheriff's dick, it had risen to its full six inches. For the first time in his life Pete realized he didn't require a big dick to enjoy a man fully. Sultan choked him but the sheriff's cock seemed perfect for sucking. It was easy to handle and he was loving riding up and down on it with his succulent lips.

With his hard-on buried inside Pete's mouth and throat, Claude was obviously enjoying the ride as well. "Yeah, boy," he said, rearing his hips up as if to feed more of himself into Pete, although there was no more dick to swallow. "My boy's got a pussy mouth. Better than any pussy I've ever had. Oh.... *Oohhhh shit!* I'm gonna cum. I don't want to cum! I want this to last a *long* time." He reached for Pete's head, clamping the boy tightly onto his pulsating dick. "I'm fucking creaming. Your mouth's just too hot. I can't take it no more."

Claude's cock felt hard as steel in Pete's mouth as it exploded. The sheriff seemed to be going into convulsions. Long after he'd exploded, Claude continued to force Pete's head down on his deflating cock. Pete didn't want to pull away. As far as he was concerned, he could remain buried between Claude's legs forever. Even in his fantasies about Claude, he didn't expect the man to taste that good.

Pete gently kissed and licked the sheriff's cock until it had returned to normal. Finally, Claude released his head and let him sit up in the passenger seat.

Pete couldn't look Claude in the face. Even though he'd enjoyed what he'd done, he felt deeply ashamed.

"I guess I have up and forgot all those charges I had against you," Claude said, slapping Pete on the leg. "You're one good boy. I know why the Riddles are proud of you, son."

"Does that mean I can go?" Pete asked, as a sense of great relief swept across him.

"You'd better go," Claude said. "That big-tit Rosacoke will be wondering where her boyfriend's been all this time. Mind you now. The next time you see my daughter, Wanda Mae, you be real nice and gentlemanly to her."

Pete thanked the sheriff and blurted out several promises. Confused and his mind a blur, he didn't even know what he was saying. "Thanks, sheriff," Pete said before heading back to the dance. He wiped his lips. He could still taste Claude's semen in his mouth. He never wanted to brush his teeth again.

After telling the sheriff good night, Pete walked toward the clearing and the path that led back to the square dance hall. Before he'd gone twenty feet, Claude called him back to the squad car.

Fearing he still might arrest him, Pete obeyed the sheriff but couldn't help but notice how shaky his knees were as he headed back.

"There's one thing I forgot," Claude said, making eye contact with him for the first time tonight. He reached for Pete's wrist and held it in a firm grip.

"What's that?" Pete asked, trying to conceal the fear in his voice.

"Meet me at Blowing Rock Falls at four o'clock tomorrow afternoon." Claude released Pete, turned the ignition to his car, flipped on the lights, and headed down the bumpy dirt road.

Pete stood for the longest time watching him drive away before walking up the hill to where the sounds of country music filled the night air.

That and the sound of a distant whippoorwill.

*** 

Rosacoke was waiting on the large verandah in front of the barnlike hall. "I thought a snake had got you," she called out to Pete when she saw him coming from the river.

"Took longer than I thought," Pete said, blushing. "Ran into someone I know. Sorry to be away from you for so long."

"You were gone just long enough for me to get into trouble," she said. "I guess it was the white lightning talking, but I went up to ol' Sleepy Eyed John when his boys took a break. I told him that he was just no good when it came to singing country music—and that his Brushy Mountain Boys were

not much better."

"You did what?" He was horrified.

"I told him they might play at some little hick shindig, but that was about it. I told Sleepy Eyed John he couldn't even carry a tune. So you know what the bastard did?"

"Slugged you in the mouth."

"No," she said. "He asked me did I know anyone in these parts who was any better. Pete Riddle, I told him. I said to him that he ain't heard country singing until he's heard Pete Riddle."

"You told him all that?"

"I sure did. Not only that, Sleepy Eyed John said that if you were so darn good, he's gonna give you a chance to prove it. He's gonna announce you. Let you get up there and sing."

"You mean get up there and make a big fool out of myself," Pete said.

"Pete Riddle, if you let me down this time, I'll never speak to you again. You can sing real pretty. Here's your chance. Go for it."

At first he looked hesitant but then a devil-may-care grin broke across his handsome face. "I'll go for it. Maybe some sad ballad with a bluesy guitar break. None of that right-way-to-skin-a mule shit that Sleepy likes so much. Fetch my guitar from my car."

When she came back from the parking lot with his guitar, Pete was already on stage chatting with Sleepy Eyed John and the boys in the band before he was introduced to the suddenly silent crowd, all of whom knew Pete, although few had heard him sing, except those who attended the same church.

Taking off his suit jacket and borrowing a large, dirty cowboy hat from one of the Brushy Mountain Boys, he reached down to retrieve his guitar, winking at her as he did. He looked nervous, the way you'd expect a singer to be making his first record. "I'm just a backwoods cat," he called into the microphone. "Just like the rest of ya."

Rosacoke could tell that he'd deliberately made his voice sound more hillbilly than it was, which gained him an immediate rapport with his young audience.

As Pete launched into his sad song, a love ballad, his voice was filled with a harshness and raw power she'd never detected in it before. The number he'd selected was "Sparkling Blue Eyes," and in it he sang of a "ramshackle shack down in old Caroline that's calling me back to that gal of mine." Unlike the lackadaisical style of Sleepy, Pete was much more sincere, giving it his all. Honest emotion came forth from his vocal cords, as he sweated heavily under the lights. His back bent, he half sang, half yodeled his song, as he hunched over the microphone. As he closed his eyes his notes sounded almost painful, as they bounced off the walls of the roller rink.

Suddenly, he dipped his knees forward, a rhythmic action so sexually suggestive it sent a murmur through the girls at the dance, shocking Rosacoke. At the end of the ballad, he was greeted with the evening's most thunderous applause. Hoots from mountain boys filled the air. Freed of the confines of the church and the restrictions of the Riddle home, he emerged as a natural performer, drawing immediate inspiration from a live audience.

"And now I want to bring up, as the songs says, that gal of mine. Rosacoke Carson. For a duet."

Although she recognized her name, it seemed so distantly related to her as to have no bearing on her at all. It took moments before she could even believe that he'd called out her name, publicly identifying her as his gal. She was so struck by that pronouncement she still hadn't gotten it into her head that he'd asked her to get up and sing with him in public, completely unrehearsed. With his coon-dog keen ear, he just seemed to know they could sing a smashing duet.

Reaching for his hand, she felt his comforting presence. He whispered so close to her ear his lips brushed against her lobe. "Don't worry. They'll love you. Let's do *You Are My Sunshine*. I know you know that."

Woodpeckering her head, she snapped her fingers to the beat. The moment her voice launched into the song with Pete, she knew her own sound was a natural blend with his. Although she cut off a word when he didn't expect it, and sometimes placed the emphasis on the wrong syllables, he was able to follow her and cover for her if she ended a sound before he did. Even though it was a love song, her voice seemed fervent with fundamentalist religion, an Appalachian purity, as she took the melody and he sang tenor harmony.

At the end of the song, he kissed her on the mouth, right in front of everybody, as the dance hall erupted into applause, demanding more from them. But Sleepy Eyed John wasn't having any more numbers from these amateurs. He got the Brushy Mountain Boys to switch to their loudest song.

"We sound close enough to be blood kin," Pete told her as he led her off the stage.

After the duet, he needed a swig, and invited her along, his guitar strapped across his back. On the way to the verandah, Sleepy Eyed John caught up with them.

"What'd you think of our act?" Pete asked, all smiles.

Sleepy turned down his lower lip. "If I didn't see how white the two of you was, if I had my eyes closed, I'd swear two niggers was up there singin'."

"I'll take that as a compliment," Pete said.

"I didn't mean it as such."

Rosacoke tugged at Pete's arm, wanting him to break away, fearing a

brawl.

"You're good enough to get a group together," Sleepy Eyed John said. "You know the type of boys. A harmonicist and a washtub bass-player. Maybe somebody will toss you a few coins, like we do the nigger shoeshine boy on Main Street."

"You son of a bitch!"

She tugged even harder on Pete's arm, pulling him toward the verandah, as Sleepy Eyed John turned his back on them, mounting the stage.

"He don't mean what he said," Rosacoke told Pete. "He's just jealous."

"Fuck him!" Pete turned and glared at her. "I told you to stop saying, 'he don't.' Now that you're my gal, I'm gonna make a class act out of you."

"I'm sorry." Tears welled in her eyes.

Out on the verandah again, he swigged down more moonshine, and she volunteered to have another stiff drink herself, feeling she needed it. It staved off the cold, and she'd also gotten a case of the shakes after singing in public like that. Her duet with Pete had taken place so fast she didn't have time to get nervous before going on.

He was drunk, and getting drunker, and filled with a kind of spite, and, strangely, also an overriding ambition which the corn whiskey had seemed to fuel within him. "I'm not gonna end up here with some tobacco-spittin' crew of ne'er-do-wells. Singing songs comes natural to me, but what I really want to do is argue law."

"You will. Just give it a little time,"

"Let Sleepy get a kick out of sticking a go-to-town shoe up to some little pickaninny to shine. That's about the only person on Main Street he can feel superior to. That's not for me. One day I'm gonna leave that Main Street so far behind they'll speak of me, and everybody will claim to have been my friend, even though I hardly knowed most of 'em."

Without warning, he grabbed her and kissed her. Not a light stage brush this time. A full fledged kiss. As she gasped in surprise, he inserted his tongue between her teeth on a mission of discovery of her mouth. Completely caught off guard, she didn't know that men put their tongues in your mouth when they kissed you. It didn't seem quite right. Indecent somehow. Still, it was thrilling as he held her tight. She enjoyed his strong embrace, the masculine scent of him. He had the kind of arms a girl could lose herself in.

"Let's clear the hell out of this dive."

In the Ford, he offered her some more moonshine, which she turned down. Her head was already swimming, not only from the liquor, but from the passionate kiss. As his brakes screeched, he drove the coupe forward, hitting the open road and speeding. "What you gonna remember about

tonight?"

She wanted to tell him to slow down, yet didn't want to nag either. Nervous as she was, she tried to answer his question. "It was the first night of my life I felt really grown up. Singing with you for the first time." She blushed in embarrassment. "Getting kissed and all."

"You mean you've never had a man kiss you?"

"Never!"

"I can't believe that."

"It's true," she said. "I wouldn't lie about such a thing."

"I believe you're telling the truth. My God!" An excitement was reflected in his face, which was illuminated by the glare of the headlights. It was as if he were thrilled to be the first. Other thoughts seemed to form on that face. "Hot damn!"

"You know I'll sure remember tonight. "How good it was."

Leaning closer to her, he pulled her toward him with his strong right arm. "Baby, I want to give you something to really remember it by."

She pulled away. "Don't you go spoiling it. It's been good up to now. Don't ruin it for me. Please."

"Since when is a man giving his gal some lovin' ruining it?"

"I didn't mean it that way."

"You want me to take you home then? No place is open this hour, 'cept the Blue Note."

"Are you gonna go there after you drop me off?"

"Maybe. You may be my gal, but you don't own me. I'm a man who has to have some lovin' when I need it. I can't wait around one year, two years. I got needs now! It's not natural to wait."

She burst into tears. "If being your gal means giving in to your wants, then I'm not gonna be your gal. I'm not like Narcissa. I'm a good girl."

"Any gal who denies her man some lovin' is not a good gal in my book."

"You better read that book again, 'cause I'm no pushover."

"Okay, okay, forget it!" The tires squealed as he speeded around dangerous hairpin curves, taking out his frustrations at the wheel. He remained silent for the rest of the ride.

To break the monotony on the way home, she read the road signs out loud.

Near Sultan's shanty, he pulled the car off the road and into an abrupt stop that jolted her forward.

Bracing herself on the dashboard, she said, "Thanks. For taking me to the dance. Singing with me…and everything. I truly enjoyed it. I really did."

"I'll see you around."

She opened the door for herself and got out, and without a good-bye he reached over and slammed it behind her, leaving her standing there in the

cold night in the cotton patch. His headlights jiggled and bumped, fading into the night.

As she made her way across the dead, brown field, she found herself crying, and the tears wouldn't stop.

A kerosene lamp burned in the front room, making shadows on the croaker sack covering the window. Had Narcissa remained home for one night of her life? Rosacoke hoped she wasn't in that room with Hank. Fixing her face and wiping away her tears, she adjusted her dress under her coat before going in.

When she opened the door, she spotted Sultan, lying drunk and half naked on the battered old couch. He'd come home from one of his mysterious trips, and his being here, with so little clothing on, frightened her.

"Get your sexy white ass in here, woman, and shut the God damn door."

# Chapter 3

Sultan's big eyes seemed to stare right into her, like a house dog's, as she took off her coat. Those eyes then moved up and down her body, as if absorbing her with a terrible intensity.

A primitive fear spread through her, and she wished Narcissa were in the house. She was embarrassed not only by the way he devoured her, but by his lack of clothes.

Wherever he'd disappeared to this last time, he'd come back with a different look. His dark hair had been clipped to a crewcut, a thick brush that made him appear older and tougher. Rippling with muscles, he was ruggedly attractive, his body like that of a young superman. Just as his eyes moved up and down her body, she, too, took in his tall, sculpted frame, pausing only for a second at the nest of dark hair revealed through the opening of his thin cotton shorts, which also framed blatant evidence of his masculinity.

"I've never seen you made up like that," he said. "You're like a dirty filthy slut. Just couldn't wait, could you? Mama's hardly cold in her grave before you're running around painting your face and showing off your tits to everything in pants."

She swallowed hard, "Night. I'm gonna go to bed. I'm real tired."

"Not so fast, woman." He rose from the sofa. "Bring me another jug of Herb Hester's moonshine."

Reluctantly obeying him, she went to the cupboard where she knew he stored his liquor and brought him the last jug along with a clean tumbler. She sat both down on a broken-legged table next to the sofa, and, as she turned to leave, he grabbed her by the wrist, imprisoning her in his grip.

"Narcissa told me you were out with that whorechaser, Pete Riddle."

"We went to the dance—that's all." She tried to break free of his hold, only to have him tighten his grip.

"What went on with you two? Did he get into your bloomers? Pete don't go out with no woman 'less she puts out."

"Nothing like that." The way he talked, so accusing like, hurt her pride. "We sang a duet, danced some, and came right home."

"So if he didn't get your cherry, did he make you go down on him?"

"That's disgusting! Let me go."

He released her, and she yanked her arm away from him, rubbing her wrist to ease the soreness.

"Pour me a drink, bitch!"

Not wanting to arouse his anger, she poured some of the homebrew into the tumbler and handed it to him. In one swallow he gulped down the entire contents. "Another one. And have a swig yourself. You're old enough."

"No thanks, like I said, I'm gonna go to bed." She poured him another drink.

In one sudden move, he tossed the tumbler on the floor, the liquid running down a crack in the crude planks. "Listen to me, and listen good. You're gonna do exactly what I tell you. I've kept my hands off you, even though I know you're hot for it. I've seen the way you've looked at me. You've lured me, too, with those big tits just busting out all over the place and that blonde hair. Now that ain't very nice, is it? To get a man worked up and out of control and everything."

Flushed and breathless, she drew her lips tightly against her teeth, glaring at him fiercely, almost daring him to harm her.

His neck swollen with a rising surge of blood, he looked down at her with flaming anger. "You little blonde hell-cat! You've put me off long enough."

She backed away from him, moving toward the kitchen, wanting to break into a run, but fearing he was too quick for her. Wishing she'd kept her coat on, she felt completely vulnerable and exposed in Narcissa's dress.

He slapped her, and the sting had hardly stopped smarting before he hit her again. He advanced toward her, grabbing her shoulder in a fierce grip, pushing her back into an old armchair.

She scratched at his face, and, as she did, his fist crashed into her jaw, sending her sprawling into the chair. It was such a bone-jarring shake she was nearly blinded, as he came crushing down on her with such force she felt she'd be smothered.

He ripped off the top of her dress, exposing her breasts. Instinctively her hands reached to cover her nipples. It was then that the sweet-sour shock of his tongue invaded her mouth.

She bit down.

He yelped in pain, drawing back, rubbing his lips. With a balled fist, he pounded into her nose. Blood spurted out. In shock, she could taste it. Moments passed before the full impact of the blow hit her.

Holding her down, he twisted powerful fingers into her curly hair. Before a sound could escape from her mouth, he caught her sharply across the lips with the back of his hand. Her protest was silenced, reduced to a muffled gasp.

She'd fallen to the floor, and as she gazed up at him, his cock stood out from his underwear, long and thick, demanding relief. The violence with her had stirred up his lust. "I've got a big fat lollipop for you, cunt, and

you're gonna take care of me. If you bite me again, I'll kill you."

He yanked her to her wobbly feet. Her breasts bounced wildly as she struggled and kicked, trying to free herself of the nightmare. Throwing her back against the armchair again, he took his rough hand and plowed it up her dress, pawing her. His cruel, insistent fingers slid up and down her thighs.

With his free hand, he caught her neck in a hammerlock. She felt her stomach roll violently, as she fought to keep from puking. Tears ran down her face, as an excruciating agony shot in bursts through her.

His voice trembled with rage and obsession, and she couldn't make out what he was saying, not that she wanted to know. The room swirled around her, as she sagged into the chair. She wanted Pete to come and rescue her.

Strong fingers dug into her bruised flesh. Her throat constricted, and nothing came out but a high-pitched whine.

She was able to cry out only when he dragged her to the couch, dumping her down like a sack of feed. He clawed her pants down over her squirming legs. Her eyes rolled around in their sockets, as her body trembled.

With her legs up in the air, she kicked him savagely, one foot landing in his face. Screeching, he staggered back.

Her pathway cleared, she darted to the kitchen like a young colt. Recovering quickly, he ran after her, throwing himself against the back door to block it. His shorts had dropped and he was fully nude. She too was partially undressed, still clutching remnants of her torn dress.

He was now moving step by step toward her, and the look in his drunken bloodshot eyes told her he was going to kill her. It was useless to scream. No one would hear her.

Her hands behind her, she felt a bag of flour on the counter. Just as his nails had dug into her flesh, her own nails clawed through the bag, scooping up a handful of the flour. She gripped it tightly to keep it from filtering between her fingers.

"I'm gonna thrash the living hell out of you. When I'm through with you, no man will ever want to look into your beaten-up face again."

When he was close enough, she tossed the flour into his eyes and ran past him, back into the front room and out the door. Flashing through her mind was a vision of him standing there, blinded by the powdery stuff, digging at his eyes with both hands.

She darted through the barren cotton patch, almost enjoying the bitter whipping of a wind that blew through the holler. She didn't stop running until she'd come to a pond where she'd gone swimming last summer.

Here she dared catch her breath. She looked back but didn't need to, knowing he wasn't going to chase after her. He was too drunk.

Never again could she go back to that shanty. That part of her life had ended.

Looking up at the sky, she searched for the moon which was half hidden by the ragged pine trees that formed an umbrella over her. It cast a faint glow over the lusterless dark water of the pond.

Even though it was cold and she was only half dressed and freezing, the thrill of having freed herself from that place warmed her body.

***

Toward the west the land appeared bleak and foreboding, needing the summer sun to make the fields green again. Dark clouds moved slowly over the pine trees in the distance. The heavy wind from the holler kept on howling through the woods, causing the branches to sway.

The time had come for her to make the break with Sultan and Narcissa. She'd never really belonged with them in the shanty, and she knew that all along. What she didn't have up to now was the courage to strike out on her own. Sultan's attack on her had left her with no choice other than running away. Rather than have it come about that way, she wished she'd had the gumption to go right after her mama died. Narcissa had warned her that Sultan might make a lunge for her. The warning was not needed. Rosacoke knew in her heart he would go after her one day. She'd stayed around too long, growing too fast right in front of Sultan's eyes, putting ideas into his head.

To her surprise, she didn't hate Sultan for what he'd done to her or had tried to do. After a night with both Pete and Sultan, she'd come to believe that men had desires that rose up in them, causing them to erupt in a temper fit like Pete or violence like Sultan.

She suspected that a woman held a tighter rein on her emotions than a man, although she wasn't at all sure about that. She didn't know anything about sex. Her awareness of how the coupling between a man and a woman took place was based on no first-hand observation.

As a farm girl, she'd seen animals in heat copulating in the fields, and the sight with all its brutality had upset her so much she wasn't looking forward to her first time alone with a man. There were limits, however, to her restraint insofar as the opposite sex was concerned. She wasn't going to end her days a virgin like that old maid, Mary Hemphill, who'd sold her the dress at Belks. Everybody talked about her and made fun of her for living alone, and Rosacoke had her mind already made up that that horrible fate wouldn't overtake her. She was equally determined that her first sexual experience wasn't going to be a brutal attack like a bull mounting a cow in the field.

She needed some loving, and wanted to feel she belonged to just one

man. If she felt that man really loved her, then she was willing to go all the way. It just had to be the right time—nothing rushed—and the right place with the right kind of feeling in her heart. Was that too much for her to ask?

Her whole body shook as if she were coming down with chills and fever. Narcissa's pretty dress was so ripped and torn it looked like it had been made from a rag sack. Rosacoke feared she'd never earn enough money to replace the dress.

Steering clear of the Negro cemetery, she shivered in the night air, as she headed east across a sharecropper's field, going in the direction of the only place in the county where she felt she'd be welcomed, and, if not exactly that, taken in at least.

The strong muscles of her back tensing, she found herself crying, her tears blinding her and causing her to stumble on a mound of red clay. She reached down and grabbed her ankle, fearing a sprain.

Limping along, she kept on crying. Her face was so chilled that the stream of hot tears burned her cheeks as they trickled down. She felt sorry for herself, and had tried to teach herself not to do that. Self-pity got you nowhere. She was certain that Sweet Jesus blessed only those who helped themselves. At least she'd been taught that at Sunday school.

Knowing that didn't help matters much right now. In this cornfield on his dark night, she resented losing both her papa and her mama, something she shared in common with Pete. Two orphans. Even though Mr. and Mrs. Riddle were hard on her, they doted on Pete. He certainly got better guardians than she'd ended up with in Sultan. "Guardian, hell!" she said out loud, talking to the night wind. Sultan was never her guardian. The only reason he took her in was because he was going to bed with her mama, and for no reason but that, other than the new one that might have occurred to him tonight.

All the tensions that had mushroomed inside her bubbled to the surface, and she flung herself into a bank of dead weeds and bushes. Even though life had long passed from this vegetation with the coming of autumn, it was something to hold onto.

Curled on the ground, face down, she lay motionless, her arm twisted behind her. The same feeling of isolation that had swept over her at Aunt Clotilda's funeral returned, stabbing at her gut worse than before. What had started out to be the greatest night of her life, her emergence as a good-looking, buxom woman out on the town, holding onto the arm of the handsomest boy in the county, had ended up a disaster for her.

In the weeds she buried her face and let herself have a long cry. She recalled that deep at night Aunt Clotilda used to do that whenever a sense of despair overtook her. "Child, when you feel you can't go on in life, let yourself have a good one. Get it all out. Then wake up the next morning, irregardless of how creaky your bones might be, and take one step forward

and go into another blessed sunny day the Lord's given you, thanking him for it."

Following that advice, Rosacoke cried as she'd never cried before, and when she was completely drained, she forced herself up off that hard ground. There were no more tears in her. If a person possessed a tear well, hers had run dry. She figured it would be a long time before it filled up again. Right now, she had to be on her way.

Hugging herself to stave off the wind, she walked as fast as she could, going around a fallen tree that stretched out on the bank of a creek, laying half submerged in the water. With a bitter resolve, she limped to the rise of a hill, where she could look down on the holler. Not one sign of life.

All the problems that had made her cry she tried to wipe from her mind, telling herself that what little brainpower she had must be turned to getting her through right now.

A sudden rustle in the bushes made her feel like jumping out of her skin. It was probably only a jackrabbit, but it could be anything. The night had grown menacing, and she conjured up that every creepy thing in the forest was advancing upon her from its lair.

Panting painfully, she stopped again to catch her breath. But not for long. She inched along, as the sound of her heart beating against her chest was the loudest noise to be heard.

Ducking her head under the low-hanging branches of a hickory thicket, she fell headlong into some briars, scratching herself. Picking herself up, she didn't care how she looked anymore. Earlier in the night, her appearance had meant everything. Now, getting to where she was going was all important.

With her next advance, she emerged into a clearing, where the moonlight illuminated the old gingerbread house.

For a moment she just stood there, afraid to go on. She'd made a big decision, and she risked getting turned away. That didn't stop her. She'd come this far, and she was going every step of the way.

On legs torn and bleeding, she came up to the back porch. The dog was accustomed to her, and he didn't even bark. Rising slowly, he wobbled over to her to lick her cold hand. She enjoyed the warmth of the animal's tongue. His trusting greeting, his familiarity with her, made her feel welcome at the homestead.

It was huddled up with the dog under several bags of potato sacking that Mrs. Riddle found her asleep on the back porch in the early dawn light, when she'd gone out to the smokehouse to fetch a slab of salt-cured bacon.

\*\*\*

All glamour that Rosacoke had evoked the night of the dance had

disappeared as Pete tended to her and nursed her back to health. She was bruised and disfigured. It would take several days for her wounds to heal. She was not only black and blue but badly scratched. Worse than that, she'd come down with pneumonia. Well, maybe not that, but a bad chest infection. The Riddle family doctor, R. V. Fletcher, came every day to check on her condition.

Pete had been all fired up and had wanted to barge into Rosacoke's bedroom and demand that she tell him what had happened to her. He'd wanted to know who it was who had attacked her. Mrs. Riddle tried to calm him and asked him to step out onto the back porch with her. O n c e there, his mama had reached for his arm.

"I don't want to hear you asking that gal what happened to her." Mrs. Riddle's face was stern. "It's clear to me what happened to her. She was raped."

Her words stunned Pete. "Raped? Then we should call the sheriff."

"Hold onto yourself there," her mama cautioned. "I figured this whole thing out. If you sleep with dogs, you're gonna catch fleas."

"What in hell does that mean?"

"To be blunt, Rosacoke lived down there with the niggers. She's a beautiful blonde girl with large breasts. I think some nigger attacked her and raped her. Going to the sheriff is the last thing to do in a case like this."

"And why not?" Pete was adamant, his blood boiling.

"If word gets out that Rosacoke was raped by a nigger, she'd be run out of the county. Everybody would say she enticed some nigger buck into raping it. Her whole life would be ruined. She'd have to go live in another part of the state. You've got to trust me on this one."

"I guess you know best," Pete said.

"Of course, I do. Even if she was raped, she's not gonna press charges."

"Okay," he said. "I guess it's okay. But I'm still going to go over to Sultan's shanty and see if he knows anything."

"Suit yourself but it ain't gonna do no good." She looked toward her kitchen. "I don't want to hear no more about this. I've got to go into that kitchen and make some creamy gravy and biscuits. Your pa is hungry. You can take something up to the gal and try to see that she eats. That one needs to regain her strength. I need help with the chores."

Pete followed her into the kitchen and poured himself a cup of black coffee.

"Is your back better?" his mama asked.

"Still hurts," he said, lying.

"Time is running out on getting someone to gather up the hay," she said. "The days are getting colder."

"I asked Sultan but he won't do it," he said.

"Then go down in the holler and get those Adams boys," she said.

"That Hank is a no-count but his younger brothers hire out to work the fields. They did a good job last summer for the Millers across the way."

The mention of Hank and the Adams boys brought a sudden excitement to Pete. He needed an excuse to call on them, and his mama had just given him one. "Right after breakfast and after I drop by Sultan's to tell that buck Rosacoke is staying here with us, I'll drive over to the Adams place. Their shanty is no better than Sultan's."

"See that you do." She turned from him and busied herself preparing breakfast as he drifted off to the living room, listening to country music on the radio until she told him his gravy and biscuits were on the table.

After he'd carried a tray to Rosacoke and checked on her condition, he went out into the yard and started his coupe. The sound of the motor running sent chickens scurrying across the brown yard, which had lost all of its summer green because of the frost the other night.

He drove to Sultan's shanty, parking on the ridge above. He headed down the washed-out gully that led to the little house. Smoke rose in curls from the chimney, making him realize how much colder the nights had become. People were chopping wood for the winter and building fires to take the chill off. He hoped that a few more days of Indian summer would come before the blast of winter completely enveloped the Carolina hills.

Sultan spotted Pete coming. As Pete came up to the door of the shanty, Sultan was there to greet him. Clad only in a thin pair of white boxer shorts, Sultan looked obscenely enticing to Pete, as memories of that afternoon at Blowing Rock Falls flashed through Pete's mind. He tried not to but Pete's eyes immediately focused on Sultan's ample crotch.

Pete lifted his eyes up to Sultan's to find him smiling mischievously. Sultan lewdly cupped his crotch. "It's all there for you, white boy, any time you get a shiny ten-dollar bill." He stepped back. "Come on in."

Pete went inside. There was no real front door, only a blanket hanging over an opening to keep out the wind from the holler.

Sultan invited Pete to come and stand with him by the fire to warm himself. "I had to come over to tell you that Rosacoke is staying with us," Pete said. "We think she was attacked but she's saying nothing."

"I wondered where she was," Sultan said. "You did say she is saying nothing."

"Not a thing," Pete said. "Do you have any idea who might have attacked her?"

"Could have been any one of a hundred guys," Sultan said. "You know a lot of field hands from out of state come in at this time of year to harvest the apples. All sorts of horny men—all of them strangers—are roaming the county. Whoever attacked her is probably all the way to Tennessee right now."

"I guess you're right." Pete looked around the shanty, sensing the

presence of someone else but saw no one. "Is Narcissa here?" he asked.

"Did you come to see her or did you come for another repeat performance with the master fucker himself?" Sultan asked.

"I came to see you and tell you about Rosacoke."

"A walking newspaper, huh? Narcissa was here last night. But she left his morning to go to town to buy her some more slut rags." He went over to a chair and put on his pants, reaching for a flannel shirt. "I've got work to do myself in town this morning. Gotta make a duty call on Herb Hester's place."

Pete knew Herb very well. So did every other young man in the county. Herb was the county bootlegger. "Picking up some moonshine, huh?"

"I might do that too," Sultan said, sitting in the chair to put on his shoes. "Ole Herb is heading for Tennessee right now to deliver some of his moonshine. When he does that, his wife always sends for me. Herb makes the best moonshine in this part of the world, but he's also known for having the smallest dick. His wife is one horny bitch. I have to go over there to give her a good stuffing when Herbie leaves town. I get not only my usual fee of ten dollars, but often a free quart of moonshine."

"She's a very ugly, fat old sow," Pete said. "I don't know how you can get it up for her."

"That's never been my trouble," he said. "Getting it to stay down is my problem. Right now if you was to reach into that wallet of yours and pull out a ten-dollar bill, you'll see about a foot of nigger dick rise out of my fly in a flash."

This sexual talk sent shivers through Pete. He almost was tempted to test Sultan on that boast. He wanted this sexy man.

Sensing that something was about to happen, Sultan studied him closely, as if anticipating earning ten bucks before rushing off to service Mrs. Hester.

Just as Pete was about to reach for his wallet, a noise from upstairs distracted him. "I thought you said Narcissa wasn't home."

"That's not Narcissa up there in that bed," Sultan said, standing up and tucking in his shirt. "It's Hank Adams. With Rosacoke gone from her bed, Hank and Narcissa shacked up all night. You should have heard them. That Hank can really fuck. Almost as good as me. He had Narcissa screaming in ecstasy most of the night. He really pounded that pussy."

Until that moment, Pete had never heard another man talk that way about his own daughter.

"I know you've slipped it to Narcissa too," Sultan said, "But I bet you didn't drive her crazy like that Hank. I keep telling you. You should sample Hank yourself. I told him about you and what we did at the falls. He said to tell you that he's ready, willing, and able." Sultan paused before pulling back the blanket and heading out the door. "That is, if you've got ten dollars. See you around, stud."

In the yard Sultan called back to Pete. "I forgot. Hank told me to wake him up before nine. He's gotta get back home. Go upstairs and wake him up."

"Sure thing," Pete said. "Then I gotta go myself. Got a lot to do today." As he waved good-bye to Sultan, who headed off through the woods, Pete was shaking nervously, remembering his rendezvous with the sheriff, Claude Billings, at four o'clock that afternoon.

He knew that he could call out to Hank and maybe wake him up. But something told him he wanted to climb up to that loft and shake him awake.

Slowly, trying not to make a sound, he climbed up to the loft and stood looking at the bed where Rosacoke and Narcissa usually slept.

The morning sun shone brightly through the window. Sprawled out on that bed, Hank lay completely nude, the blanket kicked off his body.

Never in all his life had Pete seen such an enticing sight. He'd been powerfully attracted to Sultan, but Hank Adams was the all-time prize. Pete's eyes drank in this sullen but beautiful face resting under a mop of blond hair. If Pete had a mirror, he knew his hunger would be registered on his face.

Hank's long, muscled legs were spread apart in an almost defiant sprawl. His thick, uncut cock lay against his left thigh. It was full of meaty promise. To his surprise, Pete discovered that Hank's cock was very similar to his own. Hank and he could have been brothers.

He bet Hank's cock was truly impressive when hard. His balls were low hanging and swollen. They rested like two large eggs in a fleshy, velvety sac. Pete wanted to bury his nose in Hank's scrotum, just losing himself in the folds of flesh, filling his lungs with the pungent odor. The sight of Hank's nudity made Pete feel drunk.

So intense was he on concentrating on the wonder and glory between Hank's legs that it was a long time before his eyes traveled up to the young man's face.

When he did, he saw that Hank's eyes were wide open. He had a slight look of contempt on his handsome face which, if anything, made him look more erotic than ever.

Hank stretched out on the bed, spread-eagling himself before Pete as if to invite Pete to look and inspect everything.

Pete started to stammer out an apology to Hank for spying on him.

But Hank spoke first. "Know what, Pete Riddle? It tastes even better than it looks."

*\*\*\**

Hank sat in the front seat with Pete who was driving him back to his own shanty. Hank was whistling and looking nonchalant in spite of all that

wild animal action that had just transpired between them. He seemed unconcerned as if it hadn't really mattered. To Pete, it had been a defining moment in his life, as his encounter with Sultan at Blowing Rock had been.

His hands on the wheel shook as he relived the moment when he'd taken that bold step in the loft of Sultan's shanty. Like a predator stalking its prey, he had moved toward Hank's bed where he'd leaned down and reached out for the young man's thick cock. Pete had gripped it tightly, pulling back the foreskin and absorbing the sweaty man-smell of Hank's crotch. With a life and determination of its own, that cock had started to grow, swelling in Pete's hand. When Pete had bent over to kiss the big, round head of it, the cock had shot up to its fullest and most impressive length and width.

Slowly, ever so slowly, Pete's lips had descended on that cock, taking more and more of it into his mouth. Encouraged by Hank's moans of pleasure, Pete had made love to that cock. It had tasted even better than Sultan's. Wanting more, he'd descended lower, burying his nose in Hank's balls where the smell had been riper. With his tongue darting out to lick the loose folds of flesh, Pete had entered heaven.

"Keep at it!" Hank had called down to him. "No one's ever sucked my balls before."

Pete had taken one ball at a time in his mouth, washing and tonguing it before releasing it to attack the other one.

His tongue had wandered down the hairy path to Hank's asshole. Once there, he had taken both of his hands and had pried Hank's cheeks apart, exposing the pink rosebud. As he'd looked up at Hank, he'd noted great surprise on his face.

He didn't seem to know what Pete was going to do to him next. There had been both suspicion there and anticipation. That earlier cocky look of contempt had gone to be replaced by a sense of wonder. It'd been obvious to Pete that he had stirred Hank up.

In doing that, Pete had also realized that he'd had the young man in his power. Pete had felt that he was directing the show, and, if he had his way, he'd been determined to make it a long run before he was finished with Hank. He'd planned to satisfy Hank and even more than that he'd been determined to fulfill himself. Every part of Hank's body would be assaulted and explored by Pete. Only when Pete had been completely satisfied would he grant Hank his release. In the meantime, Pete had been hell-bent on virtually cannibalizing the young man who'd succumbed to him, becoming his prisoner of sex and passion.

Pete had looked into Hank's face. His eyes had been dreamily half-shut, and his sensuous mouth was parted as he'd breathed heavily, anticipating Pete's next delicious assault. A lock of blond hair fell carelessly across Hank's forehead. The young man's beauty had sent a shiver up Pete's spine. He'd wanted more of Hank.

Pete had leaned down to lick Hank's sculpted torso, encircling each nipple with his tongue and exploring every inch of the washboard stomach. The more he'd tasted, the more he'd liked it, tracing a wet path all the way up to Hank's armpits where he'd burrowed in, lapping up the pungent sweat which had been intoxicating to him in this early morning. Up close to Hank's lips, Pete had descended to kiss him but Hank had pushed him away, directing Pete's head back to the major target—his cock.

As Pete descended on Hank's dick, it had been red, hard, and shiny with both saliva and pre-cum. Pete had swallowed Hank whole, letting the thick, protruding cock enter his throat. The moment he'd done that, Hank had cried out and arched his back, trying to cram more of himself into Pete. His dick had jerked, thickened, and then burst forth.

Pete had dislodged Hank's cock from his throat so he could taste every drop of the spewing juice. Spurt after spurt had been swallowed by Pete. Even when Hank had shot his last gusher, Pete had stayed glued to the cock, wanting more and more, even though his belly already felt full of cum.

At least five minutes must have passed before Hank had gradually reached for Pete's neck, taking it in his firm hands and removing it from his groin. "I never knew anybody could suck cock like that. The old shitheads who've gone down on me before didn't know how to do it. Some of them even make teeth marks on me."

Pete parked his Ford at the top of the dirt road as Hank's shanty came into view. Hank turned to him and from the look in his eyes, Pete knew he'd been wrong about Hank's lack of interest in the sex between them. There was almost an eagerness in Hank's face as he looked over at Pete.

"I ain't ever had an experience like that," Hank said. "You found parts of my body to love where no one ever did. I didn't even know I had fucking armpits until you found them for me. The idea that I would let a guy stick his tongue up my ass never crossed my mind. Not only that, I enjoyed it like I've almost never enjoyed nothing before."

"I want a repeat show," Pete said, smiling at Hank. "Again and again."

"You've found your man," Hank said, taking the ten-dollar bill Pete handed him. "I got to have your special kind of love every afternoon. I'll still fuck a lot of pussy at night, but me and you have got to get together every afternoon."

"I've got to have you," Pete said. "I'm addicted to you, man."

"And me you," Hank said. "I'll even lower my price 'cause I like it so much. For you it's going to be only five dollars a throw."

"You've got yourself a deal," Pete said, flashing his smile again, "and I've just made the best bargain of my life. Thirty-five dollars a week for prime grade-A meat."

"I'm gonna be your main man," Hank said before getting out of the car. "And I'll even sweeten the deal."

Pete looked puzzled. "What does that mean?"

"You've seen my three brothers, haven't you?"

"Seen and jerked off thinking about them," Pete said. "Except when I cum. When I cum, I always picture you with a big hard-on. As I beat my meat, I dream about what your cock looks like. In your case, my jerk-off fantasy came true. I was right on target about what that thing looks like between your legs. Now I know and can have it and I don't have to dream any more."

"Just call me your dream man," Hank said, looking cockily smug. "But let me warn you. Any money passing from Pete Riddle to the Adams family goes into the pockets of Big Daddy. I'm the man of the house and I control the bucks. I'm their big brother but I'm also their daddy. They do what I tell them. Don't go giving them money on the side. That way, I'd lose control over them."

"Everybody says you're the man of the family," Pete said. "But everybody always wondered what happened to your parents."

"After mama died," Hank said, "my fucking old man ran off with a low-down woman and left me to bring up my three brothers the best way I know how."

"I want you real bad," Pete said. "In fact, I'll never be able to get enough of you. But I want that Tracy too. He must be nineteen by now."

"He's just turned nineteen, and Karl is coming along too. He's all of seventeen."

"They are two teenage hunks if you ask me, but not with the full body you have."

"Wait until you see what's between their legs," Hank said. "Not quite up to my standards, but there is one thing our daddy left all of us boys. Each of us inherited a big dick from him. Mama used to scream out in pain every time he fucked her. Us boys were in the next room and we heard everything."

"What about John?" Pete said. "I know he's only fourteen but can I break him in too."

Hank laughed and leaned back in his seat. "Too late. My brothers and I have been corn-holing John since he was nine years old. That kid knows how to suck cock almost as good as you do." Hank frowned. "I take that back. No one knows how to suck cock like you do."

"My lucky day," Pete said, smiling at his good fortune. "For a guy who last week knew only pussy, I've now got the prize of the county. The Adams brothers. A lot of people put you down, and make bad remarks about how lowdown you guys are, but all the girls agree on one thing. The Adams boys are the sexiest family of brothers who ever popped out of any womb in western Carolina."

"You've got that right," Hank said. "Me and my brothers are going to break a lot of hearts in our day."

Pete reached for Hank's arm as if to restrain him. "You and I have come to—how shall I put it? A financial understanding. You've promised me what every good cocksucker dreams about. A stable of teenage boys. Plus a stud daddy who's twenty-four. What's the catch?"

"First, my brothers need relief, and it's about time we gave Johnny boy a break. Let up on him so to speak. My brothers will do it with you for the fun of it. But I'd like to get something as the agent for setting it all up."

"What might that be?" Pete asked, growing skeptical.

"Herb Hester has an old car that's just sitting in his yard," Hank said. "Finally broke down and bought his wife a new one. I've driven that car and it runs real good. He wants only one hundred and fifty dollars for it."

"I think I can get my hands on that much money," Pete said. "After all, the whole county knows that I handle the Riddle family money."

"The whole county knows the Riddle family is rich."

"I can slip that money out of my papa's savings, and he'll never know," Pete said. "The old geezer hasn't read one of his bank statements in the last two years."

Hank's face lit up. "Hank Adams is going to have wheels under his ass by tomorrow night. I can feel it."

"Not so fast," Pete said. "One hundred and fifty dollars is a lot of money. I want to sample the merchandise and see what I'm getting for my money before I drive over to Herb's and buy that car for you."

"My brothers are just waking up now," Hank said. "All of them wake up with hard-ons, so you're in luck."

"You mean it?" Pete said. "Right now?"

"Let's walk down into the holler," he said, getting out of the car.

Pete got out and ran to catch up with Hank as he headed down the red-dirt hill. "I mean I was coming over here to see them about the mowing job."

"They'll do that for you do," Hank said, walking briskly in the morning sun. "They'll mow your hay." He turned back to flash a smile at Pete. "They'll also plow your ass."

"Hot damn!" Pete shouted into the woods. He felt his heart beating faster as he neared the Adams shanty.

Hank laughed softly. "You look happier than a pig in shit. Come on inside and find out what my brothers are made of."

\*\*\*

Back at the Riddle household, Rosacoke lay in her bed, dreaming and fantasizing about Pete. Ever since he'd carried her—raging with fever—to this upper-floor bedroom, she'd found a new life for herself, even though sick and still badly bruised. Her bedroom was right over the kitchen, from

which the heat rose, making the little room with its yellowing, stained wallpaper warm and cozy. The wallpaper design consisted of faded cabbage roses, and it was the first time she'd ever slept in a room that someone had even vaguely tried to decorate.

She recalled the first time she'd awakened in this new bedroom where Pete had carried her. The first sound that she'd heard was that of rain. Water had leaked through a crack beside the battered old window, and the raindrops splattered on the sill, lulling her into a kind of comfort and security, something she'd never known before.

When she'd first awakened in this new room, she didn't know where she was. She'd bolted up in bed, trembling as she'd remembered how kind the Riddles had been to her, taking her in and all in that early morning when she'd fled Sultan's shanty.

Not one word of the attack did she plan to breathe to a soul. Certainly not to Pete. If she ever ran into Narcissa again, she wouldn't tell her either, although Narcissa had predicted such a thing might happen if Rosacoke weren't careful. She was just too ashamed to talk about it. Over the past few nights, she'd tried to blot out the whole episode.

Her eyes tightly closed, she lay in the soft bed, listening to the first winds of autumn blowing around the corner of the house. The mattress had that old-man smell of pee and tobacco, but what a safe haven it was, like being in a boat on a stormy sea. An empty feeling inside her was so strong she felt part of her heart had been eaten away.

On her first morning in the house she'd worked herself up for a good cry, like the kind Aunt Clotilda had told her about. But before one tear could be shed on that first morning, the creaky wooden door to her room was thrown open. There stood Pete, dressed in denim and a flannel shirt, his face beaming as fresh as the morning sun. To her bed, he carried a breakfast tray loaded with eggs scrambled with brains, strips of crisp bacon, buttered grits, and a bowl of oatmeal with fresh cream.

"How's my girl?" he asked, bending over to kiss her forehead.

"I'm fine, mighty fine." That heart that had felt so empty just a little while ago, a piece of it gone forever, miraculously had pulled itself back into shape and started beating like it was supposed to. In fact, it had beaten so hard and so fast she'd felt she couldn't breathe for a moment. A lump rose in her throat.

He still considered her his girl, in spite of the tiff he'd had with her after the dance. His forgiving her made her feel so happy. It meant everything to her that he'd chosen her. The next time he needed her, she'd be a lot more understanding. She wanted to be possessed by him, someone she loved, and not brutally attacked by the first man who got a hankering for her.

He leaned over the bed, setting the tray down. This time he tenderly

felt the forehead he'd just kissed. "Fever all gone?"

"Yeah, I'm okay." Her stomach was foundering, not because of her recent fever, but owing to the nearness of him. "I'm gonna get up off my lazy butt and help your mama with the house work."

He shook his head hard from side to side. "There'll be plenty of time for that later."

Feeling like some princess in a fairytale, she reached for a hot biscuit and buttered it. Until he'd brought her this tray this morning, she'd never been served breakfast in bed before. A fear had crossed her mind. She hoped she didn't look like a gal between pukes, spoiling the impression she'd made on him when she'd gone so dolled up to the square dance.

As if to answer her question, he lay down on the bed beside her, his cheek against her shoulder. The scent of him in her nostrils made her so nervous she could hardly swallow the bread. She felt strange all over, defenseless against him, as if she'd worn some protective armor up to now, and he'd gently removed it from her whole body, leaving her vulnerable. The muscles deep in the small of her back felt disconnected, as if she were coming apart.

"Now tell me," he said, cuddling closer. "Just why did you run away from your home? Why didn't you wake us up, instead of spending the whole damn night out there with the dog, catching your death?"

She put down her knife and looked at him serious like. He was her man, and she didn't want to fib to him, but felt that under the circumstances a little white lie would be better than the truth. Why stir up trouble when she'd escaped unharmed?

"After you left me in the car, I walked over to the shack. Inside that low-down Emma Lou Hayes was with Sultan, and they were carrying on something awful. She spotted me and chased me out of the house, throwing a stick of stove wood at me. I ran off into the woods but fell into a ravine. A lot of rocks. I didn't know where to go other than to you people. I just knew you'd take me in."

His face grew very determined. "It's my own fault. I shouldn't have let you stay on in their damn shanty after Aunt Clotilda died."

She reached out to caress his hand, as he looked up into her eyes. Those eyes of his could melt any girl. At night when she couldn't really see their intensity, she might be able to say no to him. But in bright daylight she didn't reckon she could go denying him any favors he'd ask.

"You're mine," he said softly. "I'm gonna look after you. Take care of you the way a man should look after his woman."

Her hand was shaking badly. No one had ever said words like that to her. She'd longed to hear them, never dreaming she would. It was too good to be true. Life didn't always grow worse and worse. Sometimes things got better, too, probably at the moment you'd lost all hope.

"About the other night," she said tentatively. "What I mean…"

"Hell." He rose from the bed and strolled over to the window, looking back over his shoulder and giving her that prize-winning, sweet-as-strawberry-jam smile of his. "I've forgot all about that."

A sense of relief swept over her. "My, what a nice breakfast this is. I don't deserve it." She picked up a piece of crunchy bacon, biting into it. It tasted good to have some real food going down. "You know, I feel as worthless as a scrip penny. I mean, I'm gonna stay here only till I can find a place of my own."

Tall and lanky, he just stood there by the window, looking over at her like she was still in some kind of delirium. "She-it, you say. You've moved in, woman. From now on, this house is yours, too."

In all her sixteen years, she couldn't remember being happy a day in her life until now. Just as she'd felt small and frail, he was so much stronger. She seemed to feed off his manhood, his very essence, and it made her feel so much better. Then a troubling doubt crossed her mind. "Your parents? They probably want to speak their mind about all this."

"They know you've got no place to go. No parents. Nothing." He smiled at her again. "You wouldn't be the first orphan they ever took in. Remember, that's how the kid here ended up."

Recalling that, she felt more secure and planned to work even harder as soon as she regained her strength so she wouldn't wear out her welcome.

"When you're well enough, I want you to run around the county with me a bit," he said. "I'm taking Sleepy Eyed John's advice and putting together my own band. If you behave, I might make you my gal singer."

She was stunned. There was nothing she wanted more than that.

"And I've got another surprise for you." He rushed over to the door to open it, reaching out to retrieve a Silverton guitar. "I bought it yesterday at Sears and Roebuck, and I'm gonna see that you learn how to play the thing."

"I feel right proud." She put down her fork to reach for the guitar, fondling its smooth surface the way she might precious lace. She strummed her first chords.

"A woman and her guitar," he said. "Like a horse and carriage, the two of you just belong together."

"I'll learn to play it, and I'll sing real pretty, too. I won't disappoint you ever again, the way I did the night of the dance. And that's one promise I'll keep."

***

As Rosacoke wondered where Pete Riddle was, he lay on the top floor of the Adams shanty much as he'd lain on the top floor of Sultan's shanty.

The shacks with their upper-floor sleeping lofts with the timbers exposed were very similar, almost like the same ramshackle house.

When Hank had taken Pete inside, the three other Adams boys were just waking up and getting out of bed. They were in a state of only partial dress, and Pete thrilled to the sight of their half-clothed bodies.

Before leaving for the morning, Hank had whispered something in the ears of each of his brothers. Whatever he'd told them obviously had met with approval to judge from the grins on the brothers' faces. John, the youngest, was the most bashful, but Karl and Tracy were practically leering at Pete. Hank had told Pete to go upstairs to the bed and get undressed. He'd claimed that each of the brothers would climb upstairs one at a time for "servicing."

Before leaving for the morning, Hank had turned to Pete. "Since he's the oldest, all of nineteen, Tracy wants to go first."

Looking over at Tracy, who was a slightly younger version of Hank himself, Pete had eagerly approved of Tracy having first go at him. From that look on Tracy's muscled body, it would be just like having Hank himself when he'd been nineteen and giving his good stuff away to God knows who, maybe even some stinking older women.

Tracy stood before him in his underwear, his perfectly sculpted chest revealed. "How do we go about this queer stuff?" he asked Pete. "I've corn-holed John before but other than that I don't know a lot about this shit. Hank tells me you're a sucker and a licker."

"You can begin by dropping those drawers," Pete said, "Showing me what kind of man you are."

Tracy dropped his drawers. To Pete's astonished eyes, he had virtually the same cock as Hank in both width and length. No doubt about it. They were brothers.

"C'mon over here," Pete said. "I want to suck that big thing."

"No one's ever sucked it before," Tracy said, moving toward him. He stood directly over Pete, who took his hand and skinned Tracy's cock back, exposing the large, succulent head. Pete's mouth was already drooling.

He directed Tracy to lie down on the bed, placing a pillow under his head for comfort, as Pete's tongue attacked Tracy's nipples, descending lower over the rippled muscles of his beautiful, tasty stomach.

Pete wrapped his long fingers around the base of Tracy's cock, watching in amazement as it burst forth to its full and impressive length. His tongue darting out, Pete's lips descended on the vein-hatched cock, sliding along the velvety ridge of it, as he swallowed inch by inch of it. The cock moved closer and closer to his throat. Only when the throbbing cock penetrated his throat and Pete's lips touched the boy's sand-colored pubic hair did Pete pull up for air.

He slid his lips slowly back and forth along the thickness of Tracy's

cock. The boy squirmed on the bed and ran his fingers through Pete's wavy hair. When Pete looked up into Tracy's face, the boy's eyes were closed, his mouth open as soft moans escaped from his throat. He was clearly in the throes of passion. The enthralled look on Tracy's face inspired Pete to greater accomplishment. With one hand he felt the fat orbs below Tracy's cock. They were large and full of promise.

Suddenly, Tracy came alive, bucking his hips and fucking Pete's mouth in a slow but steady rhythm. His chest was heaving as his breath came in short gasps.

Pete's hands were reaching out, feeling and teasing any part of Tracy's body he could touch. The full length of Tracy's inflamed prick rammed between Pete's lips, demanding to be satisfied. "I'm gonna cum," Tracy shouted out. "I can't hold back."

Pete didn't want Tracy to explode. He wanted to slow down, but the boy had needs that could not wait. He plunged for one final time deep into Pete's throat, as he continued to pound his cock into Pete's mouth in rapid, forceful strokes. The dense golden bush of Tracy's pubic hair ground again and again into Pete's face.

Tracy gasped so loudly Pete knew that John and Karl downstairs could hear every word. Tracy jerked back until only the bulbous, saliva-slicked crown remained within Pete's mouth. He grasped the back of Pete's head, holding him down as the first spurt of his scalding cum blasted into Pete's mouth, splattering so forcefully the explosion reached the roof of Pete's mouth. He went wild. The cum was sweeter than the much older nectar of Sultan and even Hank himself. It was the single most delicious cocktail he'd ever known in his life.

As the sticky juice filled Pete's mouth, he swallowed the musky tasting liquid in gulps. He was in incredible ecstasy even as his own prick demanded relief but got nothing.

When Tracy's spasms finally let up, Pete kept the deflating cock in his mouth as long as Tracy let him. Pete licked, kissed, and slurped until their love-making was interrupted by seventeen-year old Karl calling up to them in the attic.

"Shit, Tracy," Karl shouted. "You've had that Pete Riddle a long time. Hearing you guys is driving me crazy. I've got to get up there and at him before I shoot off like a firecracker."

Tracy seemed reluctant to leave Pete's bed. Pete tried to kiss Tracy but he pulled away. "You can have all of me but only below the neck."

"I've got to have you again and again," Pete whispered to him. "I've not tasted a lot of men before but you're the most delicious thing God ever put on the face of this earth. I want to do a lot of other things with you, too."

"You've got your man," Tracy said, flashing a mischievous smile at

him. "Hank said you suck a lot more than cock."

"I suck everything," Pete said.

"After you've had your fill of that, can I corn-hole you next time? I'm a fucking man, myself."

"You can do anything you want to me."

As if in a trance, Pete watched Tracy put on his pants and grab a shirt before heading down the steps.

He was replaced almost instantly by Karl who stood before a nude Pete who lay on the bed looking up at the boy.

"Do you want me just to whip it out and feed it to you or what?" Karl asked.

Pete looked the teenage boy up and down, trying to imagine what his body was like without his clothes. He wasn't as muscled as Tracy but showed every bit of promise of becoming another Hank.

Pete was also thrilled that he and Karl were the exact same age. He looked up into Karl's face. The boy had the potential of being the handsomest of all the Adams boys, although Young John was mighty cute.

There was a slightly rugged look to Hank and Tracy but Karl was almost movie star pretty—in fact, far better looking than any actor Pete had seen at the moving picture show.

"Well," Karl said, growing impatient. "You gonna answer me or not?"

"No way are you just gonna whip it out and blast off," Pete said, reaching out for Karl, cupping his buttocks and pulling him toward the bed. "I let your brother blast off and head downstairs long before I was finished with him. I'm not going to let that happen in your case."

"Exactly what have you got in mind?"

Pete was unbuttoning Karl's pants as he looked up into his face. "I'm gonna get you jaybird naked, and then I'm going to lick, slurp, and suck every part of your body from your big toe to your cute little ears. I'm gonna pay special attention to your toes, fingers, armpits, tits, asshole, balls, and that cock of yours."

"You gonna do all that?" Karl asked in astonishment. "No one's ever touched those parts of me before."

"You're in for a treat," Pete said. He pulled the boy's pants down, exposing his white underwear. He reached up and unbuttoned his shirt, reaching inside to feel the baby smooth muscles of his incredibly beautiful chest. The boy was a strong, Nordic type, muscular and broad shouldered with slim hips. He appeared in perfect shape and had the potential of filling out to become genuinely spectacular.

Pete removed the shirt from Karl's physique, letting it drop onto the wood planking of the floor. The boy was now nude except for his underwear.

Pete reached to pull them off him. "It's show time, my friend," Pete said to Karl. "Let's have a little unveiling. It's time I found out if you live up

to the reputation of the other Adams brothers."

***

The next morning Rosacoke had awakened feeling miraculously healed. She could breathe deeply without coughing, and she was eager to get up and about. Inspecting her body in the mirror, she appeared badly bruised in some places, but nothing that clothing could not conceal.

Pete had been gone all day yesterday, and she wondered what he'd been up to. She feared he was slipping off to see that low-down Narcissa. Even Mrs. Riddle kept inquiring several times about his whereabouts.

Pete was mysterious. He liked to come and go at all times of the day and night and didn't want to explain to anybody where he'd been. She could only imagine what he was up to.

When he'd appeared with her breakfast tray that morning, he'd been as bright-eyed as ever. She told him that he didn't have to carry food up to her any more because she was feeling fit as a fiddle.

"In that case, I've got a surprise for you," he'd said, his eyes lighting up. "I'm gonna take you into town."

"Now what would the two of us do in town at this hour of the morning?"

It wouldn't be a surprise if I told you, now would it?" he'd said. "C'mon, get dressed. I'll be ready to go in an hour." He'd looked out her window. "I'm picking up the Adams brothers this morning. They're coming to do the mowing."

With that pronouncement, he'd left, but had returned an hour later to knock on her door to see if she was ready.

She was fully dressed and looked much better than she had in days. She felt bad leaving Mrs. Riddle to wash up the breakfast dishes, but Pete insisted she leave with him at once. She'd quickly learned that Pete got his away around the Riddle household.

Pete's coupe with its wide-open muffler squealed rubber, as it skidded around the corner, coming to an abrupt halt at Deal Street in Shakerag, where no white woman was supposed to be seen, daytime or night. Rosacoke checked her makeup in his rear-view mirror, wiping a dab of red from her white teeth with a Kleenex. She rubbed on a second coat of lipstick as if it were war paint.

The color matched her fingernails which she'd painted last night. She'd also painted her toenails, a first for her, by spreading her toes with cotton so they would dry easier. While doing that, she'd turned on an old Philco radio Pete had brought upstairs, enjoying a country and western program broadcast from Memphis. As she listened intently to the radio, she picked up her Silvertone guitar and improvised.

In the car, he leaned over, giving her a little kiss on the cheek so as not

to spoil her makeup. The smell of Sen Sen chips was on his breath, and she wondered when he'd sneaked his first beer of the day. "Here we are," he said.

Getting out of the car, she looked around suspiciously, seeing almost no activity. He handed her her guitar, and strapped his own on his back. She didn't understand why he'd insisted that she bring her shiny new guitar to this place. Pete didn't like his reasons questioned. She never knew why the place was called Deal Street, unless perhaps any deal you might have ticking in your head could be made here if you whispered what's on your mind in the right ear, and had either cash or else something—almost anything—to barter.

The street wasn't very long. People referred to it as a block, but it looked more like half a block to Rosacoke, who'd never been there before. She didn't dare go until Pete talked her into it. When he told her he was taking her here "for a surprise," she just didn't want to refuse, even though the idea of being seen on Deal Street by anybody she knew sent shivers up her spine.

Pete gave her a lot of security, and when she got out of that sick bed after he'd taken her in from the cold, and had been so loving and kind and everything, she was stubbornly determined to follow him anywhere. How was she to know that on her first day up he'd invite her to the notorious Deal Street?

Her sense of adventure finally got the best of her frightened self, and she followed along after him, catching up to grab hold of his arm as if he were getting ready to duck around a corner and out of her sight. After all, he might have to take a leak and couldn't be with her every minute.

Deal Street began down at the abandoned docks where slaves had once loaded cotton. The pier was rotting on broken piling, and it was dangerous to walk out on it any more, although teenage Negro boys still fished from it. The red-brick warehouses, built before the Civil War, had long ago decayed, and vandals had broken out the windows by tossing rocks. The place was rat-infested. Turning her back to it, she could smell the breeze from the river.

The only holdout down at the docks was Miss Prissy, an eighty-three-year-old Negro woman who still ran her little diner shack there, as she'd done since she was fifteen.

Catfish fanciers would drive for miles around to taste one of her suppers with her own special cole slaw, crowder peas, and her crispy hush puppies, all of which were said to be the best in this part of the state. She did all the frying herself, and used some secret ingredient in the batter she claimed she'd divulge only on her deathbed and then only to the Angel Gabriel himself.

The wafting aroma of catfish sizzling in an iron skillet lazily drifted up the muddy cobblestone street to Tenderhook Road, the beginning of

Shakerag's Negro shanties that swept over the hill and down into the holler.

Stretching from the waterfront up the hill stood some dilapidated old storefronts, once used by white merchants when pier life was bustling in these parts. Now these decaying relics—ghosts of a vanished time—formed the heartbeat of Negro mercantile and night life in this section of the county.

If you wanted a recording of "St. Louis Blues," some special Old Bay seasoning shipped up from New Orleans, or a flashy suit of clothing, you could find it here. Strutting in and out of these dark storefronts, often with black curtains draped over plate-glass windows, were a lot of high nutmeg-brown belles and plenty of fancy-stepping dandies.

Rosacoke knew that Narcissa came here to buy some of her more outrageous clothing. Where else in the county could she pick up what was known as whore's rags?

Pete took her hand and led her into one storefront with a lot of clothing mostly piled up on tables and exposed by a glaringly nude electric light bulb dangling from a dangerous looking cord overhead. Against the wall, a pile of cowboy boots was tossed, as if thrown here without any regard to mating them. Shirts in brilliant hues, like lemon yellow and lime green, hung on wire hangers on creaky racks.

"We're gonna get dressed up." When seeing the look of apprehension on her face, he assured her, "Don't worry. I got money on me."

From out of the back emerged a Negro albino, who'd apparently shunned the flashy clothing he sold in favor of a frayed black suit that looked as if it might have been new in 1914. Up close she detected that he had one blue eye and one brown one.

"This is Skeeter," Pete said.

"Right glad to meet you," she told him, feeling nervous in the dank, musty shop.

Skeeter looked her up and down, as if mentally trying to fit her for an outfit, before turning to Pete. "Hit's come in."

Rushing to the back of the store, Pete called out to her. "Pick yourself out some real pretty cowgirl outfit. I'll be right back. After I change into my new duds."

She wandered through stacks of clothes, all of which struck her as vulgar. She just couldn't see herself looking like some cheap Saturday night piece of white trash, prancing around in a red silk dress, slip up to where it shouldn't be, and wearing a pair of stilt high-heel shoes which were likely to make her topple over and break her neck.

In the cowgirl section, she decided that when in doubt it was better to stick to simple white. She selected a white suede jacket with fringe and searched for a white suede skirt to match. Finding one, she was also drawn to a candy-striped blouse to wear with it. She felt this outfit might look real nice on her—that is, if she had to get herself all made up like this in the first

place.

As she sought some place to try this outfit on, Pete emerged from the room in back, trailed by Skeeter.

His appearance stunned her, as she'd never seen him look so sexy and glamorous. His mauve-colored silk shirt was just like an autumn sunset she'd once witnessed. Around his neck, he'd tied a lilac-purple scarf. A wide-brimmed black felt hat rested jauntily on his head of hair, and holding up his pants was a leather belt clamped together by the biggest silver buckle she'd ever seen. It was those pants that made her blush and look away. Made of shiny charcoal pin-striped fabric, they were the tightest pants in the county. It was like advertising everything you had, things best left private in her mind.

"How do I look?"

"Just great! You'll sure attract a lot of attention in that outfit."

"That's the whole idea," Pete said. "That's what show business is all about." He strutted around the store, seemingly annoyed that Skeeter was too cheap to install a full-length mirror. Go on back there. Let's see you get into something."

Skeeter directed her to the little dressing room in the rear of the store, and once she carefully pulled the burlap curtain shut, she took off her cotton dress. She slipped on the blouse first, finding it a little too tight, although she was able to button it. She didn't like the feel of it, as it emphasized her big breasts, reminding people she had too much up top. Wiggling into the suede skirt, she scotched the back down a little to adjust the hem line. The fit was tight on her rounded rear end. Then she put on the jacket, with tiny rhinestones on the scooped neckline. She, too, wanted a mirror, but found none.

At the front of the store, Pete held up a pair of white leather boots with high heels. "Wow! My honky-tonk angel. Every other woman out there will be poor, pitiful Pearl."

Skeeter, in the meantime, had snatched up a white leather hat for her which he dusted off. His blue eye squinted, and his brown eye bulged, as he took in her low neckline. His tongue touched his stained yellow teeth.

"I feel funny," she said. "The blouse is a little tight. Maybe we could find something a size larger."

"Not on your life. I believe if you've got something to show, don't be shy."

Recalling the tightness of his crotch, she said, "I know you believe that. But I don't like to exhibit myself like some prize steer."

"Hell with that! At the roller rink the other night, you loved showing off."

"But..."

He seemed to silence her, and she went along with him, because she

truly did want to sing with him. She suspected he had some grand plan, and somehow he'd fitted her into it. That made her feel happy and proud to be at his side, regardless of what outfit he wanted her to parade around in, making a spectacle out of herself.

Once she'd put on the boots and fitted the cowgirl hat onto her long blonde hair, she felt much better, kind of like an eagle poised on the edge of its nest, ready to spread its wings and fly.

But there would be no singing today. Pete had an almost demonic look on his face as he drove faster than he should. He claimed he had to get back home to oversee the Adams boys in their mowing, but the way he drove and his nervousness didn't seem to match up with what he said. What did it matter if he arrived half an hour late or not? The boys were only mowing hay. They'd done that for many families before and hardly needed Pete to be their foreman.

On the way back to the Riddle house, Pete stopped off at Herb Hester's place. Rosacoke knew this is where all the boys went to get bootleg hooch. Pete had told her that the Adams brothers were likely to be hot after all that mowing and he was going to take them some cold beer to go with the lunch that Mrs. Riddle was preparing right now for them.

She viewed all this concern for the Adams brothers as proof of what a sweet nature Pete had. He even looked after the field hands, whereas some other dirt farmer in the county would probably treat them with contempt. Hiring out as a field hand was the lowest worker on the food chain.

When she pulled up in Hester's driveway, Pete told her the bootlegger was still in Tennessee but that his wife sold beer from their back door.

She sat forlornly in the coupe as Pete went around to knock on the back door. He was gone for about five minutes as she sat patiently waiting for him to return with that beer. She hoped nobody would drive by and see her sitting in a car parked in front of Herb Hester's house. A gal could get a real bad reputation hanging out here.

In about five minutes, Pete came around the corner of the house, carrying what looked like two six-packs of beer.

"Guess who I ran into?" he called to her.

"Who, pray tell," she said.

Following Pete around the corner of the house was Sultan himself.

"Hi there, gal," a familiar voice called out to her.

In the mid-morning sun, she gasped, at the sight of her attacker.

It was Sultan himself, flashing a smile and heading right toward her.

*** 

Pete felt that he must surely be mistaken but Rosacoke actually seemed

to be afraid to have Sultan in the back seat. Maybe she was just embarrassed over that last encounter when she'd come across Emma Lou Hayes rutting around in the bed with Sultan. A young, innocent gal like Rosacoke could get real red-faced over something like that.

Sultan didn't seem in the least embarrassed to run into Rosacoke. Pete suspected that Sultan wasn't even familiar with the word shame. He carried on a breezy banter, talking about how his daughter, Narcissa, was getting better looking every day. He predicted a big show business career for her.

"It's hard for a nigger pussy to make it big in show business," Sultan said. "But there are openings for the lucky few. I just feel it in my gut that Narcissa Cash is going to see her name up in lights one day. She won't be playing maid's parts either like Hattie McDaniel in *Gone with the Wind*."

"I bet that Narcissa has got a hell of a lot of show biz talent," Pete said. He looked over at Rosacoke and feared she might be getting jealous of all this talk of Narcissa. "Of course, my gal Rosacoke here is a real good country singer herself. Real talented."

"I'm sure she is," Sultan said, as Rosacoke remained silent, her eyes glued to the dirt road they were traveling down.

Pete felt that Sultan wasn't much interested in exploring the subject of Rosacoke's talents, and Pete understood that. Narcissa was Sultan's own blood. Rosacoke was just some blonde-haired white girl her mama brought to live with them one day.

As soon as Pete pulled up in his front yard, Rosacoke thanked him for taking her to the store. Without saying another word, not even a good-bye to Sultan, she jumped out of the coupe, claiming she had to get into the house, change her clothes, and help Mrs. Riddle with the household chores. She turned and flashed a nervous smile at Pete. "Now that I'm up and about again, I've got to earn my keep."

As Pete drove Sultan back to his shanty, they passed an old farmer who was taking his wagon, pulled by two broken down old mares, into town to sell his corn in the autumn market. As they turned the bend heading down to Sultan's shanty, Pete passed Claude Billings speeding past in his squad car.

If Pete weren't mistaken, that was Emma Lou Hayes riding like some uppity smart thing right in the front seat of the sheriff's car. Spotting Pete, Claude honked his horn and waved at him. Pete just knew that friendly greeting was reserved for him and not for Sultan. The sheriff just plain didn't take to Sultan at all.

As the squad car roared by, Pete recalled his last session at Blowing Rock Falls with the sheriff. Claude had been waiting for Pete at four o'clock just like they had agreed upon. Claude had parked his car on the dirt road about half a mile above the falls. Seeing Pete, he had gotten out of his car and walked silently down the pathway that led to the falls.

Neither man had said a word. It had just been understood why they were here. Both of them had appeared deadly intent on committing the act that was about to transpire between them.

Once at the falls, Claude had signaled Pete to get down on his knees in the sands. The sheriff had towered over Pete, as he'd reached to unbutton Claude's green-striped sheriff's pants. Taking out Claude's dick, Pete had looked at it with lust. It was hardly the biggest cock in the county but it was the prettiest. Until he'd seen Claude's dick, he didn't know that any man's cock looked that pretty.

Thinking of Claude and how good he tasted, Pete was dreaming about their next meeting. Claude had even held out a promise that two of his sexiest deputies might like to join them for some nighttime fun in a log cabin up near Banner Elk. Pete was sure looking forward to that little session if it ever came about. He felt that Claude was a man of his word—stern, strong, and reliable, and that Claude would come for him one night and drive him away in his squad car for the rendezvous.

Pete couldn't wait. In the meantime, he had a lot of other meat to cram down his throat or up his ass. Only a few days ago he'd been a kid dreaming about having sex with men. All that had changed now. He was hell bent on giving Emma Lou Hayes and Narcissa Cash competition for the top studs of the county. No doubt the three of them were sampling all the same men—Claude Billings, Hank Adams, and at least in the case of Emma Lou, Sultan himself. Pete hoped that Sultan wasn't fucking his own daughter. In Sultan's case, you couldn't be sure. Pete thought Sultan capable of anything. Instead of repelling Pete, that made Sultan all the sexier and more alluring in his eyes.

Apparently all Pete had to do was let just one man in the county know he was queer. After that, the word had spread pretty quickly. Pete suspected that there were very few good male cocksuckers in the county. Those who were were probably portly and middle aged like W.G. Gabriel. Pete was young and good looking. Surely guys who liked their dicks sucked would prefer him to those other assholes.

Pete smiled at Sultan, who reached for his crotch. "Herb Hester's wife didn't satisfy me at all," Sultan said. "I've got plenty left for you. C'mon down to the house with me."

"I really shouldn't," Pete said. "I've got to get back and oversee those Adams brothers out mowing our fields."

Sultan chuckled rather smugly to himself. He reached over and took Pete's hand and placed it between his legs. Once there, Pete didn't want to pull his hand away. His fingers lingered between Sultan's legs, massaging and fondling until the thick penis began to lengthen.

"You really shouldn't," Sultan said, mocking his earlier words. "But you really are going to. Get your white ass out of this car. Sultan wants to

plow it."

Inside Sultan's shanty, he stirred the coals of the fire in his pot-bellied stove before throwing on some more wood.

"I'm up here," a man called down.

Pete immediately recognized the voice of Hank Adams.

"Hope you don't mind," Hank said to Sultan. "I came on in. Needed a place to plow this little Mexican spitfire I picked up. Doesn't speak a word of English. She's the daughter of one of those migrant workers passing through."

"Save some for me," Sultan called up. "I love Mexican pussy. Tastes hot like Tabasco. I gotta surprise for you. Pete Riddle's with me."

"Send him on up," Hank called. "Hi, Pete. I was gonna look you up later."

Pete felt awkward and at first didn't know what to say. "How you doing, Hank."

"I'm doing just fine," Hank yelled. "Haul ass. Get up here. You can have any part of me not engaged in satisfying this Mexican spitfire."

Slowly Pete climbed the ladder. As he stood up in the dusty loft with its exposed wooden beams, he spotted Hank lying nude on the bed, going down on a painfully thin black-haired girl with olive skin. She looked no more than fourteen. Hank interrupted his slurping long enough to look up at Pete.

"Join the fun," Hank said.

Pete didn't have to be asked twice. His eyes gazed dreamily at Hank's big cock in its full glory. That impressive shaft was left unattended. Stripping off his own clothes, Pete moved toward the bed and Hank's groin.

Hank moaned and cried out in passion as Pete's lips engulfed him. "My first load of the day belongs to my pretty boy."

Pete's fingers took delight in sliding up and down Hank's cock, exposing the head of the purple, plum-sized knob and smelling the savory scent of a natural man before plunging it down his throat. Hank's hips lunged instinctively forward, grinding his crotch hard against Pete's welcoming face.

Pete clamped his lips down hard, just behind Hank's trigger-ridge. The skin along Hank's cock felt incredibly soft to Pete's slurping lips. The food he was feasting on was sweet and thick, reminding him of molasses with just a touch of sweat. No doubt about it. Hank Adam's cock was the best thing he'd ever messed up his mouth with.

He felt Hank's pre-cum dripping its precious offering onto the root of Pete's tongue. He reared back to get a better taste of the clear, jewel-like cargo of pre-cum. The tip of his tongue darted around the cock, as Hank's body jerked in mounting excitement. He was enjoying this a lot. If anything, it caused him to attack the little girl with even more tongue savagery.

Unable to keep his greed in check, Pete descended on Hank with

mounting passion, wanting the full offering. He glided across the smooth head and descended lower, wanting every inch whether he choked or not. Hank shivered in delight at what was being done to him.

Like Sherman marching through Georgia, Pete sucked and lipped Hank harder and harder, at one point sliding his teeth across Hank's tender cockhead and sending shivers through Hank's bulking broncho body.

Hank cupped Pete's neck holding him down in an iron-fisted grip. Pete knew what was coming as that huge man meat rammed deep into his throat. Pete desperately wanted to give Hank the tonguing he needed but in such a position he couldn't. He sucked like a starving lamprey. Deeper and deeper into Pete's throat Hank pounded, his hips moving in perfect rhythm as he raced toward his climax, his ballbag rising. When Pete grabbed Hank's balls, that did the trick. He blasted into the back of Pete's throat, load after load.

Although he was far from satisfied and was rock-hard himself, Pete basked in the afterglow of Hank's orgasm. Pete looked up at Hank, finding him lying almost in sleep on the young girl's stomach, his mouth open and his eyes closed as if reliving the powerful emotions that had built up in him before exploding.

At a sudden movement from the stairs, Pete jerked his head to stare at the nude body of Sultan. His cock jutted out from his body like some obscene thing, an attachment that was strapped there like some gigantic dildo having no connection to the rest of his massive physique. That Sultan was one big man.

"You gals have had your fun," Sultan said, his face grim with some deep unsatisfied need. "Now it's my turn."

Moving toward the bed, Sultan reached down for Pete, pulling him by the hair and almost throwing him in a spread-eagled position next to the head of the Mexican gal. Pete turned and looked into her eyes. She appeared frightened. Hank seemed to scare her enough, but the sight of Sultan evoked panic.

Sultan raised Pete's legs into the air as he positioned himself at Pete's rosebud. With no prep work, Sultan lunged into Pete, burying his massive cock deep within the boy's guts.

Pete screamed out in pain at this sudden invasion but Sultan's lips descended over his. The mulatto's long thick tongue seemed to reach to the back of Pete's throat to silence him.

Sultan's virtual rape of Pete seemed to inspire Hank into another chance at orgasm, although Pete wondered how there could be anything left after the load Hank had dumped.

Pete had tried to jerk free of Sultan's attack, at least until the pain stopped. But Pete's movements had brought only more pleasure to Sultan. Pete's asshole was on fire. He'd had Sultan before but never like this.

Maybe since he had an audience of two on the bed beside his, Sultan was inspired for a special performance. After all, he had a reputation in the county to live up to.

Pete's cock remained rock hard and he knew if Sultan kept pounding him like that, he was going to explode jizz all over the Godlike body that was towering over him. Sultan's big balls slammed against Pete's, causing an extra tingling sensation to engulf Pete's body.

Sultan continued his attack on Pete until he lost all sense of time and space. When Pete would open his eyes, he would look adoringly into Sultan's brown eyes before glancing over at Hank who was riding the young girl with a fast-pounding action. The sounds coming from her throat weren't those of pleasure. She seemed to be hurting, not enjoying the experience at all. Pete suspected that the ramming she got from her daddy or her brothers wasn't as severe as that propelled by Hank. Pete had heard stories about what male members of these Mexican families did to their young daughters brought along with them to work the fields.

Hanks lips were parted in pleasure as he ground against the body that lay helpless underneath him, enduring his assault.

An indescribable sensation of almost unendurable, sensual joy surged through Pete's body. His rigid prick jerked wildly. Sultan was reaching all the right spots, and Pete couldn't hold back any more. He cried out as his fingers dug into Sultan's back. As if on cue, Sultan blasted off deep within him. Sultan's prick seemed to plunge through some virgin territory deep within the recesses of Pete's body. Pete's ecstatic moans and groans mingled with those of Sultan's into a chorus of pleasure.

As if not to be outdone, Hank rushed toward his second orgasm of the morning. Pete looked into Hank's face, distorted into a kind of grotesque passion. The girl still lay passive, enduring the ramming, but Hank was wild. His lips were wide open, his pink tongue darting out.

Hank had never let Pete kiss him before. Pete was determined to change that this very moment. As Sultan's lapping tongue nuzzled his neck, Pete impulsively reached out for Hank.

He pulled at Hank's ears, moving him toward Pete's mouth. At first Hank tried to draw back when he saw what was happening. But he too was far gone. As Pete's lips locked onto Hank's, he felt Hank's tongue dart into his mouth. Pete voraciously sucked the tongue he'd wanted to taste ever since he'd first spotted this sexy man. Pete gave Hank the longest, sloppiest kiss ever recorded, as Hank plunged into the Mexican gal and exploded.

Long after he'd finished the splash of his second orgasm, Hank continued to surrender his mouth to Pete's loving. He licked and sucked Hank's tongue and lips like a kitten going for fresh cream.

A half hour later Pete was on the road again, heading back to the

Riddle farmstead. He looked at himself in the rear-view mirror and flashed a cocky smile of triumph. He'd had Hank. He'd had Sultan. And, most importantly, Pete had devoured Hank's mouth.

Pete stepped on the gas. That Indian summer day had come. The Adams brothers would be mowing in the fields, probably with their shirts off. Pete had beer for them and lots of plans.

He'd take Tracy first, then his brother Karl. But those special moments when Pete could be totally fulfilled and satisfied would be experienced only with John. He'd been there before, and he knew that special thing that John could offer him that the other boys couldn't or wouldn't.

In time Pete planned to make not only Tracy and Karl do what he wanted done to him, but also Hank himself. Right now for that special kind of love-making, he had John. In time he'd get all of them any way he wanted. Those brothers could be had.

****

With Pete grabbing her hand and pulling her along, Rosacoke raced up the street, past tar-shingled juke joints in front of which Negro men hung around, swigging drinks from bottles or pints wrapped in paper pokes. Music blared from nickel machines inside the dark holes.

In her new duds and with a guitar strapped on her back, she hit her white boots against the wooden boards of the elevated sidewalk, feeling like a woman ready to take on anything. At her side Pete gave her a lot of confidence.

At first she didn't like the way some of the men stared at her, looking her up and down. But Pete had told her that if she were ever going to perform in public, she had to get used to being stared at. "That's what it's all about."

Parked in front of one of the juke joints was a '32 Ford which looked as if it had been cross country several times, and wasn't about to make the trip again. Caked with red clay, it was filled with five black men, drinking moonshine and eating sardines out of the tin and soda crackers. When one of them finished a can, he'd toss out the tin for a stray cat to lick clean.

"Those men may not look like much," Pete whispered to her. "But they're some of the best musicians in these parts. I know 'em."

He yelled at them and got a friendly greeting in return. She was scared, knowing she didn't belong hanging out in Shakerag, dressed the way she was. Her confidence waned.

One drunk approached Pete, squinting his eyes to avoid the sunshine. "What you doing running around here, white boy? Squirrelin' 'round like you do with a woman dressed up in such a way as to get a man in trouble."

Instinctively she reached to cover her breasts. She felt cold, wishing

Pete had let her wear her overcoat.

"I'm looking for Moss and Fry," Pete said.

"You've got to wade through a mess of tore-down niggers to get to those two," the drunk said. "They're in the back room over at Butterbean's place."

Pete thanked him for the tip, and taking hold of her arm, crossed the muddy street to a juke joint on the other side. Trembling slightly, she went inside the damp, dark hole with him. Along the way, she passed a few tables of Negro men who looked as if they'd slit your throat as quickly as they'd castrate a hog.

"Listen," Rosacoke said, catching up with the ongoing Pete. "We don't invite them to our places, and I suddenly got the bright idea they don't welcome two white upstarts barging in on their private club like they owned the place."

He turned and looked her square in the eye with the peeved expression he always had when he didn't get his way. "I wouldn't take you no place I couldn't handle, okay? Do you trust me or not?"

Giving in, she said in a barely audible voice, "I trust you."

In the back room of Butterbean's, she spotted Moss and Fry, those two old minstrels whom she hadn't seen since Pete invited them that time to play with the Riddles, much to his daddy's displeasure. Hoping Skeeter's price tags weren't hanging all over her store-bought clothes, she stepped inside the rear bar which smelled of stale beer and a tobacco like none she'd ever smelled before.

Under his slouchy hat, Fry sat in a corner, and silvery-haired Moss stood at the far end of the bar, chatting with his washtub bass-player.

Before going over to Fry, Pete turned to her. "Honey, it wasn't mama and papa who taught me to sing and play. Ever since I was eight years old, I've been slipping away to Shakerag to take my lessons from Moss and Fry."

This didn't surprise her, as she remembered how well he'd sung and played with the men at the hoedown. What amazed her was that an eight-year-old boy had enough instinct, gumption, and secrecy to do such a thing.

Joining Fry at the table, she felt more at ease. He had that way of making you welcome right away. "You don't look like no kitchen help I ever laid eyes on," he said, recalling their first meeting at the Riddles. "Not in that outfit."

"That's mighty kind of you to say so."

"Fry, it's good to see you, ole boy," Pete said.

"You're a sight for sore eyes, too. Man, where have you been? I thought the boll weevil done carried you off."

Never taking her gaze off Fry's rolling eyes, she learned that he used to be billed as "the only colored singing cowboy."

"I came up from Shakerag from living down on the Yazoo River," Fry said. "I taught your man, Pete, the Delta blues. Down there, we think white music is trash. Every time it came on the radio, my old ho would turn it off. When I started getting a few paying jobs, I had to play that damn cowboy music for my white audiences. That's the only shit they wanted to hear."

In a few minutes, Moss joined them at their table, ordering a round of beers. To be sociable, she decided to sip hers, pretending to like it. At least it was a lot smoother going down than corn liquor.

"I used to play in the dance halls of Alabama," Moss said. "That is, when I could land a job. Most of the time it was those cotton fields for me. Then one day I made up my mind to get the hell out. How long can a man go on living on baloney and crackers?" As he talked he seemed to find every situation in life amusing. His quivering jaw often broke into nervous laughter, his lips trembling with old age. However, when he laughed it came from deep within his heaving bosom.

"So what can we do for you?" Fry asked, turning serious, as if donning his business hat.

"I want you to hear Rosacoke sing and play with me," Pete said.

She nearly fell over in her chair. "I just couldn't. Really, I couldn't. Not in front of Moss and Fry. I play so bad my picking would send a dog under the house."

"You'll learn," Pete said. "That's why we're here."

At Pete's urging, she agreed to sing "You Are My Sunshine" with him in front of Moss and Fry. It was the duet she'd done with him at the roller rink, the number he knew she found the least threatening.

Before going into the song, Pete turned and, up real close to her ear, said, "Now sing like you know every teardrop and have felt each and every pain real lowdown in your gut."

At the finish of the number, she thought her singing had been okay, although it hadn't attracted any attention from the rest of the customers. She knew her picking, however, was strictly amateur night.

"Fried potatoes," Fry said, getting up to come forward and squeeze Pete's arm. "I think she's got something. A sound. Something. Moss ain't so sure."

If the floor had suddenly opened up, she would gladly have jumped in. She'd rather do that than stand around listening to hard-to-please men talk about her singing like she wasn't even here.

"The guitar—that's another matter," Fry said. "It'll take a lot of lessons."

"I want you to teach her, man," Pete said. "Just like you taught me."

He frowned. "It'll cost you, Mister Pete. At least two dollars a session. Money up front. Me and Moss don't come cheap."

"It's a deal," Pete said, sticking out his hand.

She was left standing here, holding her guitar. No one even asked her if she wanted to take lessons from Fry or anybody else for that matter.

Later, after agreeing when to meet Fry for the first lesson, she was out on the street and cold again. This time Pete let her put on her overcoat.

"We've made a deal now," he said. "And a deal on Deal Street is the real thing. We don't sign contracts around here. A man's word is all that's needed. If you don't live up to your word, they kill you. Simple as that."

She shuddered, wondering what she was getting herself into.

"Just keep it from mama," Pete said. "If she heard tell I picked up singing and strumming the guitar from Moss and Fry, she'd denounce it as the devil's doings."

On the way home, she settled back in the seat and started to feel real good. Pete wasn't forcing her to sing and play. She'd always wanted to do that but had been afraid of a commitment on any level until she'd met him. "I've always liked to sing," she told him, reaching over to take his broad hand. "'Cause I've got a lot of feelings bottled up inside me. Music is the only way I know to express myself. Get it all out."

"Music is like a good woman to me. It'll cuddle up to you and send a thrill racing up your spine. In return you've got to treat it with respect. Just the kind of dignity you bring to church. Music is also something you've got to work at. That means lessons, gal."

She'd never thought of it that way. "I don't get it. It's too much fun to be called work. To me, work is scrubbing floors, picking cotton, washing out dirty workpants, and making beds—not strumming on my guitar and belting out a song."

"It's also a business. People make good money singing and playing. At least some folks do."

"Not me. Not someone like me."

He slammed on the brakes. She feared she'd angered him again. He sure had a quick temper.

"Now listen, don't make me madder than hell. I don't ever want to hear you put yourself down like that. It's people like us who make country music real. You've got a natural talent. It's got to be worked on—that's all."

As Pete's coupe turned a bend in the road, heading for home, she knew in her heart that surprises—maybe even big surprises—were waiting around the corner for her. Maybe some of those surprises were bad enough to hit her like a big fist in the gut. She glanced over at Pete, looking so handsome and virile in the Carolina sun. He was the strongest, most masculine man she'd ever known. A real man and not one of those pasty-faced weaklings like W.G. Gabriel at Belks Department Store.

No matter what was coming down the pike, no matter the tears that would be shed, no matter what shit hit the fan, Rosacoke just knew that

there were two things that were going to eat up her time in the days, weeks, and months ahead.

Pete Riddle and country music, and in that order.

# Chapter 4

The big day for Hank Adams had come. He was going to get his first set of wheels, a gift from Pete Riddle. As Pete drove to Herb Hester's house, it was not for bootleg liquor this time. Herb had to leave last night for Tennessee again—obviously that was where he got his moonshine—but his wife had been told to turn the car and its papers over to Pete for the sum of one-hundred and fifty dollars which Pete had secretly withdrawn from the Riddle bank account.

As the morning sun of a crisp autumn day shone into Pete's Ford coupe, he glanced over at the handsome blond-haired beauty sitting up front in the seat beside him. It was not blonde Rosacoke Carson but blond Hank Adams.

The whole county was gossiping about Pete taking up with Rosacoke, and even speculating what went on upstairs in the top bedrooms of the Riddle home at night. Rosacoke had turned out to be the best insurance Pete could ever have. With Pete seen driving Rosacoke around the town, who would imagine that he was queer?

A few men had talked and murmured things in whispers, and there had been a few loose lips here and there, but secrets like the kind Pete had didn't get mentioned too much. Those secrets were real private things. A man could get himself shot for getting drunk one night and saying the wrong thing to the wrong person. Besides, no real strong he-man indulged in gossip. Idle talk like that was for women. Strong men saw everything but said nothing. It was the male code of the hills.

Pete beamed at Hank who sat idly looking out the window. Once Pete had captured Hank's tongue that morning in the same bed with Sultan and the Mexican *puta*, getting the rest of Hank had been as easy as eating a piece of Mrs. Riddle's apple pie.

The following morning he'd gotten Hank to go down on him. Hank had not only gone down on him, but had taken to it like a calf sucking the teat of its mama. There was only one barrier. Hank still refused to get cornholed. "You can go up there with your tongue, and go as far as you want, but that's it. You hear me now?"

Hank didn't want to get cornholed himself, but he sure liked to cornhole Pete. As the days had passed by, Hank couldn't get enough of Pete's ass. Only yesterday he'd given Pete the thrill of his life when he'd taken to eating out Pete's ass before fucking it. Hank had offered only a meager excuse. "I figure I might as well try that too. You're always slurping at my hole. I figured there must be something to it." He smiled, flashing those

perfect white teeth. "And there is. Tastes just like pussy. The more I eat your ass, the more I want to fuck it."

Hank had certainly earned that car they were picking up today. Pete was pleased with all the Adams brothers, but admitted he had a lot of work yet to do on Tracy and Karl. They were still in the stage of letting Pete have them from the neck down but he wanted more. Even if he didn't get to cornhole the brothers, he wanted to share love-making with them to the extent he did with Hank. Pete wanted a lot of kissing and tongue sucking before he got fucked by either of the brothers. So far both young men steadfastly refused to do that. But Pete had a scheme how he was going to win over each teenager to his way of loving. It was just a matter of time.

With John there was no problem. From the first time fourteen-year-old John had come to that bed in the Adams family loft, John was willing and able to perform any act on Pete that he desired. Hank and his other brothers had taught John well. He'd been getting cornholed since he was nine years old, and it was a perfectly natural act for him.

Of all the Adams brothers, John was his favorite. Even as he thought that, Pete wasn't so sure. John might be his favorite in the sense that he gave Pete more personal pleasure than all the other brothers. Pete liked to fuck as much as he liked to get fucked, and John practically begged for it every day.

But there was no man who was as sexy as Hank Adams. Pete suspected that in all the world God didn't make men as sexy as Hank Adams. If God had done that, no woman or no queer would get any work done on earth. They'd spend all their time chasing other men who looked like Hank Adams.

Pete was mighty pleased with his arrangement with the Adams boys. Buying Hank the car was just the first step. He planned rewards for all the other brothers as well—maybe not a car, but something real nice for each of them too.

If Pete had a problem, it was Rosacoke herself. She'd been looking at him with those calf-like eyes of hers. She practically swooned when he walked in the front door. The first time he'd taken her out on a date he'd deliberately put the make on her. He knew that Rosacoke was a nice gal and would refuse his advances. She did exactly like he thought she would. That had given Pete the excuse he needed not to hit upon her again.

Lately he felt Rosacoke had regretted not giving in to him. She was practically throwing herself at him, and he knew she wanted it badly, even if she couldn't admit to herself that she had needs that only a man could satisfy.

Sooner than later, Pete knew he had to take Rosacoke to bed. Men like himself dated for fun but occasionally had to fuck women to keep up appearances. Pete knew that was the rule. He couldn't get around the rules

any more than W.G. Gabriel at the Belks Department Store could. Pete knew that he would be expected to get married one day. When that time came, Pete was going to carry out his duty like a good soldier. He sure wasn't looking forward to it. It was just something you had to do and you did it.

In another five minutes Pete would be at the Hester house. He turned to Hank. "Did John tell you I'm getting him into the Boy Scouts?"

"He told me all about it," Hank said. "Sounds good to me. Something about you being his big brother."

"Yeah, the older boys have been instructed to recruit and bring in younger guys. Once you get them in the Scouts, we're supposed to look after them, especially if they are poor like John is and live down in the holler. I'm gonna be a Big Brother to John-John. That's my new nickname for him."

"Sounds like a good excuse to me," Hank said, winking at him.

Pete smiled back at Hank. "I need some sort of excuse. It's awkward for me to be seen hanging out with a fourteen-year-old. But with the Boy Scouts as my cover, I've got it made. We're even being encouraged to bring some of the poorer kids home with us. Show them how decent people live. Table manners. Shit like that. Under this Big Brother plan of the Scouts, I can even have John-John spend the night in my bed. No one will be the wiser unless he screams out when I plug him. Even my mama and pappy think it's a good idea. They feel I'm doing my civic duty."

"You're doing your duty all right," Hank said, laughing at the absurdity of all this game-playing. "It's all about appearances, isn't it? That's so God damn important to you."

"Hell, yes, it is," Pete said. "I've got my reputation to think of."

"Don't mean shit to me," Hank said. "I ain't got no reputation to protect."

No sooner had Hank made that accurate self-assessment than Pete pulled into the driveway of the Hester household. Before leaving on one of his hooch runs, Herb had polished and shined the black Ford for them. The car had been sitting in his driveway for months with a FOR SALE sign. The sign had been removed. Pete had already deposited the one-hundred and fifty dollars into Herb's bank account.

Hank was eager to get in his new car, tell everyone to "eat my dust," and head for the open road. But Medora, Herb's wife, had other plans and insisted that the two young men come into her kitchen to have morning coffee and a ham biscuit. Reluctantly Hank agreed but it was obvious he was very impatient.

In her late forties, Medora was dressed in a red purplish dress with six sets of beads around her neck. She wore thick glasses but was heavily made up. Even Narcissa didn't wear lipstick as bright red as Medora's.

Herb seemed to adore his woman, although Pete had heard that most

men shunned her except Sultan and one or two others. She was a disgrace in the county, though Herb often spoke of her as if she were the Virgin Mary herself returned to earth.

Sipping his coffee and looking at Medora across the breakfast table, Pete didn't see where the flame was. To him, Medora was a grotesque, and he didn't know how she managed to get a rise out of Sultan. If it weren't for the money, Pete didn't think Sultan could manage to perform with this one. Her fat belly showed through the clinging silk dress she wore.

Pete felt Medora's sagging breasts belonged more on a cow. Those massive jugs didn't have a brassiere holding them up either.

Hank seemed unconcerned and totally removed from their little morning coffee chit-chat. Medora eyed both young men as if she wanted to slurp them into that volcano of hers. Sultan had told Pete that he practically fell into a giant canyon every time he mounted Medora, and Sultan had the biggest dick in the county. Pete suspected that it would take both Hank and him entering Medora at the same time to get her off, and even with two big dicks inside her they would probably have room to roller-skate unless Sultan had exaggerated.

Medora threw back her head and laughed. About what exactly Pete didn't know. When she offered Hank a cigarette, he took it, though Pete turned one down.

"I know you young bucks can have all the women you want in this county," Medora said. "And I'm sure you take advantage of your good looks." She looked first at Hank, then at Pete. It was obvious that she viewed the more mature Hank as the far sexier of the duet. "I'm not exactly beauticious," she said. "But bold bodied and bountiful." She sucked in the air deeply which made her breasts lift up, although there was no way in hell such massive weight could become airborne.

"What did you have in mind?" Hank asked abruptly, not concealing his irritation at being denied a chance to get behind the steering wheel of his new car to take it for a spin.

She didn't answer him, at least not directly. "You know, the women of this county put me down. But my Herbie brings in more money every week than any of the no-good skunks in this part of the world. Nothing is too good or out of the price range of his Medora. When he goes away, he always leaves me with a big bundle of cash."

She drank her coffee, then leaned back in her chair, making Pete think she might topple over at any moment. "I know you boys are a little short of cash. You probably aren't opposed to having some extra money in your pocket."

"Are you offering to buy us?" Hank asked.

Medora just looked at Hank calmly, blowing smoke rings into the air.

Pete felt that he'd die on the spot. He'd never heard a man ask a married woman that question before. That's something you might say to a queer like W.G. Gabriel, but not to a married woman.

Medora didn't seem in the least insulted by Hank's question. If anything, it amused her. "It don't exactly have to be in the form of cold, hard cash," she said. "After all, you are white boys. Not some buck nigger like Sultan who can raise a foot-long hard-on at the sight of a ten-dollar bill. With you boys I could be more subtle. What say I offered you free white lightning any time you got a hankering for it? Hank, your name. Hankering. I didn't get the connection." Her garish and over-painted face lit up again, and she leaned dangerously back in her chair.

Hank rose from the table. "I'd say that was a pretty fair deal. But I can't right now. I gotta go. Me and Pete will be by some night to take you on. If you'd like we'd stick both of our dicks in you at the same time. How would twenty inches of dick feel going up your cunt at the same time?"

This time Pete felt Hank had gone too far, even with a woman like Medora. Pete wasn't even sure you could talk that way to a nigger whore.

Once again Medora wasn't insulted. If anything, Hank's dirty talk had inflamed her. "Boys, I've got to have both of you. I met up with Narcissa Cash one day when she was in the back seat of Sultan's car. She told me she'd fucked both of you and that you had big dicks but she didn't reveal the exact measurements. Narcissa wasn't sure. My pussy is on fire at the thought of taking both of you on at the same time."

Pete too rose from the table. "Catch me later. I've got to get back. I promised to do something in town for my mama."

Hank headed toward the door, and Pete was hot on his friend's heels. There was no way he wanted to be left in that kitchen alone with Medora.

As both boys raced into the autumn noon-day sun, Medora stood at her front door, calling to them. "Let me at least suck you guys off before you go."

Hank was the first in his car. Off he headed down the graveled road leading to the open highway. In his Ford coupe, Pete was close to follow. He turned once to see Medora standing in her front yard calling to him.

The last words that came from Medora's gaping mouth was, "I swallow."

\*\*\*

Rosacoke could not believe her eyes when Pete Riddle showed up at his parents' home with that low-down John Adams tagging after him. Getting the Adams brothers to mow the fall hay was one thing, but actually inviting one of them in to eat supper with his family was quite another matter.

Didn't Pete know what kind of reputation the Adams boys had? If he didn't he could find out for himself. She certainly wasn't going to tell him. If there was one thing she wasn't, it was a gossip. She would leave that loose-lipped talk to Narcissa Cash.

Pete flashed his Oscar-winning smile at her and asked her to show John where to wash up for supper.

Rosacoke had never really looked at John carefully until now. Every time she'd seen him before, he was with one of his brothers. If that brother happened to be Hank Adams, no one looked at anybody else. She had to admit to herself that Hank was sexy. Yes, even sexier than Pete. But there was something so menacing about him you couldn't look at anybody else when Hank was around. It was as if you had to keep an eye glued to Hank to figure out what his next move against you might be.

John seemed downright bashful around strangers. He sure wasn't aggressive like his other three brothers. Not only Hank but Karl and Tracy stared at a woman like they were undressing her. When she ran into them, they gaped so long, hard, and longingly at her big bosom she wished she could make her tits shrink. She feared what would happen to her if one or both of them ever caught up with her alone.

She showed John upstairs to the bathroom and gave him a clean towel. Everybody else in the household used the same towel which she changed daily. But she was instructed by Mrs. Riddle to give all guests a clean towel. Of course, Rosacoke knew Mrs. Riddle meant *real* company, like when the preacher came over for Sunday dinner. Rosacoke figured she could also extend this privilege to John himself, even if he were one of the Adams brothers. After all, she didn't want to dry her hands on the same towel where John had dried his. The boy was low-down white trash in her eyes.

John was fascinated by the bathroom, the first one he'd even been in. "I've never seen nothing this pretty before," he said. "Everything so white and so shiny new. You gotta show me how everything works."

"Maybe Pete Riddle might show you," Rosacoke said. "It ain't exactly proper for a white gal to show any boy how to use a bathroom. I know you were brung up like me. I hadn't known a bathroom neither—only outhouses like you Adams boys—until I came to live with the Riddles."

"Please, show me," he said, reaching for her arm.

"I'll ask Pete Riddle to show you," she said. "It'll be another hour before me and Mrs. Riddle get supper on the table." She looked him up and down. He was not as clean as he should be. "I'll go downstairs and get Pete. Maybe he'll show you how to take a bath in a real tub and get all clean and shiny faced before you sit down with the Riddles. They are mighty respectable folks, and it would be polite of you to show up at the table all fresh and clean, not looking as if you've come from the back yard

slopping the hogs."

"Tell Pete to come on up here," the boy said with the eagerness of a youngin' opening up some wonderful new present around the Christmas tree.

When she shut the door, she had to admit to herself that the Adams brothers might be the trashiest white family in the county, but those brothers were certainly good looking. That John with his delicate skin, almost like porcelain, was prettier than most girls she went to school with. The other Adams brothers were sexily handsome but John was downright beautiful. She felt beauty like that belonged to a girl—not a boy. When God was handing out the good looks, he must have made a big mistake and gave a boy like John looks like that. It didn't seem right somehow.

She believed girls should look like girls and boys should look like boys. She didn't know what to make of a boy who was prettier than any gal.

John was real slim, as his body hadn't filled in like the other Adams brothers. He had blond curly hair and the most dreamy baby blue eyes she'd ever seen. His lashes were long, golden, and silken. There was something luscious about the corners of his mouth which seemed to curl up at times. When he asked a question, he blushed crimson as if he'd said something wrong, even though the question might be as harmless as a fly buzzing around your nose.

Downstairs Pete was sitting in the living room listening to the radio. The news being broadcast out of Charlotte wasn't good. There was talk of war. Everybody felt that England was going to fall to the Nazis. She didn't know where England was and wasn't even sure who the Nazis were, but Mrs. Riddle had warned her that if they ever took over a country, they would gather up all the pretty gals and rape them like bulls mounting cows.

She dreaded what would happen to her if the Nazis ever brought their tanks into her county. Yet she thought about them a lot. Narcissa said that Nazi soldiers were big, blond, and beautiful, and that they wouldn't have to rape her. She'd give it away to these soldiers. Rosacoke had warned Narcissa to hush up with such talk since someone might overhear them.

Rosacoke came into the living room downstairs, and Pete seemed real glad to see her. He was always so polite and friendly to her. She hated to admit this to herself, but she wished he didn't treat her with so much re-spect, even though he knew she was a good gal. Sometimes even a good gal might like to get manhandled a bit. She'd made herself up real pretty for him tonight and had worn a new flower-patterned dress she'd sewn for herself out of feed sack.

"John's upstairs," she said. "He's in the bathroom, and he wanted me to show him how to use the plumbing. I figured that was no job for a gal. I think he wants to take a bath. That's where you come in."

"Pete Riddle to the rescue," he said.

His eagerness to show John how the plumbing worked came as a surprise to her. He always liked to listen to the news broadcast at night and seemed to resent it if interrupted. Not tonight. He bounded up the steps and was gone. She stood looking at the stairs that led to the upper bedrooms. Her mind was trying to ponder something but she didn't exactly know what it was.

She went into the kitchen to help Mrs. Riddle with supper and to set the table. When the food was ready, Mrs. Riddle turned to her. "Would you ask Pete and his young friend to come on down and eat? They are taking the longest time up there. Both of them must be getting real clean."

She walked slowly up the steps as if afraid to knock on the bathroom door. Both Pete and John had been in there a very long time, far longer than it took a decent person, regardless of how dirty, to take a sudsy bath. She heard laughter and giggling inside that bathroom. The two of them were just like little boys playing in bath water. She rapped on the door, calling out to them that supper was ready.

Pete hadn't seemed to resent her interrupting him as he'd listened to the news broadcast. But the sound of his voice indicated he was pissed off at this latest invasion of his privacy.

"Tell mama we'll go down directly," he shouted at her. "We haven't finished yet." The only sound that came from John was another giggle. She turned and headed down the stairs. She felt jealous that John, a boy, was in there getting to see Pete naked and all. She tried to blot out the image from her mind, but she constantly dreamed of seeing Pete naked. Now John was getting to look at more than one kind of plumbing—not only the white porcelain fixtures but the equipment Pete carried between his legs too. It didn't seem right somehow for a little fourteen-year old boy to have that chance. To John, Pete's plumbing meant nothing. How could it? To her, it was the stuff of dreams. She bet Pete had something real special hidden in his pants.

Wiping her mind of such dirty thoughts, she waited and waited in the kitchen, keeping supper warm for the Riddles. Just at the point Mrs. Riddle asked her to go back upstairs again and fetch them for supper, Pete bounded down the steps followed by a shy John. He might have been giggling and carrying on in that bathtub with Pete, but once he was back in polite company he retreated into a shy shell again and didn't have much to say.

Over vittles, Mrs. Riddle told Pete that she was real proud of him for taking interest in a fourteen-year-old boy and trying to set him on the right path in life.

"You've been real lucky, son," Mr. Riddle said to Pete. "Me and your mama are right proud to see you wanting to share some of your good fortune with this Adams boy here."

Rosacoke felt they spoke of John as if he weren't even at the table.

"You'll have to teach him the way of the Lord," Mrs. Riddle said. "I know he ain't getting the right teaching at home."

"If he's getting any teaching at all," Mr. Riddle added.

Rosacoke had pounded tough steak and fried it country style for the family. It was one of Pete's favorite dishes. John looked confused. "I ain't had steak before," he told Pete. "Hank says we can't afford it."

Pete reached over and showed him how to cut the meat into bite-sized pieces. On his first bite, John had practically lifted up all the meat on his plate.

"Just watch what Pete does," Mrs. Riddle told John. "If you do like my son does, you'll grow up to be a boy to make us proud like we are of Pete."

"I will," John said, glancing down at his plate before looking lovingly into Pete's eyes. "I'll do everything my Big Brother tells me to do."

Pete reached over and chucked him under the chin. "And I wouldn't have it any other way."

John giggled as he had before in the bathroom.

Rosacoke decided these two boys were gigglers. Up to now Pete had radiated a strong masculinity far beyond his seventeen years. But somehow around John, Pete reverted to being just a boy again.

"What do you eat at the Adams home?" Mrs. Riddle asked John.

"Hank keeps a pot on the stove," the boy said. "It's like a stew actually. We call it Hungarian goulash. Anything we can find we throw in that pot. A possum. Root vegetables. Sometimes we skin a squirrel. Hank every now and then comes home with a chicken. We never ask him where he got it."

"He probably stole it from some farmer," Mr. Riddle said. "I've heard stories. The Millers said you boys raided their watermelon patch a lot this past summer."

"We get hungry," John said defensively. "Hungry people do what they can to fill their gut."

"Let's drop the subject," Pete said, seemingly uncomfortable for the first time this evening. He reached over and felt the muscle on John's arms. "We'll fatten him up this winter. Put some meat on those bones. I bet John-John here is going to grow into a man just as big as his brother Hank."

Rosacoke seemed astonished that Pete was calling him "John-John." What kind of name was that for a grown boy?"

After supper, the family retired to the living room to listen to the radio. There was going to be a broadcast that night from Hollywood with Louella Parsons. Pete always liked to hear programs about Hollywood and claimed that he was going to go there one day.

Before the show came on, Mr. Riddle looked over at his son and beamed. "Me and your mama have made a big decision today. There's all this war

talk. I hear from everybody that if a war comes they are not going to make any more cars until after it's over. All the plants will have to make tanks and guns. We figure that Ford coupe we bought you won't last through a long, drawn-out war that might rage on for years. We're going to buy you a new Ford. You can go pick it out yourself. Sell your other one, but I don't think you'll get too much for it."

Pete looked like he'd miraculously gone to heaven. "A new car? I can't believe it. I'm so happy."

Rosacoke couldn't help but notice that he reached over and hugged John, almost clutching him and pulling him to his bosom. She felt Pete was sure mixed up on who to thank for his new car. John Adams sure wasn't buying that new vehicle for Pete.

Pete was filled with such joy that he couldn't listen to the broadcast of Louella Parsons from Hollywood. Usually he stayed up until ten o'clock. It was only eight-thirty when he announced he was turning in. "I'm too tired to drive John-John home," he said. "I've asked him to spend the night with me up in my bedroom."

"That's real thoughtful of you, son," Mrs. Riddle said.

John politely thanked the Riddles and Rosacoke too for what he said was "the best supper I've ever had in my life. Hank sure can't cook like you folks."

Pete finally got around to kissing his mama's withered cheek and shaking his daddy's hand and thanking him profusely for the car. After saying good night, Pete headed up the steep wooden steps to the upper-floor bedroom. Rosacoke noted that he'd playfully patted John on the ass. Boys horsed around like that.

She decided that she wasn't interested in the Parsons broadcast either and by nine o'clock she excused herself, seeing that everything was put away in the kitchen, before turning in herself.

As she passed the door to Pete's bedroom, she heard more giggling like the giggling that had come from the bathroom. Those two boys sure had a lot to giggle about.

Alone in her own room, she felt isolated, lonely, and depressed. Life wasn't much fun. But then who ever said life was meant to be fun?"

It was amazing how things worked out. Here was that John in Pete's bedroom sleeping with him and sharing a mattress. A perfect stranger had just appeared overnight in their lives and was sharing this most intimate moment with Pete. Night after night she'd dreamed of lying in that same bed and sharing intimacies with Pete.

John was where she wanted to be, smelling Pete's freshness, listening to his breathing, and basking in the glow of his masculinity. Of course, John was only a young boy, and throughout the county younger brothers were sharing beds with older brothers. To her, it was a kind of intimacy forced

upon young boys before they got rooms of their own or else found a woman with whom to share their bed. It didn't much matter, she decided. John— or "John-John" as Pete affectionately called this pretty boy—would be gone tomorrow, and she'd have no more reason to be jealous.

*** 

In Pete's chilly bedroom John snuggled into the older boy's arms. "You smell real good," John whispered in Pete's ears before planting tiny little kisses on the more masculine older boy's neck.

Pete reached out for John, pulling him even closer into his chest, as he rubbed the boy's baby-smooth asscheeks, knowing where he was going to take his pleasure later in the night. This night with John-John was going to be long and drawn out, not like the rushed sex they'd had before.

"Can I ask you something and get you to answer me all honest and true?" John said, whispering softly in Pete's ear.

"I promise to tell you the whole truth," Pete claimed. "Whatever you ask me."

"I'm real young," John said. "What I'm gonna ask may sound a little silly but I'm gonna ask it anyway. I know what I want."

"Ask away," Pete said, as his forefinger found the delicious rosebud he'd been anticipating all night. In just moments from now, he planned to spend an hour tonguing that delectable hole before fucking it all night.

"Can I be your girl?" John said.

Pete was taken back as if not hearing right. No person had ever asked him that question before. No girl, certainly. Most definitely no boy. Pete chuckled softly and pulled John closer into his body, as Pete's dick hardened. The very question was causing his dick to thicken and lengthen, knowing he had this pretty little boy in his total control. "How can you be my gal since you're a boy?"

"You know what I mean," John said, sounding disappointed at Pete's response. "I can do for you what no gal can do or would do for you. You know that's true."

There was a certain truth to that, Pete figured. He thought about John's offer. It excited him.

"I've already told my brothers, especially that Hank, that no one is ever gonna cornhole me ever again," John said. "Only Pete Riddle." He wiggled as Pete continued to finger him. "You're the only man I'll ever let get up in me again."

The idea that John-John would belong exclusively to him and would service him and only him made Pete's cock shoot up to its full and impressive length. As he fingered John, the boy was also playing with Pete's balls and testing and measuring the full length of his Big Brother's erection.

"John-John," he whispered into the boy's ear before darting his tongue in that ear to bathe it, as he'd soaped and bathed the boy in the bathtub. "You've found your man."

John took his hands off Pete's cock long enough to reach for his head, pulling Pete's mouth close to his. His little pink tongue darted into Pete's mouth to savor and taste. Pete's longer tongue shot out, burying itself deeper and deeper into John's sweet mouth where it got the sucking of its life. A little yelp escaped from John's throat as Pete's finger invaded the boy's rosebud and probed hard, preparing it for the long, deep penetration that was to come.

After about five minutes of exchanging saliva, slurping, and sucking, Pete broke away. "I'm real horny," Pete said to the boy. I've got to cornhole you."

"I only feel alive when you're buried deep inside me," John said.

Pete was about ready to flip John over and fuck him but the kid had other ideas. "Tonight's different," John said. "It's real special to me."

"How's it different?" Pete asked. "What do you have in mind?" He smiled down at John and kissed his tender cupid lips.

"Before you plow me, I want to lick and suck every part of your body," John said.

Pete lay back in bed, stretching out. "I feel I'm really gonna enjoy this."

As John scooted down into Pete's large, comfortable bed, Pete just knew he was going to be treated like some Viking God being serviced by a slave boy. That suspicion was confirmed as John's succulent mouth descended on his big left toe, sucking it as John had just sucked Pete's tongue.

The kid was like some sucking machine. As the boy worked from toe to toe, Pete's pleasure intensified. He was amazed at how much joy a human mouth could give him. He'd had impersonal sex with women before, especially Narcissa, but he'd never known and felt love like this before. Even with the Adams brothers, it was just raw sex, the way it'd been with Sultan and Claude Billings. The love-making of John was unlike all other experiences.

It was clear to Pete that John had found the man of his dreams. John was clearly in love with him, and providing pleasure to Pete seemed almost as important as the love-making itself. John had moved upward now after sampling all ten toes and licking the balls of Pete's feet. He was spit-licking and polishing Pete's legs. Pete just tingled as he knew that John was moving closer to the goodies. Pete fondled his own balls anticipating the bathing they were to get.

Pete's balls tightened as John descended on him with that pink little tongue and those cupid lips. Before the balls, John had another target to attack. His lips traced a trail to Pete's ass, as Pete reared up in bed know-

He knew that John's agony would soon ease up and that the boy would be filled with the most delicious sensation. It'd been the same with Pete when Sultan had fucked him. He just knew it'd be that way for John too.

When he felt he'd stifled any scream from John, Pete's lips eased off John's mouth and slipped across the gooseflesh of the young boy's shoulders and neck, biting him gently yet forcefully. The boy was completely in Pete's spell, and he loved having another human being chained in his complete control.

Pete's lips sucked on the boy's tender ear lobes, bringing shivers to his body. John's lips were parted in pleasure as Pete ground into him.

John's little hands reached back to cup Pete's ass and pull him harder into his own butt. As the moonlight streamed through the room's lone window, it shone on John, giving the boy a luminous glow. His face was contorted into a monstrous rapture. Pete knew he was giving John as much ecstasy as he was taking from him, and that made Pete proud.

His strong farm hands pinched the boy's hard tits. Pete's forearms pressed tight against John's chest, holding him a complete prisoner as he rammed deeper into him. He stroked and slammed John's ass, no longer caring even if he hurt the boy. Pete was too far gone for that.

Pete bit into John's neck with a savage fury. He'd never gone this far before with any other person. The boy had unleashed some primitive beast within Pete that he didn't know lived within his soul.

Pete's teeth locked into John's neck, and Pete's lungs threatened to explode for lack of air. He knew he was engaging in some ancient jungle ritual. It was a rutting rite that had passed down through the ages to descend and take demonic control of his own body tonight.

Pete felt his powerful orgasm building. In moments streams of hot cum shot deep within John's guts, coating his insides. Pete felt John exploding for the second time tonight, coating Pete's stomach with the kid's own jism. As soon as he could breathe properly again, Pete planned to descend and lick up every drop of it like it was some precious nectar. None of the Adams brothers tasted as sugar sweet as John.

Pete crushed his lips against John's as he fell on top of the boy. When Pete was breathing again, he began to lick John's neck and young chest, going lower to lap up everything, the night sweat with the jism.

Then he raised himself up and fell on John again, inserting his tongue for the boy to suck. When the boy had cleaned out Pete's mouth, he moved his lips close to John's left ear. "Before the rooster crows," he told John, "I will have fucked you three more times. *At least.*"

"I belong to you," John said, running his fingers up and down Pete's muscled back. "Just to you. I'm the happiest boy on God's green earth. I didn't know a person could be this happy." He wove his fingers into Pete's wavy, thick hair, and looked deeply into his older lover's eyes. "Tell me

what I'm begging to hear. What I'm dreaming to hear. *Please.*"

Pete knew what John wanted him to say, but held back as if deliberately keeping the boy in suspense. Finally, Pete spoke. "From this day forth and forever more, you are my steady gal. I don't want any man but me to have you."

***

Rosacoke checked herself in the mirror for one final time. She'd made herself up all pretty like for her date with Pete. Since Mrs. Riddle had already gone to her bedroom downstairs with Mr. Riddle, Rosacoke decided to apply some scarlet red lipstick since Mrs. Riddle wouldn't see her. The old woman objected to "painted women," and certainly didn't want "a heifer who painted her mouth" around her son. Rosacoke figured that what Mrs. Riddle didn't know wouldn't hurt her.

Tonight Rosacoke was determined not to reject Pete like she'd done on her first date with him. Ever since she'd turned him down when he'd wanted some loving from her, he'd been respectful, but a little distant. The way she looked at it tonight, a healthy, red-blooded male like Pete Riddle was ready and raring for some action. If she didn't give it to him, someone else would.

Narcissa Cash always seemed available to any good-looking man in the county, especially that no-count but sexy Hank Adams. Did Rosacoke want Pete turning for his loving to that whore, Emma Lou Hayes, who screwed anything that had a pair of pants on? Rosacoke did not. She feared that Pete might catch something from Emma Lou, something real bad. She'd heard of a family who lived down in the holler, the Mintons. The daddy had caught syphilis when he was just a young man like Pete and had had nine kids, all of them retarded. She shuddered at the prospect of Pete bringing home some disease like that. If she ever married him, their kids might be retarded too. To keep that from happening, she was going to send a sign to him tonight that she'd held out against his advances long enough. If he moved toward her tonight, he'd find that her borders were not defended.

Maybe Pete wouldn't want to go all the way. Narcissa had told her that on certain occasions when she wasn't attracted to one of her dates, she managed to get through the evening by jacking him off. Rosacoke wasn't exactly sure how a gal went about jacking a man off, but she knew she could learn. After all, it wasn't that long ago that she didn't even know how to apply lipstick.

From the looks of that dazzling blonde-haired creature staring back at her in the mirror, she could apply makeup just as well as that Lana Turner on the silver screen. She also knew that she had a bigger bosom than Lana.

What she didn't have was Clark Gable or Robert Taylor making love to her. The way Rosacoke saw it, Pete Riddle was better looking and probably even better at love-making than Gable or pretty boy Taylor would ever be.

The only thing that bothered Rosacoke about Pete was that cute little Adams boy he insisted on calling "John-John." She'd passed by his door last night and had heard strange sounds coming from Pete's room. The walls were real thin upstairs at the Riddle house. Those two teenage boys weren't asleep in that room. They weren't exactly giggling either. The sounds were different but the bed was moving. She figured they must be having a pillow fight. She'd been told that boys liked to horse around and do things like that, although she had to admit to herself that her knowledge of what boys did alone in their bedrooms was very limited.

Narcissa claimed that when young boys went to bed at night, they jacked off thinking of what they would like to do with gals. Rosacoke figured that was what John-John and Pete were doing.

For all she knew, Pete was in that bedroom jacking off thinking of her big tits. What John-John was thinking about when he'd jacked off she didn't know. She wasn't even certain that John-John was old enough to jack off. How old did a boy have to be before he could jack off? She suspected it was around sixteen or so, maybe earlier. If she was determined to fill her head with this useless information, she could always ask Narcissa. That little hussy seemed to know everything there was to know about the male sex.

Rosacoke had fully suspected that when morning came Pete would put John-John in his coupe and drive him back to the Adams shanty where the little rascal belonged. It hadn't worked out that way.

At the breakfast table, Pete had even given John-John two extra strips of bacon from his own plate. After breakfast, they'd wandered out into the fields somewhere after Pete had placed a call to the local Ford dealer telling him that he was coming in to buy a new car.

When John-John was still around to eat the midday dinner at the Riddle table, Rosacoke had reckoned that Pete would drive the boy home in the afternoon. Not so. When she'd found John-John reading a magazine at five o'clock in the living room, while listening to the radio, she'd suspected that he was going to be around for supper too.

And so he was. Not only that but John-John was going to spend the night again in Pete's bedroom. She wasn't sure but she'd detected anger in John-John-s face when Pete had invited her out. The boy had become sulky as if he were mad at Pete. Why on earth would that no-count boy be mad if Pete invited a gal out on a date? She guessed it was because John-John was lonely and had wanted someone to play with that night, maybe to have another one of those pillow fights with.

With John-John retreating upstairs, Pete had kissed her on the cheek,

leaving a tingling sensation, and had gone off on a drive by himself, claiming he'd be back in twenty minutes. He kept his promise. Right on time, she heard his car coming up the driveway. He honked his horn for her. She ran out the door fearing that Pete would wake up the Riddles.

Jumping in the front seat with him, she was startled to see Narcissa and Hank Adams sitting in the back seat. Pete hadn't told her that this was going to be a double date.

As Pete headed down the road, Hank and Narcissa seemed real friendly like. Narcissa had never asked Rosacoke why she'd run away from Sultan's shanty, and Rosacoke had no intention of telling her. Even Hank was especially nice tonight, not leering at her like he usually did. He even thanked her for looking after his brother, John, and feeding him well, although that was a job Rosacoke would like to see come to an end sooner than later.

She'd been shocked when she found out that Pete was driving all of them to the Blue Note Café. No respectable white gal ever went there. The local men referred to it as "that nigger joint up on the pike" outside the town limits. She'd heard a rumor that the only reason it was allowed to keep open was that its owner, Big Mama Sadie, regularly paid off the sheriff, Claude Billings.

She'd also heard that the sheriff and two of his most trusted deputies, Junior Grayson and Ronnie Key, not only came around every month to get some cash from Big Mama Sadie but also to avail themselves of some of the nigger gals who hung out at the club. Narcissa told her that Hank and Pete were regular customers at the Blue Note Café.

Big Mama Sadie always claimed she turned no man away if he had cash in his pants. "White or black," she always said, "it's all the same to me at night when the lights are out." At least that's what Narcissa had told Rosacoke that the club owner said. For all Rosacoke knew, Big Mama Sadie was a God-fearing Christian woman who went to church every Sunday and didn't talk dirty like that at all.

At the Blue Note Café the joint was jumping. Rosacoke clearly recognized the sound of the Andrew Sisters playing on the jukebox. Those gals could really sing. Next to Dinah Shore, they were her favorite singers. She hoped no one she knew would see her sneaking into the Blue Note.

At the door Big Mama Sadie—all three-hundred pounds of her—greeted them. "My two favorite white boys in the county," she said. She was wearing a cheap, slutty-looking red silk dress sewn with rhinestones. It was cut real low revealing her big bosom. Her breasts were larger than Rosacoke's, and up to then Rosacoke figured she had the biggest tits in the county.

Hank leaned over and kissed Big Mama Sadie right on the lips. Rosacoke was shocked. She'd never seen a white man kiss a black woman on the lips before, but she figured the rules at the Blue Note were different

from anywhere else in the county.

"When I was just fourteen, Big Mama Sadie here taught me what to do with that thing growing between my legs," Hank said, winking at Rosacoke.

Such talk! Rosacoke knew she was in for more than one shock that night. Her next surprise was when Pete leaned over and kissed Big Mama Sadie right on her painted mouth too. Had Big Mama Sadie broken in Pete too?

The club owner turned to Rosacoke and took her hand. "Welcome, blondie. I find that most white boys aren't worth messing up my pussy with. But Hank and Pete are different than most. I think they've got nigger blood in them."

With that strange pronouncement, she headed up to the bandstand and to a group of black men to signal to them to start the music. No more jukebox. The club was going to dance to live music.

Rosacoke was swept into the club and down to a table in the rear. She didn't know what was happening. She'd never been in a club so dark before. In fact, she'd never been to a night club at all.

Most of the room was filled with black couples, but she noted a white man or two talking at table with black girls and swigging down moonshine. Narcissa had told her that Mama Sadie wasn't allowed to serve liquor but she offered Coca-Cola at two dollars a bottle. Her patrons poured moonshine into the coke. That's how she got around the law—that and a little payoff each month to Claude Billings and his boys.

At the sound of the live music, couples jumped up on the floor for a wild jitterbug. She'd never seen such dancing. Pete grabbed Narcissa by the arm, not even asking her if she wanted to dance.

Up to now, Rosacoke had never known if Pete even knew how to dance. The way he was throwing Narcissa up in the air made them look like professionals. She'd never seen anything this wild even in the movies.

"Wanna dance?" Hank asked her, taking her arm.

"I don't know how," she said shyly. "Besides, I ain't got no intention of getting up there and showing off like that Narcissa. I've never seen a gal carry on like that one before."

Narcissa and Pete had been so good that the other dancers parted and eventually formed a circle around them. They were clearly the stars of the night, providing the entertainment for Big Mama Sadie's jive-talking customers. Many of the men wore zoot suits making them look like hepcats.

"It's cool, cool, man," was all that Hank could say.

She didn't think it was cool at all. The club wasn't well ventilated and was filled with smoke and the smell of liquor and sweaty bodies. If anything, she felt the room was stifling even though the autumn night outside was chilly.

After an hour of hot dancing, Narcissa and Pete got tired. Hank had

drifted off somewhere but returned to smoke a strange-smelling cigarette one of the black musicians had given him. Rosacoke had smelled cigarette smoke all her life—after all, she'd grown up in tobacco country but she'd never smelled smoke like Hank blew out. He told her it was a "Turkish cigarette." She'd never heard of Turkey but felt it must be some Arab country over near the Holy Land. She had absolutely no conception of world geography, and didn't even know what state North Carolina bordered except for Tennessee in the west.

Big Mama Sadie announced that she was going to appear as the "Head-liner" of the night's show going on at one o'clock. Never in her life had Rosacoke stayed up this late. Secretly she wanted to hear Big Mama Sadie sing. If there was one dream Rosacoke had other than Pete, it was to get up and sing to a group of people, even though the thought of such an appearance filled her with such dread she feared she'd shake all over if given the chance.

Pete invited all three of them to walk down by the water to cool off. He was sweating heavily and so was Narcissa. Rosacoke was thankful she'd taken a sweater. She'd sat at her table all night and hadn't worked up a sweat. She hadn't even tasted the white lightning and coke offered her.

As the four of them stood looking down at the mountain lake, Narcissa chose this occasion to tell them her big plans which so far she'd concealed from Sultan. "I've got big news, big, big news," she said, flashing her bright teeth in a wide smile, her eyes burning with a fierce determination Rosacoke had never seen there before.

"Not now," Hank cautioned her, looking over at Pete.

"Why not now?" Pete asked. "Spill the beans."

"Me and Hank here are gonna run away to Chicago next week," she announced with pride.

"I told you not to tell them," Hank said, glancing sheepishly over at Pete.

This was old news to Rosacoke. Pete had a different reaction. His face burst into fury. "You're out of your fucking mind," he shouted at Narcissa. "You bitch!" He turned and walked so rapidly it was like he was half running along the path by the water's edge.

"Hey, Pete, wait up." Hank ran after him.

"What's all this about?" Rosacoke asked Narcissa. She didn't understand why Pete would be so upset at the news. He surely wasn't still involved with Narcissa, was he? If he were, he wouldn't go out on a double date with her and invite Hank along. Nothing made sense to her.

"I don't think Pete wants Hank to go away?" Narcissa said a little too smugly. "I think he'll miss ole Hank."

"I don't get it," Rosacoke said. "Pete knows Hank but why would he care where he went?" An idea snapped in her brain like walking on a brittle

twig. "It's because of John. That's it. Pete will be left to care for John. The boy's too young to look after himself. Karl and Tracy are grown-up boys. They can fend for themselves. But if Hank runs off with you, he'll be saddling Pete with the raising of his kid brother. I can see why Pete's pissed off. I would be too. It's unfair somehow."

Narcissa looked more smugly than ever as if she were in possession of some real hot information that she was keeping to herself. "Something like that, I guess." She smiled. "Did you know that Pete went and bought Herb Hester's car for Hank?"

"I did not," she said. "Why would he go and do something like that? For a no-count white skunk he hardly knows."

"Men do strange things when they're alone together," Narcissa said. "Things women aren't allowed to be privy to."

"I can sure believe that," Rosacoke said, looking down the lone trail where Pete and Hank had disappeared. She'd heard Pete shouting at Hank but nothing more. Either Pete had stopped shouting or else the men had moved out of hearing range.

She stood in the cold waiting for Hank and Pete to come back. Almost thirty minutes went by. Narcissa got tired of waiting and went back to the Blue Note. Rosacoke wrapped her sweater around her body and stayed by the lake, shivering in the cool breezes blowing across from the other side. When she'd almost given up hope, Hank came walking up the path, smoking another one of those cigarettes. There was no sign of Pete.

"Where is he?" Rosacoke asked, fearing something might have happened to him.

"Claude Billings and two of his deputies, Junior and Ronnie, pulled up," Hank said. "Pete gave me the keys. He wants me to drive you and Narcissa back home. The sheriff took Pete off to sober him up. He didn't want him going home drunk, maybe having an accident, or upsetting his poor parents. Mrs. Riddle is a bit delicate, I hear."

"Yeah, I guess so," Rosacoke said. She felt despondent. She wasn't being fed the whole truth.

"C'mon," Hank said. "I'll drive you home."

"That'd be mighty nice of you." The sound of a whippoorwill in the forest seemed to mock her plight.

Some date this turned out to be.

*** 

As drunk as he was on white lightning, Pete tingled with excitement thinking about what was about to happen to him. Up front, the deputy, Junior Grayson, was driving the sheriff's squad car. In the passenger seat, Claude Billings sampled some of the moonshine Pete had brought to the

Blue Note. The sheriff was getting drunk himself as he so often did.

In the back seat, Pete sat next to Ronnie Key, the youngest of the town's three law-enforcement officers. He kept glancing over at Ronnie remembering what a terrific football player he'd been only four years ago at Pete's school. Ronnie was one of many boys Pete had a secret crush on, and Pete couldn't believe his good fortune. Within the hour he'd be getting into Ronnie's pants, something he never thought possible before.

Ronnie leaned over in the squad car and whispered to Pete. "Claude up there tells me you really know how to take care of a guy. Do things to him no woman will do."

"You got that right," Pete said with all the pride he could muster. He was glad that Claude had become a stalking advertiser for him, especially if such talk led him to get to sample the wares of Ronnie Key and Junior Grayson.

The squad car tilted toward the edge of the mountain road, and Claude yelled out to Junior, "Stay on the fucking road. If you keep driving like that, we'll go over the fucking mountain." Tipped toward the edge, the car straightened and got back on the paved highway and not the gravel.

It was an unlit shotgun house—two narrow rooms and an open passage between them—that Junior had taken them too. The unpainted clapboard house was perched on a hill, the cabin slanting under a massive heaped-up wisteria vine that blanketed the tin roof. It was still light and green as if lingering from the past summer, refusing to die.

Inside the house Ronnie built a fire, and Claude went to lie down on the sofa, as Junior busied himself lighting kerosene lamps.

Pete stood awkwardly about, wondering which man would go at him first and how. As the room warmed up, getting all cozy like, Claude showed that he was clearly in charge. He called for Pete to come over to the couch and remove his black leather boots. With mounting excitement, Pete approached the sheriff, taking off his boots and his black socks too.

Claude raised up on the sofa, unbuttoning his shirt and pulling it off. He kept on his undershirt but ordered Pete to pull off the striped pants of his sheriff's uniform.

"My drawers too," Claude ordered him. Pete nervously reached for the sheriff's white underwear, slipping it off and exposing the world's most beautiful dick. The moment Claude's cock was revealed, it started to rise to its full length of six inches. Pete glanced up at Junior and Ronnie who stood by the fire watching with complete fascination what was about to happen.

"I ain't never seen a boy suck a grown man's dick before," Junior said to no one in particular, perhaps only to himself.

Pete reached for Claude's erection, and lapped the head with his tongue before plunging all the way down on it. From time to time he deserted the

cock to wash and bathe the balls, taking them one by one in his mouth to savor their flavor. Claude was moaning. Occasionally he muttered something about, "How good it is."

Abandoning the balls, Pete descended momentarily on that rock hard offering of the sheriff. Pete made his way to that special spot he'd just learned every man has. It was just below the piss slit. He tongued and licked at that tiny patch of soft, sensitive skin. Every flick of Pete's tongue caused the sheriff to moan. He was running his fingers through Pete's wavy hair, holding him down, not that Pete needed to be forced down. Pete plunged deeper, taking every inch and holding the dick in his mouth like a suction pump. He was getting to Claude, and he knew the sheriff couldn't hold back much longer.

As Pete sucked, he ran his hands up Claude's muscular, hairy legs. Pete marveled at the masculine contours, as he fondled the muscled calves. The thighs felt like armor. Pete wished he'd taken off his own pants since he felt he was dripping with pre-cum.

Pete's reward came in a fiery blast from Claude that hit the back of Pete's throat. He tasted and slurped the offering and never wanted to take his mouth off the sheriff. He felt he belonged here forever deepthroating this man. Pete Riddle might go on to become a country lawyer, but he also knew that his true calling in life was that of a cocksucker, the more the merrier. One dick could never satisfy him. He needed at least three or four a day, maybe more, and was determined to go after them.

When the sheriff could take it no more, he yanked Pete by the hair, pulled him off him. "Your turn, boys," he called over to Junior and Ronnie. "Give this queer what he wants. He's a hungry one."

When Pete glanced over toward the fireplace, he was startled to see that both Junior and Ronnie had stripped buck-naked, each supporting a monstrous erection. Claude might be the big man at the sheriff's office, but his deputies had him beat in the meat market.

Claude got up on the sofa and went over in the corner to sample some more white lightning. Wearing only his undershirt, he sat down in an armchair to oversee what his boys were going to do to Pete.

Junior was the first to approach Pete. If Pete's eyes were a ruler, Junior measured up to an impressive eight and a half inches, maybe more. He had big balls too. Pete wrapped his fingers around the delicious looking uncut cock. It was rock hard and throbbing hotly.

Junior jammed his dick against Pete's face, hitting him in the eye. Pete backed off and took charge himself, skinning back the big head and reaching out to sample it.

He felt Ronnie removing Pete's clothing. Pete backed off Junior's prick and unbuttoned his shirt as Ronnie pulled down Pete's pants and underwear. Pete too wanted to be completely naked for the workout he was

about to get.

Junior hissed through clenched teeth, "Get to it." Pete slurped down every inch of Junior's cock, the long meat penetrating his throat. He opened his mouth wide to take Junior with his eager tongue. Pete's nose was buried in the dense tight curls of Junior's black pubic hairs which ground into Pete's chin. "Too big for you," Junior asked when Pete gagged. Junior backed off until his pulsating prick almost slipped from Pete's throat. Then he shoved it down Pete's throat again, filling him with an enormous penetration. Pete loved being manhandled like this. His scalp was pulled tight as Junior twisted a large fistful of hair.

Ronnie was moving in closer and closer to the action. His own cock loomed before Pete's eager eyes. It wasn't as thick as Junior's but Pete wanted it too. Ronnie's cock looked nearly as long as his partner's, standing straight out from his body, all marble-white with bluish veins. Pete's grasping fingers reached to touch the dick he'd dreamed about when he'd watched Ronnie on the football field. Pete had always imagined what Ronnie looked like nude and hard when his football uniform came off. Pete's fantasy had come true.

"Suck my balls," Junior suddenly ordered. Pete withdrew from the prick, as his hot tongue lusted over the deputy's big balls, tonguing and swabbing them. He sucked the larger right orb into his mouth before bathing the left ball. After about five minutes of that, Junior growled, "Okay, cocksucker, enough of that." He got up from the sofa, ordering Ronnie to take his place.

Ronnie eased down under Pete, as he inspected Ronnie's dick before skinning it back and plunging down on it like he'd done with Junior. At first Pete had forgotten all about Junior but not for long. All of a sudden Junior came to Pete's attention again. Without any preparation, Junior lunged into Pete's tight ass with his lust-enflamed cock. The big head of the cock plunged through the outer sphincter into Pete's anal canal. At first Pete was filled with such a searing pain that he rose momentarily off Ronnie's dick to scream. Ronnie grabbed his hair as Junior had just done and forced his cock back into Pete's mouth.

That initial pain was soon replaced with a sensation of almost unendurable sensual joy that surged through Pete's body. Junior was about twenty-four and was ruggedly handsome, not quite as pretty as Ronnie but a real outdoors man. Pete had seen him on many an occasion walking around town in his shiny uniform. Pete had wondered what it would be like to be Junior's gal, and now he was getting a preview. Pete's armpits, crotch, and forehead were wet with sweat. He was being stuffed at both ends, and Claude was getting quite a show.

As Ronnie plunged deep toward Pete's throat, Junior's huge prick forcefully and repeatedly rammed up Pete's ass. Pete clamped his mouth tightly

around Ronnie, giving the young deputy the blow-job of his life, savoring the salty taste of him. "Suck it," Ronnie hissed, pushing his groin harder against Pete's face.

As Pete's head moved up and down on Ronnie, he thrilled at the rough-house pounding Junior was giving him from the rear. Both deputies showed their pleasure by their guttural, muttered syllables. They were punctuated with moans and gasps, as Pete discovered sensitive areas within both men.

Pete felt a rapid fire swelling in Junior's prick. A sudden hot burst of cum shot deep within Pete's gut. As if knowing what was happening, Ronnie too rewarded Pete with a sticky, milky, and slightly salty explosion of his own. It wasn't as sweet as John-John's but Pete wanted all and more. Junior pounded into Pete's undulating rectum with powerful, staccato bursts of hot juice. Both men seemed to be having spasms above and below Pete.

He was thrilled that he'd provided both deputies with such pleasure. He knew they'd have their girl friends or even wives in the future but would return to him for more of what he could give them. He could tell that they didn't find pleasure like this every day. There as so much more he wanted to do to both men, and at each session in the future with them Pete would provide a little extra surprise as he explored their bodies more fully. With the Adams brothers and Sultan, and now the three police officers, Pete's male harem was expanding rapidly.

He reached below to fondle his own cock. It took only a few jerks of his prick before he too erupted. The men had made him that hot. Pete remained a sandwich between both deputies until their orgasmic spasms had long faded. Junior was the first to pull off the naked pile. Pete rose up over Ronnie's dick to see the sheriff sitting in the corner jacking off.

"Junior's got it all nice and lubed for me, and now I want to fuck that cute ass, too," Claude said, getting up with his full erection.

After having taken Junior's cock, Pete felt the sheriff would be a cake-walk. While Claude had him, Pete wanted Junior and Ronnie to rest for another round. He felt he'd had only a part of both men and Pete wanted it all, every inch of them from their toes to their ears. He hadn't even explored their rosebuds yet with his tongue. It meant a lot to him to sample and taste the rosebud of every man he seduced.

As Claude was about to enter Pete, there came a loud knocking on the door.

"Sheriff, sheriff," came the man's voice from the porch.

"There's big trouble. It's Sultan."

*** 

There are panics that come in the middle of the night that can change

your life. Rosacoke feared such an emergency had fallen in on her when she looked out her bedroom window and spotted the sheriff's squad car depositing Pete in the front yard of the Riddle household.

Her bedroom was built into a bay extending out over the front porch, and she could hear everything. After Pete got out, she spotted Claude Billings slamming the door after him. With his alarm siren sounding, Claude and some other men headed up the road, probably waking up all the neighbors.

Rosacoke leaned out the window and called to Pete. "What's wrong?"

"Get on your clothes, woman," he shouted up to her. "It's Sultan. Come with me."

She didn't know why anything to do with Sultan would get her to rouse herself from bed, but she blindly and obediently dressed hurriedly and raced down the steps.

Pete was in the hallway telling Mrs. Riddle something. She stood looking forlornly and a bit disheveled. "You be careful, boy," she warned him. "I'll tell your pa where you're gone." Seeing Rosacoke, she cautioned her, "Look after my boy. Don't let him get into trouble."

On a signal from Pete, Rosacoke raced out the door with him. "Hold onto your horses," she yelled at him. "I'm coming."

In the cold darkness of Pete's coupe, her chest rose and fell with her heavy breathing. She was glad he'd tossed his hunting jacket to her as they'd run out the door. She snuggled inside it as she faced the dewy Carolina morning.

"We've got to go over to Sultan's shanty," he told her.

"Count me out on that little social call," she said. "I've seen enough of that place to last a lifetime."

"Sultan won't be there," he said. "Some men came for him."

"What does that mean?"

"They took him away in the night."

"What are they going to do to him?" she asked.

"Claude Billings and his boys are on their way to find out where these guys took Sultan. They were dressed like Klansmen."

"Oh, my God," she shouted. "They're gonna kill that buck nigger. He was probably caught with one of their wives. I knew his fast living was gonna catch up with him."

"No time to worry about him now," Pete said. "Claude is gonna try to rescue Sultan. Take him to the state line. Get him out of the county."

She looked over at her man. Pete had sobered up since she'd last seen him drunk at the Blue Note. His eyes in the early dawn light were like blue morning glories, and what gal wouldn't follow a man like that anywhere, even if it were to Sultan's shanty at this hour of the morning?

The coupe rattled and shook along washboardy stretches, as Pete gripped

the wheel, a stern look on his face. "I think it's big trouble."

She felt her heart had stopped beating. Sultan had a lewd meanness to his soul, but that didn't mean he should become the victim of some revenge-seeking mob hot on his trail. "What has he done now?"

"Herb Hester came home a day early from one of his bootleg runs in Tennessee," Pete said. "He said he caught Sultan in his house attacking Medora. Medora is down at the sheriff's office right now. She claimed that Sultan broke into her house and raped her."

"Who is gonna believe that lie?" Rosacoke said. "Everybody in the county knows that Medora pays Sultan to go to bed with her. Gives him white lightning too."

"Southern white men believe what they want to believe," Pete said. "If Medora says she was raped, then an all-white jury will say she was raped. That's the way white men do business in the South."

After taking the pig-track that led to Sultan's shanty, he braked the car in a fallow cotton patch. She jumped out as he slid from behind the driver's seat. With her tailing, he raced across the field past the place where she'd tried to grow watermelons last summer until the drought got the best of them. An old stray hound came looping by after a night up to no good. Wisps of fog rose from the dew-damp earth.

Once at Sultan's shanty, he called out for Narcissa. There was no sound from inside. "I'm coming in." Sultan never had a rear door, just a blanket, but someone had placed a barricade, perhaps a piece of broken-down old furniture in front of the door. Pete called out to Narcissa and Rosacoke did too. She heard footsteps racing across the creaky planks, and a chair crashed to the floor.

"Sweet Jesus," Rosacoke said as Pete pushed the barrier away. Like a banner in defeat, her old green blouse had slipped out of her skirt. "I pray she's okay."

"Narcissa," Pete called again. "It's me. Rosacoke is here. We want to help you." He paused only slightly, surveying the front yard of rusty fenders and worn-out tires. "I sure hope you don't have a gun pointed at this door. Here I come."

***

From the dark depths of the piney woods, the morning sun came up full and bright, revealing Narcissa's bloodshot eyes. Only the sound of the old hound dog barking in the far-off distance filled the air, as Rosacoke, with Pete behind her, stared eyeball to eyeball at Narcissa.

Narcissa glared back suspiciously at her. Rosacoke knew at once she was in bad, frazzle-assed shape. In just her flesh-colored petticoat, she stood shivering in the air, her right hand held up to conceal the cleavage of

her breasts, something she usually liked to show off. Swollen and bruised, her face looked like gadfly blows had rained down. Her cut brow had been caked with dried blood. Puffed up, her right eye was all but closed, yet her left eye exuded raging contempt.

She stuck her neck out the door, scanning the yard, as if to check to see if anybody waited there to pounce on her. Her cheeks were tear-streaked, her hair looking as if chickens had made a henhouse nest of it.

Satisfied that Pete and Rosacoke were alone, she stepped back cautiously into the shanty. "Might as well haul your white asses in here. A lot of good you all are gonna do me now." In red-hot impatience, she commanded Pete to barricade the door behind him, the way she had it.

Painful memories of her last night here came rushing back to Rosacoke, and, as if seeking protection, she cuddled deeper into Pete's hunting jacket. "Where's Sultan?" She asked that as if expecting him to jump out from behind a curtain at any minute.

Wetting her lips, Narcissa leered at Rosacoke, as if blaming her for all her recent trouble. "How in hell do I know? When word got to us from Shakerag that a mob of Klansmen was coming together to lynch him, that nigger didn't even bother to put on his pants he got out of here so fast. The bee-gee-zes scared outta him, he was off in a cloud of dust. Not even a fuck-you. I don't think we'll see that buck's hide in this county ever again."

"At least he got away from them," Pete said.

"He did," Narcissa said contemptuously. "I didn't."

"They hurt you?" Rosacoke asked, a look of real concern crossing her face. She moved toward Narcissa to comfort her, but Narcissa backed off as if afraid. Rosacoke had never known Narcissa to be afraid of anyone, even Sultan.

"Kee-ryess," Narcissa said. "Hurt ain't exactly the word for it."

"Why didn't Hank help?" Rosacoke asked. "He was with you, wasn't he?"

"He'd had his fill of bootleg liquor and me too. He don't know what went on here. He'd gone home. We're getting the hell out of this stink-hole."

Pete picked up pieces of tattered furniture that had been turned over, setting them on their legs again. "What happened?"

"What didn't happen is more like it," Narcissa said. "Fool that I was, this yalla-hided wench—that's what they called me—got it into her noggin' to stay here. You know me? Afraid of nothing. But when a whole gang of 'em came roaring down here, seeking to string up a nigger, I was scared alrighty. The sons of bitches found me crouched wild-eyed in the wood-shed, hiding under some old feed sacks you used to have for your chickens before Sultan sold 'em."

Sick with the realization of what must have gone on, Rosacoke still

didn't want to believe it. "They were after Sultan—not you. Even though we both know Sultan didn't rape Medora."

"She-it, gal you are dumb at times. Those men wanted to string Sultan up. I'm Sultan's kid. A pot liquor substitute, maybe, but when white people want to string somebody up, and they can't catch 'em, they've got to get their rocks off some way."

The old clock that Aunt Clotilda left behind ticked inexorably on the mantle. Rosacoke, and apparently Pete, too, had decided not to force the story out of Narcissa, but to let her tell it in her own way.

"One of them pulled out a gun and slammed the stock against my head. I thought I was staring at Almighty Lucifer. Then one of the shitheads grabbed me by my hair and dragged me into the shanty, with me kicking and screaming like a wild bobcat you've got by the tail."

Rosacoke shook her head confusedly, huddling closer to Pete and thanking her maker she wasn't around at the time. What would those men have done to her? She dreaded to think.

"They got me inside, and I'm in a terrible sweat. I was straining so much I was farting. It took three of the creeps to tie me up to that rickety bedstead there. I fought like they'd just dumped me in hellfire, but what chance did I have against all of them big bruisers?" She burst into tears. "I just lay there on the bed, shaking all over with fright, waiting for their next move."

Pete advanced toward her, and she let him lay his broad hands on her naked shoulders. He just clenched and swayed there a bit with her, as if holding her up.

Still sobbing, she said, "When I went to open my big mouth, no sound came out. Not one damn chirp. I looked at those men, and it didn't take no college diploma to figure out I was gonna get raped. That fucking Hammond Duffy, the rottenest piece of sub-human flesh ever to pop out of a woman's womb, came toward me. I can just see his ugly red face right now, and smell his bootleg liquor breath. Sorta like fermented rat's piss. Right up close to my mouth, he says, 'Sultan, that no good nigger, is so hot to rape white women. I wonder how he'd feel if white men raped his own yalla gal. He's probably broken you in long ago from what I hear tell.'"

In sympathy, Rosacoke moved toward Narcissa, as Pete stepped back. No longer spurning her, Narcissa gave in this time, cradling herself in Rosacoke's arms, and she burst into violent sobbing again.

After a few hysterical sobs, she drew back. Bubbles of saliva shot from her agitated mouth, as she went on, her voice filled with fury. "With me cringing there, all tied up to that damn bed, Hammond ripped my clothes off. One of 'em even poked my thing with the barrel of his shotgun. He threatened me he was gonna pull the trigger. 'Yalla bitch, you're gonna lose your money-maker,' he shouted at me. All the white mothafuggahs laughed

at that one. With my head buried in the pillow to hide my sobbing, they took their turns with me. One by one. Each one like a bale of hay with a pitchfork stab in it. As each one shot into me, I hated the bastard more than the one before."

Now tears came to Rosacoke's own eyes. It was as if by hearing this, a mad, spinning collapse of their old world had taken place.

"When they'd finished their business," Narcissa said, "they still wasn't done with me. One of them went out to his pickup truck and brought back a bottle of turpentine."

"Oh, please," Rosacoke said, "I don't want to hear it."

"Go on," Pete ordered.

"They poured it over me," Narcissa said. It burned like hell. Hotter than putting your hand on an iron stove with full flames going. If my hands hadn't been tied, I would have ripped and clawed at my belly until I brought blood. The pigs just stood there, watching me writhing and screaming. One of them got so hot again he had to jerk off." She collapsed into a chair and stared blankly at the door. No tears, No emotion. Just a terrible emptiness seemed to have moved in around her heart.

There was a long silence in the shanty, broken only by the scurrying of a rat in the overhead bed loft.

Pete was the first to speak up. "Get dressed. We're taking you to a doctor."

***

After checking Narcissa into a tiny local hospital, Pete drove Rosacoke over to the jimcrow jail of the sheriff, Claude Billings. Junior Grayson was in charge. The deputy took Pete into the backroom and Rosacoke could hear the two men talking in whispered tones.

Pete came back into the front room and told her to get into his car. Behind the wheel, he said that the sheriff and his other deputy, Ronnie Key, were looking all over the county for Sultan. He'd learned from Junior that a mob of men were assembling at Fuzzy Seeger's homestead. Word had spread that a "nigger hunt" was on. Rumors were flying that Sultan was going to be strung up, and the white men of the county didn't want to miss entertainment like that.

"Do you think Claude can find Sultan in time and save his life?" she asked.

"If I know Sultan, he's already crossed the county line by now." Pete said. "He's not gonna let those KKK bastards fuck with him."

On the edge of her seat, she felt smothered by the events taking place around her. Certainly she had no control over them. Head down like a spent animal, she feared the world of men and their potential for violence.

As it passed in review before her, the countryside looked so peaceful that it was hard to believe that somewhere up the road farmers were gathering with shotguns.

In an old sorghum field, between Fuzzy's house and his rotting 1903 barn, a mob of white farmers—noisy, excited, and cussing—had gathered. As Pete braked the coupe, he turned to her, and she was touched by a look of sadness in his eyes. She knew Pete was different from the white men gathering in the early morning. Pete wouldn't lynch anybody even if he knew the man was guilty. Like the future lawyer that she knew he would one day become, Pete believed in fair trials, justice, things like that, the kind of things that would make a woman proud to have Pete as her man.

"This sure isn't gonna be a Saturday night possum hunt," he told her. "Stay in the car. It's not safe for a gal to be running about this place."

Over her protests, she remained in the car, and, when he'd faded into the group of men, she rolled down the window so she could hear what was going on.

In pairs of three or four, the men began to disband, heading for Fuzzy's front yard, where his wife and three grown daughters ran in and out of the kitchen with pots of freshly brewed coffee served with buttered sourdough biscuits.

In their brogans, some of the farmers stomped their feet on the frosty earth to keep warm. Thick as bees, the farmers clustered around the porch.

In spite of Pete's warning, she slipped out of the car, easing up to the back of the crowd to hear what he was saying. In the midst of the men, she sensed their anger and hostility. They were like mad ants sore that someone had stepped on their hill.

Fuzzy barged out of his house, slamming the screen door behind him. He stood before Pete, almost but not quite shoving him down. "Get the hell off my porch and stop butting into our affairs, you fucking nigger lover."

"We got the rope," came a voice from the back of the milling farmers. Rosacoke's eyes met the source of that rebel yell, Stringbean Tillis. Spotting her and knowing her connection with Sultan, he sheepishly dropped his eyes and faded into the mob. She'd heard awful stories about him, one particularly bad one about him and his own daughter. If what she'd been told was right, Stringbean was the one who should be strung up.

"We're gonna kill that nigger," another man shouted. She didn't see who called that out.

From the front porch, Pete talked to the crowd, ignoring Fuzzy. "Everybody moves slow around here. I've seen many of you hoe your corn in July. My God, do you take your time doing that. But when it comes to lynching, everybody gets the lead out. If Sultan is guilty, the courts can decide."

To her, he talked more sense than all these older men, even though he

was just one teenage boy against the whole of them. But she could tell that his words made no impression on these backwoods farmers in their bib overalls and flannel jackets. The guns and rifles they used to hunt animals in the woods they now wanted to direct at a man. Mostly she knew they wanted to catch Sultan alive. There hadn't been much entertainment for them that autumn, and she was fully convinced that they'd enjoy seeing Sultan hanging from a tree as much as they'd like to look at Betty Grable at the picture show. Pete had told her there hadn't been a nigger lynching in these parts since 1933, and, until the party formed to hunt Sultan, she'd been convinced that such events belonged to the shadowy past of the county.

Pete refused to be hushed. "Guilty or not, you guys want to get rid of Sultan, don't you. Now you've found an excuse. He threatens you—that's what it's all about, isn't it? Any excuse will do, won't it? Even a lie!"

The farmers seemed impatient with such talk and were easily distracted by two pickup trucks turning the bend, heading up the hill to Fuzzy's homestead at breakneck speed. Piling out of the first truck, Buck Anderson, a tenant farmer from Miller's Creek, raced up to the men. "They got the nigger," he shouted at the mob. The farmers turned their back on Pete, crowding around Buck. "He's being held in Josh Rover's barn over at Boomer. They're gonna cut his balls off, then string him up. That nigger's gonna holler more than my pigs at castration time. If you fuckers don't hurry, you'll miss seeing him dangle in the wind."

Losing all control of herself, she went crazy, pressing into the crowd, imploring the men not to go. "He's innocent," she shouted at the top of her lungs. "He didn't do it. Don't go there. Don't kill him. Please." She pounded Stringbean on the chest, but he pushed her aside.

No one heard her. Shoved and jostled, she separated herself from the farmers, searching for Pete. In a mad stampede, the men raced to every available vehicle, piling in like cattle. The sound of spinning tires filled the noon-day air.

She gazed up at the sky as dark clouds moved over her, obscuring the sun which failed to break through for the rest of the day.

***

It was one o'clock that very afternoon when Pete got a call at the Riddle house to go to the sheriff's office. Claude Billings wanted to see him.

At first his mama protested that Pete shouldn't go if the sheriff wanted to see him in connection with Sultan. "He's no kin to us," she said. "We don't need to go getting mixed up in other folk's business. Especially nigger business. That Sultan was no count and maybe got what was coming to him."

Pete kissed his mama good-bye and gave Rosacoke a peck on the cheek. If Claude wanted to see him, he knew it must be important. Maybe Claude and his deputies had heard some news about Sultan. Maybe he'd crossed the state line and fled to Tennessee before Herb Hester's men could catch up with him.

On the way to the sheriff's office, Pete speculated that he had fully expected to be buying a new car today, not going to visit some broken down jail.

It was a little awkward confronting Junior Grayson, Ronnie Key, and even Claude himself on official police business. After he'd known all three men in the most intimate of ways, he didn't know how they'd respond to him. Would they be embarrassed about what had gone down between them? Would they pretend it had never happened? Or would they—and this is what Pete wanted—request a repeat performance?

Ronnie was outside on the front porch waiting for Pete. He was the cutest of all, and Pete genuinely liked the young man who was closer to his own age than either Claude or Junior. Ronnie flashed a smile when seeing Pete and put him at ease. If Pete had worried that Ronnie would be embarrassed to see him after what had transpired, he realized he didn't have to be. Ronnie was friendlier and more natural acting with him than he'd ever been. He called Pete over to the corner of the porch and reached for his hand. "Me and you are real close," he said in a low voice to Pete. "You might go so far as to call us asshole buddies."

"You might say that," Pete said looking into Ronnie's beautiful, trusting face. Ronnie Key with his full sensual mouth, chestnut brown wavy hair, and his powerful build was one delectable piece of male flesh.

"I'll give you a call this weekend," Ronnie said. "Let's slip away somewhere. The way I figure it, without Claude and Junior overseeing the action, me and you might try a lot of things together."

Pete leaned closer to Ronnie. "I want more." He touched his arm. "I want you. Everything you've got to give me."

"That's a lot," Ronnie said.

Pete wanted to lean over and kiss Ronnie but held back. The front wooden porch of the sheriff's office was no place for that kind of shit. Things like that should be done in private. He didn't know if Ronnie would even let him kiss him. Pete loved sucking men off and getting fucked by them, but he seemed to like kissing them even more. He vowed to eventually kiss every man he seduced, even if he had to get the stud drunk before doing the dirty deed.

The screen door to the sheriff's office opened up and Junior Grayson called for Pete to come inside. "Catch you later," Pete said to Ronnie.

Inside the sheriff's office, Pete looked around expecting to see Claude. Junior shut the door and smiled at Pete. He didn't seem embarrassed at all

about what had happened between them in that shotgun house. He reached into a drawer and took out a key. "Here's the key to that house up at Banner Elk. Claude said you could go there any time and use it like your own place."

"That's mighty nice," Pete said, looking intently into Junior's face, trying to gauge his reaction to Pete in the broad daylight.

Junior always reminded Pete of a Marine recruiting poster. Handsome and strong-jawed, he had black hair and long lashes that softened his rugged, masculine features. He wasn't pretty like Ronnie, and didn't look like Gary Cooper the way Claude Billings did. If anything, Junior resembled a more masculine version of Tyrone Power who enthralled Pete every time that handsome actor appeared on the silver screen at the moving picture show.

"Me and you connect real well," Junior said to him, smiling. "We're going to have a lot of good times together. Ronnie boy out there and me were talking about you this morning. You got a lot of talent where it counts. I'm tired of being horny all the time and chasing after some pussy to satisfy me. I'll still go for my pussy, but if my squad car pulls up in front of the Riddle house, you'll know I've come for you and I want you to rush out the door and get in."

From the desk, he looked up at Pete. Junior's gray eyes were so beautiful and expressive that Pete at that moment could even forget Hank Adams. When Junior looked at him with such sexual aggression and promise, Pete experienced melt-down. He'd do anything Junior Grayson commanded him to.

"You've found your boy," was all Pete could manage to say.

A severe frown crossed Junior's face. "That's not why I called you here today," Junior said. "We got ourselves a real shit case."

"It's Sultan?" Pete asked. "You found him."

"We got him alrighty," Junior said, "and he ain't gonna go nowhere. I was just at the hospital. Talked to Narcissa Cash. Some arrangements have got to be worked out with Sultan. She told me she ain't prepared to help out at all. How can she? She's got not one God damn dollar."

"Is he alive?"

Junior looked up and shook his head. "He's dead. A fucking brutal death. The Klan got 'em."

"Herb Hester's behind it, right?" Pete asked.

"Claude is sure of that," Junior said. "But not directly. Herb Hester was playing cards with three of Claude's closest buddies when Sultan was killed. The perfect alibi. As for the other white men in this county, those who know what was going on, no one has seen or knows anything. To hear every man tell it, he was home fucking his wife when they got Sultan."

"Was he strung up?" Pete asked.

"Worse than that," Junior said. "Worse than that." He shook his head in despair. "What no man on earth, even Sultan, should have happen to him. Claude will fill you in on all this."

"What can I do?"

"Glad you brought that up, boy," Junior said. "Narcissa wants you to reclaim the body. Give it a proper burial."

"Sultan ain't no kin to me," Pete protested.

"We know that, now c'mon," Junior said. "The whole thing can be handled for two-hundred dollars. Narcissa Cash ain't seen two-hundred dollars in her whole life."

"I guess I could do that," Pete said. "I got the money."

"Are you kidding? Your stingy old dad has got more money hidden away than any other man in the county. He's still got the first dollar he ever made."

"He's got quite a bit," Pete said. "Guess he won't miss two-hundred dollars. You won't tell him."

"Hell, no," Junior said, getting up from the desk and coming over to stand close to Pete. They were about the same height, although Junior, being an older man, had a far more developed physique. "Me and you got something real special between us," he said. "Junior Grayson and his pretty boy, Pete Riddle. In a few months I might be going and getting married." He chucked Pete under the chin. "Now don't you go start bawling on me. Just 'cause Junior is getting married doesn't mean you're gonna be denied Little Junior."

"It's not so little," Pete said. "I'm still sore."

"Music to my ears," Junior said. "I wish I could take you back into one of the cells right now, but we've got police business to take care of. The gal I'm gonna marry is real nice. She'll never do to me the things I'm gonna get you to do to me. I'll bang her once or twice a week but when I want to get real down and low, I'm gonna come to you."

"You'll be glad you did," Pete said. "I wish I was marrying you. Any woman who marries you is in for a treat."

"Yeah, but sometimes gals in this county don't know how lucky they are. They think sex is dirty and want no part of it. Me and you are gonna find out just how dirty sex can really be when you ain't got no inhibitions at all."

"That's my kind of sex," Pete said, "I'll do anything a man wants."

"That's why I'm gonna make you my boy."

After telling Ronnie and Junior good-bye, Pete drove over to the county morgue where Claude was waiting out front for him.

Claude looked nervous and agitated as if he wanted to get this thing over and done with. "I just hope one of those big city papers don't hear about this," Claude said. "There's an election coming up. I got to get this

over with and in the ground."

"Junior told me what you wanted me to do," Pete said. "I'll make the arrangements. Reclaim the body. Whatever it is Narcissa wants."

"Thank God," Claude said. "Have a quick funeral. Maybe no funeral at all. We got to get Sultan buried. There's sure gonna be no open coffin for this one." He took Pete inside and led him back into the tiny morgue room. At the door. Claude hesitated. "What you're gonna see is not a pretty sight. I hope it don't make you throw up. When I first saw the body, I puked. You man enough to take what you're about to see?"

"Yeah, I'm okay," Pete said nervously. Claude made him real scared.

When Claude opened the door, the room was dark. The sheriff reached over his head and pulled on a light switch, as a naked electric bulb of dim wattage came on, casting an eerie glow.

It was just enough to illuminate the giant of a man lying on a slab. It was Sultan. Stark naked.

But more than that. Pete stared first at Sultan's groin. No sign of his big cock and large balls, his pride in life. There was nothing there but a gaping hole.

It was only when Pete looked into Sultan's face that he realized where his genitalia had been stuffed. They hung out of his mouth like some monstrous bloody gut.

# Chapter 5

Like an old puppet hurled down or kicked over, Rosacoke lay in bed the next morning, not wanting to get up, even though she smelled bacon frying in the iron skillet downstairs. She knew she should jump up and go downstairs to help Mrs. Riddle feed her husband and Pete, but Rosacoke was afraid to get out of bed.

Her heart ached—not exactly for Sultan, but over everything. Pete was a little vague when he'd told them of Sultan's death. She figured he was leaving out a lot of gory details.

Sultan was a mean man, and Mrs. Riddle still claimed he deserved what he got, although Rosacoke didn't want to speak of the dead in such a way. She knew he didn't rape Medora, even though he'd attacked Rosacoke. Rosacoke had wanted to protect her innocence from Sultan, saving it for Pete. But Medora was known for screwing any man who'd go to bed with her the moment Herb Hester had crossed the state line heading for Tennessee.

Rosacoke had learned that Pete, at the urging of Narcissa, had reclaimed Sultan's body. He'd invited Rosacoke to the funeral parlor to view Sultan's cleaned-up remains before the wooden coffin was sealed. But she'd refused. He'd told her that Narcissa had also turned down his offer to view her daddy in death.

"I think Narcissa is more hurt than she makes out to me," Pete had told Rosacoke. "Ever since that attack, she's built a shield around herself. She always was one tough bird but now she's tougher than ever. As tough as old shoe leather. I don't think any man's ever gonna hurt her again."

When she came downstairs, Rosacoke learned that Pete had eaten breakfast and left—not to get his new car but to bring Narcissa back to Sultan's shanty after checking her out of the hospital. He also planned a small funeral for Sultan in the morning. Rosacoke would only attend if Pete asked her to. She felt she had no place at Sultan's funeral.

As she ate her bacon and eggs, Rosacoke looked over at Mr. Riddle. He was withered and withdrawn. He said almost nothing at table—that is, if he got up to eat at all. Mrs. Riddle usually served his food in bed. If he did come to table, about all he said was, "Hand me another biscuit." Or else he'd ask for more gravy. That man sure liked his country cream gravy. It was hard for Rosacoke to imagine Mr. Riddle as ever having been a young

man. He seemed to have popped out of his mama's womb an old man.

Mrs. Riddle looked up the stairs when she heard John-John walking across the creaky floor to the bathroom. He'd spent another night in Pete's bedroom.

"When that Adams youngin' comes down those steps this morning," Mrs. Riddle said, "I'm gonna ask him to leave our house. Staying over one night was okay but we didn't tell Pete he could move that no-count kid in with us as a permanent boarder."

"I guess Pete's been too busy to take him back home where he belongs," Rosacoke said.

Mr. Riddle stopped eating and glared at his wife, a look of defiance on his face. Rosacoke had never known him to challenge his wife before. Until she'd seen the old man's belligerence, Rosacoke didn't know if he had any emotions at all. All feeling within the man seemed dead.

He slammed down his fork and reached over and grabbed his wife's arm, yanking it hard. "The boy stays in my house. The last time I checked, my name was still on the fucking deed—not yours. I'm still the man of the house. If you kick that boy out, you'll be the next to pack up." He turned over his plate of unfinished food on the table, slid back his chair, and tottered off to the living room.

Mrs. Riddle didn't say anything for a long moment, and Rosacoke didn't know what to do. She rose from her chair to clean up Mr. Riddle's mess.

At that point John came down the wooden steps ready for breakfast, his hair still wet from where he'd tried to comb it in the bathroom, hoping to get rid of a cowlick.

Later that morning, as Rosacoke was coming back from slopping the hogs, she spotted Mr. Riddle walking the barren fields with John-John, his arm around the boy. That shocked her. Mr. Riddle almost never left the house. This display of affection for John-John amazed Rosacoke. Mr. Riddle didn't even show affection for his own son—that is, his adopted son, Pete—and here he was under God's blue sky with his arm around that no-count Adams boy. This cozy scene coming so soon after his outburst at the table in defense of John-John puzzled Rosacoke all the more.

She watched as a big black crow flew over, searching for its morning breakfast. The vulture-like bird frightened her and sent an ominous chill through her body. Aunt Clotilda always said that "one bad thing will be followed up by another." The woman had always seemed to possess some intuition that her ancestors coming over on a slave ship from Africa had imparted to her.

As if to prove Aunt Clotilda right that trouble comes in pairs, Rosacoke looked up the road and saw a car fast approaching the Riddle household. Tires screeched as it pulled into the driveway. Since the car was shiny new, Rosacoke felt it might be Pete showing off in his new car. But when the

driver came to a halt in the Riddle driveway, out popped Medora. Rosacoke would know that whore anywhere. She'd be the only woman in town wearing a red dress on a Monday morning. Only nigger gals like Narcissa wore red dresses, and even they didn't wear them until night came and they were going out whoring and clubbing.

Spotting Mr. Riddle and the boy, Medora ran toward them in the field. Rosacoke hid around the corner of the house, hoping to learn what was going on. Medora had never visited anybody's house before, at least as far as Rosacoke knew. Why was she pulling into the driveway so brazen like at the Riddle household? Everybody knew that Pete's parents were the most respectable in the county. Rosacoke feared that Mrs. Riddle was looking through lace curtains at what that heifer was doing driving up to her house? At any minute, Rosacoke expected Mrs. Riddle to emerge on her front porch. Maybe she'd even take a shotgun to threaten Herb Hester's wife.

No woman in the county wanted her man left alone with Medora even for one minute. Rosacoke was glad that John-John was with Mr. Riddle in the field. What could Medora do to a man with a little boy looking on?

Rosacoke sneaked up as close as she could to the trio and didn't go any nearer for fear of being spotted.

Studying Medora from afar, Rosacoke felt the woman looked as if she'd been beaten up. The way Rosacoke figured it, Medora ripped up her own dress and messed herself up, still hoping someone would believe her about that rape story, even though Sultan had been killed to protect that woman's honor.

She didn't know what kind of messy business a whore like Medora had with a decent man like Mr. Riddle. The three of them stood talking in that field for a good five minutes. At one point Mr. Riddle raised his voice and shouted at Medora. But the big-tit thing stood her ground, as she seemed to be making some sort of demand. When Medora turned from Mr. Riddle and started stalking toward the Riddle house, as if she were going inside to confront Mrs. Riddle, the old man called after her. He sure didn't want her going inside that house and upsetting his wife.

After more field talk, Mr. Riddle, trailed by John-John, turned and headed toward Medora's car. Rosacoke watched as Mr. Riddle got up front in the passenger seat with Medora on his left, and John-John climbed into the back seat. Without even telling Mrs. Riddle where they were going, they headed out into the day, going in the direction of town.

It was at that moment that Pete's coupe turned a corner coming back from town. He waved Medora's car down. In the distance Rosacoke could see Mr. Riddle get slowly out of Medora's car and walk with Pete toward a red clay embankment. Medora and John-John remained in her spanking new car.

A good ten minutes must have passed by as Pete stood talking with his daddy along the side of the road. At one point she heard Pete shout, but then he quickly lowered his voice. Finally, the two men parted and Mr. Riddle went and eased back into the car with Medora, who had never turned off her motor. Pete stood in the road for a long time watching them go, even long after they had faded from his view.

He then got back in his car and headed to the Riddle driveway. Rosacoke ran to meet up with him, hoping he would fill her in on what was going on.

He called out to her to get in his car. She looked back at the house, noticing the lace curtains move. Mrs. Riddle must be standing in the living room spying on them.

Sitting up front with Pete, she waited for him to say something. He was driving toward the Blue Ridge Parkway. "I wanta go up in the mountains," he told her. "To look up at the blue sky. Clear my head."

She said nothing but huddled in the seat beside him. She was glad he'd invited her along. It made her feel part of the family. She reckoned that he would tell her what he had to lay on her when he was damn good and ready.

At a lookout point, Pete got out of the car, and she opened her door and ran out to stand next to him, taking in the beauty of the mountain panorama. She was glad she was wearing his old hunter's jacket because the air and wind were much colder this high up.

"You'll find out sooner than later," he said. "Herb Hester has kicked Medora out. He's ordered her to leave the county."

"Then he didn't really believe that story about Sultan raping her?"

"Shit, woman," he said, flashing his anger and impatience at her. "Who would believe a tale like that? The bitch tried to seduce Hank Adams and me only the other day. She's a nymph."

Rosacoke wasn't sure what a nymph was, but was too afraid to ask.

"She's Herb's third wife," Pete said. "'Bout time that old bootlegger wised up to women."

"Where is Medora gonna go?" Rosacoke asked. "And why did she come to see Mr. Riddle?"

"I'll let you in on a family secret," Pete said. "Before Medora got Herb to marry her, she carried on an affair with my daddy."

Rosacoke looked astonished. It was inconceivable to her that Mr. Riddle could ever have had an affair with anybody. Rosacoke could not even imagine Mr. Riddle having sex with his wife, even if they kept their clothes on during the act which she was sure they'd do, at least on Mrs. Riddle's part. Rosacoke had heard that many men in the county had never seen their wife's body completely naked, even though married for decades.

"Medora is demanding five-hundred dollars from my daddy," Pete said. "He'd gone into town with her to the bank to withdraw the money. With that dough, Medora is going to drive to Charlotte and start a new life for

herself. She'll probably end up slinging hash in some diner. She's getting a little long in the tooth for most men."

"Why would Mr. Riddle give her money?" Rosacoke asked. "Just because they had an affair a long time ago? Was she threatening to go into that house and tell Mrs. Riddle all about it?"

"She was indeed," Pete said, "and that bitch would have done it, too." He looked at her in his leather jacket, its collar turned up to protect his neck from the winds that came down from the Blue Ridge. "She's got more on Daddy than that. It seemed that my daddy, who is really my adopted daddy, is the actual daddy of John-John."

"My God," Rosacoke said. "That's why Mr. Riddle doesn't object to your bringing that kid into his house. It's his own son you dragged in."

"Yeah," Pete said, his face reflecting his own amazement. "I guess that makes John-John my half-brother."

"Something like that," she said. "I don't know how these things go. Mr. Riddle ain't your actual daddy, so I guess John-John ain't your actual half-brother."

"I guess you're right," Pete said. "Thank God we're not related or anything like that. Actually being related to John-John would bother me."

"You call yourself his Big Brother," she said. "So I guess you're a lot closer to him than you thought."

"What a fucking coincidence," Pete said. "Life is like that. I invite one of the Adams brothers into our house, and it turns out his daddy is my old man. You can't make up shit like that even at the moving picture show."

"I always felt that John-John wasn't like the other Adams brothers," she said. "He seems more tender-hearted. The other brothers, especially that Hank, are a bit crude."

"Don't you go bad-mouthing Hank," he said, his face flashing anger again. "He's my friend."

"I'm sorry," she said. "I didn't mean anything."

"You're right," Pete said. "John-John is different from his other brothers. Even physically different."

"What's Mrs. Riddle gonna think about all this?" she asked. "She was watching all those goings-on in her front yard."

"I think she's always suspected something between Medora and my dad," Pete said. "Ma never said a thing but there was talk in the county. Medora was sleeping with Hank's daddy about the same time she was carrying on with Pa. I think she paid Adams to take John-John in right after he was born and pretend that the boy was his own son. When that bastard thought Hank was old enough to raise the rest of the brothers, the shithead split the county. Ran off with some whore."

"I'm not a great fan of Hank Adams," she said, "even though he's your friend, but he did act like a man and brung up those boys by himself."

"You gotta admire that," Pete said. "But I'm gonna be helping out the Adams boys myself. I know it's a bit far-fetched, but I feel related to them somehow. Like we're all kin."

She didn't quite follow that reasoning, but knew that Pete had a mind of his own and listened only to his own drummer.

He drove back in silence to the Riddle household. "At some point I gotta go in and see mama about all this. She's gonna have a lot of questions."

"What are you gonna say?" she asked.

"At the moment I don't have a clue," he said. "But I've always been good at thinking on my feet. Frankly, I think Pa should do all the explaining. Leave me out of it."

When they got back to the Riddle homestead, neither Mr. Riddle nor John-John had come back from town.

She trailed Pete into the house. Mrs. Riddle was in the kitchen cooking collards and looking as if nothing had happened. Pete went over and kissed her on the cheek before heading upstairs to his bedroom, leaving Rosacoke alone with the old woman.

"The cat got your tongue?" Mrs. Riddle asked.

Rosacoke tried to blurt out something but felt shy and awkward. For a moment she wished that Pete hadn't introduced her to the family skeletons.

Mrs. Riddle looked at Rosacoke. The old woman's face was pathetic, almost as if she were about to start bawling. "I want you to go in that bedroom that I share with Mr. Riddle. I want you to pack up all my clothes and all my things in that room I shared with him for more than a quarter of a century. I want you to take all my things and put them in the guest room upstairs. The one at the far back of the hallway. That way I'll be as far from my husband as this house will allow."

"Yes, ma'am," Rosacoke said. "I'll go right now and fetch your things and tote them upstairs."

As Rosacoke headed for the ground-floor bedroom, Mrs. Riddle called to her back. "About what went out in this household this morning, we never need speak of it ever again, even with Mr. Riddle."

"I understand," she answered the old woman before heading back to this mysterious bedroom where this long-married couple had spent a good hunk of their lives together. Until this morning, it had been almost like a shrine to their love for one another.

*** 

Pete smashed at his brakes and sounded his honk on the ledge above Hank's shanty. He could see the handsome stud walking back from the broken-down old outhouse with a half-moon carved in its door. Seeing it

was Pete, Hank ran up the hill to get into his coupe.

The actual physical presence of this young man in the car with him made Pete's brain simmer. He checked out the slender, muscled body stretched sensually in his car. Hank's face was still dark from the raging sun of early autumn. Pete's mouth could vividly recall the taste of the hairs on Hank's legs. That hair was gold, the same brown gold as his pubic hair.

As Pete headed up the road, Hank settled back into his seat. "I don't know where you're taking me, but I'm real horny. Thank God you came by. I was going to have to jack the big ol' thing off if I didn't get relief somewhere."

With no specific target in mind, Pete decided to head up the road toward Banner Elk and that shotgun house. He fingered the key in his pocket, finding it and fondling it like some tantalizing prize that would open the door to a treasure trove of precious gems.

"I can't let you go to Chicago with that Narcissa," Pete said.

"You can't let me go!" Hank said in astonishment, as if not believing his ears. "Some seventeen-year-old kid still wet behind the ears is telling Hank Adams what he can do and can't do."

"I love you too much, man, to let you go," Pete said, trying to conceal the desperate pleading tone of his voice. "I gotta have you every day."

"That's just too God damn bad," Hank said. "Fuck man, I'm leaving you my three brothers. In a year or two Karl and Tracy both will be every bit the man I am. As for John, you've got your own special pleasure with that one. I broke him in for you."

"It's not the same," Pete said. "I'm crazy about your brothers. But you're the special lollipop I want to suck on."

"If I'm here, you can have me any time you want—day or night," Hank said. "I'm a guy who enjoys giving it. I gotta admit that. Your kind of love-making gives me a more intense cum than anybody else's. Even that of Narcissa. You've been there, done that. Narcissa is pretty good. At least she was. Before that thing happened the other night."

Exactly what does that mean?"

"After what came down on her, Narcissa has locked up her pussy and thrown away the key."

"If that's true, we both know why. Shit, man, she's been to hell and back. Those creeps could have killed her just for sport."

"She'll get over it in time," Hank said. "Give her a few weeks up in shiny Chicago, and she'll be brand new. The streets up there are made of gold, I hear."

"I can't believe you're leaving me," Pete said, flooring the gas as his coupe headed up the steep mountain road.

"I'm gonna talk turkey with you, boy," Hank said. "I like you a lot. I like even better the money you give me. But do you think for one minute I

want to spend the rest of my life living in some nigger shanty and earning ten bucks here and there with some vile pig like W.G. Gabriel? I want to go to Chicago where the big bucks are. If I'm gonna fuck somebody, man or woman, I want that person to be rich and pay for what I've got by the inch."

"You're nothing but a whore," Pete said. "A male whore."

"W.G. Gabriel once told me, after he'd sucked me off, that there have been male whores down through the centuries," Hank said. "I'm just following a time-honored profession."

"But why Narcissa?" Pete asked. "Are you in love with her?"

"I'm a little scared to go up there alone to the big city," Hank said. "I need a brassy gal like Narcissa. She's got the hustler instinct. I bet in no time at all, she'll get us a place to live. Find a job for herself. One for me too. You just wait and see. Lickety-split, me and Narcissa will be working the circuit. Both of us will have them lining up to sample the special goodies that each of us has got."

"But I thought you said Narcissa has locked up her pussy," Pete said, understanding nothing.

"Don't you know that's temporary?" he asked. "She'll get over that gang-bang in no time and will forget about the Klan, Sultan, all that shit. Only yesterday she told me she had this gift of not remembering. She said if she put her mind to it, she could wipe out all bad memories from her head. She's just got to try. On the bus to Chicago, she's gonna put her mind to erasing all the crap that's gone down."

"I don't see how this Chicago thing is going to work," he said. "I want you to stay here with me."

"Wishing and getting are two different things," Hank said. "The only way you can keep my dick in you is to go away to Chicago with us."

"You mean, run away? I can't do that."

"Of course you can't, and I know that. You're waiting around for those old stepparents of yours to die. Everybody in the county knows you're gonna be filthy rich when they pass on. Old man Riddle looks like he's going to croak any minute now. With him out of the way, you'll easily get around that mama of yours."

Pete looked over at Hank as they neared the shotgun house. "You know everything?"

"Hell, yes, I do," Hank said. "My old man, before he ran off, spilled the beans. John belongs to your papa, and it seems right and proper that he's living under the Riddle roof. It's his birthright."

"Let me ask you something," Pete said, braking his coupe in front of the shotgun house where he'd been sexually assaulted by the sheriff's deputies and had loved every minute of it. "Say I've got John-John's welfare covered. What about Karl and Tracy? You're just gonna up and leave them?"

"Maybe a few weeks ago I might not have felt so good about splitting. That's before we got this thing going with you. I'm leaving the boys in your care. I told 'em you'd take care of them and provide for them like I've done—more or less—in the past."

Pete could feel his heart beating faster at the prospect of having Tracy and Karl in his complete control, the way he now dominated John-John. He decided to press his advantage. "Strike while the poker's hot," his mama told him. "You're going all the way with me now," Pete said. "John-John goes even farther, as you know. But Karl and Tracy are holding back. Not going the full trip with me."

"They'll come around," Hank said. "I've already talked to them about it."

"What did they say?" Pete asked eagerly.

"They're thinking about it. All this shit is pretty new to them. Give 'em a little time. After all, they're just boys. Young boys have to have time to get used to this queer stuff."

"I want to go all the way with your brothers."

"How far?" Hank asked.

"All the things you're doing with me now that started when you let me kiss you."

"Shit," Hank said, getting out of the car and stretching his muscled arms in the mountain breezes. "The way I look at it, when I opened my mouth and stuck out my tongue for you to suck, I was only a minute away from sucking your dick too. I also look at it this way. If I'm gonna get rich hustling the daddy warbucks types up in Chicago, I'm not gonna always get off so easy—I mean, just lying back and getting done. I figure I'll be presented with a few dicks to suck to earn my paycheck. What better way to break into sucking cock than Pete Riddle's dick. You're the cutest boy in the county and you've got a great dick. I don't expect to meet up with too many like you in Chicago. They'll be fat with ugly, puny dicks. But I gotta do what I gotta do. If you wanna get rich, you gotta do a lot of things to get there. Narcissa told me that's true, and she's gonna go all-out to get her own dough using her money-maker."

"Sounds to me like you two have got it all planned out," Pete walked up three steps to the front porch and unlocked the door. "C'mon," he called back to Hank. "I'll build us a fire. After that, I'm gonna heat some water and give my mountain boy here a scrubdown. Considering what I'm gonna do to you, I want every surface of your body squeaky clean."

Inside the shotgun house, Hank stood idly by, watching Pete build a fire. "What you're gonna do to me today, and what you're gonna expect me to do back to you, is what you're going to expect from Karl and Tracy? Right?"

"You got that right, big boy?"

"With the right kind of training, you can break in those broncos and

have them ridin' your ass."

"Do you think they'd ever let me fuck them?" Pete asked, looking up from the fire and then getting up to go heat the bath water for Hank.

"Maybe they won't go that far," Hank said. "Hell, I won't go that far, 'though I sure do like cornholing you. They're younger than me and not so hardened like I am. You might get them to do everything you want. They can learn to give you their tongues and go down on you and slurp up your cum. As for fucking, you got John's hot ass for that. That boy loves it. If you've got the stars, man, don't ask for the moon. At least that's what Narcissa says."

An hour later Hank was nude in the old zinc tub. Pete was giving him the scrubbing of his life, paying special attention to the nether regions. He didn't know how many more chances he would have to go all the way with this stud, and he wanted to spend the afternoon taking full advantage of Hank while he had him here. There was nothing he didn't want to try and do with Hank. If it felt good, Pete wanted it.

As he bathed and fondled the young man's prick and balls, he couldn't believe he'd be losing him so soon to those Yankee bastards up there in Chicago. He bet all of Hank's future conquests would be creeps. If a guy were good-looking and well-built, he didn't have to pay for sex. It just stood to reason that those guys paying Hank would be so repulsive they'd been reduced to buying studs like Hank on the open market.

As he dried Hank off, Pete asked him, "How are you paying your way to Chicago?"

"I figured you'd handle the bus fare for both me and Narcissa. Also I planned to sell that car you gave me. It won't bring in a lot of money but I'll start hauling in the dough once I get up there in the Windy City."

"I'll buy the car back from you and help with the bus fare and all," Pete said.

"That's mighty nice of you," Hank said, bending over and giving Pete a wet, sensual kiss.

When Pete finished drying Hank, he led him over to the big sofa where Ronnie Key and Junior Grayson had stabbed him with their delectable swords. "My old man is buying me a new car before the war comes. I'm gonna give your car to Karl and my old coupe to Tracy."

"Hot damn!" Hank said, bucking up. "You give both of my brothers cars, and they'll come around to your way of loving so fast you won't know what hit you."

"You think so?" Pete asked, looking deep into Hank's blue eyes. Pete's lips were only an inch from Hank's delectable mouth.

He stuck out his tongue. "Let's forget about my brothers right now. You've got Hank Adams hisself sprawled out on the sofa all jaybird na-ked." He moved his head slightly and nibbled at Pete's ear. "Think of

everything you've ever dreamed about in your whole life. Everything you've ever wanted to do to a man in your jack-off fantasies with the moon streaming through the window of your bedroom."

A sigh escaped from Pete's throat, just thinking about what Hank told him to think about.

"Do those things to me this afternoon," Hank said. His big, broad hand reached for Pete's neck, cradling it in a powerful grip as he opened his mouth and lunged forward to press Pete's sensual lips against his own.

It would be a long afternoon.

One that Pete Riddle would never forget.

***

It was one of those gray, rainy days that often bathe the Blue Ridge Mountains in a foggy mist. Just the kind of day one needed for a funeral. Pete remained bathed in gloom and silence as he drove Rosacoke to Sultan's funeral. Mrs. Riddle had given her a black dress and black coat that she'd worn as a much younger woman in the 1920s. The outfit didn't fit but Rosacoke wore it anyway.

Rosacoke had suggested that Sultan be buried on that lonely hilltop site overlooking the holler where Rosacoke had buried her own mama and the stillborn infant fathered by Sultan. To her, the graves would form a kind of link of three people united in death but unfulfilled in life.

This site had been selected because the black preacher wouldn't let Sultan be buried alongside his mama, Aunt Clotilda. "Aunt Clotilda was one of the finest women who ever lived," the preacher had told Rosacoke. "She couldn't help it that she got saddled with a son like Sultan. The Devil hisself must have sired Sultan. I'm not gonna disturb that poor woman's eternity by placing Sultan next to her in God's earth."

When Pete drove up at the grave site, there were no mourners, not even Narcissa. Only the county grave digger, Haydon Eller, who'd dug Aunt Clotilda's grave. Along with Pete, he hoisted Sultan's wooden coffin from the pickup truck and toted it up the hill.

Rosacoke stood forlornly looking down the road waiting for Narcissa to come to her daddy's funeral. Hank Adams had agreed to drive her.

In the cold and the rain Rosacoke waited in silence under a large black umbrella with Haydon and Pete. It must have been an hour or more before she spotted Hank's car driving up that hill. By then, Rosacoke feared she'd caught her death of cold.

The rain had stopped when Narcissa got out of the car with Hank. He'd dressed in a dark blue suit he'd borrowed from Pete, since no Adams brother had ever owned a decent suit of clothing in their no-count lives.

To her shock and surprise, Rosacoke saw Narcissa get out of that car

wearing a white dress. Rosacoke didn't know where she got it since white was about the last color of dress Narcissa would wear. Over her dress she'd worn an imitation leopard-skin raincoat that looked so tawdry and tacky Rosacoke felt Narcissa must have paid all of fifty cents for it at the five-and-dime.

Rosacoke walked over to Narcissa and reached for her hand, telling her how sorry she was about her daddy's death.

Narcissa looked her so straight in the eyes that Rosacoke felt at first rays were going right through her head. "He's dead and that's that," Narcissa said. "In case no one ever got around to tellin' you, life is for the living."

Rosacoke leaned over to Narcissa to whisper. "You're supposed to wear black at funerals. A sign of respect."

"I'm not showing up at some God damn funeral in widow's weeds," she said. "I'll wear what I fucking please. White is a symbol of celebration. A renewal of life. With Sultan gone, I'm a free woman for the first time in my life. Free, black, and twenty-one."

"In that case, why not the real color that symbolizes the renewal of life?" Rosacoke asked. "Spring green?" Turning her back to Narcissa, she headed up that bleak hill for Sultan's burial.

Pete had been whispering to Hank, and it looked as if they were arguing over something. At the sight of her, Pete stopped talking and looked somewhat guiltily at her. Hank stared absently into the muddy grave Haydon had dug.

There had been too many funerals lately for Rosacoke's taste. She felt Sultan's immortal soul deserved some sort of sendoff, but she could get no preacher to perform the services.

Pete had brought along his guitar which he retrieved from his pickup truck. Before Haydon had covered the pine box coffin with red clay, Rosacoke asked Pete if she could sing "Peace in the Valley" with him playing for her. He agreed.

On what she felt was her last legs, she stood here in the cold, biting wind of the mountains. At this desolate spot with the bones of her own mama rotting in the ground with the baby half-brother she'd never know, the soothing words of the song and her own voice carried a haunting, melancholy ring as it sounded across the mountain like an echo. You couldn't get much sadder than she sounded today.

It was no longer a question of going back to that awful world she'd known with Sultan, her mama, and Narcissa. That life, tawdry as it was, simply didn't exist any more. It was like that novel that had come out, the one written by Margaret Mitchell. It was *Gone with the Wind*. Rosacoke figured she now belonged right where she was. Standing side by side with Pete, even if it were at a grave site.

Muscles taut, her body felt empty that morning and drained of emotion.

What feelings she had escaped her body and went to her voice. At the end of her song, she felt someone should say a prayer. She really didn't know how, and she was sure Hank Adams had never said a prayer in his whole rotten life.

Instead of looking after Narcissa, the way he was supposed to, Hank kept glancing over at Pete. She felt there was some issue between them that these two boys just couldn't agree on. The tension between Pete and Hank was something fierce. Without knowing what it was about, she could sense there was some powerful disagreement between them. She suspected it was because of John-John and Pete inviting the boy to live permanently at the Riddle homestead. But that didn't make sense either. If Hank were going to run off up there to Chicago with Narcissa, wouldn't he be grateful that Pete had taken John-John in? She was sure that Karl and Tracy wouldn't look after John-John the way Hank in his own sloppy way had provided for the youngin'.

She waited for Pete to say a prayer. But he remained stone-faced and silent. She hardly expected anything from Narcissa other than her behaving herself. She'd already disgraced the memory of her daddy by showing up in that cheap imitation leopard-skin raincoat that belonged more on a Saturday night whore than it did on a dutiful daughter at the grave site of her daddy.

Out of embarrassment, if for no other reason, Haydon volunteered to say a few words. "I've been digging graves ever since I was fourteen years old. Followed in the footsteps of my daddy. I've been near every funeral ever held in this county since I was a boy. I should know one by heart now, even if for a nigger."

Narcissa looked furious at Haydon for calling her daddy a nigger, but she kept her overly painted mouth shut.

Rosacoke tried to ignore Haydon's remark and bowed her head, feeling sorry in her heart that poor Sultan could get only a gravedigger, Haydon Eller, to say a few words over his coffin. Rosacoke feared if she said something, her throat would choke up.

Haydon said a prayer and ended with some words he'd heard repeated often about "dust to dust." Before the last "Amen!" had rolled off his tongue, Haydon appeared eager to shovel the red clay over Sultan so he could hit Pete up for the money he'd earned digging the grave. She knew the cash would go to buy paregoric for Haydon. He was addicted to it. Rosacoke hoped no one else died in the county any time soon because until that money ran out, Haydon would be in no more shape to dig any graves.

After the burial, Rosacoke stood before the big uncarved rock that marked her mama's grave and her stillborn child. Pete linked his arm with hers, as they made their way down the pebble-strewn hill to the pick-up truck. Narcissa and Hank trailed behind them.

The scraggly pines that could grow this high up on the mountain—hardly the pick of the litter—bent over, laden with the burden of the rain. It was as if these trees had witnessed too many deaths and too much violence.

\*\*\*

Riding back with Rosacoke at his side, Pete's mind wasn't on her at all, even though he told everybody she was "my woman." He had to keep up his image, and at some point he guessed he would have to make love to her. He couldn't keep her dangling forever.

That dead man, Sultan, was sending so many images through Pete's brain it was like going to the motion picture show.

Right now his mind wasn't on Rosacoke but on Sultan. Somehow, and he knew in his heart how unfair this was, he blamed Sultan for dying, for leaving him like he did.

Pete was counting on many years of enjoying Sultan until his virility and manhood eroded. With Sultan gone, Pete could only imagine how much pleasure had been denied him. Sultan was one of the handsomest men who'd ever been born in the county. God only knows who his white daddy was, and what that man must have looked like. He'd passed on his genes to Sultan, turning his son into a buck of awesome masculinity. No white boy, not even Hank Adams, measured up to Sultan's stature and grandeur.

Pete was just getting to know Sultan before the Klan took him away. If Pete could get away with it, he wished he could murder every member of that Klan, making each and every killer pay for what they'd done to this prince of a man who'd carried in his blood all the beauty and nobility of the jungles of Africa.

At first, Pete didn't even know where he was going but found himself at the top of the embankment that led down to the falls. He asked Rosacoke to wait in the pickup truck until he got back. "It's something personal I've got to do."

As he headed down to Blowing Rock Falls, the land had changed from that hot day where Sultan had broken him into the pleasures of male love. The dusty trails and parched grass that had known the violent green of late summer were now barren and cold, denuded of life.

The fierce blaze of the sun on his naked body as Sultan had taken him and had given him the greatest pleasure that Pete had ever known up to then seemed a distant memory. The memory, though distant, was hardly fading. The feeling of Sultan's penetration would be in his gut forever.

That hot, steamy afternoon and the secretive meetings that had followed had lit a fire within Pete that would never go out. He'd need many men, and not just Hank Adams, but many others, to dampen the flame that

Sultan had lit within him.

Pete dreamed dreams that could never be. He wanted Sultan back among the living, making love to him the way he'd done that first afternoon and all the many times since.

At the falls, Pete gazed down in tears at the sand where Sultan had caused Pete to realize his own desires. Sultan had awakened deeply buried feelings and emotions in Pete that he'd never known dwelled within him.

He was glad that he'd told Sultan that he loved him. At the time it seemed like a bold, reckless thing to blurt out. Considering how few days they had left together, Pete was happy to have whispered that into Sultan's ear. For all Pete knew, Sultan had never heard the word "love" from anybody. He felt both men and women had used Sultan like some God damn fucking machine. He was all that and a lot more.

Pete stood looking at the big rock where he'd first spotted Sultan sunbathing in the nude. The dread chill of winter was upon Pete now, but he still felt the summer sun's rays.

Without meaning to, he burst into tears calling out for Sultan. Even as he did, Pete knew his cry would not be heard. An image of Sultan lying mutilated in that morgue flashed through Pete's mind. He just knew that horrible image would remain to haunt him for the rest of his life.

Still fighting back his tears, he headed up that embankment again to the pickup truck and Rosacoke.

***

When Pete drove up to the Riddle homestead, he spotted his old man sitting bundled in a heavy coat on the front porch. This surprised him since his daddy no longer sat outside even on the hottest day of summer, but stayed secluded in his bedroom.

Pete told Rosacoke to go inside and see if his mama needed anything. Seeing Pete, the old man rose from his rocker and headed toward Pete's car. "Get inside," he instructed Pete. Mr. Riddle slowly climbed into the passenger seat of the coupe. Pete got behind the steering wheel and glanced at his daddy who did not look back at him, keeping his eyes glued to the windshield in front of him. "We're goin' to town, boy."

Without any more talk, Pete started the motor and headed in the direction of town. It was at least five minutes before either of them spoke.

"I've never known you to go to town, except for the other day," Pete said, fearing that his daddy might have learned that he'd made some unauthorized withdrawals at the bank, such as taking out the money to buy Herb Hester's old car for Hank Adams.

"We're gonna go to my lawyer's office," Mr. Riddle said.

"You mean, Bevil Perdue?"

For the first time the old man looked at him harshly. "Who else in hell is my God damn lawyer?" He seemed raging with a fever in his blood, his eyes squinting in fury. "Me and your ma just had the biggest fight of our lives. Things were said to me that no God damn woman should ever say to a man. For years I've let the bitch boss me around, tell me what to do, run things. No more. I'm still alive. Still the man of the family."

Pete was filled with an awful dread. He'd never seen his daddy like this. Just when Pete had come to feel that all drive had disappeared from his daddy, he seemed to be asserting himself with the kind of vigor he must have known when he was much younger.

Mr. Riddle said no more until Pete pulled up in front of Perdue's office. "Let's get out, boy."

Inside, the front office was empty. Perdue had to let his woman assistant go last year because of lack of business. Hearing Mr. Riddle and Pete come into his office, Perdue called for them "to come on back."

Mr. Riddle always said the portly, bald-headed lawyer was a "glad-hander." True to his reputation, Perdue shook hands, asked about Sultan's funeral, offered coffee, and chatted about the weather.

"Shit, man," Mr. Riddle said, a sharp bite to his voice. "I'm here to get business done. I ain't got that much time left. All of us can feel it's fucking cold outside."

Pete looked in surprise at his daddy, as he'd never heard him use words like that. Mr. Riddle was talking like Hank Adams did.

Perdue cleared his throat and looked over at Pete, as the fat attorney settled down comfortably at his desk, leaning forward and staring at some documents on his desk. He looked up at Mr. Riddle. "Sure you want to go through with this?"

"Hell, yes, I'm sure," the old man said. "That's why I drug myself here in the dead of winter."

"Your daddy here is a very rich man," Perdue said, turning to Pete. "The richest man in the county. Far richer than anybody knows. I've heard Mr. Riddle's fortune put at two-hundred thousand dollars. It's a lot more than that. Half a million dollars is more like it."

Pete was flabbergasted. He knew that Mr. Riddle was worth at least one-hundred thousand dollars. But half a million! Pete couldn't even imagine money like that. He said nothing, trying to imagine a big pile of gold somewhere.

"Most of the money is tied up in land," Perdue went on, looking at the documents and glancing up at Pete frequently. "You know yourself that your pa's own parents left him all that farmland in Elkin County. It wasn't worth all that much when they passed on, but with a war coming on, with the economy taking an upturn, land prices are rising again. That land is worth a fortune. Also, the bonds he was left are worth a lot of money. A

gift from Mr. Riddle's mama—a fine lady from New York. I knew her and liked her a lot even if she was a Yankee. Her own mama who lived on Long Island left her a bit of jewelry. It's in the bank vault. I've had it appraised for your daddy here. That jewelry is worth a lot of money, too." He leaned back in his chair. "After I added up everything up, it came to half a million dollars. The estate is gonna grow. By the time you're thirty, the way things are going, your good-looking pa here will be worth at least two-million dollars, maybe more."

Pete listened to Perdue like he was reciting a fairy-tale, the kind Mrs. Riddle used to read to him by the fire.

"Get to the point," Mr. Riddle barked at Perdue.

Perdue cleared his throat again. Pete thought he must have a frog in it. "Up to now Mr. Riddle's sole heir has been your mama," the lawyer said. "I've drawn up this new will for him. He's leaving your mama one-hundred dollars. That will show the probate judge that he considered her when drawing up this will. Other than that one-hundred dollars, he's made you his sole heir. He left the provision that you're to provide for your mama and let her live at the homestead until the day she dies. But you'll get all the money. The will doesn't specify that you provide a certain amount. Just see that she has what she needs until she passes on." Perdue turned to look at Mr. Riddle. "Did I state the case correct?"

"You stated it exactly the way I told you to state it," the old man said. He looked up at Pete. "After today, you're gonna be a rich man."

"Oh, Daddy," Pete said, his mind a blur of confusion and conflicting thoughts. He felt he was betraying his mama by just being in this office. He didn't know what to say, so he said nothing. He was so nervous in this unheated office he was shivering. Suddenly, he heard the front door open. He looked down at the black booted feet and then up into the face of the sheriff, Claude Billings.

He was followed by his deputy, Junior Grayson. Pete fully expected Ronnie Key to come in too but figured he was back at the sheriff's office, holding down the fort.

Claude and Junior shook Mr. Riddle's hand but the old man remained seated, still wearing his heavy coat which seemed much too big for him. It was as if his whole body had shrunk since that long-ago day when he'd bought that overcoat.

Claude patted Pete on the back, and Junior smiled knowingly at him. For law-enforcement officers, Pete felt these were real friendly guys. Try as he must, he instinctively looked at their crotches. Of all thoughts he should be having right now, he knew that thinking of the size and taste of their dicks was about the last thing that should be on his mind. But he couldn't help it. Claude and Junior were two sexy guys, not in the same league as Hank Adams, but nothing a cocksucker would turn down.

"The sheriff here and junior boy are going to witness your daddy sign his new will," Perdue said.

"Let's get on with it." Mr. Riddle said. "Before I freeze my ass off in this Kelvinator. Haven't you heard of heat?"

Mr. Riddle signed the will, as Claude stepped up, putting his signature under it as a witness, followed by Junior.

The next ten minutes passed as in a blur for Pete. He just didn't know how to handle himself. After all, this was a world of grown-up men, and he was just a seventeen-year-old kid.

After the men had signed the will, Perdue turned to Pete. "When I was going over your daddy's assets, I left out one thing. Now that you're his heir, you'd better know about it."

"What's that?" Pete asked, fully expecting anything at this point.

"Some time back Mr. Riddle here signed a contract to buy Bleeka Walker's mansion," Perdue said. "The grandest estate in the county. It was built by her tobacco farmer parents in 1885."

"Yeah, yeah," Mr. Riddle said. "Everybody in the county knows the place."

"Hot damn!" Junior said. "I go there all the time. There must be forty rooms in the fucking place."

"More if you count the outbuildings," Claude said.

"Walker's a greedy bitch," Perdue said. "Wanted one-hundred thousand dollars for the place and the land. We finally settled for sixty-thousand dollars. Mr. Riddle here instructed the bank to pay off the loan at ten thousand a year. He's got only ten-thousand to go."

"So it's almost paid up?" Mr. Riddle said. "So what? I'll never live there. I want it for you, son."

When Mr. Riddle looked into Pete's eyes, the boy discovered a love and a bond between them that he'd never known before. Up to that very moment, Mr. Riddle had been rather cold to Pete, who was, after all, an adopted son, not his true blood. Pete jumped up from his chair and went to hug his daddy. Pete realized he'd never been hugged by his adopted daddy before. The old man was not a hugger. Nor did he believe in showing affection even toward Mrs. Riddle.

When the men broke apart, Perdue cleared his throat again. "Claude here has something to tell you good folks."

"Miss Walker took a fall the other night," Claude said. "Me and my boys rushed her to the hospital. She doesn't want it to get in the papers. But her daughter has come down from Richmond. She wants her mama moved back to Virginia. If she gets over this fall, her mama will be put in a nursing home. Hell, the old hag is ninety-two years old."

There was a sudden silence. "The daughter wants to see you, Mr. Riddle, sir," Junior said. "About settling the final claim. Taking over the

estate. They're moving out her personal possessions today. The daughter wants to know if you people want to buy her furnishings. There's silver there. Lots of antiques."

"I can't see any Walkers," Mr. Riddle said. "The bitch broke me into fucking three or four centuries ago. I was only eighteen, and she must have been a hundred even back then. I don't want her to see me in this condition." He took Pete's hand. "You drive up to the Walkers. Perdue is giving you the power of attorney to act on my behalf. Just get a good price for everything. I bet they're anxious to sell. Nobody else in the county has got the money to buy all that junk she's collected over the years. Her parents were from England and they brought all this crap from an estate they used to own in Buckinghamshire. Get to it, boy."

"First I've got to take you home," Pete said, assisting his daddy from the chair.

"Junior will run him out there," Claude said, signaling to his deputy.

After more hand-shaking, Pete walked with his daddy through the front office and out the door, helping the aging man into the sheriff's squad car.

After thanking Perdue who stood watching them go, Claude put his arm around Pete, giving him a squeeze. "I'll take you over to the Walkers to talk to the daughter." Once in the sheriff's own car, Claude turned to him and placed his hand on the boy's knee.

"I need it real bad today," Claude said. "Can we stop off at our little love-nest?"

"There's nothing better that I would like to do than suck on that pretty little dick of yours. It's the tastiest piece of meat I ever came into contact with."

Claude floored his gas pedal. "Shit, boy, talk like that is giving me a roaring hard-on."

Three hours later, after a jaybird naked sheriff had gotten the loving and licking of his life, including some spots that had never before been touched by human lips, Pete plunged down on Claude, eager to drain a second powerful blast from the tall, lanky man.

It was Junior Grayson who pulled up in front in a squad car. He barged right in, catching Claude and Pete in the act.

"Save that for later," Junior said.

Stark naked and still maintaining his hard-on, Claude followed Junior into the back room of the shotgun house.

In five minutes Claude came back, a towel wrapped around his nude body.

"Something wrong?" Pete asked.

"Get your clothes on, boy," Claude said, going over to retrieve his own uniform. "I think in a case like this it's better to come right out with it. Get it over with." He turned to look over to Junior who stood awkwardly in the

doorway.

"After I took your daddy home," Junior said, "I got a call an hour later. It seems that Mr. Riddle went back into his house, got his shotgun, and took it out into his front yard. Once he got there, he turned the gun on himself. Blasted his head off."

***

Everybody said it was the most spectacular funeral ever held in the county. Rosacoke felt that she'd never sung "Peace in the Valley" with such tenderness. Even though she'd faced hundreds of people, some of whom had driven in from neighboring counties, her voice hadn't failed her. Pete had smiled and had seemed right proud of her final tribute to his daddy.

The preacher, L.T. Younger, had extolled Mr. Riddle as a giant of a man and an American pioneer. Pete had also addressed the audience. In his black suit, white shirt, and gray tie, he'd looked far older. It was as if he'd grown into a man overnight after his daddy's suicide.

If he were proud of her for singing so pretty, she was rightly proud of him too and for the fine words he delivered over the closed coffin. Considering the condition of Mr. Riddle's head after the shotgun blast, it had to be a closed coffin funeral, although that had clearly disappointed the mourners, many of whom had asked for one final glimpse of their departed acquaintance. Over the decades Mr. Riddle had known or been involved in some way with about everybody in the county. He was known for his fair and honest dealings with everybody, so he had few, if any, enemies, or at least that was the way it appeared to Rosacoke.

She felt she'd had enough funerals to last a lifetime. Aunt Clotilda. Sultan. Now poor Mr. Riddle.

Every funeral has its disappointments, and Mr. Riddle's was no exception. She'd been shocked to see Hank Adams wearing a black suit drive up to the funeral with John-John, also in a black suit. That hadn't been all. Even Tracy and Karl had gotten out of Hank's car, and they too wore black suits. She didn't know where these no-counts got suits all of a sudden. These were not hand-me-downs. These were store-bought suits. She'd never known one of them to have any decent clothes to wear at all.

As reluctant as she was to admit it, the Adams brothers in their new clothes were the best-looking quartet of men she'd ever seen. Karl, Tracy, and Hank looked alike. Each one was handsome enough to be a star on the moving picture screen.

John-John looked different from the rest, because he wasn't their real brother, but the son of Medora and Mr. Riddle. Since Mr. Riddle was his real daddy, Rosacoke on second thought felt that the boy had as much right attending the funeral as did anybody else in the county, maybe more reason

than most.

When Pete spoke his kind and thoughtful words about Mr. Riddle, John-John's sobs could be heard throughout the church. A memory of the boy walking through the winter field with Mr. Riddle flashed through her mind.

Rosacoke had been real sorry that Mrs. Riddle didn't attend the funeral. Everybody had asked about her. "She's grieving too much," Rosacoke told anyone who asked her. Pete told more or less the same story. If anyone asked him, and most of the mourners did, he claimed his mama was too weak to come to the funeral. "The doctor's with her right now," he'd said.

Mrs. Riddle had taken to her bed upon hearing of her husband's death. She hadn't even come out into the front yard to view the body before the county's only ambulance came to take it away. After watching as two attendants from the hospital had hauled away Mr. Riddle's body, Rosacoke had gone back into the Riddle household. She'd offered her condolences to Mrs. Riddle.

The woman had looked at her sternly. "Don't you ever mention the name of Mr. Riddle to me for as long as you shall live." With that command, she'd turned and walked toward her bedroom, slowly climbing the steps. At least for today, she had no intention of moving back downstairs now that Mr. Riddle had gone on his way. At the top of the steps, Mrs. Riddle had called down to her. "From now on, I want you to bring all my meals to my room. I won't be leaving that room until Gabriel calls for me."

Rosacoke was sorry for the woman, but on the other hand felt that was just some idle threat. Rosacoke fully expected Mrs. Riddle to be up and about in a few days or so. The old woman was much too curious about everybody's business to stay in bed forever. Rosacoke didn't like Mrs. Riddle but was grateful and all that the family had taken her in after she'd fled from Sultan's shanty. She'd wait on Mrs. Riddle hand and foot if called for, because Rosacoke was mighty glad to have a roof over her head. She knew from certain times spent with her mama what it was like to have the open sky as your roof and some dirt farmer's field to be your only source of food.

At the gathering at the grave site, Rosacoke had never seen so many beautiful flowers in all her life. She wasn't quite sure where somebody got all these flowers. In December you didn't see many flowers in full bloom. The grave digger, Haydon Eller, had told her that the flowers were shipped up from Charlotte.

After the ceremonies at grave site, Pete had told her to go over and get in the back of a large black car. She'd come to the funeral with Junior Grayson driving her in his squad car. Apparently, in an act of kindness, the sheriff, Claude Billings, had sent the car for her, since Pete was still involved at the funeral parlor with last-minute arrangements and couldn't

make it up to the Riddle homestead to pick her up.

As she approached the limousine, she studied it carefully, recognizing it at once as the grandest car in the county. It belonged to Bleeka Walker. Rosacoke had spotted it several times when the grand old dame was driven to town by a woman driver. The rich old hag was probably the only person in the Carolinas who was known for hiring a woman chauffeur. Mrs. Walker must have lent the car to Pete so he'd have something decent to drive to his daddy's funeral.

Rosacoke opened the car door and got into the front seat. To her astonishment, two of the Adams brothers, the black-suited Karl and Tracy, were already waiting in the back seat, their faces beaming with excitement even though they'd just attended a funeral.

"Get on in, gal," Tracy called up to her. "I bet you never parked your ass in such a chariot before. The last time I saw you you were in Sultan's broken down old wagon being pulled by a mule that should have been sent to the glue factory a long time ago."

Rosacoke said nothing but got into the limousine anyway. She didn't like to be talked to in such an uppity way.

"Pete told us this is a Rolls-Royce," Karl said. "A Phantom V. I never dreamed I'd be riding around in the world's greatest car. Hot damn! We're in the money now."

Finally, she decided to say something. These boys were just too much for her. "How did you come into money all of a sudden? I ain't heard of nobody dying and leaving you no fortune."

"Pete believes in sharing the wealth," Tracy said. "He's not stingy at all. He's gonna give me my own car. Nothing like this fucking Rolls-Royce. But I'll have wheels under me."

"I wanta drive too," Karl said. "I'm old enough." He looked up at Rosacoke, "Don't worry. Pete is giving you wheels too. He told me he's gonna give you his coupe to drive around in."

"He ain't told me that yet," Rosacoke said. "Besides, I don't know how to drive no car."

"I'll teach you," Tracy said. "I can drive. Hell, I bet I can even drive Bleeka Walker's car here but Pete won't let me. He's saving this baby just for himself, although he told me that the sheriff's deputies can drive around in it."

"I was expecting him to stop by and pick me up in this thing," she said. "Although it looks like a hearse to me. But he got held up with funeral arrangements in town."

"Where did you hear shit like that?" Karl asked. "Pete was in town making a deal to buy a 1940 Lincoln Continental. It was bought by this rich fart down in Asheville. Before the car could be shipped to him, the old geezer up and croaked."

"You mean, Pete was buying a car on the morning of his daddy's funeral?" she asked in astonishment. "I had no idea."

"You ain't got no idea about a lot of things that go on in this world," Tracy said. "Unless Pete has the key to your goodies, you should hang out with me some night. I'm even better than my brother Hank. Hank told us he busted your cherry. Broke you in for that wicked ole Pete."

"Shut that kind of talk," she said, turning in anger on Tracy. "Your brother Hank ain't never touched me and never will. As for you two whippersnappers, you might grow up to have all the gals in the county. But this is one gal you'll never get any closer to than you are right now sitting in the back seat of this car, which is so grand it's probably against the Lord's teachings to drive around in anything this sinful. What a waste. Spending so much money on a car when families in the holler go to bed hungry at night."

From seemingly out of nowhere, Pete opened the door to the limousine on the driver's side and slid in behind the wheel, leaning over to kiss her on the cheek. He glanced back only briefly at Tracy and Karl. "How's it hanging boys?"

"Real low," Tracy said, smiling lewdly at him. "But ready to stand up and salute."

"Getting better every day," Karl said.

She wasn't really sure what that kind of talk meant, as Pete seemed to communicate with the Adams brothers in some kind of code language.

She hoped that Pete was going to drop the Adams boys off at their shanty and head back home to the Riddle homestead with her to comfort his mama. But he had other ideas. He was steering the Rolls-Royce toward town. Once he got to the little dirt town, if it could be called a town, he headed up the hill and entered the private gates of the Walker estate. She'd never been here before, nor had she ever seen the Walker house because it wasn't visible from the main road.

Anybody coming on the property was likely to be shot. Mrs. Walker had a reputation for being afraid of getting robbed of all her precious stuff, and the word was that she'd hired a sharpshooter to fire at any unauthorized person who came onto her private property.

Claude Billings, the sheriff, and his deputies, Junior and Ronnie, also hung out at the house a lot. Rosacoke had heard that the men received extra bonuses to stop by frequently. Mrs. Walker liked a police presence at her estate. Rosacoke had also heard stories that the rich old woman stocked the best liquor cabinet in the state, and no bootleg hooch either.

Before Rosacoke's eyes emerged the most magnificent house she'd ever seen. A steamboat Gothic plantation built in 1849, or so she'd heard. Dreamed up by a tobacco baron, the house was majestic, light, and gay. Imbued with architectural fantasy. Getting out of the car, she stood looking

in awe at this fantasia. It looked like it could sail down the Yadkin River.

It rose three stories with broad galleries like double decks along with twin stairs, much like those seen on pleasure boats. Great wooden stars were cut into its lintels. The verandahs were held up by Corinthian columns with iron acanthus leaves and volutes. Towering above were mullioned dormers and a glassed-in belvedere surmounting the hipped roof like a pilot house.

As the Adams brothers leaped out of the back seat of the Rolls-Royce and ran toward the house as if they owned it, Pete took her by the arm. He leaned over and planted another kiss on her cheek.

"This is what Pete Riddle now calls home," he said, taking her by the arm. "C'mon in and feast your eyes on it. I call it 'Heaven on Earth.'"

***

Even though he'd just buried his daddy, Pete couldn't help but feel a sense of power and glory as he paraded Rosacoke into the grand foyer of Heaven on Earth. Bleeka Walker had called her mansion Belle Reve, but that name didn't make much sense to him. He could tell that Rosacoke was so in awe of the joint she was nearly speechless. It looked like it was all too much for her to take in in one day. The Rolls-Royce he'd acquired for only two-thousand dollars was enough excitement to generate talk for three months in these parts.

Karl and Tracy headed upstairs to get changed into more comfortable clothing. After they'd gone, Rosacoke turned to him. "Those Adams brothers look like they own the place. I saw the way they headed up that spiral staircase."

"I moved them in last night," Pete said, wondering if Rosacoke suspected anything. "It takes a lot of upkeep to keep this house and grounds going. The boys need jobs, so I figured."

Rosacoke frowned as she asked the next question, "Are you gonna move John-John in, too?"

"Sure thing," Pete said. "Mama doesn't want him at her place. The boy would be a daily reminder of daddy's sin with Medora. In this house John-John will grow up into a fine man and will be a great help to me."

"What kind of help?" she asked skeptically. "From what I've seen, all he does is look at magazines and listen to the radio."

"I'm going to send him to secretarial school," Pete said, taking her by the hand and guiding her into the most magnificent parlor she'd ever seen in her life. It was filled with antiques and red-velvet upholstery and draperies with a huge black marble fireplace. He flipped on the giant crystal chandelier overhead, as she gazed at the porcelain and paintings once owned by Mrs. Walker's family in Buckinghamshire.

"This is a fine room," she said. "Looks like it would be mighty hard to keep dusted, though."

"I'll have people to do that for us," he said. "Don't worry. C'mon, I want to show you the rooms in back. You won't believe how many rooms this place has."

After an exhaustive tour, and tiring of her gasps of wonder, he took her into the kitchen to pour her some orange juice.

She looked a little pathetic in these grand surroundings. "I want to go upstairs and have a look-see, too," she said.

"For the moment, I'm keeping that private," he said. "There are nine bedrooms up there."

"What are you planning to do with all those bedrooms?" she asked, slowly drinking her juice.

"They are sort of guest rooms," he said, concealing from her the fact that he'd already assigned the rooms. He'd taken the master bedroom, of course, with its luxurious marble bathroom. John-John would have the small bedroom next to his, where Mrs. Walker had stashed her personal maid. Karl, Hank, and Tracy would be assigned to each of their own bedrooms, and when Claude and his deputies, Junior and Ronnie, drove over this afternoon, Pete was going to offer each of these young law enforcement men a room of their own and a key to the front door to come and go any time they pleased.

"Does Mrs. Riddle know you're moving out?" Rosacoke asked.

"I told her this morning," he said. "She said it was better that way. She told me I should go live in the grand house and leave her where she is. She said she never planned to leave her house until the hearse came for her."

"I know she's real bitter like over Mr. Riddle and all that went down before he up and killed hisself," she said.

"A lot has happened," he said, kind of distracted and eagerly awaiting the arrival of Hank and John-John from the funeral.

Bounding into the kitchen was a bouncing mass of blubber, Tara Jones. Pete had met her only last night and had asked her to stay on as the overseer of the property after Bleeka Walker had left with her daughter for Richmond.

He liked Tara. She was thirty-five years old. In her late teens and twenties she'd worked the backwoods tonks of north Georgia as a country and western singer. She called all men "hoss." There was something about this heavy-drinking, rough-living tank of a woman that delighted him. He'd felt an immediate rapport with her. Tara's hard drinking eventually led to her failure as a country and western singer. She'd gone on one drunk just too many times, and soon the word got out that she was unreliable.

When she'd drifted into town and had gotten a job as a waitress at the local diner, Tara had met Mrs. Walker one rainy day when the grand dame

had asked her driver to stop in and get her a bowl of hot potato soup. For some reason, this elegant woman with her quiet dignity and refinement had taken to brassy Tara. After visiting the diner for lunch on several more occasions, Mrs. Walker had offered Tara a job at Belle Reve. In time Tara worked herself up to overseer of the property.

When Pete introduced Tara to Rosacoke, she said, "I know you from some place. You're the gal who used to drive Mrs. Walker around town."

"The best God damn chauffeur in these parts," Tara said. "I can drive anything, especially the Rolls that now belongs to Pete. I can ride hosses, plow fields, grow turnips, cook possum, castrate a pig, and love a hoss of a man like he's never had no loving before."

Rosacoke flushed with embarrassment. "That's an awful lot of accomplishments. I'm mighty impressed."

"Welcome to the renewed and renamed Heaven on Earth," Tara said. "I've been out back telling the cook what to fix for lunch. We're gonna have a houseful. A lot of hungry men to feed. I like that. Things were a little dull around here with Mrs. Walker. From now on, the place is gonna be lit up at night. Filled with country music and good times."

"Sounds like you all are shore gonna have a lot of fun," Rosacoke said.

"Fun ain't the half of it," Pete said, his eager eyes lighting up with the anticipation of what lay in store for him that night. He felt on top of the world.

Upon hearing some people come into the foyer, Tara cocked her head and walked over to the doorway and looked up the long corridor. "It's Hank and John-John."

"Good," Pete said, taking Rosacoke by the arm and gently urging her to come with him, even though she hadn't drunk her orange juice yet.

Pete ran up to Hank and gave him a hug. 'Thanks, man, for everything."

"Your wish, my command," Hank said.

John-John looked at Pete and walked over to him and brushed some lint off his black suit. Every day that boy was acting more and more like he owned Pete.

John-John just lived for Pete and seemed to anticipate his every wish. The kid had even taken to bathing Pete, laying out his clothes, and shining his boots. He'd never known such devotion from anyone, and it was a bit hard to get used to at first, but Pete was now lapping up such undivided attention.

He turned to Rosacoke. "Mama is gonna be all alone, and she's gonna need you to run the house for her, fix her meals, keep the fires going. Shit like that."

He noticed, but only briefly, a look of disappointment that came over her face. "Don't think such devotion to my mama will go unrewarded. I'm

gonna put you on salary. Give you thirty-five dollars a week."

"That's a whole, heaping lot of money, and I don't think I could take it," she said, tears welling in her eyes. "I mean, you provide me with room and board and all."

"Hank or else Tracy will teach you to drive," Pete said. "You're gonna need to go into town to get provisions and everything. Also, if mama gets sick, you might need to rush her to the hospital. I'll give you fifty dollars every week to pay for groceries and run the house. Don't let mama want for anything. Promise?"

"I promise," she said in a weak voice, looking up that grand spiral staircase again, which Pete himself was eager to ascend.

"I'll be back in 'bout an hour," Hank said. "Get out of this damn black suit. I'm not much of a suit-wearer. That damn corridor upstairs is so big I think I'll take all of my clothes and run naked through the house."

Tara called from the rear of the house. "Glad to meet you, Rosacoke. You come by for lunch one day, ya hear?"

"That's mighty nice of you," Rosacoke called back to her.

Pete leaned over and kissed her gingerly on the cheek. He grabbed Hank's arm in an affectionate squeeze. "You take care of my gal," he cautioned him. "Don't you go putting the make on her. She's my private property." He flashed his award-winning smile at Rosacoke. "Thanks for everything. Tell mama I love her."

He gave John-John a pat on the ass, and the boy ran ahead up the spiral staircase and into the mysterious chambers overhead where Karl and Tracy had already disappeared.

Without looking back at Hank and Rosacoke, Pete headed upstairs and into his new life as master of Heaven and Earth.

***

In the early light of the following morning, Rosacoke tiptoed from her bedroom where she'd cried herself to sleep the previous night. With towel in hand, she headed for the bathroom. A sense of relief had come over her when she awoke this morning, as if the worst had already happened and things were going to start looking up from now on.

A feeling of hope had filled her heart, and she'd started to count her blessings instead of looking at how dark her life was. After all, Pete still called her his gal, even though he didn't spend much time with her. She was still a servant girl, but she felt that she was lucky to live in the Riddle homestead, even though it was a lonely life. It sure beat living in Sultan's shanty with that poor wretch and with Narcissa herself.

Rosacoke had understood why Pete hadn't invited her to live at Heaven on Earth. It wouldn't be proper for her to live there unless she was married

to Pete. When Pete lived at the Riddle home, and she did too, that was considered all right by the neighbors as Pete's parents could be chaperones.

She was at a loss why Pete wanted so many men living at the mansion with him. She thought she'd never understand his strange attachment to the Adams brothers. She found one Adams tough enough to take, much less four of them under one roof along with Claude Billings, Junior Grayson, and Ronnie Key running in and out of the place. These were the best looking men in the county. If the gals wanted these bachelors, they would sure know where to find them.

As she slipped off her clothing in the cold room, she figured she was mighty lucky to have a real bathtub, right in the house, with running hot water. She'd never known such luxury before. It had taken some getting used to, and she'd finally mastered the faucets.

Sneaking into the bathroom while Mrs. Riddle was asleep, Rosacoke wanted another total dunking. She'd already had two baths this week. She'd be happy to take at least three baths a week, but she feared Mrs. Riddle would object to her using so much hot water which cost good money.

Yesterday Hank Adams said that he'd be by the Riddle homestead around nine o'clock to pick her up and take her over to Sultan's old shanty. He was going to drive Narcissa into town to the bus station, and Narcissa wanted to say a final good-bye to Rosacoke.

Running a tub of hot water, she put her foot in to test how hot it was. It was just the right temperature for her. She submerged herself in the deep tub, long blonde hair and all. Yawning from morning fatigue, she relaxed in the bath water, luxuriating in it, loving the feel of the sudsy bath over her porcelain skin.

After Sultan's murder, she'd longed for a period of calm, a cooling of tempers, but got Mr. Riddle's suicide instead. Claude Billings had made no arrests in the Sultan case, and none was anticipated. Even though Sultan's death was recent, his name was no longer mentioned. Narcissa had seemed to want to forget the whole thing.

Rosacoke's pulse raced, and her whole body throbbed from the impact of the hot water on her satiny skin. She lay back, letting a curtain descend in her mind to blot out all bad thoughts. The veil was only momentary. Her mind suddenly went wild with an explosion of thoughts. Instead of her gray and murky past, she wanted to think of the future, of the day Pete might up and ask her hand in marriage. As his bride living in that Walker mansion, she knew a perfect life lay in store for both of them. They'd also have perfect children—a boy and a girl.

Thinking of marriage to Pete made all the pain and suffering she'd gone through to date worth it somehow. She wasn't that bad looking herself, if she did say so, and Pete was dynamite handsome. Any kid they produced would be a mighty good looker himself. She knew that to be true. It'd be

easy for Pete to father a boy. He'd probably have a hard time fathering a daughter, though, as she figured he was too ruggedly masculine for that. She secretly suspected that only weak men fathered daughters. Her son would have a large, bobbing head, a strong pair of legs, and he'd grow up to sing even prettier than Pete and her, because he'd inherit both of their voices, a perfect duet.

Even though long dead and buried, an image of her own mama crossed her mind, blotting out the perfect son she'd one day have with Pete. Rosacoke regretted that any woman had suffered as much as her mama during her short time on this earth. If only her mama had gotten to take a hot bath in a real tub in a good home. If only...

Rosacoke knew that she'd turn blue in the face thinking "if only." She was determined not to end up like her mama did. If her mama taught Rosacoke anything, it was how not to live. Rosacoke's eyes stung and a big lump came in her throat, as she sank back into the sudsy water, trying to blot out her mama's image.

Finishing her bath, she stepped out of the tub to rub herself dry in the brisk air. She put on her robe and slipped back toward her bedroom to get dressed. She wanted to get breakfast for Mrs. Riddle and carry it up to her room.

As Rosacoke buttoned up her sweater, the date on the wall calendar stuck in her mind. December 6, 1941. Christmas would be coming soon and after that 1942 would burst upon them. Her heart told her that 1942 would be the greatest year of her life.

It would be a year of happiness and a year devoted to Pete Riddle like all the other years of her future life.

\*\*\*

Pete stirred in bed, slowly opening his eyes onto the opulent master bedroom. At first he didn't know where he was. This was not his familiar room at the Riddle homestead, which was still filled with some of his old toys, including a broken-down rocking horse. That was the room of a young man who hadn't left the nest. His new bedroom was a chamber worthy of its former tobacco baron owners.

As he moved, Pete sensed he wasn't alone in his king-sized bed. Still sound asleep, Hank was breathing heavily on his neck. Pete looked down, reaching to feel John-John's head, which rested between his legs. Pete practically had his cock in the boy's mouth. Pete's last memory of the night, somewhere around three in the morning, was being on the receiving end of a deep, long drawn-out penetration from Hank. While Hank fucked him, John-John had sucked him off. For Pete, it had been pure rapture.

The whole night had been the most glorious of this life. He'd done Karl

and Tracy before Claude and his deputies, Junior and Ronnie, had come by. Before midnight, Pete had had the finest trio of law-enforcement officers in the county. Far from tiring him out, each man made him hungry for the next one. He couldn't get enough. Each one had tasted different. He wanted to suck each of their cocks endlessly until he could be blindfolded and tell which man was invading him. He wanted to know each of these young studs by their taste alone. He was truly the luckiest man in the world. Surrounded by great guys, he was determined to figure out ways to hold onto each of them. That didn't seem possible last week. Back then he'd be lucky to have sex with each of them a few times before they drifted off to relationships with women, maybe marriage eventually.

But with the power and money he'd inherited, Pete was determined to convince each man, even the sheriff, that his future lay with Pete. He'd let them have their gal friends, maybe even sanction a wedding here or there, but Pete wanted first claim on what each man had in his pants. Pete had a hunger for dick that was even greater than the addict aching for his drug or the alcoholic wanting his moonshine.

Before waking Hank and John-John, Pete relived last night. As the men drank and played loud music in the parlor, he'd taken his boys one by one up to his master bedroom. He'd insisted that each of them strip completely naked for his workout. He didn't want to have a man just with his dick sticking out of his fly. He wanted to see and experience everything they had, including stretching out their rosebuds for his inspection, to be followed by an attack from his lusty tongue.

Karl especially seemed to go crazy with that kind of love-making, and Pete had already singled him out as the first man he was going to fuck. He'd get the kid drunk enough and one night it'd happen. If his luck still held out, Pete knew it'd be just a matter of time before he was pounding Karl like he was plowing into John-John.

In time Pete felt he'd have all of these men in any way he wanted them. He assured himself all of them would come around and give him all the love-making he wanted any way he desired it. It'd be like breaking in a stallion. It couldn't be done overnight. He was going to spoil these guys rotten and make them totally dependent on him.

He smiled to himself and looked up at the ceiling, imagining all the black slave girls that must have lain in this bed looking up at that same ceiling, as they got pounded by their white masters whether they liked it or not.

In a much more modern sense, Pete felt that he was carrying on in the tradition of those horny old slave masters. The tobacco barons may have had their stable of black women to choose from, with an occasional bang-bang to their long-suffering wives. Imitating them, Pete had his own stable, except his choice was not young gals to deflower, but young men.

He could have all the gals in the county he wanted. Maybe any gal in

the county he took a hankering to, except he didn't really want any of them. Except for Rosacoke. He liked her but really didn't relish the idea of going to bed with her, although for appearance's sake he'd tried to put the make on her one time. He was grateful when she'd turned him down, although the actor in him tried to look disappointed at her rejection.

He felt John-John waking up. When the boy saw where his head was, he planted tiny little slurpy kisses on Pete's dick and stomach, going lower to lick Pete's big balls. He wasn't quite ready for that, as he hadn't taken his morning piss yet. He yanked the boy's hair, pulling him up to Pete's own mouth, where he planted a tongue kiss deep within the little cherry-red mouth.

All the commotion brought a stirring of life to Hank too. After waking up and seeing where he was, he gently nibbled on Pete's neck, as he enjoyed the early morning stubble of Hank's blond beard. Pete knew he could easily turn this early morning wake-up call into a sex marathon, but they were running late and had things to do today.

"To the showers, boys," he said, raising up. Pete was the first to hit the bathroom followed by a nude John-John. Hank stayed in bed as if not wanting to get up. John-John came up to the toilet bowl and stood across from Pete. The boy reached over and skinned back Pete's dick, exposing the big head. Possessively he held Pete's dick as he pissed. Pete found this erotic.

He was the first in the shower, trailed by John-John who got the soap and began to lather Pete's body. The shower curtain pulled back, as Hank with a semi hard-on joined them. He was in a playful mood. He held his dick up and showered them with a golden stream, as both John-John and Pete screamed at him. Their screams quickly turned to giggles as they reached out for Hank, bringing him under the shower with them for a good soaping and lathering.

Fully dressed, but in work clothes—no more black funeral suits—Pete was the first in the dining room. Tara was here to pour his morning coffee, telling him that Claude, along with Junior and Ronnie, had already driven over to the sheriff's office for a day's work.

"Hank and John-John will be down in a minute," Pete said to Tara, kissing this big hunk of blubber on the cheek as she handed him his morning coffee.

"I guess Tracy and Karl will be down a little later," Pete said. "I think they're pretty tired from last night."

As he said that, he remembered his final call at Tracy's room. Before turning in with Hank and John-John, Pete had been determined to suck a third load from Tracy. That nineteen-year-old was at his sexual peak, and Pete wanted to enjoy every minute of him. Tracy had been only too willing to oblige. Before falling into sleep, Tracy had rewarded Pete with the

sweetest mouth of nectar he ever hoped to taste in life. Almost immediately after Tracy had fallen asleep, Pete had gently kissed his rosy lips, knowing that one day his tongue would be inserted deeply into that beautiful open mouth.

That afternoon after the football game, he planned to take Tracy up to his bedroom where Pete would strip the boy down, spending at least two hours tongue-bathing every inch of him, including his ears and his toes. There was something about the boy's taste that drove Pete wild. He loved all his boys, especially that Hank, but Tracy was something special.

It was a gnawing feeling Pete had deep in his gut. He felt that he had endless time and endless years to make love to the other men. But for some reason he felt he didn't have all that much time with Tracy. Would Tracy be the first to leave him? Pete hoped not. He'd do anything to make Tracy stay with him. Spoil him rotten. Buy him off. *Anything*.

Forgetting where he was, Pete came back to the reality of the dining room and Tara who stood looking bemused.

"Listen, gal," Pete said. "I gotta come clean with you. I don't know what you heard or saw last night, but it's liable to continue. I mean this place isn't called 'Heaven on Earth' for nothing."

"Hoss, I see nothing," Tara said. "I do my job. Whatever is wanted and needed from me."

"I mean there are certain people—ignorant hillbillies to be sure—but certain folks who might find some of the goings-on here." He paused. "Shall we say, unnatural?"

"When a gal like me goes on the circuit playing rotting honky-tonks, she's seen and done it all. I myself have to admit that sometimes when I needed five dollars real bad, I've let the muff-divers get at me."

"You're one of those?" he asked in astonishment. To his amazement, he'd never met a lesbian before.

"No, I just did that when I needed a place to crash for the night," Tara said. "What I really like is a man with a foot-long dick, but there ain't many of those around any more."

He winked at her, sitting down at the lace-covered breakfast table as the cook arrived with bacon, ham, livermush, and fried green tomatoes.

After the cook had gone back to the kitchen, Pete looked up at Tara who went over to pour him some orange juice. "If you find one of those stud hosses with a foot-long dick, you won't be stingy, now will you?"

"I'll share him with you," Tara said, coming back over and putting Pete's juice on the table. As Pete dug into his plate, Tara rubbed his head fondly. "I'm gonna love it here. You're the nicest boss a broken-down old hag like me could ever hope to find."

"I think you and I understand each other," Pete said, looking deeply into her sad eyes. It was as if they had established some silent communication

between each other. Instinctively he just knew she'd be the best keeper of his secrets he could hope to find.

When Hank and John-John came into the dining room, Pete motioned for them to sit next to him. He asked Tara to join them too. "We're not gonna treat our big mama like a fucking servant," he said.

"Should I go get Tracy and Karl up?" John-John asked, digging into his food.

Pete looked at him carefully. "Let 'em sleep. First thing, boy, we're gonna teach you how to eat with a knife and fork real proper like. This is a grand house and you're sitting at a grand table. Lace tablecloth and everything. A little table manners are in order."

Hank too dug into his food. "You tell him, Pete."

"While we're at it, we're gonna teach you the same lesson," Pete said to Hank, softening his words with a flashy smile.

"Fine with me," Hank said. He looked over at Tara. "Since hooking up with Pete here, I've learned a lot of things. Before that, I thought I knew it all."

"We're missing a few at table this morning," Pete said. "Karl, Tracy, Ronnie, Junior, and old Claude himself. But I've got the makings of my own family. One I created all by myself."

As an afterthought, Pete noted silently that he'd left out mention of Rosacoke.

\*\*\*

Hank pulled up at the Riddle homestead right on time to take Rosacoke over to Sultan's shanty to pick up Narcissa. He looked freshly scrubbed but not like a man about to leave the Carolina hills for the big city of Chicago. She figured he must have a lone suitcase resting in the trunk.

Hank didn't have much to say this morning, although she was eager to ask him how all of them had settled into Heaven on Earth that night. It was Rosacoke who broke the silence. "I guess you're really looking forward to going up to Chicago."

"Something like that," Hank said, his eyes glued to the road. A light rainy mist was falling, making a gray day even grayer. "As you know, a lot has happened since me and Narcissa made those plans. A hell of a lot."

She could only agree, knowing that there was something he wasn't telling her. She just sensed it. That Hank was one mysterious boy.

When he came to a stop at the embankment overlooking Sultan's shanty, he told her, "Go on down and fetch her. I've got to take a piss and have a smoke."

Since she had no intention of watching him take a piss, she got out of the car and wrapped Pete's jacket tighter around her body as she made her

way down the dirt path to the shanty.

Seeing her coming, Narcissa pulled back the blanket covering the door. She looked up at the embankment and Hank's car with a look of contempt on her face. "That's a white boy for you," she said. "If you're a nigger gal, they won't even come down and carry your suitcase for you."

Rosacoke walked into the foul-smelling shanty as a memory of Sultan's attack flashed through her brain.

"Actually I'm not a nigger gal at all," Narcissa said. She was wearing her red silk dress. "I read in a movie magazine that my type of beauty is called 'café-au-lait.' Isn't that a high-falutin' expression? It means coffee with cream. The magazine article was about Lena Horne."

"That sure is one fancy term, alrighty," Rosacoke said. The weight of Narcissa's recent attack spewed up through Rosacoke's chest, and she wanted to sympathize with Narcissa and tell her how sorry she was. "How you feeling today?" she asked, genuinely concerned even though amazed at how fast Narcissa seemed to have recovered. Rosacoke felt if she'd been in Narcissa's place, the memory of what those men did to her would haunt her for the rest of her life.

She glared contemptuously at Rosacoke. "All the white mothahs in this county ain't gonna get me down. You see, I look at life like a big poker game. Up to now I've been dealt some bad hands. But I'm a heavy player, baby. I'm gonna stick in there and fight 'em to the fucking end. All the white daddies from this moment on, starting with that smug, big-dicked Hank Adams, are gonna be left pop-eye wondering when I pick up all the chips. Up there in Chicago, I'm gonna squeeze dry a lot of those pale pink type of little balls that white men have nesting under their even tinier dicks."

Rosacoke flushed red in embarrassment. She'd never heard anyone talk about men the way Narcissa did.

She blotted her scarlet lipstick with a tissue, saying nothing for a moment, as she stared intently at her reflection in the broken old mirror, as if self-enchanted. "I've been thinking. Where I'm gonna go, I'm gonna have a lotta grattooidies droppin' down on me. I've got a lot to sell, baby." She ran his hands down her waist, as if cradling her hips. "This package of goodies—if any white sucker wants to pick it up at a shop—is gonna carry a high price tag. You see, I know that except for my slight coppertone tan I live up to the ideal perfection of American galhood. Of all the beauties who've strutted their stuff before a bunch of gaping-mouthed whities, no one in show business has ever looked just like me. No one, except that Lena Horne. When audiences see me, they'll forget about that other black pussy."

"You are mighty pretty."

"She-it, bitch, I'm gorgeous. I compared myself to a check-list in a magazine, and I came up top score. When stacked against what that damn

magazine called our culture's beauty standards, I more than measured up. Certainly more than that pale-face piece of yesterday's custard, Bette Davis, and she's a bigtime Hollywood movie star. My hair's straight. My face is God damn perfect, and I've got a figure that would stop an eight-day clock. Nice tits too. Just the right size. Not those cow jugs you haul around. When I get my first singing job, I'm gonna tell them I'm Puerto Rican. It sounds better than nigger cunt. I guess I'll do that unless I change my mind and decide I'm gonna become the biggest black pussy star of all time."

"Sounds like a mighty big ambition to me," Rosacoke said, "but with your guts of steel I just know you'll make it."

"Don't give me that bull she-it," Narcissa said. "You think I'll fall on my ass in Chicago and end up a broken-down whore, peddling my pussy on the street corner."

Rosacoke looked through the dirty paned window at Hank having his smoke beside the car. She could hardly imagine the tough life facing Narcissa in Chicago. From what she knew of Hank Adams, Rosacoke was certain he would not be there for Narcissa if she needed him. "I've heard lots of tales about what happens to southern gals up there on the streets of Chicago."

Narcissa stood in a defiant stance, running her hands caressingly up and down her slinky figure. "Oh, yeah. Well, can you imagine something worse happening to me up there in Chicago than what those white mothah fuckers did to me in this little red-dirt cotton patch?"

"I can't say I can." She felt sorry for Narcissa, and knew that her grandstand performance was covering up a broken heart. "I'm ashamed I ruined that dress I borrowed. Pete is going to pay me thirty-five dollars a week for looking after Mrs. Riddle. When I get my first paycheck, I'm gonna send you the money to pay you back. I'll mail a money order to you in Chicago if you send me your address when you get up there."

A smirk crossed Narcissa's brightly made-up face. "That hot-ass Pete must have chased you through the briar patch. From the looks of things, he couldn't wait for you to undress."

"Nothing like that." Rosacoke shuddered, remembering what had really happened that night with Sultan. "Come to think of it, how will I get in touch with you?"

"General Delivery, Chicago," Narcissa said. "Not an address to be proud of, but it's all I've got for the moment. After I take the air out of The Windy City, my next address will be a mansion in Beverly Hills, even if I have to kick Lana Turner out of hers. She's too bleachy blonde and pasty-white anyway. This *café-au-lait* pussy's gonna go to Hollywood and make it big in the movies, even bigger than Lana Turner herself."

Taking one final look at the shanty where she was raised, Narcissa spat on the floor. She asked Rosacoke to carry a battered old suitcase, which

had once belonged to Aunt Clotilda, up the slippery hill.

When Rosacoke reached the car with Narcissa's heavy suitcase, Hank didn't get out to help her but told her to put it on the back seat. For two lovebirds, Hank didn't seem all that pleased to be hauling his lady-love into town.

Narcissa did most of the talking, mainly gabbing about all the night clubs she was going to go to when she got to Chicago, and all the big, fancy restaurants she was going to make appearances at in her dazzling new wardrobe, which she was going to have made to order in all the deluxe fashion houses. Narcissa did not fully explain where she was going to get all the bucks to do all these grand things, and no one asked her.

Hank seemed sullen and didn't have much to say. Rosacoke felt she understood. He'd made plans to go to Chicago with Narcissa, but didn't have a pot to piss in . Now he was living off Pete's money in the finest mansion in this part of the country and with cars of his own and new clothes.

In town Hank pulled into the little clapboard-framed bus station so dirty and decrepit it looked like the worst sharecropper's house in Shakerag.

Through a screen door with a faded Dr. Pepper sign on it, Narcissa went inside the waiting room, standing idly by as Hank went over to the counter to purchase her ticket. Narcissa pulled Rosacoke over to the water fountain, one marked white, the other colored. "I'm the best looking piece of ass in this part of the Carolinas. The only one with class on that bus I'll predict. Yet I've got to sit at the back of the bus. Me, a first-class pussy. This time I'll bite the bullet. I've had enough trouble with white people around here. Next time I arrive in this hogwash holler, I'll be in the back seat, alrighty, but it'll be the back seat of the biggest, slickest limo you're likely to feast your eyes on." Her face reflected a bitter determination. "It won't be no black limousine even. The fucking color will be *café-au-lait*. I'll have the curtains drawn in back. No one will be able to take a gander at me unless they pay, baby."

All this big, brassy talk made Rosacoke want to cry. She didn't really believe that it would be so easy up there in Chicago for Narcissa. Rosacoke reached out to touch her hand. "I know we ain't meant much to each other. But I'm still gonna miss you. I can't believe you're gonna go away. All the way to Chicago. It must be the biggest city in all the world. I never thought this day would come."

"I'll miss you too, baby," Narcissa said, glancing impatiently at Hank. The Greyhound was already being loaded. "What about you?" This was the first time today Narcissa had actually inquired about Rosacoke's well-being. "Gonna marry that Pete and raise a house full of snot-nosed white kids?"

Rosacoke lowered her voice to a whisper. "I've been thinking about it. Dreaming is the better word."

"Honey, you're a natural born housewife," Narcissa said, "unlike me. "I know you can sing a bit. But you don't have the gut-smashing drive it takes for show business. Tend the kids, slop the hogs, and lay down at night and get hammered by that stick of stovewood Pete carries around with him. That's my career advice for you."

"I guess so." Put that way, Rosacoke's dream of marriage didn't sound all that exciting.

"Tell you what," Narcissa said, her eyes brightening. "If things don't work out with Pete, I'll find a job for you up there in the big city of Chicago. Not where I'll be working of course. In some super supper club. But not slinging hash to a lot of hungry, stinking men just coming in from the slaughterhouse in blood-soaked aprons. Hank tells me he heard a lot of southerners gather at night in little clubs up there. They get homesick for some good mountain music. Maybe I can get you a job singing in some joint catering to these uprooted hillbillies."

"I could never do that," Rosacoke protested. "Just couldn't."

Narcissa looked hesitant. For a moment, her bravado look was gone and she seemed afraid and vulnerable, as if sensing something had gone wrong. "Have you noticed anything peculiar?" she asked. "I ain't exactly seen Hank with no suitcase."

When Hank came back from retrieving something in his car, he still wasn't carrying a suitcase. He handed Narcissa a one-way ticket to Chicago and leaned over and gave her a little peck on the cheek, hardly touching the flesh.

"Where's your luggage, boy?" Narcissa asked, her bravado mask back on her face. Instead of answering her, he picked up Aunt Clotilda's old suitcase and handed it to the bus driver who stowed it away in the bowels of the bus.

"Now's not the right time to tell you," Hank said. "I know I misled you by waiting until the last minute to lay this shit on you. But I ain't gonna go to Chicago with you."

"What the hell?" Narcissa asked, not seeming to believe him, although Rosacoke felt Narcissa had suspected this might be coming.

"Ole Pete's come into big bucks," Hank said. "He's made me an offer I can't turn down."

Impulsively, Narcissa reached out and slapped Hank so hard the noise resounded across the waiting room. Without looking at him again, she bent over and kissed Rosacoke on the cheek before scurrying onto that bus, heading for the back seat where she didn't even look out the dirty, mud-splattered window for one final good-bye.

Rosacoke stood forlornly on the oil-slickened pavement waiting for the Greyhound bus to pull out. She waved a limp good-bye to Narcissa whether she saw it or not. Hank didn't look at the bus pulling out but at Pete Riddle's

new Lincoln Continental coming into the bus station, with its brakes slammed on.

She figured Pete might be driving it, but he didn't get out from behind the wheel. Instead the front door of the passenger seat opened. It was Tracy Adams walking toward Hank and Rosacoke.

As soon as he saw his brother, Hank tossed his car keys to Tracy. "I'm gonna drive you home," Tracy said to Rosacoke. He then looked at his brother and smiled. "Pete wants you to go to the game with him. I'll catch up with you guys later." He turned to Rosacoke again. "After I drop this one off."

Rosacoke reached to brush something off her cheek. It was wet. Had Narcissa been crying when she'd kissed her cheek? Or was it Rosacoke's own tears?

She watched as Hank went over to the Lincoln and got into the front seat with Pete. The windows of the limo were dark, and Rosacoke couldn't see inside. She didn't know who was in the back seat, suspecting that it might be Karl and little John-John who was like no fourteen-year old kid she'd ever known.

Even though Tracy was urging her to get into the car, Rosacoke stood for a long moment watching the Greyhound go one way, and Pete's Lincoln Continental disappear over the horizon in the opposite direction.

\*\*\*

For the rest of her life, she'd remember exactly what she was doing when the news came over the Philco radio of the Japanese attack on Pearl Harbor. She'd been listening to her favorite Memphis station, as a bulletin interrupted Uncle Dave Macon's "Wreck of the Tennessee Gravy Train." Shocked and not really comprehending, she sat up in her chair, wishing Pete were here to tell her what all this meant. Where was Pearl Harbor? She'd never heard of it before, figuring it must be down in Florida some place.

Pete had gone to the football game with the Adams brothers. He was headed there yesterday in his new Lincoln Continental. After the misty rain had turned into a raging downpour, the game had been called off. She didn't know why grown men liked watching someone chase a pigskin around a football field anyway. She understood football about as much as she did Jap history. Until their sudden menace, she wasn't sure what the difference was between the Japs and the Chinese. She'd just never thought about the Japs until now, as they had nothing to do with her life. It was like a stranger who collides into your car, injuring you for life. That person from out of nowhere becomes important.

In the living room, she waited with Mrs. Riddle who had roused herself from her bed to call Tara Jones, telling her that she wanted to see her son at

once. Rosacoke knew that Pete would come, as the game had probably been called off when the spectators heard the news of the Jap attack. Who could go on playing football when the Japs might be dropping bombs on your head at any moment? If the Japs had already seized Florida, they might push north through Georgia and into the Carolinas for all she knew.

Mrs. Riddle stayed glued to the radio, listening to bulletins coming out of Washington. It was announced that the president, Franklin D. Roosevelt, would soon be addressing the nation.

In tears, Mrs. Riddle perched nervously in her favorite rocker, knitting furiously. She'd raised an altogether new and frightening prospect for Rosacoke to consider. Pete might soon be drafted into the army to fight the Japs.

The thought of losing him on some Jap battlefield made Rosacoke's throat swell. His loss would break her heart into so many little pieces she might not be able to put it together again.

What would happen to her? With Pete gone off to war, Mrs. Riddle might not let her live here any more. Rosacoke wasn't exactly sure just how welcome she was around Mrs. Riddle. The old woman increasingly regarded her with a certain hostility.

To take her mind off Pete, Rosacoke's thoughts drifted to Narcissa. She wondered how far that bus had gone on its way to Chicago. Narcissa had learned that she'd have to change buses in some city somewhere and get on a bigger bus. In spite of her sass, Narcissa wasn't all that familiar with bus stations in big cities. Rosacoke wondered if she'd get on the right bus. Narcissa might end up somewhere other than Chicago.

Rosacoke knew her dreamy plans of marrying Pete had come apart that afternoon in the chilly draft following the bulletin out of Memphis. What had seemed so vital in her life—marriage to Pete—became a frill. It was like running after a cluster of brightly colored balloons, trying to grab hold of a red one, but having it slip from her hand to float upward to the clouds, never to come within her grasp again.

The sky was growing dark before Pete drove up in his Lincoln Continental at the Riddle homestead. From the smell of his breath, she knew that he'd been drinking. She could see in Mrs. Riddle's eyes that she too knew her son was drunk. The old woman often lectured against the evils of hard liquor. Tonight her concern for her son overrode her objection to alcohol, and she warmly embraced Pete. He paid more attention to Mrs. Riddle than he did to Rosacoke, and this hurt her. She wanted to be alone with him, far away from his mama, so Rosacoke could talk over both of their futures together.

Pete stopped talking every time a bulletin came out of Washington. Mrs. Riddle seemed to resent Rosacoke's presence in the living room. "Would you be a nice gal," Mrs. Riddle asked, "and go into that kitchen and fix us

something to eat? Pete looks like he could use a good, hot meal."

Getting up, Rosacoke went to the kitchen and cooked Pete's favorite dish, spicy spareribs and greasy collards. Maybe if he liked the food, he'd pay her some attention. Pete stayed in the living room talking over something with his mama. Because the radio was on, Rosacoke couldn't hear what they were saying.

Over dinner Pete never said whether he liked the food or not, but when he asked for second helpings, she knew he must have enjoyed her cooking. At the end of the meal, his eyes lit up and a strong determination seemed imbedded in his jaw. "I'm gonna go and enlist—first thing tomorrow morning. I'm old enough. Almost old enough if you'll sign for me, mama. The Adams brothers, even Ronnie and Junior, are going to go and enlist with me. Everybody but Claude. He's the sheriff and will probably be deferred."

Mrs. Riddle remained stonily silent listening to her son's plans. Rosacoke didn't know what she thought. Her mind was caught in chaos as a chunk of sparerib caught in her throat, lingering there for a painfully long time before she could swallow it.

"I want to be in that first bomber attack to fly over Tokyo," Pete said. "There's gonna be a hell of a lot of dead Japs when Pete Riddle gets through with them. It's pay-back time."

She wanted to ask him, "What about me?" Yet she feared that was a selfish attitude. Here Pete was patriotically pouring his heart into the war effort, thinking about his country, and here she was lost in her sentimental dreams at a time everybody was talking about nothing else but the national crisis. Ashamed of herself, she got up and cleared the table of the supper dishes.

Pete took his guitar and drifted out of the kitchen and off into the far corner of the living room, from which emerged some very sad picking.

On looking back, she guessed she always knew it would happen before marriage. Now with his going off to war, maybe to get killed by some ugly, yellow-faced, gold-toothed Jap, she wanted to give him something of herself.

When he asked her to go up to his bedroom to pack some personal possessions to move over to Heaven on Earth, she gladly agreed. Mrs. Riddle announced that she was going to bed. In a complete change of plans, she said she was going to sleep in the ground floor bedroom she'd shared with her husband. "I'm getting too old to climb those stairs no more." Pete kissed her good night and headed up the steps with Rosacoke following him.

They'd eaten their supper at twilight time, as was their custom, and the sun had set but it left enough illumination to provide a faint light through Pete's lone window. The wooden floor of his old bedroom creaked as he walked across it.

The smell was musty. She hadn't aired out the room since he'd left for his new home. It smelled like bedrooms occupied by men, all dirty socks and that peculiar aroma that always hung in the air when boys slept together, doing naughty things she suspected.

Like thunder, the threat of growing up frightened her. When he closed the bedroom door behind him, she knew something was about to happen, even if she didn't know the exact nature of it.

She remained silent, waiting for him to tell her what to do. Better yet, to show her so she could follow his lead. Never before had she been ready to deliver herself up to any man. Now she felt completely under his control and wanted to be, feeling it was right. She only hoped he'd be kind—nothing violent like the attack from Sultan.

A panic came over her, as she conjured up all the hot hussies waiting to spread their legs for him when she'd been reluctant to. If he joined the army, how many temptations would lie in his path? She knew he wasn't the kind to turn down one temptation, and for a moment the idea of other women knowing, fondling, loving, and kissing her man made her feel that a giant fist had twisted her stomach all out of shape. The sick feeling soon passed, leaving an empty ache in its place.

"It's good to be up here alone with you, shut off from the rest of the world," he said. "I love you a lot, Rosacoke."

That made her melt into his arms. He'd never told her he loved her before, and those were the words she most wanted to hear come across his lips, far prettier than any love ballad he might have sung.

"I love you, too," she said, "So much that it hurts some time."

He moved over to kiss her hotly on the mouth, and, agitated, she kissed him back real hard, as his tongue darted inside her mouth. Like a battle of serpents, his tongue grappled with hers. She retreated, advanced, ultimately surrendering to his more penetrating thrust.

A powerful weakness of real desire came racing through her so strong her knees knocked. As winter's darkness blanketed the house, she had a hard time breathing, as her air came in short gasps. She planted quick little kisses on his ears, his forehead, his nose.

He was busy taking off her blouse. As he did, he squeezed her breasts. Her lips still parted, she murmured and looped her arms around his neck. "Hot damn, they're big, bigger than I dreamed," he said softly. With his fingertips, he played and teased the nipples, sending a delightful tingling sensation through her. He nibbled at the burgeoning nipples, sucking on them, making circles with his tongue. His lips were gentle, incredibly tender, causing her to feel warm all over.

His hand slid slowly downward, and she raised her hips, helping him remove the rest of her clothing. Determined fingers crisscrossed her smooth stomach, as she buried her face in the cradle of his neck, where her tongue

shot out, licking him. A shudder flashed through her body, as those long fingers plunged into her wet interior, making her moan, her hips arching upward. She bit her lip to keep from crying out.

His thirsty mouth withdrew from her as he took off his own clothes. As if perched on a lily pad, she lay in the darkness waiting for him to bury his head against the incredible softness of her breasts, which so obviously fascinated him. So vulnerable, she trembled as he sucked on her breasts like a baby will do its mama's. He gently pinched her nipples, making them larger, as they stood up like little hard acorns.

A sigh came from deep within her, and a little swallowing sound escaped from her throat. Her breathing was different, too, a sound she didn't recognize as her own. She responded reflexively to his touch, reacting without thinking. She'd lost control of her actions, giving in completely to his manly power.

Like a bloody sabre, that part she most feared in a man lunged forward, hot and red, seeking its reward, as their hips gyrated together at a maddening tempo. Their bodies pressed and slid. At first the pain was there, hot and searing, and she felt she was bleeding. But the joy of providing him with so much pleasure eased the hurt until it just seemed to go away, replaced with a thrill she'd never known.

Her legs rose and clamped around his narrow hips, as he pinned her shoulders back against the bed. A sweet, incandescent fire consumed her. She cried out as he throbbed inside her, plunging deeper. An excruciatingly wonderful sensation spread through her at his eruption. She clamped her thighs tighter around him, rolling and pressing with a savage intensity in their final shiver of ecstasy.

Even when his movement stopped and she felt the dead weight of him, he continued to lie on top of her.

Her only concern was that through it all, his mind was somewhere else. Even though making love to her, he'd seemed strangely detached. She could understand that. A man going off to war to fight Japs had a lot more things on his mind and lot more important duties than busting the cherry of a sixteen-year-old gal.

With deft fingers she traced ringlets on his sweaty back. She couldn't see his golden body but only remembered how broad his shoulders were as he'd stood in front of his bedroom window in the dying light to pull off his shirt so she could take in the fullness of his chest.

To her, he was not a mortal man but some God-like statue.

He raised himself up off her body, and instinctively her arms reached to clutch him and pull him closer. A kind of panic seized her body. She feared if her link with him were broken, she could never really bond with him ever again.

# Chapter 6

If the attitude when he left was one of indifference, she didn't remember it that way. He'd clearly claimed her as his own, with orders that she was to wait until his return from the war. When that would be, he couldn't be sure. She was to continue to stay with Mrs. Riddle and look after the frail woman while he was away.

As winter drifted into spring, and buds formed on the dogwoods in the backyard, she became resigned to his being away, accepting his going as one of those burdens that had loaded her down ever since she popped out of her mama's womb. She wasn't alone in her grief, as she knew that war was making women all over the country give up their loved ones.

She devoted an hour every day to writing him, filling him in on the most minute details of everyday life back home. He'd occasionally write back. Only yesterday a letter came in from where he was stationed in Norfolk, having decided to join the Navy instead of the Army.

*Dear Rosacoke,*

*So far we haven't seen any Japs, but I've had my tail dunked in enough water to cure me of skinny dipping at Blowing Rock forever. I don't know when I'll see the old homestead again, but I was hoping you might catch a bus and come up to see me this Easter. That's if it would be okay with Ma. I mean, if she'd understand and all.*

*People come and go around here so fast I can't make any real good buddies.*

*I miss my pals something awful. I was pretty much of a loner growing up. Just when I started to make friends, the damn war comes. Claude and Tara are taking care of both John-John and Heaven on Earth. I can't wait to get back home. Tracy is in the Navy same as me. I was hoping we'd be bunk-mates, but no such luck, even though he's being transferred to Norfolk in a few days. I can't wait. It's all I think about, really. Ronnie is down in Jacksonville. That's in Florida. He joined the Navy too. Hank said he's no fish. He signed up for the Army instead.*

*Karl was the lone hold-out. He was having such a good time at Heaven on Earth he didn't want to go into the military, war or not. But he was drafted into the Army a week or so ago.*

*Junior Grayson joined the Air Force. He wants to be a pilot and fly over to bomb Tokyo the way the Japs bombed Pearl Harbor. All the old gang split up but we keep in touch by mail. I can't wait for mail call. There's not a day goes back I don't get some letter from one of my old pals. John-John writes three times a day, sometimes four. Course, you write too, and I'm grateful for news of Ma.*

*The nights are so lonely here I cry myself to sleep many a time. With Tracy stationed in Norfolk, I hope to get to see a lot of him. I pray they don't ship us overseas. But who knows?*

*The training is sure hard here, and already I'm sorry I signed up for the Navy instead of the Air Force. In the Air Force, I might have become Junior's co-pilot and fly off on bombing raids with him. Hank says the Army sucks. He hates it. After the war is over, and we've whipped the Krauts and the Japs and busted in Mussolini's skull, I hear talk I might get my education paid for by Uncle Sam. Not that I need his money. I could go to college like I planned and on to law school. MAYBE. One hell of a maybe. For that to happen, we've got to hope some Jap submarine or German U-boat doesn't have our number on it.*

*Hope you are well. Take care of Ma. Tell everybody hi for me.*

*Got to turn in early tonight cause we get up before the roosters here. The fat guy in the bunk above me snores all night long, and I can't get much shut-eye. You know me, I need my ten hours. He also eats a lot of beans, and I sleep directly under him. Ha-Ha!*

*Keep up those guitar lessons.*

> *Your friend,*
> *Pete*


Instead of "your friend," she'd much rather he'd written "love." She had a powerful reason for wanting him to write that.

Starting last week like a little fear in the back of her brain, the idea had grown and grown into full bloom. She wasn't sure, as she didn't know a damn thing about such matters, but she felt that she was pregnant with Pete's child.

***

It was only two days before Tracy Adams hit Norfolk, and Pete was literally counting the hours. Surrounded daily by handsome young men, often half dressed or else jaybird naked, he was feverish with sexual heat. So far, he'd approached nobody, although he had his eye on three hot prospects he'd been entranced with in the open showers.

On board ship anchored in harbor, he noted the stillness of the air of a Virginia spring night. There wasn't even a breeze stirring. He recalled fondly the cool breezes that used to blow up from the holler into his upstairs bedroom window, bringing relief on the hottest of summer nights.

He missed his Carolina home, the moon at night, the pot liquor left over after the collards were cooked, but mostly he missed his men. Every night he went to bed, he jacked off as images of Claude Billings, Junior Grayson, Ronnie Key, Hank, Karl, Tracy, and John-John Adams flashed through his brain.

He remembered with amazing accuracy what each of their pricks felt like either crammed down his throat or buried in his ass. He loved each man, even though wondering how one man could love so many. Was he just being a male whore and calling it love? He rejected that notion outright. He did love his men.

After the war ended, if it ever did, and America wasn't carved up by the Japs and Nazis, he wanted to live at Heaven on Earth with all his boys. His mansion would be open to each and every one of them. Each man would have a bedroom and a key to come and go as he wished.

In some way, he knew that the war would change all their lives. Junior, Ronnie, Tracy, even Karl, would find women, or maybe men, to love. For all Pete knew, Claude himself might find himself a wife. Pete hoped his boys would fuck these new conquests and leave them. It was called sowing wild oats. Maybe the war years would get this experimental streak every man has out of a guy's blood, and at the end of the war each of his men would be willing to settle down with him.

Even though Pete knew this was but a pipe-dream, and life didn't exactly work out the way you planned it, he dared dream what might never be. It was all he had left now that he was in the Navy. The military world around him was just too bleak, and he longed for the freedom of civilian life.

The stillness of the night was broken only by an occasional shrill shriek of a whistle. The sky was dark but still had a faint glimmer left over from a day that refused to die.

The spring and summer of 1942 were about to come upon him. The Pacific fleet had almost been wiped out by the Jap attack on Pearl Harbor, but Pete had heard that all over the country factories were being converted into defense plants.

Guys like Pete were going to get not only the Japs but string Hitler up by his Gestapo neck too. The fucking bastards would pay for what they did, if Pete had any say about it.

He knew that Rosacoke was waiting for him when he got back home. He feared that she even felt she belonged to him. He didn't want to own her, and in his secret heart he hoped she'd find some sweetheart and get married before he came back to the Carolina hills. He didn't look forward

to the day he'd have to get married and settle down with a house full of screaming brats. That was not the future he wanted.

No woman would ever satisfy him. They didn't have the right plumbing. Yet he fully expected he'd have to marry one day. It was what was expected of a man. He wanted a woman who would not be sexually demanding. For his own sexual pleasure, he just knew he'd have a lot of men, maybe the men already in his life. He didn't need a wife for sex. To him, wives were about keeping up images. Men like him didn't marry a woman for love. They married out of duty. After all, Pete planned to go far in this world. For all he knew, he might become one of the most powerful men in the Carolinas. It would be expected of him to have a wife. Even W.G. Gabriel had to take a wife, and he was only the manager of the town's department store. The kind of future that Pete envisioned for himself would require a woman at his side, maybe even a kid or two tagging along.

All that property he'd inherited from Mr. Riddle would surely become even more valuable when this damn war ended. With his newly acquired wealth and power, Pete would keep all his boys at his side. What would they do otherwise? Come home and become a gas jockey? Work in the local hardware store at twenty-five dollars a week

He'd have his own airplane one day. He'd fly his boys anywhere in the world. He'd offer each of them a life of such adventure and glamour that each man would want to stay with Pete and not burden himself with some woman. From what he'd seen, women ended up looking like Medora Hester. When she'd become so broken down and hag-like she could get no white man to sleep with her, she'd turned to buying black meat on the block— none better than Sultan himself. Both Medora and Pete had shared a mutual interest in that Mandingo.

Pete looked down the deck of his ship, finding it almost deserted. He wondered if he'd ever have to ship out from Norfolk and see action in the Atlantic. There was talk of that but nothing definite.

While in Norfolk, he'd rented a small three-room apartment upstairs over an old lady by the name of Mrs. Rhodes. She ran a boarding house downstairs, with a little rental apartment upstairs. It was reached by climbing rickety wooden steps. The apartment had a kitchen and private bathroom. More than that, it contained a small bedroom with a double mattress that Pete was aching to put to use.

Even though rents had gone sky-high since the coming of war, with all those newly arrived people flocking to Norfolk, both civilian and military, Pete could well afford the rental. He wanted the little top-floor apartment to become a love nest for Tracy and him whenever Tracy was in Norfolk.

In the back of his mind, Pete also hoped to bring some sailors back to the apartment if he got lucky on ship. He'd noticed at least two pretty boys who wouldn't take their eyes off his big dick when he showered.

As darkness crept over the distant horizon, Pete buttoned up his pea coat. The night was growing colder, and he longed to be in bed with a hot man who'd warm him up.

He knew that down below the enlisted men were lying on their bunks in their skivvies. Some were reading, and others were dozing. Pete wanted to go from bunk to bunk, reaching inside each man's white skivvies, sampling, sucking, feeling, fondling and weighing what goodies they had.

As blackness inked the gray sky, he swallowed a lump in his throat. He was lonely. He wanted loving and was getting nothing.

It was nearing nine o'clock when Pete felt the first breeze of the evening. Black clouds were moving across the already black sky. Where was the moon? On the far horizon, he took in a streak of faded light. Maybe that was a reflection of the moon hanging over the side of the earth. But it gave no hint of light to the black murky waters enveloping the ship.

With just his thoughts and dreams, time passed slowly, and it was almost midnight when Pete went off duty, making his way down into the bowels of the ship. At one point he climbed down a narrow ladder and headed toward his own sleeping quarters along a passageway lit by a lone, exposed bulb which burned all night. He sat down on his bunk, untying his shoes. Unbuckling his belt, he slid out of his pants.

In deep slumber on the bunk next to him was Josh Harnell, a long, lean, muscular young man from the Outer Banks of North Carolina. He was entirely nude, although the other men in the cabin wore their skivvies. Josh was snoring but gently so, nothing offensively loud like the blubber butt, Arlie Rae Minton, on the upper bunk above him.

In the dim light Pete stared in fascination at Josh's dick and balls. The nut sac was a nice set, like large eggs. The uncut dick showed a meaty promise. In its soft state, it wasn't the longest dick Pete had ever seen. After all, he'd known Sultan and Hank Adams. But Josh's equipment was one of the thickest.

Josh had a fair complexion and light blond hair, almost corn yellow. Under the sheet, Pete as quietly as he could began to jack his cock. He wanted to cum while taking in a view of Josh's dick. The sexual thrill of watching a nude man in an unguarded state was enough to give Pete a roaring hard-on. Even if some of the men woke up and heard Pete masturbating, it wouldn't matter. All the guys did that.

Pete tried to hold back his climax as long as he could. He even imagined that in sleep Josh's dick had extended itself an inch or two. Maybe the young man was having his own sexual dreams. After all, what could a sailor dream about at night? Going off to war and having your ship sunk by some fucking Nazi submarine? Sex was a better nighttime fantasy than that.

Pete couldn't hold back any longer. He exploded into his white hand-

kerchief, catching the precious stuff in linen that he felt more properly belonged down the throat of some guy. He imagined John-John in bed with him, lapping up every bit of jism and begging for more.

After he'd wiped himself off, Pete still hadn't taken his eyes off Josh's cock. It was a thing of beauty, just made for sucking or even worshipping. Pete didn't like the shape or size of many of the dicks he'd seen in the Navy, but to him Josh was male perfection. Pete felt he was the handsomest man on the ship. Not movie star handsome like Tyrone Power. A little bit too rugged for that.

Josh had stopped his light snoring. Still staring at the young man's crotch, Pete noticed a slight shift of movement in the boy's body. It was only then that he looked from Josh's dick and into his eyes. They were wide open, staring at Pete. A panic swept across him. How long had Josh been awake looking at him?

The young man smiled at him before reaching for his sheet to cover his nude body. "Night, buddy," was all Josh said before turning his back to Pete and drifting off into sleep again.

For Pete, sleep didn't come that easily. He didn't know just how he was going to go about it, but his mind was made up.

He was going to taste every inch of Josh Harnell, or else he'd die trying.

***

Rosacoke didn't know what to do. There was no one to turn to, not even Narcissa any more. Rosacoke and she alone knew about her pregnancy. But how long could she keep the secret from the world? Mrs. Riddle was the last person Rosacoke wanted to know that her son had fathered a baby.

With the thirty-five dollars a week that Pete still paid her, she knew she could easily afford the Greyhound bus fare to Norfolk to see Pete, maybe at Easter time.

Although Pete had seemed eager for Tracy to be shipped to Norfolk, Pete had not seemed that eager for her to go up there. She wasn't sure that an eighteen-year-old boy in the Navy, likely to be shipped off anywhere any day, would want to hear that he was soon going to be the daddy of a little baby.

With her pregnancy, everything familiar became strangely different: the spittoon in which Mr. Riddle used to deposit his tobacco juice, the stamping of heavy-shod feet—covered with red mud—on the front porch, when a delivery man arrived, the chicken-fried steak that was Mrs. Riddle's Sunday night favorite, the pastor preaching on the evils of sin, the morose, tragic old mountain ballads she played on the gramophone, the fields coming

to life with spring green.

Always there were her dreams. They came in vivid Technicolor, just like the movie she'd slipped off to see at the local cinema where Narcissa had worked. It was called *Gone with the Wind*.

The movie had played to packed audiences around America but was very, very late into coming into their town. The owner of the cinema showed only old movies that had long ago played out elsewhere. He'd told Narcissa that he got them cheap that way. Even so, he still charged four dollars for *Gone with the Wind*. Up to then, she'd never paid more than a quarter to get into the movies before.

Mrs. Riddle claimed Margaret Mitchell had gone shopping around this part of the country to gather material which she later used in episodes falsely set in Georgia. When Clark Gable took Scarlett O'Hara in his arms, Rosacoke had swooned, imagining Pete and her playing those same parts.

The dreams that came at night when she was asleep in her old iron bedstead rushed through her mind with the ferocity of the melting winter snow that turned into roaring water as it gushed down the Brushy Mountains.

She owed it to her unborn child to get him a proper daddy and a real name. She wasn't going to give birth to any bastard and have him carry that stigma against him for the rest of his born days. A kid had enough trouble to face without starting off with a strike against him. Besides, what child could forgive its mama for doing such a thing to him?

The only pleasure she had in life, the only time she could take her mind off motherhood, was when she slipped off for her guitar lessons from Fry. He filled her with the spirit of music, and when she'd get back to the Riddle homestead, she'd want to retreat to her room to practice, the way Pete had hidden away to read those thick law books. But always Mrs. Riddle had some duty waiting for her—feed the hogs, wash some fresh spring greens for supper, or poke her finger into the ground to make holes for some plant going into the freshly upturned red clay.

Twice in the past three days she'd written Pete a letter, telling him of her condition. Each time she'd torn it up, feeling she'd made it seem that he must come home at once and do his duty by her. She wouldn't be happy getting him as a husband that way. She wanted him to marry her, even if he were sailing for Europe and would be gone for years. Who knew how long it would take to beat those Nazis, much less the Japs. Yet she hoped he'd ask for her hand because he loved her, not because some seed he'd planted was growing day by day in her womb.

She'd been able to conceal her condition up to now, although each week became harder. She noticed Mrs. Riddle looking suspiciously at her stomach, yet the old lady said nothing. Heaven only knew what she thought. Mrs. Riddle might think Sultan had something to do with implanting that

baby inside her.

If Rosacoke didn't have the heart to tell Pete, she had to confide in somebody other than Narcissa. The only person close enough for her to tell such a secret to was Fry. Tomorrow afternoon when they'd finished their lesson together, she was going to let him know she carried Pete's child. Surely, his survival-keen instinct, as sharp as a hound dog's, would come up with some way out for her. She feared if Mrs. Riddle found out, and she was bound to any day now, she'd ask Rosacoke to leave her home.

And then what would Rosacoke do?

***

When they were both off-duty, in the bar where they'd gone for beers, Pete was mesmerized by Josh Harnell. It was like they were brothers or something. Pete found he had much more in common and more to talk about with Josh than he did with any of the other men he knew, including Claude, Junior, Ronnie, or any of the Adams brothers, even Tracy who would soon be popping up in Norfolk.

Both Josh and Pete were from North Carolina, Pete from the hills in the west, Josh from the Outer Banks in the east. He spoke of how lonely he'd been wandering the wintry coasts of Carolina. "There's a cold light there in winter that's like no place on earth. At times you think spring will never come."

Josh said he didn't have that much time to be lonely once the warm weather came. His family rented out tourist cabins, and Josh had to do everything around the complex—making beds, carrying out the garbage, tending the yard. "It was a relief to go into the Navy. I might get killed but I figured I'd come alive a few times before the Japs get me."

"I was like you," Pete said. "Same lonely feeling. I didn't have the Outer Banks and the cold ocean to stare at. But I wandered the hills alone and lonely." He smiled at Josh. "Everything changed right before I went into the Navy. I started to find out more about myself. I started to reach out and take what I wanted. What I had deprived myself of for much too long."

"You're gonna lay it on me what that means?" Josh asked, looking intently into Pete's eyes.

Pete felt embarrassed, feeling he might have gone too far. "It was sort of sexual. What I mean is, I found out that I need a lot of sex. I mean, not like the average kind of guy. What I mean to say is I need sex more than most men. You might call me an addict."

"I saw you were having to handle the problem for yourself last night," Josh said, his eyes brightening.

"You saw that?" Pete looked down into his beer. He wanted to say

more to this young sailor, but felt tongue-tied. He didn't know how far to go with Josh.

Josh seemed more confident and aggressive. He moved closer to Pete at the bar until his right leg was touching Pete's. "I hope I helped you get your rocks off. I mean, while you jacked off, I wanted to give you something to look at."

"What?" Pete asked, understanding Josh exactly but hoping to draw him out a little more before Pete revealed more about himself.

"I figured that by looking at my dick, you'd get even hotter," Josh said in a low whisper close to Pete's ear.

Having Josh so close to Pete caused a tingle to race through his body. He desperately wanted this young sailor.

"I deliberately had pulled off my skivvies so you could see everything I had," Josh said. "I wanted you to want me like I've wanted you the first day I laid eyes on you in that shower." He downed the rest of his beer and ordered another round for the both of them. "My, oh my," he whispered to Pete again, "They sure grow some big boys up in those Blue Ridge mountains. You sure beat us guys down on the Outer Banks."

Pete finally got enough courage to look Josh in the eye. "From what I've seen, no person who went to bed with you would have anything to complain about."

After the bartender placed the beers before them, Josh flashed his brilliant smile and toasted Pete. "Here's to the start of a beautiful friendship. I even have a goal in mind. A purpose to our friendship."

"What might that be?" Pete asked.

"I don't know when we'll have to ship out, or where we might go, but I sure don't want you wasting that good white stuff in no handkerchief any more. Not when it could be deposited down my throat for me to drink or else shot deep in my gut."

Pete looked on in astonishment. He felt deliriously happy. Josh had made it easy for him. He'd been right about the sailor. Josh wanted him as much as he wanted Josh who was his own age and height.

The two sailors retreated to a booth in the back of the bar where Pete ordered hamburgers for the both of them. It didn't seem right to talk of sex over food. Not proper somehow.

Pete was halfway through his hamburger before he learned that Josh's secret dream was to write country songs. Pete leaned back in the booth. "You've found your boy."

Josh winked at him. "I know that. We'll deal with that later."

Pete smiled. "I meant that too. But I also meant something else. I could be your boy in more ways than one. If you know how to write country songs, I know how to sing 'em. I'm a country singer. Better than Roy Acuff."

Josh looked at him in surprise, reaching under the table and squeezing Pete's knee. "I'm gonna hold you to that. I brought some of my songs with me. I want you to sing 'em for me. Let's see how good you are."

"Sounds like you'd like to audition me." Pete said.

"In more ways than one."

Within the hour, Pete was leading the way up the rickety wooden steps to his little top-floor rented apartment. He felt the greatest guy to come out of the Outer Banks was hot on his heels.

Once inside the privacy of the apartment, Pete undressed so fast he practically ripped his own clothes. He was stark naked before Josh. Too impatient to wait any more, he helped Josh pull his undershirt over his head. By the time he'd tossed Josh on his bed, his tongue was already licking the sailor's beautifully formed red lips. Pete had never had a piece of candy that tasted as sweet as the lips of Josh Harnell. Shooting his tongue deep within the boy's throat, Pete got the sucking he so desperately wanted.

With his left hand, Pete felt every inch of the boy's balls and rigid cock. Last night he'd only dreamed what it would look like in its full glory. Tonight he got to feel and touch, eager to taste all of Josh.

In the meanwhile, Josh was running his one free hand over Pete's back, testing his muscles. The sailor's other hand had grabbed hold of Pete's cock with a grip so strong Pete felt he'd never escape from Josh's clutches. Not that Pete wanted to.

Once Josh broke from Pete's mouth, he said, "I can't wait no more. I've got to have it." Scooting down, he swallowed Pete's cock in one mighty gulp. The boy was damned good. Pete's pulsing, quivering cockhead slid all the way to the back of this Carolina boy's throat.

Josh's tongue was licking the tender tissue he found as he'd slid around Pete's meat. Pete let him suck, grinding Josh's cute little pug nose into Pete's pubic hair. He couldn't take a lot more of this without exploding, and he had far more ambitious plans for Josh this night.

He tried to pull Josh off his cock, but the sailor practically mutinied, locking his hands around Pete's firm butt and sucking harder. With cock completely engulfed in Josh's throat, Pete knew he no longer had the will-power to break loose even though he desperately wanted to plow into Josh's delectable ass.

With a life of their own, Pete's hips took control of his body, as he pounded his cock harder and deeper into Josh's suction pump of a mouth. Pete reached out and grabbed huge fistfuls of Josh's hair. Pete didn't want to hurt the boy, but he was driven.

Pete reared up in the air, arching his back. "Oh, fuck," he cried out. His balls rose to deliver their cargo. It was a heavy load. A real gusher. The boy had got to him. Josh sucked and slurped, wanting every drop. Long after Pete was spent, and lay gasping for air on the bed, Josh still

would not release his prize.

Finally, Pete pulled Josh's head off him and raised the boy up to his lips. "Like my prime, Grade-A USN jism?"

"I have found my drink of choice for life," Josh whispered, as Pete gently kissed him, licking and tasting the rest of the cum that rested in the boy's mouth.

"You know we aren't through yet," Pete said, whispering in his ear before darting his tongue in to taste that ear. "You know I'm gonna eat every inch of your body, suck your cock, lick your balls, and tongue your asshole before giving you the best fucking of your life."

When Josh didn't answer, Pete yanked his hair and bit hard on his ear. "Answer me, bitch!"

"I'm yours," Josh said, his lips desperately searching for Pete. "You're my sailor man. The man of my dreams."

As Pete's tongue began a slow, sensual lick of Josh's smooth neck, the boy's moans were like country music to Pete's ears. He felt he had Josh completely in his power. He could do anything he wanted with this golden specimen of manhood from the Outer Banks.

The next three hours passed as in a blissful dream. Pete was determined to have Josh in every way he could possibly conjure up.

Before he'd finally let the boy go, before he'd attacked him for one last time, and before he saw it was time both of them returned to their ship, Pete knew he'd found his sea-pussy for the duration of the war.

What Pete didn't know, at least not until he was boarding the ship with his sailor boy, was that he'd fallen in love with Josh Harnell.

***

Fry's verdict about Rosacoke's singing was flat and bold. "Pretty woman, you ain't got true pitch and, unlike us colored folk, you ain't got a good sense of rhythm. But, I'll tell you this, you got a nasal twang—right straight from the hills—that could give you one of the most distinctive female sounds in show biz. You'll never make it up in the big cities like your friend Narcissa plans to do. But if you'll stick to the backwoods, singing to the down-home folks, you could be booked on one-nighters across the South— even as far away as Texas." He lit up that strange-smelling cigarette, sucking the smoke into his lungs in quick, short gasps. "Now I want to teach you a few tricks with the guitar."

As patient a teacher as a bream fisherman, he didn't make her nervous, the way he had that first day. She got scared only when Moss came into the backroom of the juke joint. Unlike Fry, he continued to regard her small, fragile talent as just that, holding out no big hope for her at all.

"Before I finish with you," Fry said, "I'm gonna teach you how to

nigger-pick the guitar instead of just strumming it."

From the gospels in the church choir, she'd actually gone to thinking about the possibility of making a meager living singing country songs, if only she could learn to play the guitar real good. She might have to earn money if Mrs. Riddle fired her. As each day went by, her hope of marrying Pete faded. She certainly couldn't support herself hiring out as a servant girl, and in a few months she'd have yet another mouth to feed. The thought came back again that a good Christian woman like Mrs. Riddle wouldn't tolerate having a servant around the house with a little bastard baby boy growing inside her womb, even if her own son planted that seed.

At the end of her jam session that day, Fry gave her a quick hand-clap. "You're okay, yes you are. You're gonna do just fine irregardless of what Moss says. But you've gotta have a goal. A big dream, if you're gonna make it as a chicken-lickin', guitar-pickin' gal singer. "What's your dream?"

She hesitated. The idea had crossed her mind several times in the past few weeks of heavy dreaming. In a confidential voice, she said softly, "For me, the end of the rainbow would be to become the first female Roy Acuff."

"Crackerjack!" he shouted so loud he embarrassed her, "That's a mighty fine dream."

He invited her to have some home-brewed beer, and she agreed, gulping it down too fast and asking for another one before it was offered. She felt the alcohol would make her tongue come a little loose, as it hurt to tell him what was on her mind.

"I got a kid in my gut," she finally blurted out, slamming down the beer on the stained, soiled table. "It's Pete's."

"I figured you two had been going at it like jackrabbits. Does he know?"

"I haven't been able to write him yet. I've been thinking about hopping the bus up to Norfolk. But then that would be like trapping him. I don't want to do that."

"He trapped you with a baby when he was getting his jollies. Was he thinking about you? Go after him. Make him marry you."

"I can't do it that way," she said. "I just can't. I figure he'd end up hating me. He's got plans, too. Big plans. A teenage mama and her snotty-nosed young'in could get in the way of those dreams."

"There's more than one way to skin a possum." He gave a long, hard stare, as if brutally sizing her up.

"What do you mean?" Anxiety gripped her as the beer had settled heavily on her stomach.

"I know an old granny woman I can take you to. She gets rid of those mistakes people make in the back seats of cars."

A panic overcame her. "I'd never do that. Take a human life. I just couldn't."

"Okay, forget it! That's what I do with mine." He suggestively grabbed

hold of his crotch. "Better correct myself. That's what I used to do with mine. Ain't cutting the mustard that much no more."

"I'm gonna have Pete's kid. I've made up my mind about that. At first I got the idea I'd find a husband for it. When I woke up this morning, I decided I was gonna have it with or without a daddy. Besides, Pete's already done his part. The kid's growing inside me. I take over from here on in."

"You're very mule-headed, and I wish you luck," Fry said. "You're gonna need it. But you've got to call Pete. You owe him that much. I'll get through to him in Norfolk and have him call here tomorrow when you come for your lesson. You promise to do that much?"

Dreading to make the call, she felt that Fry was right in insisting that Pete know. He might never forgive her if she didn't tell him. After all, it was his kid, too, and he had some say in the matter. She reached for that beer again and slowly sipped it this time, as a bitter determination crossed her face. "I promise," she said faintly, looking vacantly about the bar, avoiding contact with Fry's searching eyes.

***

"You're a sight for sore eyes," Pete said as he eyed Tracy Adams from his sailor cap to his newly shined black shoes. Even though only an hour ago Pete had slipped away to a hidden compartment on the ship where he'd proceeded to go down on Josh Harnell, Pete's appetite was gargantuan again.

"I'd like to grab you and give you a bigger hug than any bear about to eat you," Tracy said. "Guess we'll have to save that for later."

Tracy had already turned twenty since joining the Navy, and Pete thought he looked more like his brother Hank every day, except a little younger and with less wear and tear than Hank had on his face.

"Are we gonna stand here all night and let you look at me like a piece of beef dangled before a hound dog that ain't eaten in a month?" Tracy asked. "Or are you gonna buy me a beer and catch up."

In the same back room of the same bar where he'd eaten the hamburger and drank the beer with his newly discovered Josh, Pete smelled the clean, masculine aroma of Tracy. Pete had glanced down several times at the sailor's crotch, recalling in vivid detail the length and thickness of the boy's dick, the sweet taste of his cum, like a vaguely scented apricot nectar.

"It's been hell, man, without you," Tracy said. "Several queers have come on to me, but I figure I have 'Private Property, Pete Riddle,' stamped on my government-inspected meat."

"You've never talked this way before," Pete said, astonished at Tracy's comment. "I mean, I figured you'd let me cop your joint from time to time.

That is, when you weren't out chasing some skirt."

"I don't know," he said, sipping his beer and looking intently into Pete's eyes. "I went with one God damn whore since joining the Navy, and it didn't do much for me. I shot my load. That was it. No feeling. No love like you put into it. In fact, when I came inside the bitch, my mind flashed on you."

"I can't believe you're saying this," Pete said, breathing heavier and sliding closer to the boy. "We haven't even gone all the way yet. What I mean to say is, I haven't even kissed you. You've been really swell letting my tongue taste everything but I haven't gotten to kiss those pretty red lips of yours and suck your tongue."

"Stop that fucking talk," Tracy said. "You're giving me a hard-on." In the back booth with no one looking, Tracy reached for Pete's right hand and placed it on his crotch. Pete eagerly felt the promising mound, and wanted to rip off Tracy's uniform right in the tavern and go down on him.

"In about an hour, that big thing is going to be down your throat and then up your ass," Tracy said. He removed Pete's hand from his crotch. "I'll fucking cream my pants if we don't stop right now."

"I guess what you're telling me is that our relationship is about to take a new turn," Pete said.

"You heard that right," Tracy said. "It's not your becoming rich and everything, though deep in my heart I've got to admit that has something to do with it. You took me from the dirt shanty that was no better than Sultan's. You moved me into a mansion. I didn't know beds came that comfortable. You got me a car. You gave me everything. And when you came to my bed, you made me feel like I was the most special guy in all the world. You were the one who made me feel in parts of my body that I didn't even know could be aroused. It was you. Night after night of that began to get to me. Over these past few weeks, I'd lie in my bunk and jack-off just thinking of what you used to do to me." He reached for Pete's hand. "And what you're gonna continue to do to me."

Pete felt an agitation growing within him. When he was with Tracy, he wanted to forget all about Josh, and certainly all about the other Adams brothers. He knew he might love other men, but not tonight. Tonight that good-looking mother-fucker, Tracy Adams, was at the center of his universe.

The sailor boy in his uniform was prettier than Pete had remembered him. After his basic training, Tracy seemed more sure of himself, more assertive, more willing to reach out and take what he wanted.

"Leaving Heaven on Earth was the saddest day of my life," Tracy said. "I had truly found my Heaven on Earth, and it was in that mansion with you. That's how I want to live. I remember the night Tara cooked steaks for us. You know up to then I'd never had a steak before?"

Signaling the waitress, Pete ordered two steaks for both of them cooked rare. "You're gonna have one tonight, sailor boy."

"Thanks," Tracy said, leaning back in the booth after the waitress had left. "I'm gonna feed you some prime Grade-A meat too."

"My life depends on it," Pete said, almost meaning it.

"I haven't jacked off in two weeks," Tracy said. "I've been saving it for you. All for you. Sometimes I thought I'd go out of my mind, and couldn't hold back no more. But I did. It's all yours, buddy."

Over the steak dinner, Tracy kept looking up into Pete's eyes. "Even though I ain't been in the military that long, it's done me good. All my life I've compared myself to Hank. I felt my older brother had a better build on him. I felt all the gals wanted him instead of me. I used to feel his dick was bigger than mine, but I caught up to him in that department. Hank was the first one who got you. I felt I was thrown in as some fucking consolation prize. Hank was your main man. Me and Karl—forget John—were like some whipped cream on the cake. The cake was Hank. I'm gonna change all that."

"Tell me more," Pete said, feeling his heart beating faster. "I mean, how are things gonna change between us?"

"Before the morning comes, I'm gonna become your main man. But more. So much more."

"I think I'm getting it but I might not be getting it at all," Pete said, wanting to draw his buddy out.

"Let's put it this way," Tracy said, reaching for his beer. "I'm gonna become all the man you will ever need in all your life. My brothers can work for you. The sheriff's deputies can come and go. If you do any cocksucking in the future, it's gonna be my dick rammed down your throat. If you need to get fucked, and I suspect you will once or twice a day, it's gonna be my big dick shoved up your ass."

If there was one thing that drove Pete wild, it was masculinity in a man who was still a boy. No man had ever taken possession of him before. He loved the way Tracy was staking his claim. Pete had no idea how he'd fit the other men into his life if Tracy took control like he threatened. For Pete, that would be a problem for tomorrow.

Tonight he was going to haul his ass out of that tavern as soon as his boy finished off that steak. Pete was going to take him to his secret hide-away. He was going to go at Tracy tonight like no other person had ever devoured the boy. Regardless of where he was going in this fucking war, where he would be shipped off to, Pete wanted Tracy to remember this night for the rest of his life. Pete felt that all his love-making with Tracy up to this moment had been foreplay. Tonight would be the real test of their love.

On the way to his apartment, Pete suddenly realized something about

himself. He had an infinite capacity for love. At this moment Tracy was the main man, maybe the most important man in Pete's life. Tomorrow afternoon on the ship when he'd slip away with Josh, that Outer Banks specimen would be the man whose flesh Pete wanted to devour.

How could men chose just one mate and settle down to a permanent life? Every man brought something special to him. Every man from Josh to Claude, from Junior to Ronnie, from John-John to Karl, and especially that Hank, thrilled him in some way.

Inside the apartment, Pete didn't bother to turn on the light. He took Tracy's hand and led him over to the window where the Virginia moonlight shone on the young man's face.

He looked into that face, finding it filled with wonder. Tracy seemed eager to experience what was about to happen to him. "You know," Pete said, "I've dreamed about it, but I've never had the chance to kiss the most beautiful lips that God ever put on a man, and that man is Tracy Adams."

"Why don't you make up for lost time?" Tracy asked.

Pete moved his lips until he was only a half inch within striking distance of Tracy's succulent lips. He felt he was breathing for Tracy. The boy's breath, slightly tainted by beer, was like a spring flower garden for Pete. His tongue flickered out for a quick taste of Tracy's upper lip. When Pete's tongue darted out again, he caught the tip of Tracy's tongue.

Pete was like a sadist with himself, denying the pleasure that had so long eluded him. Stalling as if to tantalize himself until he couldn't stand it any more. Pete's arms went around Tracy's muscled back, pulling the sailor boy into his clutches.

Pete's tongue darted out and plunged deep inside Tracy's mouth where it launched World War II with Tracy's own succulent tongue.

Tracy fell down on top of the sofa, burying Pete underneath him. Pete ran his hands through Tracy's wavy blond hair and felt everything he could, as he deep-kissed this beautiful man, loving the thrill of it and loving the man himself.

Nobody in Pete's universe existed right now except Tracy. How could there be any others? What could any other man ever give him that Tracy could not provide?

Ten minutes must have passed before Pete felt he'd drained a quart of saliva from Tracy's mouth. He was the most liquid kisser Pete had ever known, and Pete drank every drop of it like he'd drink every drop of Tracy's cum later that night.

When he finally broke from Tracy's mouth, Pete hugged him close, kissing his ear lobe before whispering into it. "Very, very slowly, I'm going to take off all your clothes. There's no part of you that I don't want to taste tonight. From your big toes to your big dick, from your beautiful asshole to your armpits, I've got to undress you for the blow-out night of your whole

life."

Tracy lay back on the sofa, as Pete descended to remove the boy's shoes, finally pulling the black socks down over the big beautiful feet. Slowly his hands moved up Tracy's legs, descending on his crotch which was practically bursting through his sailor pants.

As Pete slowly unbuttoned those pants, he felt that he might have left his home, Heaven on Earth, but he'd found it again in this darkened apartment.

The lone, lonely sound of a ship heading for sea blasted from the port, reminding them of a fate that no doubt awaited both of them when they would be shipping out.

As Pete pulled Tracy's pants down and reached to unfasten his skivvies, he felt that their eventual separation would be years and years away in some distant future.

That didn't matter right now. What mattered was the young man underneath him. When he had Tracy's clothing down to his knees, he looked at the prize he'd uncovered as it reared its head in the moonlight. It looked bigger and more frightening than Pete had remembered it. It needed to be tamed, and Pete was the man to do it.

He had this night. He had this boy. Could he ever want anything else in his life?

\*\*\*

Rosacoke was right proud she'd paid off her obligations. With money from her salary that Pete had given her, she went to Belk's Department Store and settled her account and even bought a new dress, paying cash for it. W.G. Gabriel beamed with pride at his good judgment in trusting her. But his snippy clerk, Mary Hemphill, seemed put off with her, having predicted she'd never earn the money to pay the store what she owed.

After each guitar lesson with Fry, she paid for it with her newly earned cash. Not only that, but she'd sent money to Chicago to pay for Narcissa's dress that she'd ruined. Like Narcissa instructed, Rosacoke sent the money to "General Delivery," hoping that she'd pick it up. So far, Rosacoke had not heard one word from Narcissa since that day she'd left Sultan's shanty and had boarded the Greyhound bus to the Windy City.

In the past few weeks, the sheriff, Claude Billings, had showed up faithfully every day to teach Rosacoke how to drive. The lessons had gone so well that in six weeks Claude had granted her her driver's license. With that license, she was able to drive the Riddle's pickup truck, running errands for the old woman who'd become a complete recluse after the suicide of her husband and Pete going off to war.

The only person Rosacoke had written to about her baby was Narcissa.

To everyone else, it was a dark secret, although Claude had commented that Rosacoke looked as if she were putting on weight. Because of the size of her stomach, she feared that any day she'd have to drop out of high school. She was just a few weeks from graduation, and, to cover herself better, she'd abandoned the sexy clothes Pete had wanted her to wear. In baggy dresses, she'd reverted back to her old look, the way she'd been seen before Narcissa's transformation of her image.

On the way to Shakerag, she stopped in at a filling station to buy herself some orange pop. Drinking it, she found herself shaky all over. The past night had brought not one wink of sleep. She'd been up until dawn, thinking about that call to Pete at the Norfolk base. Several times she'd mulled over not showing up, but she'd promised Fry, and she was a woman of her word.

What compelled her to make the call was a memory racing through her head of a skinny little boy at school, Freddie Perkins. The other boys would beat the tar out of him, and once he'd been thrown down a flight of stairs and badly injured. Someone was always popping off at him, calling him "bastard" or "little son-of-a-bitch." She never felt that way toward Freddie, and had tried to make friends with him. He'd have nothing to do with her, trusting no one, suspicious of everybody. Rosacoke didn't want to bring another little bastard into the world that other boys would beat up on.

Fearing she'd be late, she, nevertheless, stopped by the side of the road to pick the first wildflowers she'd seen there this spring. After she'd talked to Pete, she was going to take them and put them on her mama's grave. As she was soon to be a mama herself, she'd grown much more sympathetic about how hard it must have been for the poor dead woman to make her way in the world.

Since Rosacoke faced almost the same hardship herself, she'd been thinking about her mama a lot lately, wishing she'd given her more love and understanding, instead of nagging and complaining all the time the way she did. She was afraid of ghosts who traditionally haunt graveyards and old houses, but the spot where Sultan, her mama, and her little baby brother lay under the ground wasn't a real cemetery, like the one where Aunt Clotilda had been buried.

Her mama used to collect wildflowers in the spring, bringing them back to the shanty, as they formed her only token of decoration. She favored one spot near some pecan trees where just about every kind of beautiful wild-flower grew. Her mama knew just when each flower would bloom.

Her own flowers resting on the seat beside her, Rosacoke headed over to the juke joint to see Fry. There would be no guitar lessons today, as the phone call would provide too much excitement for her to put her mind on her picking. She'd hardly talked to anyone on the phone in her entire life, as she viewed the instrument as something you used in a real emergency, like summoning a doctor when a person is dying. Long distance made it even

worse.

As she came into the backroom of the juke joint, Moss and Fry were doing a fast, driving, cut-time boogie. Something about what fate awaited at the end of the road. Even before making that call to Pete, she figured that after she'd traveled down some long, lonesome highway, there still would be no wedding in sight. Bracing herself, she came up to Fry at the finish of their number. Moss took one look at her and sauntered off to join some black musicians in the far corner, drinking beer and smoking those strange-smelling cigarettes.

"I got in touch with him last night," Fry said after Moss was out of hearing range. "I told him the whole story, even about the granny woman and how you wasn't so hot on that brainstorm."

Her heart seemed to rattle upon hearing that. "What did he say?"

"He wants to talk to you personal like. He's waiting for us to put through the call exactly at four o'clock."

"Please do it for me," she said. "I'll speak to him when he comes on the line."

In the far corner of the room, she waited for Fry's signal from the operator. Her whole body shook as he motioned for her to come over. Nervously she took the receiver from Fry.

"That you Rosacoke?"

At first Pete's voice made her not-too-steady heart jump, until the reason for the call rushed through her mind. "It's me, Pete. *Both* of us."

"I heard the bad news from Fry last night." He sounded dejected.

She trembled, knowing all along that he'd consider the news bad. How else could he look upon it? It's hardly what an eighteen-year-old boy, on the dawn of his adult life, wanted to hear, especially in wartime.

Instead of asking her about her condition, he seemed more interested in learning if Mrs. Riddle knew. "She doesn't know anything, I mean about your condition?"

"If she does, she ain't said one word to me about it."

He paused, as if reluctant to say what he was about to. "I think Fry has the best idea." That was followed by another long pause. "I mean. You know. The old granny woman."

She burst into tears. It was as if all the forces that had kept her contained for the past twenty-four hours had been unleashed. He muttered what comfort he could into the phone until she could regain control. "Pete Riddle, don't go asking me to take a human life. I'll have the baby myself. I don't need you or your folks. It's *my* baby, and I'm gonna have it."

"Okay, okay," he said, an edge of irritation in his voice. "I was just tossing it out as an idea. It was a joke, you know. I wasn't really serious. Can't you take a joke?"

"I don't think yours was very funny."

"Listen."

"I'm all ears," she said.

"What do you want from me? To marry you?"

"I'm not asking for that," she said. "You brought it up."

"You know I've got plans. About going to college—and all. Becoming a big-time lawyer. I just can't throw away all my dreams and get saddled with a lot of kids running around."

She couldn't stop crying. Between sobs, she blurted out, "I'm not asking to let the baby keep you from getting an education. Going to college and everything. I don't want to be a burden to you, and I don't want *my* baby to be a burden to you either."

"It's not that." The irritation faded from his voice, and he spoke in more consoling tones. "Tell you what. I have an idea. I'll write Ma. Tell her the whole story with lots of apologies and promises to the Lord it'll never happen again. You go ahead and have the kid. But in the next county right in a hospital. Hide yourself during the final weeks. It'll be my kid, but we won't tell anybody. We can get Tara to bring it up at Heaven on Earth. Tara can pretend she dumped the kid—not you. That way, your reputation will be protected. The more I think about it, the more I know my idea is great."

"I was hoping to keep the kid myself."

"Forget that!" His anger exploded. "Goddamn it, do what I tell you to. It's the only way out. I'm agreeing to provide for the kid and protect your reputation. That should be enough for any teenage gal still in high school. A lot of boys wouldn't go so far as I'm going. I'm really putting myself out for this one since you're begging to keep the kid and not let the old granny woman do her job."

"I don't want to give up my baby to Tara," she protested. "Just like that."

"Fuck that! What makes you so selfish? Do you want the kid to grow up and be called a bastard? Like Freddie Perkins?"

"I'd die. I'd just die."

"Then you've got to do it my way. We'll get married one day after I get out of the Navy. If I ever get out alive. Times are too uncertain right now for anybody to think of marriage. I've got to go to college. We're talking years before I can settle down. Besides, you can't bring young-ins into the world."

"It's too late to think about that now."

"Okay, I'll write Ma tonight. I'm sure my idea will work. No one will know, except Ma and Fry, of course. Naturally, Tara, too. I've had a long talk with Fry. I'm gonna pay for him to make all the arrangements for you to have the kid and everything."

Pete yelled at somebody in the background. "Hey, I'm tying up this

phone," he said to her. "Can't talk any more. There's a war on."

"Pete." Her voice was hesitant.

His was impatient. "What is it?"

"I love you."

"That's good. Well, take care of yourself, you hear?" He hung up.

For a long time she held onto the phone, listening to the dead receiver. Then she suddenly flinched, shrank, and turned with a spasm-like motion to the bar. There was a lot she wanted to say to him, all about what was on her mind. There was much to reveal that was in her heart.

After thanking Fry, she headed back in the pickup truck to the Riddle homestead, forgetting her way and getting lost once. The spring land was bathed in a golden twilight.

A light rain began to fall, and she pressed her angry, tear-smeared nose flat against the windshield, as the wiper wasn't working too good. She tried to see out, but the rain, though gentle, formed a misty fog, blocking her vision. Blindly she drove on, as if following the trail of the road by instinct.

She pulled into the Riddle driveway beside the house, and the dog ran out, barking with joy and jumping up on her to greet her, getting her clothes muddy. Looking back at the pickup truck, she feared she could have died, killing not only herself but her baby if she'd run off the road down a mountain. She vowed to take that pickup truck to the filling station in the morning and get those wipers fixed.

Forgetting her flowers, she returned to the truck, opening the door. She'd meant to put the flowers on her mama's grave but had forgotten to do so because she'd been so upset about that call to Pete. When she saw the wildflowers lying on the front seat, she sighed.

They were real wildflowers, all right. Once plucked from their stems, the flowers had died almost instantly.

***

Pete tried to carry out his duties, but he was obsessed. He had Tracy. He had Josh. It was all too good to be true. Even at this young stage of his life, he was beginning to suspect that when things were too good, you attracted the jealous attention of the gods. Like a bolt of lightning from heaven, a blast would be sent to take away your joy. When he was living with his boys at Heaven on Earth, his lonely world had changed and turned idyllic. That didn't last for long. Alone came Pearl Harbor uprooting everybody and changing all their lives.

He couldn't have sex with both men all the time he was off-duty, although at times he wanted to. He was convinced that no two men ever received more loving than Tracy Adams or Josh Harnell. In just a short while, he'd become more familiar with each of their bodies than he was

with his own. He'd become so familiar, in fact, that if he were blindfolded and allowed to stick his tongue into the armpit of either boy, he'd know exactly who he was tasting. Each of them tasted different, and he couldn't get enough of either one.

Josh had given of himself willingly from the first night he'd been with Pete. For Tracy, it had been a greater struggle to go all the way. But he'd known that Pete had wanted to penetrate him, and Tracy had finally surrendered. If anything, Pete enjoyed fucking Tracy more than all the men he'd known. It was because Tracy had considered his rosebud virgin territory, except for allowing Pete's tongue to invade.

That first night in his reunion with Tracy, the boy had let him go all the way. Tracy had sobbed but Pete couldn't stop himself. The greatest music to his ears, even better than one of Josh's songs, was when Pete had taught Tracy not only to love getting fucked, but to beg Pete to fuck him. Beg wasn't exactly the right word. Pete was always willing.

As much as he loved penetrating Tracy, Pete also loved getting fucked by the young sailor. The greatest sexual night of Pete's life was when he'd lain under Tracy, after the boy had vowed not to "take it out until I've shot three times in you, even if it takes me all the God damn night." Tracy had kept his promise. By the third climax which had come shortly before five o'clock in the morning of a Norfolk dawn, Pete had surrendered completely to Tracy.

Pete didn't know how or when but at some point, a day he dreaded, he was going to tell Josh that it was all over between them. As hard as it would be for him, he planned to swear fidelity to Tracy Adams. He was going to write Claude, Hank, Karl, Ronnie, and Junior, and even John-John, telling them to get on with their lives. Each of his boys would be welcome to come and go at Heaven on Earth for as long as they wanted, but Pete's heart forever more would belong to only one man, Tracy Adams.

In Tracy, Pete had found a man tall, lean, and lithe. He lived to make love to Tracy in the silvery pale moonlight. The boy was mythologically perfect in form and grace. As Pete fell deeper and deeper in love with Tracy, the young boy assumed almost Godlike dimensions in Pete's eyes. Before leaving one morning, Tracy had crushed out a cigarette in an ashtray. Pete could not bear to part with something that had touched Tracy's lips. He had carefully wrapped up the cigarette and stored it away in a drawer, as a kind of souvenir.

He loved Tracy even if his body seemed unfinished. Tracy was on the threshold of manhood, yet clung to the innocence of boyhood in some way. He was like a piece of sculpture waiting for the sculptor to apply the final carving. Pete wanted to have Tracy's body in his arms, watching him grow and develop into the fine man he would one day become.

Tracy and he both knew that they could be shipped out any day. It was

just a matter of time. Pete felt he'd die a little bit when he had to say good-bye to Tracy. The more Pete thought about it, the more he felt it was beyond the realm of possibility. It was like something that even though you knew it would happen, you couldn't think about it. It was like waking up and thinking that you were going to die instead of getting on with your life. He wanted Tracy to be on the same ship, but there was no way that was going to happen. The US Navy had a mind of its own.

Even though falling more and more in love with Tracy every day, Pete still held onto Josh. He loved the boy and didn't want to imagine Josh in the arms of anyone else but him. When he was drinking Josh's sweet juice, or fucking him, he felt he loved him too. It was thrilling. It was wonderful. But it lacked that special magic he had with Tracy.

All Pete's boys had been spectacular performers in bed. Each of them from Junior Grayson to Hank Adams had totally satisfied Pete sexually.

It was a cold Tracy had caught in the damp weather that brought a new reality to Pete. His young man felt sick and was hardly in the mood for sex. At first Pete had been disappointed, even angered, as if he were blaming Tracy for catching cold.

As the night had lengthened with Pete alone with Tracy in his secret apartment, Pete had experienced a kind of bliss waiting on Tracy, cuddling and protecting him, giving him an extra blanket, massaging his feet, and making a mean old bowl of vegetable soup for his main man.

As a surprise to himself, Pete found that he was loving waiting on Tracy and helping him get well again. Pete was being a nurse and getting off on it. That was a side of himself he never knew existed. He almost wanted to breathe in Tracy's germs and share his cold with him.

What he loved most of all was running a hot bath for his favorite man on the planet and soaping and bathing every inch of the boy's body. Pete loved the pounding of Tracy's heartbeat. There was no part of Tracy's body that Pete didn't touch, fondle, love, and bathe.

It was as if he were storing up a vast memory bank that he could recall at any time when he'd lose Tracy to the vast Atlantic Ocean. Both of men knew in their hearts that their time together was only temporary, and that the vast ocean would eventually separate them.

As he dried Tracy off and put him to bed, Pete ran his hands through Tracy's still damp hair. "This war is not gonna go on forever, although right now we sure seem to be losing the fucking thing," Pete said. "But America will win. It'll just take some time."

"Hell, yes, we'll win," Tracy said with a kind of bravado that brought a stab of joy to Pete's heart. "But I've already won my battle."

"Lay that on me again." Pete said.

"My battle was to win your heart," he said, reaching for Pete's hand and squeezing it. "To grab you up and take you away from all the others,

even my own brothers. Karl and Hank have known you and even been inside you. And John has sucked you like an all-day lollipop. I can't go back and change any of that shit. But I've staked my territory. Pete Riddle's throat and Pete Riddle's ass are private property and off-limits to one and all. You belong to me and only to me."

"You're all I want," Pete said, running his hand over Tracy's feverish brow.

"Hell, man, why shouldn't I be the only man for you?" Tracy said, his fingers digging into Pete's arm with a fierce grip of possession. "You like big dick, I've got a big dick. You like a pair of man-size balls. Just feel mine. You like a hot asshole. You told me yourself that getting inside me had been the greatest thrill of your life. You like getting fucked by me." He put his fingers to Pete's lips. "You don't have to answer that. I see how you moan and come alive when I'm fucking you. I know I'm getting to you. Giving you the thrill of your life. That night you came twice when I was pounding into you was all the evidence I needed. I know how I make you feel. We're right for each other. It's good. It's true. I never thought I'd say this to any man. But I'm saying it to you. I'm in love with you. So much in love it hurts me."

"I'm in love with you, too. Any time I'm away from you, all I think about is Tracy Adams. In my mind I go over every inch of your body. I can't wait for the hours to go by until I'm with you again."

"It's not just about sex," Tracy said. "I need to be with you. I don't know where to go with my life. I'm nothing without you. Some white trash kid living in a shanty and hunting possum to put in the pot. If you want to know what po' is, it's eating greasy possum pot liquor. It's shit, man. But it keeps you alive. With you, I'm something. We're gonna get through this war, and we're gonna go back and live at Heaven on Earth. It's the grandest place that ever was. It's what I want. When I take you into that master bedroom at night, I'm locking the door. No one gets to Pete Riddle but his husband."

"You know I want that more than anything in the world," Pete said. "Nothing matters but you. Until I met you, I thought I needed a lot of men. How wrong I was. There's only one man in the whole world who's for me. You're it, buddy. I love you with all my heart. You're everything I've ever wanted."

Pete took both his hands and cradled Tracy's head in their firm grip. He knew he shouldn't but he couldn't restrain himself. Even if he caught a cold, he couldn't hold back.

He moved his mouth over Tracy's as Pete's lips descended, his tongue probing at the doorway to a pleasure he could no longer deny himself.

***

Without ever seeing it, Rosacoke just knew when Mrs. Riddle got that letter from Pete. After learning about her pregnancy, her attitude—never friendly—altered completely, growing into stone-faced hostility. On Friday afternoon when Rosacoke drove the pickup truck home from the hardware store, Mrs. Riddle was sitting in the living room, reading about the war in *The Journal-Patriot*. She looked up as Rosacoke came in, her face a mask of bitterness. "I never knew you was another Emma Lou Hayes, or I would never have moved you into this house with my boy. Pete's a good boy, and I always tried to steer him away from bad women."

To keep from bursting into tears, she'd run from the room, retreating to the smokehouse for a good cry, and she'd been having quite a few of those lately. The dog joined her, licking her hand, as if trying to ease her humiliation. When she'd dried up, she looked up at the hanging hams as if they held the secret to her next action.

She dreaded the coming weeks, and, though nobody had said anything, driving about town was an ordeal, as she suspected people were pointing at her and snickering at her behind her back. Sucking in the stale, musty smokehouse air, she mustered up enough courage to go back into that house to face Mrs. Riddle. She was a good woman in her own way, and she lived by a standard Pete hadn't matched.

When Rosacoke did come in again, her smile was firmly set on her face. If she were going to bear the child growing inside her, she'd made up her mind to do so with all the dignity she could summon. Her boy would have Pete's good looks, hopefully some of his talent, and regrettably, maybe some of his ways. But she was sure the boy would grow up to be a fine and noble man even if Pete didn't want to give him his own name. Still in all, the boy would be a Riddle one way or another. How did she know it would be a boy and not a girl? She just knew.

Clad in her bathrobe, Mrs. Riddle came into the kitchen the next morning, paused, and gave Rosacoke a disappointed look but said nothing, heading for the table where she dutifully and silently served herself some buttered grits and country-fried ham with her favorite red-eye gravy.

In the weeks ahead, no word came from Pete, although Mrs. Riddle still got letters from him, none of which she cared to share with Rosacoke. The elderly woman kept her distance from Rosacoke, as if she'd been contaminated. At times she felt Mrs. Riddle was staring at her when she wasn't looking. When Rosacoke came into a room, and said something, Mrs. Riddle's voice would fade to a mumble, as if she could not bear to speak.

When Rosacoke wasn't looking, she felt Mrs. Riddle was staring at her belly, which seemed to grow bigger every day. To catch her, Rosacoke whirled around, as Mrs. Riddle averted her eyes from Rosacoke's gaze.

The old woman retreated quietly to the solace of her bedroom without even telling Rosacoke good night.

With her belly as big as it was, Rosacoke had been forced to drop out of school. She wasn't alone. At least two other girls had to drop out too. With the men of Wilkes County going to war, a lot of gals had surrendered their virginity. When those same men came home on leave, Rosacoke suspected that even more gals would be knocked up. Surrendering your virginity in times of war was easier to do than before. Rosacoke was real sad that she wouldn't get her graduating diploma when the other kids in her class did. She'd have to read about the ceremony in *The Journal-Patriot*.

Life was stirring within her day by day, and she could feel Pete's baby boy growing bigger and bigger. When she got home from her music lesson with Fry, Mrs. Riddle was up and about, knitting in the parlor. She told Rosacoke that there was a letter waiting for her on the kitchen table.

Her heart beating faster, Rosacoke just knew it was from Pete in Norfolk. To her surprise, it was from Narcissa in Chicago, and it had a real street address on it. No more "General Delivery."

*Hi Rosacoke!*

*I got the money for that dress. You didn't have to send it. Your mothah up here ain't on relief or some shit like that. You were welcome to that old slutty glad rag of mine. I ain't against 'cepting gratooidies from time to time, but only from men. This café-au-lait pussy has got a high price tag on it now that I landed in Chicago.*

*When I got here, I found the town swarming with big fish, every one of the fuckers trying to take a nibble out of this brown-skinned belle. Then the shit hit the fan. I found myself pregnant. Just like you. Pete Riddle knocked both of us up before heading off to war. He got into my pants months before he got into yours. But I've done and had my baby.*

*I was caught in a real jam. With a God damn kid growing inside me, I couldn't use my money-maker, and that was how I planned to make my living up here. I got a piece of good luck, something I ain't much used to in my life. I was taken in by this black family. I'd met them when I went to an agency to apply for a job.*

*All the fucking maids in Chicago are going into defense work. It's hard to keep a maid now that everyone is rushing off to make the big bucks in the defense plants. This man and his woman can't have children of their own. They wanted me to live with them until I dropped my kid, and they wanted me to give them the kid, which they planned to adopt. I said okay.*

*I sure don't want some little brat messing up my plans. The kid popped out of the oven looking like an uncooked biscuit. He's sort of*

a combination of Pete Riddle and Sultan all rolled into one package. I got five-hundred dollars for giving him up.

Since birthing that baby, I've gotten three jobs singing in clubs. I ain't no big movie star yet like Lana Turner. I'm not even Lena Horne. It's gonna happen. It's just gonna take longer than I figured.

I can even get you a job if you come to Chicago. Dump that kid at the Riddles and get on with your own life. I'm sure you've saved up enough money to come to Chicago if Pete is paying you thirty-five dollars a week. Where in Shakerag are you gonna spend that kind of money? The town up here is full of soldiers, and some of the stud hosses I've seen would make both me and you forget that Pete Riddle forever.

By the way, I know you're asking why do I know it's Pete Riddle's kid and not Hank's. Hank always used a rubber. Pete told me he liked his pussy natural like.

Since landing my shapely ass in Chicago, I have saved up one-thousand dollars, and that's more than Sultan ever saw at one time in his whole wasted life.

Too bad to hear about your shit with Pete. Frankly, I have some advice for you—just strictly from one pussy to another. I like white dick as much as anybody else—maybe more so. But I ain't met a white man yet that's worth a good goddam in no other department. Those mothahs will tell you any lie they can think up jest to get in your pants. I let em lie all they want, providing they keep those gratooidies rolling in. Before any white fingers wrap about my coffee-colored butt for the big squeeze, I tell em I like to hear the rustle of paper—not the jingle of coins. That's a line I heard a woman preacher say before she passed out the collection plate.

So let me know if you want to come to Chicago after dumping another one of Pete Riddle's brats. That is one virile white mothah-fucker. Come on up here. I've got an extra room in this apartment I've rented. One of my gentlemen (B.S.), admirers runs a club that goes in for that hillbilly shit. He'll hire you if you don't mind mixing with the customers, nearly all men, and tending a little bar on the side. At least it'll get you out of that stink-hole back in the mountains where we was born and a place I never want to set my gold slippered foot into ever again. It's a pile of shit down there. Get out while you still can.

Your loving "sister"
Miss Narcissa Cash
(Soon-to-be international movie star and major recording artist)

Rosacoke neatly folded up the letter. Mrs. Riddle must never know that her son had brought a kid into the world. One that was birthed by a black woman..

That feeling of helplessness that had come over her like a cloud for the past few months began to lift, as an idea took root in her mind. She'd been waiting for other people to make her decisions for her, to run her own life. While doing that, she'd been weak and submissive, and she was getting tired of that.

In spite of some of the words in Narcissa's spicy letter, which shocked her a lot, she still admired that girl's spirit. Narcissa had been hit with some reeling blows, far worse than anything that had ever befallen Rosacoke. Yet Narcissa seemed hell-bent not to let any big tragedy get her down. Equally determined, Rosacoke set her face to look strong, no matter how spongy weak she felt inside. It was about time for her to toughen up.

She couldn't make it in the world with a kid, and she knew it was only fair and proper to let Tara take the boy, although such a thought grated across her very soul, filling her bones with a quiet despair. But she had to give the boy up. If she couldn't offer her son a real name, a home, and a running chance in the world, she owed it to his unborn flesh to let Pete do that for her. But parting with her kid was the only major concession she planned to make to anybody.

When the rooster crowed at daybreak, Rosacoke Carson—the woman, not the servant girl—was going to take her own life in her hands and see what surprises the future held for her.

\*\*\*

When Fry came for her in his old Chevy, it was still dark at the Riddle homestead. Only the dog got up to wish her good-bye, as Mrs. Riddle chose to stay in bed. Hardly saying a word, Fry drove her into the oncoming dawn, past the streets and alleys of Shakerag which were littered with empty moonshine pints and garbage. A huge rat jumped out of a pile of garbage, scurrying across the street and into an abandoned cotton warehouse.

The road that Fry took into the next county had only recently been paved, and, once Shakerag had faded into the distance, the well-kept farmland became richer, good for raising dairy and beef cattle along with burley tobacco. Ginseng and wildflowers covered much of the mountain, and lots of gingerbread and porch posts passed in review before her.

Fry coughed and spit, "I've come down with the flu, and I hope I don't give it to you and your baby. My old mama had a home remedy every time one of us youngins got the fever. She'd rub our chest with polecat grease."

"What's that?" she asked. "It sounds awful."

"Grease rendered from a skunk."

"I think I'd rather keep the fever."

She tried to take her mind off giving birth, feeling her health wasn't too good, as she hadn't been eating properly for weeks. Fry was taking her to a friend of his, an old black washerwoman, Ruby Green, who lived about a mile from the hospital. Rosacoke's baby was due in two weeks, and Mrs. Riddle felt it was time Rosacoke left her home to await the birth. If the baby should be born before that, Mrs. Riddle could not keep the secret from the folks in their parish. The local doctor wasn't very good, and, when drunk, he revealed the medical embarrassments of all his patients.

When Rosacoke gave birth, Mrs. Riddle had made two demands—one, that Rosacoke not return to her household, and two, that she not look at the baby "so you won't go forming no unnatural attachments to the poor unwanted thing." Reluctantly, Rosacoke had agreed.

She, too, had been afraid of seeing her baby boy—she was still convinced that it'd be a boy—fearing that she might not be willing to give it up if she gazed upon his tender, still unformed face.

She'd sent a telegram to Narcissa in Chicago, taking her up on her offer, and true to her word, Narcissa had responded with another invite. Rosacoke had never really thought much good of Narcissa until now, but when she'd come through like this for her, Rosacoke was forced into an upgrading reappraisal.

As Fry turned at the crossroads, heading up the road and over a mountain to Sparta, she felt a rush of water running down her legs. Confused at first, she thought she'd wet her bloomers. When the second rush of water ran down, she sobbed.

Fry looked over at her and seemed to know at once what was happening. "Honeychild, I think your water has just broken. She-it! She-it! She-it! Remember what that Butterfly McQueen said in *Gone with the Wind?* Well, Miss Rosacoke Carson, I don't know nothin' 'bout birthin' babies. I sure don't—that's the God almighty truth."

As the water kept on pouring out, Fry pulled into a filling station, and, after a hasty chat with the sleepy owner, he rushed back with some old towels from the shanty at the rear where he lived with his wife. "Balls of fire!" Fry said. "I had to pay for these damn things. These rags look like they was used to dry the backs of hound dogs after a flea bath."

After handing her the dirty, smelly towels, he hit the road again, stepping on the gas. In desperation, she placed the towels all around and under her, holding her legs clamped together as if that would prevent another rush of water. At first she'd been so embarrassed she'd wanted to scurry off like that Shakerag rat, hiding in his dark hole in the warehouse. But Fry was so comforting and accepting of the basic facts of nature that he put her at

ease, like he'd done when he gave her guitar lessons.

She cried out, as stabbing pains shot through her. "They won't let me in the hospital, I just know it."

"Don't worry. I talked to Mrs. Riddle on the phone yesterday when I was agreeing to pick you up this morning. Everything's been taken care of. If you was a nigger gal, that'd be another tale to tell. Any ole cowfield would do for giving birth."

By the time he'd screeched his brakes at the entrance to the ratty-looking hospital, Fry looked more scared than she did. "She-it!" he said. "I made it. Before we turned that last bend in the road, I thought I was gonna have to birth the baby myself. I never asked the good Lord for a personal favor before. This time I did."

With pains shooting through her body about every fifteen minutes, she was wheeled through swinging doors into the labor room.

Here, as she sprawled on a bed, a doctor examined her and gave her some medication. The pains were coming so sharp and fast she just knew her baby boy was going to pop out at any minute.

By six o'clock that night, she knew how wrong she was. Still strapped on the bed, she was bleeding.

"I think she's in false labor," the doctor told Fry, thinking he was the daddy. "Better take her home."

"She-it!" Fry said. "I've put enough women in her condition to know she's hemorrhaging. False labor, my ass. Where did you get a license to practice medicine? Through the Sears catalogue you picked up after wiping your lilywhite dunghole in an outhouse?"

The new medication the incensed doctor offered, she spat out, as her head spun and the worst stomach ache of her life caused her to knead her muscles down there, hoping that would ease the agony.

When the baby did arrive at nine-thirty that night, the doctor Fry had angered had gone home for the day. A big nurse with burly arms delivered it in the labor room, then took it away quickly before she could see it. She wheeled Rosacoke into the delivery room where a night intern, just coming on for duty, cut the cord.

The next day Rosacoke woke up bright and early, thanking God she'd survived that ordeal. All night a strong feeling had come over her that she'd made a mistake in agreeing to Mrs. Riddle's terms. She wanted to keep her baby, and had almost made up her mind. As soon as the baby was old enough to travel, Rosacoke was going to get on a Greyhound bus bound for Norfolk. She felt that if Pete actually saw his own kid, he'd want to marry her and give the boy his name before going off to war.

When Fry came into the room, he talked her out of what she eventually came to see as nonsense of the night. He won her promise to stick by her original deal for the sake of the kid. "They're gonna check you over later

this morning, the doctor told me. If nothing's wrong, they're gonna send you on your way. They don't like healthy women taking up bed space once they birth babies. I'm driving you over to the bus station. You're leaving at four o'clock for Chicago and those bright lights Narcissa always talked about. Forget about the kid."

She clutched his hand, her fingernails digging in without her meaning to. "I've got to know one thing. I know I promised to ask nothing. But I've got to know something. I mean, I don't doubt it, but I've got to hear it from you. Is my baby a boy?"

Fry reached into his back pocket and pulled out a large red handkerchief, and, drawing out the tension, spent a long time coughing in it. "Still got the flu." He smiled, showing his yellowing teeth. "It's a big white mothah-fucker with a long dick on it like its daddy."

She burst into tears of joy.

"And I'll make a prediction. If the two of you passed on your voices to that little Buster, he's gonna grow up to be the hottest act country music's ever seen."

***

It was Thursday morning. Tracy had already shipped out days ago. Their final night together had been the most memorable of Pete's young life. He was deeply in love with Tracy.

In each other's arms, they'd pledged their devotion to each other. The war was just something to get through. Their real life at Heaven on Earth would begin when the war was behind them, and the Nazis and Japs defeated.

Pete had awakened that morning with a steely resolve. As much as he cared for Josh, he was going to tell him that the physical side of their relationship had to end. Pete hoped to continue as Josh's friend. He also wanted to sing the country songs that Josh wrote. But Pete's heart now belonged to a young man sailing the cold waters of the North Atlantic as part of a convoy hauling supplies to a beleaguered Britain.

Pete had seen Josh two or three times on the ship that day, but at no time did Pete feel that they had the privacy needed for such a talk. He kept postponing his moment of truth with Josh until he was off-duty. He asked Josh to meet him later, and the young sailor readily agreed. Pete could tell from the look in Josh's eyes that he was expecting it would be another one of the many evenings of passion they'd shared together in each other's arms. Pete had not given Josh the slightest indication that their love-making would soon be winding down.

In the mess hall Pete had been having dinner with Josh when a chaplain came over to their table and asked Pete to go with him to the front office.

On the way there, Pete was nervous. He felt that somehow the Navy had found out about his carrying on with Josh aboard ship. Pete feared that he'd been spied upon by someone during his private times with Josh and their having had sex together reported.

He was shown into an outer office where he was told to wait. Time dragged on. He must have sat there an hour before he was summoned into the chaplain's office where papers were piled high on his desk.

"I've got some bad news for you," the chaplain said. "You were listed as next of kin on these papers. That's why I'm having to break the news to you first."

"Is my mama dead?" Pete asked, nervously perched on the edge of his chair. "You've heard something?"

"I haven't heard anything about your mother," the chaplain said. "It's about a fellow member of the Navy. Tracy Adams listed you as his next of kin."

Pete jumped up from his chair. "He's dead! Tracy is dead."

"I'm so sorry but he is," the chaplain said. "He was part of a convoy. It was attacked by a German submarine. Twenty-eight men on board were killed. Mr. Adams is missing. There's no hope. We fear the worst."

# Chapter 7

Far from her mountain home, she felt like a refugee in some strange, foreign country when the Greyhound bus pulled into the Chicago depot. The ride had been bumpy, and she'd cried most of the way, thinking about her little baby boy, whose name she didn't even know. Mrs. Riddle, she feared, was too cold in the heart to give the kid much love.

Fry had assured her that Tara at Heaven on Earth had warmly taken the kid to her bosom and had promised to give it tender, loving care, as if it were her own child. This brought comfort to Rosacoke's heart, that and the hope that Pete would one day get back from the war alive and would become a real daddy to the little boy.

She'd heard that thousands of hillbillies were flocking to the big cities in the wake of Pearl Harbor, hankering to get jobs in defense plants. Even so, she was scared. She'd found that she'd been able, just barely, to live off the land. How could she learn to survive and face the harsh new experiences of city life?

Like some migrant worker, she got off the bus with just enough money to live on for a week. Narcissa had promised to meet her, and if she failed to show up at the terminal, Rosacoke didn't know what she was going to do.

The sweaty wartime mobs of milling people—with lots of men in uniform—made her feel claustrophobic. Used to wide open spaces, she felt hemmed in, as she was jostled and pushed when trying to pick up her battered old suitcase. In panic her eyes scanned the anonymous faces, hunting for Narcissa. Of one thing she was certain: if Narcissa did show up, she knew she'd spot her at once. That was one lady who knew how to stand out in a crowd.

Clutching her bag, Rosacoke just stood there on the platform, as her heart sank. She felt Narcissa might have tricked her, as that gal always did have one weird sense of humor.

Rosacoke's hair was tied up in a bun for comfort in the summer heat. All of a sudden she felt someone come up behind her and pull out the pin holding it up. As her blonde hair fell down over her shoulders, she spun around to stare into the face of Hank Adams in his soldier's uniform.

He'd never been her favorite person—in fact, she hardly knew him. But here in Chicago, with her not being on a speaking acquaintance with

one familiar soul, he was like the biggest, nicest present that ever waited under a Christmas tree.

"Hi." His face broke into a smile. "What's a dumb hillbilly like you doing in a place like this? I hope you didn't bring up no cooties with you."

"Hi, Hank." Tears of relief welled in her eyes. "It's mighty good to see you. That's the longest ride I ever took in my whole life."

"Narcissa couldn't come to meet you. She's got a club date and is working out with some musicians. She's invited us to go hear her tonight. Her opening."

"Oh, my God. I ain't got nothing to wear."

"Don't worry about it. Narcissa has got plenty of clothes, and I'm sure she'll let you wear something. After all, she calls you her sister. You sure don't look colored to me."

Grabbing hold of her bag, he hailed a cab and gave directions. On the way to wherever she was going, she looked him over closely. She'd never paid much attention to him before. Unlike Narcissa, she'd tried to stay clear of all the Adams boys, considering their reputation and all. It was funny how her feelings about somebody could undergo such a dramatic change. In the new world of Chicago, she was downright glad to see a face from back home.

Hank had two weeks leave and, though he said he'd wanted to spend it in Norfolk with Pete, his friend had sailed to England as part of a convoy. With sad eyes, Hank told her that his brother, Tracy, had been killed in a similar convoy a few weeks earlier. "Me and Pete are real broken up. I can't believe I'm not gonna see my kid brother no more. He was just beginning to live his life. Full of piss and vinegar. If anything, ole Pete is taking it harder than I am, and Tracy was my own brother. I never knew how close Pete was to Tracy. But when Tracy was stationed in Norfolk, those two guys really bonded."

"I'm so very sorry to hear of your brother's death," she said, reaching for his hand to extend her sympathy. "I hardly knew him. It don't seem right for God to take away someone so young."

"I just pray that nothing will happen to Karl," Hank said. "Also, that the war won't last long enough for John to be drafted and sent to fight."

She was eager for news of Pete, figuring that Hank knew a lot more about him than she did, as his letters had dwindled down to none. She knew he was writing Tara and Claude, but they never shared any news of Pete. He'd fathered her baby boy, but was a man of mystery to her.

In her loneliness and in this shared cab with Hank, Rosacoke took real notice of him for the first time in her life. Up to now she never allowed her mind to dwell on him. With his thick hair and clear green cat eyes, the color of her own, he was the kind of tall man who could saunter down the street of any town and get noticed. She was sure that his well-formed mouth had

charmed many a woman, probably ever since he was twelve years old. Hank, she'd heard, had broken in early, perhaps with Emma Lou Hayes. His lips turned up at the edges, revealing strong white teeth in total contrast to many country boys she'd known with their yellowing, rotten mouths. Unshaved stubble of beard appeared as golden flecks against his sunburned face.

Long, lean, and muscular, his body radiated power. Even though a country boy in a different environment, he moved his arms and legs with grace, revealing none of that awkwardness she'd noted in the young men at that roller-rink dance Pete had taken her to. Hank's eyes were searching, as if eager not to miss out on anything. He took it all in. She found herself liking him, and was no longer horrified that Narcissa had once wanted to run off with him. Sometimes Narcissa was a lot smarter than Rosacoke gave her credit for.

"We're holed up at this place in the hillbilly ghetto," he said. "The colored live there with the white, but that don't mean they always get along. I've already been in a knife fight. The other guy got cut up—not me. The landlord hates Narcissa. They charge like hell for the joy of sharing our beds with rats."

The taxi pulled up at a seedy, furnished accommodation with bulging garbage cans stacked up out front. He explained that a lot of Chicago band men lived here with their wives, girl friends, or boy friends.

Inside, she was disappointed, as the little apartment showed the dismal effects of a thousand vagabond occupancies. She could scrub and brush all day and into the night, and she knew this apartment would never be any less dingy than it was now. It was almost like being back again in Sultan's shanty. With all Narcissa's newly found money and everything, Rosacoke suspected she'd be living high off the hog in some really elegant place.

"I'm going to bed," Hank announced, taking off his shirt to expose a powerful chest, muscled as if a sculptor had worked to perfect it. Contrasting with the rich tan of his body, a thin trail of golden hairs trickled from the center of his chest to his navel. In embarrassment, she looked away.

"Make yourself at home," he said. "The other bedroom is yours." He stood at the door to the room he shared with Narcissa and tantalizingly unfastened the top two buttons to his soldier's pants. "Unless you want to come in here and see what drives the girls crazy."

"Oh, no," she said, retreating to her own little bedroom, with its frayed rug, creaky old brass bedstead, and exposed electric light bulb.

Closing the door, she stood by the lone window, and through a smudged pane looked down below at a gang of white kids tossing rocks at the dirty glass of an abandoned warehouse. Two boys swung from a fire escape, as their pals down below busted coke bottles in an alley.

This was the ugliest slum she'd ever seen, far worse than anything in

the South. Even if you're poor in the mountains, you still had the pretty countryside to enjoy. Here there was nothing to look at but a rat-infested urban blight, with broken windows opening onto desolate elevator shafts.

She sucked in the stale hot air, and somehow in spite of things didn't feel depressed. All the warmth, strength, and courage she'd brought with her on that Greyhound bus from the Brushy Mountains marched with her on this fading afternoon.

Without Pete, she was going to fight her way through this city jungle, searching for her own special place in it.

***

Coming from somewhere in the Tennessee Hills, Captain Don Crook was a brute of an officer. Rumor on the base was that "something had happened" to Crook's balls back in 1939, and he'd undergone a personality transformation, becoming meaner and nastier than he'd been before when his sac was intact.

In Southampton, England, from his barracks and the bunk beds he shared with Josh, Pete tried to have no direct dealings with Crook, even though a fellow Southerner. To an enlisted man, a captain was an awesome sight, to be saluted if encountered, but avoided at all costs.

When Crook was on the base and found the slightest infraction, he ordered punishment so severe that men talked about it for weeks to come. One fat recruit was exercised so brutally he'd had a stroke. His sin? The young man from north Florida didn't make up his bed properly.

When Pete was summoned to the captain's office, he went with a heavy heart, once again fearing that he'd done something indiscreet with Josh and had been spied upon. Ushered into the august presence of this military warlord, Pete approached the captain's desk with trepidation.

After Crook had ordered him to relax and sit down, Pete felt less intimidated. The captain seemed downright friendly today. About five minutes of chitchat ensued, mostly about their common origins as Southerners. With no transition, Crook abruptly changed the subject. "Some of my boys tell me you are one hell of a country singer. A regular Roy Acuff. He's my favorite."

"I do my best, sir," Pete said.

"Don't give me that shit," Crook said as if angered. "Your best is the best there is—or so I hear. I also hear you sing songs written by Josh Harnell, and that he's as good a song writer as you are a country singer.

"He's real good, sir," Pete said. "Really good."

"I'm glad to hear that," Crook said, leaning back in his chair. "There are gonna be many jobs that have got to be filled to win this fucking war. All the guys can't be out dropping bombs on Berlin or blowing Kraut subs

out of the Atlantic."

"I don't understand, sir," Pete said.

"I'm gonna ask you and this Josh boy to work in a special unit," Crook said.

Pete's heart jumped, fearing it was some dangerous suicide mission being dangled before him.

"You might call it an entertainment corps," Crook said. "We've been asked to help set up a series of Red Cross Clubs near our bases in England. It's for our boys. They are gonna need entertainment. We can't turn thousands of oversexed and overfed American boys loose on a small English village with one or two pubs. We're gonna have to provide some after dark clubs for them ourselves."

"How can I help, sir?" Pete asked.

"Since you're a Southern boy, I can talk more openly with you than I could a Yankee boy. We're going to be sending over a lot of troops, and some of those troops are gonna be black. Before a final build-up, there may be as many as 150,000 black bucks in the military over here in England. We won't be able to keep them on the base at night. They're entitled to entertainment too, and there's the problem."

"In what way, sir?" Pete asked.

Crook seemed angry again. "Picture it," he said, leaning forward and slamming an inkwell down on his desk. "Back home the white boys had their clubs, the niggers their clubs. Over in England we ain't gonna always be able to keep the black boys segregated from the white boys at night. I predict trouble."

"What kind of trouble, sir?" Pete asked.

"I'll tell you what kind of trouble. Can you picture black guys standing at the same bar with whites? There will be fistfights. Definite trouble. If a nigger antagonizes a white man too much, that coon may even get shot. We've got a lot of hot-tempered boys on this base. What if one of our white boys is putting the make on a British woman, blonde no doubt, and some buck nigger moves in on his turf?"

"She'd probably turn the black guy down, I would suspect," Pete said.

"Think again," Crook said. "In England there seems to be no color line. We've got reports that a lot of horny English gals like to get fucked by black dick." He looked down at his papers. "Not only that, but a lot of English queers too perverted to serve in the King's army are getting jobs near our bases just so they can suck off our boys. I hear some of the faggots even prefer black men to white men cause the niggers have got bigger dicks."

An hour must have gone by as Crook outlined in detail what Pete's new duties were. He was to be assisted by Josh. The captain handed Pete a study to read. It was from the U.S. Army War College, and was summarized in two paragraphs. Pete read the report marked "Top Secret."

"The Negro is docile, tractable, lighthearted, care free and good natured," the report stated. "If justly treated he is likely to become surly and stubborn, though this is usually a temporary phase. He is careless, shiftless, irresponsible and secretive. He resents censure and is best handled with praise and by ridicule. He is unmoral, untruthful and his sense of right doing is relatively inferior. The Negro is cheerful, loyal and usually uncomplaining if reasonably well fed. He has a musical nature and a marked sense of rhythm. His art is primitive. He is religious. With proper direction, Negroes are industrious. They are emotional and can be stirred to a high state of enthusiasm."

Pete placed the report back on the captain's desk. So much for the secret opinion of the U.S. military about thousands of its fighting men.

At that moment Pete speculated what Captain Crook would think if he knew Pete had sucked off a black man and had taken it up the ass. In his heart, Pete still missed and longed for Sultan.

Crook was telling Pete that Negro soldiers would be used mainly for unloading ships or driving trucks. "They're no good for combat."

He also told Pete that it was impossible for the military to provide separate clubs for both blacks and whites, and that in many cases blacks would have equal access to these Red Cross Clubs.

Crook wasn't too clear in defining Pete's new job. He suspected the captain didn't really know that much about these new duties himself. Pete was to set up a small unit that would coordinate entertainment for black men and deal with their access to clubs.

"You can also put them in charge of clean-up details at these clubs," Crook said. "Let them serve food and drink. Stuff like that. We'll try to issue passes to our white boys one night, and passes on other nights to the colored. But it won't always work that smoothly. There will be nights when they mix."

Pete eagerly took the job offer, not really sure how to go about it. He knew more about entertaining troops than the captain did. Pete wished that Moss and Fry were close at hand to get him started. Actually, Pete was thrilled with the assignment. He was also glad that he'd be working with Josh as well. Pete predicted that before the war was over, he'd come back to the hills as the best country singer in the Carolinas. He just knew he'd learn more from the black musicians than they'd learn from him.

Before he left that day, the captain assigned Pete an enlisted man who'd serve as his coordinator with the Red Cross. That's how Pete came to meet a tall, muscular, strapping young Navy ensign who looked more like a model for a recruiting poster for the Nazi army than he did a U.S. sailor.

Before meeting Frederick Raubal, Crook had already filled Pete in on the background of his new partner. Born in 1920, in Düsseldorf, Germany, Frederick had joined the Hitler Youth as a teenager. But when his aunt had

wanted to marry a German soldier in Hamburg, her past had been investigated. It was discovered that the founding father of the Raubal clan, the great-grandfather of Frederick, was Jewish.

That quickly led to Frederick being kicked out of the Hitler Youth. Two years later, when he was 15, his mother, fearing for his life, had shipped him off to live (she thought temporarily) with relatives in Chicago, where he assimilated into U.S. culture. But because of his German birth, when Frederick had tried to enlist in the U.S. Army in 1940, he was classified as an "enemy alien." Appealing through a local congressman, a friend of his adoptive family, to J. Edgar Hoover of the F.B.I., Frederick was eventually granted U.S. citizenship and accepted into the U.S. Navy.

Crook said he was still suspicious of Frederick, regarding him as a spy, but the officer had figured that Frederick could cause "the least damage to our war effort" by being confined to an entertainment unit.

Pete liked Frederick at once, finding him remarkably handsome and virile. He was even sexually attracted to Frederick, but Pete suppressed any obvious feelings. For all he knew, this exiled Hitler Youth detested homosexuals, as did his former Nazi chums.

"You'll be working with my buddy Josh and me," Pete said. "We're gonna sing tonight at a pub on High Street. Called the Red Lion. What say we hook up with you there at eight o'clock?"

Frederick readily agreed. As Pete was heading back to his barracks to tell Josh the news of their assignment, Frederick ran and caught up with him. "Hey, guy," he called to Pete. "Didn't I say that just like a Yank? Thanks for letting me come aboard. Until I met you, all the other guys call me the Kraut. Shit like that. I'm just as much an American now as anybody else. I have more reason to hate Hitler and the Nazis than any of you. My parents and my Aunt have been exterminated by the Nazis. I loathe the bastards."

Pete shook Frederick's hand and embraced him in a manly, non-sexual way. "See you tonight," he said, leaving the young German standing there watching him walk away.

Instead of heading immediately to the barracks and to Josh, Pete decided to wander down by the pier. He came here to walk this vast stretch every day. It was his time to be alone with his memories.

He looked up at the darkening sky. The skies were always darkening in England. You'd wake up and think it was going to be a beautiful day and before noon you'd be in a flood of rain.

A lump rose in his throat. As he slowly made his way along the pier, Pete's thoughts were with Tracy. Pete looked out at the port and the vastness of the sea beyond, figuring that in that bowl of murky water the man he'd come to love had found a terrible grave.

Tears welled in Pete's eyes. He knew that although he had Josh, he'd

go on to love other men. But with even more certainty, Pete knew that Tracy Adams would always occupy a special place in his heart. He'd never find a replacement for Tracy. In their last days together he'd come to love Tracy as he had no other. Other men wouldn't have that special touch that Tracy did, that magic, that tender look he had in his eyes when he met Pete's own eyes.

"Tracy, Tracy," Pete whispered to the breeze, telling the wind and no one else. His tears were falling faster now, as he closed his eyes, remembering in vivid detail the feel of Tracy's nude chest upon his own naked flesh. He could literally feel the beat of Tracy's heart.

That heart had now grown silent but would always beat inside Pete's mind and memory.

***

The club where Narcissa was slated to open, The Gilded Grape, stood on the outskirts of Chicago. In the most conservative dress she could find in Narcissa's wardrobe, Rosacoke, along with Hank, piled in the back seat of a Ford. The car belonged to two guys, Frank, a trombone player, and Jeff, a bass fiddler. They shared a tiny one-room apartment directly over Narcissa and Hank. Earlier Hank had told her the men were lovers, and she had understood that to mean that they were considered good in bed and liked to have a lot of sex. She hoped they wouldn't make a pass at her, since they shared a mutual hallway bath.

On the way to the club, Rosacoke felt that Frank and Jeff must be real hard up, as they passed a thinly wrapped, lone cigarette between them, even offering to share a drag with Hank and her. Hank accepted but she refused. The men sucked the smoke deeply into their lungs, as if direly in need of it, and the heady smell filled the car, reminding her of the tobacco Moss and Fry enjoyed in Shakerag.

After a 90-minute drive, the Ford pulled into the back of a parking lot. Eagerly, Rosacoke scanned the brick structure, its upper windows broken by vandals, like those her bedroom opened onto. It didn't live up at all to her conception of a Chicago night club, and, before its present reincarnation, The Gilded Grape had been a warehouse for grain, she'd learned. Even so, this was her first time out at a genuine big city nitery, and she was secretly thrilled, although she concealed her enthusiasm, not wanting to call attention to herself, as she was still too young to patronize clubs where alcoholic beverages were sold. During the ride here, she'd said little, fearing Frank and Jeff, two Yankees, might make fun of her hillbilly accent.

Inside, The Grape wasn't very gilded, with bare wooden chairs and unadorned metal tables. But it was crowded and noisy, and more patrons arrived every five minutes or so. Rosacoke was delighted that Narcissa

had drawn such a big wartime mob. The patrons, like Frank and Jeff, were white, although Hank had told her that except for some boys in the band, all the performers, mainly women, were Negroes. That signaled Rosacoke that Narcissa had decided to introduce herself as a black woman, apparently having rejected the plan to go Latin.

A special air of excitement flooded Rosacoke's whole system. Being taken out to a nightclub on her first night in Chicago more than made up for the disappointment of the shabby tenement dwelling she'd be living in with Narcissa.

Hank told Rosacoke she could go backstage to say hello to Narcissa before the show, and Frank led the way. She found Narcissa, along with a bevy of scantily clad brown belles, slipping into a tight-fitting chorus girl outfit, all gold and silvery colored with glittering sequins.

"Welcome to this crapper!" Narcissa squealed out, as she rushed over to plant a kiss on Rosacoke's cheek. "This used to be where all the men workers at the warehouse went to drop the big load before some faggot decided to turn it into a dressing room for us stars."

Rosacoke kissed her back and was genuinely glad to see her. "Thanks muchly for letting me come up here."

"Forget that. Come on back while I make myself even prettier than I am."

Narcissa led the way past the milling chorus girls, none of whom looked as beautiful or was as shapely as Narcissa. Rosacoke could easily understand why Narcissa had been made the star of the show. Paint buckets were scattered about the floor, and loose plaster still hung from the ceiling.

"There's a war on, honey, in case you ain't heard," Narcissa said. "They tell me in hard times people need entertainment. Those Jap bombs launched me into show business."

Rosacoke stared in astonishment at the girls in their gaudy makeup and costumes that made them look as if dressed in underwear. She was shocked that many of the beauties ran around without a stitch on, apparently not in the least embarrassed even though a couple of male stagehands came through.

"We'll meet for hamburgers and drinks after the late show, baby," Narcissa said. "Don't let that Hank drink too much. He won't be able to get it up for me tonight."

Rosacoke blushed. "I can't believe how fast you became a success. I mean, just overnight."

In the middle of applying another coat of scarlet red lipstick, Narcissa paused, her eyes searching Rosacoke's in the mirror, outlined by tiny little light bulbs. "Yeah, yeah, sugah. Overnight! Better run up front. The show's about to begin."

Rosacoke started to give Narcissa another kiss, but she told her to shoo.

"Don't spoil your mothah's war paint."

On the way back up front, Rosacoke lost her way until the stage director showed her. Narcissa hadn't minded Rosacoke borrowing one of her dresses. "I don't wear that number often," Narcissa had said. "Only when one of my johns asks for the librarian type. Would you believe there's an actual demand for that type?"

Settling down in the seat Hank had held for her, Rosacoke felt that she didn't understand a lot of the talk up here, like that remark about the librarian. It seemed that people like Frank and Jeff meant a lot more by what they said than she caught onto.

As it turned out, The Gilded Grape wasn't Narcissa's opening, but the debut of a new revue, *Blackbirds of 1942*. To Rosacoke's disappointment, Narcissa wasn't the star of the show. She was just one of the girls in the chorus line.

When the curtain went down on the first act, Rosacoke turned to Hank. "She didn't get to sing or nothing. Just strutting around showing off her ass. Aunt Clotilda would die for the second time."

"Don't worry. She's got this number in the second act. She'll bring down the house."

Hank's prediction came true. In the middle of the second act, the house lights dimmed before going entirely black. The band struck up a number, and a cold yellow spot, the only light in the room, was turned on to reveal Narcissa standing in front of a microphone in a skin-tight red silk gown split up to the thigh to show off her *café-au-lait* leg. The gown was low cut and very revealing, exposing far more flesh than Narcissa had ever dared to reveal back home—and that was one hell of a lot even then.

Unlike the down-home, Ipana toothpaste smiles the country music performers she'd known plastered onto their faces, Narcissa didn't aim for that kind of friendly rapport with her audiences. In total contrast, she projected a hypnotic coldness, and this seemed a deliberate, calculated attempt on her part to turn herself into some sultry, unobtainable black goddess. As she gyrated and twisted around the stage in her gown, she exuded sexuality. With her petulantly pouty mouth, she was the ultimate temptress, not bothering to conceal her arrogance, but making it a part of her act, as if the men in the audience might dare look at her, but none could touch, feel, or smell.

When she opened her mouth, the club quieted down. She hesitated a long time before speaking, building the anticipation. Before going into her bluesy song, she made a few comments to the audience, cleverly mixing sex with humor. She got a lot of laughs until she held up her hand for the patrons to quiet down, as if they'd laughed enough and it was time to get serious.

Launching into her song, she was a steamy performer with a four-octave miracle of a voice. That voice, so smooth and vibrant, was filled

with tension, and she seemed to spit out every word. With her gleaming white teeth, her fiery eyes, and her magnificently shaped mouth, she immediately went over with the audience.

Perhaps because she was so startlingly new and different, and because she obviously felt superior to many of the blue-collar white patrons, she aroused resentment. It was so strong that Rosacoke could sense it from some of the other tables. Unlike what they were accustomed to from most black performers, Narcissa imitated the white goddesses of the silver screen.

From down front a drunken heckler called out to her. "Hey, Miss Prissy, be a good little coon and show us your tits."

At first Narcissa tried to ignore him, but when he wouldn't stop heckling her, she walked down from the stage toward his table. A hush settled over the audience.

Filled with concern for Narcissa, Rosacoke leaned forward, straining her neck, not believing what was taking place. She reached for Hank's hand, as if to calm him down. Jerking away, he stood up on the balls of his feet to see over the heads of the other tables.

In front of the heckler's table, Narcissa picked up a bottle of catsup and poured it in blurping gobs over the middle-aged man's bald head. The audience burst into wild applause, cheering her on. She made the wartime victory salute with her long fingers and turned to go back up on the stage. As she did, the offended heckler leaped from his chair, wiping the guck from his face. He ran after Narcissa, slapping her and sending her sprawling into the band, where she fell into Frank's trombone.

Kicking his own chair back, Hank darted to the front of the room where he grabbed the heckler by the throat, as if he had every intention of killing him. To Rosacoke, who'd raced after Hank, the heckler appeared to be in mild shock, the sneer long gone from his catsup-saturated face, replaced by a panic, as Hank's fingers squeezed tighter and tighter. Within seconds the neighboring patrons had cleared a small section of the club, as if making an arena for the battling men. The drunk was no match for Hank's power, until two big waiters who looked like bouncers rushed over to pull Hank off his victim. Still propelled by rage, Hank was dragged kicking and yelling from the club. Rosacoke ran after him to see if he were hurt.

Hauled back on stage, Narcissa seemed in command of the situation, straightening her dress and adjusting her hair. "I drive men crazy," she told the audience. "Usually they have knife fights over me." With the skill of a veteran who'd been in show business for years, she launched into the final bars of her song, finishing the number to thunderous applause.

Rosacoke, holding onto Hank's arm, led him out to the parking lot where she suggested that they wait out the rest of the show in the back seat of Frank's Ford.

Hank said nothing, slumping down in his seat and sulking. The night

that had started out with so much promise for Rosacoke turned sour. She feared Chicago wouldn't be the fantasy she'd dreamed about on the bus ride there, and a sinking homesick feeling swept over her, until she faced up to the fact she had no home to go back to.

***

The next day as Pete headed for his lonely, daily walk along the pier, he was surprised to see Josh running toward him, as if he had some urgent message. When the handsome young man caught up with him, Josh's only urgency was to be with Pete and walk with him. Pete affectionately put his arm around Josh and invited him along, although for the first few minutes no one spoke.

It was Josh who broke the stillness. "I'm really afraid I'm losing you, man," he said.

Pete turned to him and smiled. "You've got me. I belong to you and no one else."

"That's what I want to hear," Josh said, "but somehow I can't believe it. I've met this Frederick Raubal. He's gonna be working with us, and he's twice as good looking as I am. Looks like he's got an even better build. I don't know if I can compete if he goes for you."

"How do you know he's homosexual?" Pete asked. "You know that some guys in this war actually prefer women."

"I don't know for sure," Josh said. "He struck me like a man carrying around some dark secret. I guess I just assumed."

"I don't even know the guy," Pete said. "I guess you are filled in on his background. Hitler Youth and all that shit."

"Yeah, but he's a Jew."

"Forget about Freddie boy," Pete said. "Let's talk about us." He nudged Josh under the chin. "What's all this shit about losing me? Don't I put out?"

Josh gently pulled at Pete's sleeve, causing him to stop walking. He looked into Pete's eyes with a plea for understanding. "You're the greatest lover I could ever dream about. Your technique is perfect. You take me to places I've never been before, and probably will never go again. You're all I want. All I could hope for and dream about. But something's missing."

"Another inch on my dick," Pete said. "But no one's ever complained before."

"Don't kid me," Josh said. "You could lose three inches and still be too big. That's not it. When you're making love to me, even though it's as good as it is, I feel you're not thinking of me, but of someone else. Like some love you've lost."

"I haven't lied to you," Pete said. "I didn't pretend to be a virgin when

we met. There were other men before you."

"I guess that's what I'm afraid of," Josh said. "That one of those other men from back out of past is gonna show up and take you back. You're too good a catch for someone to let you go easy like unless the war tears you apart."

At first Pete was tempted to tell Josh about Tracy, but decided not to. He wanted to keep whatever had gone on between them at Norfolk to himself. "I've got a surprise for you," Pete said. "C'mon." On the way to the Red Lion, Pete told Josh his secret. He'd rented a room over the pub where he sang Josh's songs. "We can be private there. The Red Lion's owner, Reginald Wake, is one of us, at least I think he is. If not, at least he's very friendly to our kind of love. He said he was a young man once, and he knew how important it was for young men to be alone together off the base. Behind a locked door where no one can pry into their business."

"If that's not an invitation to do naughties, I don't know what is," Josh said, his eyes filled with eagerness. He had seemed to forget his earlier challenge to Pete about not being there when he made love to him.

Pete reached for Josh's hand, touching it gently before dropping it. He never knew who was looking and spying on them. "When I get you to that room, and make love to you, you'll change your tune. Pete is going to be there for his boy."

"Thank you for calling me your boy," Josh said. "I want to belong to you. I want to be your private property. When I see other guys checking me out, I want to hold up a sign, Pete Riddle's boy. No one gets my pretty ass but the master himself."

"You love me, don't you?" Pete said. "Forget I asked that. I can tell you love me. The way you look into my eyes tells it all." He reached into his jacket and pulled out two Lucky Strikes, lighting both of them and handing one to Josh.

"A Lucky Strike for a lucky man," Josh said. "At least I feel safe for the moment even though we're in England. I'm scared, though, about the future. I heard England can't hold out much longer."

"Don't worry," Pete said. "The Yanks and us Southern boys will save the day."

Alone in their secret love nest, Pete removed all of Josh's clothes, saving the skivvies for the last unveiling. Fully clothed, Pete pulled the nude boy to him. Josh had a sexy smile, and Pete wanted to taste his kissable lips. It wasn't Tracy he was kissing, but it was the second best thing in all the world.

Pete put his arms around Josh and pulled him close to him, as close as he could get, and ground his crotch against Josh, producing an instant erection in him. Slowly the boy helped Pete get out of his clothes. As Pete picked him up to lay him gently on the bed, Josh was kissing and nibbling at

Pete's neck. Pete felt Josh's body trembling at the prospect of what Pete was going to do to him.

Pete lay Josh on his back and eased on top of him, looking deeply into the boy's eyes. He pressed his body into Josh's. Slowly, ever so slowly, he moved his mouth to cover Josh's, pressing his lips tightly against the boy's own lips before inserting his tongue for Josh to suck.

As Josh satisfied him that way, Pete ran his rough hands along the boy's smooth body, sampling all the flesh that he was going to lick and kiss before finding deeper satisfaction. He was making Josh so hot that boy was about to explode. Pete didn't want that. He planned to drag out his love-making. He had at least three hours before meeting Frederick in the club, and he wanted this time with his boy to last forever.

When he stopped kissing Josh's mouth, Pete moved his lips lower, sampling the hairless chest, gently biting his nipples. Pete ran his hands over the boy's smooth thighs and washboard stomach, sticking out his tongue to sample his navel but only momentarily skirting Josh's excited cock. Josh jerked in anticipation, and Pete felt if he descended on Josh's cock right at this moment the boy would erupt.

Pete let his fingers wander down to Josh's nut sac. He teased the bags lightly before his mouth descended on them to lick and devour. He liked taking each one at a time in his mouth. Josh went wild at that. He knew that was but a prelude to Pete's next move. Josh's rosebud was quivering as Pete attacked it. He wanted to get Josh in his spell and completely relaxed until he was begging to be penetrated. This was his favorite way of taking the boy and subjugating him.

On a signal from Josh, Pete scooted his body around. He could still attack Josh's rosebud but now Josh had access to Pete's own cock for a deep throating. Josh applied a powerful suction action, and Pete moaned in delight.

When Pete could hold back no longer, he withdrew from the boy's mouth and rearranged himself, letting Josh's feet rest on Pete's broad shoulders.

Josh reached up to hold and fondle Pete's neck, inviting his body to move down on his own. Josh's eyes were closed like he was in some dreamy trance. They opened wide with a kind of terror when Pete penetrated him, but those trusting eyes closed again when Pete descended on the boy, biting his lips and his ear to distract him from the pain.

Pete arched his back in pleasure after he'd achieved the final penetration of Josh. He let the boy squirm until he got used to the invasion. Josh spread his legs even wider to accommodate Pete and wrapped his thighs around Pete's waist, pulling him as close as he could get.

Pete started a slow in-and-out motion, rocking gently against Josh's body. He gripped tighter with his legs, inviting Pete to pump away. When Pete had found his rhythm, he lowered his head to Josh's face. Pete's

tongue darted out to lick Josh's lips, neck, and ears as he fucked him. Pete felt Josh's left hand enclosing his balls, fondling and loving them as Pete continued to pound into the boy.

As the minutes drifted by and Pete managed to hold back, he felt Josh was giving him the ride of his life. He was thinking of no one but his boy and how much he loved him. Right now no other man, not even Tracy, existed for Pete Riddle. He couldn't even imagine wanting another man. He had what he wanted, and it was beneath him.

Pete's stomach kept brushing against Josh's rigid cock, and he knew that his boy was fighting a losing battle against reaching his own climax.

Pete tried desperately to hold off his explosion but feared he couldn't go on much longer this way without an eruption. He ground his power tool into Josh and after that deep thrust he felt Josh spurting loads of hot cum onto Pete's stomach.

A kind of dizzying heat washed across Pete's body. He shut his eyes as tight as he could and then let go.

Nothing existed in the whole world for Pete but Josh Harnell.

It was going to be a long war, and he'd found the boy who was going to help him get through it.

*** 

In the weeks ahead, Rosacoke learned quickly that the slums of Chicago weren't exactly Hillbilly Heaven. Hunting a job wasn't quite as easy as Narcissa, in spite of her "contacts," had suggested. Rosacoke was too afraid to try to get a job in a defense plant, considering that man's work.

One day, just two blocks from her tenement dwelling, she wandered by chance into a bar-café-grill. Attracted by its name, My Old Kentucky Home, she sat down on a stool and ordered a cup of coffee.

The couple who ran it, Owen Hawkins, and his wife, Daisy, were born in the mountain hollows of Eastern Kentucky in Southern Appalachia. Rosacoke found them downright friendly. "We serve home-style cooking here," Daisy told her, trying to get her to order something. "Even the colored people come in here and buy food to take out. We can't serve them at the tables, though. Our other customers would raise holy hell!"

When Rosacoke told her that she had money to pay only for the coffee, Daisy offered to give her—"compliments of the house"—the Blue Plate special of smothered collards, fried pork chops, and black-eyed peas. After hungrily downing the meal, Rosacoke, to show her appreciation, volunteered to help out in the kitchen that afternoon, washing dishes. "I ain't got nothing else to do—'cept look for a job, and I ain't having much luck doing that."

Within a week, Rosacoke was hired full time, and she felt right at home, mingling with resettled mountain people who'd come to Chicago to work in

defense plants where the pay to them was the highest they'd ever heard of. Some were born and bred in the coal camps of Eastern Kentucky; others, who'd rarely finished the eighth grade, arrived from the dreary mill towns of North Georgia, hoping to strike it rich in the big city. At times it seemed to Rosacoke that every man or woman had one of two afflictions—either "black lung" from the coal mines or "brown lung" from the mills.

Tips were small, rarely more than a dime, most often only a nickel. Sometimes nothing at all. In many cases the displaced hillbillies had never heard of the custom of tipping, as eating out in public places was a novelty to them. Rosacoke didn't mind too much. She got all the food she wanted to eat for the first time in her life, and Daisy's cooking was good and tasty, especially the sirloin steak which Rosacoke sampled from the stockyards of Chicago.

Daisy and Owen guaranteed her five dollars a day if she couldn't make that in tips. She was completely honest in her accounting to them, and on slow days Daisy often had to give her a dollar or two from the cash register.

Her popularity, especially among the men, grew. When she'd take a day off, which was rare, many of the customers complained, Owen told her. That made her feel real good. A few of the male defense plant workers, often ones with wives still back in the South, asked her out on dates, and some of them came right out and propositioned her. At first she'd been afraid, not knowing how to respond to such offers. Once or twice she'd retreated to the women's room where she'd burst into tears. But, after a while, she learned how to handle the more aggressive customers. Not to insult any of the café's loyal patrons, she used humor to turn them down, and found this didn't rile them as much as a flat rejection from a woman.

The place was jam-packed every Saturday night, and the crowd would often get rowdy, as if wanting something to do other than sit around swilling beer. An idea came to Rosacoke. She had continued to play the guitar, and, although she didn't have Fry around any more, she felt she'd become pretty good at it. One night she proposed to Owen and Daisy that she be allowed to get up on Saturday night and pick and play for the customers. "By the time I go on," she said, "most of 'em will be drunk on beer anyway. So I guarantee they won't jump up and run for cover."

Owen liked the idea right off, but Daisy wasn't sure. Finally, she consented, agreeing to give it "a try for just one night. If it don't go over, you're back slinging hash at early breakfast on Sunday."

Delighted and grateful for the chance, Rosacoke agreed. Back at the apartment later that day, she found the place empty, as was usual.

She didn't know where Narcissa was, but whatever free time she had it wasn't spent in this shabby apartment. Hank's leave was up, and he'd already been called back to duty.

After taking a bath in the hallway, she went back to her bedroom and tried on the cowgirl outfit Pete had bought for her in Shakerag. For a moment her mind dwelled on Pete, and she wondered if he'd been sent to sea. Her thoughts also turned to her little baby, and she wanted to send him a present. However, Mrs. Riddle had asked her to avoid any contact with the child, once they had taken it from the hospital and put the boy in the care of Tara.

Rosacoke brushed aside such thoughts, which would only send her into a morbid depression, and instead she concentrated on her singing debut that night. Only last year she would have died of embarrassment before asking Owen and Daisy if she could get up and sing in public. Weeks of working as a waitress had given her a lot more confidence in dealing with the public, especially men. She was still afraid of the natives of Chicago, but the back-home folks who came in to eat at My Old Kentucky Home held no terror for her.

Nevertheless, she was still plenty scared. The customers might like her as a waitress, but that didn't mean they'd take to her picking and singing. She knew everybody from down South had his own ideas about how country music was to be played and sung, and she wondered how she'd live up to those preconceived notions they'd taken with them to Chicago.

She sucked in the stale air in her bedroom until the mirror over a broken-down vanity table revealed that doing so inflated her breasts. Exhaling quickly, she knew if there were anything her breasts didn't need, it was inflating. That thought left her jittery about wearing the blouse Pete had bought for her, as it made her breasts more prominent than she cared to. "Hell with it!" she finally said out loud. She'd been a sissy long enough. The time had come for her to take the big challenge.

That night the joint was jumping, mostly with beer-drinking men. Over a microphone installed only that afternoon, Owen announced her appearance. As he did, she tried to think not of the patrons out there but of what Pete had once told her when they were singing together. "Don't think of singing to a whole audience. That'll scare the shit out of you. Just single out a very special person, and then imagine you're singing in his ear." That night the special person she'd selected to sing to was Pete himself, whatever strange sea he was sailing.

She'd selected songs that meant something to her, and she instinctively knew that everybody in the house was just like her, feeling homesick and wanting her to bring back memories of the places they'd left behind, and, if this damn war kept on, mountain shanties they might never see again.

Before going on that night, Owen had told her that he'd pay her five dollars for singing. That had thrilled her, as this was her first professional engagement.

Standing up on the hastily assembled wooden platform, she was greeted

with cheers and rebel yells, as most of the customers knew her.

"Baby, when I order cantaloupes for breakfast, now I know where you grow them," one of the men called out. The other patrons hooted and laughed.

A paralyzing fear came over her. She'd not warbled a note, and already a room full of men were laughing at the size of her large breasts. Her first impulse was to turn her back on the audience, run and hide. She hated herself for wearing such a tight-fitting blouse. Determined, she stood her ground, not letting them get her goat.

In front of a roomful of people eating and drinking, she had trouble drawing her breath. Once she got over that, she filled her lungs with enough air to launch into "Rye Whiskey." For the first few bars her voice sounded unnatural. But the more she sang, the more that voice came unthawed. By the time she'd reached the bridge, she felt she was more herself.

Mild applause greeted her first number, and that was okay and expected. She was just getting used to being up on a stage, picking a guitar, making a public spectacle out of herself, and the patrons were still making up their minds if they liked her or not.

For her next number, "Roll in My Sweet Baby's Arms," a traditional, crowd-pleasing Grand Ole Opry favorite, she found she really liked singing in front of an audience. By the end of the evening, to judge from the applause and foot stomping, the customers liked her, too.

She soon realized that she was able to communicate her own sense of enjoyment to the audience. Singing gave her a sense of release from the anxieties of the move to Chicago, and the people who listened to her seemed to know that and felt the same way themselves, as her music brought back fond memories for them.

Later, back home in her room, she held the five dollars up to the light coming in through her lone window from the street. That was the proudest money she'd ever earned. Even though tomorrow morning, she'd be back slinging those ham and grits over the counter, she wouldn't really be a waitress any more, but a singing star. Well, a singer.

Owen and Daisy had invited her to perform again next Saturday night, and she'd agreed, barely able to conceal her bubbling glee. From now on, if anyone asked her how she made her living, and regardless of how she actually did, she felt that she was entitled to introduce herself as a singer. If only Pete were aware of what she was doing, he'd be right proud of her. She just knew that.

***

Even though Pete suspected that country music was hardly Frederick Raubal's favorite kind of tune, the former Hitler Youth, who probably pre-

ferred Wagner operas, had immediately made himself an integral part of Pete's newly formed entertainment corps. Perhaps he'd learned such efficiency working for the Nazis, but "Freddie," as he was now called, turned out to be a dynamite organizer.

Just two days after hearing Pete sing at the Red Lion, Freddie assembled the raw elements of a band. Once he did that, he invited Pete for a "bluegrass picking party." It provided the opportunity for Pete to scope out the musicians, and for the members of the ragtag band to get a good look at him to see if he had any talent as a singer. It also provided insights into whether the mostly black group could make music with white boys like Pete and Josh. The fate of the canteen hinged on their creating harmony together, both musically and in their personal relationships.

In gratitude for the U.S. military presence in Southampton, the city had offered them the use of a broken-down, derelict house, a many-gabled early-Victorian structure that had seen much better days. It was within this semi-derelict building that Pete and his group were instructed to set up their canteen. The house and at least some of its battered contents had been bequeathed to the city of Southampton by an aging eccentric, Maude Cooper, who had no known kinfolk, and who had died about a year before the outbreak of the war. Both Pete and Josh were grateful to have the use of any building with a roof over it. In deference to her memory, they posted a sign near the building's entrance, respectfully acknowledging Maude's contribution to the establishment of their new club.

The piano player who Freddie recruited, a good-looking sailor of twenty-one from Chicago, was Nipsey Smith. Pete couldn't help but notice the color of his skin: It was beautiful, what Narcissa called *café-au-lait*. He was a strikingly sexy young man, filling out his uniform to perfection, especially his tight-fitting sailor pants.

Even though a former member of Hitler Youth, Freddie quickly developed an immediate rapport with Nipsey. Pete felt that he could work with both men just fine. Josh, however, remained a bit skeptical and a little standoffish.

Sitting in the rear kitchen of Maude Cooper's former home, Nipsey was telling them how rough it had been on him since joining the Navy. "There's nothing but Southerners in my barracks. Some of us guys have a knockdown-drag-out fight every day or so. Growing up in Chicago, I was always good with my fists." He held up one of his broad hands for inspection. "The scabs on my knuckles didn't come from Chicago, or even from fighting the Nazis. They came from fighting my fellow sailors. These white boys get their kicks out of needling me and some of my black brothers. Those white boys won't give us any peace. I think they use us for their own amusement."

"From the looks of you, I wouldn't go picking no fight with you, man,"

Josh said.

"I can take care of myself," Nipsey said. "But regardless of how big you are, there's someone out there a little bigger. On my first day here, I stepped up to the wash basin with my shaving gear. This big Texan grabbed me by my T-shirt and yanked me back so fucking hard I fell on the floor. 'Back in Texas,' he drawled, 'niggers wait at the back of the line.' I jumped up and plowed my fist right into his face. I bloodied his nose. He was bleeding real bad. At first I thought he was going to attack me back. I stood there, fists ready to pound him again. He just looked at me. 'In a few minutes,' he said, 'my nose is gonna stop bleeding. But tomorrow when you wake up, you're still gonna be a nigger.'"

Pete had brought some beer, and he enjoyed sitting and talking to Nipsey and Freddie, feeling he could work with these two remarkably different men.

As a Southerner, Josh didn't readily take to a Chicago black and an ex-member of Hitler Youth. Pete felt these two men were a bit exotic for Josh, but Pete liked the guys and felt a bond with them.

Everybody had ideas about how to turn the old house into a club, giving the blacks on the base a place to go to in the evening. Nipsey felt he could help Freddie put together a hot band within twenty-four hours.

Nipsey smiled, flashing perfect white teeth. "Us niggers not only eat watermelon, we've got rhythm, baby."

Pete and Josh had arrived at the club an hour earlier and had inspected every nook and cranny, noticing how derelict everything was. Maude Cooper must have not opened a window since before World War I. Everything smelled stale and musty. He even inspected the closets, noting that this English lady must have been a flamboyant dresser in her day. From the looks of things, she hadn't parted with one item in her wardrobe since she was in diapers. She had saved virtually everything.

Downing his beer and waiting for his boys to come downstairs, Pete heard a knock on the back door. Getting up, he opened the door to stare into the face of a rather elegant-looking English queen wearing a very bad black wig. He definitely wore too much mascara. "My, oh my," he said, "they do grow big hunks of beef in the colonies."

"England certainly produces some beautiful ladies," Pete said, smiling at this stranger. He took in the outfit of this Englishman, which was an original design that seemed to have been pieced together from both men's and women's clothing.

"Flattery will get you my pussy tonight," the queen said. "Tell me, why did you put two socks in your crotch? Wouldn't one have been more tasteful?"

"It's all prime Grade-A meat, and all me," Pete said. "Who are you, my fair maiden?"

"I'm Gladys Gregory," he said, inviting himself into the kitchen. He turned on his wedge heels and looked back suggestively at Pete. "That's Lady Gregory to you."

"How can I help you?"

Gladys looked down longingly at Pete's crotch. "If a big boy like you doesn't know how to put out a five-alarm fire in me, I'm the gal to teach you."

"Seriously, aside from the obvious, why are you here?"

"Reginald Wake from the Red Lion told me what you're gonna do here," he said. "I came over to volunteer my help. A lot of my girl friends would be only too willing to volunteer our services to run this canteen for you. We'd serve drinks, keep the place clean, even cook for you boys. After all," he paused, smiling seductively at Pete, "you Yanks have come over here to save us from the Nazi rapists, and we figure we owe you a favor."

"I might take you up on that offer," Pete said.

"I'm also an entertainer," Gladys said. "Back in the West End, I was known as the greatest female impersonator there. Especially at the Black Swan. I come out dressed as Queen Mary."

When Josh came downstairs with Nipsey and Freddie, Pete introduced them to Gladys. Nipsey and Freddie seemed amused at the queen, but Josh once again was a little reserved and put off. Apparently, the Outer Banks of Carolina hadn't exposed this Southern boy to such an exotic crowd.

Gladys had brought more beer over from the Red Lion. He willingly shared it with the sailors, as Pete told them of his serious plans to get the entertainment launched, the house fixed up, and everything turned into a canteen for black military men as soon as possible.

"It's nice of you English to offer us all this help," Nipsey said. "I have never found white people too accommodating to me. Especially those on the base."

"We want to do our part for the war effort," Gladys said. He arched his mascara-coated brow. "Naturally, my sisters and I will hope to find our own rewards by working here. The reputation of the black American male has preceded him." He pursed his lips. "I was, in fact, known as the fellatio queen of the West End. Most of the young British soldiers I used to service have left England. But I'm sure I'll find many replacements now that the Yanks have arrived."

Pete noted the sudden silence at the table. He wasn't sure what the tolerance level toward homosexuals was by Nipsey or Freddie. But the men appeared at ease with this blatant queen. Only Josh seemed embarrassed.

After another round of beer, Pete, along with his fellow sailors, was getting drunk and drunker. Under the influence, Gladys became even more outrageous.

"I noticed that there's a toilet in the hallway over there," Gladys said. "I'm going to go and sit on that toilet." He pursed his lips again. "I'm sure some of you men need relief." He darted his tongue out succulently, indicating exactly what he was prepared to do for the war effort. "Will you gentlemen excuse me?"

When Gladys headed for the hallway and the toilet, the men sat looking down at their beers. No one said anything. It was Nipsey who broke the silence. "I don't know about you guys, but I'm horny as hell and desperate. The way I feel tonight, I can't let no opportunity pass me by even if the offer is from a drag queen." He rose from the table and headed for the toilet.

Josh got up and went over to the kitchen sink where he started to clean up the mess. Gladys had also brought some fish and chips from the Red Lion.

During the time Nipsey disappeared into the toilet, Freddie kept glancing apprehensively toward the hallway. He appeared extremely agitated. Not looking at Pete, he rose to his feet and headed at once to the hallway. Pete heard the door of the toilet creak open.

"Come in and join the fun," Nipsey called out to Freddie.

After five long minutes, Pete could stand the suspense no more. He got up without looking at Josh and walked slowly to the hallway toilet where he opened the door.

Gladys was on the toilet seat, servicing one dick while holding the other. After a minute or two of sucking, he left one cock to devour the other. Pete looked up at Nipsey and Freddie. The two sailors were seemingly unaware that there was anybody else left in the world, not even Gladys. A foot of Nipsey's tongue seemed to have been inserted down Freddie's throat where it was getting the sucking of its young life.

Pete gently closed the door and headed back to the kitchen and Josh.

***

It took some doing, but Narcissa finally persuaded Rosacoke to go out with her one Sunday night on a blind double date.

"I'll let you wear one of my real slinky dresses," Narcissa said. "Not that damn cowgirl outfit that makes you look like Annie Oakley. Honey, that buckaroo garb don't go up here in Big Town."

Faced with the vast choice of Narcissa's wardrobe, Rosacoke had a hard time making up her mind. Narcissa came in and dressed her in a tight-fitting white skirt like she'd seen Lana Turner wear in a movie. She also selected a white silk blouse that Rosacoke felt did not do a good job of covering her ample breasts. But she decided to wear it anyway, not wanting to piss off Narcissa, her benefactor.

Hailing a cab with a new, commanding authority, Narcissa made Rosacoke right proud. Narcissa didn't look like some small town hick. Somehow she'd seemed to throw off her humiliation and torture back home, and the experience, if anything, made her tougher and more self-assured. She appeared eager to assert her newly discovered rights.

The apartment she took Rosacoke to was luxurious and sensuous, its windows overlooking a body of water. Opening the door for them was a Negro maid in a black uniform with a dainty white apron, just like in a Claudette Colbert movie. Once inside, Rosacoke felt she was going to drown in a deep-pile red carpet. Up to now she didn't know carpet came that thick.

Narcissa excused herself to go fetch her friend, while Rosacoke stood here, quietly breathing in the exotic male atmosphere. The maid asked to take her wrap, and nothing like that had ever happened to Rosacoke before. She felt absolutely pampered, living like the rich people do. What a difference, she thought, from carrying out Sultan's slop jar every morning to dump in an open field for fertilizer. It wasn't hard to understand why Narcissa liked to spend so much time at this place.

Wandering deeper into the living room, she was shocked at some of the nude marble statues. One in particular seemed to depict a sex act, but Rosacoke felt she was surely mistaken, as she knew nothing about art. The furniture dripped with gilt and was upholstered in leopard skin. Over the fireplace mantle hung a mirror, shaped like a heart and framed in wood, which had been coated with glistening Chinese red lacquer.

She searched the ceiling for some electric light bulbs, finding none. Only three small table lamps provided the illumination for the whole big apartment. She didn't understand that. To her, someone with as much money as this apartment owner evidently had could afford more electricity and didn't have to be such a cheapskate. "My God," she said in a whisper barely audible to herself, "we had this much light at night in the shanty."

"This place is lit for lovin'!" Narcissa said, as she marched back into the room as if she owned the place.

Trailing her was a tall man with a large mustache and heavily oiled, raven-black hair which he wore long and slicked back. Slender as a riding crop, he wasn't even dressed to go out, wearing a pair of red bedroom slippers, black silk pants that looked like pajamas, and a black velvet jacket fringed with gold threads and open at the neck to reveal a caramel chest, as if he'd just gotten back from some tropical island. To Rosacoke, he would look downright handsome if he weren't decked out in all those sissy clothes.

Upon seeing her, his eyes lingered too long on her tight-fitting blouse to make her feel comfortable. "It's champagne and strawberries for you two good-looking pieces of tail," he announced.

Rosacoke blushed in embarrassment and was deeply offended at being

referred to in any such way, but she held her ground, as much as she could on that deep pile, and acknowledged him politely, figuring that's how certain sophisticated people talked up here in Chicago. There were many customs she'd have a hard time getting used to.

"Silky, meet Rosacoke Carson." Narcissa presented her as if she were introducing an act on stage.

He eyed her up and down, taking in her whole figure this time, although his attention kept straying again and again to her breasts. She told him she was glad to meet him, which wasn't the truth at all.

"Never in my whole life have I met a man with the name of Silky," Rosacoke said.

He burst into laughter. "That's not my real name. That's how I'm known in the business. You see, I have this fondness for silk suits and silk shirts. That's the main reason I'm against the war. Our silk supply from the Japs has been cut off."

That struck her as the most unpatriotic remark she'd ever heard in her life.

"That's not the only reason they call you Silky," Narcissa said, coming up from behind him and wrapping her long, tapering fingers around that caramel chest, digging in and gently pulling a patch of hair.

He laughed again in that lowdown, vulgar way he had of doing. "I smelled you coming up on me, bitch," he called back to Narcissa, flicking out his tongue as if trying to lick her.

Rosacoke turned from this disgusting display and gazed out at that body of water. In the moonlight it was sure prettier than anything going on inside this dimly lit apartment. She was sorry she'd accepted the invitation from Narcissa, wondering if she could bow out, pleading a sudden headache as her excuse. Silky was obviously Narcissa's date, and she dreaded seeing what hers looked like.

"I like my girls to massage me daily," Silky said. "Twice a day I get lotioned down. I use only baby lotion on my skin. It makes my skin real silky like. I get massaged all over if you know what I mean. I really live up to my name, especially when I guide Little Silky to home base in some furry nest."

"You mentioned your girls," Rosacoke said, trying to change the subject. "I hope you weren't referring to your daughters giving you massages. *All over*."

He turned around, catching Narcissa and kissing her as if expressing gratitude. "The innocent type. You know what I like."

At that moment the maid came back into the room, carrying the champagne and strawberries Silky had promised. "Take a seat, Rosacoke," Silky said. "You've probably had nothing but corn liquor up to now. Wait till you get a taste of this stuff. It's from France. Probably the last I'll get until

the war's over." He blew her a kiss. "I like you."

Wishing she could return the compliment, she sat down in the corner farthest from Silky and Narcissa, as if fearing contamination.

"My girls aren't my daughters, although in some ways I feel that protective of them," Silky said. "Like a father. I've got seven in tow, including your friend here." He reached over and planted a wet kiss on Narcissa's lips which was returned with even more force. "That's good," he said, breaking away as if she'd tasted enough. "I like to get nigger-lipped when I'm kissed whether it's by a white gal or a colored one. I rent my gals out except I spend one night a week with each of them. That's their time to get their chance at me. I throw them a mercy fuck. Tonight Narcissa is the lucky bitch."

The maid was chubby and could easily be someone's grandmother, and, to Rosacoke, she looked like a good woman, totally out of place in such a sinful setting. Yet she seemed oblivious to Silky's talk. On the other hand, Rosacoke could hardly ignore it. As she took the stemware glass from the maid, she rose to her feet. "Frankly, Mr. Silky, I don't like this kind of talk. You're wasting this here champagne on the wrong gal in inviting me up to this fancy apartment."

"Now, wait a minute," Silky said, alarmed that she might leave. "A lot of women coming up from the South are whores. Only they don't know it yet. They're out sleeping with every Tom, Dick, and Harry in town, giving away the goodies for free. It takes a guy like me to come along and wisen them up to the fact that they've got something to sell. I'm an agent, taking fifty percent commission. I get well paid for what I do, but I've got my responsibilities, too. I earn my paycheck. After all, you've got to work real hard to put the whore in a woman."

"I'm not a whore, mister," Rosacoke said defiantly. "And I ain't got no intention of becoming one. I'm a singer, and a damn good one at that."

"Okay, okay, have it your way," Silky said. "Sit down and drink your champagne. Every time I see a well-stacked broad like you I've got to make the old pitch. You can't blame a professional like me for trying to recruit, now can you?"

"I ain't blaming you for nothing. I just want no part of it."

"Sit down, goddamn it!" Narcissa commanded. "You're so top heavy you're gonna fall over anyway."

"I got to be going," Rosacoke said. "Tell my date, whoever he is, he just got stood up. Thanks for the hospitality, Mr. Silky, but I ain't having one bit of it."

"Listen," Silky said. "Don't get your feathers all riled. Enjoy the champagne and the strawberries, and I'll stop coming on to you like a German tank." He smiled real sweet-like, but to her it was a sickening grimace.

Very reluctantly, she sat back down and slowly sipped the champagne.

She liked the taste of the bubbly, and she reached for one of the fat, juicy strawberries, dipping it into sugar. Just as long as this creep got the message, she figured she might as well go along for a good steak dinner, which had been promised by Narcissa earlier in the evening.

"You'll soon see what you're turning down by insisting on keeping those shapely legs of yours crossed," Silky said. "If you was one of my gals, I'd pay for an apartment for you, a real nice big one. Think of the pretty clothes you'd have. Everything you'd need. You'd live it up in style, gal."

"Oh, yeah," Rosacoke said, no longer bothering to be polite. "If you fix up your gals in such nice apartments, why is Narcissa ducking out to the slums with me while you're living here like the queen of Sheba?"

Narcissa smiled in that catlike way she had of doing and sipped her champagne with such feline grace you'd think she grew up on bubbly instead of clabbered yellow milk.

"The reason's simple," Silky said. "Narcissa doesn't care where she lives, providing I furnish her with the best wardrobe in town. The money that would go into a luxury apartment is put instead on this black pussy's back. Speaking of that..." He signaled to his maid. "Autumn's coming on, and it gets mighty cold up here in Chicago. Sorta like a deep freeze. Southern gals especially freeze their tits off up here. Of course, in your case that would take a big Arctic blast."

"Listen, mister," Rosacoke said, slamming down her fragile, tulip-shaped glass onto a marble-topped surface. "Keep your wiseass remarks to yourself. It gets mighty cold back there in those Brushy Mountains. I can take the chill."

This time when he smiled, his expression seemed to carry a begrudging respect. "I believe you can."

The maid came back into the room, carrying a big box gift wrapped in white tissue and tied with a flashy red ribbon.

"Narcissa is one high-class broad," Silky said. "I'm giving her a mink coat, and I don't usually give my gals mink."

Narcissa squealed with delight. "If it's rabbit, you beast, I'm gonna cut off your white dick. I saw enough rabbit back there in those hills."

Grabbing the box from the maid, she tore off the ribbon and pulled out a silver floor-length mink. "Oh, Silky, it's divine, gorgeous, stunning, and *the real me*." She fondled it, making a purring sound. "The most beautiful thing I've ever owned in my life." She slipped into it and pranced around the room, just like she was Alice Faye.

Rosacoke had to admit Narcissa looked stunning, and, for a moment, she was downright happy for her until she recalled how she'd earned it. For some reason she found herself remembering poor dead Aunt Clotilda, wondering what that good woman would think about all this. "It's right pretty on you," Rosacoke said, a lump rising in her throat.

Snuggling into the fur as if losing herself in it, Narcissa stuck out her hand, letting her ring finger tower into the air. "My hand, though, looks so bare. From now on, I'm gonna have a new slogan. No ice, no dice."

"Hell with that, bitch!" Silky said. "You ain't earned the fur yet."

In front of the heart-shaped mirror, Narcissa burst into tears. "All my hopes and dreams are coming true," she said. Then that bitter, determined look she always got crossed her face. "This mink coat don't make up for what I'm hungry in my gut for. I want to be a big Hollywood movie star, and you can shower all the minks in the world on me—and it won't make up for that."

"Be patient," Silky said. "Everything will happen in time. If you're a good, obliging, legs-apart gal, I'll introduce you to the right types. All in good time, my pet."

"Bull-she-it!" Narcissa said. "Try out that line on one of your *innocent* types. The only way I'm gonna be a Hollywood star is to do it myself. No one's gonna make me a star 'cept this divine *café-au-lait* beauty you're feasting your bloodshot eyes on right now."

The doorbell rang, and the maid went to answer the urgent summons.

"You say you're a singer," Silky said to Rosacoke. "You'd better play up to your date, Larry Hunt. He books acts all over the country."

\*\*\*

Larry Hunt was not at all the man Rosacoke had expected and dreaded meeting. Walking into the room with an easy stride, he was friendly, warm, and clean-cut. Unlike Silky, Larry seemed the perfect gentleman and was one of the best-looking men she'd ever laid eyes on. Blond, blue-eyed, and broad-shouldered, he was almost a match for Pete or even Hank. His face was as wide open as the American grain fields of the Middle West, from which she soon learned he'd originated. That made her trust him more. She felt people from the Middle West or the South were more honest than people from the Northeast, and she definitely didn't trust anybody from California. She'd heard terrible stories about what went on out there on the coast.

Silky went over to Larry and gave him the same wet-lipped kiss he'd given Narcissa. He lingered so long at Larry's lips that Rosacoke went into shock. She'd never seen two men kiss like that. In fact, she'd never seen one man kiss another on the cheek, much less suck his mouth which was what Silky was doing to Larry. Looking at the men, Narcissa only giggled.

Rosacoke turned her head away in embarrassment. She didn't really know what was going on. Finally, freeing Larry's lips from bondage, Silky let him go but reached to squeeze his crotch. "How's it hanging tonight?" Silky asked.

Rosacoke didn't know what that meant. Larry seemed to know what Silky was getting at. "All ready, willing, and on the rise for you, sweet cheeks," Larry said. "Although I must admit that soldier boy, Hank Adams, is one tough act to follow." He turned to look over at Rosacoke. "They sure grow them big down there in those hills."

She said nothing, only looking down into her champagne.

"You're out of luck tonight," Silky said to Larry. "I'm in the mood for some poontang. But tomorrow afternoon I've got absolutely nothing to do. I'll expect you at three. I'll be pre-lubed."

When Narcissa disappeared into the bedroom with Silky, Rosacoke offered Larry some strawberries. He poured his own champagne. As he slowly sipped the champagne, he spoke in a slow, relaxed way, totally devoid of Silky's sleazy quality. At first she was terribly shy with him, until she came to realize that he wasn't the aggressor Silky was, treating her like a young woman who was entitled to some respect.

Silky was gone for one complete hour in that bedroom with Narcissa. Rosacoke kept glancing at the clock. Larry, on the other hand, seemingly paid their disappearance no mind, concentrating on Rosacoke with genuine interest.

When Silky finally did come out of that bedroom, he at least was dressed in a proper suit and not his pajamas, much to Rosacoke's relief. He looked completely refreshed and revitalized, as he invited all of them to join him at The Gilded Grape for Narcissa's show. Rosacoke was glad to escape Silky's apartment, feeling he would cause less harm in a public place.

Outside the canopied entrance to his apartment house, a black limousine waited for them, again just like she'd seen in the movies. Up to now she'd thought movies were just fantasies, but after tonight she'd become convinced they were a depiction of real life after all. *Some* people's real life—certainly not hers. Hers was more like *Grapes of Wrath* than *Grand Hotel*.

On the way to the club, Narcissa dominated the conversation, telling all of them what a hit "Blackbirds of 1942" was. Having heard nothing else from her, Rosacoke was aware of the favorable press the show had received, especially the attention called to the appearance of the heretofore unknown Narcissa Cash.

"In every review," she told her back seat limousine audience, "I was cited for my stage presence and voice. One reviewer called me 'daringly different.' Another critic, 'an original.'" In her new mink, she snuggled up in the well-upholstered seat like a contented tiger. Suddenly, her head stuck up out of the fur. "I've got those reviews in my purse in case somebody don't believe me."

"We've read them!" Silky said, raising his voice in impatience. He bellowed new instructions to the driver who'd taken a wrong turn.

Rosacoke had long since ceased to listen to Narcissa's chatter, as she, too, settled in, enjoying the first limousine ride of her life. It sure beat Sultan's horse and wagon. Yet she wondered if it'd be her last. A person, she decided, could easily get used to the good things of life—champagne, strawberries, and limousines. She didn't dare spoil herself, remembering the dingy apartment she had to come home to and the job of slinging greasy eggs and bacon in the morning. Larry sat close to her in the back seat, making no move to get fresh. He had the chance to hold her hand but didn't.

At the club a doorman opened the limousine for them, and Rosacoke was escorted out onto the carpet, wishing all the time she'd had a fur to wear like Narcissa, although there wasn't much chill in the air. Impulsively Narcissa grabbed her arm, pulling her toward the stage door. Rosacoke called to Larry and Silky that she'd join them later.

The stage manager greeted Narcissa and whispered something in her ear. The news made her squeal with delight, and she gave him a big juicy kiss on the mouth. Like a schoolgirl in a confidential whisper, Narcissa told Rosacoke that there was going to be a big nationwide tour. She broke into an ear-to-ear grin of sheer delight. "First to New York, then on to the coast. And *me* the star!"

In the dressing room, Narcissa learned a different part of the story from the girls of the chorus. Rosacoke watched in sadness as Narcissa's bubbling enthusiasm fizzled.

Because the show was doing such big box office, the producers had brought in America's leading black diva, LaDonna Jones, to headline the show. Up to that point, Narcissa's solo had been the spotlight of the revue.

Again in a huddled conspiracy, Narcissa took Rosacoke aside. "That cunt's mastered every cheap trick in show business. What chance do I have?"

"You're different from her," Rosacoke assured her. "Be yourself. People will notice you plenty."

Narcissa hissed and looked like she was spitting tacks. "They'll notice me all right." A bitter determination came across her face.

The Grape was still under construction, and in the dressing room Narcissa made herself up in the midst of open pans of turpentine, used brushes, and even a container of silver radiator paint left by some workman who hadn't finished his job before the chorus girls came in to change.

Narcissa looked over at Rosacoke with a funny smirk on her face. "Honey, when you're competing with legend stuff, you've got to come up with a surefire gimmick!"

Before Rosacoke's astonished eyes, Narcissa walked over and took the container of radiator paint, dabbing the silvery liquid all over her head. Rosacoke was convinced Narcissa had lost her mind, but she heeded her

call for help. Standing behind her as Narcissa sat at her dressing table, Rosacoke brushed the silvery paint into Narcissa's hair, then pulled it into stiff but sweeping plaits with the help of a hairbrush and hair dryer, transforming her image completely.

From one of the other entertainers, Narcissa borrowed a tight-fitting silver lamé gown. Then she painted her long nails with the silver radiator paint, putting on the floor-length silver mink Silky had already given her.

After washing her hands, first with turpentine, then with soap and water, Rosacoke stepped back to appraise Narcissa. "You look like a stick of dynamite. Fiery hot and ready to go off."

"Thanks for the vote of confidence. Now go join the studs while I strut my stuff."

Later, with Larry and Silky at their ringside table, Rosacoke waited eagerly for Narcissa's solo appearance. Because of the good reviews, she no longer had to dance in the chorus line.

When she appeared on stage, the audience was stunned. At first there was a long silence, which eventually broke into spontaneous clapping. Even before she opened her mouth, the audience rose to its feet to give her an ovation. She stood at the edge of the stage looking regal in front of a microphone.

Rosacoke felt pride in knowing her. She wondered what Sultan, if he were alive, would think of his little Narcissa now. Rosacoke could just imagine what Aunt Clotilda would say.

At the end of her show, Narcissa slithered toward the wings. The audience's response was so overwhelming, she was forced back for five curtain calls.

Finally, the "living legend," LaDonna Jones, could stand it no more, having waited impatiently in the wings for her cue. In the midst of Narcissa's sixth curtain call, LaDonna walked in rapid strides onto the stage, waving her hands to quiet the audience. "Enough, already!" she shouted at Narcissa, signaling the band to strike up her own opening number.

About half an hour later, Narcissa, smelling ever so slightly of turpentine beneath a haze of cologne, joined Rosacoke, along with Larry and Silky, at their table. A photographer came up and snapped their picture. "I showed that bitch," Narcissa said. "Didn't I? I stole the whole fucking show right from under her."

You sure did," Rosacoke said. "You looked great. Sang great. Everything was great!"

"I know." Narcissa wanted to celebrate her silvery success, and she gladly accepted Silky's invitation for an all night on the town.

In spite of her being surrounded by these glamorous trappings, Rosacoke remembered that she was still a waitress, and she'd soon have to be slinging hash to her fellow rednecks at My Old Kentucky Home. She politely

declined Silky's offer to join them, as she did all his other propositions. Since she was caught without transportation in the environs of Chicago, and Silky and Narcissa were headed in a different direction, Larry agreed to take her home.

"Darling," Narcissa called as a parting greeting, "a star walked out on that stage tonight, and I sure don't mean LaDonna Jones. Speak of yesterday's tired mullet wrapper reeking of cat piss!"

Rosacoke blew her a congratulatory kiss, and, after thanking Silky for his hospitality, headed for the exit. This time Larry reached out to hold her hand, and she willingly extended it, as she'd come to trust him. That is, if a girl could trust any man up here in Chicago.

***

Larry tipped the doorman after he promised to call for a cab. Since there was a war on and a gas shortage, they were forced to share a 1935 Ford with three other drunken men, who quickly entered into the spirit of it, singing songs from the Blackbirds revue.

Rosacoke didn't join in the singing, yet welcomed the company on the ride. In spite of his good manners, she still felt Larry would make a lunge for her the first time they were alone, the same way Pete had done on their first date. She'd come to expect such from men. They were lungers, she was convinced.

Once delivered to her tenement, after the cabbie had dropped off the other men to another club, Rosacoke tried to persuade Larry to stay in the taxi and go back to his own apartment. He insisted on at least walking her to her door. "I've got to make sure you're not attacked. A lot of crimes in this area."

Still expecting a sexual advance from him, she was surprised as she neared the door to hear loud radio music coming from their apartment with its cardboard-thin walls. Surely Narcissa hadn't come back to the apartment so soon.

Unlocking the door, she opened it to find Hank sprawled on the ratty sofa. As he looked up, he reached to flip off the radio, not bothering to get up.

"Hank, what in heck are you doing here?" she asked. "How come you got another leave so soon?"

"I'm on permanent leave," he said, rushing to embrace Larry. "Good to see you again, old buddy."

"God damn it," Larry said. "Now we can be together every day. I've got memories. In all of Chicago, there's not another Hank Adams."

"What happened?" she asked, amazed that the Army would discharge him.

"You know," he said, looking at Larry as if some unspoken communication was going on between them. "I went to the men's room on the base hoping to get some…" He paused for a long moment. "Relief. There was another young soldier there seeking the same kind of relief I was. While there, an officer walked in on us and caught us unaware. We were both discharged. Dishonorable they call it."

"I don't get it," she said. "Don't the Army allow men to go to the toilet? That's the craziest story I've ever heard."

"I'll explain it to you some day," Larry said to her.

She was going to make coffee for the men, but Larry spotted a half empty bottle of gin left over from one of Narcissa's parties. She poured both men a drink and went to the refrigerator to get some ice.

She was put off by the brazen way Hank paraded around the apartment. He was completely nude except for a pair of very thin cotton skivvies, which did little to conceal his ample endowment. When he sat back down on the sofa, he propped a leg up. It all fell out.

She averted her eyes. Being a man, Larry took a good look. In fact, as he talked to Hank, he couldn't seem to take his eyes off this former soldier's equipment. Narcissa had once confided in Rosacoke that men liked to check out each other's equipment to see how each measured up. She figured that was what Larry was doing with Hank.

Larry pulled out a tiny packet of tobacco wrapped in brown paper and rolled a cigarette for Hank. He offered her the first drag on the cigarette but she turned it down. Hank was only too glad to puff in the smoke deep into his lungs. She knew it was different from regular tobacco, as she recognized the smell as the same smoke Moss and Fry used to enjoy back in Shakerag.

As the night wore on, Larry and Hank seemed to take a genuine delight in each other's company. The gin and the tobacco had put them in some dreamy state, making her feel left out of the party. She got up, excused herself, and headed for her own bedroom after telling them good night. Neither one of them seemed to care whether she stayed or went.

Shortly before she fell asleep, she heard a shuffling noise from the living room and wondered what those two guys were doing now. Paying it no mind, and fully expecting that Narcissa would be gone for the rest of the night, she drifted off into a deep sleep.

The next morning she woke up with a start, noticing that she had only fifteen minutes to get dressed and get to work. Not even time for a shower. In the living room, she paused to look about only briefly. Larry and Hank had left the place a mess.

Seeing the door to Narcissa's bedroom shut, she figured Hank had gone in there to sleep. She was surprised to find Larry's jacket on the sofa, figuring he must have forgotten about it. Then she spotted his shoes. How

could a man leave and forget his shoes? She was also mildly surprised to find the thin cotton skivvies of Hank on the sofa. That mountain boy was putting on one big show for Larry last night. She guessed Hank had decided to remove his drawers completely once she'd left the room.

A glance at the clock, and she wiped her mind of such matters, as she raced out the door in her waitress uniform, heading for the café-grill up the street. A troubling image came to her mind, and she quickly blotted it out. There were a lot of hungry men waiting to be fed at My Old Kentucky Home, and she was in good form, raring to sling those Blue-Plate specials.

She was a long way from her dream, and there had been a lot of compromising, but Chicago was one hell of a better place than Shakerag.

At least Narcissa was on the way toward becoming a star. How unlikely that had seemed when Rosacoke had put her on that bus heading out of the Brushy Mountains.

Dreams do come true, she felt. They weren't merely to be dreamed. She would have to be more patient and wait a little longer, as she wasn't willing to take the shortcuts to stardom that Narcissa had.

***

With the songs of Josh, his lover-man, in his heart, Pete knew he was singing better than ever. The band assembled by Nipsey and Freddie taught him something every day. It was just like being back in Shakerag with Moss and Fry "We'll make a nigger musician out of you yet," Nipsey promised.

Smokey Wetter was picked as the banjo player. A slightly pudgy Texan, Smokey was a pioneer in the style of Western swing, a combination of fiddle music, jazz, and country blues. "No one could have named me better," Smokey said. "My real name is Wetter. I've been wetting the bed every night since I was eight years old. Old habits are hard to break. I always get the lower bunk. Nobody wants to sleep under me."

Nipsey was also a friend of a remarkable bluegrass musician, Maston Mastin. He could play the fiddle like no man Pete had ever heard. Maston had a homespun personal philosophy. When the music wasn't playing, he regaled the men with his talk, especially his adventures on the riverboats that navigated their way up and down the Mississippi. He'd been born in northern Louisiana, and he'd lost his daddy to a lynching by the KKK. Like Josh, Maston promised to write two or three songs for Pete.

Maston was a hardened survivor of barn dances where he performed for white folks and of rough-and-tumble honky tonks where he played for his own kind. The first song he was working on was about a hobo riding the rails during the Depression and reminiscing about the lost loves he'd left behind in Louisiana.

He was a thin runt of a guy, with blue-black skin, and Pete liked him a lot. "You won't beat me up, will you?" Maston asked Pete when he first met him.

"Hell, no," Pete said. "Why did you ask that?"

"Usually when I get around white boys, they always beat me up 'cause I'm small. I'm an easy target."

"You're not gonna get beat up, not while I'm around," Pete said.

"I'm a jack of all trades when it comes to music," Maston said. "Not just the fiddle, but I can also play guitar and banjo. I can do clog dancing and tell stories. My picking parties used to attract white folks to some black taverns along the river. After I finish this song, 'Riding the Rails' for you, I'm gonna write one called 'Mark Twang' about a guy who performs on showboats telling his tall tales and picking and playing."

Rounding out the group was a tall musician from Alabama, named "Guitar Red," an albino Negro who knew the guitar so well he could even play it with his feet. Guitar Red told Pete he'd never eaten regularly until he joined the Navy. "On most nights my mama didn't even have a bit of fatback to put in the beans. We were po. If we managed to get baloney we didn't have bread. If we got bread we didn't have baloney. We never got baloney and bread at the same time."

"Gladys and her gals will feed you plenty," Pete said the first night he'd met Guitar Red at the club.

Pete didn't know if these black men from the South would take to all these English queens, as he suspected they had the typical black attitude toward homosexuals that most men of their region did. But somehow the menace of war had broken down barriers, and everyone, except for some belligerent white Southern men, had come to realize that they were fighting for the same cause against a menace from hell.

Pete sensed that Guitar Red and Smokey Wetter were more than tolerant of the English homosexuals. Both men didn't mind slipping off to one of the upstairs rooms with one of the English canteen workers "for a little relief," as Smokey put it.

Maston told Pete, "I never had to worry much about the queers hitting on me. I'm not the pick of the litter. Queers go for big guys like you and Nipsey. They figure I'm not worth messing up their mouths with."

"You'll find some fair British maiden over here who'll be crazy about you," Pete said, slapping him on the shoulder as a way of encouragement, although doubting his own prediction.

Day by day the reputation of Pete's singing and his band grew on the base. Even some of the white sailors asked Pete if they could attend one of the sessions. "Since we're in Britain and not in America," Pete said, "I guess it's a free country. We're not looking for trouble. There have been no fights at Dixie's. That's the name of our club. I just named it last night."

Some of the brighter white sailors, mostly from Chicago and New York, showed up at Dixie and mixed freely with the blacks. Pete's favorite was a pair of blond-haired twins, Troy and Dale Anderson. When those two hit the dance floor as a couple, Pete had never seen two guys jitterbug as wildly as they could. The boys literally threw each other in the air.

Pete couldn't help but notice what cute, sexy guys they were at eighteen. They wore tight white sailor pants as if to showcase their perfectly developed asses. Even with Josh at his side, Pete got hot watching Troy and Dale dance. He wanted to get to know them better, but no chance came to him.

In the past few weeks, Josh had become increasingly possessive. He followed Pete around most of the time, not even allowing him to go to the toilet unescorted. Actually Pete loved the attention from Josh. More than that, he loved the young man. Josh surrendered himself completely to Pete's needs. In bed, Pete had never known anyone as responsive as Josh, not even little John-John back home. One day Pete got a little impatient with Josh hovering over him, "Shit, man, to you my farts smell like perfume."

"I like everything about you," Josh said. "One morning when you kissed me, I loved having my skin reddened by the stubble of your beard. Even your stale morning breath of leftover beer from the night before is like ambrosia to me."

"You've got it bad, kid," Pete said.

Later that day Pete took his daily walk along the pier. Originally he'd preferred to walk alone as it was his private time to think about Tracy and what might have been in their relationship. But Josh insisted on tagging alone.

"You've got to understand something," Josh said. "I've found in you all that I've ever wanted and dreamed about. I ain't gonna let you go, and I'm not gonna let anybody move in on my turf."

"Is that why you won't let me out of your sight?"

"You got that right," Josh said. "You belong to me. No one else. All those English queens, especially Gladys, want to sample those mighty inches of yours. If you want to stick it into someone, I've got a wide mouth and a wide ass. Besides, I'm the prettiest sailor in Southampton. What would you want with anyone else?"

That night Josh had duty. It was a Sunday, the one night the canteen, Dixie, was closed. Having nothing to do, Pete wandered over there, thinking one of his band members might be there. He was tempted to try out Maston's new song, "Riding the Rails." Pete thought it had the potential of a hit.

When he got to Dixie, all the lights were out. Everybody was gone. At first he was tempted to go over to the Red Lion. Gladys and her "girls" were going to put on some drag acts that night. But he'd seen all their

routines countless times.

Pete decided to get his guitar and rehearse by himself in the cold, deserted canteen. He went and got himself a beer and tried to learn the new song Maston had written for him. In some ways he felt that Maston was a better songwriter than Josh, but he certainly was not going to tell that to his lover boy.

He counted himself damn lucky to have Josh in his life. Pete got all the loving he wanted. Josh was good. He'd learned all Pete's secret sexual zones. Josh knew what turned Pete on. When he was pumping it to Josh, Pete had long ago learned just the right touch, just the right spots to hit. In giving Josh a good time, Pete was experiencing sexual thrills he'd never known before with anybody. In his heart, he longed for Tracy but couldn't help loving Josh more and more every day in spite of the boy's clinging quality.

Pete stopped his guitar playing. Angry at himself, he slammed down his beer. "I want more, God damn it! More. More. I need to suck some other dicks. Fuck some other asses."

He went to the back of the kitchen and walked out the back door and into Mrs. Cooper's deserted garden. With the old lady gone, the garden was sadly neglected, as if in mourning for its previous loving owner. Nobody at the canteen took much interest in gardening.

Coming back into the house, Pete felt lonely and at loose ends. He wished Josh didn't have duty tonight. He wanted to be with him. At times like this, he thought of Rosacoke, wondering what she was doing up there in Chicago with Narcissa and Hank Adams. He missed Hank and wanted to be with him again, now that he'd been discharged from the Army.

Pete didn't know when he'd get to see his boys again, especially that John-John who continued to write him every day. If Pete survived the war, Josh fully expected Pete to invite him to Heaven on Earth where Josh just assumed that Pete would take him almost like his bride, forsaking all other men.

Pete had told Josh about the other men in his life. Upon hearing about them, Josh had been dismissive. "I'm glad you got that out of your blood," Josh said. "You were searching for me and had to make some mistakes along the way."

Pete missed everybody, as he was homesick. He eagerly read letters from his mama, from Junior, Ronnie, Claude, and Karl. John-John wrote a letter every day, sometimes two or three. The letters that meant the most to him were from Tara, telling about little Buster Riddle growing up without Pete.

He hated the war, tearing him away from the people he wanted to surround himself with. After the war, he wanted to hold onto everybody, creating one big happy commune at Heaven on Earth. He'd be the center

of everyone's attention and he preferred it that way.

Only the other day, he'd written to Hank, inviting him to come back and live at Heaven on Earth now that he was out of the Army. Hank had a stubborn streak in him, and Pete suspected Hank wanted to have a few wild times before returning to the quiet life of the mountains.

Back in the kitchen, Pete heard a loud knocking on the front door. Since the canteen was closed, he didn't know who it could be.

Going through the large living room, which had been converted into a bar with a small stage, Pete came into the foyer and turned on the porch light. He opened the door. Here lit by the porch lamp stood those twins from California, Troy and Dale in civilian clothes.

"We're closed tonight," Pete said, smiling at the boys. "We'll be up and running tomorrow night, though."

"We know you're closed," Troy said, easing by Pete and into the house. At least Pete thought it was Troy. It could have been Dale. Pete couldn't tell them apart. They were identical.

Dale (or was it Troy?) stepped inside the foyer too. "We heard on the base that you'd come over here," Dale said. "I hope you don't mind our dropping in."

"We thought you might be lonesome tonight," Troy said. "Thought we'd keep you company."

"Yeah, that's right, Dale said. "Entertain you." He smiled provocatively at Pete.

"A country boy like me can always use some entertaining from two hotshots from California like you guys." Pete flipped off the porch light. He didn't want anyone else showing up on the doorstep.

***

The next night Pete lay in his upstairs bedroom over the Red Lion, cradling Josh in his arms after their love-making. He'd tried especially hard to put more love into their sex than he'd ever done before. He wanted to show Josh a real good time because Pete felt guilty about what he'd done the night before with those twins, Troy and Dale.

The canteen wasn't set to open until an hour from now, and Pete wanted to hold onto Josh for as long as he could before both of them went over there. Pete's heart wasn't into singing tonight, but he was determined to give it his best shot.

Why couldn't he be satisfied with just one man? He'd asked himself that repeatedly. Somehow it was just assumed from his raising that a man was supposed to settle down and be faithful to his mate forever and forever. When Pete was with a loved one, as in the case of Josh, he wanted to be true and faithful to him. Yet Pete could never resist temptation, espe-

cially when it presented itself so delectably as in the case of Troy and Dale.

The twins reminded him of varsity athletes he'd seen in school. They stood just under six feet tall and had developed powerful physiques surfing off the California coasts. Just past their eighteenth birthdays, their identical bodies formed a perfect V-taper from their broad shoulders to their narrow waists. Their eyes were a soft turquoise blue like the California surf they'd known. Those eyes were set off by long lashes that made them look almost too pretty for a boy. After the war was over, each man wanted to go to Hollywood and dance in movie musicals with the likes of Betty Grable.

Their bodies were beautifully tanned, their skin of such delicate smoothness that Pete had wanted to run his tongue over every inch of them. He could not detect one imperfection, no moles, not even the occasional freckle. Without the slightest blemish, Troy and Dale were almost too perfect. Their bodies were a homosexual man's dream fantasy. How could Pete have summoned the willpower to turn down their offer of sex? He wasn't that strong. Far from it. He'd practically wanted to eat both boys after he'd removed every stitch of their clothes. He'd wanted both of them jaybird naked for the workout he had planned for them that lonely night.

Even as he cradled Josh closer to his chest at the Red Lion, Pete's mind drifted back to the previous evening, as he'd moved his mouth first over Troy's lips, then over Dale's. It was almost the same kiss from either twin. Even their breath smelled the same.

It was only when Pete had begun to taste their bodies that he'd discovered a difference in the two men. Troy had kept wanting Pete to return again and again to attack his large, pinkish nipples and his tempting belly button on the surface of his narrow, washboard stomach.

Dale had screamed with joy when Pete had licked his hairless legs and had probed his tight little ass with his tongue. Pete had quickly decided that Dale would be his bottom for the evening. Surprisingly, Pete had accurately perceived that Troy was a topman. Pete had based that assessment on how Troy was fingering Pete's hole, probing with his finger.

Pete had gotten a deep penetration from Troy, while Pete had sucked off a squirming Dale who had seemed the most sensitive man Pete had ever known. Pete's love-making had seemed to drive the boy into fits of wild passion. Pete had feared he'd have a hard time holding him down to finish the act.

Troy and Dale had blasted off at the same time, as if they'd trained themselves to do that. Pete had thrilled at getting shot full of cream at both ends. When he'd drained both boys dry, he'd fallen over in bed in exhaustion. But Troy and Dale had other plans for him. They'd attacked his body with their mouths and didn't let him up for air until they'd drained him twice. Both of those very determined young men had wanted a taste of Pete and he'd rewarded them amply.

As all three of them had lain in total fulfillment on the bed, Pete had contemplated their recent love-making. One didn't fall in love with Troy and Dale. They were not giving love like Josh. The twins provided sex. Both men were like well-oiled love machines.

It was as if they could no longer function in life if they didn't get their daily quota of hot cream. Pete had been convinced that Troy and Dale turned to each other's bodies for sexual gratification when they didn't have some other man such as himself readily available. In a way, he guessed that their love-making was like making love to yourself. Even their thick seven-inch dicks were exactly identical.

As he'd fondled the bodies of the twins, Pete had fantasized that the sex between them so far was a mere tantalizing appetizer of what was to come. He'd felt that this pair could teach him a lot about sex, and Pete was eager to learn from them. Maybe people out in California knew a lot more about sexual games than men from the Carolina Mountains.

Pete's reverie about Troy and Dale were interrupted as Josh's lips sought his. The brushing of Josh's lips against Pete's brought him back to the reality of the only man he truly loved. Pete wrapped a hand behind Josh's head and held it in place as he pried his lips apart with his tongue. As Pete inserted his tongue into the boy's sweet mouth, he was rewarded with a powerful suction action. It caused Pete to harden again for the second time within the hour. Pete's cock throbbed against the boy's rock-hard stomach. Josh was sucking Pete's tongue with an incredible brute force. As he did that, Pete's fingers probed the boy's smooth body, one index finger making its way to the boy's tiny, puckering hole. As he felt it, Pete still couldn't believe that it could open up big enough to take all of him. It not only could, but did.

Josh reared up as he opened himself wide for Pete who descended on his neck to lick it before nibbling on his delectable earlobe. "You're my boy," he whispered into that ear when he wasn't tonguing it.

As Pete hit sensitive spots deep within Josh, the young man dug his fingernails into Pete's back. "For the rest of my life, I'll let no other man get inside me. Just you, Pete Riddle." His fingers dug deeper into Pete's back as he speeded up his rhythm, enjoying the absolute power he had over this beautiful young sailor.

"I belong just to you," Josh whispered between gasps of joy. "Only you. No other."

\*\*\*

It was amazing how something so new and different could become routine after a few weeks. Rosacoke sure didn't want to spend the rest of her life serving spareribs and mustard greens. Her customers were nice,

and that eased the drudgery somewhat. By now most of them had lived in Chicago long enough to learn to tip, at least a dime. A few of the more extravagant ones, earning lots of defense plant dollars, left a whole quarter. She liked those best of all.

She'd come to live for Saturday night when it was time for her to sing. Along the way she'd developed a small but loyal following of displaced Southerners, and many of them had told their friends about her. It was strictly standing-room only on Saturday night, and Owen and Daisy couldn't have been happier. The cash register rang all night.

Rosacoke liked going on stage in a noisy, crowded room of beer-drinking men, then listening as a hush fell over the audience. She felt the power of a performer with a command over an unruly crowd. As she'd sing, familiar faces would come into view, but always her mind was on Pete, particularly in the love songs. Singing made her happy—the only time really when she could say that about herself—and it made the homesick men who listened to her happy, too.

Larry became a frequent visitor to the apartment, and, though he saw a lot of her, made no attempt to move in on her as she'd feared. She was lonely and almost wished he would, thinking a new boy friend might help her forget Pete and the infant son she'd left behind in the Brushy Mountains.

When she was at work, Larry spent a lot of time at the apartment with Hank. They had developed quite a friendship, and, though she was sorry Larry never asked her out on a date, she was at least glad that Hank had some companionship. Narcissa came to visit them less and less until, almost without Rosacoke's knowing it, she realized Narcissa had moved. If it weren't for Larry's company, Hank would spend all his time sulking in the apartment, drinking and listening to the radio.

Finally, Rosacoke despaired of waiting around for Larry to ask her out. On Friday night in their apartment, when Hank left to go to the corner grocery store to get a package of Lucky Strikes, she looked over at Larry. He smiled politely, a look that made her feel merely tolerated. He didn't seem to find her attractive as a woman and she just couldn't understand that, because she was dressing much sexier.

"You know I sing every Saturday night down at the café," she said. "I really was hoping you might drop in some night. Considering you're in the business and everything. It might help for me to get a professional opinion."

"You got yourself a date."

That Saturday night she didn't expect him to show up, but Owen and Daisy told her he'd come in in time for dinner and had asked for the best table in the house, right down by the platform where she sang.

More nervous than usual, she went on to loud applause, avoiding making eye contact with Larry. She knew he'd heard so many singers in his business, and she feared unfavorable comparisons.

Before her first words came out, she had a cramped feeling in her throat. She felt she'd made a horrible mistake in inviting him. He'd just laugh at her and take bad stories back to Narcissa and Silky. She wanted to crawl under Daisy's table and die, but rejected the idea as unprofessional.

Bracing herself and trying to erase Larry from her mind, as was her way, she stepped in front of the microphone. She'd selected two Hank Snow tunes, "Lonesome Blue Yodel" and "Prisoned Cowboy," both new songs for her rapidly growing repertoire.

The audience's response was so good that by the time she'd launched into her more standard numbers she'd forgotten all about Larry. The café was jumping, and she showed everybody a good time. She quit worrying over whether her breasts bounced and jiggled too much. No one else out there in that crowd seemed to mind that either; in fact, she felt it was part of her show.

At the finale, she was brought back to sing three sentimental favorites, including "My Old Kentucky Home," before the now-drunk men would let her go.

After a final bow, she rushed toward the kitchen, wondering if Larry would ever speak to her again. He caught up with her in the toilet, as there was no dressing room. She was taking off some of her more garish makeup.

"You were terrific," he said.

"You really mean that?"

"I sure do. To tell you the truth, I'd never come over here before 'cause Narcissa told me you were no good. How wrong she was!"

A sharp pain struck Rosacoke. She was real sorry to hear that Narcissa had put her down like that. "You really mean it?" she asked again. "About my being good and all."

"I not only mean it, I'll put my money where my mouth is."

"In what way?"

"I'm putting together a carnival band of outlaws and outcasts to tour western Canada. Those farmers up there will have their pockets bulging with money earned from their summer crops. Those crops are more valuable than ever now that there's a war on. The carnies I'm booking will know how to help them spend it."

"That doesn't sound like a very appetizing job."

"I need a cowgirl singer for my traveling show," he said. "You've got the job providing you'll stick to songs by Tex Ritter and Gene Autry in their singing cowboy movies. Not so much of this Kentucky home shit."

"You got yourself a deal."

"Silly girl, you didn't even ask what it pays," he said.

"I bet a hell of a lot more than I'm making here slinging hash."

"Seventy-five bucks a week."

"That's more money than I've ever earned in my whole life," she said.

"Not only that, but I'll give you three cowgirl costumes—covered in rhinestones," he said. "They were made by a guy in Hollywood. Nudie. They're worn a bit but still good enough for those farmers."

"That's fine with me. When do we hit the road?"

"Two days from now," he said.

"Oh, damn. I've got to give notice to Owen and Daisy. They've been like parents to me. And it's not much of a notice."

Even though she dreaded telling them, she was secretly thrilled at the offer. She didn't have to wait tables any more. For the first time in her life, she'd earn her living entirely by her voice.

***

In her Chicago kitchen Daisy ladled out a big bowl of chili for a customer waiting at the linoleum-covered counter. "Get him some crackers, honey," she called to Rosacoke as she came into the steam room.

"Sure thing!" Rosacoke called to her boss. That steaming bowl of chili brought another request and yet another from the beer-drinking men out front. At a wooden block, Rosacoke's eyes watered as she chopped raw onions for the men to sprinkle on top of their chili bowls.

It was after three o'clock in the morning when the last customer had gone and she was able to be alone with a tired Owen and an even more worn-out Daisy. All three of them sat sipping cups of stale coffee, surveying the wreckage of Saturday night's show. All the tables had to be cleaned and the floor swept and mopped in time for Sunday breakfast.

"I'm quitting," Rosacoke blurted out. "I don't mean to but Larry offered me a job singing with a carnival in Canada. It's a big break, and I'll be real sorry to leave and all."

Owen and Daisy didn't respond at first, but then the news registered and both of them looked real hurt, as if they'd personally been betrayed. That didn't make Rosacoke feel any better.

"God damn it, Owen," Daisy spoke up. She turned to Rosacoke in exasperation. "I've been poking him for weeks now to give you a raise. I mean, you've increased our business a whole lot, and we're right grateful and all. Starting tomorrow morning, we're upping your pay to ten dollars a day."

"I appreciate it and all—I really do—but I've already given my word to Larry," Rosacoke said. "I promised and all."

"In other words, your mind's made up?" Owen asked.

"Afraid it is," Rosacoke said.

"Then let's get the most out of her while we can," Owen said to Daisy.

"We'll spread the word. We'll have a big farewell performance for Sunday night. The place will be jammed. Our last chance to clean up."

The news surprised Rosacoke, and she really didn't want to do it, but she felt that she owed Daisy and Owen that final favor.

After cleaning up that morning, Rosacoke walked the streets alone, heading for the apartment she still shared with Hank. She didn't know how he was going to take the news either, because he counted on her for half the monthly rent now that Narcissa had moved in with Silky.

When she came into the shabby living room, she looked into Hank's bedroom, finding it was empty. On the coffee table lay a note. She recognized Narcissa's scrawl at once. Opening it, she read an invitation to visit Narcissa at Silky's that afternoon at three.

That little piece of paper was yet another first in her rapidly changing life: she'd never received a written invitation before to go anywhere.

***

The following afternoon, the maid showed Rosacoke into Silky's apartment, where Narcissa, under a mass of silver hair, lounged on the red-satin sofa. Clad entirely in white, including a turban, she was a stunning bird of prey. Since going into show business, she'd learned a lot more tricks about grooming and glamour.

"I'm considering changing my name from Narcissa Cash to Tijuana Cash. The Cash I definitely want to keep. I like the sound of it."

"Better stick to Narcissa. It sounds pretty. Tijuana sounds cheap."

"Maybe you're right. If there's one thing I'm not, it's cheap." As if to prove her point, she ordered the maid to bring in a bottle of Silky's vintage champagne.

Narcissa got up to put on some fancy jazz tunes with mariachi overtones. She clapped and hooted with delight at the sound of the music. Before settling down again, she did a few bumps and grinds.

"You sure have changed," Rosacoke said. "Sexier than ever if that's possible."

Narcissa nodded as if agreeing. "I guess you know I'm leaving Chicago with the Blackbirds revue. Before we reach New York, I assure you LaDonna Jones will be retired from show business. Then we're gonna go to Los Angeles. In no time at all you'll be reading about me in my big mansion in Beverly Hills. Complete with a swimming pool and Silky's maid— just to show *that* one!"

"I guess this is good-bye then. I'll sure miss you, and I sure do thank you for helping get me to Chicago"

"Forget it." She paused for a moment, then raised her eyebrows, making a purring sound like a cat. "Someday I'll collect—not now."

"I've got a big break, too," Rosacoke said. "Oh, nothing big like yours but it's still show business. Larry has hired me as a cowgirl singer traveling with his carnival act."

Narcissa looked disdainfully at Rosacoke, almost as if she resented her getting a job. "A carnival! How nice." She sipped the champagne the maid poured for her, spitting out its contents. "Take it back. Tastes like vinegar."

"But Miss Cash, it's Mr. Silky's finest...."

"You saying I don't know bad champagne from good?" Under Narcissa's steely eyes, the maid retreated. Settling back on the sofa, Narcissa returned her attention to Rosacoke. "I didn't call you here to talk show biz."

"I'm not working for Silky if that's the question."

"It's not," Narcissa said. "After this week, I'm not working for Silky neither. I called you here to tell you me and Hank are through."

"I'm just a country girl and pretty dumb about some things, but I figured that one out. I never knew why you took up with him in the first place."

"He was the only guy I knew striking out of the Brushy Mountains. I had plans for him until he joined the Army. Men are to be used. They use us, so why can't we use them? I thought I needed him, but I wised up soon enough. I gave you Pete with a ribbon tied around it. Now I'll cough up Hank."

Rosacoke jumped up, splashing the tulip-shaped champagne glass she'd been handed. "A gift I've got to say no to. I never thought of Hank that way before. Thanks but no thanks."

"Perhaps you'll change your mind. I just wanted to let you know another one of my discards is up for grabs. Still carrying a torch for that Pete?"

"Yeah, I guess so, But somewhere up in the wilds of Canada, I'll forget him. I just know I will."

"Sure, you will." Narcissa couldn't dwell on any subject other than herself longer than a minute or so. Soon the talk was of her big plans for a career in show business. She jabbered so much and so incessantly it was nearly six o'clock before Rosacoke became aware of the time.

"I've got to get out of here. I go on at seven, and I'm not even dressed."

"Speaking of that, I had the maid pack some of my hand-me-downs for you. They're in the hall."

"I sure could use 'em. Thanks muchly."

At the door she gave Narcissa a kiss on the cheek, and Narcissa wished her all the luck. "I know you'll become a big star and everything," Rosacoke assured her. "I always felt that about you."

"I know it, too." Narcissa gave her a parting kiss on the cheek, and, as Rosacoke turned and raced from the apartment with the used clothing, she felt a pang in her heart. She doubted if she'd ever see Narcissa again.

It was twenty minutes before seven when she got to My Old Kentucky Home. An impatient Larry waited there, and he helped her change into her costume and put on her makeup.

Her final concert earned her the first standing ovation of her life. Her act was constantly interrupted by rebel yells. She'd never felt more wanted before, and she just knew that her voice was in rare form. She was glad Larry had come to the club to provide moral support.

At the end of the show, Owen passed the hat around for her, and it filled quickly with fresh, crisp dollars her fans had earned in defense plant work.

After the show, Owen counted the money for her: a nest egg of two-hundred and fifty dollars, the most money she'd ever seen in her whole life.

The only disappointment came when she told Daisy good-bye. "Honey, can't you stay over and clean up this mess with me? After all, the show was just for you, and on Monday morning, breakfast comes early."

# Chapter 8

Riding the Canadian rails on a show train painted a violent purple and vomity chartreuse, Rosacoke quickly became involved in the wide, weird milieu of the carnies. A tattooed lady, a woman sword-swallower, a geek, an anatomical wonder who exposed his body in a cage kept behind a tawdry red curtain, Rosacoke met all of them in this hurly-burly world.

Alberta, Manitoba, and Saskatchewan passed in review before her. A carnival wasn't exactly her dream of a show business career, but she'd decided it was a start and she should be grateful for that.

As the sound of the merry-go-round's calliope filled the air, she sang "Tumbling Tumbleweeds." To a crowd of ruddy-faced wheat growers and cattlemen, she found her most successful number was the wartime hit, "Have I Told You Lately That I Love You?"

Larry had invited Hank to join them on the tour, placing him in charge of the one-armed bandits. When he wasn't conning the farmers out of their money, Hank was the barker for the show, ballyhooing the carnival's many attractions.

For Rosacoke, it was an atmosphere of gaudy magic, with bright lights and the smell of cotton candy and roasting chestnuts. In her new but worn cowgirl outfits, she was giddy with excitement.

As autumn gave way to November, the nights grew cold. The show train moved deeper and deeper into western Canada, past miles of open range and clear, clean rivers. In time, the landscape became denuded, and Larry said he'd never worked the carnival this late. "The crowds are bigger than ever," he said. "The war's going bad. They want to forget."

At first when the country was blanketed in autumnal colors, Rosacoke was at her peak of excitement. But as the nights turned long and dreary at the first signs of winter, her spirits sank. Indians came out of the woods, pitching their tents around the carnival, although they never paid to hear her sing. "They just don't like my kind of music," she told Hank one night.

Larry kept busy coping with the problems of the show. The rest of his free time he spent with Hank. Occasionally he found some time for her, advising her on how to improve her grooming and teaching her tricks to use on stage.

A new feeling of her own femininity took over, as she became more and more aware of the striking impact her recently acquired glamour had

on audiences. One man told her he'd pay good money to see her act "just to gape at you even if you couldn't carry a tune." At first embarrassed by such excessive attention, she eventually became seduced by it. Her confidence grew week by week.

Before the trip to Canada, she'd never thought much about Hank. At least nothing good. Increasingly and to her surprise, she was drawn more and more to him. A warm, glowing feeling came over her when she was around him. He was also protective of her, and she came to rely on him. Gentle but firm with her, he was her last link to her roots back in the Brushy Mountains.

One day, almost without her realizing it, she came to believe she was in love with him. And she'd never even kissed him.

She remembered the exact moment she came to that conclusion. He had argued with some slick pitchman who wanted to travel with the carnival, peddling his own brand of rattlesnake oil. When Hank had gotten rid of the huckster, he turned to her with a roguish smile on his face that was invincibly impish. He winked at her, as if indicating he wasn't really as tough as he sounded. It was like a secret she could share with him, making her feel closer than ever to him.

The next night when he asked her to have supper with him, she melted with delight, spending an extra long time with her makeup and dress. To her disappointment, Larry joined them, and all his talk was of business. Later when Larry went to the men's room, she told Hank she wasn't doing anything after the show in case he was free.

"Shit, I think Larry has something planned." He looked like he didn't want to go through with it, cracking his roguish smile again. He leaned over the table and gave her nose a little kiss. "I'm worth waiting for. Hold onto your horses."

Hank bunked with Larry, and Rosacoke was assigned Gypsy Day, the woman sword-swallower, as her roommate. Gypsy told her that she could swallow a twenty-five-inch long, three-quarters-of-an-inch wide sword easily. "When the tip of the blade touches the lining of my stomach, it's just like a pinprick, the way a needle feels when you get a splinter out of your finger. A doctor once told me that I have the longest esophagus he'd ever seen."

A tap on the door interrupted Gypsy's story. Rosacoke went to the door, finding Hank, who pulled her outside into the corridor.

He glanced nervously up and down the hall. "Larry's gotta fly to Toronto tomorrow morning on business. I want you to run away with me for a day or so. You've got to promise to tell no one. Not even Gypsy."

"Okay," she agreed, her excitement mounting. "I don't know why we have to keep it a secret. We're both grown-ups."

"Trust me, okay?" He gave her a quick kiss, a promise to meet in the morning, and then he was gone.

Filled with wonder and confusion, she went to bed that night eagerly awaiting tomorrow.

***

As the first snow flurries of winter filled the air, Rosacoke ran away from the carnival for a weekend alone with Hank. Nervous at the prospect, she was also excited and thrilled. From one of the gypsies traveling with the show, Hank had learned about a summer fishing cabin which was always abandoned at this time of year.

He'd borrowed a 1933 Ford and had managed to acquire enough gasoline for the trip. His ability to pick up whatever supplies he needed impressed her. Hank was a real man, used to fending for himself. He was no sissy—that was for sure.

The road was bumpy, rocky, and desolate, but taking a break from the carnival atmosphere filled her with excitement. "I feel like a human being again," she said. "Thanks."

"Before the night is over, you're gonna feel like a woman." He reached over and cupped her around the neck, giving her a masculine hug and a big kiss.

The cabin wasn't much, just one bare room with a stone fireplace and two bunk beds. It definitely wasn't geared for winter living. In the forest he gathered stray logs, some covered with moss, and with some dried twigs he found under a shed out back he got a fire going. He kept tossing logs on, and as the snow continued to fall the place warmed up. He'd brought along a can of beef stew, and, after they'd heated and eaten it, they rubbed pure sand over their plates, washing them in the icy water of a nearby stream.

As darkness came early, she sat by the roaring fire, which provided the only illumination in the cabin. To her, he'd never looked handsomer, wearing his cheap long-sleeved plaid shirt and denim. On his right cheek was a large dark mole, which if it did anything made him even sexier.

He'd brought along some Canadian whiskey, which she shared with him, the alcohol combining with the fire to give her a mellow glow. The heat from the flames steamed the small panes of the glass in the cabin's one meager window.

After dinner he asked her to go for a walk in the twilight. The snow had stopped but a wind had come up, blowing down fiercely from the north. A flashlight lit their way. Hugging her close, he guided her with a firm hold on her arm. The chilling wind cut into her face.

At the crest of a hill, he came to a stop. Shivering in her parka, her teeth chattering, she moved toward him, as his mouth pressed down on hers. She stopped shaking at once, losing herself in his powerful embrace. Her legs were unsteady, as they made their way back to the cabin and their

sleeping bags. She knew what was coming.

Dizzy from the whiskey and the passion he'd aroused in her, she didn't know what to do next until he whispered, "Take off your clothes." She no longer cared whether it was right or wrong to go to bed with him. She just knew she wanted him very much.

His shirt fell beside the bedding. As he leaned down to take off his boots, she watched in fascination as the muscles in his stomach rippled as he bent over.

She slipped off her clothes and jumped under the matting before he had a chance to get a good look at her nude body. In the sleeping bag with her, he held her close, and she loved the feel of his hairy chest pressing against her nipples.

Exploring her neck with his tongue, he descended lower, sucking her breasts, nibbling and biting hard. At first she'd wanted to protest the rough treatment, until she found she loved it. She put her hand on the back of his neck, holding him in place over her heaving chest.

Rearing up, he took her by the shoulders and pushed her back. He felt her body grow tense. "Relax, relax," he said. "You'll love it."

"Oh, Hank," she cried out as he pressed down on her. Tears rolled down her cheeks as he entered her. She was gasping for air, as he rode her hard. She didn't want it to end. He leaned down and gave her a long hot kiss. Her guts were on fire, as memories of Pete came racing back. She yelled in pain as his last powerful lunge pushed her naked back against the matting. She held on to him as he lay motionless on top of her.

"Don't ever leave me," she said. "Please."

"Don't worry, baby. I'm going nowhere. We're gonna stay like this all night."

***

In the middle of the night, she got up to put more wood on the fire while Hank still slept. As she tossed two logs on, she sat wrapped in a blanket for a long while, getting lost in the dancing flames. Her mind was confused.

Hank was a hard-driving but good lover, and she really cared for him. But sometimes she couldn't keep her mind on him like she should. Her thoughts kept drifting back to Pete, wondering what he was doing tonight. She wasn't even sure it was night wherever the hell Pete was. For all she knew, he was sailing somewhere in the noonday sun. She didn't know until last week that time was different throughout the world. She'd read it in a newspaper bulletin out of London, where morning came a lot earlier than back home.

Getting up, she stared vacantly and without any particular purpose out of the little lone window. She peered down through the snow-covered trees

at the valley below, where she imagined she saw an occasional flash of light. Or did she imagine that? Wiping the steam from the windowpane, she looked out, concentrating her vision in the murky darkness. Sure enough, yellow lights were flickering. Headlights. Someone was coming up the old logging road at this time of the night.

Wondering who could be visiting them at this hour, she dropped the blanket on the floor and slipped into her heavy clothes.

"Hank, get up." She shook him real hard. "Company's coming."

Jumping up, he rubbed sleep from his eyes. "Who in hell? No one knows we're here 'cept Shorty at the carnival. And he wouldn't tell nobody."

"I see headlights." She returned to the window. Those lights were getting closer. "Maybe it's the owner of the cabin. Maybe he likes more than fishing. A little hunting at this time of the year."

Stark naked, Hank jumped up and slipped on his shirt and pulled his pants up, not bothering with underwear.

At the window she could see somebody getting out of a carnival truck. With a flashlight he made his way to the door and, without knocking, barged in.

It was Larry.

For a long moment, all three of them stood looking at each other, saying nothing.

She didn't know why, but she felt guilty at Larry catching her with Hank. She didn't want him to think she was the type of girl who'd run off with any man who asked her.

Larry paid her no mind, concentrating his entire attention on Hank with ferocity.

It was Hank who broke the silence. "Seeing you're here you might as well come in and have some whiskey. It's mighty cold out there, especially when you stand there with that God damn fucking door wide open."

She'd never heard Hank talk to Larry with such hostility.

Larry slammed the door. "I was bumped from the plane. The military needed my seat. I got back to the carnival. It didn't take me long to figure out where you'd gone. Especially when I threatened to fire Shorty."

"Now, Larry, I don't know why you're carrying on like this," she butted in. "I mean, there's no work this weekend, and me and Hank ain't had a day off since we left Chicago."

"Shut up, you God damn stinking tramp!" He turned to her with such a burning hatred in his eyes she felt he wanted to bash her face in. She didn't understand any of it. Larry was like a crazy man.

"You don't own me," Hank shouted. "Your hillbilly hoss likes a mare now and then."

"You promised, God damn you," Larry said. "I told you what would

happen if I ever caught you out with another tramp."

"Listen, mister," she said. "No matter what you think, I'm no tramp, and I don't like being called one."

"You're fired," Larry yelled at her. "You can't sing anyway. I don't know why in hell I even hired you. I must have been drunk. As for you...." He turned to Hank again.

"What about *me*?" Hank had a mean sneer on his face.

She knew Larry was pushing him too far, because Hank had a bad temper that occasionally flared. Slow to boil, he became a raging cauldron when mad. Back home he had a reputation for beating the hell out of anybody who crossed him.

"I could kick your ass for doing this to me," Larry told him. "After all I've done for you."

"You got yours," Hank yelled. "I'd say you were more than amply repaid. I'm leaving. I've had it with you and the carnival. It didn't crack up to be what I thought it was. All that excitement I was promised for some favors. I ain't seen no excitement yet, faggot!"

"You son of a bitch!" Larry lunged at Hank, but he was too quick for him, side-stepping the blow. He punched Larry in the jaw real hard, knocking him back against a chair. Larry's nose was bleeding, and she moved to help him. But Hank grabbed her arm. "Get your things. We're clearing out."

"You're not walking out on me like this, shithead," Larry said. "With what I know about you, I could have you arrested."

"Don't try it!" Hank threatened. "You might be in the same cell with me."

"I could kill you, you bastard!" Larry tried to raise up from the floor.

By now Hank had his boots on. With one quick kick in the groin, he sent Larry sprawling on the wide-planked floor, squirming and holding himself as he moaned and sobbed.

Outside the door to the cabin, she turned to Hank as he slipped on his parka. "You didn't have to go and do that, even though he carried on something awful."

"Shut up! Get in the car."

Hank had trouble starting the old Ford's cold motor, and she was glad Larry stayed in the cabin. When Hank got the motor running, he pulled out his pocket knife.

Panic came over her. "What you gonna do with that?" She was afraid he was going back to the cabin to stab Larry. She watched in horror as Hank slashed the tires to the carnival truck.

Back in the car, Hank headed down the hill in the Ford along the logging road. "Let the fucker walk back to his carnies."

"It's miles to the next house," she protested. "He could freeze to death."

"It'll teach him a lesson. Cut the lip! I've got to think."

The rest of the ride back to the carnival was in silence, and she was afraid to say one word.

She was shocked how in the course of one night her own life had seemed to become irrevocably linked to Hank's. She wasn't at all sure how she felt about that. Too much had happened too soon.

With no job and no prospects, she rode with him in the cold light of a pre-dawn into an unknown future. She just hoped he knew what he was doing, because she sure as hell didn't.

***

Through the foggy gray murk, the old Ford delivered them to the carnival train at what looked like an abandoned railway station outside Edmonton, Alberta. "Get your clothes," Hank ordered. "We're heading for Ontario."

"In whose car?" she asked, totally puzzled.

"I forgot to tell you. I didn't borrow the car. I bought it. It broke me, too. You got any money?"

"I've saved up eight-hundred dollars."

"Great! We'll need that. Gas. Food. Some fleabags. With the war on, the price of everything has gone crazy."

In her compartment, she unintentionally woke up Gypsy as she packed her battered old suitcase, lent to her by Mrs. Riddle who'd once used it to travel to Atlanta in 1923.

"What's up?" Gypsy asked, rising from her bed and rubbing sleep from her eyes.

"Larry fired us. Me and Hank are driving to Ontario."

"I knew you shouldn't have run off with Hank. Larry's jealous as hell of that boy. He caught us together once. You know all the men in the carnival are attracted to me because I'm a sword-swallower."

"I don't want to hear it. I really don't. I'm worried and afraid."

"You've got yourself a hell of a man in that Hank. He knows how to show a girl a good time."

Slamming the suitcase shut, Rosacoke turned to tell Gypsy good-bye. "This show business is something else. Take care of yourself. I don't know if I'll ever see you again."

"Don't worry. I'll catch your cowgirl act in some town somewhere, and you come to see me when you hear the carnival's in town."

"I sure will. Good-bye, Gypsy. I hope you get out of Canada before you freeze your butt off."

Without saying another word, Gypsy turned over and seemed to go right back to sleep. Rosacoke stood for a long moment looking at her, not wanting to think about Hank and her together, then she turned and hurried

toward the Ford.

Hank was there waiting impatiently. With a grim face, he set out on the road. That day they passed through desolate, dusty towns and lots of barren land. The now dead wheat fields made the terrain look like one vast checkerboard.

Away from the carnies and the excitement they generated, Rosacoke began to reevaluate Hank, fearing she'd made a terrible mistake in impulsively running away with him.

Almost too late she'd discovered another side of his personality. At times in the past he'd been kind and understanding, easing some of her homesick feeling. But he could also be cold and uncaring. Based on her limited experience with men, she'd begun to feel that those movie star magazine romances she'd read about were flimsy illusions.

The trip to Ontario lasted too long for her comfort. Now that she slept with Hank every night, he'd come to treat her like a newly acquired possession, to be protected and guarded. She suspected he'd been seriously hurt by Narcissa, and he didn't want his latest girl to run out on him with other men.

Living in seedy, half-furnished lodgings, whatever was available in wartime Canada, he'd abandon her for long periods of time, ordering her not to leave the room. These rooms were always drafty and unheated, and she spent most of her time huddling under blankets, fighting off the cold. He'd taken all her money, and she had nothing left for food.

Once when he'd disappeared for a whole day and night, leaving not one slice of bread, she thought she was going to starve to death until she remembered she'd once hidden a five-dollar bill in her rhinestone-studded cowgirl outfit, the money representing her pay for the night. Searching through the suitcase, she took out the dress and found the money. Nothing had ever looked so good to her before.

Disobeying Hank, she slipped out of the dreary bungalow and headed for a local diner she'd spotted as they'd driven into town. There she plopped down on the nearest stool, ordering herself a big juicy hamburger with lots of fries and a giant coke.

Seated next to her were a friendly American man and his pale, sickly looking wife. They'd been to visit relatives in Regina, Saskatchewan, and were driving back to North Dakota.

Waiting for her hamburger, she chatted casually with them, enjoying having friendly souls to talk to. Hank certainly wasn't much for conversation. The woman excused herself to go to the toilet, and Rosacoke continued to chat with her husband.

As Rosacoke's hamburger was served, she glanced toward the rear of the diner, spotting Hank as he enjoyed a big steak dinner near a blaring jukebox.

Just as she discovered him, he looked up, spotting her. An uncontrollable rage came over his face. Pushing his plate back, he walked in rapid, angry strides to the front of the diner. Up close to her, his face was drawn and tense, as he was consumed by rage.

In front of the astonished man from North Dakota, he grabbed her by the arm, practically dragging her to the courtyard outside the diner. Opening the car door for her, he shoved her inside.

On the short ride back to the bungalow, he said nothing. She sat near the far edge of the seat, trembling. It wasn't the first time she'd seen him mad, but never this out of control.

Throwing open the door to their bungalow, he pushed her inside. She fell down across the bed. For the second time in her life, she experienced overwhelming fear at being trapped alone with a man, that memory evoking her attack by Sultan.

Locking the door behind him, Hank spun her around, hitting her in the face. Covering herself with her hands, she cried out for him to stop. But he hit her again and again, shoving her against the wall. "You fucking whore!" he shrieked at her. "A two-bit tramp. Just like Narcissa."

Only seventeen, she didn't know how to handle such an assault. She felt she'd done nothing wrong. She collapsed on the floor, sobbing in the cradle of her arm. Fists clenched, he stood over her, menacing her. He kicked her and walked away.

She didn't know for how long—maybe it was for hours—but she continued to lie there in that crouched position on the floor. Her whole body ached, and her head pained her so much she felt it would explode.

He'd turned off the light and had sprawled out on the bed. She felt she was a prisoner, knowing how foolish it was to give him all her money. Throughout the long night, she plotted about running away the first chance she got. If only he would take her to Chicago, she'd go back to work for Owen and Daisy at My Old Kentucky Home, a safe haven she shouldn't have left in the first place.

Shortly before daybreak, she heard Hank sobbing on the bed. His rage seemingly gone, he was filled with remorse. Like a helpless, errant boy, he begged her to forgive him. "I love you so much I was just jealous. I thought you were trying to pick up that guy. Narcissa pulled that trick on me. I couldn't stand for it to happen again. I went crazy. Please. I'll never beat you again. I promise."

It was a long time before she went to join him on the bed, and when she did, her heart was filled with despair.

***

"I didn't figure you for a queer," Captain Dan Crook was telling Pete,

as the toughened sailor glared at him on one of the few sunny days Southampton had seen in a month. "You are a queer, ain't you?"

"Sir, I like pussy as much as the next man," Pete said, telling a final lie before facing the inevitable dishonorable discharge.

"Do you want the charges, all the evidence we've accumulated against you, aired? Do you want this mess to get in the papers? Fuck up the rest of your life? Or do you want to let the Navy hush this up? Sweep it under the carpet. Kick you boys out of the Navy and ship you home real quiet like. There's a war on. This man's Navy has something bigger and more urgent to worry about than sailors sucking each other's dicks."

Pete hardly hesitated. "I think it would be better if we hushed it up. We'll go peacefully. I don't want to deny or admit anything. I thought we were doing a damn good job of running the canteen. Entertaining the boys."

Captain Crook practically spat out his next words. "If you ask me, you were entertaining them too well." He rose from his desk, and Pete stood up too. "Two guards are going to take you down to a debriefing room. Your fellow queers will be there. We want to make sure we've rounded up all the pansy boys who have been into this shit."

The next few hours passed as in a bad dream for Pete. Someone at the canteen who seemed to know everything that was going on turned their names in. Josh Harnell. Freddie Raubal. Nipsey Smith. The twins, Troy and Dale Anderson. Pete's backup musicians, Smokey Wetter and Red Guitar.

After the first grilling, when their break came, Pete stood next to Maston Mastin at the urinal, relieving himself. "Maston, why are you here? I never saw you with anybody at any time."

"As I once told you," Maston said. "No one wants me. Both the gals and the queers are after good-looking guys like you."

"Then why are you with us?" Pete said. "You shouldn't be getting a dishonorable discharge. You're a good and fine man."

"There's a thing I call loyalty," Maston said. "My buddies are in trouble. Hell, if that's the case then I'm gonna share trouble with them. We blacks are hounded in the South. Queers are hounded in the Navy. It's all part of the same shit."

Pete was due back into the "grill chamber" with the other men, but he had ten minutes to slip away for a walk in the fresh air with Josh. He shared a cigarette with his lover. "I can't stand this," Pete said. "I want this to be over. I want to forget there is a war, that I was ever in the Navy. I feel like my life's come to an end. I'm so ashamed. They're humiliating the hell out of us before they kick us out on our asses."

"It's gonna be fine—just fine," Josh said, taking the cigarette from him for a puff or two. "This crap will soon be over. We'll be civilians again. We can start our life over. I can hold you in my arms all night long and not

be afraid someone will discover our love."

"You seem happy about going home," he said. "You're not ashamed?"

"Hell, no," Josh said. "Why should I be? What have I done wrong? Love another human being. So what if that human being happens to be a man? I'm proud to love you. I don't care if the whole fucking world finds out. I'd be proud to stand with you in battle but the Navy doesn't find us worthy. The war will end in two or three years. It'll have to. All the men not killed will be returning home. We're just going to be returning home a little earlier than most. At least we'll be alive."

"Thanks for reassuring me," Pete said. "I wish I could grab you right now and hold you in my arms before going back in there to take more of their shit. I need you, boy, real bad. I'm hurting and it's gonna take a lot of your loving to get that hurt out of my heart."

"You've found your man," Josh said. "I'll always love you. I remember the first night I pulled off all my clothes in the bunk next to you. I wanted you to see me and want me. From that very night, I swore I would belong to you and to no one else."

"You've got me, man," Pete said crushing out the cigarette. "I want to kiss you right now but I can't. They'd probably throw us in the brig."

"Just so long as I'm there with you, mate," Josh said.

"What's this mate, shit?" Pete asked.

"All the Brits say that, and I sort of like it too. Mate. It fits me and you."

The hazy night of grilling seemed to drag into eternity, as the Navy officers sought more and more names from Pete and his boys. The Navy wanted to know the names of all the enlisted men who had indulged in homosexual acts on the upper floors. Neither Pete nor any of the others revealed one single name. The Navy's informant must not have known as much as Pete had first suspected.

Finally, at midnight, Pete and Josh, along with Maston, Guitar Red, Nipsey, Freddie, Troy, Dale, and Smokey were released. The discharged men were confined to base, except for Pete who was granted permission the following day to go to the canteen to remove musical instruments and other personal effects. The other men had to remain behind.

That afternoon in the loneliness of the canteen, Pete read the notice posted by the Navy. The center had been closed down indefinitely. It was a sad day to him. He remembered all the good times here. He was singing better than ever, and the boys were playing their hearts out to men who were going off to war, maybe never again to be entertained and maybe to die. He knew what had been going on upstairs, especially among the black sailors and the English queens brought over by Gladys. It had gone too far. Someone was bound to turn tattle-tale. Someone had.

Pete heard a car pull up out front and looked out the window, seeing

Gladys get out. He was wearing his daytime clothes, a mixture of both male and female dress.

Pete had come to genuinely like Gladys or "Lady Gregory," as he liked to be known. Pete was going to miss Gladys and all her "gals." He went to the door, opening it and ushering Gladys in.

"I'm so sorry," Gladys said, coming in and shutting the door. He hugged Pete. "If only you were staying behind with us in England. If only you could be my man."

"Sorry, old gal, but I belong to Josh," Pete said.

"I know that," Gladys said, kissing Pete on the cheek. "Josh is one lucky sailor, discharged or not. You're one lucky sailor to have him, too."

"Thanks for coming over here to say good-bye," Pete said.

"What's gonna happen to Josh?" Gladys asked. "And the boys in the band?"

"Josh's future is all taken care of," Pete said. "I'm not gonna let that discharged sailor out of my sight."

"You really love him, don't you?" Gladys asked.

"I've loved only one man more," Pete said. "His name was Tracy Adams. He lies at the bottom of the Atlantic."

"The only man I've ever loved also lies out there somewhere, probably not even in a grave. He died at Dunkirk."

"I'm sorry." Pete reached for his friend's hand and held it up to his lips where he tenderly kissed the inner palm.

Gladys lovingly ran his fingers through Pete's hair. "There is only one man in the world who could replace Dirk, and that's Pete Riddle. And he's already taken."

Gladys walked away, looking forlornly at the stage where he used to entertain the black troops. "Of course, it seems that Josh has found the pot of gold at the end of the rainbow." Gladys spun around on his wedge heels. "But you and I both know it won't be that easy for him, will it?"

"What do you mean?" Pete asked.

"You'll be there for Josh, but you're not going to give up other men. Are you?"

"You know me too well," Pete said. "You know about Troy and Dale."

"Of course, I do. You can't fool your mother here. I hope Josh doesn't find out."

"I'll try to keep it from him," Pete said. "I want to be true to just one man, and in my heart I guess I'll love only Josh, but there will be others. I've got some romantic complications waiting for me when I get back home. The one man I want to return to is my son. I told you about Buster. He's growing up without a daddy and I need to be with him."

"Guess the poor kid will have to get used to a queer daddy."

"I guess he will," Pete said. "He'll have to learn to put up with me, bad

habits and all."

Gladys walked over to Pete again, this time kissing him on the lips. "Adieu, my darling American man."

Pete ran his hand along the cheek of his new friend. It was painful to leave Gladys. There were promises they'd write.

For Pete and his buddies, the war might as well be over now, except for the final humiliation of sailing back as part of a convoy.

In the foggy dawn of a Southampton morning, Pete, Josh, and the boys were sent aboard a supply ship returning to America. The officers knew these men were being dishonorably discharged, but no one wanted to make too much fuss about that.

Since the war was raging and going badly for both Britain and America, news of such discharges were considered demoralizing for the troops who stayed behind to fight the war. Pete fully expected to be treated with utter contempt while sailing back home to America.

To his surprise, he spotted Captain Crook arriving at the pier in his Jeep driven by an enlisted man. Pete, signaling Josh he'd meet him on board, walked over to the Jeep to face the captain.

"I have to sign this document," Crook said. "To make sure you boys are all aboard and being shipped back to Norfolk. You can go aboard. I have no more business with you."

"I'm sorry, sir, about everything," Pete said. "I was the man to open those canteens in England. I feel I could have made a real contribution."

"The Navy doesn't need men like you," Crook said.

"Good-bye, sir," Pete said before turning his back to the captain and heading for the gangplank.

"Riddle," Crook called to him. "Come over here a minute."

Fearing the worse, Pete walked over to the captain. "What is it, sir?"

"That ship you're going on is one of ours," he said, "and God knows we need every tub we can get in this man's Navy. But if a Nazi submarine somewhere out there in the Atlantic has to blow up one of our ships, I pray to God it's the one hauling your queer asses back to Virginia."

\*\*\*

Winter had hit Canada, and the nights were long and cold. Somewhere in the back of a truck stop, Hank came up with the idea of driving all the way to Florida. "Man, that sunshine. I can just feel it now. The hot sun beating down on you all day long."

"We can't live off coconuts," Rosacoke said. "We gotta make some money."

"Don't worry about it." Her reminder had made him mad.

She figured she'd better worry about it. So far, she was the only one

who'd brought any money into their relationship. When she demanded to know how much of her bankroll was left, he told her, "Enough, baby, enough."

As they headed out into another one of those bleak dawns, she urged him to go back to Chicago but he bypassed it, heading toward Detroit instead. "That's where the good-paying jobs are."

"I thought you wanted to go to Florida."

"Yeah, that, too, but I've got to stop off in Detroit to take care of business."

"What kind of business?"

"Let me worry about that, okay?"

When they crossed the border into the United States, she felt more relieved. At least this was her own country, and she'd have a better chance of surviving.

In a fleabag hotel in the heart of Detroit, he found a seedy room with yellowing wallpaper that looked like urine stains. He brought her two cans of pork and beans and a can opener before disappearing for three days without one word of explanation. She never left the room during the whole time, except to venture out to the rickety hallway toilet shared by all the vagabond tenants.

She was afraid to go out into Detroit, knowing she'd get lost. If she only had money, or knew how to earn some, she'd get the next Greyhound bus heading for Chicago.

When Hank came back to their room, he didn't bother to say hi or anything. "Get your things. We're heading for Florida."

"There's a gas rationing."

"Listen, bitch, I'm the man of this family. That means I clank balls. Make the decisions. I've got the coupons we need."

"How did you manage that?"

"Would you shut up and get your fucking clothes packed? We're heading out."

With no enthusiasm whatsoever, she drove south with him from Detroit, the road seemingly endless. She hadn't realized how big the country really was. Along the way there were frequent outbursts from Hank, in spite of his promise of no more violence.

She washed in the women's rooms of filling stations. They took turns driving, sleeping in the back seat of the car.

Over a hamburger and Coke at a truck stop, she voiced alarm that they might not have enough money to make it to Florida. "Would you get off my fucking back?" he asked. "I know what I'm doing."

There were nights, only rarely, when he treated her like a human being, and she always knew those were the nights he wanted some loving. He called it "sweet-talking a gal."

She wasn't sure that she could call sex with him lovemaking. Every-

thing was for his own pleasure, and he'd quickly withdraw, turn over in bed, and go right to sleep. She didn't expect a thank-you note, but she thought there ought to be a hell of a lot more to it than that. Pete was a lot better. Not a hell of a lot better. But better. She feared young men didn't really know how to make love. Not that she did either.

There were also the violent nights when the day had gone bad, and she'd done something to upset him. Often it was just a simple thing when she begged him to stay somewhere for one night so she could take a real bath in a tub. "I've taken so many whore's baths I'm beginning to feel like one."

For that one, he slapped her face. When morning came, he always asked her to forgive him, and she did. But as the days rolled by, forgiving became harder and harder for her.

One night in the back of a truck stop, he attacked her, knocking her down on the oil-streaked gravel. She jumped up and ran toward a house out back. He chased after her, tackling her. She fell down, skinning her knee. She just lay there crying, totally defeated, almost not caring if any more blows rained down.

She found him kissing her neck instead. "I can't help myself, baby," he said. "You've got to understand. I've had these outbursts since I was a kid. Something comes over me. I want to strike back at life. I hit those I love."

"It's okay." She reached around to caress him, running her fingers through his hair, and that made her feel like a real whore. He took her right on the cold ground, and she endured it, moaning softly, whispering to him how good it felt. Actually each stab cut into her like a wound.

Instead of Chicago, she'd work in Miami. She bet it would be easy getting a job there as a waitress. After all, she'd had experience waiting tables. Maybe one day she could be a singer again. Some day. For all she knew right now, her career was over.

He finally reached northern Louisiana, and her hopes soared a bit. She wasn't sure but she thought Louisiana was somewhere near the Florida border. A few more nights, and she'd be in the Sunshine State. To her Florida sounded like the promised land.

\*\*\*

On the long and dangerous voyage across the Atlantic from Southampton back to Norfolk to face dishonorable discharge from the Navy, Pete had to think of something to keep him from going out of his mind. Josh offered him all the comfort he could. He wanted Pete sexually but all the men were closely watched, and Pete felt none of them needed any more trouble.

To forget his humiliation, Pete dreamed of going back to the hills to see his son, his mama, and his new mansion tended to by Tara. Sometimes he thought of Rosacoke but not often. He spent more time thinking about that sexy Hank Adams, wondering where he was. Hank had stopped writing, and Pete feared he was in some kind of trouble. If he could locate Hank again, Pete was determined to put him on a leash. That handsome stud couldn't be trusted out on his own.

Pete's most faithful letter writer was John-John. When Pete returned to Heaven on Earth, he knew that John-John would want to spend his nights with Pete. But, in fairness, Pete had to let Josh sleep with him. Pete saw trouble right away, and he didn't know how to resolve this romantic triangle. Claude, Junior, and Ronnie, if they still wanted Pete, would be just fine, as he knew that trio actively pursued gals most of the time. Karl Adams was the one brother Pete never thought much about. Since joining the Navy, Pete had received only two letters from Karl. Pete thought that potential relationship had died even before it got off the ground.

Every day Pete thought lovingly of Tracy, especially when his ship passed a point in the mid-Atlantic where Pete figured Tracy's convoy was fatally attacked. Pete stood out on the deck and wept bitter, lonesome tears for his departed comrade. Of all the men he'd known so far in his short life, Pete felt that Tracy had been the one. If Tracy had lived, Pete knew that Tracy, not Josh, would be his real mate. He'd found a chemistry with Tracy that he'd found in no other man. God had taken Tracy away from him, and sometimes Pete just didn't understand God. If he ever came face to face with God, Pete had a bone to pick with that one.

After a dinner of canned pork and beans, Pete met with Freddie, Nipsey, Maston Mastin, Smokey Wetter, and Guitar Red. He was going to invite all of them to come and live at his compound at Heaven on Earth. If he didn't have enough room for everybody right away, Pete figured he could build more houses. He certainly had the money, although he feared wartime shortages would make it difficult to get building supplies.

As the men drank bottled orange pop instead of their usual beer, Pete spoke of his civilian dreams with his boys. All the black men were talented musicians. The only white one, Freddie Raubal, was a brilliant organizer. Freddie would fit in just fine with his scheme, especially since he still wanted to live with Nipsey after their return to America. Those two beauties—one an ebony color, the other a blond—were truly in love. Pete figured opposite colors do attract. Freddie told Pete that Nipsey was the love of his life, and Nipsey called Freddie "My blond Nordic God."

As the men sat around in cramped quarters, Pete told them that after a week or two of rest back on his estate, he wanted all of them to join with him in forming a band with a new sound. "I want to bring white music together with black music, and I don't know how just yet. But I bet we can

learn. I own this beautiful barn. I'm gonna get it insulated. We'll work out there. Before we go on the road, we'll be the best band there is. And I ain't talking Glenn Miller either."

The idea excited each man. No one had any prospects waiting for them back in America, and all seemed eager to sign up with Pete.

Nipsey shared with the men some of the lyrics of three songs he was working on for Pete, which he hoped that Pete would one day record. "Six Pack of Trouble" was Pete's favorite in Nipsey's repertoire.

"I'm not like my black brothers here," Nipsey said. "I mean it was a bit odd for my black family to listen to Opry, Hank Williams, Minnie Pearl, Roy Acuff, and the like. But we did every weekend when I was a kid. Country music is rooted deep in my heart. Take away my songs and I would die."

As Nipsey talked, Pete wished that Josh could be here with them. But he felt seasick as they were sleeping deep in the bowels of the ship, the captain having assigned them Spartan quarters usually reserved for black sailors.

Dale and Troy weren't interested in joining the band. Pete had promised to help them get to Hollywood where the twins wanted to try out as dancers for MGM musicals.

"This country stuff is not for us," Troy said. "We want to be dancing around Judy Garland."

At his "orange pop summit," Pete was asking for a commitment from each man and was getting it.

"Count me in, man," the pudgy Texan, Smokey Wetter, told Pete. "I think I've got some vague idea running through my head about what sound you're after, and my banjo will be right there backing you."

"You're a hot musician," Pete said. "You know how to make the banjo talk and people listen."

"I believe in plucking the strings instead of strumming them," Smokey said. "I've been playing that banjo ever since I was four years old. As a little black Sambo, I'd sit with my daddy's banjo and pick for hours and hours. Time didn't have no meaning. Instead of the usual two fingers, I believe in playing with three fingers—my index, middle finger, and thumb."

"It sure makes for a different sound," Maston said, "and I know a lot about banjo picking myself."

"I want our music to be the music of the people," Pete said, his eyes lighting up at the prospect. "Let's sing to the poor working class stiffs, the factory workers, and the truck drivers. Even the outcast and those in prison. I want to write for oppressed America, not just the beaten black folks but down-trodden white folks too."

"I used to think all white folks was rich," Nipsey said, "but there's a lot of poor white trash out there too."

Guitar Red finally spoke up. "I especially liked the part you said about

singing for those in prison. If there's a lonesome person on God's earth, it's a guy in prison. I should know. Me and three other guys were getting drunk one night and talking big. We couldn't get work playing in an outhouse. We decided to rob this honky-tonk café. We were so damn drunk we didn't know what we were doing. We got arrested and sent up. I entertained my fellow convicts with my guitar when they let me play in the warden's band."

"You told us a lot about that fancy estate of yours," Smokey said, "and I'm really looking forward to living there with you guys. I was born in a converted boxcar and ain't had many fancy places to live. Ain't had no fancy places to live, in fact."

"You've found your home," Pete said, wondering what Tara would think of the sudden invasion of Heaven on Earth. Knowing Tara, she'd be ready and willing to receive each and every one of the men with her generous heart and spirit.

"Until I met you guys," Freddie said, "I didn't know a damn thing about country music. Wagner, I know."

"He didn't know a lot about a lot of things," Nipsey said, chucking Freddie under the chin. "I taught him." Nipsey smiled at Freddie. "A fast learner."

"And how!" Freddie said. "You won't believe this, but the Hitler Youth I was with left out a few lessons in life. Nipsey is helping me catch up and fast."

"It'll take some getting used to our sound but I know you'll learn how to look after our band," Pete predicted. "Hitler's loss. Our gain."

Later that night when "lights out" was called, Pete huddled close with Josh who was still feeling sick at his stomach.

"How's it going, sweet man of mine?" Pete whispered in his ear.

"I'm afraid about going back to the Carolinas with you," Josh said.

"Hell, man, I thought you were looking forward to it."

"As long as I had you with me in the Navy, I felt I could hold onto you," Josh said, reaching for Pete's hand. "But back at your home, a lot of temptation will be thrown at you. What if some of the guys from your past want to get it on with you again?"

"Not likely," Pete said. "Most of them like pussy and have forgotten all about me. Besides, that thing I had with them was just fooling around in the hayloft. That's before I met the real thing."

"Do you mean that?" Josh asked, looking deeply into Pete's eyes.

"Like I never meant anything in my life," Pete said.

"I hear you and I want to believe you," Josh said. "I'm still afraid, though. If I ever lose you, I'd die. You mean that much to me."

"C'mon now," Pete said, flashing his smile which always seemed to win Josh over to his side. "No one's gonna go losing anybody. We might have lost each other if the Navy had kept us on. But they sure don't want

our kind."

"Guess they'll have to win the war without us," Josh said.

A bitterness about his discharge was reflected on Pete's face. "Don't see how they can, but I wish them luck." He tenderly reached for Josh's arm. "Let's get some shut-eye. I'm counting the hours until we're off this tub."

***

After two and a half hours of riding in Louisiana, Hank slammed on the brake. In her search of his face, she saw only grimness. The early evening was gray, dark, and chilly, and she sat swathed in a smelly blanket, as there was no heat.

"We're about out of gas, and that plate of gumbo we shared a little while back took the rest of our loot," he said.

She felt a sense of panic. Things hadn't worked out at all the way she'd planned. She wanted to be in Miami where she had a fighting chance—not stranded out here in some wilderness with no money and no hope of getting any.

"'Member that little gas station we passed about two miles back?" he asked, a determination coming over his face.

"Forget it! You're a fool to try to break in there. I bet there's not a red cent there, and you'd end up getting caught even if there was." Before she could go on, he took the back of his hand, slapping her face, knocking her against the right window. Her nose ached as if it had been broken.

"Now cut the lip!" Turning the car around, brakes squealing, he headed back up the road.

Her mind confused, her head aching from the blow, she felt that she'd lost control of her life. In the pitch-black night, she didn't know what to do. "Count me out of any robbery."

"Listen, bitch, you'll either go along with it or I'll let you out on the road. I'm tired of taking care of you. 'Bout time you started fending for yourself."

The prospect of being turned out into the night terrified her even more than the upcoming break-in. Without saying another word, she sat stiff-backed, feeling as if she were rolling along to some horrible fate beyond her control.

He parked around the corner from the gas station near a field of scrawny pines. "You sit in the car," he ordered. "This will be as easy as taking candy from a baby."

She didn't share his optimism. Shivering, she stayed glued to her seat, knowing she was about to begin one of the longest vigils of her life. Seconds felt like hours. She'd never done anything like this before. Tears

bubbled over and ran down her face, and she'd never felt so cheap. She bitterly resented the circumstances that had placed her in such a position. What would Pete think of her if he could look in on this? Thoughts of her baby flashed through her mind, and she tried to blot them out.

Suddenly, the rear-view mirror framed the approach of a Louisiana highway patrol car. Hysterical, she threw open the door to the car and rushed to the gas station, screaming Hank's name. If she reached him in time, he might never commit the robbery and get arrested. He'd already told her that if a car "or anything" passed by, she was to act natural. In her anxiety she'd forgotten that command, and, when it was too late she realized her impulsive action had signaled the attention of the highway patrol.

The sound of a siren split through the night. Her sobs blinded her as she fled into a nearby meadow, stumbling into the darkness.

Before he'd spotted the patrol car, Hank had already broken the glass at the door to the station. Seeing her split, he chased after her, running into the field, as a spot was turned on them.

Catching up with her and gasping for breath, he grabbed her and shook her. "How stupid can you get?"

She fell back into a ditch, as his booted foot kicked her shins.

It happened so fast she wasn't sure what took place next. Tears of fright blinded her, and her leg hurt something awful. She'd also fallen on rocks, which had cut into her breasts.

Strong hands reached for her, the fingers digging into her flesh. She walked and was pushed toward the waiting patrol car. Handcuffed, she was shoved into the back seat of the car along with Hank. She couldn't stand to look into his face.

The three-mile ride to the nearest station was like one of those long, seemingly endless trips everybody takes once or twice in a lifetime. Cringing with embarrassment, she wanted to sneak off and hide somewhere. Wild animals had the right idea.

The dilapidated old station house smelled of stale cigarette butts and cat piss. Even though she'd only recently eaten some gumbo, her stomach felt totally empty, as if all the food had been miraculously cleaned out of it. Only a dangerous, bubbling acid seemed to be fermenting there. Her stomach knew how serious her trouble really was.

Booked and finger-printed, she was scared. She heard the sound of loud voices around her, but was so terrified she couldn't make out their meaning. All the voices sounded alike to her, threatening, menacing. Cruel words with equally cruel voices.

Beads of sweat formed at her hairline and temples. What were these men going to do to her? She'd warned Hank that he'd make a terrible mistake if he robbed that gas station, but by sitting in his car—probably stolen—and running after him, she knew she was deep in the whole mess

herself.

After about an hour of sitting outside and watching the patrolmen as they meticulously searched her suitcase, she was taken to a tiny jail block out back, which was separated from the main building. She feared that the echoing clang of the closing of that door would haunt her for the rest of her life.

"How long have I got to stay here?" she asked the guard.

"Shut up, you God damn whore!"

Like a little child, she crouched in that cell all night, the longest she'd ever remembered spending anywhere. An exposed electric light bulb in the corridor illuminated the narrow little bandbox, with its sagging cot of broken springs. Stacked to one side was a smelly blanket and a yellowing pillow, both of which she suspected were infested with vermin. On the far side of the bed was a leaky toilet without a seat and a zinc sink with a drippy faucet, whose endless and monotonous sound was like some form of water torture.

She didn't feel like a criminal, but guessed she was after all. Why else was she locked up? Good girls didn't get thrown in the slammer.

Sleep was out of the question. She lay here, trying to figure things out, what had gone wrong. She'd seen a heap of trouble in her life, but nothing like this before.

Someone had pasted an old calendar in her cellblock. Having nothing else to do, she studied the dates. Without realizing it until now, she found out last night was her eighteenth birthday. What a way to celebrate it!

About two hours later the guard came back, bringing with him a frail, gray-haired woman in a dress with a high-button collar in the style worn at the turn of the century and locking her in a nearby cell. In some way she reminded Rosacoke of what Mrs. Riddle's mother looked like, to judge from the fading, yellow photograph Pete's mama always kept in the living room gathering dust.

"You've got to spend the night here, Mrs. Roosevelt," the guard said. "In the morning the President will send a limousine for you to drive you back to the White House."

"When Franklin hears about this outrage, he'll have you fired," the old woman said. "If you don't know now, you'll learn the meaning of the expression, 'the long arm of the President.'"

Rosacoke shivered, realizing at once that the woman had clean lost her mind. She thought she was Eleanor Roosevelt.

Throughout the long night, Rosacoke heard the pathetic old woman mumbling. It appeared that she felt she was entertaining distinguished guests, everybody from the King and Queen of England to Clark Gable.

Right before dawn, Rosacoke started to pray. She hadn't prayed much lately, but she figured that if ever there was a good time for prayer it was

now. She did more than pray: She begged God to save her, promising in return that she'd never get mixed up in such a mess ever again. Her prayer came from deep within her gut.

"Lord, I need a second chance. Grant me that."

At dawn two men from the state mental hospital came for "Mrs. Roosevelt." She paused at Rosacoke's cell, peering in. "Don't worry," she said in a kind, gentle voice. "When I tell Franklin about the conditions of this jail, he'll have it closed down. I'll see to it that you're granted a presidential pardon. I don't care what you did."

"Thank you kindly," Rosacoke said, her face flushed.

A new guard brought grits with red-eye gravy, some stale bread, and bitter black coffee.

An hour later two guards came for her, and because she'd prayed so hard and hadn't done wrong before, she felt that she'd be forgiven without punishment for this one mistake.

***

In the corridor Rosacoke met an old lawyer with tobacco-stained teeth. Hard of hearing, he introduced himself as Sebastian C. Crabtree. "The C is for Calhoun," he told her. "Your boy friend retained me to represent him, and I thought I should look after your interests, too."

"Thanks a lot, Mr. Crabtree," she said, "but I ain't got a penny."

"Sweet child, I'm the only man you'll ever meet who became a lawyer to help people, not to make money."

She almost burst into tears, remembering that Pete had once claimed that as his ambition.

Hank joined her in the corridor, and, after a huddled conference with Crabtree, he came over to her, his eyes filled with remorse. "I should have listened to you. Too late for that now. Crabtree says we'll both get off on probation. First offense and all that shit."

"Good luck," she whispered to him before a guard broke them up. Handcuffed, they were walked to the courthouse down the main street. She avoided looking into the eyes of passers-by, but obviously she and Hank were the center attraction in the little town.

As she was seated next to Hank in the courtroom, he leaned over. "I'll tell the judge it was all my fault. That you begged me not to do it. That I threatened you if you didn't go through with it."

"You shouldn't go all that far," she said, pleased that he wasn't being mean any more. If his badness came in streaks, so did his goodness.

The courtroom, including a number of idle curiosity seekers with nothing to do that day, rose as the judge entered. Jehosat Ball was a bit stocky, with graying hair and a ruddy face with lots of crinkles, in particular crow's-

feet. His eyes were slightly popped, and he looked as if he'd spent a lifetime glaring down into the faces of the children of Satan.

Nothing seemed to go right that day. In spite of his promise, Hank didn't have a word to say. After the charges were aired, the prosecution making a particularly damaging case against Crabtree's weak defense, the judge gave his opinion. He spoke slowly and deliberately, as if enjoying holding the audience in suspense.

"I know the good man who runs that filling station. Randy O'Neal, one of the finest boys you'll ever meet up with. Works twelve hours a day trying to support his family. Eight kids. Breaking and entering we call a felony. If the parties were local citizens, I might could set bail. *If* they could raise it. Seeing that they're from up north, I order them confined to the local jailhouse for fifty-three days and nights until their case can come up for trial."

It was as if a great big hand had reached out and grabbed her heart, squeezing it hard. She was so light-headed she stumbled, as she was taken from the courtroom and walked back to the city jail. Once there, the crossbars and steel rods of her cell—her new home—slammed shut.

The guard seemed to enjoy locking her up. Filled with mockery, he had a sneer on his face. "Ole Jehosat's known in these parts as a hanging judge. Normally you might have got off, but the prison where he'll send you, Mozambique, is short on workers. He's got to fill a quota." The guard grabbed himself obscenely. "I know you've been used to getting it regular from your boy friend and all. When you can't stand going without no more, I'll take care of you."

"Get the hell out of here!" Rosacoke shouted at him.

"Okay, you don't know what you're missing. Down there at Mozambique they'll shave all that pretty blonde hair of yours. What a shame! And when that pack of Mozambique bull-dykes get a load of your big tits, a gang-rape is about the brightest thing in your future."

Desolate, alone, filled with despair, she sat on the cot, conjuring up all the future horrors that would descend on her, including many she'd never heard of before. How could a gang of women rape her? Some things just weren't possible—said only to scare her.

There was nothing to do but wait, and it would be a long one.

***

On the overcrowded wartime train taking them back to the Carolina hills, Pete lay in a cramped berth in Josh's arms. They were free at last, having been officially discharged from the Navy once they'd left the "captain's mast" in Norfolk.

"The Navy pins medals on you for killing a man, but kicks you out on

your ass if you make love to one," Pete said, "You figure it out."

"It's a crazy world out there," Josh said, whispering in his ear. Even though he was a free man, he still seemed afraid, as if someone were spying on Pete and him. "I'm with the man I love. His warm cum is still in my belly. I'm free to love my man and take care of him. What more can I ask?"

"We're gonna go back to the good life," Pete promised, huddling closer to Josh and smelling his sweet breath. As he kissed the young man, Pete could still smell the tantalizing aroma of himself as he tasted Josh's lips and tongue. "I love you, sweet man of mine." He ran his hands up and down Josh's smooth back, cupping his succulent ass cheeks. "I hope this pretty little thing is prepared to take a lot of pounding."

"It is, but only from you, baby," Josh said, gently nibbling on Pete's ear.

Even as he held Josh close to him, Pete's mind wandered to Tracy. He belonged on this train with them, but he was dead. Pete wanted to keep Tracy's memory alive, even if it prevented him from truly giving himself to another man.

Later, after Pete and Josh had dressed, they joined Freddie for a drink in the club bar. "I miss Nipsey," Freddie said. "Over in Europe we hear America is a free country. But I can't ride in the same compartment with Nipsey, my lover. He's back there with the boys."

"It won't always be that way," Pete said. "I think the war will break down a lot of barriers. That goes for the color line. Black people won't always be treated second class the way they are now. You mark my words."

"What about homosexuals?" Josh asked in a discreet whisper so as not to be overheard.

"I don't think the world will ever be able to accept them," Pete said. "Not in our lifetime. Perhaps some time in the middle of the 21st century. Not before."

"Why do we frighten people so?" Freddie asked. "Jews, homosexuals, and gypsies, Hitler's three least favorite people."

"Fuck all that," Pete said. "When I get back to Heaven on Earth, we'll have our own compound. I've got a big house there. Plenty of room for everybody. There are three other smaller houses on the grounds, and lots and lots of land. If I need more houses, I'll build them. If I need more land, I'll buy it. I want my family with me. We'll have no back-of-the-bus shit at my house." He turned to Josh. "Freddie here can hold Nipsey's hand, or hold anything of Nipsey's and live together in sin at my place. At Heaven on Earth, love will not be restricted. On the other hand, hatred will be definitely off-limits."

"I can't wait to get there," Josh said. "You've told me so much about it."

"I just hope I won't be bitten by a rattlesnake," Freddie said.

"We're wild, but not that wild," Pete said. "Of course, a poisonous snake does get inside a house every now and then, but not that often."

Over their second drink, Freddie grew more confidential. "Growing up, I knew I was attracted to other men, But I thought I liked blonds. I swear I never fantasized about getting seduced by a black man. I never thought anything like that. But the moment I laid eyes on Nipsey, I felt I not only wanted him, but had to have him. I think I fell in love with him when he was kissing me and both of us were getting blow-jobs from Lady Gregory."

"What a perfect way to fall in love," Pete said. "I miss old Gladys. I'm gonna write him a letter before I get off the train. When I get back home, I won't have time."

"What's the first thing you're gonna do when you get back there?" Josh said.

"Rush to see my son," Pete said. "What else? Imagine having a son and not knowing how he looks, how he smells, or how he feels when you lift him up in to the air."

"You got that one picture," Josh said.

"Tara writes me that he's changed a lot since that was taken," Pete said. "Claims I wouldn't recognize him. I bet she's wrong. I bet I could walk into a kindergarten with a hundred different boys and go right to Buster. I just know it."

"You've never told me who his mother was?" Freddie said.

"A good and decent gal named Rosacoke Carson," Pete said. "She deserved a lot better man than I could ever be. If I'd asked her, I know she would have married me. But it didn't seem right somehow. I can never give myself over to a woman's love, at least not completely. I knew in my heart I'd never really be there for her. When I feel the chest of another human being, I want it to be the rock-hard chest of Josh here. Not the softness of a woman. I can perform with a woman, and I have in the past, but my heart wasn't in it. I wasn't thinking of the woman under me but of someone else." At that pronouncement, Pete got up from the table on the moving train and went over to the bartender, an old man from Virginia. He whispered something to the bartender and slipped him a bill, then returned to join Josh and Freddie.

"What was that all about?" Freddie asked.

"I slipped him twenty bucks to take two bottles of rye whiskey to my good buddies in the back—namely Nipsey, Smokey, Guitar Red, and Maston."

"Thank you for doing that," Freddie said. "We'll be reunited soon."

Pete was feeling wild and impulsive that night on the train as it roared out of Virginia and into North Carolina heading west. The train was filled with defense plant workers returning from Norfolk for a brief vacation at their homesteads in Appalachia and with servicemen home on leave.

"Get my guitar from the back," Pete told Josh who willingly obeyed. Freed from the rigid control of the military, Pete felt like a new man in charge of his own life. He was still a teenager, but when he got to Heaven on Earth he knew he'd be the boss man. Everybody would depend on him for their livelihood, and he'd be giving the orders, although he would run things in a kind and loving way. He knew Claude would be there at the station to pick him up, probably in a squad car.

Pete could handle everything except John-John. The boy wanted exclusive rights to Pete, and he couldn't grant him that. He wanted to confine that thing he had with John-John to what they did as kids. Pete needed the kind of loving Josh could provide. Almost overnight Josh had transformed himself from a boy into a young man. Pete desperately wanted and needed that more mature kind of love, not the total adoration of some kid.

Pete vowed he'd be loving and kind to John-John and would help launch him into life.

Pete knew from John-John's letters that he was growing more and more possessive of Pete in his dreams, and he didn't want to disappoint the boy, yet knew he must. If anything, Pete wanted to be more like a daddy to John-John than his male lover. Even as he thought that, he knew that would be a hard-sell with John-John. The boy desired Pete's body and wanted Pete to make love to him. Pete wanted to turn to Tara for her help. She seemed like everybody's earth mama. Surely Tara, who had faced about everything in life, would know how to handle a complicated triangle like he had with Josh and John-John, the two "Js" in his life. Or was that three Js?

Brushing aside those thoughts, Pete thanked Josh for fetching his guitar. With permission from the conductor, Pete sat in the corner of the bar and began picking and playing. If he wanted to be a country singer, he'd better seize every moment. In this compartment filled with lonesome strangers on a moving train, he knew all the numbers to play. "Carolina Moon." "You Are My Sunshine." All the crowd pleasers. The men and women on the train gathered around Pete. "Who knows?" he thought. These same passengers might one day be buying his records.

It was in the early dawn hours that the train pulled into the station in Pete's hometown. He found his heart beating faster, as he held onto Josh's hand looking out into the dense fog.

The first thing he spotted was the flashing dome light of Claude's squad car. The sheriff had gotten out of bed early that morning and had driven down to meet them. There were two other cars parked behind the sheriff's vehicle, and Pete wondered what passengers were inside?

Pete was the first one off the train. He practically leaped off onto the platform while the train was still moving. Claude was the first one to catch up with Pete. Claude stood tall, lanky, and as handsome as ever. He seemed so glad to see Pete that he practically lifted him into the air as the sheriff

gave him a big bear-hug.

From the squad car emerged John-John screaming Pete's name. The boy ran up to him with tears of joy. "You're home," John-John said. He wrapped his arms around Pete. As Pete embraced the boy, he noticed a look of concern on Josh's face.

But Pete wiped that from his mind as he saw Tara getting out of his Rolls-Royce and walking toward Pete. He reached for Claude's hand and gave John-John another hug and a quick kiss on the lips.

Instead of running toward Tara, he walked slowly toward her, seeing the tears running down her cheeks. "Welcome home, hoss." She held out an offering to him, bundled in a blue blanket.

"This here is Buster Riddle," she said, looking first at Pete and then down at the baby in the blanket. "Meet your son, the prettiest baby ever born in the Carolina mountains. He's gonna grow up and break a lot of hearts in his day."

***

For Pete, his homecoming had been a long night. He missed all his boys, and wanted to be reunited with Hank, Karl, Junior, and Ronnie, but they were away at war. At least Karl, Junior, and Ronnie were. He didn't know what had happened to Hank, who had stopped writing.

Both Rosacoke and Narcissa had also disappeared. Claude was still here and still the sheriff. He was filled with stories of what had happened in town since Pete had gone away.

Upon reaching his homestead, Pete had called his mama but she said she wasn't feeling well, and had asked him to delay his visit with her until in the morning. He was saddened when she'd told him, "And don't bring your bastard, son," before putting down the phone.

In one of the upper rooms Claude was left alone with Pete for a few minutes. The sheriff pulled Pete close and gave him a long, lingering kiss with tongue. "I've missed you," Claude said. "Every day of my life I think about you. Needing you and wanting you."

"I thought you would have forgotten all about me," Pete said. "You must have some steady gal by now."

"Nothing steady, but I run around with some women," Claude said. "As much as I carry on with you, I'm still a woman's man."

"And you always will be," Pete predicted.

Claude pulled him close again, taking him in his arms and kissing him. "The gals in my life come and go, but ole Claude will always be there for you. I want you to know that."

When Pete broke away for the second time, he wasn't sure about his feelings for Claude. The sheriff seemed to want to keep everything the

same between them, as if the war hadn't really changed things. "You don't mind my having Josh?" Pete asked.

"I'm glad you got a steady, though how you plan to deal with John-John is another matter," Claude said. "With us, it's just a casual thing for fun. With John-John, you're his life. Did you notice him looking at Josh most of the night? Saying nothing. Just staring grimly?"

"Everybody noticed that," Pete said. "I've got to talk real private like with John-John. He's got to be made to understand that I'm a man now and he's just a kid. The games are over."

"You're making John-John out to be a play toy you had as a boy," Claude said. "Something to toss aside now that you're grown up."

"From what you know of things, don't you think there's just a little bit of truth in that?" Pete asked.

"More than a little bit of truth," Claude said. "But you've got to go easy on the boy. He's held his breath all the time you were in England waiting for you to come back. I fear this long-dreamed-about homecoming is a bitter pill for him to swallow."

"Maybe we can work it out," Pete said. "But Josh—not John-John—goes into my bed tonight."

"I'll keep the thing I have between us real private like," Claude said. "But I want it to go on  whenever we're off somewhere together."

"I'm sure we'll have many chances," Pete said. "You've still got the prettiest dick I've ever seen."

"No one ever appreciated it more than you," Claude said, kissing him tenderly on the mouth.

There was a knock on the door. Pete called out for whoever it was to come in. It was Tara. "I'm putting Buster to bed," she said. "Please come and kiss him good night. Let him know daddy's home."

"C'mon, Claude," Pete said, walking toward Tara and giving her a kiss on the cheek.

It was getting late when Pete asked Tara to show each of the men a bedroom for the night. More permanent living arrangements would be decided tomorrow when Pete figured out where to house all his band so that each man would have complete privacy to lead a life of his own. Earlier Pete had whispered to Tara to show Josh into the master bedroom where he was to unpack his things.

After kissing his son, Pete headed down the steps with Tara. All the men, including Maston and Smokey, had been put to bed, each having been given a private room upstairs. After thanking Tara for raising Buster while he was gone, Pete kissed her on the cheek again.

"See you at breakfast, hoss," she said. "I've got a million stories to tell you about what Buster did while you were gone."

"We'll catch up over some good bourbon," he promised her.

"Claude wants to see you in the kitchen," she whispered before heading for her room in the rear wing next to Buster's. John-John is also waiting for you in the living room. All the other guys are upstairs."

In the kitchen Claude was sitting at the wooden table drinking some bourbon. "I had planned to be with you on your first night back," Claude said, "although John-John might have had something to say about that. Seeing that you are taken care of, I accepted another offer and I hope you don't get pissed."

"Who with?" Pete asked. "Surely you're not going to join Freddie and Nipsey. Those love-birds don't do three-ways."

"I got an offer from Dale and Troy," the sheriff said. "One that I couldn't turn down. Those are two hot pieces of ass. You must have had more fun in Southampton than I knew."

"Go to it, man," Pete urged. "You're in for a treat. I mean, *they're good.*"

"I knew you'd see it that way," Claude said, getting up to hold Pete in his arms, and giving him a passionate good night kiss with a lot of tongue sucking the way both men liked to kiss.

"If those twins leave anything left over for me," Pete said, "me and you will slip off tomorrow some time."

"You got yourself a deal." Claude kissed him another good night before heading upstairs to the bed shared by Troy and Dale.

Alone at last with John-John, Pete sat across from him in front of the black marble fireplace in the library. "Welcome home," John-John said, staring intently at him. "It's a day I've been waiting for, but things didn't work out the way I planned them in my dreams. Your friend, Josh, is very handsome."

"Let me explain," Pete said. "I never wanted to hurt you."

"I think I would have liked you to take a butcher knife to stab me in the heart," the boy said. "That would have at least shown me more mercy."

"Let's don't get too carried away here," Pete said. "Even though the Navy discharged me—dishonorably at that—it helped make me a man. I'm not a boy any more. When I was in bed with you, we were just boys. Let's face it: All the boys in the county do shit like we did."

"Shit?" John-John practically rose up in his chair in fury. "My love for you is shit?"

"I didn't mean it that way," Pete said, trying to calm him down. "What I meant, we were just horsing around."

"You might have been horsing around," John-John said. "I sure wasn't. I was falling in love with you, and I love you more every day of my life."

"That's bullshit!" Pete said. "You're just fifteen. You are fifteen, aren't you? Something like that. You'll grow up to have other boy friends if that's what you want. For all I know when you turn sixteen you'll find some

pretty little gal that catches your eye."

"Fuck that!" An anger unlike any Pete had ever seen before flashed across John-John's face. "Can you picture me with a gal? I can't stand them. I don't want another boy friend. I want Pete Riddle. I will never want no man for the rest of my life but Pete Riddle. Don't you understand that? Who's being the fool here?"

"God damn it." Pete was angry too. He got up and went to the bar at the far corner of the room and poured himself some Tennessee whiskey. His talk with John-John wasn't going the way he had wanted it to. He downed a hefty swig of the liquor before turning to face John-John, who sat rigidly in the chair as if ready to pounce up at any moment. Even though mad at him, Pete couldn't help but be enthralled with John-John's beauty. He'd filled out, lost some of the gangly quality of an adolescent boy, and was turning into a dazzling specimen of a young man. In a year or maybe two, Pete sensed that John-John would be a catch for somebody, even though Pete knew that the love object couldn't be him.

"I won't be the first enlisted man—Marine, Air Force pilot, sailor, or soldier—who went to war, left some sweetie behind, and hooked up with someone else while overseas," Pete said, "and I won't be the last. This God damn war is uprooting people, changing their lives. Yes, and changing their lovers too. Wars do that."

"What are you trying to tell me?" John-John asked, getting up and walking with a certain manly pride toward Pete. John-John stood only two feet from Pete, staring him intently in the eye, as if defying him to say the inevitable words that hadn't yet been spoken.

"Do I have to spell it out?" Pete asked. "Is that what you want?"

"You got that right."

"Okay, have it your way," Pete said. "I'm not only with Josh now, I'm in love with him. He's my mate. I still love you. I want you to go on living here. I want to send you off to school. I want you to work with me and be a part of my family. But I'm not going to be your man—and that's that."

"You finally said it," John-John said. "I didn't think you'd put it so strong like. But you did." He turned his back to Pete and headed for the main door that led from the library into the foyer.

"Where are you going?" Pete called to him, as a sudden undefined alarm spread through Pete. John-John wasn't going to do something drastic, was he? Like stab Josh?

At the doorway John-John turned and looked back at Pete. It was a melancholy look, like he was saying good-bye. Pete suspected that he might be planning to pack his clothes and head off into the night.

"I'm not exactly sure where I'm going," John-John said in a barely audible voice. "Some place." He turned and left the parlor. Pete finished his drink, but felt the issue with John-John was hardly resolved.

This was Pete's homecoming night, and instead of the joyous occasion he had planned, it was a time of pain. Even so, he was glad to be back home. Everything seemed right with his world except John-John. The boy cared too much, the way Pete felt about the dead Tracy, and Pete could easily understand loving someone as much as John-John loved him.

Pete slammed down his empty glass and headed upstairs to the master bedroom with Josh. Pete at first thought he should knock on John-John's door, but decided another confrontation with his young buddy wouldn't be good.

At three o'clock that morning, a loud rap sounded as Pete lay in Josh's arms. Tara was calling out for him. Jumping up stark naked, Pete headed for the door, thinking in panic that something had gone wrong with Buster in the middle of the night.

Pete threw open the door, not bothering to cover his nudity. "It's John-John," Tara said, her face in anguish. "He tried to kill himself. Claude rushed him to the hospital."

***

During Rosacoke's confinement, the guards wouldn't give her anything to read. She thought she'd die of boredom until she decided to get to know herself better. She tried to relive every experience she could remember since childhood, and when she'd run through all those memories, she began to plot her future. She'd get a better education, resume her singing, and mainly restore her pride.

Being caged like some animal in a zoo was a time of major humiliation and sadness for her, but it also gave her a strong and fierce resolve. She knew that there was no one in the world to help her but herself, and no longer would she depend on anybody. If she made mistakes, they would be her own errors, and she'd know exactly what she was letting herself in for. Never again would she go along with a man just for the ride. Regardless of her age, she knew in her heart she wasn't a girl any more—but a woman.

On her second week locked in the cell, she came down with a virulent case of dysentery, which left her immobilized. Unable to move, she lay on her cot for days, getting up only to crawl over to the stinking toilet bowl. She begged the guards not to stick that awful plate of grits and red eye into her cell, as the very idea of food made her vomit.

On the fifth day she had recovered a bit and was able to drink some foul-tasting broth. She knew if she didn't swallow it, she'd die. She forced down whatever the guard gave her, hoping there was some nourishment in it.

Since she wasn't provided with a change of clothing, she tried as best she could to keep herself clean. She washed herself daily, cringing as she

did, in the cold water coming from the faucet in the old zinc sink. She'd discard one garment at a time and wash it, although it took far too long to dry in the cold, damp air.

Time spent in the city jail seemed endless, but eventually it, too, was over. On the way to the courthouse walking behind Hank, she caught the first glimpse of herself in weeks in a storefront mirror. She looked a fright. Her long blonde hair was straggly, her eyes bloodshot, and she'd lost fifteen pounds. Her breasts were no longer as full and prominent as they were. Her clothes were mussed, looking as if she'd slept in them for more than fifty days which she had.

Mentally groggy and visibly nervous, she was marched into the courtroom, where her attorney, Sebastian C. Crabtree, waited for her.

Surprisingly, she learned that charges against Hank had been dismissed. Crabtree had worked out a plea-bargaining arrangement, whereby Hank was allowed to go free, providing he would accept immediate induction into the army. In his slow southern drawl, the sanctimonious Judge Ball had said, "A life in the military will put you back on the straight and narrow path."

She was petrified after the arresting officers' testimony and Crabtree's meager defense. She nearly cried at the indignity of having to face punishment for a crime she didn't commit and that wasn't her idea.

She was taken before the judge for sentencing. His stern face looked down at her, obviously not liking what he saw. Crabtree had told her the judge had kept referring to Hank and her as Yankees—presumably because they'd lived in Chicago—although they were just as southern as he was.

"Young lady, I feel you need to be taught a lesson," the judge scolded her. "I'm gonna teach you one. One day you'll thank me for what I'm doing. Just as the army will make a good man out of your traveling companion, we have no suitable institution for you. With one exception. I'm sentencing you to serve one year and one day in the state penitentiary, Mozambique."

Shocked and stunned by the severity of the sentence, she was taken back to her cell to await transport. Crabtree told her good-bye at the entrance. "I didn't expect to win for you. I've never won a case in front of that judge. Thank God I've got a pension, as I sure could never make any money in law. I guess that's why they let me represent all you people who get arrested and have nothing. Usually I get only niggers. You and Hank were the first white people I've represented in two years. Maybe if I charged, my luck would change. Good luck to you. You'll need it at Mozambique."

She thanked him for what help he'd been, feeling if she'd had a really good lawyer she'd been freed long ago. Crabtree was a senile old drunk,

but she didn't have anybody else to turn to at the time.

Before she was to be taken to Mozambique, she was allowed a final visit from Hank. Given five minutes to talk to her, he spoke in a low voice so the guard standing nearby couldn't hear him. "I just had to see you to tell you how sorry I am about how everything turned out."

"You seem to be doing fine," she whispered. "What if the court finds out you were already in the Army and had been let go?"

"Crabtree told me not to worry about that," he said. "He claims the court never checks these things. The old fart told the judge that he'd handle my induction in the Army when I went back to the Carolinas."

"What are you really going to do?"

"Head for the hills," Hank said. "This life on the road is not for me. Pete said I could come home to Heaven on Earth any time I wanted."

The mention of that caused her to tremble. "You'll get to see my son."

"I guess I will."

She wanted to ask Hank to take a picture of her son and send it to her but decided not to.

"I'm real sorry Crabtree couldn't get you off on some plea-bargaining deal like he did with me," he said.

"I'm real sorry about that too," she said with bitterness.

"I know you don't owe me no favors, but I'm gonna ask you for one anyway."

"You must be joking," she said. "What kind of favor could I possibly do for you?"

"You won't always be in jail, and one day you might even run into Pete again," he said.

"What if I do?" she said. "He is the daddy of my boy."

"I can't explain every single little detail," he said, sounding slightly irritated. "But I'd be mighty grateful if you didn't tell Pete what happened. I mean leave out all mention of me and you being together on the road. The robbery. All that shit."

"Why should I do that for you?" she asked.

"For your keeping your trap shut, I'll keep mine shut too. I mean, I won't breathe a word to the folks back home about you being sent off to prison for highway robbery. You know how the kids would taunt your son growing up if anybody found out that his mama served time in jail."

"I don't have much power to make deals with no one," Rosacoke said. "But if that's the best deal I can get with anybody, guess I'll go for it."

"I mean your son has to live with the reputation of being a bastard," he said. "To have folks calling him a bastard like Freddie Perkins is tough enough. Added to that, he'd have the added problem of knowing his mama was a jail-bird. That's too much for any kid to have to live with. You understand, don't you?"

"I understand more than I've ever understood in my whole life," she said, noticing the guard signaling to them that their time was up.

"Now you take care of yourself," he said. "You hear?" He didn't look her in the eye.

"Yeah, you look after yourself too," she said, turning her back to him. Under the watchful eye of an armed guard, she headed down a long, dimly lit corridor into her future behind bars.

\*\*\*

Pete had had a tough morning. What was left of the night was spent at the hospital with Claude and Tara waiting for news of John-John's condition. The hospital had pumped his stomach. He'd swallowed a bottle of Tara's sleeping pills, which he'd stolen from the medicine chest of her bathroom.

By ten o'clock that morning, Pete had been assured by the local doctor that John-John was in satisfactory condition. He'd been given a sedative and wouldn't be able to see visitors until later in the day, perhaps around five o'clock.

Before getting into his car to go to the sheriff's office, Claude hugged Pete good-bye and offered him all the help he could give.

Tara remained behind in the parking lot wanting to talk to Pete in private. She looked up at the hospital. "You've got to have a long talk with that boy, hoss," she said, as she reached into her purse to pull out a letter. "I woke up in the early morning and was hungry," she said. "I have to keep this blubber fed. When I went into the kitchen I found a letter with your name on it. I knew it was John-John's handwriting. My brain sometimes doesn't work. This time it did. I knew something was up. I barged into his room and found him sprawled naked on the bed. I saw the bottle of my sleeping tablets on the floor. I called Claude at once. There's something to be said for living under the same roof as the sheriff of the county."

After Tara left, Pete stood for a long time in the hospital parking lot looking up at John-John's darkened room.

Very slowly he opened the note from John-John, as the words seemed to bounce off the page hitting Pete in the eyeballs.

*My darling:*

*I wasn't horsing around. I love you with all my heart. You are my life. My only life. I live for you. If I can't have you, I don't want nobody—not even life itself. You are everything to me. I've even gone to sleep with your smelly socks pressed against my nose. I might be just a kid, but I know what I want. We could have had a great life together. Guys like Josh will come and go in your life. Your John-*

*John will go to his grave with love in his heart. That love of mine is for only one man. His name is Pete Riddle. Until we meet in Heaven, I will always be your boy and belong only to you forever more.*

*John-John.*

With heavy heart, Pete stuffed the letter in his pants pocket and got behind the wheel of his Rolls-Royce heading for his mama's house.

The Riddle homestead was cold and dark when he got there. He used his old key and it worked. He stepped inside the musty Victorian parlor of his youth where he'd listened every night to radio broadcasts.

There was a fire raging within him, and he didn't really feel the chill of the house. Why didn't she keep the house warm? He'd offered to hire her another woman to help out around the house after Rosacoke had left, but his mama had refused.

He found her huddled under handmade quilts in her bedroom. On seeing him, she slowly pushed herself up in bed. "Do you want supper?" was the first question she asked him.

Right away he knew something was wrong. In her darkened room, she seemed to have lost all sense of time. She was asking about supper and it wasn't even noon. She turned on the light beside her bed. He was shocked at her appearance. Her yellowing gray hair looked matted and she'd lost weight. He suspected that her weight had dropped to around eighty pounds.

He leaned over in bed to kiss her on the cheek. "Son, you've known the lips of whores. Don't kiss my face. I will soon stand at the Pearly Gates. I don't want my chance of entering Heaven jeopardized."

He was shocked not only at her dissipated look but at such talk. He couldn't believe this was his own mama. Since he'd joined the Navy, she had changed so much he hardly recognized her. He knew that his daddy's suicide must have hit her harder than he could have imagined.

"It's good to be home, mama," he said. "Good to see you. Now that I'm back, I'm gonna take care of you. Get you better. In no time at all you'll be out of this bed and up walking around again."

"Son, the only time I'm gonna leave this bed again is when the Grim Reaper comes for me."

"I won't hear of such talk," he said. "Tara has far more help around our house than she needs. I'm gonna get her to send over one of her gals. She'll help you bathe, cook collards for you, keep the fire wood in the stove, and the place cleaned."

"I don't want none of that trash you got living with you to come around this house," Mrs. Riddle said.

"The day daddy died, I promised him I'd take care of you," Pete said,

not remembering any such conversation at all. "I'm gonna do that. Daddy would have it no other way."

"What does it matter what that man wanted?" she asked. "I didn't care for him when he was alive. I certainly don't care for him now. He took the coward's way out of life."

"I'll never know why he did that," Pete said. "He was pretty closed off as a man. He never let me know what was going on inside him."

"I lived with him for years," she said. "But I never knew him. He never opened himself up to me. I'm sure his whores knew him better than I did. He was never there for me."

"I thought you loved him," he said. "You always seemed devoted to him."

"I could never stand for him to touch me when I learned he was running around with sluts like that trashy Medora Hester. Night after night I lay in the same bed with the stinking adulterer. I prayed every night that God would take the life from his body. Finally, God answered my prayers. Your daddy is burning in Hell's fire where he belongs. When I die, and my time is coming soon, I am going to Heaven. I can assure you that your daddy won't be there waiting for me." She turned her back to him, as he stared at the red flannel gown she was wearing. "Welcome home, son. But you don't need to come here again. I'm not here for you. I've heard tales about what's going on up at that house of yours. I want no part of it and of you. You're not my son anyway. No son of mine would have turned out like you did. I've never told you this before but your real mama was a whore. Now go and leave me alone."

Astonished and hurt at this rejection, he turned off her light and went back to the kitchen. Feeling despondent, he called Tara at Heaven on Earth. After asking if Buster, Josh, and all the gang were all right, he said, "Thanks for all the help with John-John, but I've also got another problem. I thought after the discharge from the Navy, I'd be coming home to bliss. So far, it's been hell. My mama's got to have a fulltime nurse living with her. I know they are hard to come by with a war on, but I'll pay anything. I can afford it. I feel she's ill and growing worse by the day. She looks awful. Like she hasn't even had a bath in a long time. She can't look after herself."

"Don't worry, hoss," Tara said. "I'll get her somebody. In the meantime, why don't you haul ass over here and sit down with me and the boys for an old-fashioned noon-day dinner? I'm cooking it myself. All your favorite foods."

"Kiss Buster and Josh for me, and tell them their daddy will be home soon," he said, noting the time.

Filled with confusion and dread, he tiptoed down the hallway and looked in on his mama again. The room was dark and he hoped she was resting.

Not a sound came from her bed.

Back in the front room, it seemed that the house where he'd grown up was now a funeral parlor. All life was gone from the place.

Outside in the front yard where Mr. Riddle had shot himself, Pete gazed up at the clouds. A sky ripe for storm stared back at him. He looked back once more at the darkened house that had been his home for so long. Quickening his steps, he raced to get inside his car before the rain came lashing down on his head.

Before starting the motor, he stared longingly at the house that he was leaving behind. As the rain pelted it, it looked much smaller than he'd remembered it. Compared to Heaven on Earth, the Riddle homestead was like a doll's house.

As he started the car, he looked once more at the Riddle house where he was no longer welcomed. He knew that when he pulled out of that driveway he was leaving not only his former home but leaving the boy in himself there too.

***

The following morning Pete sat alone in John-John's hospital room. He'd been there since seven o'clock that morning, and the boy was still asleep. Shortly before ten o'clock, John-John opened his eyes. He looked dreamily at Pete as if in a trance. "It's you," he said weakly. "Really you."

"I'm here for you, boy," Pete said. "I'm going nowhere."

"Then you do love me?" John-John asked.

"Of course, I do. Always did, Always will. But I don't want you going and acting stupid like. Trying to kill yourself. What kind of shit is that?"

"I thought it was all over between us," John-John said. "I didn't want to live. Without you, what would I have to live for?"

"Your whole fucking life is ahead of you," Pete said. "That's what you've got to live for."

"Now that you've come back to me, it's all worthwhile," John-John said. "I knew if I survived, you'd come to your senses and face up to the fact that you love me and only me. Not Josh. Not anybody else. You don't need anybody but me in your bed. You'll see."

"We're both gonna have to do a lot of compromising," Pete said, leaning back in his chair.

"What in hell does that mean?" John-John asked, forcing himself to sit up a bit. "You're getting rid of Josh, aren't you? Pay him off. Give him some money and tell him to hit the road. Anything Josh can do for you I can do better, and you know that's true."

"Hell, I'm not getting rid of Josh, and you'd better face up to that right now," Pete said, placing his chair firmly back on the floor. "Josh is with me

now and forever."

"How do I fit into the picture?" John-John asked, a grim look crossing his brow.

"That's what I meant by compromising," Pete said. "We'll work it out. Me and you are gonna have our own relationship. Our secret times together. Josh won't know and neither will anybody else. It'll be just between us. You're gonna get only a small piece of the pie, not the whole damn thing. Those are my terms. Take them or leave it."

"You mean that, don't you?" John-John said, sliding back down on his pillow and closing his eyes.

"Hell, yes, I mean it," Pete said. "If you love me enough, you'll take what I can give you and ask for no more. What I can give you is a lot. I can even provide a great life for you. And you'll be with me every day. But you can't lie in bed with me at night. That's where Josh is gonna be."

"You mean slip around with you and do it in the closet?" John-John said.

"We'll have our times together," Pete promised. "Plenty of time together, providing you stop doing stupid things like trying to kill your fool self."

The boy opened his eyes and stared intently into Pete's eyes. "This is the best deal I'm gonna get?"

"You got that right," Pete said. "It's our new reality. Live with it."

John-John sighed. "What choice do I have? If I'm gonna go on living, I can't live without you. But I want you all to myself."

"You're not gonna get that," Pete said. "I've already told you that."

"I'm gonna take you up on your offer," John-John said. "I'm gonna make myself so valuable to you you won't be able to stand for me to be out of your sight. Josh will leave you one day. I never will. When you're an old man on your death bed, I'll be at your bedside nursing you."

"What a grim prediction."

"We're talking fifty years from now," John-John said. "In the meantime, we're young and hot." He reached out for Pete's arm, his fingers digging in. "Please lean over this hospital bed and put your mouth on mind. And don't take your lips off mine until at least an hour's gone by."

***

On that same day Rosacoke was delivered to the state penitentiary, one of the youngest females ever sent there. Lacking any identification, she gave her name as Rose Adams, claiming she'd married Hank Adams in Canada and had lost their marriage certificate. She'd never had a birth certificate, as she'd been born in a cabin with the help of a black midwife, and her birth had never been registered in her county.

At the prison it seemed that she'd wandered into one of her childhood nightmares and that she'd soon wake up. Regrettably, that wasn't to be the case.

Mozambique was once a great cotton plantation. At the end of the Civil War, it was transformed into a profit-making prison, where conditions of brutality prevailed. At the death of Colonel Samuel Baker, who ran the prison until somewhere near the turn of the century, the state of Louisiana purchased the plantation-prison and continued to operate it in much the same way as the sadistic colonel.

The plantation contained rich bottomland, and prisoners were forced to slave-farm cotton on it. If they refused, they were horse-whipped. Prisoners were shackled, and all were overworked and underfed.

After she was fingerprinted and assigned a number, she was given a dull gray uniform, which was two sizes too big for her. Then she met the head matron, Alma Hunt, whose reputation Rosacoke had already heard about from some of the other prisoners. Once in a riot Alma had shot three women inmates in the head and gotten away with it. She was a large, beefy woman with a heavy bosom. She'd never been seen in a dress, preferring male clothing. Everything about her suggested brutality. She wore her hair short, and few indiscretions missed her beady black eyes.

Rosacoke felt uncomfortable at the way the matron appraised her from head to foot, feeling she was like a slab of beef. Alma assigned her to the cotton mill, where she was to work at a machine in the dyehouse. For her bed that night and every night thereafter, she was given a bunk in a large dormitory with thirty other women.

When Rosacoke pulled off her dress the first night there, she heard one of the women call out, "Look at the tits on that babe. What I could do to her."

Rosacoke was so shocked she nearly burst into tears, as she'd never heard one woman appraise another in such a way.

"Just pay her no mind," said a fat woman on the adjoining cot. "They're filth, those women over there. We're split up into two sections. The filth over there and us good women over here who've gone wrong. Made a mistake or two, you know."

Hazel Lowe was in her mid-forties. She wasn't a very attractive woman, but she had a kind face and a motherly air about her. She was serving time for murdering her philandering husband. Before the night was over, Rosacoke knew that she'd found a friend in Hazel, who worked during the day as a cook preparing food for the black women of the prison. "They get the worst food of all. The crap usually given to the dogs. It's a shame."

The next morning Rosacoke reported for duty at the cotton mill. Here she faced a large boiler, which had been heated up and filled with dye. After the cotton had soaked up the dye, it went through a wringer. Her job

was to stand at the wringer, pulling the damp dyed cotton out of it. The work was too much for her, and it was unrelenting. Hour after hour she pulled the cotton from that wringer until, sweaty and exhausted, she was granted a fifteen-minute lunch break where she ate a cold boiled potato. The very thought of doing this hard manual labor for more than a year was too much for her already depressed mind.

"Don't think about it," Hazel had warned her at breakfast that morning. "Think only of what you've got to do to get through one day at a time."

As the days at Mozambique became weeks, Rosacoke sank deeper and deeper into herself, as if losing herself in the swampy earth surrounding the plantation. She'd been here only a short time, and already she'd seen some of the worst and most inhumane conditions she'd ever known. Nightly she had to fight against all the old memories that marched through her mind like a parade.

She tried to control her feelings, easing the pain as if in hibernation. She suspended her life, waiting for the eventual spring which seemed a long time off in coming. Hazel, her only confidante, offered her some comfort, easing her adjustment to the harsh life.

Rosacoke's worst moments came when the power dimmed in the corridors at night. Someone was getting electrocuted. Low moans of despair could be heard coming from death house row where the prisoners there, mostly black, knew that their number would soon come up. Rosacoke shuddered at the thought of the deadly juice pouring into a human body. She'd never thought about capital punishment before, but being so close to it made her determined to oppose it for the rest of her life.

The next morning she encountered Alma Hunt. "We fried another nigger last night," she said to Rosacoke, the whole idea seemingly filling her with glee. "Convicted of raping a white woman. If I had my way, I'd string out their sentence a little longer. Castrate them first. Make them suffer one hell of a lot. Just electrocuting them is too easy and painless."

Turning from the sight of the matron, Rosacoke hurried to the cotton mill for another long and tedious day at the wringer.

The nights were even longer and harder to get through than the days. "Don't think about life on the outside," Hazel had warned her. "If you do you'll go crazy in here for sure."

Rosacoke was determined to stay out of trouble. Fights broke out all around her, but she stayed clear of them. She did whatever she was told, regardless of how unfair the command. Alma Hunt got no sass from her. Trouble-making prisoners ended up in the black hole, which her fellow sorority sisters spoke of with almost as much fear as being sent over to death house row.

Because she'd tried so hard to be a model prisoner, she was very nervous when a guard told her after supper one night to report to Alma Hunt's

office.

"What have I done wrong?" she kept asking herself. The long walk down the corridor made her feel like one of those condemned men waiting to get fried. Filled with hesitancy, she stood in front of Alma's door. With all the courage she had in her body, she knocked gingerly.

"Come in," Alma called out in a voice that almost sounded kind.

***

Alma Hunt had never looked so massive. In a deep-throated voice, she commanded, "Get the hell in here and lock that door behind you. This is a private little gathering."

Rosacoke smiled weakly at the head matron, shutting the door. For some reason, she only pretended to lock it. "Why do you want me?"

"Don't rush things, baby, or I might have to spank you. Some naughty girls like that. Do you?"

"I've never been spanked, and I'm sure I wouldn't stand for it."

"Mighty cocky talk coming from a bitch." She got up from her bed and moved menacingly toward Rosacoke. "Take off your dress. It's the wrong size for you. I've got a new one that really fits."

Hoping to be let go as soon as possible, Rosacoke slipped out of her prison uniform, standing before Alma clad only in her cotton slip. The inmates weren't assigned any other undergarments.

Suddenly, Alma lunged toward her, pressing her with force against the door. The handle ground painfully into Rosacoke's back. Her hot, thick, sweaty lips pressed against Rosacoke's mouth. Alma had locked Rosacoke's head in her arms, as she pounded her body with a brute force against Rosacoke's thin, trapped frame. Alma broke away only long enough to drag Rosacoke toward the bed by the hair of her head.

Before Alma threw Rosacoke on the bed, she ripped her slip off. Falling down on her, Alma squeezed and kneaded her breasts. Alma was almost foaming at the mouth.

Twisting, jerking, groaning, Rosacoke fought back with her last remaining energy. She thrashed her body underneath Alma's, trying to break away. The more Rosacoke struggled, the more she felt bound in some frozen hell. Alma's slurpy tongue burned her body like acid. Sucking in air, Rosacoke reared up, biting Alma's neck as hard as she could, gnashing her own tongue in the process.

Alma jumped back, raging in pain, and that split second gave Rosacoke her moment to run. She darted toward the door, which mercifully she hadn't locked. Throwing it open, she raced down the corridor until two male guards tackled her.

In her gibbering, scrambled maze, she didn't know exactly what hap-

pened next. All she could remember was Alma's booming voice, "The crazy bitch attacked me. Tried to kill me."

Hands pressed down hard into her flesh, dragging her down the corridor as she screamed, kicked, and fought back. Without anybody telling her, she knew that she was going to be thrown stark naked into the black hole. Right now that didn't matter. Escaping this hell meant everything.

***

For Rosacoke, the worst thing about going into the hole was not knowing when you'd get out. Nobody ever told you that. The first problem was passing the time of day. Nights you expected to be atrocious, but getting through a day was something else again.

She had plenty of time to think about Alma Hunt wanting to have sex with her. No one had ever told her about anything like that. Up to now she thought male rapists like Sultan were the only people she had to look out for. She wasn't even certain about how two women made love. To her, the plumbing wasn't right. Sure as hell, if she ever got out of this black pit she wasn't about to find out either.

Her living space, if it could be called that, was four feet by eight feet. Air from somewhere came in—after all, the bastards had to give her that— but not one bit of daylight. It was pitch dark from morning till the next morning, and she never knew what time it was. Not that time mattered in here. Bread and water were given to her—nothing else. There was a toilet hole in the floor, but no paper was passed to her, not even an old newspaper.

For two weeks she lasted in that black hole. Others had died here in less time than that. She didn't know how she made it. Later she suspected she'd gone crazy in there, or at least temporarily mad. She did vow one thing: If she ever got out of prison she would never wear black again, only bright colors that evoked the sunshine, even if attending a funeral.

When she did see her first sunshine, it blinded her, giving her a powerful headache. Still, she welcomed it. At least she was out of that hole where Alma Hunt had put her. Other than Alma spying on her when she went in to take a shower, the head matron gave her no more trouble. If anything, she seemed to have a begrudging respect for Rosacoke. Apparently, she never expected her to get out of that hole alive.

To Rosacoke's surprise, surviving in the hole made prison life easier somehow. After what she'd been through, the power to walk around became a luxury. The next day after her release she was back at her job at the wringer in the cotton mill. She was much too weak and exhausted to work, and many times she came near fainting. But she was determined not to give in, to stick it out.

She was equally determined to play by the rules. She never challenged

authority, and she got along with the other women prisoners, even the rough, crude ones. She'd noticed that inmate fighting often led to getting thrown back in the hole, and she never wanted to see that dark pit again.

If she found a roach in her food, she said nothing. Degradation and humiliation didn't matter much any more. She'd lost all self-respect, becoming like an animal, getting through a day at any price.

At least she felt that way until she discovered the pleasure of reading. Books and magazines brought the outside world in, and devouring these publications gave her joy. Between supper and bedtime the women had about two hours to themselves. Most of the inmates listened to the radio, and she liked to do that, too, until she found reading more satisfying. She made her mind up that she wasn't going to be an ignorant hillbilly the rest of her life, and since she'd had very little schooling, she determined that she'd best educate herself.

It was one night shortly before roll call that she picked up a copy of *Life* magazine. Inside to her amazement she saw a picture layout on Narcissa. The Blackbirds revue had landed in Los Angeles after all, and Narcissa had been cast in a Hollywood movie. A real Hollywood movie, just like Lana Turner. Well, not quite like Lana, but a genuine movie, nevertheless. Narcissa would appear in one scene. The white stars of the movie would be seen at a night club watching Narcissa sing.

Rosacoke burst into tears. Things hadn't worked out for her, but they had for Narcissa. At least one dream had come true.

Narcissa had become glorified as a national oddity with her silver hair. But, according to the article, the White House had eventually intervened, claiming that radiator paint was badly needed for the war effort, and that to waste it on one's hair was considered unpatriotic. Narcissa was back to wearing her own hair, or, unless the photograph lied, a wig. Rosacoke feared that silver radiator paint would permanently damage Narcissa's real hair. Wig or not, it didn't matter. What did matter was that Miss Narcissa Cash was setting the Hollywood Hills on fire.

Rosacoke went to bed that night, daring to dream dreams that she'd suppressed for a long time. Hearing about Narcissa's good fortune brought renewed hope to her own dismal life.

Maybe there was some bright tomorrow waiting out there for her after all. If dawn could come for Narcissa, maybe the morning light would shine on her too.

# Chapter 9

Pete felt in a safe haven walking his ranch grounds with Josh. The horror he'd had with John-John seemed removed from Pete at the moment. The vision of John-John's attempt to kill himself flashed through Pete's mind like lightning, but he tried to dismiss it. He knew the triangle was not resolved, and he was grateful that Josh wasn't pressing him for details.

The presence of Josh, the closeness of his body, the glow of his complete acceptance of Pete, were all that mattered right now as they enjoyed the oncoming summer.

With Josh at his side, Pete stood on a hill, looking down at the houses he owned below. Freddie and Nipsey only that morning had settled into the biggest house in the compound, which was once occupied by the overseer of the plantation. Guitar Red and Smokey shared a house in the distance, but Maston didn't want to live in a house by himself. He asked to stay in a room in the far wing of Pete's mansion. The small room had once been occupied by a maid.

"I've lived in cramped little hotels all my life, often bedrooms over honky-tonks, and that's what I want now that I'm here at this grand mansion," Maston said. Pete had readily granted his wish.

Josh and Pete had put the twins, Troy and Dale, on a train that would take them to Los Angeles. To provide them with a grubstake, Pete gave each of the men ten-thousand dollars to get them started on the coast.

"You're my life," Josh said, to him on the hill.

"And I'd have it no other way," Pete said, kissing him on the lips before asking him to walk back to the main house with him. "Buster will be getting up, and I want to be there when he does. Please learn to love him like he's your own son. Buster will be one lucky boy. Two daddies."

"I'll look after the kid like he's my own," Josh promised.

After spending an hour with Buster, Pete left him with Tara as Josh retreated upstairs to work on his music.

The doctor was releasing John-John that morning, and Pete wanted to be there for the boy, bringing him back to Heaven on Earth.

After meeting in the corridor with the doctor, Pete was told to see that the boy got a week or two of rest before resuming his normal activities. "It's a small town," the doctor said, "and I don't want word to get out that he tried to kill himself."

On wobbly legs, John-John was up and about when Pete came into his hospital room. John-John's face lit up as he spotted Pete. He rushed over to hug and kiss the object of his affection.

"We're going home," Pete said. "We're not going to do anything stupid in the future, like try to overdose on sleeping pills."

"I'm not gonna do that again," John-John said. "I've had a lot of time to think in this hospital bed. I've decided I'm not gonna give up the battle so easy in the future. I want you to be my husband. It's what I have to live for."

John-John said that with such determination that it sent a chill through Pete. He realized for the first time just how much John-John really wanted him. Back in his Rolls-Royce, Pete glanced several times at John-John who was saying nothing, although that look of a fierce resolve still seemed imbedded in his face. "When you're yourself again, me and you are gonna sit down and map out some plan for your future," Pete said.

John-John took Pete's hand and held onto it real hard. "You are my future."

Back at Heaven on Earth, Tara was the only one waiting to greet them. When John-John faltered at the bottom of the steps, Pete sensed how weak the boy still was. Pete picked John-John up in his arms and carried him to a bedroom just off the master bedroom close to Pete and Josh. At first Pete felt he should assign a bedroom to John-John in a far wing of the house. But it didn't feel right somehow.

After an hour spent cuddling John-John in his arms, Pete felt relieved to see the boy drifting off into sleep.

At a light rap on the door, Pete went to open it, finding Tara standing there, a look of surprise on her face. "You'd never guess who showed up on the porch just ten minutes ago," Tara said. "Looking a little worse for wear."

Pete stepped into the hallway with Tara, gently closing John-John's door.

He went over to the stairwell and looked down into the main foyer.

There stood Hank Adams.

Pete nearly fell down the slickly polished marble stairs as he rushed into Hank's arms. He raced up and gave Hank a warm embrace, feeling the muscles in his arms and back as he hugged him.

"God damn it," Pete said. "I'm glad you're home."

"I've come back to stay," Hank said, kissing Pete's lips.

Pete smelled strong body odor and was aware for the first time of just how disheveled Hank looked. His clothes were also dirty and smelly, and his Army shoes looked as if they should have been retired on some maneuver a year ago.

"I've been hitchhiking on the road for five days to get back here," Hank

said. "No sleep and only two dollars for food for the whole fucking trip. You can eat just so many potato chips."

"Where in the fuck have you been?" Pete asked. "You stopped writing and everything. I thought you were in the Army."

"The Army ain't got no need for the likes of me," Hank said.

"Ditto the Navy with me," Pete said. "You're a little ripe, fellow. Let's go upstairs."

Tara came to the bottom of the stairs, and Hank went over to kiss her on the cheek. "Welcome home, hoss," she said. "I'm so sorry to hear about Tracy."

"I don't even want to talk about poor Tracy," Hank said. "He had to give up his life before it'd even begun."

"I couldn't help but hear how hungry you were," Tara said. "Let me rustle you up some grub."

"A woman after my own heart," Hank said, kissing her again before trailing Pete up the stairs to his new room. On an impulse Pete decided to assign Bleeka Walker's old bedroom to Hank. Even though it was a boudoir all in pink, it was also the most luxurious and comfortable in the house, even more so than Pete's more masculine-looking master bedroom.

"This looks like the dream bedroom for Narcissa Cash," Hank said, standing in awe of the bedchamber which he'd never laid eyes on before. "That old rich bitch, Walker, sure liked pink."

"You'll love it too," Pete said, motioning to the canopied pink-clad bed. "Especially that delicious bed over there. That's where I'm going to extract at least three blasts of hot cum from you every twenty-four hours."

"It's all yours, baby face," Hank said, unbuttoning his shirt. Hank slipped off his shoes and socks, as Pete unbuckled Hank's pants, pulling them down on his firm, muscular legs.

Within fifteen minutes, the big claw-footed pink marble tub had filled with hot water. Pete applied the suds and invited Hank to step into the deep.

Once in the tub, Hank lay back, his head resting on a rubber cushion, letting Pete do all the work. It was a job he relished. The sensual softness of Hank's unblemished skin brought back wonderful memories. Pete lovingly washed Hank's sculpted chest and powerful arms. Pete ran his hands between Hank's creamy thighs, as he watched his friend's cock throb and pulsate in anticipation of what was going to happen to it. Pete's hands moved up and down Hank's hardening organ, pulling the foreskin back again to polish the head with soap.

As Pete held Hank's cock, Pete realized how much he'd missed it. With his left hand, he reached below to gently squeeze and fondle Hank's large balls. They were encased in a purse of fleecy skin with the feel of kid gloves. Pete's fingers made their way across that no man's land of human

anatomy until he reached the firm cheeks of Hank's ass. The young man turned over in the tub to give Pete complete access. Pete washed, soaped, and fingered Hank's rectum, loving the way his friend voluntarily surrendered the most intimate parts of his body to him. Hank's stomach heaved and relaxed, and then heaved again, writhing in the pleasure of the sudsy bath.

"It's all yours," Hank said after his ass cleaning. He turned back over as Pete moved down the strong legs washing his way toward Hank's feet.

"Out on my own I've seen a little bit of this country—in fact, a whole lot of it," Hank said. "I didn't like what I saw. This is the life for me. Everything's made easy for me here."

"We've got to keep things between us hush-hush," Pete cautioned. "I brought a jealous lover back from the Navy. Josh Harnell. He was discharged with me."

"Lies, deceit, cover-ups—you've found your man," Hank said.

Pete reached for a pink terry-cloth robe for Hank, and it was in that robe seated at Mrs. Walker's former breakfast table that Hank waited for his food.

At a knock, Pete opened the door, taking a heavily laden tray from Tara. He noted the big steak and fried potatoes, even a fresh salad and some green beans and corn. "Hoss," she said to Pete. "I also brought this wandering boy a glass of Tennessee bourbon straight. He looks like he needs it."

"You got that right, lady," Hank said.

After Tara left, Hank devoured the bloody steak as he opened his robe to reveal his nude body for Pete's eager eyes. He was amazed at the size of Hank's dick, even when soft. "We've got to make up for lost time, baby," Hank said as Pete inspected his wares.

When he could take his eyes off Hank's dick, Pete brought him up on the news, even of John-John. Pete mentioned that the boy had been sick and in the hospital but left out the reason why Hank's brother was sent there.

Rosacoke was mentioned once or twice. "The last I heard she was going to Chicago to hook up with Narcissa who told her she could get Rosacoke a job," Pete said. "Heard any news?"

"Not much," Hank said. "I don't know what happened to Rosacoke, but I heard that Narcissa was moving up in show business. Living out in Hollywood."

"That she is," Pete said.

Hank leaned back in his chair after swallowing the last piece of steak. "Good meal," he said. "I don't know whether I should tell you this or not. But you're the daddy of a baby boy."

"You mean, Buster?" Pete said. "He's the boy I had with Rosacoke. He's living here."

"That's not what I mean," Hank said "Narcissa did write me. You knocked her up, ole buddy. She had a bouncing baby boy by you. She sold him like a slave to a couple for five-hundred dollars."

Pete was shocked, so much so he almost gasped for breath. "Narcissa fucked around a lot. How do we know it's my boy? You fucked her too."

"I always used a rubber," Hank said. "Narcissa told me you liked it in natural."

"I did, but you don't think…." He hesitated for a long moment, not certain what to say. "I can't believe this. She didn't write me or anything."

"She's too much of a prideful high yellow gal for that—you know that. She wanted to have the baby on her own. She debated having an abortion but feared the ghost of Aunt Clotilda would get her. So she went ahead and birthed it."

"Feature this," Pete said. "Me the daddy of two bastard sons. I hope my second kid is okay."

"How could he not be," Hank said. "He'll grow up to be a combination of Pete Riddle and Sultan. What a man that will be."

"If you think he's okay and not wanting for anything, I'll let him grow up in peace," Pete said. "If I felt he wasn't being cared for, I'd go up there to Chicago, kidnap him, and bring him back here."

"Narcissa said he's doing just fine," Hank said. "We'd better leave it at that."

"I think we'd better keep this to ourselves," Pete said. "If I want my Ma to die tonight, let word get out that her son has fathered another baby, a chocolate-coated one at that."

"It'll be our secret," Hank said. He got up, pushing back his chair. "Are we gonna sleep together now or do you want me to get some shut-eye before the flagpole rises for you?"

"If you haven't slept in days, I think you'd better get some shuteye. I want you in top form for our first time together again."

"You're calling the shots around here, buddy."

Pete tucked Hank into the pink bed. As Pete raised himself up, Hank grabbed him by the neck, pulling him down against his mouth and kissing him long and hard before inserting his tongue.

When Hank finally released him, he said to Pete, "When I wake up, I want you here for me."

When Hank hit the pillow, he seemed to fall into a deep sleep right away. It was more than sleep, almost like a coma. Pete checked on him several times throughout the day and night. Whenever he opened the door to Hank's bedroom, he was always sleeping. Maybe he got up to go to the bathroom, maybe not.

When Hank did wake up officially, it was nine o'clock the next morning.

From his position buried in Hank's crotch, Pete looked up lovingly and

longingly into his lover's eyes before returning to his main task of the morning: the deep-throating of Hank's enticingly large fuckpole.

*\*\**

With Josh, Pete stood before his red barn, watching four black workers he'd hired begin the long, hard task of converting the building into a recording studio. Even though materials were in short supply, Pete had gotten what he needed and wanted. He'd learned that even with wartime shortages, a man could get what he wanted if willing to pay the price.

"I can't wait," Josh said. "In that barn we're gonna create a distinctive sound that will one day put Pete Riddle on the charts."

From the back porch, Tara called to Pete, saying that Claude wanted to see him in the library. As he came in, Claude was standing before the fireplace looking upset. Pete shut the double doors.

"What's up?" Pete said.

"It's Wanda Mae."

"Your daughter?" A slight frown crossed Pete's brow. He hadn't seen Wanda Mae since that night he'd taken Rosacoke to the roller skating rink for the big dance. He had never liked the girl.

"She's run away," Claude said.

"You're the sheriff," Pete said. "Why don't you track her down? Just how old is Wanda Mae anyway?"

"Only fourteen."

"Fuck, man, just how old were you when you fathered her?"

"I knocked up Betty Lou when I was just thirteen," Claude said. "But we've been separated for years. Wanda Mae stayed with her mama when we broke up. I came to live here with Bleeka Walker. She claimed she liked a police presence around this place, fearing robbers."

"I never told anyone why Betty Lou and I broke up. She caught me in bed one night fucking Ronnie Key."

"My God," was all Pete said.

"She didn't know until then that I had these tendencies. I mean, I think of myself as a lady's man. But then I've never been known to turn down some hot male action like you offered me with those twins. While you were in England, Wanda Mae started dating Ronnie in spite of the differences in their ages. The little air headed fool has fallen madly in love with him. She stole money from her mama yesterday and boarded a Greyhound bus for Jacksonville, Florida. When she gets there, she plans to marry Ronnie even before he gets out of the Navy."

"That's her choice and that's his choice," Pete said.

"You don't seem to get it," Claude said. "Wanda Mae is marrying one of my former deputies. A man I've slept with on more than one occasion."

"What does Betty Lou think about all this?" Pete asked.

"Betty Lou is as disgusted as I am with the whole mess," Claude said. "After vowing she'd never say a word, she up and told Wanda Mae what she caught her daddy doing to her future spouse."

"How did Wanda Mae take all this?" Pete asked.

"She handled the revelations with far more sophistication than I would have given her credit for," Claude said. "She told my wife that she didn't object to Ronnie playing around with boys. She said so long as Ronnie doesn't mess around with any other gal, it's okay by her."

"C'mon, Claude," Pete said. "If Wanda Mae can live with this, so can we."

"I still have this special thing for Ronnie," Claude said. "If Ronnie becomes my son-in-law, I don't know that I can keep my hands off him. You know yourself, stuff happens."

Pete got up and went over to the library doors. "I think we should go to the wedding down in Jacksonville. I'll call down there today and try to get through to Ronnie. I'll invite Hank and Josh to drive down with us."

"You mean that?" Claude asked.

"We could throw quite a bachelor party for ole Ronnie," Pete said. "We're not losing him. In fact, maybe it's better that he settles down with Wanda Mae. There's that beautiful cottage—it's quite big—on the other side of the hill. It'd be a great place for Ronnie and Wanda Mae to launch their married life when the war's over."

"You'd let them live there?"

"Course I would," Pete said. "With Wanda and Ronnie living there, you'd know where to find Ronnie when you need him. He's one cute guy."

\*\*\*

John-John threw a fit when Pete told him he had to stay home at Heaven on Earth to regain his health more fully. With Claude at the wheel, Pete headed south to Ronnie's wedding with Josh and Hank. Pete had personally fed Buster that morning and felt the little boy would, as always, be safe in the arms of Tara.

After an early morning start, Claude drove all day until they reached some dreary little hick town in North Georgia where Pete rented three cabins for the night—one for Claude, another for Hank, and the largest one for Josh and him. Hank urged the sheriff to take Josh into the neighboring town to bring back a mess of ribs and cole slaw.

While the men set out on their mission, Hank pleaded with Pete to slip away to his cabin "to give me some relief."

When Pete saw that Josh and Claude were safely down the road, Pete said, "When the sexiest man alive asks for some relief, I don't have to be

asked twice."

"I only hope that Josh won't hit on you tonight," Hank said. "Maybe the trip will have worn him out. As for you, I'm gonna wear you out before they get back with those ribs. You'll have nothing left for Josh."

When making a sexual promise, Hank lived up to his word. A little battered, but in the most delicious way, Pete was standing under a tepid shower in the claptrap bathroom washing away the evidence of Hank's assault when Josh and Claude came back with the ribs and slaw. Claude had also got them some beer for the night.

The men turned in after midnight, and Josh was in an amorous mood, even though Pete would have preferred sleep. He gave Josh a blow-job to settle him down before Pete fell into a deep sleep.

He was the first to wake up the next morning, knowing that they had to get an early start. He let Josh sleep a little longer, as Pete made his way to the front of the tourist cabin complex.

The owner's wife was there with some freshly brewed coffee. After drinking a cup and making idle chitchat, Pete asked for another cup to take to his friend. He headed for Claude's cabin with the steaming cup of wake-up brew.

Two days later in Jacksonville, Pete made all the plans for Ronnie's wedding with Wanda Mae. She was far too young to be marrying anybody, but Pete decided that if her own daddy didn't object he certainly wouldn't either.

His reunion the first night had gone beautifully with Ronnie. He looked a little older and filled out his sailor's uniform perfectly. He'd developed muscle and a certain masculine leanness in the Navy. Even though Pete had had sex with Ronnie, he hardly knew him.

Ronnie had eagerly accepted an invitation to go out with his buddies from North Carolina the night before for some heavy drinking, leaving Wanda Mae to stew alone in her hotel room.

Even though hung over the following morning, Claude had invited all the men to go out on a fishing boat with him. Such mountain boys as Josh and Hank eagerly accepted the invitation to fish in Florida waters, but after sailing that Navy tub back from Southampton to a dishonorable discharge, Pete turned down the offer. Besides, someone had to hook up with Wanda Mae and Ronnie about the wedding plans tomorrow. Pete delegated himself to do the job, especially since he was footing the bill for the nuptials.

Ronnie was still on duty when Pete went by to call on Wanda Mae at her hotel room. He planned to take her to a dressmaker to get her a bridal gown when he'd learned that she was going to get married in the same tacky dress she'd worn when riding that Greyhound bus to Jacksonville.

Before heading off on their shopping expedition, Wanda Mae invited Pete into her room for "some private type of conversation."

He sat in the lone armchair, and she perched nervously at the edge of the bed. "I want you to talk to Ronnie for me," she said. "I'm too embarrassed. He likes you a whole lot. In fact, he talks and brags about you and how much money you have to anyone who will listen."

"That's nice," Pete said, wondering where this talk was going. "What's up? Is there a sexual problem here?"

"There could be a God damn major sexual problem here if someone don't talk some sense into that lust-crazed fool, Ronnie Key."

"What's he been doing?" Pete asked.

"That sailor boy thinks that because he's putting a ring on my finger tomorrow afternoon that he is gonna be entitled to get into my bloomers any time he wants."

"You know how men are," he said. "Many guys marrying for the first time think it's an open ticket to get all the nooky they want. You will, after all, be his lawfully wedded wife."

"The sex between us might come in a year or two," she said. "But right now the only sex he is gonna get is from Minnie."

"Who in the fuck is Minnie?" Pete asked, growing impatient and eager to leave the room.

"As Minnie fingers as I can get around it."

"Let me get this straight," he said. "You're willing to jerk off your husband after marriage—and that's it?"

"For the time being," she said. "You've got to understand where I'm coming from. Ronnie is always bragging how big his is. I ain't ever seen it. Ain't seen too many naked men except for daddy. A girl friend told me that she went to bed with a boy and it hurt something awful and she bled."

"You're a virgin?" he asked.

"I'm a virgin and plan to stay that way for a long time," she said. "I saw a bull mount a cow one time, and it didn't look like any fun for the cow, believe you me. If Ronnie's got something as big as that bull has, I sure don't want him sticking that monster up into me."

"Very few men are built like bulls," he said, a smirk crossing his face. "Present company excepted. Just why are you getting married if you're not going to have sex right away?"

"I didn't say I wouldn't have sex," she said. "I'm going to play with his thing. He can do the same for me. Rebecca, my friend, has a boy friend. She lets him play with her. He even puts his mouth on her thing, but I shouldn't really be telling you this."

"Have you fully explained all this to Ronnie?" he asked.

"Hell, no, I'm too ashamed," she said.

"If you can't talk this over with your future husband, why are you telling me? You don't seem embarrassed at all."

"Ronnie says that him and you have done it," she said. "Gone at it like

rabbits. He says you've been his woman."

"His woman!" He rose with a certain fury on the edge of his seat. "That little devil. I'm a man, sweetheart. If you think Ronnie might have one big one, wait until you see what Pete Riddle has got."

"I sure don't want to see it," she said, "so you can keep it in your pants, you big show-off. Anyway, since you've slept with Ronnie, I figured you could talk sex with him. I'll go out and buy that bridal gown with you today. But remember there's gonna be no wedding tomorrow until Ronnie agrees to my terms. After all, I'm the bride and I've got some rights."

"Wanda Mae, my little chickadee," he said, getting up. "I'll explain the facts of life to my good buddy Ronnie. If he's okay with it, then the wedding goes on. If he's demanding pussy rights, then it's off. A deal? Okay?"

In the night that followed, even after telling Ronnie of Wanda Mae's "conditions" for marriage, Pete never figured out why Ronnie wanted to marry her. But the sailor was willing to go through with the marriage for reasons that Ronnie might not have understood himself.

The following afternoon, Wanda Mae looked right pretty in her bridal gown. She'd chosen pink instead of the traditional white, which pissed off Claude, until Pete said it was okay. "She comes out there dressed in pink, folks will think she's a whore," Claude said. "Virgins wear white to the altar."

"It's okay, good buddy," Pete said, trying to calm him down. "There won't be anybody here but Josh and Hank, plus some preacher we don't give a fuck about. No one from back home will know."

With everyone calmed down, the wedding went beautifully with Josh at the piano providing the music.

At the party Pete had thrown later in a hotel suite rented for the occasion, everybody, especially Hank, had too much to drink. Wanda Mae had tasted her first champagne, and had devoured three glasses of it before it took its lethal effect.

Claude and Pete joined Ronnie to return to their rooms to change out of their wedding garb.

As he was leaving, Pete noticed Hank sprawled out in a stupor on the sofa. Aided by a kindly Josh, Wanda Mae had her head thrown over the railing of her small balcony. Pete only hoped there was no passers-by underneath.

Nothing had been planned. Nothing had been set up. But in Pete's hotel room, the men pulled off their clothes after having performed their duties—Pete as best man and Claude as the father of the bride.

The sight of two hunks stripping down in front of him gave Pete a raging hard-on, which was obviously visible to both men. With a life of its own, Pete's hand reached for Ronnie's ass, still enclosed in his white boxers. "Hey, dude, I've got to eat some more of that."

Ronnie turned around to kiss him. "Why don't you fuck it instead?"

Pete didn't know or couldn't remember just how the rest of that wedding night ended. But he'd always remember the beginning of the evening.

As he plowed into the virginal canal of Ronnie, biting into his neck, Ronnie had yelped but screamed for more. Ever the opportunist, Claude descended on his new son-in-law's dick to deep throat it.

As the center of the "sandwich," the bridegroom called out, "My wedding day and I'm the happiest man alive!"

***

After driving back to the Carolina hills, Claude dropped off Wanda Mae at her mama's house. Kissing her on the cheek and wishing her well, Claude drove Pete, Hank, and Josh back to Heaven on Earth.

Following a suitcase-lugging Josh into the house, Pete was mildly surprised to see a strange-looking car in his driveway with an Illinois license plate. "Who knows anyone from Chicago?" Pete casually asked Josh and Hank.

"I've known a few," Hank said, "but none I want to meet up with again."

Hank and Josh headed up the spiral stairway to wash up after their long drive north from Florida.

Tara rushed up the corridor from the kitchen to kiss Pete. "Welcome home, hoss," she said.

"How's Buster?" Pete asked.

"Meaner than ever and missing his daddy."

Thinking no more of the car from Illinois, Pete headed for Buster's nursery to kiss his son and play with him. He found Buster sleeping soundly.

In the kitchen Tara was pouring Pete a brandy. "Let's have a little welcome home drink," she said.

"Wanda Mae and Ronnie got hitched," he said. "A disaster in the making."

"I didn't know Ronnie liked gals all that much," Tara said.

He leaned over to whisper. "I think when Ronnie gets out of the Navy, his father-in-law is going to be getting more of that good stuff than Wanda Mae."

"C'mon," she said laughing. "We live in the South. Those Yankees expect us to act like that. Incest, the works. If you've got the name, why not play the game?"

"I always say that too," he said, downing the rest of the blackberry brandy in his glass.

"I almost forgot," she said. "You've got a visitor waiting in the library. Says his name is Larry Hunt. He's a show business booking agent. Says he knows Narcissa Cash and Hank. More than that, says he's worked with

them."

"That so?" Pete said. "Hank never told me he had a job in show business."

"Come to think of it," Tara said, "Hank ain't said much of anything about what he did after he got kicked out of the Army."

"Let me go meet this mysterious Larry Hunt," Pete said.

Bursting into the library, he feasted his eyes on Larry Hunt who was sitting on the sofa reading a movie magazine with Jennifer Jones on its cover.

"I'm Pete Riddle," he said, extending his hand.

"Larry Hunt," he said, getting up from the sofa and holding out his hand as well. "I'm a hotshot agent. I've come here as the answer to your prayers."

"You look like you could be the answer to anybody's fucking prayers," Pete said. "Yankee boys who look like you get held down and raped in the South."

"If all Southern boys looked like you," Larry said, "rape would be impossible."

"Tell me why you're here, and do you really know Narcissa and Hank?"

"Hank and I were lovers. Didn't he tell you?"

"I think he left you out of his autobiography," Pete said.

"Simply put," Larry said, "I'm here to beg you for a job. I want to manage your act. Get it together. Get the sound right. Arrange bookings and take it on the road."

"I'm converting the barn out back into a recording studio. I've got songwriters. But it's not soup yet. We need work."

"Please take me on," Larry said. "I've got about ten bucks left on me. I'll work for room and board until I start bringing in the bookings. When I do that, I'll want twenty percent. I can also get you recorded."

"You're like a dream come true for me," Pete said. "There must be a downside to all of this."

"I'm not perfect," Larry said. "Gotta lot of faults. But you won't find any better agent than me."

"Let's bring Hank down here," Pete said. "I can't make you any promises until the three of us have talked and I've been filled in. I also want you to hear me sing and hear my boys play."

Without a knock, the door to the library was thrown open. There stood Hank in the steamy late morning, barefoot and shirtless. "Larry Hunt, you fucker." His face brightened before his lip curled. "Ain't we supposed to be mad at each other?"

"I've forgotten what we had a fight over," Larry said. "Whatever it was, it doesn't matter."

"I guess it don't," Hank said.

"For God's sake, please get that delectable ass of yours over here and give me a big wet kiss," Larry said to Hank. Larry turned to look provocatively at Pete.

"Carry on, boys," Pete said.

Larry came up to Hank and reached out for him, giving him a long, deep kiss.

"I guess we've got to catch up on some fucking tonight," Hank said when he broke from Larry, turning his attention to Pete. "This Chicago boy likes to get deep-dicked up the ass."

"Whatever turns him on," Pete said.

***

With Larry signed on to their rapidly expanding team, Pete drove in his Rolls-Royce to John-John's school the next afternoon.

Ever since Pete had returned from England, John-John had retreated into a shell of timidity and shyness, especially since he'd attempted to kill himself. He didn't join the evenings of country music Pete created with his newly formed, ragtag family of whites and blacks. After dinner, John-John retreated to his bedroom. Sometimes when Pete was fucking Josh, he thought of John-John lying in a bedroom nearby, wanting Pete to be fucking him instead.

After picking up John-John, Pete headed for the mountains, taking the trail to Banner Elk. On the way there, he stopped off at his favorite catfish joint. Miss Prissy was waiting with some cold beer and some hush puppies.

Later, as Pete finished off his second plate of catfish, he slid his wooden chair back and looked intently at John-John. "Is there anything you want to do in life? Anything I can do for you?"

In the afternoon sun, John-John's light-blond hair was neatly combed. His fingers were long and graceful, and he often used his hands to express himself. "To be with you," he finally answered. "Even if waiting outside your door."

"What kind of shitfaced ambition is that?" Pete asked, growing impatient with the response. "Don't you want to do anything?"

"Be in your life—that's it. That's all I want and dream about."

After a very late lunch, Pete drove John-John to Claude's shotgun house in the mountains. Pete had been avoiding John-John as a sexual partner, but having this young boy with his tight, muscular body in the seat beside him made Pete horny.

On the rotting front porch, Pete fumbled with the key and pushed the door open, listening to its screech. Inside the cabin, Pete looked around and turned to face John-John. "Want something to drink?" he asked.

"Your spit."

Pete pulled the boy close to him, planting his larger mouth over John-John's. The boy opened his mouth as if begging for Pete's tongue. John-John got his reward, as Pete pushed his tongue deep within the boy's mouth. He shoved the boy against the wall and ground his pelvis against him. "Think you can handle a real man?"

The boy seemed to go wild. His hands were all over Pete. He was feeling the muscles in Pete's back, cupping his ass, and losing himself in Pete's arms. John-John slipped his deft fingers under Pete's white T-shirt to knead his torso. When those fingers later captured Pete's dick, John-John groaned softly as if anticipating the pleasure the cock would bring to him.

He tugged at Pete's clothes, stripping off the T-shirt before unbuckling the belt and pulling down the tight jeans.

By the time he had gotten John-John to bed, Pete had stripped him buck naked too. At this point Pete's hands had felt every inch of the boy's body. It was lean and more defined than he'd remembered it, more of a young man's body. His skin, though, was just as white and as smooth as it had been before Pete had gone off to war. The boy's dick had also grown an inch or two.

John-John reached for Pete, kissing him on the mouth with such tenderness that he was almost embarrassed by the intimacy. Freeing his lips, John-John used that same mouth to travel down Pete's torso, tonguing his pectorals, swirling around his navel. While doing this, John-John's fingers were lightly flickering across Pete's heavy balls and up his rock-hard dick. Pete shuddered involuntarily.

Pete reached down to pull the boy up to him again. He wanted to fuck him real bad.

John-John pushed him back. "Give me time. First I want to get acquainted with every inch of your body." The boy kept his word. Pete felt that there was no part of him that John-John didn't kiss and explore with his tongue. He stroked and squeezed until he had Pete moaning with pleasure.

He had never had his body treated with such reverence. He felt John-John's tongue moisten his ball sac and tickle the hairs there before taking each ball into his mouth one at a time for a thorough sucking.

When he separated Pete's asscheeks, John-John flickered at Pete's rosebud with such a feathery lightness that Pete practically crawled up the bedstead in ecstasy. When he could stand no more of that, Pete forced John-John down on his dick, deep throating the boy who took every inch of it without choking. Pete got into it, pumping his hips in quick, staccato thrusts reaching deep into the boy's throat. The more he pumped, the hungrier John-John became.

He was fast bringing Pete to the brink, but Pete had other plans for their evening. He reached down and yanked John-John's long blond hair.

"Sit on my chest and drop your nuts in my mouth," Pete ordered. John-John was a compliant lover, almost like a slave boy obeying his Roman master.

In no time at all, Pete was sucking and licking the young nuts, knowing they held a delicious nectar he wanted to swallow. He rolled them around in his jaws, enjoying the boy's groans. Without Pete even going down on him, John-John exploded, his cum shooting all over Pete's face. In minutes, the boy rearranged his body and was licking Pete's face clean of the ropy white strands.

There was a look of such exhilaration on John-John's face that it made Pete hornier than ever. Tongue darting out, Pete was going for the boy's succulent little rosebud. Pete looked at the clock on the mantle. It was ten after four in the afternoon. The hands of that clock had moved to seven o'clock before Pete finally withdrew his dick from John-John's ass. The boy had been incredible. He'd drawn three loads from Pete.

Pete had rested between rounds with his dick still deeply implanted in the young body beneath him.

As he felt John-John's ass muscles tightening around him again, he pulled out abruptly. "Enough, enough, you little fucker." Pete had to push him away. "You could go all night and never get enough."

He looked down into John-John's cherubic face. No choir boy had ever appeared so innocent, yet Pete felt the boy had all the makings and desire of a brazen male whore. He would clearly have been the favorite in a Grecian brothel of classical days. Pete leaned down and kissed the boy lightly on the lips.

"Me and you have made up for some lost time," John-John said.

Pete raised himself up slightly and looked deeply into the boy's eyes. John-John's face revealed an arrogant confidence, as if knowing that Pete would return to this love nest time and time again.

***

When Rosacoke was sent away to Mozambique, her sentence seemed like forever. It was amazing how even forever eventually came to an end.

Her worst mistake came in counting the days before her release. Hazel, her cellmate, warned her not to do it, but during her last month in prison she started marking off those days. How she wished she'd taken Hazel's advice. Instead of speeding up time, it dragged it out.

Oddly, her last night in prison was as horrible as her first night there. She had to serve out the "one day" in her sentence of one year, one day. It was the longest day and night she'd ever remembered spending. Minutes went by like hours.

Hazel sat with her for most of the night. "Honey, go straight. Make a

good life for yourself. Find a decent man. Not another Pete. Not another Hank. A man who'll really love you and make you his wife."

"I'll do my best."

The next morning she kissed Hazel good-bye before reporting to Alma Hunt's office.

"I'll probably rot in here," Hazel said.

"No, you won't. You'll get paroled. One day." With tears in her eyes, she kissed Hazel again.

This time Rosacoke wasn't afraid to knock on the head matron's door. Alma Hunt came to the door, threw it open, then went over to her desk. She held out a paper for Rosacoke to sign, and, when she had, she got her clothes back, including Nudie's old rhinestone cowgirl costumes, which Larry Hunt had given her. She clutched the bag to her, and, without saying one word, turned and left the main house of the prison. As she neared the gate, she didn't dare look back, fearing a long hand would reach out and yank her back in there.

Once outside those gates, she felt like a survivor, and she just knew that no ordeal she'd ever have to face in the future would equal what she'd gone through.

She had to walk to the nearest village, about a mile up the road. Once she heard a truck pull out of the prison compound, heading up the same road. She jumped into a nearby gully, hiding behind a briar patch until the van had gone on its way. Back on the road again, she broke into a run when she saw the ramshackle wooden buildings of that bleak, dusty village come into view.

She stumbled and fell twice, but kept picking herself up, grabbing her battered suitcase and running the rest of the way.

In the new but ill-fitting dress she'd been given, she felt out of place in the hamlet. Passers-by turned and looked at her suspiciously. She wasn't the first prisoner they'd seen who'd just been released from Mozambique.

She took what little money she'd been given and headed for the local drugstore, which contained the ticket window for the bus station. The old vendor there asked her where she wanted to go. She didn't know for sure. Throughout those long months in prison, she'd always planned to head south to Miami, where she was going with Hank before her arrest. However, all of a sudden she feared it would bring more bad luck to continue to carry out a plan that had ended so badly.

"Texas," she blurted out.

"Where in Texas? It's a mighty big state."

"*Anywhere* in Texas."

\*\*\*

"You've got to do something about Buster," a shirtless Josh was complaining as he sat with Pete eating breakfast on the terrace of the master bedroom at Heaven on Earth.

Pete didn't really care to talk about Buster but wanted to look out over his green fields. Since the war ended, and since Karl Adams had come back home safely from the Army, three new gingerbread-trimmed houses had been added to his acreage, which had grown by another three-hundred acres.

Pete could not have predicted it, but Karl as the overseer of Heaven on Earth had increased his real-estate holdings and had turned into a crackerjack manager of Pete's business affairs. No one else was making much progress around Heaven on Earth except Karl. In many ways he was the most unlikely candidate to be the business brains behind Pete's operation, but he'd come back home with a take-charge attitude and Pete had given him a free hand.

"You're not even listening to me," Josh said, hardly disguising the irritation in his voice. "You've got to do something about Buster. He's five years old. Next year he'll be going to school."

"And just what is wrong with my kid?" Pete asked, slamming down his cup of coffee. When Josh complained about Buster, it always pissed Pete off.

"You've got to control him more," Josh said. "This loving of you is getting out of hand."

Pete studied Josh's face carefully. "I do believe you're jealous of a little five-year old boy."

"I'm glad he loves you," Josh said. "I love Buster, too. But it doesn't seem like the love of a little boy for his daddy. It's sexual somehow."

"What in the fuck does that mean?"

"I mean he's all over you all the time," Josh said. "I've seen sons kiss their daddies but when Buster kisses you, which is about every minute he's with you, he kisses you right on the mouth."

"Cut the shit," Pete said. "Many daddies kiss their sons on the mouth."

"It's not that," Josh said. "When Buster kisses you, I practically have to pry his lips from your mouth. It's more than that. He doesn't like to lie on your chest. He likes to place his head on your crotch and go to sleep. You're always walking around naked in front of him. You know yourself he's reached for your cock several times and has even tried to play with it and kiss the head. Only the other day I noticed he was practically giving you a hard-on."

"If I'm getting a fucking hard-on," Pete said angrily, "that means you're not doing your job of taking care of my needs. I'm a man and a virile one. I've got desires. In fact, right now just for all this smart ass talk, I'm of a mind to grab you and throw you down on this terrace and fuck you until

you're bloody sore."

"I do take care of your needs," Josh protested. "I don't want Buster horning in on my act. Also he demands to sleep with us too many nights."

"The kid gets afraid of the dark," Pete said.

"That's what he claims," Josh said. "I think it's just an excuse to get into bed with his buck naked daddy. Buster is fascinated by your big dick. I heard him ask you last week if you thought his little pee-pee would one day grow to be as big as yours."

"It's just natural boy curiosity," Pete said. "All kids are like that."

"All kids aren't like that," Josh said. "I've never seen my daddy naked in my whole life, and I sure don't want to. I don't think my Mama has seen him completely naked either, and they've been married for years."

"Buster is not growing up in a puritan family like you did," Pete said. "The war's over. It's gonna be a new world out there. My kid is following his natural instincts."

"I still say it's getting out of hand and you should put a stop to it." Josh leaned over and kissed Pete on the lips. "Promise me you'll think about what I said."

"Don't worry about it."

"I'll be in the studio working on my music," Josh said, putting on his shirt. "Come out and join me."

When he'd gone, Pete called down to Tara.

"Morning, hoss," she said.

"Thanks for breakfast," he said. "Could you send Buster up?"

"Sure thing, hoss."

In three minutes, Buster burst into the bedroom, racing toward the terrace and into Pete's arms. His lips were still warm from Josh's kiss. Buster's lips met Pete's, and he held his son tight.

Who wouldn't love this little bundle? He was the most adorable child Pete had ever seen or known of. He also happened to be the most beautiful boy on earth with perfect skin and features.

He was certainly a product of his gorgeous mama and his handsome daddy. He seemed to have some of the loveliest features of both his parents. Buster was lingering a little longer than he should at Pete's mouth. It was hard for him to pull the boy off him. How did you tell a little five-year old kid that he was loving his daddy too much? Boys were supposed to love their daddies.

While Buster still clung to him, Pete picked him up and headed for the bathroom. It was time for their morning baths. Josh objected to Pete bathing every morning with Buster, but the kid delighted in it. Pete didn't see anything wrong with it.

As he ran the bath water, Buster pulled off his clothes and looked up at his daddy. "Go on, take off your robe," he said.

Pete would be lying if he didn't admit to himself that he liked stripping down in front of Buster. Pete let the robe fall to the marble floor.

Buster's face burst into glee, as he flashed that winning smile of his, showing perfectly formed white teeth. "It's so big, daddy."

Minutes later in the tub, Pete was splashing around with his son. "Let me soap it up, daddy. Make it real big."

Pete closed his eyes and placed his head on the rim of the tub. Buster's tender little fingers were fondling him, as the little boy applied the soap. He giggled in glee as Pete felt himself hardening.

*** 

Twilight was settling over the Blue Ridge Mountains as Pete sat by himself on the back verandah eating a Hershey bar and waiting for the sight of Josh—fresh from jogging—to emerge on the distant horizon. On many of these late evenings Pete joined Josh along the jogging trail but not tonight. He welcomed these moments alone.

He'd just finished a hot rehearsal session with Guitar Red, Smokey Wetter, Maston, and Nipsey in the converted barn. Larry had thought the musicians had never sounded better, and had pronounced Pete's voice at its top form.

Larry kept pleading every day to let him take the band on the road, but Pete kept holding back. All he'd agree to was the Saturday night hoedown at Big Mama Sadie's Blue Note Café. These performances were becoming something of a legend in the Carolina hills, and fans drove all the way from Tennessee to hear Pete sing. The verdict was in, and many a patron summed it up: "That's a white boy's body but a black man's voice coming out of it."

If Pete were more comfortable with that assessment of his talent, he'd be a lot more agreeable about Larry's getting bookings for them. Pete had recorded three songs that Larry felt had tremendous potential. Two were written by Josh, one by Nipsey. Maston had told Pete, "Those recordings are hot. When they're released, folks will think you're a nigger like us."

Pete was hardly a man of prejudice, but he was still a Southern white boy, and few of that breed wanted to be compared to a black man, except maybe in the dick department.

In their deepest, darkest nights of pillow talk, Pete had never admitted even to Josh that he was just plain scared to go on the road or be heard on radio. He thought he was terrific, and he loved the sound of the boys in his band. But the fear of rejection kept holding him back.

Freddie had even gone and bought a bus for the men to travel in. Every day Pete looked at it, including last winter when it had been covered in snow. Sometimes he'd get on the bus by himself, imagining what it would be like riding the roads between the Florida Panhandle across Louisiana

and into Texas.

Not everybody at Heaven on Earth wanted Pete to go on the road. Having long ago retired as sheriff, Claude liked his life as it was, although he was ready and willing to go on the road any time Pete ordered him to, as he'd be in charge of security.

Claude and his son-in-law, Ronnie, had grown closer since that Florida wedding. Pete felt that the two men were growing more and more in love as each month went by. They were virtually inseparable, and Ronnie didn't look forward to Claude going on the road perhaps for weeks and months at a time.

Ronnie's reluctant bride, Wanda Mae, didn't seem to care very much what her daddy and her husband did. Pete had never asked Ronnie if their marriage had ultimately been consummated. For some reason, he didn't want to know.

Wanda Mae ran around a lot with her girl friends. Pete had no evidence she was cheating on Ronnie. What Wanda Mae wanted more than anything was to become a hair dresser. Pete had willingly opened a deluxe beauty salon for her in the center of town. Business had been so good that Wanda Mae had taken on three extra beauticians.

Wanda Mae was also talking about opening up the first dress shop in town. As it was, all the women of the county were forced to buy their clothes at W.G. Gabriel's Belks Department Store. Mary Hemphill, the buyer, dressed like an old maid aunt, and she wanted the rest of the women, even the young gals, to emulate her. Wanda Mae was convinced that her dress salon, geared to the youth-conscious, post-war market, would virtually wipe out the women's clothing department of Belks. Pete agreed.

After meeting with Karl, his business manager, Pete also agreed to finance Wanda Mae's venture into women's wear. Pete had never liked Wanda Mae but at least he admired her entrepreneurial spirit.

Ronnie didn't do a damn thing, except play tennis. If Claude and Ronnie got any exercise at all during the day, it was from only two pastimes: tennis and fucking.

The man who worked the least and did almost no exercise was Hank. He slept late, drank, and fucked, and was great at all three activities. Pete was amazed that Hank's body stayed in such perfect form.

Larry had fallen deeply in love with Hank, but Hank didn't seem to care all that much. Pete was left with the impression that it wasn't all that important who Hank slept with, providing it was a hot, young body.

Natural or not, Hank was the sexiest lover at Heaven on Earth, even if his fabulous love-making technique remained confined to just Larry and Pete. Hank secretly confided in Pete that he wanted to run around with women, "but I can't as long as I'm shacked up with that jealous fool. Larry hawkeyes me day and night. He likes to watch me and you get it on, but

that's it. I still want a woman from time to time."

From a distance in the field beyond, Freddie Raubal and his black lover, Nipsey, waved at Pete. They were taking a sunset walk hand-in-hand around part of Pete's property. In many respects, they were the easiest couple to deal with that Pete had moved into his compound.

Smokey Wetter and Guitar Red didn't seem to care too much whether they worked or not. Having been on the road most of their lives, they seemed happy to have a roof over their head, an easy practice session every day, and plenty of good food to eat. Smokey and Guitar Red had become good friends with Moss and Fry. Those two aging black musicians often arranged for young black gals to visit Smokey and Guitar Red.

Interrupting his thoughts, Tara came out onto the back porch. Pete knew at once it was only sad news she had to tell. "It's mama, isn't it?" he asked.

"Yes, hoss," Tara said. "Your mama passed on about an hour ago."

***

On his return from the Army at the end of World War II, Karl in his neatly pressed uniform had never looked sexier, like a young Hank without the dissipation of the years.

Within months of his return, Karl had turned the decaying old plantation around, bringing new life to it, repairing the mansion and planting the fields, bringing in a bumper crop his first few months back.

Ever so slowly he'd taken over Pete's business affairs. Other than the farm, Karl's greatest interest seemed to be in architecture. In the first year, he'd convinced Pete to build a series of affordable houses in western North Carolina for returning veterans who would surely marry and raise families. "They're gonna need a place to live and we can provide for them," Karl said.

Since Karl seemed to make everything he touched turn to gold, Pete had given him orders to go "full steam ahead."

Karl had done just that. "I want to make something of myself," Karl had told Pete. "With your help, I can. I don't want to be like my brothers."

One Sunday morning, Karl drove Pete up the mountain road and past the shotgun house owned by Claude, heading to an "eagle's nest." Pete was determined to seize the chance to press Karl into some clarification of their own personal relationship. Ever since coming back from the service, Karl had seemed to avoid Pete on a personal level. All their talk seemed to center on business. At times Pete had come to feel that Karl was a walking cash register.

Pete could only remember the nights he'd had sex with Karl as a boy.

Since this handsome hunk of a young soldier had returned from the war, Pete hadn't even seen Karl with his shirt off, much less done anything else.

It was a summer day and Karl was wearing a form-fitting white T-shirt that showed off the muscles of his upper torso to perfection. Pete could see rock-hard nipples bursting through the thin cotton material, and Pete wanted to suck them into his mouth. He'd known the boy but desired this fully grown man even more. Karl had consistently rebuffed all of Pete's sexual overtures, usually made when he was drunk.

"I'm glad to be out on the road with you away from the rest," Pete said, relaxing back in his seat but casting his eye on Karl's beautiful profile every chance he got. "Heaven on Earth is turning into Grand Central Station. You and me haven't had much chance to be alone together except in your office talking business shit all the time."

"Yeah, it's good to have you all to myself for the day," Karl said. He turned and flashed a smile so alluring that Pete felt he was getting an instant hard-on.

"This may be a delicate subject," Pete said. "But you and me used to be a hell of a lot closer before you joined the Army."

"You mean the sex stuff?" Karl asked abruptly, interrupting him. "That's kids' stuff. The Army turned me into a man. Since coming back home, I've taken up with two or three girls. In fact, I've fallen in love with one of them. Rebecca. Me and her are going steady. She's a friend of Wanda Mae's."

"I'd say that Rebecca is one lucky gal," Pete said. "I got to you long before she got to you, and I know how good you are. At least when you were a boy. I can only guess you're even better as a man."

Karl turned and smiled at Pete. "I am." A sexy smirk crossed his face. "But that's for Rebecca to know—not you. I'm gonna marry her."

"Ronnie married Wanda Mae but that sure didn't stop him from fooling around with Claude," Pete said.

"That's fine for Ronnie," Karl said. "But I'm a true-blue kind of guy. I know I've got a lot to give to a woman. It's gonna be one woman and one woman only for me. No fooling around with guys like the rest of you. I decided in the Army that's not for me."

"Does that mean that I, your best friend, your business partner, a man who thinks your shit smells sweet, is not gonna get to suck that big dick of yours ever again?"

"I don't want to say never," Karl said. "I know a little bit about life. We'll probably go off on some business trip together and will end up one night drinking in a motel room. I'll get horny. One thing will lead to another. You are the world's greatest cocksucker. I tried to get Rebecca to go down on me. She said it was disgusting. So I'm sure not gonna get all that good licking and sucking from her that I got from you."

As they neared the top of the mountain, Pete said, "I want you, man. Real bad. I wish you'd whip it out for me right now and let me suck you dry. You're prettier and sexier than Hank ever was even in his prime."

As Karl pulled over to the side of the road, he looked Pete over carefully. "You really mean that? God damn it, I think I've waited for years to hear someone say that. I always felt inferior to Hank and Tracy. They were always bigger than me. The way you make me feel today is that I'm a better man than either of them. Of course, I may not have been as good as Tracy, but we lost him."

The memory of Tracy's loss stabbed at Pete's heart, as he tried to blot it from his mind.

"C'mon," Karl said, seemingly nervous at the way the conversation was going. "I didn't bring you up here to talk personal shit like this. I brought you up here for business."

Up in the mountains with the wind blowing through their hair, Pete felt he was falling in love with Karl. "How could he love yet another?" he silently asked himself. But Pete knew in his heart he wanted Karl, and their talk in the car had indicated to Pete that Karl could be had once again.

Karl led Pete to one of the most beautiful pieces of mountain real estate Pete had ever seen. He didn't know this spot existed. Pete had been all over these mountains, and he had never seen such a setting with such a panorama.

As the day unfolded, Pete learned Karl's intentions. He wanted Pete to buy up all the acreage for miles around and construct a stunningly modern house in the Frank Lloyd Wright style. Karl had been studying a book of Wright's architecture, and he wanted to design a house for Pete as a retreat from the world.

"You're gonna be a big-time star," Karl said. "Larry Hunt told me that and Larry really knows show business. Heaven on Earth is gonna be overrun. You'll never have privacy there. You can come up here and work on your music. You'll be high in the heavens. The place will be spectacular in winter or summer. It's perfect for you. A real hideaway."

Before the afternoon ended, Pete had given Karl a green light to go ahead with his plans. His heart wasn't really into it, but Pete saw how delighted and thrilled the prospect made Karl. He owed Karl big favors, and Pete felt it would be wrong to deny Karl his dream.

At one point later that night when they'd stopped off in a mountain tavern and had downed too many beers, Pete felt he was leading the conversation in the right direction to accomplish his aim, which was to get back once again into Karl's pants. But each time Karl cleverly avoided Pete's sexual trap.

When Pete went to the men's room, he stood at one urinal relieving himself. He was thrilled to see Karl come in the toilet to join him, standing

at the other urinal. As Karl reached in to pull out his dick, Pete felt his heart beating faster. When Karl flopped it out, it was even bigger and thicker than Pete remembered.

Karl looked over at him and said, "Hell, we can piss together, can't we? I don't have to keep my dick hidden from you. After all, you've deep throated it and had it up your ass. Who am I kidding? You've had me more times than Rebecca has."

Even though too drunk to drive down the mountain, Karl got behind the wheel when they left the tavern an hour later. As he reached to switch on the engine, Pete blocked his action. "I want one big favor. I've got to have it, man."

"The answer is no," Karl said. "We're not getting back into that shit again. I've told you once and I don't need to tell you again. I'm not fucking you or letting you blow me no more, so wipe it out of your head. Josh is one good-looking guy. I'm not depriving you but sending you back to your real loving man."

"I'm not asking for sex," Pete said. "I want to kiss you. You've never let me kiss you before, and kissing you has become an obsession with me."

"I'm not into it," Karl said, once again trying to start the engine.

Pete reached for Karl, feeling the power of his muscles. Pete's fingers dug into Karl's back, pulling him closer.

When Pete looked into the gorgeous face of Karl, Pete knew he'd won. Karl's eyes were closed and his mouth open as his face inched closer to Pete's lusting lips.

The kiss must have lasted fifteen minutes—maybe more. After the first three minutes, Pete's hand, with a will of its own, had moved toward Karl's crotch, finding him rock hard. After six minutes, Karl was moaning and in heat. His cock was throbbing. As Pete reached to unbutton Karl's fly, he pushed him away and started the car heading down the mountain.

Even though his own cock was painfully hard, Pete settled down in his seat in bitter disappointment. He didn't know when he'd wanted another man more than he desired Karl Adams tonight.

His heart woke up in delight when he saw Karl turning off the road and parking the car in front of a house. In the dark night Pete looked out at the building.

"C'mon," Karl said. "I'll call down to the house and tell them we're too drunk to drive and will be home in the morning." He cut off the lights and got out of the car and went over to Pete's side, opening the door for him. Karl's hand reached inside for Pete's. "You're gonna get what you've been drooling over all day."

In the dark Carolina night, the moon suddenly emerged from behind a cloud, illuminating Claude's empty shotgun house.

Pete stood with Junior Grayson in the tower overlooking the airfield which up to now allowed only private craft to land because it was too small and undeveloped. As an airplane pilot during World War II, Junior had fallen in love with aviation and had decided to devote the rest of his life to it. "It's the coming thing for America," he told Pete, who also believed that was so.

With Karl's financial blessing, Pete had given Junior the go-ahead to invest money in a new airfield. Junior predicted that in a year Pete could buy eight planes with a loan from the bank and bring commercial aviation to this remote part of western North Carolina.

"Now all air passengers have to fly to Charlotte and then drive all the way up here," Junior said. "We'll soon have commuter planes flying. We'll make millions. This part of the world is gonna grow and grow big, and we're gonna cash in on it."

Pete knew that Junior was right on target. Only last night, Karl had predicted to Pete that he might one day be earning his living and supporting all of them from the money earned by his own private airline.

As Junior watched a bulldozer in the distance, his dreamy eyes looking toward the future, Pete seized the chance to study Junior closely. He stood tall and proud, his body fully matured after his stint in the military. His hair had darkened but his green eyes were the greenest Pete had ever seen outside a cat family. Junior still retained his boyish grin even if it were set in a warrior's jaw. He still had that youthful quality that had at first attracted Pete but it was blended with a studly sensuality.

"I've got a great idea," Pete said. "Let's fly out of here right now. I'll call Josh and Tara and tell them to hold down the fort. I'll claim something important has come up about the new airport. That we've got to fly to Nashville for the night."

Those dreamy green eyes were turned on Pete with an eager anticipation. If there were any bait to dangle before Junior, it was a request to fly somewhere in Pete's private plane. "Hell, I'd like that, man. I'll go now to make the arrangements."

Even though Junior had been back from the war for months, Pete had never spent much time alone with him. Pete had wanted to but the opportunity never seemed to arise. He was always surrounded by his hangers-on, and there was the hawk-eye of Josh to deal with. That was one jealous boy.

Tonight in Nashville would be a test of just how far Junior was willing to go sexually with Pete. Fortunately, the answer to that question had been full steam ahead in Karl's case. After that time in the shotgun house, Karl cornered Pete every chance he got, and there were quite a few private

times since the two business partners had many excuses to be alone together. It turned out that Karl wasn't too much into fucking. He figured he could do that with Rebecca. What he couldn't get were expert blow-jobs, to which he had grown addicted.

Every opportunity that arose, Karl rose to the occasion, sneaking away for Pete's skilled blow-jobs. He loved draining Karl dry every day if he could. One day Karl pulled it out four times for Pete, and each of Karl's loads had tasted as creamy as the first one. When they had more time, Karl liked to pull off all his clothes. "Almost as much as I like blow-jobs, I'm crazy about an around the world. Don't miss one single inch of my body with your tongue." Before their latest bout had ended, Pete felt Karl was the most licked-down man in western North Carolina. Karl's climax had been spectacular.

After he'd made the calls to Heaven on Earth from the airport, Pete eagerly anticipated sharing a hotel room in Nashville with Junior. He'd given Junior frequent blow-jobs since he'd come back from the Air Force, but Pete hadn't really spent long hours with his private pilot jaybird naked in bed beside him.

He was anxious to devour every inch of the handsome stud the way he had so recently done with Karl, and the way he always did with Josh. Kneeling in front of a fully dressed guy with his fly open and his dick hanging out was okay by Pete for appetizers, but he liked to taste every single part of a man's body.

On the flight to Nashville, talk was virtually impossible because of the noise of the engine. Once landed, Pete called the Peabody Hotel and booked a suite for them. At the hotel, he asked the desk clerk to get them the best seats possible for the Grand Ole Opera. Pete dropped a ten-dollar bill on the desk for the young man's trouble.

Alone in the suite, Pete wanted to take Junior in his arms and kiss him, as there had been none of that in their relationship to date. But he didn't move on Junior right away, as he sensed hesitation on Junior's part to go too queer too soon. He felt Junior liked women a lot more than he liked men. Pete suspected Junior was willing to go along with Pete's sexual requests, but only to a point. No fucking, unless Junior was on top, and no kissing ever. Before the night was over, Pete hoped to change that.

Junior said he was all sweaty from the plane ride and wanted a shower. As he undressed in front of Pete, Pete was hopeful about what the night held in store for them. Junior wasn't modest about taking off all his clothes in front of Pete, which made sense. What did Junior have to hide from a man who'd repeatedly sucked his cock?

The sight of that exposed cock made Pete want to drop down on his knees in front of Junior and taste it. Junior smiled when he caught Pete's eyes eagerly checking him out. "Looks pretty good, huh?" Junior asked

before heading to the shower. Pete took in every movement of Junior's firm butt, wanting to sample every inch of it with his tongue and maybe another organ of his if Junior would let him go that far.

On an impulse, Pete stood up and slipped off his own clothes. Totally nude, he headed for the bathroom where he pulled back the shower curtain and without an invite joined Junior under the hot spray. At first Junior had seemed surprised but then welcomed Pete.

As he soaped Junior's body, Pete was rewarded with the pilot's immense, intense erection. Pete fell to his knees, under the running water, lapping at Junior's ball sac, nudging the handsome pilot's nuts around with his prodding nose and darting tongue. His lips took time out to kiss and lick Junior's thighs before returning to those balls to suck on them like some blood-thirsty vampire.

Junior leaned back against the tile wall, spreading his legs to give Pete greater access. Deserting the balls, Pete's tongue traveled Junior's long shaft of raw meat, polishing the throbbing hardness and tonguing and slurping until he kissed the head and plunged all the way down to the pubic hairs.

Pete would bring Junior to the brink of climax, then take his mouth off Junior to make him hold back. Pete wanted to enjoy an intense sucking of this gorgeous man before letting him spurt his load.

As he sucked, Pete's hands felt the broad, muscle-knotted chest of his pilot, paying particular attention to Junior's nipples.

When Pete decided that he'd tortured Junior long enough, he swallowed him whole again. As he plunged down once more, something inside Junior's guts seemed to snap. He grabbed Pete's head this time and forced him all the way down on his dick. He wasn't going to let him escape to tantalize him any more. Heaving and ramming, Junior pounded his meat into Pete's face.

It wasn't long before Junior's balls exploded, and Pete was there to drink every drop. The frothy cream scalded Pete's mouth. It tasted delicious. Junior kept one hand around Pete's neck holding him in a tight grip until he was completely satisfied. Even when the final drops had been swallowed, Pete was reluctant to let go.

Finally he got to his feet, his face only an inch or so from Junior's. Pete's tongue darted out, licking Junior's lips, which up to now had been off-limits to Pete. Junior was still breathing heavily and offered no resistance as Pete's tongue darted inside his mouth. Pete knew that the pilot's quality cream was still on his tongue. Junior's lips were ruby and pouty. As Pete kissed him, Junior kissed back. Pete licked between Junior's lips and probed his mouth with his tongue. Junior sucked on that tongue.

At that point Pete never wanted to get out from under the shower, but they did.

Pete took Junior for a steak dinner, and felt proud at how handsome the

pilot looked in a suit. Pete didn't often get to see Junior in a suit. Both men had a full suitcase waiting in their plane in case they took off suddenly somewhere and didn't want to pack, or else didn't have time to.

An hour later, it was a big night at the Grand Ole Opry, as Pete dreamed that one day in the not so distant future he'd be up on that same stage performing before crowds of adoring fans.

The show opened with one of Pete's favorites, Grandpa Jones. Grandpa stepped on that Opry stage and started stomping his foot and playing his banjo, and the crowd went wild. In boots, an old hat, and mountain clothes, Grandpa delivered a crowd-pleasing act

The hit of the night was Eddy Arnold, who'd come a long way since as a boy he'd stood and watched as his family farm was auctioned off by his daddy's creditors. When Eddy sang his mama's favorite, "Sweet Bunches of Daisies," some of his loyal fans shed tears.

After the show, Pete and Junior had polished off a quart of Tennessee bourbon before returning to their rooms, where they stripped nude and fell drunk on the bed.

As Junior started to drift into sleep, Pete's hands felt his friend's ass. Pete eased below to taste the soft flesh of his cheeks, his tongue darting for the asscrack. Sensing Pete's target, Junior arched upward to give Pete greater access. As Pete's tongue danced about the tender pucker, Junior was moaning in delight. But if Pete thought he was going to be allowed to invade this virgin turf, he was wrong.

Junior had another plan. He caught Pete off guard when he threw him over. His cock had become a gigantic boner, as he spread Pete's legs lifting them into the air. Pete knew he was going to get fucked and fucked rough, and he wanted it. Slicking up his cock with saliva, Junior invaded as Pete's hole twitched in anticipation. He rammed his cock deep into Pete's guts without giving Pete time to get used to it. Crying out in pain, Pete just held on, scissoring his legs around Junior's trim waist.

Pete's asshole was burning as a drunken Junior fucked fast and furious. His jabbing rod plunged deep inside Pete, hitting something. No doubt it was his prostate gland. Pete blasted off into the air, and Junior didn't pause one second but kept pounding until he'd delivered his second load of the night.

Sweaty and exhausted, Junior pulled himself up and collapsed against Pete. The semen on Pete's chest seem to glue them together. Pete could hear the pounding of Junior's heart and his heavy breathing. His pilot was drifting into sleep. His smell was a manly aroma of nicotine, bourbon, and hot sperm.

Before completely falling asleep, Junior reached over and crushed his lips against Pete's who could feel the tickle of tomorrow morning's beard.

Wrapped in the arms of Junior. Pete felt he'd added another man to his

stable. This one was hot as a firecracker, and Pete planned to hold onto him until the end.

***

As the years went by, Rosacoke still thought a lot about Pete. She hoped that he was out of the Navy by now and he'd developed into a proper daddy for their son. How she wished she could take Pete's hand and watch that little boy run across a field or play ball or ride a pony. He should be big enough now. A five-year old who'd be starting school next year. She couldn't think too much about it, because if she did she'd start to cry.

It was already 1947, and she was all of twenty-three years old. She hadn't made much progress in her singing career. At least she supported herself, working the honky-tonks between Texas and Louisiana, places where men went more to fight than to listen to music.

She knew that the years had brought many changes to her life. No more could she lay claim to being the fairly innocent teenage girl she was when she was sent to the penitentiary. She'd learned to survive in what she called a world of "mean-assed motherfuckers." At first she was uncomfortable with the term, and it definitely sounded more like Narcissa than her. But Narcissa had a point. Because of all her hard knocks, Rosacoke had come to view the world that way, too.

She wasn't singing all the time. Most jobs were pretty much the same as My Old Kentucky Home. When she wasn't up there singing, she tended bar. Learning to be a bartender wasn't hard at all. No fancy mixed drinks for her crowd. They liked beer or their liquor neat.

Even the places had become pretty much the same. Big, barren beer joints with dull wooden floors sprinkled with sawdust. Along with the dust in the air, a bristling danger prevailed in many of these tonks, and sometimes her singing was interrupted by a massive free-for-all fist fight.

From pool halls in the back room, men with sharpened knives in their pockets emerged to hear her sing. In spite of her voluptuousness, many of the men referred to her as "one of the guys." That was a tribute to the fact that she'd learned to cope in code-of-the-hills country, entertaining men whose lips curled down at the corners. One night in Waco, right in the middle of her big number, she'd witnessed a guy get his stomach cut out.

She'd learned to shoot pool with the rednecks and accept beers from them, although to turn down their other requests. She didn't intend to get emotionally involved with another man, in the wake of her disastrous involvements with Pete and Hank.

That didn't mean she'd given up men entirely. There had been a few along the way. The only difference was, she didn't give her heart to the first cowboy who came along. She liked the feeling of some body warmth

and especially the whispered words of love. She accepted the body heat and enjoyed but didn't believe the words.

Mostly she selected her fellow singers and players as her boy friends. One, in particular, Manny Reno, liked her a lot, or so it had seemed at the time. Tall and lanky, just the way she liked men, he'd looked real good to her in his cowboy hat and jeans. He was more of a western singer than country, and his real dream was to become "the second Gene Autry."

Like her, he'd been thrown into jail when he was a kid. The crime, stealing cars. What had won her to him was when he'd said, "I turned twenty-one in jail." She painfully recalled her own eighteenth birthday spent waiting for her trial. "I had no daddy," Manny said. "I grew up with my mama in a converted railroad car outside Waco. I used to hitch up and down the highway looking for a gig playing guitar."

He gave her what she considered some pretty good advice. "If you're gonna make it big singing your hillbilly music, you've got to remember to present yourself in such a way that your image will sit right in the public's mind. In your case, it's okay that you had a ne'er-do-well for a daddy. But you can't let your public know your mama was like that, too. One's mama has just got to be right perfect, sitting out rocking on the front porch singing 'Rock of Ages.' Maybe she could have dipped snuff. But she can't have no sin bigger than that. She certainly could never have played around with men, and under no circumstances nigger men. So you'd better start inventing a past for yourself. From what you've told me, you could never tell any of your fans the real truth."

Manny was real courteous around women. He treated them like they were something special, like the type of food that should be served only on Sunday. He had a disarming way about him of making her feel she was the only woman in the world. But, as she discovered one night when she returned unexpectedly to their bungalow, he practiced that same knack on other women. In this case, two women.

Along with a bitter pang in her heart, she'd learned something else she'd never known. Men not only cheated—she knew that—but they even went to bed with two women at the same time. She didn't understand the logistics of that and never wanted to.

It was good-bye to Manny after that. He'd run after her with his pants down, begging her to forgive him, but she felt she'd best travel along. Her romantic Manny had come to look ridiculous, especially with his pants down.

The men she'd met after that were pretty much the same. Whatever their backgrounds—roughnecking it on oil rigs, hopping freights, juvenile arrests—there was a similarity. They'd all come up the hard way, and there existed in most of them an immaturity she felt would always be there. "Isn't there one good man for me in the whole wide world?" she kept asking herself. If there were, she was yet to meet him.

Mostly she didn't think about men. She thought about work, accepting whatever jobs came her way, providing it was honest. Regardless of how disappointing the response, how small the pay, how bad the working conditions, she kept singing and playing the guitar. Even on a Saturday night when the noise of drunken revelers almost drowned her out.

Occasionally on some nights, as she wallowed deep in quiet despair, she wanted to give up, feeling there was no place for a woman in country music, that it was strictly a male-dominated showcase.

The next morning after one of those gloomy sessions, she would will her spirits to perk up again, and she went back to singing, continuing to add to her repertoire and trying, always trying, to get people to listen. She knew she could sing, and she hoped that one day the world—or at least a little bit of it—would come to appreciate that.

*** 

Nights on the road were long and lonely. She remembered one gig outside Dallas when she'd been booked into an orange-colored bar that had the name of Crazy October. In all that cavernous tavern, only eight customers had braved the cold winter weather that night to listen to a girl singer in an unheated arena. She hoped that the manager would cancel the show, but he'd insisted that she go on.

For the next hour, in front of the sparse, shivering audience, she'd worked her way through her standards. At curtain call, she spoke to the audience. "Thanks a whole heap for coming out on a night like this. This place gets very, very lonely when nobody shows up." To scattered applause, she'd turned and walked off.

At the rear of Crazy October, an old woman had approached her to thank her. "My son and daughter brought me here for my seventy-fifth birthday. You were just fine. Remember, it's not the number of the crowd you sing to, but singing right for the folks who showed up."

Upon hearing that, Rosacoke had burst into tears, kissing the woman's withered cheek. "Happy birthday."

After she'd leave a club, she was almost afraid to go to sleep early. She'd closed many a coffee shop at three a.m. or lingered long in an all-night diner. The earlier she went to bed, the earlier she got up. Spending a day alone in a bleak hotel room never appealed to her. Often she wasn't due at a club until nine o'clock that night. Afternoons loomed like vast chasms.

Month after month she lived in old cars and even older hotels, eating what she could. If she never saw another hot dog again she'd be happy. But she'd end up buying one any way when she got hungry again. After all, they were cheaper than hamburgers and who could afford steak?

The one thing she had to guard against was having another child. That wasn't easy as she traveled the country byways, always in the company of a rag-tag band. All the men figured that any woman running around with professional itinerant musicians was up for grabs. She wasn't. Making that clear got pretty tough at times.

There was the occasional fellow she went to bed with. After all, not all men are rotten. But those nice guys were few and far between, and most likely married in spite of what they claimed. Usually they were one-night stands. Once or twice an affair lasted a little longer. But on many a morning she woke up to find that the man of her dreams had gotten up in the middle of the night and gone back to his real life, probably with a wife and three kids. One man she felt she could really fall in love with had lied to her. He too was married. He finally confessed. "I've got nine kids. I've been having one a year since I turned fourteen."

As hard as life on the road was, she suspected life as a married woman wasn't all roses either. She'd seen more than one overworked, barefoot, pregnant woman with kids toddling and crawling around the floor, cooking her husband's supper in case he might chose to come home and demand it. Rosacoke wasn't a slave any more, the way she'd been at Sultan's and with the Riddle family. Hard times or not, she was out on her own, making her own way and her own decisions. That meant growing up early and learning to cope.

She tried to make a home where she could find it, and to do that she carried around her own personal memorabilia. The Christmas before he went to war, Pete had given her a cigarette case with a Confederate flag design which played "Dixie" when opened. She always carried that around, along with a few other items.

Her outfits had changed. Nudie's rhinestone cowgirl classics had long worn out, but she'd settled for cheaper imitations. Those imitations, if anything, were even flashier. A club manager had told her one night, "Honey, you look like a Texas cowgirl who's just struck oil." She had liked that comparison.

Nearly everything was a one-nighter. If she ever got a job for more than one night, she practically felt she was living in a town. She'd sing anywhere—school gymnasium, tent, barroom—wherever she could get a gig.

All these places blurred in her mind, like the bleak hotel rooms. Some things you could count on: lumpy beds (always with chenille spreads) and drab, smelly hallway toilets. The rooms had witnessed a string of either broken heads or broken hearts. The menus in all those little diners were always grease stained, the fried food indigestible.

Summertime was the worst, as she rode along in the back seat of a car, crowded in with three or four other musicians and God only knows how

many instruments. Her bones ached, and she was a mess of wrinkles. Sometimes she'd arrive for a date so late there was almost no time to freshen up before she went on. Still, she endured, glad to be working in a man's world.

There were good moments, too, like the deep, dark nights spent riding the back roads of Texas. A person, usually a stranger or a musician she'd just met, would sometimes open up his heart, and the most intimate secrets and deepest fears would be revealed. That made for a bittersweet camaraderie that in some small way filled the vacuum caused by her lack of friends and lovers.

***

Looking for a big break, Rosacoke decided to stop off at Reba's Orchid Lounge in Austin, Texas. She knew that Reba's place drew a slightly better clientele than most of the dives where Rosacoke had worked previously. At least she'd been told that the men at Reba's wore checked sports shirts and western string ties, and they often actually listened to the music, at least when they were picking pieces of fried chicken out from between their teeth with toothpicks.

If you traveled the honky-tonk circuit in Texas and Louisiana, you knew who Reba Crawford was. A bit of local legend, she liked country and western music, and had a reputation for always booking the best acts.

On Sunday afternoon Reba auditioned new talent. So short on money she'd spent the night sleeping in the Greyhound bus station, Rosacoke hitched a ride over to Reba's lounge. There, she had to wait her turn, listening to a group of acts that ranged from Jimmie Rodgers imitators to old-time banjo pickers. To her acute discomfort, Rosacoke noticed that she was the only woman there. If Reba liked to hire members of her own sex, that would be a breakthrough for Rosacoke, but if she didn't, Rosacoke would be scrounging for her next meal.

When Rosacoke's time came to go on stage, she was nervous. A piano player accompanied any of the singers who wanted it. Stepping up to the man's side, Rosacoke asked him if he knew "Walking the Floor Over You."

"Does a bear shit in the woods?" the old-time player asked.

As she stepped up to sing, Rosacoke knew that Reba was in the room, although the club manager remained seated in a dark corner, her face buried in a newspaper. "The bitch," Rosacoke hissed to herself. She felt Reba could at least give her a chance.

Halfway through the song, Reba slammed down the newspapers. "Next!" she shouted, her booming voice echoing through the cavernous lounge.

Hungry and also desperate for work, Rosacoke burst into tears. "God

damn you," she yelled at Reba. "I'm starving to death. I need this job real bad. You wouldn't even listen."

"I listened, you big tit heifer," Reba yelled right back. "I heard enough to offer you a job beginning tomorrow night. When someone's good as you are, I don't have to sit here all afternoon listening to shit. I've got a stud waiting upstairs who's gonna fuck me silly. Go back to the kitchen and fetch yourself a plate of ribs. Then come and see me. Next!"

Shocked and stunned, Rosacoke staggered to the kitchen, almost crying with gratitude. After devouring the ribs, she went over to Reba's table. She had just finished listening to a group of cowboy singers. "Get the hell out of this building," she yelled at the singers. "You stink! Don't even come back as customers."

Rosacoke studied Reba closely. With her wind-whipped red face and burnt-orange hair, cut in a wild, electric way, she was no beauty. Though not good-looking, at least by traditional standards, she was built most satisfactorily.

"I know I ain't much to look at, honey," Reba said, catching Rosacoke staring at her. "But many men have fallen in love with me over the years. One of my former lovers, a guy named Marty, said I was wonderful only as a woman can be wonderful. He was speaking of me in bed. But that's all the details I'm feeding you until I get to know you better."

Rosacoke was embarrassed at Reba's frank talk.

"When did you last eat?" Reba asked.

"I had a chili dog the other night."

"Thought so. This is no place for a woman, but I think you're a refreshing change of pace. With your figure and those knockers, you should go over big with the boys."

"I sure hope so."

"Where you from?" Reba asked.

"The Carolinas."

Reba immediately interrupted. "I was born in some holler back in Tennessee. Your next door neighbor."

As Reba talked, Rosacoke carefully observed this tiny, high-spirited woman who appeared to be in her early thirties.

"I've owned quite a few bars and night spots in my day. Got my first one when I was just twenty-one. Don't ask me how. I grew up to the sound of throbbing jukeboxes and pinging pinball machines."

Rosacoke was clearly fascinated by Reba's dynamic personality and her violent, snatching gestures. Her face was slightly pocked, owing to a girlhood skin problem. Deep-set intense eyes of inky black stared back at Rosacoke.

"You got any place to stay?" Reba asked. "I'm sure you haven't. I've got an extra room upstairs I'll let you have."

"I'm right grateful and all."

"Say, you haven't asked about the pay. It's fifty dollars a week, seven nights a week. And you get three free beers every night."

After taking a shower, Rosacoke unpacked her possessions and fell asleep for several hours. When she awoke, the joint was rocking. She dressed in one of her cowgirl outfits, going downstairs. The bartender, Charlie Starrett, had already been told she was to have her beers on the house.

She drank them slowly, as she listened to a group of cowboys singing not very well. She mentally rehearsed her own act for tomorrow night.

Reba was nowhere to be seen, but at last call she appeared. "Okay," she shouted into a microphone. "Drink up, you suckers, and then get the hell out of my hair."

Rosacoke was surprised that Reba talked to her customers that way, but they seemed to like it. Those who lingered too long at the bar got a jab from her three-inch, diamond-headed hairpin.

Rosacoke wheeled around to stare into Reba's face, half hidden behind her thick glasses with diamond-flecked rims. Reba bent over and whispered to Rosacoke. "If you want to pick up some extra money, I know some guys who want to bed you. Only problem is, I take in fifty percent of the outside action."

"No thanks," Rosacoke said. "I was hired to sing, and that'll be just fine. Good night."

\*\*\*

Night after night Rosacoke's popularity grew at Reba's place. Rosacoke could almost feel it. Slowly but steadfastly, she began to pick up some loyal fans—truck drivers from Wheeling, plain women in thin cotton Sears dresses from Port Arthur, sharecroppers from the West Texas plains.

Five tough years were now behind her, years of backseat sleeping and country music-making. She still took her standard songs from the repertoire of Bob Wills, Roy Acuff, and Ernest Tubb. But she also wrote and sang many of her own songs, having found her unique voice after going through her sentimental period and getting that out of her system.

Her rapport with audiences grew nightly and, at times, seemed uncanny. She learned to sense if a crowd was in the mood for a sad song or an upbeat one. Between numbers she learned some philosophical throw-away lines.

At Reba's, Rosacoke felt she had at last developed a stage personality. She virtually pulsated with energy in front of an audience.

Offstage she remained a loner. Pensive and quiet, she saved her "explosion" until she appeared on the orchid lounge stage.

In her private life, there remained a yawning emptiness. No one had

filled the void left by Pete, and that was a long time ago. She'd hoped to forget her son, but late at night she found herself trying to conjure up his image. She felt she would never settle down with anyone, be understood and loved—that she was sentenced just like in jail to spend the rest of her years as a drifter. The more intense her presence on stage, the more she feared she was becoming less and less a woman in real life.

Nowadays as she sang, her voice seemed to have a tear in it, and there was an almost violent lonesomeness in her eyes. She transmitted much of that same feeling to her audience, particularly in her most popular song, "Far, Far From This Lonely Hotel." Her fans, mainly drifters themselves, seemed to understand and respond at least to the onstage version of Rosacoke Carson.

At Reba's a major difference came in Rosacoke's act, a new dimension of romantic intensity. Up to now she'd tried to play down her obvious sex appeal, but, as she felt more secure with her fans, she imbued her songs with strong sexual overtones. In that, she received massive encouragement from Reba. "There's not a woman performer in country music doing that, honey, and you might as well be the first," Reba had said after watching her one night when Rosacoke just knew she was "hot."

Rosacoke often self-assessed herself. She was aware that she had both the voice and physical intensity to communicate that sex appeal. Some of the women in the lounge were frankly offended, and on occasion quite a few of the men, especially those who believed that women should know their positions. However, the large number of male members in her audience liked her message.

She was a woman who sang that if you loved her, you'd have to love her on *her* terms—not on yours—and she wasn't looking for forever. After a few nights with you, she was likely to be on her own again, leaving you before you ran out on her.

"Baby, your own songs are electric," a drunken Reba had told her one night. "Women just don't sing this way in country music, at least they haven't until you came along. I mean, the reason I didn't hire women before you is that they all stick to those 'home-and-hearth-songs,' always with an overkill on religion."

With Reba's encouragement, Rosacoke continued her song writing, and from her words a message evolved. She wrote of the newly emerging post-war woman who'd grown up in defense plants, welding Liberty ships, a person who'd learned to live without men, knowing she could make it on her own.

In her off-duty hours, when Rosacoke should have been resting up from her strenuous performance that night, she wrote more and more music for herself. She continued to hit upon this new approach in country music, singing about women who were self-assured, who reached out and took

men as their lovers, instead of waiting around for the male to make his selection.

Her crowds grew bigger and more responsive, as her songs took on added intensity and maturity. Through all the saloon stages and fistfight encores, she'd come to develop her own distinct styling. One night Reba came out and introduced her before a packed audience. "This little gal, who's not so little…" The audience burst into clapping, interrupting her. "I've seen 'em all come and go, and tonight I give you an original in country music. Rosacoke Carson. One hot tamale who's going places!"

In the spring of 1948, Reba announced that she was driving down to station KWKH in Shreveport, Louisiana. "They're gonna reinstate their own barn dance show, the Louisiana Hayride. I hear one guy's really hot. He's been playing dates in Alabama and Georgia, and he's stirred up quite a storm. I want him for Reba's. A guy by the name of Pete Riddle."

Rosacoke felt paralyzed at the mention of his name. It had to be the same Pete.

*Her* Pete.

On an impulse, she asked, "Could I go? I mean, I've been working here for months, and I'd really like to take a break."

Reba looked up at her, debated the issue in her mind, and said, "Why not? I need the company. I was gonna take David, but he slipped down to Tijuana one night and caught lethal clap."

Deliberately masking her enthusiasm, Rosacoke asked, "When do we leave?"

"'Morrow morning. Who knows, I might get a booking for you on that show. Texas is a big state, and everybody in Texas eventually makes it to Reba's. But you want to get known somewhere else, don't you?"

That may have been true, Rosacoke thought, kissing Reba on the cheek and rushing upstairs. She could hardly contain her mounting excitement, as she kept checking her image in the mirror. Had she changed that much? Gotten too old for him? After a jail sentence and thousands of nights in smoke-filled barrooms, she didn't have that milk-maiden freshness any more. But she still thought she looked pretty good. At least the men in Texas thought so, and they judged female flesh like they did steers.

That night she tried to get some rest, knowing it would be a long and arduous ride, and she didn't want to make Shreveport looking anything less than her best.

Shortly before dawn, she almost burst into tears as a thought occurred to her. Pete was one hell of a hot-blooded male. He probably had a new girl. Worst, several girls if she knew Pete. For one fleeting moment, she was tempted not to go, fearing rejection. But when morning came, she jumped out of bed and packed her suitcase.

She looked at herself in the mirror, not disguising her expectation. "I've

got to see that long, lanky shitkicker one more time."

The trip to Shreveport seemed almost as long as her jail sentence. As Reba's Ford neared the edge of the city, Rosacoke feared the beat of her heart sounded too loud. Along the way she'd been seriously tempted to tell Reba that she was in love with Pete and was, in fact, the mother of his son. But she decided against that in case things didn't go right after his show. Even now, she wasn't sure that she'd have the courage to go backstage to greet Pete after his act.

Reba checked them into a dreary downtown hotel, so reminiscent of all those Rosacoke had known on the road. Reba was immediately on the phone making deals, while Rosacoke smoked and tried to listen to the radio. Even the steak dinner that Reba ordered for her in the restaurant downstairs went untouched.

"I never knew you to turn down a steak before," Reba said, biting into a blood-red piece.

"Lost my appetite, I guess."

"Well, perk up! When I introduce you to the director of the show, I want you to look lively."

Broadcast live, the Louisiana Hayride drew people from Texas, the Mississippi Delta, and the Southeast. Rosacoke was so excited that she was bursting with joy and could hardly contain herself until Pete's turn at the microphone. Reba glanced over at her. "You sure took my advice. You look like a time bomb about to go off."

"I just love the music," was Rosacoke's weak excuse.

When Pete bounced on the stage, she didn't know where to look first. He practically stood in front of the mike for five minutes, letting the women in the audience soak him up. Then he hit his guitar a lick, breaking two strings. The crowd went wild, even though he hadn't sung a note. Moving his hips real slow like he had a thing for his guitar, he had some of the women in the audience practically fainting.

Rosacoke felt as if her hair was grabbing at her collar. She'd never known anyone in country or western music who brought such excitement to the stage.

Over the years, he'd matured, and as he got into his first song she realized his music had grown up with him. The softness and sensitivity of boyhood had faded from his features, to be replaced by a somewhat rugged, expressive face of a young man. He had a winsome half-smile.

Reba leaned over to her to whisper. "That's one hot stud. Christ, I'd like him to shake those hips over me some night. Each and every night."

Rosacoke immediately felt jealous.

At the end of his song, pandemonium broke out. The fans loved Pete. So did Rosacoke, all over again.

"Pete's face could only be put on a Southerner," Reba said. "The face

alone will win him a whole lot of loyal fans. He's one of 'em. I met this guy once who was called the writer's writer. Hell, Pete is the hillbilly's billy."

As Pete went on with his act, Rosacoke found in him the eternal lonesome cowboy. In his boots and wide-brimmed hat, he stood tall in his skin-tight pants that left little for the imagination.

"Those pants are so tight you can tell he's not Jewish," Reba said, downing her beer. Rosacoke stared into Reba's face. The woman looked as if she were in heat. That was the affect Pete had on women.

His down-home speech and warbling "tear" in his voice—so similar to Rosacoke's own—won him an immediate rapport with his biggest audience to date. In his cutting-edge voice, when he sang lo-o-onesome, Rosacoke felt his lovesick blues personally, relating them to her own. The patrons howled after every number.

His voice went through Rosacoke like electricity, sending shivers up her spine. Glancing again at Reba, Rosacoke could tell she was clearly mesmerized. Usually Reba was disdainful of most performers, and wasn't easily impressed, but Pete had clearly won her heart.

Ignoring Rosacoke's shyness, Reba pressed backstage after his act. "I'm gonna go right up to him and introduce myself. Hire him to come to Austin for a show date."

Backstage there appeared to be even more people than out front. From the dressing rooms poured a host of musicians along with their friends and relatives. Not only that, but promoters, fans, and agents roamed freely through the crowd. Whiskey and beer flowed in every dressing room, and the air was smoke clogged.

In such a heady atmosphere, Rosacoke felt dizzy. If it weren't for Reba pulling her along, she wouldn't have the courage to face Pete.

When she spotted him, her heart skipped a beat. He was surrounded by a bevy of young women.

Reba snorted under her breath. "Snuff queens."

"What does that mean?"

"Those girls like to fuck stars—that's how they get their kicks. I'll have to come on like a bulldozer to break through."

Reba plowed through the free-hearted females, while Rosacoke remained discreetly in the background. From what she could observe, Pete and Reba were getting on fabulously. He'd obviously heard of Reba's place in Austin.

"Come over here," Reba called out to Rosacoke. "Step right up and meet Pete Riddle."

From out of the shadows of the stage wing, Rosacoke emerged into the bright lights of the studio.

At first Pete didn't seem to see her, but when he did he stared at her in disbelief. She felt weak, almost wanting to turn and run.

Sweating heavily after his hard workout in front of the microphone, Pete took a step toward her, his shock fully registering on his face.

She still couldn't judge his reaction. Was it one of pleasure or embarrassment at running into her again? Up close to him, she could smell him. That intoxicating aroma, along with the titillating presence of him, thrilled her as never before. Wavering, feeling like she was standing on legs of jelly, she grew faint in the heat of the studio.

Reaching out, he grabbed her in his arms, crushing her against his strong body. He kissed her, not just a polite kiss of a long-lost friend, but a soul-searching probe of her mouth. His hunger for her seemed stronger than ever.

Leaving her gasping for breath, he glanced over at an astonished Reba. Rosacoke held onto him, afraid to let go.

"Reba, this here is my long-lost lady. 'Bout time you sent her home to take care of me and our little boy."

# Chapter 10
## (The Fifties: Gaining Fame)

Rosacoke's maroon-colored Studebaker crossed her home-county line on her return from a singing engagement in Louisiana. She was anxious to get back to Heaven on Earth to be with Pete and Buster. Even though they lived in the far corner of the county, she knew it wouldn't take long for her to get there. The county stretched for only forty to forty-five miles across in any direction.

Before her life on the road these past few years, she used to think of the county as so much bigger. As a little girl growing up here, she imagined it was God's country. Some of the old folks still called it a state, based on the long tradition of claiming that the county once swept west to the Mississippi. That was just so much idle talk.

Rosacoke had taken two weeks off honky-tonk hopping to spend time with Pete and Buster. Her long separations from them were hard on her. She couldn't understand why Larry Hunt didn't get her more bookings with Pete, instead of sending her off in entirely different sections of the South from where her husband appeared.

As her Studebaker rolled along, she passed patchworks of brown and green fields, with cool hills in the distance. A steam train puffed along, heading for Virginia with its freight of timber and cotton. Mules kicked up the soil, and the red clay hills and pine trees beckoned, stirring up long-suppressed memories.

Past bright-leaf tobacco fields and apple orchards, she longed for a glass of refreshing cider—the real kind, made by some old farmer from a time-tested recipe, not the bottled variety sold in markets.

In the county seat, nothing much had changed since her last visit. Flies still buzzed around the old men who lounged on the courthouse benches, telling tall tales of the exploits of their Confederate grandpappies charging up the slope at Gettysburg.

Heading out of the sleepy town, on the highway winding its way toward Heaven on Earth, she sucked in the fresh air. She cut down a dirt road, spotting blackberry bushes along fencerows. Two little girls picked them, their hands as black as if covered in dried blood. Crows circled over a neighboring cornfield. A red bandana tied around its neck, a pathetic scarecrow did little to keep them away.

An old farming couple rolled by in their wagon pulled by a mule. Snuff on her gums, a poke bonnet on her head, the Gothic American woman was a scene straight out of Rosacoke's childhood in the Thirties. She wondered how long these tableaux would last before they were swept away in the post-war craze overtaking the country.

She rolled down the other window, enjoying the dog-day scents of the fading summer.

Her heart was beating faster as she drove up the long driveway leading to what was now a mansion familiar to her, Heaven on Earth. As the house in all its ornate architectural richness came into view, she was thrilled to be living in such a grand palace far removed from Sultan's shanty. Her heart only grew sad when she saw eight cars parked in the driveway.

Her new home with Pete and Buster seemed to have all the privacy of a bus station. She was almost never alone with Pete. Everybody in the household, from Larry to Hank, not to mention Claude, Ronnie, and Junior, competed for Pete's attention. Karl seemed to be the real boss man of the place, and Rosacoke didn't really feel like the mistress of the mansion. Tara was clearly in charge of the house and made all the decisions, even to what rooms the household crew, including Rosacoke herself, was assigned.

Tara had placed Rosacoke in a luxurious bedroom suite in the far wing of the house. She felt isolated and alone there. Her finest times spent were in the former barn—now a recording studio—where she worked on her routines, with Guitar Red, Nipsey, and Maston Mastin. The men were incredibly skilled musicians and had taught her many tricks of the trade.

Upon seeing her again, Hank and Larry had made no mention of their having traveled on the road with her. To her knowledge, Pete didn't know of her romantic involvement with Hank. She didn't want Pete to know, fearing he'd explode in a jealous rage and kick Hank out of the household.

For all Pete knew, Rosacoke had never even met Larry before. When Pete had introduced her to Larry, Rosacoke pretended she was meeting him for the first time, and Larry had gone along with the deception. She didn't like lying to her husband, but felt that under the circumstances it was better for everyone to keep her shared past with Hank and Larry a secret. The two men seemed to want to hide the extent of their former involvement with her as well.

Early in the marriage Pete had insisted that he could not sleep with someone else in the room, even his wife. He'd demanded complete solitude and had ordered black velvet draperies to be placed over his tall French windows. He stayed up virtually all night and preferred to sleep through lunch. As was her custom she always rose at six o'clock in the morning, regardless of how late she'd stayed out the night before.

To her, the only real mystery person of the household was Josh. She couldn't understand why Pete spent so much time with him. She was told

that Josh shared the room next to Pete with a connecting door in case they wanted to get together for a sudden song-writing session.

Josh seemed to go to bed when Pete did and get up for breakfast at the same time. It was as if the two men were on the same time clock. She longed to be as close to Pete as Josh seemingly was, but was nowhere as near to her husband. Pete respected her and lavished gifts on her, buying her a new car, new clothes, and seeing that she always had plenty of money. For a gal who'd lived in Sultan's shanty and went to bed hungry at night, Rosacoke felt she should be grateful for what she now had. She had almost everything except Pete himself. She wanted her man, but he rarely came to her bedroom except on Saturday night.

Although he at first had come on strong in the marriage, his visits to her bedroom were growing more infrequent. She feared she wasn't attractive to him. Not wanting to go to seed and blubber like Tara, Rosacoke dieted to keep her weight down, feeling that Pete would find her more alluring if thinner. But even her reduced self could not entice him to visit her bed more than once a week.

He always seemed to want to get through the sex act as quickly as possible, in spite of her wish to draw it out. He'd bring her to climax but as soon as he did, he'd rush off to her bathroom to clean up. He used a rubber and would always thank her for "the terrific sex." She wondered if he'd found it that great. He'd flush the rubber down the toilet. One night when he'd been with her and was drunk, he'd dropped the rubber on the tile floor of her bathroom and hadn't flushed it. She'd picked it up to examine it, finding no liquid inside. She wondered if he'd climaxed at all but decided to give him the benefit of the doubt. Maybe he'd tried to fit the rubber on himself and had had difficulty, discarding it and reaching for another condom. At least she hoped that was what had happened.

Just once she also hoped that he'd approach her bed to have sex with her when sober. She'd never known him to want sex unless he was fueled by alcohol. During the few times she'd tried to come on to him when he was sober, he'd spurned her.

"Listen, honey," he said, "I'm not some sex fiend who can get it up any time it's requested. I love you. I love our son. But if you want a fucking love machine, you'd better find yourself another guy. When I want it, I want it. But I don't want it most of the time. I've got a low libido. Many men are like that."

She'd found the subject of sex so uncomfortable with him she'd never brought it up again. Over the past few months, she'd tried to make peace in her turbulent heart about her husband's lovemaking, and had decided to accept it and take what she got. She didn't understand this kind of marriage, and it wasn't what she wanted, but she was prepared to live with it. Of all the men she'd ever known, including Hank, none had turned her on

like Pete. She'd rather spend fifteen minutes enjoying the pounding he gave her than every night locked in the arms of any of the men she'd known before.

Even before she'd parked her car, Tara ran out of the front door and across the wide verandah to greet her. Spotting Ronnie, Tara ordered him to help bring in Rosacoke's luggage. "Welcome home, hoss," she said.

After catching up on the news, Rosacoke retreated to her wing of the house, taking a long, sudsy bath in an old claw-footed porcelain tub. She wanted to get herself prettied up for Buster and Pete when they came back. Tara said Pete had left with Josh and Buster about three hours ago, not telling her where they were going.

"I guess they didn't know I was coming back so soon," Rosacoke had said, trying to save face.

After dinner with Claude and Tara, Rosacoke wandered off by herself, sitting on the front verandah. As she rocked, she listened to some descendant of a whippoorwill she'd heard as a girl. Even though Claude and Tara had turned in early, Rosacoke wanted to wait up for Pete and Buster.

In the quiet of an oncoming night, her favorite time of the day, her mind drifted back to that night at the Louisiana Hayride when she'd had her reunion with Pete and he'd asked her to marry him.

\*\*\*

She recalled so well how Pete had slowly brought her back home to Heaven on Earth. The trip had taken a long time because of their frequent stops at little motel cabins along the way. More than ever, Pete had been in the mood to make love. He couldn't seem to get enough of her, or she of him.

On their way home, she remembered waking up after their first night together. A sliver of light had cut through a stained, yellowing window shade in their shabby motel room. The light had revealed his nude body, as she'd followed its pattern, exposing first a strong, muscular thigh. The light had crawled to his slim, long fingers that lay gently on her bare stomach. Innocent and relaxed now, that hand last night had been an imaginative, feverish tool of lust. His fingers had probed, pinched, and touched every inch of her body, sending her into a whirlpool of excitement.

She'd loved searching out the charms of his body in such unabashed secrecy while he slept. His arms were tanned and muscled to perfection, and the hair on his chest was soft and curling in the cleft between his flat, brown nipples. Her eyes continued their search across his skillet-hard stomach with its wide, winking navel to his cock, which was in a slight curve, like a snake lounging in the sun. Thick veins ribboned down to the roots. As he'd awakened, it was the hungry gaze on her face that had greeted him.

He'd licked his lips wickedly and grinned. "You gonna get it one more time, baby doll." His voice, carrying with it such carnal suggestiveness, had produced just the effect he'd wanted. She'd begged for it again.

His love-making had acquired such expertise over the years that she'd been jealous at first, wondering how he'd managed to pick up so many tricks. Admittedly, he'd thrilled her with his newly acquired knowledge, and she'd never known such sexual excitement could exist with any man. Nevertheless, his skill had created a troubling anxiety within her.

She'd been so happy to be back with him after all these years that she'd tried to release her fear about the past. A hot-blooded young man like Pete would never be completely faithful to just one woman, and from the very beginning of their reunion she'd faced that. Those long separations that Larry always arranged hadn't helped matters these past few months. Still, Rosacoke figured that if she gave of herself, then gave a little more, he wouldn't have such passionate longings for other women, even though they sure made themselves available to him.

On that hot ride back home after the Hayride show, there had been almost no talk of what had gone wrong with their relationship in 1942. The war had been raging at the time, and he was just a teenage boy, eager to set out on his own adventure in life. She didn't blame him for his reluctance to settle down with just one girl, even if she were pregnant.

He'd matured a whole lot since those days, and she'd noticed that in his growing up his love for his son had deepened as well.

On their first night together, he'd told her, "I never found another like you, honey. Besides, Buster needs his own mama. Right now he thinks Tara is his mama. She's not and it's not right the boy should get so attached to another woman like that."

As Rosacoke was to learn, "Tara" referred to a dynamic blockbuster of a woman who looked after Buster when Pete was on the road, which was most of the time.

It was important to both Pete and Rosacoke that Buster's illegitimacy be kept a secret. Not only for the boy's sake, but their own as well. Larry kept alive in them the dream of eventual stardom. He didn't want it to leak out that they'd had a son out of wedlock. "It might ruin our careers," he said.

Larry told them to announce back home that they had been married in the Christmas of 1941, when Rosacoke reputedly took a Greyhound bus to Norfolk where Pete was stationed with the Navy. Because that in the opening days of World War II, many lives had been uprooted, people displaced, and basic milestones such as births and deaths obscured, the story gained creditability, going unchallenged. Rosacoke had been gone from the county for so long that not too many people remembered her anyway, although everybody knew Pete.

Before Rosacoke had laid eyes on her son for the first time, Pete had assured her, "with us back together, and with Buster tagging along, it'll be like a new start for everybody. Let's forget the past. It wasn't the kind of thing a man would want to remember anyway."

***

As Pete drove Josh down from the mountain heading for Heaven on Earth, Buster was asleep in the back seat. Pete and Josh didn't need to talk. Over time they had developed a silent communication. Pete reached over and placed his hand possessively on Josh's knee. When he'd impulsively married Rosacoke, Pete had come dangerously close to losing Josh, and he never wanted that to happen again, regardless of what came down in their lives.

It had been Larry who'd strongly urged marriage onto Pete. Before Larry introduced Pete as a big player in country music, he wanted him safely married. "If you don't go ahead and get married, you might as well kiss your career good-bye," Larry had said. "We'd be wasting time to even launch you. Word will get out that you're queer."

"I don't want to get married," Pete had protested. "I'm married to Josh."

"Same-sex marriages don't go over big in country music," Larry had said. "Leave that to J. Edgar Hoover and his FBI pal. We've got to get you a wife."

After having the idea pounded into his head day after day, Pete had at least accepted the prospect that he'd have to get married one day. That day appeared to be coming up sooner than later. Although Pete had women throwing themselves at him almost nightly, none of them intrigued him.

He only vaguely had thought of Rosacoke. That is, until he'd seen her that night at the Louisiana Hayride. He'd acted on an impulse and had reached out for her, not even certain she'd agree to marry him. He really had wanted her to say no, and was shocked at how quickly she'd accepted his proposal.

The disaster had come after Larry had arranged a hasty wedding at a chapel in Tennessee. Pete had not prepared Josh for the sudden news. All during the time Larry had been urging marriage onto Pete, he'd never told Josh that Pete's hooking up with a woman was even a consideration. With good cause, Josh rightly considered himself Pete's wife, and for all practical purposes functioned as such day and night.

Right after the Tennessee wedding, Pete had called Josh with the news, hoping to be given the chance to explain what had happened. Josh's reaction had been violent. He'd slammed down the phone. When Pete had called back to Heaven on Earth, Tara had picked up the phone, telling Pete

that Josh had fled from the house, taking one of the cars. She didn't know where he'd gone.

Once he got back to Heaven on Earth, Pete had told Rosacoke that he had to postpone their honeymoon and head across state on a business trip. He'd warned her that he might be gone for a few days and was totally uncertain when he'd come back.

While wandering a lonely sand dune near the house of Josh's parents on the Outer Banks, Pete had caught up with him. On seeing Pete, Josh had turned and run, but Pete had chased after him, tripping him and landing on top of Josh, holding him down in the sands as he'd struggled to free himself. "Let me go," Josh had yelled. "I don't ever want to see you again."

When he'd sensed that Josh wasn't going to bolt, Pete had raised up from his young friend. "That's bad news to hear since I'm gonna be sleeping next to you every night for the rest of my life. If you don't want to look at me, you'd better put on a blindfold when I fuck you two or three times a day."

Josh had looked pouty but Pete had felt he was willing to listen. "Why don't you fuck your new wife?" Josh had asked.

"I only do that when I absolutely have to and then I fake a climax," Pete had said. "Any juice in ole Pete Riddle is reserved for his loving spouse, Josh Harnell."

"Yeah, right!" Josh had said, getting up and brushing the sand off him. He had walked along the beach but wasn't running. Pete had genuinely wanted to get Josh back with him, but as punishment Josh had seemed to make him beg for the privilege. Pete had been more than willing to oblige.

"Christ, this is a bleak place," Pete had said, catching up with his lover and falling in step.

"Stick around until winter if you want to see some desolation," Josh had said. "The tacky place lives only for summer and sunshine. Without that, it's as empty as my heart is right now."

Pete had reached for Josh's hand, bringing him to a complete stop. Pete had looked deeply into Josh's eyes. "I'm gonna kiss my boy," Pete had said. "Kiss him long and hard. You can bite my tongue, bite my lips, or punch me in the nose, but I'm taking charge with you. I'm back with you where I belong."

Josh had made no attempt to prevent Pete from kissing him. At first when Pete's lips had met his, Josh had stood motionless. The longer Pete had kissed and tongued him, the more Josh's stonewall resistance had faded. Pete's kissing lips and sucking tongue had warmed Josh's heart. He had reached out and had hugged Pete as tightly as he could, pulling him closer and closer into his arms. With one hand he'd reached to open his jacket, granting Pete greater access to his chest.

Both men had held each other, unaware of time passing. Pete had looked up at the gray clouds moving over and knew that in a few minutes raindrops would be falling. He had been prepared to stand here for the rest of the day and night if Josh had wanted to be held. Finally, it was Josh who had broken free. He'd taken Pete's hand and had walked slowly with him along the sands heading for the shelter on shore that both of them would soon need to escape from the pelting rain.

"How could you do this to me?" Josh had asked, breaking the silence between them.

"I hated to," Pete had said. "It was the most God awful feeling I'd ever had in my gut. Larry forced me into a marriage I don't want. He says if he's gonna promote me in country music, I've got to have a wife. Already people are asking too many questions."

"Fuck!" Josh had said. "I hate it. When is the God damn day gonna come when two guys like us can live openly as lovers the way we were meant to be? Why must we always conform to some asshole's rules?"

"I didn't make the rules, baby," Pete had said, slipping his arm under Josh's jacket and around his waist. "If I want to be a player, I've got to follow the game. Guys have been doing this since the dawn of time."

Josh had said nothing as he'd continued to walk along with Pete, who was convinced that he was getting his lover back. Pete had felt in time he could get Josh to accept his new status as a married man. Confident he'd won Josh over, Pete had whispered in his ear. "I've rented a cold motel room for the night. Please come back with me and help me warm it up."

When Josh faced him, tears were running down his smooth cheeks, turned a ruddy color from the biting wind. The first raindrops had fallen on his face. As Pete had looked at him, he could no longer distinguish between Josh's tears and the falling raindrops.

A half hour later in that motel room, an almost magical experience had unfolded for Pete. It had even surpassed his final night with Tracy in Norfolk before he was sent off on that convoy to his death. The thought of losing Josh had filled Pete with such fear and dread that he was determined to mend his cheating heart and treat Josh like his little darling now and forever more. Life without Josh was a life Pete didn't want to live.

As the night unfolded, Pete had felt he'd never made love to another human being with the tenderness and devotion he did in his reunion with Josh. There had been passion but more than that there was an overwhelming outpouring of love and bonding that had made the men so close to each other that Pete felt nothing, not even his indiscretions and betrayals of the future, would separate them again.

Before the morning had come, Pete had worshipped every inch of Josh's body. Pete had figured that no man on earth could thrill Josh the way Pete had satisfied him that night. Morning had found Josh clinging to Pete as

he'd never had before. One look into Josh's eyes had told Pete his man was a lovesick puppy who'd never leave him again.

On the drive back to the western hills of North Carolina, Josh couldn't take his hands off Pete who was driving. Josh had kept constantly reaching for Pete to touch, fondle, and kiss as if to convince himself that Pete had really returned and would never abandon him again.

Josh had insisted on some new rules in their relationship even though Pete was married. "I come first, not Rosacoke Carson," Josh had said. "That has to be understood. I don't know what she knows about our relationship, if anything. If you must fuck her, you've got to use a rubber. The idea of you sticking that big beautiful dick in a woman makes me really want to throw up. I've got to know when you're fucking her. Make it as infrequent as possible. I want you to return immediately to our bedroom when you've done the dirty deed. I'm gonna suck the cum out of you and I want to get a full load. Not have you deposit it in some cunt. I'm gonna put you to the test every time."

Pete had leaned over in the front seat and had kissed Josh. "Put me to the test, man. The big load will be there for you."

***

As Pete drove his Lincoln into the courtyard of Heaven on Earth, he was shocked to see Rosacoke sitting in the light of the front porch veranda. He had not expected her until tomorrow. "Time to wake up," Pete called back to Buster. Josh said nothing but it was obvious to Pete he didn't want to see Rosacoke and was sorry to have her back.

Getting out of the car, Pete called a welcome greeting to Rosacoke, who rushed over to greet them. Pete kissed her on the lips but gently so. Buster got out of the back seat. As she reached to embrace him, he held out his hand and shook her hand instead. "I hope you had a good trip." He turned to Pete. "I love you, daddy." Buster kissed Pete long and hard on the mouth. Buster hurried to the door and into Tara's arms who was waiting in the foyer for him.

"Good evening, Miss Carson," Josh said, before racing past her and heading up to the master bedroom he shared with Pete.

"Honey, I'm bushed," Pete said, wrapping his arm around her and walking her toward the front verandah. "You must be tired too. We'll catch up on your road trip tomorrow when I've got some shut-eye. I wouldn't be any good to you tonight. You'd get no rise out of me."

"I was hoping we could sit up and talk," Rosacoke said. "Have a bourbon or two."

"If anything I've already had my quota for tonight," Pete said. "My head is reeling." Actually he felt fine. He kissed her good night again and

headed up toward his bedroom. At the top of the spiral staircase, he watched as she walked down the lonely corridor to her wing of the house.

As he opened the door to his bedroom, his eyes feasted on Josh lying in the middle of the bed. He was stark naked. Pete felt that he'd never seen a more delectable human body in his born days.

As he moved toward the bed, Pete was already unbuttoning his shirt. By the time he'd descended on Josh, his shirt was off, and Josh took immediate advantage to feel his rippling muscles before reaching below to unbuckle Pete's leather belt.

As he kissed, licked, and nibbled at Josh's ear, Pete said, "Did I ever tell you you look good enough to eat?"

"What about eating me and fucking me both?"

"You've found your man," Pete said, as his lips returned to Josh's succulent mouth. Pete just knew it was going to be a long night. Right now he wanted to hold back the dawn.

He could just feel that it was going to take a lot to satisfy him tonight. He was going to have Josh in every known way he'd ever had him before and maybe even think of a new trick or two before the rooster crowed.

\*\*\*

Alone in her bedroom, Rosacoke was slated for a sleepless night. It wasn't just the lack of sex. She could see that Pete was tired, maybe drunk too. What she longed for was the warmth of a human body next to hers.

She felt doubly sad, not only at Pete's indifference to her most of the time, but by the way her son treated her as well. She was a long way from winning his love, and regretted not being there with Buster in her arms during all those years he was growing up. When Pete had brought her home and had introduced her to her own son, Buster had seemed to have a tremendous grudge against her. Even though he treated her with great politeness, he did not welcome her presence at Heaven on Earth.

When she'd first laid eyes on Buster, he was already five years old. She knew she would never be able to make up for those lost years, that precious time that a little boy really needs his mama. If anybody was his mama, it was Tara. Buster's eyes lit up whenever Tara came into the room, and he always rushed to her arms, kissing her and wanting to be cuddled. Rosacoke could only stand idly by watching the scene unfold, wishing that Buster would love her the way he loved Tara.

Even more than Tara, Buster loved his daddy. In all her life Rosacoke had never witnessed such devotion from a child directed at a parent. It was more than love, bordering on worship. When Pete walked into a room, Buster ran to his arms. He was constantly kissing Pete on the lips and demanding to be held. The boy seemed to resent Pete paying attention to

anybody else, especially Josh. With Josh, Buster always had a chilly reception although the boy was polite and well mannered with his elders.

Once when Josh was pouring Pete a glass of bourbon, Buster rushed over to the bar and took the drink from Josh, wanting to deliver it directly to his daddy. Every chance he got, Buster piled into his daddy's arms, wanting to be held.

When Pete was around, Buster would pretend he was having trouble fastening a button so Pete would do it for him. "Thank you, daddy," Buster would say before rewarding Pete with a lingering kiss on the lips.

"My daddy is the most beautiful daddy in the world," Buster once told Rosacoke. "When I grow up, I want to look just like him." Rosacoke was pleased that Buster loved Pete so much, yet such excessive devotion disturbed her. She couldn't quite nail the source of her anxiety, but Buster's love seemed unnatural somehow.

Whenever Rosacoke returned from one of her tours, she lavished expensive gifts on Buster, hoping to buy his love. She had presented him with a red bicycle and even a cut-down Gibson guitar, which he was much too young to play. She called him "my little prince." But her gifts meant little to him. She couldn't help but notice that the simplest gift from Pete would be treated like some precious relic, to be hoarded away in his bedroom and fondled for hours.

Buster spent all his time in adult company, not caring to form any friendships with children his own age. Except for Tara, he didn't relate to the rest of Pete's houseguests. Rosacoke called them "the boarders." Hank and Larry were always loving and supportive of Buster, who usually ignored them, as he did Nipsey and Freddie. Too concerned with Pete's business interests, Karl had almost nothing to do with Buster. Junior Grayson seemed to love only airplanes, and both Wanda Mae and Ronnie claimed that they didn't want to have kids around. That left Tara and Pete, of course.

Buster always seemed clever at avoiding being alone with Rosacoke. Whenever he saw her, it was always in the presence of someone else, especially Claude, who spent more time roaming the house than anybody else. Now that he was no longer sheriff, Claude didn't seem to have much to do. He often went for long drives or walks with his son-in-law, Ronnie. Claude always made himself available if Pete wanted him for anything.

Of all the people in Pete's strange new family, Rosacoke liked Claude the most. He seemed more aware of her loneliness and isolation and was kinder to her than the rest. No one, not even Josh, was rude to her. The members of the household were distant somehow, not seeming to embrace her as part of the Pete's extended family, even though she was his wife. From the first day she'd arrived at Heaven on Earth, she'd been a stranger, not the mistress of the household. That role clearly belonged to Tara.

From the first moment she'd spotted him, Rosacoke had been awed by

Buster's startling physical beauty. Platinum blond and hazel-eyed like herself, he was the most strikingly handsome boy she'd ever seen, and up to that moment of her reunion with Buster, Rosacoke had always felt John-John was the winner of any boy beauty contest.

Buster had the most hauntingly expressive eyes of any child she'd ever seen. For reasons known only to him, Pete called his son's eyes "those of a jack hawk." Rosacoke found in his heavy-lidded eyes a lucent, inexplicable power. Buster's pupils were so big they gave him a deep, penetrating look, which was at odds with his round cherubic baby-face. His incredibly red lips were distorted by a curl. In that feature, he took after his daddy. Buster's lips twisted into a lopsided leer, giving him a mischievous look, which Rosacoke found irresistible in one so young. She longed to hold him in her arms, hoping he'd bestow kisses on her like he delivered to Pete.

Buster was slim and somewhat docile. He always wore long-sleeved white shirts, open at the neck, and baby trousers tugged up over his stomach by suspenders. He was sweet and unfailingly polite.

As she'd seen him grow, Rosacoke watched in fascination as Buster took to the guitar. He'd long ago discarded the guitar she had given him in favor of a shiny new one presented to him by Pete.

It was through music that she hoped to develop a relationship with her child. But even in music, Buster turned to Tara for help, as Tara had many valuable tips to give the young boy. As sad as it was for her to admit, Rosacoke felt that Tara knew more about how to present a song that she did. So even in the one thing Rosacoke could offer, her love of country music, she had been replaced by someone else.

When Pete wasn't around and when he'd tired of Tara, Buster seemed to be a loner. Rosacoke noticed that he spent hours picking and playing on his guitar as he listened to hillbilly stations on the radio. Jimmy Rodgers was Buster's favorite singer, and he also listened in awe to the sounds of Otis Span, Big Billy Broonzy, and Booker White.

The following night Pete invited Rosacoke to go with Buster and him for "supper and a few other things." Rosacoke eagerly welcomed the occasion to be alone with her two men and was disappointed when night came to find Claude, Josh, Larry, and Hank joining them for the outing. She had grown used to unwelcome company. Wherever she went at Heaven on Earth, she discovered at least one member of Pete's so-called family. There was no escaping them.

An ominous feeling had come over her on her return to Heaven on Earth. She felt that all their lives were about to change for all time in ways that were new and frightening to her. It was as if their private little world was about to be invaded by forces from the outside. None of these thoughts made much sense to her. It was just a feeling.

At times she wished Aunt Clotilda would tell her tales of her past. "These

forces are out there ready and waiting for us. The moment we let our guard down, that's when they come for us. They can even take over the soul of a man or woman. They've invaded Sultan's soul, and I can't get rid of them. They'll kill that nigger. He's gonna have a short life. When the forces get you, you don't live long. They up and see that you die. Then they escape the body of a dying person and seek out their next victim. That's what the forces do. Mark my words."

Rosacoke feared those forces were about to move in on her family and her, and she didn't know how to ward off their evil influence.

Pete was hauling them to his favorite eating place. Once there, Miss Prissy, now past ninety, seemed as spry as ever, as she bustled about, frying her famous catfish and hush puppies. Imitating his daddy, Buster gobbled up everything on his plate. If Pete liked something, then Buster was sure to like it too. Claude had brought a bottle of bourbon from the house and poured drinks for all at the table. Buster looked up at Pete. "I can't wait until I'm old enough to drink bourbon like you, daddy."

"Give it time," Pete told him. "I'm sure you'll drink up a few breweries in your day."

After the greasy supper and on an impulse, Pete ordered all of them back into the car where he asked Claude to drive them to Deal Street. Once there, Pete banged on the door of the Negro albino, Skeeter, who had originally fitted Rosacoke for her first cowgirl outfit.

Waking Skeeter, Pete demanded that he dress Buster in his first cowboy suit with rhinestones. Finding a pair of black and white two-toned pants and black boots to fit, Buster looked so good that Pete wanted to have his son's picture taken.

After Buster was fully dressed, Pete picked him up in his arms and carried him over to the pool hall across the street. There in the back he had a black man, the owner of the joint, photograph Buster, for which Pete gave the old man a dollar.

A red silk cravat dangled from Buster's neck. In front of the camera, he knew instinctively how to wear his hat with a brim at a cockeyed angle. Seeing him posing and all dressed up, Rosacoke became aware of the changes that had taken place in Buster's face in the past three years. It was as if she were seeing him for the first time after a long absence.

His eyes were more shadowed, and his face had lost its baby-fat, becoming leaner and even more beautiful. There was no doubt about this: Buster Riddle was a stunner. She could only imagine what a gorgeous man he would eventually become. She even believed that he might become more beautiful than Pete Riddle, and her husband was the handsomest man on the earth.

As she mulled over the beauty of men, she also was aware that Pete had surrounded himself with good-looking men. With the exception of that

startling good-looking Nipsey, the black musicians, especially Maston Mastin, didn't bring home many beauty cups. All the other men—Claude, Hank, Larry, Ronnie, Karl, and Junior—were among the best-looking men in the county.

Pete sure knew how to pick a male staff, she figured. She felt that the eligible girls of the county should be beating on their front door. But they weren't. She didn't know what the men did for sex. Guitar Red and Smokey had their women, and Ronnie was married to Wanda Mae. All the rest didn't seem to date too much.

Of course, Rosacoke didn't know what these men did when she was on the road. All of their worlds seemed to revolve around Pete Riddle. She once expressed this concern to him. "I think everybody in this household seems to think the sun rises and sets in Pete Riddle."

He'd only winked at her and lovingly chucked her under the chin like she was a child. "Doesn't it?" he asked, getting up from the table and heading to his studio out back. Seeing him going there, Josh had gotten up immediately and had trailed him. Only Tara had been left at the table. Motioning toward Josh as he'd headed out the back door, Rosacoke had said, "There goes Pete's shadow." Tara had only looked at her, saying nothing, as she'd begun to remove the dishes.

Her evening "out on the town," if this sleepy little hamlet could be called that, wasn't over yet, though Rosacoke eagerly hoped that Pete would return home early without too much bourbon floating around in his gut. She wanted him to visit her bedroom.

Pete had other plans. He asked Claude to drive them over to Fry's house. Rosacoke was eager to see her old-time friend who had helped her so much when she'd wanted to become a girl singer. It had been months since she'd seen him, although she secretly sent him a money order every month for a hundred dollars, and he always seemed eager to get it. He'd aged badly since she'd last seen him, and had trouble getting about. Moss had died the year before.

"Miss Rosacoke," Fry said, "you are sure a sight for sore eyes. Mr. Pete, oh, Mr. Pete. I'm so proud of how things turned out."

Pete warmly embraced the old man and stepped back, making way for Buster as he came into the house. "Introducing..." Pete said like the MC at the Grand Ole Opry.

"Don't tell me," Fry said. "I can feel it in my bones." He looked Buster up and down carefully, his eyes taking delight in the new rhinestone-studded cowboy outfit. "I'm gonna go out on a limb. This boy here is gonna become the biggest name in the history of country music."

***

On the way home that night, Rosacoke was disturbed at Buster's first solo performance at Big Mama Sadie's Blue Note Café, where Pete had insisted they go after calling on Fry and taking the elderly Negro with him to the club. Even though the mostly black crowd had loved Buster's song and clapped for an encore, the whole evening had left a disquieting note resounding within Rosacoke's head.

Buster had only a little eight-year-old voice, and had never appeared in public before, but he'd seemed completely at home on stage, as if he'd been performing for years. That had been in total contrast to the acute anxiety Rosacoke had felt when she'd first had to get up and sing in public.

Buster had been a natural performer. Since he was somewhat reticent in private, she was shocked at how quickly he took to performing, loving all the attention. It had seemed to her that Buster had been waiting all his life for this chance to sing in public and was terribly impatient to grow up and go on the road.

Considering that her career or even Pete's hadn't made much money for either of them, she was reluctant to have Buster follow in their footsteps. She hoped to encourage him to go to school, maybe pursue some career other than working the tonks.

When she'd once cornered Buster for a serious talk about this, he'd dismissed her concern. "Tara says music is in my blood. You of all people should know that. Look who my parents are. I'm gonna be a big star just like Fry always predicts. Don't worry, I'll make lots of money, and I'll take care of you and Pete."

Faced with his relentless drive, she'd given in and hadn't pursued the subject. She felt she didn't have a right to interfere, and Pete seemed to want Buster to devote his life to music. Rosacoke could only hope that the world of music would be a kinder place for Buster to live than the one she inhabited.

As Claude drove the drunken gang toward Heaven on Earth, it was way past midnight. Buster was still wide awake, even though it was long past his bedtime. Try as she might, she couldn't shake the image of Buster at the Blue Note Café.

On stage her son had seemed to mimic Pete. In spite of Buster's young voice, the impersonation was amazingly accurate. At the end of Buster's debut song, Fry had pronounced, "That sure is his daddy's boy. A chip off the old block. Hot dang!" Of course, Buster hadn't been able to hit the high notes and when he'd tried to break into his daddy's familiar yodel, he'd fallen short of the sound. Otherwise, Buster sang not with his own voice, but Pete's. It was eerie, the stage presence and delivery hauntingly familiar and derivative.

Buster sounded all of Pete's notes, even the slight mispronunciations. Buster's voice was imbued with that lo-oo-oo-oonesome quality in singing

the blu-OO-OO-OO-ues. He also had the same break in his voice that Pete did.

Rosacoke recalled that whenever Buster was around Pete, even as he watched as his daddy related to other people, Buster seemed to be giving Pete the once-over. Her son imitated Pete's mannerisms, as if he wanted to turn himself into a carbon copy of his daddy. The one time Rosacoke had voiced that concern to Pete, he'd dismissed her fear and had even seemed to have been flattered by his son's imitation. "One Pete Riddle is enough," she'd said to Pete. "I want Buster Riddle to grow up to be his own man."

Occasionally professional singers they knew from the road dropped in unannounced at the Riddle homestead, and Buster was immensely intrigued to meet some "greats" he'd known only by listening to them on radio. The stars gave him many pointers about singing and guitar-playing, and also taught him how to tell jokes to establish a rapport with the audience.

One day everybody's favorite, Uncle Dave Macon, had showed up on the doorstep, sadly announcing he'd finally stopped touring, although he would keep appearing on the Opry. The corpulent singer from Tennessee had entertained Buster with stories of his early days in medicine shows and old-time fiddling. "Listen, don't worry about your daddy. He's got plenty of time to make it in show business. He's not even thirty yet. I embarked on my career at the age of fifty."

After singing "Take Me Back to My Old Carolina Home," Uncle Dave had asked Buster to fetch him his black satchel in the car. From it Uncle Dave pulled out a bottle of Jack Daniels. Downing a hefty swig right from the bottle, he'd said, "I recall when me and my boys used to haul this stuff to Woodbury at twenty-five cents a gallon. As we drove along, I'd stop and entertain with my banjo at the stations."

When Tara had served a crawfish dinner that night, Uncle Dave had ordered his satchel again. From it, he'd removed a checkered bib and, later, after he'd tired, he'd taken a nightcap from that same satchel, even a pillow, and had gone upstairs to bed.

Afterward, Pete had turned to Buster. "Son, you've met one of the greats of country music."

As Claude drove the Lincoln up that private road that led to Heaven on Earth, Rosacoke still felt a pang in her heart about her night out. At the end of his performance at the Blue Note, Buster had run up to Pete, sitting on his lap and giving him a long, hard kiss right on the mouth, as if demanding Pete's immediate approval. She could not help but notice that Buster didn't even glance at her for her reaction to his song.

In the Lincoln on the way back, Josh had seated himself next to Pete, but Buster had interfered, asking Josh to move over so that Buster could sit next to his daddy. Josh had seemed to take offense at that and hadn't said one word on the way home. Buster had done all the talking.

Regardless of what Buster did, Pete always seemed to approve. "How can you expect him to act like a normal child?" Pete had asked Rosacoke one afternoon as they'd sat on the back verandah of the mansion. "With us as his parents?"

Even so Rosacoke wished that Buster had some friends his own age, as everybody he knew was twenty years older than he was. Buster just didn't seem to fit in at school. His teacher had told Rosacoke that he was very sulky, sitting by himself and not relating to the other kids. "All he seems to do is listen for the sound of the school bell, so he can get up, run out the door, and go home." Once back home, he'd practice his guitar instead of doing his school homework.

Over the years Pete and Rosacoke had long stopped going to church, and Tara had never set foot inside one. No one around the compound was religious at all, even though all of them had grown up in the Bible Belt. Rosacoke worried that the boy's religious training had been sadly neglected. She knew she didn't set a good example, as she had "backslided" after spending too many Saturday nights as a honky-tonk angel who was too tired to get up on a Sunday morning and go to church.

Feeling guilty, she'd urged Tara to take Buster to the First Assembly of God Church. No church-goer herself, Tara had only reluctantly agreed.

When he'd come back home from church, Buster had actually seemed excited at how "the preacher cut up all over the place." Rosacoke knew that wasn't the stern-voiced L.T. Younger who never seemed to even move his lips as he delivered his staid sermon. The preacher that day had been a traveling "fire and brimstone" evangelist.

"The preacher moved every which way," Buster had told Rosacoke. "He jumped up on the organ and shook his legs. He even wiggled his ass, claiming he was filled with the spirit of God and was shaking off the Devil. The women in the front row got all worked up. The preacher went over like a firecracker."

Instead of any spiritual message the preacher might have imparted to her son, Rosacoke had suspected that Buster had studied the evangelist's movements, viewing the pastor not as a messenger of God, but as a performer whose show business tricks Buster could copy the way he always imitated Pete. Rosacoke never asked Tara to take Buster to church again.

Even though tanked up on bourbon, Pete had gone to her bed that night when Claude delivered them back to Heaven on Earth. When Pete had come out of her bathroom, he was already rock hard with a rubber on his big dick. He'd apparently jacked himself into a full erection in the bathroom.

She would have preferred him to indulge in a little foreplay before mounting her, but he didn't. He'd entered her the moment he hit the bed as if he feared he might lose his hard-on. She wanted to suck his dick to its full

glory the way she'd done with Hank, but she was grateful for any intimate contact with Pete. He did his job well, pounding into her until she'd reached a spectacular climax, calling out his name. Mission accomplished, he withdrew from her so abruptly it had left her panting and feeling a terrible loss at his abrupt withdrawal. She wanted him to stay in her until dawn broke. He gave her a quick kiss and got up, heading for her bathroom. She was uncertain whether he'd gotten his rocks off or not.

She begged him to come back to bed and sleep with her, but he turned and blew her a good night kiss. "You know me, babe. I sleep alone." He put on his robe, heading back to his own master bedroom.

Long after he'd gone, she lay bathed in the moonlight, wondering about this mysterious man she'd married. If she didn't know better, she felt that Pete was heading for other arms and another bed tonight where his lovemaking wouldn't be as quick on the draw as it'd been with her.

Turning over into her pillow and praying for the comfort of sleep, she dismissed the fear from her mind. Whose bed could Pete be heading to since fat Tara was the only other woman in the house?

The next morning she woke up with a headache, feeling frustrated and unfulfilled even though Pete had made love to her that night.

Larry was the only one at the breakfast table that morning. Rosacoke didn't know where everybody else was. "I've been on the phone all morning to Nashville," Larry said, his face brightening. "Something big is about to break. But I can't give you the details right now. I don't want to jinx the deal."

"What do I do in the meantime while waiting for this big break?" she asked, not bothering to disguise the note of sarcasm in her voice.

"I've arranged for you to go on a tour of the tonks again," he said to her bitter disappointment.

***

Pete knew he had been neglecting John-John. When Josh eventually left for a long weekend to visit his parents on the Outer Banks, Pete had whispered to John-John that he'd visit his room at ten o'clock that night.

After supper and a few drinks, Pete told everyone good night and headed up the steps. Instead of going to the master bedroom he shared with Josh, he knocked on John-John's door. There was no answer. Thinking John-John might be in the bathroom, Pete opened the unlocked door and went inside.

The room was softly lit, but there was no sign of John-John, even when he searched the bathroom. Back in the bedroom, he called out for John-John.

The curtains to the boy's dressing room were suddenly pulled back.

Standing before Pete was one of the hottest blondes he'd ever seen.

The flaming red lipstick would put both Lana Turner and Betty Grable's to shame. Alarmingly sexy in "bad girl" curls, John-John stood high in Joan Crawford fuck-me heels with straps. The boy had transformed himself into a slutty Cinderella of overwhelming sex appeal. He wore a pink gown cut low to reveal what appeared to be a burgeoning bosom. The gown was split to showcase one of the shapeliest long legs Pete had ever seen. It was encased in nylon hosiery.

Pete's mind was all confused. It was as if John-John was a virginal whore, the type of nymphomaniac who will fuck you to death, but still retain the allure of a teenage vamp with her cherry intact.

"As I live and breathe, let's go over the mountain and see what we can see," Pete said.

"How's it hanging, stud?" John-John asked, wetting his lips with what had to be the world's most delectable and tantalizing pink tongue.

"It ain't happening, baby, but it's starting to rise like a flagpole," Pete said. "Looking at you has made me realize I ain't queer after all—not if the sight of a woman turns me on like you do."

On those high heels, John-John propelled himself toward Pete. "What you see is what you're about to get."

It was an erotic new adventure for Pete, fucking a man who looked, dressed, and talked like a woman. He needed this variety to spice up his sex life.

The clock on the mantle told Pete that it was two o'clock in the morning when he rose from John-John's bed to put on his jeans. He'd lost count of how many times he'd penetrated the boy. The kid couldn't get enough of Pete's dick. "Give me one deep-throat kiss before going back to your room," John-John said. The boy sucked Pete's tongue so ravenously that Pete had a hard time retrieving it.

John-John's hands reached out, cupping Pete's crotch through his jeans. "Tonight has convinced me that Pete Riddle is the only man who will ever satisfy me."

"You shouldn't be so hung up on me," Pete cautioned him. "I still have Josh, though God knows why he puts up with me, and I've got a wife."

"Your marriage to Rosacoke is a sham," John-John said with contempt. "Not a real marriage. As for Josh, I'll be with you long after he deserts the nest. It was all you could do to get him to accept your marriage to Rosacoke. What if she finds out you're not sleeping alone like you say?"

"I like to keep it pretty quiet," Pete said. "Be a little discreet."

"Time will catch up with you one day," John-John predicted. "In the meantime, I'm getting my beauty sleep. You've made me cum three times and I'm wiped out."

"Glad to help out," Pete said, blowing him a kiss before heading back to

the master bedroom. On the way there, Pete figured that John-John was the best fuck of his life. He loved Josh but could never turn down a piece of ass offered by John-John in drag.

Pete didn't know what it was: Maybe it was the way John-John moved his muscles. But when Pete plunged into that boy's butt, it—and not his mansion—was Heaven on Earth. It seemed to be John-John's "thing" in life to get fucked, and he poured his entire reason for living into the act. That was one hot boy, and, if anything, he looked even more beautiful than he did on that long-ago night when Pete first mounted him.

In his own shower, Pete figured that John-John was wrong about his prediction.

Time would never catch up with Pete Riddle. Every day of his life proved that he could get away with anything.

***

A place for walking and wandering, dreaming and drowsing, the acreage around Pete's mansion was the same kind of country Rosacoke had grown up in. It brought back memories to her. Painful ones. She remembered the coves and crannies she used to get lost in, and wished she'd lived at a place like this instead of in a dump like Sultan's old shanty.

She'd been invited to Tara's for lunch. Tara wanted to show off her new little gingerbread cottage that Karl had built for her. On the way there, Rosacoke passed a weathered old ox yoke and an iron bear trap of menacing proportions, both like artifacts of her own past life.

At the door to Tara's house, Rosacoke called out her name. Within minutes Tara was at the screen door, welcoming Rosacoke inside.

Rosacoke was a little nervous about being alone with Tara. Up to now, Rosacoke had always seen her in the presence of others.

Tara looked like some wild creature yet to be discovered and catalogued among the human species. Long hair flailing, she'd dyed a blonde streak in her otherwise red hair, whose frazzled ends looked as if they'd been struck by lightning. Her eyes bulged like black purple grapes, as she led Rosacoke on a tour of her new home, the only one she'd ever had in her life.

Leading Rosacoke to the kitchen, Tara barged in like Mother Courage barreling through hell with a wagonload of cotton. In beat-up sandals, she wore a pair of men's bib overalls and a loose-fitting red blouse. She'd wrapped a wide, brightly colored man's tie like a sash around her bulging middle. Everything she wore looked as it were acquired from a Goodwill store going out of business.

A gutsy, raunchy, yet vulnerable woman, Tara had prepared a lunch of pig's liver, corn bread, green beans with ham hock, and fried yellow squash.

Over lunch, Tara said in a gravel-throated voice, "When I was little, mama said my fat was caused by a thyroid condition. I say it's caused by excessive eating and bourbon drinking."

Deliberately avoiding talk of Pete or Buster, Rosacoke shared her own experiences of growing up with those of Tara. Tara claimed she'd been born "wan and tiny," weighing only five pounds, but even before she was a teenager her weight had shot up to a two-hundred and thirty pounds. Rosacoke felt that Tara's face was still pretty, except for the chubbiness of her cheeks which had become bloated to a hefty hog-jowl size. A bad skin condition as a child had left her otherwise peach-colored skin pock-marked. Little girl freckles were still sprinkled across her face.

No one knew Tara's exact age, and she'd never shed any enlightenment on the subject. Rosacoke figured Tara was at least thirty-four, maybe a whole lot more.

Born an Army brat and kicked around from one Southern base after another—from Key West, Florida to Port Arthur, Texas—Tara claimed she was part Cherokee and "part God only knows what." She related how her great-grandmother had told her tales about how the Cherokees were driven to Oklahoma in 1838 on the infamous "trail of tears." Tara claimed that her own ancestors hid out in the Carolinas, their homeland, refusing to go on the march.

As Tara overloaded her plate at her wooden table, rivers of sweat streamed from her face. Rosacoke ate her food and studied Tara carefully, hoping to learn something. Rosacoke no longer resented her as she had at first, feeling that Tara was stealing Buster's love. She'd come to accept Buster's intimacy with Tara and was appreciative of all the love and help she'd given Buster during Rosacoke's long absences. She was convinced that Tara deeply loved Buster as if he were her own child.

"I know Buster's coming home from school soon," Rosacoke said. "I wanted us to have a little private talk before he got here." She bit into a pig's liver, finding it fried just right. Among other talents, Tara was a good Southern cook.

"I told Buster to let himself go with his music," Tara said. "I have a funny feeling about him. He'll be more alive on stage than he is off stage."

Rosacoke was mesmerized by the sound of Tara's voice—not just when she sang but when she talked as well. The voice was that of a survivor of hundreds of honky-tonks from Florida to the Gulf Coast of Texas, with lots of North Georgia and South Alabama towns thrown in. It was a voice aged in Southern Comfort and filtered with untold numbers of cigarettes. Even in the middle of a meal, Tara had to stop eating to light up a Lucky Strike.

"I appreciate all the help you're giving Buster—and everything," Rosacoke said. "But I don't want him imitating Pete."

"And why in hell not? We begin by copying, then break away and

develop our own styles. Frankly, I don't think you're bothered by Buster. You're worried about yourself."

Rosacoke was startled. "What makes you think that?"

"You're the one who's imitating Pete. Or Roy Acuff. Or one of those male fuckers. You're still not a woman singing like a woman up there on the stage. You're copying the guys."

Rosacoke stopped eating. She was clearly disturbed, as if Tara had hit a sore point. "You know more about how to perform than I do, huh?" Rosacoke didn't bother to disguise the fact that her feelings were hurt.

Slamming down her plate, her mouth still stuffed, Tara heaved her fleshy body from the chair, kicking it back. She went over to the record player and put on some country music as background. Then she sang one of Rosacoke's own songs.

Uninhibited and unbridled, Tara was bawdy, sexy, lusty, and sensual as she went into her act. Energized by the music, her raspy voice shrieked in mournful mutations. It was the voice of back country blues sung by a hard-living, hard-drinking, hard-loving gin mama of the swamps.

Her head thrown back, Tara was impulsive, hot, and temperamental. She had the earthy qualities of a whorehouse singer, yet in some strange way she weaved a web of softness. Her bass notes were gutturally frightening, and her high shrieks filled the air with the terror of a small animal pursued by hunters.

At the finish of the number, Rosacoke impulsively rushed over to her, hugging and kissing her. She understood exactly what Tara was trying to teach her. In her appearances, Rosacoke had held back, as if afraid to let go. As much as she'd tried in the past, she knew she'd delivered only a small part of herself to her audiences. "Help me, mama," she said to Tara. "I've got only days before I go on the road with Pete. I want to make it big. Help me, *please*."

\*\*\*

After lunch Rosacoke and Tara relaxed over a bottle of Southern Comfort.

"Hoss, I fucked up my career," Tara said. "You've still got a chance, but you've got to hit it soon. On the road with Pete, there's got to be a big change in your act. You've got to open up your music. Open yourself up."

"I get scared, real scared. Sometimes I feel I'm a stupid hillbilly up there making an ass out of myself. My deepest fear is that I feel it's unnatural to be up there letting a lot of drunken men undress you in their minds. I feel like some cheap stripper."

"I don't want to hear no more talk like that," Tara said. "You've got to get out on that stage and shout—'I'm here to have a party, boys.' You've

got to make them feel it. Have a sound a little like Leadbelly. But you've also got to evoke a train whistle late at night, all lonesome like. Your throat's got to give off notes like you've drunk too much rotgut bourbon and you've lost your virginity long ago somewhere between Baton Rouge and the Florida Panhandle. Make a racket like Calamity Jane galloping in on her horse to rescue Bessie Smith from a burning Harlem tenement, from there to race off into the sunset to find love forevermore. Be all raunchy and hayseed. You've got to get out there and fuck the men in the audience. The more sterile the room you're working, the more you've got to tighten those vaginal muscles and really give them a good roll in the hay. Top it all off with a great big pussy fart!"

Once Narcissa shocked Rosacoke with her blunt talk and advice. In Tara's presence, Rosacoke was no longer shocked. She'd heard too much of such talk working the "tonks." In spite of the crude gutter language, Rosacoke was challenged by Tara's projection of what she could be on stage.

Tough and butch, Tara covered up her sensitive core as best she could. "And shake those tits," she called to Rosacoke. "If I had 'em, I would have. I not only grew fat, but when I used to jiggle my bee-bite boobies at the red-blooded men in the audience, they'd laugh. They won't laugh at yours, hoss."

Standing in the doorway of her new house, Tara spotted Buster coming across the field. Rosacoke looked out and saw him, too, his hair sleeked back like yellow sealskin.

"That Buster is gonna grow up to be one hell of a bee-yute-ee-full man," Tara said. "He's also gonna grow up to be a silver-throated devil." Tara turned to Rosacoke for one final word. "Get your ass over here first thing 'morrow morning. I'm gonna teach you everything I know about performing. Trouble with you, hoss, is you've been tailgating while Pete's been boomeranging around the room. 'Bout time you changed all that."

Rosacoke couldn't help but notice that Buster's kiss of Tara—wet and long, right on the lips—was far more passionate than his affectionate brush on her cheek. She tried to blot it from her mind.

After Buster was fed, Rosacoke invited him to go for a walk with her. Tara wanted to sleep off too much Southern Comfort.

Rosacoke drove her son up to the hillside site of the grave of her own mama, her little baby brother, and Sultan. She explained—or tried to—how she'd become involved in such a bizarre life before meeting Pete.

It was twilight as they headed down the hill for home. Buster opened up to her for the first time.

"I've got these needs in my gut," Buster said. "Feel like I'm gonna bust sometimes. I don't get on with the kids at school. They want to be dumb things when they grow up. Firemen, crap like that! I want to go on the road

with you and daddy."

She sensed what a very unhappy child he was, filled with a limitless sadness that somehow found release only in music. She was glad he had some outlet, remembering how she had no pastime as a little girl. Music would have assuaged her loneliness.

"I got a ball of fire in me," he said. "It's burning. My tummy hurts, it burns so much. I want to get out there on stage and sing."

"I hope Tara isn't putting too many big ideas into your head."

"Don't worry. She gives me high hopes. I mean, about where I'm going and everything."

"When I was a little kid, the future frightened the hell out of me," Rosacoke said.

"You'd been hurt a lot," Buster said. "I know how that feels." He reached for her hand. "I can't wait to grow up."

"I'll help you, son. But don't rush growing up. You'll get there soon enough. I'm gonna ask you once more—and never again. Do you really want to be a singer?"

He squeezed her hand tightly. "I ain't got no choice, mama. My gut's made up my mind for me. I can't talk much about it. I've just got to do it!"

***

On the top of the mountain where Karl wanted to build that dream house, Pete had never seen his friend this excited before. Karl told him, "It's a done deal. The papers are gonna be signed in the morning."

Without asking him, Karl came toward Pete and took him in his arms, giving him a long, deep kiss, inserting his tongue for Pete to suck. "Hell, man, in addition to being a great country singer, did anyone ever tell you you're a great kisser?"

"You're the first," Pete said, his face indicating he was joking.

Karl looked deeply into his eyes. "Yeah, right. When I want you these days, and I'm wanting you more and more, I have to fucking go wait in line for my turn."

"That's not the kind of talk I heard from you last time we were up on this damn mountain," Pete said. "If I recall, you were into giving up all this shit. The Army had made a real man out of you."

"That was before we went to that shotgun house together," Karl said. "That was the best sex I've ever had in my life. Thank you for letting me be the man. The Army has turned me into a man, and you made me feel that my balls were so big they drag the floor. I came out of that session with you feeling more manly than I've ever felt in my life. The biggest bull in the pasture."

The masculine aroma of Karl was intoxicating. Pete pulled him close,

grinding his body into Karl's as his tongue darted for Karl's mouth. One hand held Karl's back in firm position as Pete kissed him, the other fondling his hardening cock. "That Lincoln is one big car," Pete said. "I don't think I'll be the first guy to get fucked in the back of a limousine."

"Nor the last," Karl said, nibbling at Pete's ear. "I'm hotter than a firecracker. I've got to have it."

The next few minutes were blurred, and Pete wasn't exactly sure how he got his clothes off and into the back of that Lincoln. It happened so fast. Pete knew that sucking off Karl's cock would not be enough for him today. Pete's sucking was good and Karl was moaning but he wanted more.

Within minutes, Pete felt Karl's large cockhead pushing against his still closed sphincter. He could see the rippling muscles of Karl's chest as he prepared for the big push. Within seconds, he'd plunged into Pete who shouted out both his pain and pleasure.

When Karl started thrusting, hitting Pete's prostate, he was licking Karl's neck and urging him ever onward. There was a combination of almost unbearable pain and pleasure. One hand cupped Karl's large balls, and Pete's other hand roamed Karl's body, feeling everything he could. Karl was one muscled boy.

Karl's hips were moving in a beautiful rhythm. Pete was thrilled at the penetration, even excited at Karl's contorted breathing. He fucked wildly the way Pete liked it, with no slowing of rhythm. Pete figured Rebecca was going to be one lucky gal to get this stud in her bed every night. Karl continued to plunge the monumental length of his big meat into the deepest recesses of Pete's ass. Karl would draw back, almost pulling out completely, then would lunge powerfully into the depths again.

Pete couldn't stand much more of this. When Karl repeated that action one more time, Pete blasted off without even touching himself. A scalding load of manjuice splattered against Karl's washboard stomach. Pete's explosion seemed to send Karl over the top too. His orgasm was the longest Pete remembered getting from any man ever. It seemed to go on and on, never softening, the pace never flagging. Karl fell on Pete, kissing him and licking his face. "Christ, that was hot! You've turned me into a queer just like yourself."

An hour later, back at the same tavern where they'd gone before, Pete sat alone with Karl in the far corner of the room. There was only the bartender, talking to an old mountain climber up front. With such total privacy, Pete felt he could get personal. "What did you mean, I've turned you queer? You're not queer. I mean, you're gonna marry Rebecca and all."

"That marriage will never be," Karl said. "Me and Rebecca broke up."

"May I ask why?" Pete said.

"It's a little personal, and if you tell any of the guys I'll beat the shit out of you. Unlike Wanda Mae who doesn't like sex with Ronnie at all, Rebecca

can't get enough. She's not for me. Me and her did it a few times, but she's a fucking bitch in heat."

"How so?"

"She wants more than I've got to give," Karl said.

"You've got plenty to give, boy," Pete said, still feeling the soreness of his ass.

"Yeah, when I'm around you my dick grows an extra two inches. But the last two times with Rebecca, I went soft inside her and had to pull out. Not only that, the very last time when I failed her, she asked me to go down on her. I have no trouble sucking you off and even swallowing it, but one time down on Rebecca and I threw up. I guess I'm more of a cocksucker than a pussy-licker."

"These things happen."

"You're too kind," Karl said. "I'm not gonna shame myself with no woman again. And I sure don't want no man either." He leaned over toward Pete, a lock of his beautiful straight hair falling over his forehead, which made Pete want to grab him and kiss him. "You're all the man I'll ever need."

"But I'm not always with you," Pete said. "There's Josh. And a lot of the time, I'll be on the road."

"And I'll be waiting for you until you come back," Karl said. "If you're gone too long, I'll fly or drive to you. After all, everybody knows me and you have got a lot of business to talk over. Speaking of that, come and get in the car. I'm gonna start that mountain house for you but I want something for myself."

Back in the Lincoln, Karl was behind the wheel, and Pete enjoyed watching him take charge. Except for his show business career, Karl controlled all of Pete's business interests and was doing a fantastic job, unlike his older brother, Hank, who continued to do absolutely nothing. At least the other brother, John-John, would soon be doing gigs as a drag queen on jobs arranged by Larry, all of them safely outside the Carolina hills, in such places as Atlanta and Miami.

For some reason, Karl was driving Pete into town. Karl pulled into a driveway along Peachtree Lane, heading for a large white elephant of a house. "Without asking your permission, I went and bought this place. Paid twenty-thousand dollars for it."

"That's a lot of house for twenty-thousand dollars," Pete said, getting out of the car. "The gardens are beautiful too."

"Wait until you see inside," Karl said. "The place is gorgeous. Stained glass. Terrific woods. It just needs to be restored—that's all."

After showing Pete every room in the house, Karl led him out onto the back verandah, which like the house was built on a hill overlooking the town and the mountains beyond.

"One hell of a place," Pete said. "So you bought it. Fine with me. You have power of attorney. But what in the fuck are you planning to do with it?"

"I want to fix it up just for us," Karl said. "Me and you. I'm building and fixing up houses for everybody else, and I want a place of my own. A place where you can come and conduct business with me. A lot of business, including monkey business?"

"And what do you plan to do when I can't come here?"

"First, I'm not some little housewife sitting around peeling taters waiting for her man to come home. You've given me so much work to do I have to go at it seven days a week. Not only that, but I know I ain't got enough learning to run your business in the future. I'm gonna take correspondence courses. Even some private tutoring if I have to. All your business would fall apart if I went away to college. So I'm gonna educate myself here."

"That's a God damn good idea," Pete said. "And I love this house. I'd love to slip away here with you."

"Only thing is, once you walk into this house, you belong to me. I don't want anybody else coming here. It's just our place where we can have our time together. When you go out that door, everybody else will be clamoring for a hunk of your flesh. But when you're here, you belong to me."

"Did anybody ever tell you that you're the type of man a guy can fall in love with?"

"Cut the shit, man," Karl said. "You're already in love with me." He moved toward Pete with his mouth open.

As Pete felt the nearness of Karl's cherry-red lips, he pulled him as tight as he could into his firm body. "Rebecca's loss. My gain."

***

"Hoss, we've got to talk," Tara said, guiding Pete down the long corridor that led to Buster's room. "Our boy's at school now and I want to show you some things."

At first Pete hesitated. He didn't want to hear the revelation he feared Tara was about to make. It felt like a violation of Buster's privacy. As a boy, Pete had always guarded his own privacy, and was always relieved that his mama never came into his own bedroom where he stashed magazine tear-out pictures of John Payne in a bathing suit or a shirtless Tyrone Power in a rowboat.

As Pete came into the room with Tara, he took her gently by the arm. "All young boys have their secrets. Why don't you let Buster keep his?"

"That's the way to go in most cases," Tara said. "I love Buster dearly but I think before you go on the road again, hoss, you've got to face up to a big truth."

He'd never really been angry at Tara before, but this afternoon he was pissed off. He instinctively knew what she was about to reveal, and he didn't want to hear it.

"Everybody at Heaven on Earth, with the possible exception of Rosacoke, knows the truth about Buster," she said. "In your heart you know it too, but for some reason you can't face up to it."

"What's this God damn truth I can't face up to?"

Tara stood her ground, confronting him. "Buster is madly in love with you."

"A lot of sons love their daddies," he said, "Last time I checked there was no law against that." His face was stern when he stared at Tara. "Don't tell me you're jealous. You want the kid's love just for yourself. You aren't his mama though I feel you forget that sometimes. Why can't Buster love you and me both? Nothing wrong with that."

She looked at him for a long moment as if reluctant to go on with her mission. Slowly she walked over and opened the bottom drawer to an antique piece of furniture that had belonged to Bleeka Walker, the former owner of the house. She held up a pair of underwear. "Recognize this?" She held up another pair, then another pair. "A little big for Buster, don't you think?"

He recognized the underwear at once. It was his. He was always missing personal items, and figured one of the guys around his compound was taking stuff for his own use. At the drawer, he rifled through the clothing. All of it belonged to him. His fingers retrieved a soiled jock strap.

"He stole that from that exercise room where you and Josh work out."

He didn't know what to say, as his mind was confused.

Like a relentless prosecutor, Tara headed toward a night table beside Buster's bed. "There's more." She opened the door and pulled out a picture.

Without looking at the photograph, Pete knew immediately what the subject was. Tara handed him the photograph. "Mighty impressive," she said.

He glanced only briefly at the picture Josh had taken of him fully erect at Blowing Rock Falls. They'd been drinking beer and had been in a fun-loving mood when Josh had asked Pete to pose for his camera. The pictures had been secretly developed on Deal Street.

He handed the picture back to her, and she put it back in Buster's drawer. "The other morning when I came in to wake him for school, he was jacking off to that picture. Yes, Buster is of the age where he's beating his meat."

"The kid has a crush on me—that's all," Pete said. "A lot of boys are like that. I was the same way when I was his age."

"You call it a crush," she said. "I call it an obsession." She led Pete into

the living room of Buster's wing. There were three rooms in addition to the bedroom. One had been turned into a playroom.

In that room Tara opened a trunk, inviting Pete to look inside. "He even collects cigarette butts you discard. An empty beer can or two. Anything that's been at your lips. Here are some bars of soap used to scrub you down. Buster seems to want anything that's been in intimate contact with your body."

Pete was doing a slow burn. More than the revelations, he resented Tara for exposing them to him. She just wouldn't give up, walking over to a large closet and turning on the light. "Look inside."

Pete peered inside, not really wanting to see what he was likely to find there. Buster had taken photographs of Pete and wallpapered every inch of space with the images.

"I think he comes in here, where pictures of you are everywhere, to jack off," Tara said. "I've done my duty. I felt I had to call it to your attention. But it's your problem now. If you want to let the boy make love to you every night and kick Josh out of your bed, that's your life and I'll go along with whatever you tell me to do. I love it here. I want to live and die here. It's the first real home I've ever had. So please remember that if there's anything you want me to do, I'll do it. You can count on me."

His earlier resentment of Tara had faded. He viewed her as a welcoming ally again. "Okay, I've faced up to the truth, although Josh has been warning me about this shit for the last two years. Buster really wants to sleep between us and take baths with me, stuff like that. At first I loved such devotion. I didn't want to think of it as sexual, but the most loving son and father in the Carolina hills."

"Instead of me picking him up at school today, why don't you go for him?" Tara asked. "A chance for you guys to clear the air a bit before going on the road with Rosacoke."

"She doesn't know anything about this?" Pete asked.

"She's never said anything to me," Tara said. "I think there's a lot that Rosacoke don't know, but she's catching on to more every day."

Driving to Buster's school, Pete didn't know what to say to him. He wondered if he should say anything. Didn't all children go through periods? Pete recalled vividly his own libido when he was Buster's age and how he'd dreamed of all the things he'd do if Tyrone Power, Errol Flynn, or John Payne—his favorites—crawled into bed with him.

When Pete had seen *Gone with the Wind*, he had wished that Clark Gable as Rhett Butler had picked him up in his arms and taken him to a bedroom upstairs to rape him instead of Scarlett O'Hara. Pete figured that he'd been attracted to Claude initially because of the sheriff's remarkable resemblance to movie star Gary Cooper. The difference was, and Pete was acutely aware of this, his own sexual fantasies were usually about the

reigning male movie stars of his day—not his own daddy.

In the school yard, Buster seemed surprised and then delighted that Pete, not Tara, had come to drive him home. Pete asked Buster if he could take him to Breazeale's Drug Store for a banana split.

"I'm not a kid no more, dad," Buster said defensively. "I've also out-grown the ice cream cone stage, and I don't play with dolls no more. I can't wait till I start drinking beer like you and the boys do."

"You're growing up mighty fast," Pete said, looking over at the increas-ingly handsome Buster, as Pete stepped on the gas and headed for the open countryside to be alone with his son. In the bright light of a mid-afternoon, Buster had become remarkably beautiful, even more than John-John who was considered the male beauty of the county.

Pete reckoned that Buster was far more attractive than Pete had been as a kid. With handsome Pete Riddle and the stunning Rosacoke Carson as his parents, how could he not grow up movie-star gorgeous? It wasn't beyond Pete's imagination to picture Buster a movie star right up there one day on the silver screen with Robert Taylor, Van Johnson, Guy Madison, and William Holden.

When Pete later approached a belvedere up along the mountain park-way, he leaned over toward Buster. "Let's stop here. I used to come up here when I got my first car. I'd go for a long walk down yonder along a mountain trail. I did so to figure things out. I thought today we might have a little come-to-Jesus talk between a daddy and his son."

"I'd like that," Buster said. "I don't get enough time alone with you. I almost never get to see much of you when you're alone. There's some-body hanging on to you all the time. That Josh can't seem to let you out of his sight. The other day he told me he gets really pissed when you're off seeing one of the other guys, like Freddie and Nipsey with your music or Karl with your business."

"He's a little possessive," Pete said, taking Buster's hand as he led him down the trail that would in a few weeks be covered with snow and not passable.

"I don't see how Josh helps you out all that much," Buster said as they made their way along the trail with its panoramic views in all directions. "I mean, he writes a few songs. But I don't see him doing much work, other than dogging your trail like a lovesick puppy." He came to an abrupt stop. "Why don't you ask him to go? I could do everything he does for you. Only better."

"What exactly does that mean?" Pete said, looking deeply into his son's eyes.

"Anything he can do, I can do better," he said, gazing into Pete's eyes with a ferocity of feeling that sent a shiver through Pete. "I can work out with you. My body's growing every day. I can sleep with you and look

after you. I can give you better massages than Josh. I know you like how I bathe you. I can lay out your clothes, take care of your outfits when you go on the road. Polish your boots."

"You're picturing some slave role for yourself," Pete said. "You're my son. I don't want that for you. I want you to grow up and lead a life of your own. Be your own man."

"What if being my own man meant becoming your boy like Josh is?" Buster asked.

In the golden light of the fading day, Pete looked at Buster as he never had before. Almost overnight he'd grown prematurely. It was as if he'd gone from being a child to developing a young man's passion without going through a transition period. Pete said nothing.

"What were you like at my age?" Buster asked. "Try to remember. What did you think about at night when you went to bed?"

The images of all the naked men Pete thought about at Buster's age came racing through Pete's mind. Had Buster become a young Pete?

"You don't have to answer me," Buster said. "I know the answer. I'm just like you when you were my age. The same thoughts. The same feelings. The same powerful urges."

"Okay, okay," Pete said, growing intensely uncomfortable. He walked ahead rapidly, as Buster rushed to catch up with him. Buster grabbed his arm, forcing him to stop in his tracks.

"Why are you walking away?" Buster asked. "Why aren't you facing up to things like a man?"

Pete stopped and looked deeply into Buster's eyes. "Exactly what in the fuck do you want from me? What is it I'm supposed to face up to. Even Tara is demanding that I face up to the truth. Okay, God damn it, spill the beans. Hit me with the fucking truth I can't face."

Buster stood tantalizingly close to Pete who was now shaking all over. Pete feared the next few moments with his son.

"I'm in love with you, fucker," Buster said. "You're all I think and dream about. And in my thoughts you're always naked. God, you're got a big cock."

"Stop this kind of shit talk," Pete said, turning from the sight of him.

Buster wouldn't stand for that. He walked around and stood danger-ously close to Pete. His mouth was only inches from Pete's lips.

"Admit the truth," Buster said. "You think I didn't know what was going on when we bathed together. Your hand kept going back to my smooth butt time and time again. You were turned on by it. Come clean."

"I'll admit nothing of the God damn sort," Pete said. "You're my son. Ever heard of a thing call incest?"

"I sure as hell have," Buster said. "I heard that little bastard boy, Freddie Perkins, used to get fucked by his adopted stepdaddy all the time. The

stepdaddy liked fucking Freddie, and Freddie loved it so much he begged for it."

Out of control with his own feelings and emotions, Pete slapped Buster so hard he knocked him down. In a flash, Pete kneeled down and took the boy in his arms, holding him tightly and crying into his neck. "I'm sorry. I've never hit you before. I swear I didn't mean to."

Buster's face was so close to his that Pete could smell his sweet breath, the sweetest breath he'd ever smelled on anybody in his life. Pete's whole body was trembling.

"Look at my lips," Buster said, "Aren't they the sweetest cherry-red lips you've ever seen on a boy before? Wouldn't you like to put that big dick of yours between my lips and invade my virgin mouth while my little pink tongue licks the head of your dick? You've felt my butt. Wouldn't you like to get naked with me and play with me day after day, inserting more and more of yourself into my ass until one day you've loosened me up until I can take all your inches? Don't you know what would happen? The first night you plunge all the way into me you'll cum right away 'cause it'll be the most sensational feeling you've ever had in your life. The first time you fuck my virgin ass, you're not going to let go. You're going to stay in me all night. Fucking me four or five times before you'll dare withdraw from my ass. You know why? Because when you break me in, it'll be the greatest fuck of your life. When you teach me how to suck and fuck, I'll be better at it than anybody."

Not able to hold back, Pete burst into tears at Buster's words. This was more truth than any man wanted to face for one day.

Buster's hand moved toward Pete's crotch. "You're getting hard. Hard and big. You want me, fucker, and you're gonna get me. I can't wait to get my sweet mouth over every inch of your body."

Pete reached out and pressed his face against Buster's, licking his lips before inserting his tongue. Buster sucked greedily.

It was the single most thrilling kiss Pete had ever experienced, but he knew it was wrong. He had to force himself to pull away from Buster who clung to him desperately.

Rising to his feet and using all the willpower he had, Pete broke away and ran back up the hill.

"Come back," Buster yelled after him. "You know you want it."

*** 

After a communal breakfast at Heaven on Earth, Pete left to drive Buster to school. He also planned to call on Karl and Junior before heading on the road for his first trip on their as yet unused bus. Freddie was busy getting it ready, and Maston, Smokey, Nipsey, and Guitar Red were check-

ing their instruments.

Claude was going to do most of the driving. He hadn't joined them for breakfast, having it instead with Wanda Mae and Ronnie.

Alone in the Lincoln with Buster, his son turned to Pete. "Our time alone together on the parkway didn't exactly end like I wanted it to."

"It's gonna have to end that way every time," Pete said harshly. "What you're talking about is wrong. It's against God's teachings."

"When did you ever pay any attention to anything you learned in church?"

"That's beside the point," Pete said. "I don't pretend to be a religious man. I've done a lot of things that are wrong."

"Done," Buster said sarcastically. "Isn't the word do instead of done?"

"Both are true. Done wrong and doing wrong." Pete gripped the wheel nervously. "Even I draw the limits somewhere."

"Face facts. I'm a queer son with a queer daddy with a ten-inch dick. Things are bound to happen. If not today, then when you get back from the road in that stupid bus."

"Things are not bound to happen," Pete said. "I get all the sex I want from Josh."

"Bullshit!" Buster said. I think you're also getting it from Karl."

"Hell, no!" Pete was getting angry. "I've never touched Karl."

"I'm getting prettier and prettier every day," Buster said. "You're gonna get real curious. You're gonna come to my room to sample what I've got." As Buster said that, Pete pulled into the far lot of the school yard. He was the only daddy who delivered his kid to school in a limousine.

"Be a good boy while I'm away on the road," Pete said. "Keep up with your homework and do what Tara tells you."

"Cut this playing daddy crap," Buster said. "You're not thinking about my homework at all right now. You're thinking I have the most beautiful lips in the world and you're hot to taste them."

"God damn you!" Pete said, his whole body shaking. He reached over and pulled Buster to him, crushing his lips against his son's and licking and tasting them before inserting his tongue into the boy's mouth. The sweetness of Buster was overpowering. The more he kissed Buster, the harder he got. Buster's hand was in Pete's crotch, feeling every inch. Finally he had enough willpower to break away from Buster.

"No one can give you a hard-on faster than I can," Buster said, resting his head back on the seat. It was obvious from the look on his face that he felt a sense of triumph mixed with the passion Pete had aroused in him.

"Get out of the fucking car and go to school," Pete said. "Don't you ever tempt me like that again."

"You don't want me to go to school," Buster said, opening the passenger door. "You want to take me up to that shotgun house of Claude's and fuck me all day."

"Get out!" Pete shouted again at him.

Buster slammed the car door and walked rapidly across the school grounds to the main building. Still shaking violently, Pete watched him go as a feeling of awful desolation swept over him.

Buster had stirred up Pete's passion this morning, and it had to be satisfied before he headed back to Heaven on Earth to hook up with Josh, Rosacoke, and his boys.

Pete steered the Lincoln in the direction of Junior's new apartment. Karl had built a small three-story apartment right at the airport so Junior could "live, breathe, and sleep" airplanes. Junior still kept his bedroom at Heaven on Earth, but increasingly he spent all his time at the airport. Within a year he predicted that he'd be able to launch his commercial aviation venture with Pete.

Junior's apartment was almost like a tree house. Although there was a garage and a workshop on the ground floor, and a guest bedroom, kitchen, and dining area on the second, the real living space was on the third floor. From there, Junior had an eagle's eye view of the airport day and night.

Pete climbed the steps to Junior's new abode and knocked on the door. Looking disheveled, Junior came to the door wearing a pair of blue boxer shorts. Most men wore white underwear, and Pete believed that Junior in blue was the sexiest looking man he'd ever laid eyes on. Junior liked to wear his shorts real tight, and his big bulge was clearly prominent. The fly of the shorts was open, giving Pete a tantalizing preview.

Junior pulled Pete inside, giving him a long, deep kiss. Pete enjoyed the stubble of Junior's morning beard rubbing against his smooth cheeks, feeling his rippling muscles as the pilot kissed him. When he could stand it no more, he reached inside Junior's fly, feeling every hardening inch before descending to fondle and weigh the balls.

"You're my favorite pilot," he whispered into Junior's ear. "Wanna fly me?"

"Hop aboard," Junior said, leading him over to a rumpled bed.

"If I didn't know better, I'd say this bed was the scene of some wild action last night," Pete said.

"You got that right. Rebecca got pounded. Since Karl dumped her, I figured her pussy was up for grabs."

"What you did to Rebecca last night, I want you to do to me," Pete said. "Only harder."

"You got it, big boy," Junior said before descending on Pete.

An hour later, Pete had had a hard time breaking away from Junior for a final mission.

\*\*\*

At Karl's new house in town, Pete came in through the back door, finding his friend alone in the kitchen drinking freshly brewed coffee. Karl was wearing only a pair of white underwear. Pete had never seen him look more gorgeous, a true golden boy.

Karl sensed what Pete wanted by merely looking into his face. Within fifteen minutes Pete had been stripped down and was in Karl's bedroom getting a fierce pounding. "I won't be seeing you for a while, and I've got to make this last a long time," Karl whispered into his ear. Karl held back as long as he could, but Pete's fondling of his balls, kissing his neck, biting his earlobes, and tonguing his mouth had gotten to him. He erupted with a blast so powerful Pete felt he was going into orbit.

During their fuck session, Pete had had an incredible experience. Karl delivered almost the same fuck that his brother, Tracy, had come through with in Norfolk. It was as if Tracy had come back and lived anew in Karl's magnificent body. The two brothers even looked alike. Hank also resembled Tracy and Karl but he'd matured more than his brothers, and his looks had changed into something more rugged, more dissipated, than before. The glow of youth still shone over Karl, who was in his physical and sexual prime.

Karl had not wanted to pull out of Pete. Collapsing on him, Karl breathed heavily on Pete's neck when he wasn't kissing and licking it. He must have lain like that for fifteen minutes until Pete felt Karl hardening inside him once again. Karl reared up, then pressed his lips against Pete's. Karl parted only slightly from those lips to tell Pete. "This second one is for the road, music man."

# Chapter 11

At long last Rosacoke went on the road with Pete and his musicians, now called the Foggy Mountain Boys. Pete didn't really like the name, but Nipsey, Maston, Guitar Red, and Smokey seemed pretty determined, so he gave in to their wishes.

Riding in their shining new bus, Rosacoke had wanted to sit next to Pete but Josh seemed to have taken that permanent seat. At times she felt Josh was more like Pete's wife than she was.

She'd been disappointed when they stopped off for their first night on the road. Freddie Raubal had rented cabins in a trailer camp for them. Rosacoke noted that she'd been assigned a room alone. "Josh and Pete are going to double up," Freddie had told her. "It cuts down on expenses." Claude was off in his own room, and Hank and Larry were sharing, as were Nipsey and Freddie. Smokey and Guitar Red had their own cabin, although Maston, as always, preferred to sleep in a room by himself.

When Pete studied the tour schedule with them the next morning over a breakfast of grits, country ham, and red-eye gravy, he turned to Larry. "Hell, man, you're going to one-night us to death."

"It's what you've got to do when you're starting out," Larry said.

Rosacoke didn't complain. Traveling on that bus was so much more comfortable than what she'd been used to when working the tonks on her own.

The first night on stage, the Foggy Mountain Boys were hot, and their bluegrass instruments, including a fiddle and a banjo, sizzled. She too planned to set the stage on fire.

Night after night they played to the poor audiences of the Deep South, sometimes entire families who were willing to spend hard-earned money to escape from the dreariness of their lives. The audiences for their music had grown familiar to her—pale mill workers from the towns of North Georgia, weather-beaten farmers from South Louisiana, off-duty cops from Jacksonville, and a jakeleg preacher or two from the Carolinas. On stage she could feel a kind of hope that good country music brought to these people. At times she felt she was at a prayer meeting. Their music seemed to stir up memories and even desires in their downtrodden fans.

Pete's sound was true grit, and hers was, too. "Baby," Pete said one night, "our stuff is full of life."

Sometimes, instead of open-air arenas, they worked the honky-tonks—

called "blood buckets"—and on many a night more heads were broken than guitar chords. "They're a lot of loners out there like ourselves," Pete said. "We've got to reach out to them every night."

And she did. In her hot colors and rhinestones.

Coming off the stage after one of her better shows, she rushed over to kiss her man. "I'm flying," she almost shouted. "Like a bird who's just grown new wings."

There had been an invitation to come to her room that night, but he didn't show up. He did show up the following night, though. He had sex with her only in darkened rooms, and still preferred to come out of the bathroom with a rubber covering his impressive hard-on. She still couldn't understand why he wanted to work up his erection by himself before coming to her. She much preferred to do it for him.

On the road again, she worked on a new song for herself. It was about a love affair that was cracked up beyond repair, only to be followed by the undiminished wonder of getting back together again and betting your life it was going to work out the second time around.

Pete was not writing music but singing it, especially any song—good or bad—that Josh wrote. The best number Josh had written, and he'd done it on the road, was "One Wrong Turn Too Many." It told the story of all-night trucker barreling down the highway after he'd just learned his wife had walked out on him and into the arms of his best friend.

"The song is great," she told Pete, even though a bit jealous of Josh for writing it. "But I'll never walk out on you."

"Life is long," he said.

As the tour deepened, and to her surprise, she found out that Pete actually had fans. Not in any great number. Many of his small but loyal band of followers drove across two or three counties to hear him sing and play. Pete appreciated their response, yet he called many of the clubs Larry had booked them into "the chicken shit circuit." Having to get all dolled up in some of their crappers, Rosacoke felt that was too kind an appraisal.

At one dance hall she was nervous about the crowd, as the smell of booze and violence was in the air. The aging manager of the place, Bubba Short, informed her: "After our big Saturday night, I have to hire a nigger come Sunday morning to sweep up the eyeballs."

Pete fitted perfectly into this rowdy world, and, to her, he seemed to drink more heavily than ever. Once or twice she had to fill in for him when he was unable to go on. He was very nervous the next morning, hoping his failure didn't upset Larry too much.

The nights became a blur for Rosacoke who felt her songs were just background to the saloon fistfights.

However, day by day she slowly became aware that Pete had developed his own highly original style. He'd gone through his stages of imita-

tion, and he didn't sound like Ernest Tubb or Roy Acuff any more. He sounded like Pete Riddle, and that was real music to her ears.

His blues numbers became lowdown and dirty. Both Rosacoke and Pete interjected sex into music, as it had never been heard on country and western stages before. Their church choir sentimentality was behind them. They no longer sang of mama sitting out in a rocking chair on the porch of her old mountain shack, waiting for her drunken husband to come home. Their new music reflected the aspirations, problems, and changing morality of the post-war generation.

Night after night she watched as Pete strutted onto stage in a pair of tight-fitting pants, encasing his muscular legs that she wanted to see more of. He closed his heavy-lidded eyes, let go with a moan from deep within his throat, and buckled his knees. The women in the audience, to hear him tell it later, "creamed in their bloomers."

The obvious bulge in Pete's crotch went over well with the women, but it made the men jealous. On many a night a guy waited in the back parking lot to beat Pete up after some girl friend squealed too enthusiastically at his act. Confronted with Claude and Hank, no man ever attempted to jump Pete more than once.

Pete told Rosacoke, "Ever since that day we outfitted ourselves like cowboys, I've liked tight pants. I like to show off what I've got. Those years in the Navy made up my mind for me. You know, a sailor's pants seem made to show off what's hanging. I remember once walking into a Greyhound bus station in Richmond. Back then I walked exactly to the rhythm of *Managua, Nicaragua*. A lady comes up to me— a real good looker—and says, 'Sailor, what you're swinging down there would be the answer to my prayers.'"

Watching him close their act every night, she became convinced that Larry was right. Pete Riddle was going to become a big name in country music.

Rosacoke knew the reason why, and it was based on more than just talent. Even though Pete, unknown to his audiences, was a very rich young man, he was able to convince his fans that he was one of them and had shared the same troubles and woes. Whether it was true or not, he came across as a man who'd eaten southern fried chicken every Sunday, his mama treating it like a delicacy of the type you put out on the table only when the preacher came. Even though he'd lived in the comfort of the Riddle household, Pete in his voice sounded like a man who'd hopped freight trains or had worked as a tenant farmer, praying to God he wouldn't lose his crops to bad weather. He projected an image of a man who'd cried his heart out at the death of his beloved mama.

Yet in spite of these sentimental and crowd-pleasing on-stage antics of Pete, there was another quality he projected, particularly if the audience

was more mature and not filled with families but composed of hard-drinking and even harder-fucking patrons. To them, Pete suggested that there lurked within his soul a streak of violence just simmering below the surface of his skin.

He evoked a man who'd slapped his woman around on a drunken Saturday night, then got a hard-on while beating her and fucked her four times before the rooster crowed on Sunday morning. He came off as a man who'd seen his electricity cut off as the bills piled up and he had to go out and get money somewhere to feed a pregnant wife and three bawling kids back home.

There was a vision on stage of a man who'd had his heart broken by more women than he could remember, a man who drank up most of his paycheck, and who knew how to use his fists.

For all his faults and all his excesses, she was proud to be his opening act in Memphis at the biggest and most important club they'd ever appeared at.

The crowd was usually impatient to get the girl "canary" out of the way until the big act—Pete Riddle and his boys—came on. Tonight she was determined to give them that special something Tara had talked about, something the boys would remember her by.

The club manager, Charlie Cabell, didn't give her the dignity of an introduction. She just had to go out and start singing, hoping to capture the noisy crowd's attention.

Throwing her head back the way she'd seen Tara do, she pranced out on stage in her gaudy white cowgirl outfit studded with rhinestones.

For her first number she was ignored by the beer-drinking audience. But by the second number, she'd heated up the place. Snapping her fingers, she was on fire, as she stomped her white boots down hard on the wide-planked floors. She heated up the Foggy Mountain Boys, who usually woke up only when Pete came out.

Jumping up and down in front of the bright red spotlights, she demanded and got the attention of the mostly male audience. Like an electric switch, she plugged the men into her music. All the pent-up energy she'd kept bottled up inside her was uncorked.

At the finale, her body was drenched in sweat, her outfit hugging snugly against her like a sausage casing. She was practically delirious, as supercharged herself as she'd made the audience.

Rushing toward the wings, she heard the screaming, the Tennessee-boy whistling, the pounding of fists on the bar. The rebel yells splitting the air told her she'd won them over, that they were hers. She silently vowed to hang onto them forever, as she needed them more desperately than she'd ever realized.

Backstage she practically bumped into Pete, wanting to share her mo-

ment of triumph with him. In his ten-gallon hat and "suit of lights," his eyes were ablaze with a jealous rage she'd never seen there before.

"Jee-zus!!!" he shouted at her, as the lingering applause—still thunderous—resounded in her ears. "How in hell's bells am I to follow a hotcha act?"

He strode angrily onto stage. The continuing roar was not for him, but for the girl singer who'd just vanished in air before giving the crowd its fill of her.

She burst into tears until comforted by the presence of the old stage door guardian, Uncle Darling. He'd seen the best and worst of acts and had known all the greats in country music. In some way he reminded her of Fry back home. In a bourbon-saturated voice, he told her, "You can get a rise in the pants of any stud between Memphis and Amarillo."

***

On the bus, Rosacoke came back to Heaven on Earth with all the gang. Buster was the first person to rush out the front door and race across the verandah into Pete's arms. Her son couldn't stop hugging and kissing Pete. A good ten minutes went by before he acknowledged her. He was courtly and polite to her, but, as for love, she might be saying hello to a neighbor's child.

Tara rushed to kiss both Rosacoke and Pete. At least this fat mama spread her kisses around. She told them that Fry had heard that they were coming back today, and that he was waiting for them on the back porch.

After she'd freshened up, Pete asked Rosacoke to join him for their reunion with Fry, their early mentor.

On the porch, Fry seemed to have aged greatly since their last time together. He looked frail and in poor health, and was coughing a lot. He confided to Pete that he was going to have to have an operation, and he'd written a song, which he wanted Pete to buy off him. "It's called 'Lonesome Blues.'"

"Listen," Pete said, "I'll buy the song but don't you worry about paying for that operation. I'll take care of it. You taught Rosacoke and me everything we know."

Fry asked if he could sing the words to the song, and Pete seemed eager to hear it. As twilight stole across the grounds, Fry in a broken, shattered, but still strangely haunting voice quietly sang the song for Rosacoke and Pete. Tara had already learned it and came out from the kitchen to play guitar. The whole spectacle seemed eerie. At the end of the song, no one said anything.

The look on Fry's face was one of rejection. The opposite was true. Both Pete and Rosacoke were so stunned by the song they couldn't say

anything at first. In many respects, their silence was the greatest kind of applause.

"This song would be perfect for you," Rosacoke said to Pete, breaking the silence. "Buy it. Go to Nashville. Record it. Fred Rose, Roy Acuff, move over."

Pete agreed to buy the song but he wasn't sure if he wanted to record it, even though it called for a talent to yodel, which he'd already mastered. "Let's get Larry out here and let him hear it."

Within minutes Larry was on the back porch. Pete took the music from Fry and, as Tara played the guitar again, he sang it for Larry. The song was a natural for Pete on his first try. Even without one bit of practice, he'd found new dimensions in the song that Fry might not have known was there. When Pete sang the song, he literally moaned the blues. The pupil had long ago surpassed his teacher.

Far from the simple lament of lost love Fry had sung, "Lonesome Blues" in Pete's throat became a tear-jerking lament about the gal who got away, the one that all men remember even or especially when they are in bed with another woman.

The chord progression on the guitar was a little fancier than what he'd been used to, but he handled it well. For a country song, the phrasing was also a little complicated for him, yet because he was such a natural-born performer he adapted the song to his own particular style, avoiding possible pitfalls. However, he still sounded poor as "purr," a word he'd never been able to pronounce correctly.

Strong and steady, his voice had a cutting edge, plunging out of the depths of a lovesick hell into an altitudinal falsetto register.

"Let's go for it," Larry said. "We'll record it in Nashville."

Larry's order meant more to Pete than Rosacoke's opinion, and he agreed to not only buy the song from Fry but record it as well. "It'll take some work," Pete said cautiously.

He kept singing the song long after devouring the supper Tara had prepared for them. Claude, Ronnie, Wanda Mae, Junior, Hank, Buster, Freddie, Nipsey, and Larry all joined them on the porch. Pete sent Josh to fetch Maston, and the old man heard the song and proclaimed it, "A Pete Riddle natural." Pete also wanted to have Guitar Red and Smokey to hear it, but they'd run off with some black gals for the night.

Josh was the only one who appeared less that enthusiastic. Rosacoke figured that as a songwriter he was a little bit jealous of all this attention being paid to Fry's song.

Long after his gang drifted off, Pete kept singing the blues without leaving the back porch. Fry had since departed, and even Tara headed off for her new cottage. Buster had kissed Pete goodbye at ten o'clock. Josh was the last to leave Rosacoke alone with Pete. At first she thought that Josh

was determined to stay up as long as Pete did, but road fatigue finally hit him. Before leaving, he urged Pete to turn in soon.

Rosacoke stayed up with Pete until the very end of the night, even when it was past two o'clock in the morning. Two or three times he walked off the porch into the darkness. "Even with all these fancy marble bathrooms, I still like to piss in the moonlight." He might be pissing but she knew he was also swigging some whiskey in the converted barn.

Each time he came back to the porch, he sang "Lonesome Blues" again, as if he'd become mesmerized by the song. "No, not that," he said more to himself than to her. He'd try the song another way. Shortly before three o'clock, he pronounced it, "Perfect! My God, I could have written this song myself. It's got Pete Riddle all over it."

When he was completely exhausted, she helped him up to his feet and led him down the corridor to her own bedroom. She wanted to be with him tonight, although she hardly expected much action from him. Pulling off his clothes for him, she helped lower him into her bed, as the moonlight streamed in through her big window, making him look like a golden boy.

Her nearness seemed to revive him, and he reached out to kiss and tongue her mouth, squeezing her big breasts. Even in his drunken state, he was arousing her. She felt his cock. As it hardened, she fondled his balls.

More than listening to him sing "Lonesome Blues," she wanted him to make fierce, passionate love to her.

All of a sudden the door to her bedroom was thrown open. She hadn't bothered to lock it. It was Josh silhouetted against the glaring lights of the hallway.

"So there you are," he said to Pete. "I've been looking everywhere for you."

At first, she was too startled to cover her nudity with a sheet. Finally, realizing the state he'd caught her in, she hastily concealed her nakedness.

Josh went over and tossed a robe to Pete. "Get up. I'm taking you to bed. You're drunk."

Pete obediently followed Josh's orders, as his friend put the robe around him.

In more anger than he'd ever revealed to her before, Josh confronted her. "You know I'm trying to keep him away from the bottle. He's drinking far too much. Look what you've done to him."

She didn't say anything as Josh helped escort Pete out of her bedroom.

After Josh had slammed the door, she collapsed on her bed, letting the moonlight stream in and wash her body, making it golden just like it had done to Pete.

A nagging thought that had taken seed in the back of her brain now sent its tentacles to the forefront of her mind. She no longer needed a road map to tell her what she'd known for a long time, although refusing to admit it to

herself.

Josh Harnell was madly in love with Pete Riddle.

***

Thirty minutes later in Pete's master bedroom, Josh pulled off all his clothes. Flat on his back and nude, Pete looked up at his lover. "Tonight I'm gonna punish you," Josh said. I'm changing the rules about not topping you. I'm gonna fuck you till dawn breaks."

As he said that, Pete noticed Josh's dick hardening. Without foreplay, he moved onto Pete and inserted himself, plunging deep into him with no preparation. Pete yelled out in pain as Josh's mouth descended, biting his lips.

"You belong to me," Josh said, asserting his territorial rights in ways Pete had never known him to do before. "Not to Rosacoke Carson. And not to Buster."

The pain had eased up now for Pete to be replaced by the most exquisite pleasure. Pete's hands reached up to fondle, rub, and feel every inch of Josh's body as his lover pounded harder into him. "I'm all yours, baby," he whispered into Josh's ear before licking and nibbling his neck.

It was a Saturday morning when Rosacoke faced Pete for a late lunch prepared by Tara. It was served on the same back verandah where she'd heard endless versions of "Lonesome Blues" the night before. Josh had joined them for the lunch, directing all his talk to Pete and ignoring her. No mention, not even an apology, was made for his barging into her bedroom last night without knocking.

On Pete's second cup of coffee, she asked to talk to him privately about Buster. Josh still didn't budge from his chair until Pete asked him to. That seemed to make him mad, and he stormed off toward the recording studio to join Freddie and Nipsey.

She felt that there were many ways a wife could deal with a dawning of reality about her husband. Confront him with her version of the truth? Divorce him and ask for a big settlement? Go on and suffer through the marriage and say nothing, growing increasingly bitter every night? Those seemed like options.

Instead she chose to pretend to ignore what was obvious to her eyes. She wasn't going to challenge or confront Pete in any way. She was determined to go on with her marriage regardless of how ignored she was both by her husband and her son.

What she was going to do was to declare her independence. "I'm always here if you want a wife," she said. "If Buster decides he should ever want some mama other than Tara, I'll be here for him too."

Tara came onto the porch to pour Pete yet another cup of coffee and to

bring him some freshly squeezed orange juice. "Thanks, sweetheart," he said to her before turning to Rosacoke again. "What kind of talk is this?"

"I feel your career is about to take off," she said, "and I'm happy for you. I just want you to know I'm gonna launch myself as well, maybe in a slightly different direction. But I woke up this morning and said to myself, 'Miss Pussy, you're gonna become a star, and beginning tomorrow you're gonna devote all your time and attention to achieving that one goal.' If Narcissa can do it, I can do it."

"That's the spirit, gal," he said. "My boys and I will help you in any way. And there's always Larry. He's showed us only a tiny part of what he can do to jumpstart a career. By the way, what brought on this grim ambition this morning?"

"It's been a long time coming," she said. "I've seen too many women in too many honky-tonks who devoted their entire lives to their husbands and children, only to be deserted by both. I'm not gonna let that happen to me. I hope you understand. I hope Buster understands.

"We'll manage somehow," he said.

She couldn't help but notice a slight smugness on his face. If anything, she felt that he'd be delighted to get her out of his hair. "My only wish is that you can persuade him to develop some friends his own age. I know what it's like to grow up with nothing but adults. Narcissa was around, of course, but she was hardly my playmate. Maybe she wasn't ever a child at all. Narcissa seemed to pop out of her mama's womb with a fully developed adult mind."

"Buster will work out just fine," Pete said. "Let him keep the company he wants."

"He sure adores you," she said. "Maybe too much so."

"Exactly what does that mean?" he asked, flashing anger.

"Nothing," she said. "I mean he looks real attached to you."

Slamming down his coffee, he got up and headed to the barn and Josh. "There's nothing wrong with a son loving his daddy," he called back over his shoulder. "Seems I can't convince enough people of that."

Filled with this awful emptiness, she walked down the long corridor leading to the front door and the wide verandah. She got behind the wheel of a new Studebaker Pete had bought for her and headed up to the mountains and the Tennessee border.

She needed to spend the day driving to clear her head. She knew that she was driving too fast over curvy mountain roads but somehow couldn't stop herself from pressing down on the gas. Reckless at the wheel, she plotted driving that car over an embankment. As she sailed off the mountain to her death, she figured that the brief moment of the airy plunge would be the only freedom she'd ever known in her whole life.

Not knowing where Rosacoke had driven off to, Pete headed toward Buster's bedroom later that afternoon. Increasingly, Buster lived in the suite of rooms Pete had assigned him, rarely venturing out except for school.

Pete had to tell Buster that he would be leaving in the morning for Nashville. He knew Buster would pout and throw a fit but he had to tell him.

Behind locked doors, Pete had to force Buster's mouth off his. Buster had taken to sticking his little tongue in Pete's mouth, knowing that gave his daddy a hard-on.

Pete pushed him away. "You know something, son?" he asked. "You're like a bitch in heat."

"You got that right, big boy," Buster said, looking up at him and licking his mouth as if he could still taste Pete's lips.

Pete couldn't believe how tantalizing Buster looked. Like some whore. "Get over me, kid. There's nothing there for you. I belong to Josh. Besides, even if I were so inclined, your mouth is too small and your ass too tight for the likes of me. Grow up and then get it on with some guy your own age. When you do, I'll let the two of you live here together as lovers or have Karl build you boys a place of your own."

"Is that what you think?" Buster said, taunting him. "Give me a roll in this bed and you'll see what I can do for my ole man."

Without meaning to, he reached over and slapped Buster, regretting it the very moment he did so. "I'm sorry," he said, "I didn't mean that. Something just came over me."

Still rubbing his cheek, Buster looked up at Pete. "You owe me one for that slap. A big favor, and I mean big." He reached for Pete's hand, pulling him down on the bed with him. "Kiss it and make the pain go away."

Pete reached up to kiss Buster's cheek but his son darted his head and Pete found Buster licking his lips instead. As Buster sucked those lips, his open mouth signaled he wanted Pete to invade. When Buster's hands started fingering his hardening cock, Pete in spite of himself stuck his tongue into Buster's mouth. Buster was getting to him, and Pete wanted to force himself up from that bed and out of the room. But he couldn't.

Sighing, he lay back on Buster's soft pillow, as his son unbuckled his belt and unbuttoned his fly. "I want to see it big like you make it for me in the bathtub."

Pete closed his eyes in despair as he felt Buster free his cock. Buster squealed with delight when he saw his daddy's cock rise up in the air.

He skinned back the head of Pete's cock and planted tiny little kisses and licks on the big knob, causing Pete to moan in ecstasy.

"No more lollipops for me," Buster said to him. "I've found my all-day

sucker." With his little mouth, Buster descended on Pete again, bringing an almost delirious pleasure to him.

*\*\**

On the bus to Nashville to make Pete's recording, Rosacoke was not resenting her husband, but was a little pissed off at Larry. Their manager was asleep in the back seat with Hank. Like Josh and Pete, those two never parted. She figured they must be homosexual lovers too. After all, on looking back it should have been obvious that Larry and Hank were having an affair in Narcissa's Chicago apartment. She knew from her own experience that Hank liked women too. Without naming names, Rosacoke had asked Tara about men such as Hank. "They're called double-gaited," Tara had said, "and they have more luck than anybody."

"What do you mean?" Rosacoke had asked.

"Since they'll go back to their bedrooms with either a man or a woman, their chances of getting laid on any given night are doubled."

"Yeah," Rosacoke had said, still a bit puzzled. "I guess you're right. There is some advantage to that."

"To get back at some of these boys, hoss," Tara said, "let's me and you get it on one night. I'm a pretty good muff-diver."

"No, thanks," Rosacoke said, feeling uncomfortable, and not really certain if Tara were joking. Was everybody in the whole world queer?

Larry kept telling her that it was easier for him to get bookings for a male singer than a "gal canary." In spite of that obstacle, Rosacoke had expected more to happen in her career, and the fact that it hadn't disappointed her greatly.

Growing like small seed on the dirt floors of the honky-tonks of West Texas, until reaching full flower in Memphis, her style and delivery were ready for the big time, at least according to the way she saw it. Just like Pete, she too wanted a song to record.

When Larry woke up and lifted himself up from Hank's shoulder, Rosacoke asked him to talk to her, so she could plead with this show business entrepreneur to nail down a recording for her too. She didn't know what she wanted to record, but she figured she could come up with something hot. Up to now, Larry had always kept putting her off, claiming she needed more experience before "breaking in big."

During their dialogue, Larry had a big surprise for her. Everybody had been in on the secret except her. "I'm only Pete's wife," she said to Larry in anger. "You could have told me too."

Inspired by the success of Fred Rose and Roy Acuff as music publishers, Larry, with Pete's money and the full approval of Karl, had bought a recording studio in Nashville. At least part of their decision was based on

the fact that Acuff and Rose had already established their own music-publishing firm in Nashville. Right before the jealous eyes of both Pete and Larry, Acuff and Rose had scored a big hit with country star Hank Williams. Their "stable," as they called it, also included Jenny Lou Carson, Redd Stewart, and Pee Wee King.

"Hell, I know as much about country music as those guys," Larry said. "Maybe more. Watch me go."

Rosacoke was convinced of one thing: Larry had plenty of confidence in himself if nothing else.

"I want to record music in its natural habitat," Larry said. "Right now most of the artists are recording in Chicago or Cincinnati."

In Nashville, Claude drove Pete's bus to their new studio on the ground floor of the old Tulane Hotel.

Pete inspected the studio with Josh. The two men were thrilled at what Larry had done and were eager to begin rehearsals in the morning for "Lonesome Blues."

In rooms that Freddie had arranged for them, Rosacoke found herself alone again, Josh sharing a suite with a king-sized bed where he would no doubt enjoy those mighty inches of Pete Riddle. She wasn't exactly sure how men got off with each other, and preferred to be spared some of the details.

The next morning before rehearsals, Larry and Pete made a joint visit to the office of a Nashville lawyer. Rosacoke learned later that Pete had signed a long-term management contract with Larry, giving the agent twenty percent of whatever deals Larry was able to arrange. Later, when Pete had told her about this, she'd been a bit skeptical. "I still have eighty percent," he said. "Some artists are being forced to give away a hefty fifty percent."

If Rosacoke thought Larry was going to rush Pete into recording, she was wrong. Rehearsals dragged on for two weeks. She attended the Grand Ole Opry nightly with Claude, Pete, Josh, Larry, and Hank. They'd often hit the tonks later that night, the boys preferring to stay up later than she did.

During the day Larry worked with Freddie in the sound studio, polishing "Lonesome Blues." Although this former Hitler Youth had never planned to become a sound engineer, Larry told everybody, "He's a natural."

Before the day of the recording, Rosacoke was invited to the studio to hear "Lonesome Blues" in its updated version.

Once there she learned that Larry had been on the phone to Fry and had bought the song outright for the grand sum of three-thousand dollars. That much money had seemed too little to Rosacoke. Later, she too placed a call to Fry to find out what he thought about the deal. "You won't have a grudge, will you?" she asked. "I mean if it becomes a big hit and all. By

selling it to Larry like this, it means you'll get no credit. The song will be published as if it had been written by Pete."

"I ain't seen so much money together in one pile in my whole wasted life," Fry said with joy. "Pete's already arranged to pay for my operation. With this money, I'm gonna buy myself a pink Cadillac. Make a million bucks on it for all I care. I'm happy as a pig in shit with the money I've been paid."

Rosacoke was further surprised that day to learn that Larry had demanded—and gotten—credit as coauthor. Pete only slightly resented the concession. "It's still my song," Pete said to Rosacoke. Both men seemed to have forgotten that the true author of the song was Fry himself.

Seated by herself in the studio at the Tulane Hotel, Rosacoke heard the final polished version of "Lonesome Blues" at the last rehearsal. In spite of her resentment of Larry, her respect for his craftsmanship leapfrogged. Like the sculptor of a beautiful statue, Larry had taken the basic raw materials of the song and had fashioned and shaped the words and melodies into a highly polished product. The changes were subtle but made all the difference. An inflection here, the wording of a lyric some place else, a change in a note over there. The original song was still intact, but under Larry's direction "Lonesome Blues" reached another dimension. On hearing the playback, Pete seemed to realize that too.

The final recording was scheduled for the following day. Larry was in charge of everything, giving final directions to his new sound engineer, Freddie. The Foggy Mountain Boys seemed in fine shape.

When lunchtime came and still no recording had been made, the men sent out for burgers. Josh had seemed nervous having Rosacoke see and hear everything going on. He suggested that Claude take Rosacoke into the hotel dining room for lunch. "The food's real good," he said as if to dismiss them.

Until now, Rosacoke had never paid much attention to Claude. He was always at the airport with Junior Grayson or else spending time alone with his son-in-law, Ronnie, when Wanda Mae was hard at work in town.

Over lunch Claude spoke of his daddy and growing up in the same hills she had. "He was an ole roustabout. A boozing and party man."

There was something about Claude that captured her fancy. Now that she felt she didn't have any more marriage vows to honor, she was looking anew at the men surrounding her. Nearly six feet, four inches, Claude had a long, lean body, not fully developed like Pete's at all. His pin-striped seersucker suit with full-cut pants, held up by long suspenders, seemed to hang from his body like rags on a scarecrow.

Yet she found him strikingly handsome and strangely appealing, with his dancing blue eyes, ruddy complexion, and his thick, sensual lips which, unlike the rest of his frame, seemed to have filled out to their full potential.

She might wonder at some of the other men at Heaven on Earth, but Rosacoke was convinced that Claude was one hell of a lady-killer and didn't go into this male butt-fucking like some of the other tenants at Pete's mansion, notably her husband.

"Before settling down in the county, my daddy did a lot of things," Claude was telling her. She wasn't as interested in the biographical details as she was intrigued by his face as he talked. "Daddy even sold fertilizer to farmers. It was really cowshit. I figured a man must be really smart to make money on manure. I used to help him stage going-out-of-business sales for stores in Knoxville. He made everything the biggest flood sale since ole Noah auctioned off the ark."

She hadn't met anyone in a long time that she liked as much as Claude. His thin face and wide grin that turned up at one corner made him look boyish. He was self-confident, outgoing, and treated her better than any of Pete's gang.

Back at the studio, Larry was like a child going over with Freddie the shiny new equipment he'd bought, including two tape recorders—Ampex 200s. In addition, Larry had paid for the first Scully master cutting lathe in the Southeast.

"Any sound Cincinnati can do we can do better," Larry claimed. His knowledge of the technical side of the business amazed Rosacoke. "We can be technical down here in Tennessee, too," Larry said.

The tape machines were a novelty to Pete, who'd expected to cut a disc.

At the first recording of the afternoon, Pete was stiff and a little nervous. Larry demanded that he do the song over again.

"Loosen up a bit," Larry instructed Pete. "Let's hear those big balls clank."

That made Rosacoke wonder how Larry knew that her husband had big balls.

Larry was much more pleased with the second recording and at first had been tempted to run with it. "Let's try it again anyway."

Before they left that night, Larry had forced Pete and his boys to record "Lonesome Blues" twenty times, although it was finally decided to go with the second recording after all.

"That song and Pete Riddle have got a big future," Larry said, inviting Hank, Pete and Josh out for a drink. Freddie was staying at another hotel in the black section of Nashville, since he couldn't live at the Tulane with Nipsey. The black singers headed for their own club.

Claude volunteered to show Rosacoke up to her room. "Thanks for a good day," he said, kissing her on the cheek. "Think I'll turn in early. I've got to call Ronnie anyway."

Alone in her hotel room, Rosacoke fell asleep dreaming of the day when

she'd be in that studio recording hit records of her own.

That night she also dreamed about Claude, but on awakening the next morning, she couldn't exactly remember what the dream was about. One part of her brain wanted to remember the dream, but the other part of her mind blacked it out.

\*\*\*

Two days later Pete's gang was hanging out in the living room of Heaven on Earth. Those who had stayed behind were eager for news of the recording studio. Pete had wanted everybody to hear the recording, "Lonesome Blues," at the same time. Even Buster emerged from his bedroom. At the end of the recording, Rosacoke led the applause. Buster was so pleased with the disc that he went over and kissed Pete on the lips. Rosacoke was real happy for Pete and with the way the record had turned out. She couldn't help but notice that neither Pete nor Larry had invited Fry to listen to the song he'd written.

As Tara was passing around drinks, Larry jumped up. His face looked like a light switch had been turned on inside his head.

A longtime associate of his, Frank Walker, had established a record company for Metro-Goldwyn-Mayer. "That guy has handled everybody, even Caruso," Larry said. "Frank was cutting records after the war—World War I, that is. He's been around for a long time. I think Grover Cleveland was president when he was born. He used to be president at RCA Victor. He left there after the war—World War II, that is."

Acting on his impulse, Larry called Frank Walker. Back in the living room, Larry was beaming. "Frank wants us to fly to the coast. He wants to meet Pete and hear his 'Lonesome Blues.'"

"I can't think of a better time to break in our new private plane," Junior said. "A co-pilot friend of mine who's flown to Los Angeles many times will help me wing you there."

Pete thought it was time that all his gang see California. Buster wanted to go, too, until Tara reminded him school hadn't let out for the year. He looked bitterly disappointed and retreated to his room.

Everybody accepted Pete's invitation except Wanda Mae who claimed she was too busy with "hair and clothes." Ronnie would go with Claude instead. Pete invited John-John, who was excited about the trip although he protested that he had nothing to wear. Larry claimed he could get a weekend booking for John-John at a club run by a friend of his on the Strip.

The idea of going to Hollywood excited Rosacoke as no other prospect had. She felt it would be like walking into one's dream. For all she knew she might meet up with Lana Turner or at least Betty Grable. She'd also call to see if she could get through to Narcissa Cash if that brown belle was

in Los Angeles and not New York. Based on the incomplete information about her that Rosacoke kept reading in the movie mags, it was virtually impossible to keep up with her.

It turned out that Pete's new plane wasn't new at all but was a converted military plane that the U.S. government had sold as surplus at the end of World War II. Junior had it converted to carry commercial passengers. Inside, it looked a little bleak but Rosacoke was happy to settle in. She would have much preferred to have sat up front with Pete, but Josh claimed that privilege. Junior told them that they would make two stops along the way before finally landing at the airport at Los Angeles.

When Larry could free himself from Hank, he drifted to the back of the plane. Smoking a cigarette, he told her that Frank Walker loved country and western music. He likes Eddy Arnold, Gene Autry, and the likes, and I think he'll flip for Pete in a big way. Frank is also an old homosexual size queen, so I told Pete he should wear his pants so tight he might have to get Josh to sew them on him."

Rosacoke didn't like to hear that. It seemed to make Pete sound like a piece of flesh instead of an artist, but she said nothing. After all, Pete wasn't adverse to appearing on stage in front of a live audience in too-tight pants and no underwear.

As soon as they'd landed in Hollywood, everybody had an agenda, even Maston Mastin who said he was going to look up an old black musician friend who'd settled somewhere in Orange County. Freddie and Nipsey were off on a round of sightseeing, and Claude and Ronnie were going to share a suite at the Chateau Marmont with Pete and Josh. Larry and Hank were sharing a room together, and Junior and John-John had each been assigned their own quarters.

As per usual, Rosacoke had been assigned a room of her own. The only person Rosacoke knew in Hollywood was Narcissa Cash. She'd left as many urgent messages as she could, urging Narcissa to call her at the Chateau Marmont. But secretly Rosacoke suspected that Narcissa had become too grand a star to call back.

Her first night in Hollywood, Rosacoke wandered through the city as if in a trance. Pete had hired a limousine for all of them. They had cocktails on top of the roof of some grand hotel before going to a spectacular Polynesian dinner where the waiters and waitresses wore sarongs and the lighting was from blazing torches. Pete later took his gang to the Cocoanut Grove where he danced with her throughout the evening, as Josh fumed. He had done little to conceal his resentment at Rosacoke's flying with them to Hollywood, but she wasn't going to let that man spoil her fun. Not tonight of all nights.

Junior Grayson had found himself a show gal, and from the looks of things the blonde hussy would be sharing Junior's bedroom back at the

Chateau Marmont.

Claude danced with Rosacoke three times, and she was delighted. Unlike Pete, he wasn't much of a dancer. She noticed that Claude didn't take up with any show gals like Junior had. When not with her, he stayed mostly with Ronnie, who didn't run after any gals either. She understood that. He seemed to be one married man who never cheated on Wanda Mae.

Pete expressed only two disappointments. He'd practically begged Karl to come out to the coast with him, but Karl refused to budge, claiming he had to stay in the Carolina hills to take care of Pete's many businesses. Pete was also sorry that Nipsey and Freddie couldn't come to the Cocoanut Grove with them, but blacks were not allowed. "When will that day ever come?" Pete said, eying the sea of white faces.

The next morning Rosacoke invited herself along to meet Frank Walker, although Josh assured her it wasn't necessary. "Larry can handle the arrangements," Josh said.

"Since you're going, I'm going too," Rosacoke said. "Hell, for all I know, Frank Walker might take one look at me, especially when I show up in my new Nudie rhinestone-studded cow gal outfit, and make me the next Dale Evans. I know more about cows than Miss Priss. Besides, I'd let Roy Rogers kiss me and not his horse."

Josh eyed her from the tip of her white boots to her hair-do which she wore like Betty Grable did in *The Beautiful Blonde from Bashful Bend*. "It's all a bit much," Josh said. "You can take Rosacoke Carson out of the Carolina hills, but you can't take the hills out of Rosacoke Carson. Maybe at Frank's studio, someone will cast you as Daisy Mae in *Dogpatch Revue*."

Now that she knew what the score was between Pete and Josh, she had decided not to let his insults get under her skin. Increasingly she was standing up for herself. "So sorry, Josh, but we all know you want to look like me yourself." With that insult, she headed down on the elevator and into Pete's waiting limousine.

Only Larry and Pete were ushered into the office of Frank Walker. Seeing she wasn't invited, Rosacoke pranced in any way, ducking in a step ahead of Pete and Larry. God, she was becoming aggressive. "I'm Rosacoke Carson," she said, to the aging man at the desk. "Pleased to meet you."

Frank was gracious to her until Pete and Larry followed a few steps behind her. After a quick hug of his old friend Larry, Frank focused his entire attention on Pete. As Larry had instructed, Pete was dressed in the tightest pants she'd ever seen on any man. When not looking into Pete's handsome face, Frank was practically drooling over his crotch. He couldn't take his eyes off the package. Pete sat with his legs open, giving Frank an uninterrupted view.

After coffee was served, Larry was anxious for Frank to hear their

recording of "Lonesome Blues." With his keen and sharp ear, Frank listened intently, glancing over at Pete every now and then when he hit a note that especially pleased Frank. When the record ended, Frank didn't say anything at first. "It's different," Frank said. "Different good, not different bad."

The way Frank was looking at Pete, Rosacoke just knew that the entrepreneur was going to sign her husband to a record contract.

"I'm a singer too," Rosacoke piped in. "Real good. I ain't got a recording right now but I'm gonna do one soon."

"That's nice," Frank said. He continued to eye Pete as if there were some silent communication between them.

When Pete told Frank he had flown to the coast with most of his mountain gang, Frank was delighted, especially when he asked Pete to bring Josh, Junior, Ronnie, Claude, Freddie, Nipsey, and Hank into his office. He eyed each man like a Tyrannosaurus Rex about to enjoy a tasty supper. "I've got a great idea," Frank said. "I'm gonna have a swim party tonight at my little old shack up in Beverly Hills. I want all of you guys to come." Frank eyed each man carefully, especially Hank. "Don't worry about bringing bathing suits. They're not allowed." He turned to Rosacoke. "Because all the guys will be running around in their birthday suits, no women can come. Sorry." As he left for a board meeting in another building, Frank turned to Rosacoke. "I'll have Larry send me your first recording. Maybe I can promote you as a husband-and-wife team."

He told Larry and Pete that his secretary would give them instructions about how to reach his house tonight. He looked into the eyes of Junior, Hank, Nipsey, Claude, Ronnie, Freddie, and Josh. "I'll be seeing you guys," he said with a saucy smirk on his face. "All and everything of you later." He pranced out of his office.

After he'd gone, Pete broke the silence. "Hot damn! Hank Williams, eat my dust."

\*\*\*

Pete arrived late at Frank's swim party. A fully dressed Frank came into the foyer to greet him. "Better late than never. Welcome to my party. Come on back. The gang's all here, including your friend Josh." He raised an eyebrow. "Lucky you."

Around the Olympic-size pool at least thirty young men were bucknaked. Some had jumped into the pool; others just lounged around, and a few had disappeared into tent-like structures in back. Buck-ass naked, Josh ran up to Pete and gave him a big, gooey kiss, the kind Pete liked, with lots of slurping. "I've missed you, big guy," Josh said.

"I've missed you too, baby," Pete said, holding him close. "It's a won-

der I still have you for myself with all this competition around." Pete had never eyed so many handsome men in all his life. At least five of them looked as if they could put Rock Hudson to shame.

Josh took Pete's hand and led him into a little gingerbread cottage to the side. "Here's where you can stash your clothes," he said. "Frank insists that all of us boys be dressed for skinny-dipping."

Under Josh's appreciative eyes, Pete stripped completely naked before joining the other nude revelers. Hank, Claude, Junior, Larry, and Ronnie, all naked as well, were there to greet him.

The liquor Pete later drank beside the pool only added to the intoxication of the evening. Even the air in Frank's California garden smelled camellia sweet.

It was after midnight when Pete was called to the edge of the garden by Larry. "It's a tradition at Frank's famous nude swim parties. My man Frank gets the stud with the biggest dick at each of his parties. Tonight he feels you and Hank are in a dead heat for the donkey dong prize. He wants both of you to slip away to his bedroom upstairs for a blow-job."

"He's got his man," Pete said.

"I'll keep jealous Josh distracted," Larry said. "He won't know what's going on."

Ten minutes later in Frank's bedroom, the producer fell to his knees before Hank and Pete, polishing one uncut dick before going on to lavish his mouth on the other. Since Frank was no Rock Hudson, Pete kept himself aroused by kissing and tonguing beautiful Hank.

While doing that, he cupped Hank's buttocks and felt the rippling muscles of his back. That in time had proven to be all the stimulation Pete needed to reward Frank with a big blast of cum. After slurping that load down, Frank descended on Hank for a final eruption. Afterward, he pronounced Hank and Pete "the two best studs I've ever had. I think they grow a tastier type of man back in those hills than they do out here in California."

\*\*\*

For one o'clock that day, Rosacoke accepted an invitation from Frank Walker to attend a big lunch he was throwing for them at a seafood restaurant at Laguna Beach. Her only regret was that Pete was tied up in "some promotional thing" according to Frank and couldn't make it. Josh also couldn't go, as Frank had arranged for a record producer to hear three of his best songs.

She was doubly disappointed that Frank hadn't arranged any such meeting for her. She had songs to present too. She sighed, thinking country music was almost an exclusive male turf. Freddie wouldn't attend either because Nipsey couldn't go along to the restaurant because of his color.

Freddie chose to join the black musicians instead. But John-John, Claude, Ronnie, Hank, and Junior joined in the feast by the seas.

Frank urged Rosacoke to sample some raw clams, a first for her, and she didn't like the taste or slimy feel of them as they went down her throat. But she swallowed them any way. When she got back to the Chateau Marmont, her stomach was feeling queasy and she went to bed right away. Scheduled for the same day, Frank had invited all of them to a big afternoon lawn party at his mansion between 3 and 5pm. "Lots of big time stars will be there," he told her. She had to turn down that invitation, although the idea of meeting some of her screen favorites thrilled her. Nonetheless the prospect of throwing up in the lap of Henry Fonda didn't appeal to her either.

Reluctantly she remained behind in her room at the Chateau Marmont. Josh had returned from his audition and was dressing for the party when she called Pete's room. Josh picked up the phone, informing her curtly that Pete was still tied up and would meet everybody at the lawn party. Afterward Pete was taking all of them to dinner to be followed by a drag show starring John-John. The way she felt, she couldn't attend any of these spectaculars.

It was a wise decision she'd made to remain in her room. Puke One came at 5:02pm, followed by Puke Two at 6:15pm. The second puke seemed to do the job. By seven that night, she was feeling much better, though a little weak.

Fifteen minutes later a call came in for her. She was stunned to hear on the other end of the line the purring voice of Narcissa Cash.

Within the hour Rosacoke was dressed and ready as she waited at the portico for Narcissa's sleek black limousine to pick her up. She'd been frantically leaving messages for Narcissa all over Hollywood until Rosacoke had finally given up, deciding that Narcissa didn't want to remember someone from the hills. Narcissa not only wanted to see her, but there was an urgency in her voice.

It was a long, winding ride into Beverly Hills, giving Rosacoke time to think, mainly about Narcissa. It's been years since they'd last seen each other, and Rosacoke had carefully followed Narcissa's career in the newspapers and on the screen.

That gal had made a lot of headlines over the years since she'd left Sultan's shanty in the cotton patch. This limousine in which Rosacoke was riding was proof alone of how far Narcissa had climbed the Hollywood ladder.

Settling back into the comfort of the well-upholstered, elephant-gray seat, Rosacoke poured herself a whiskey from the car's bar, softening it with an ice cube. She figured that riding on smooth, fat rubber tires in this black chariot sure beat that bumpy wagon, pulled by the Riddle mule, that

took Narcissa and her to Aunt Clotilda's funeral.

Without really meaning to, Rosacoke couldn't help but compare herself to Narcissa. For a black gal, Narcissa had made it big in show business. So far, Rosacoke's dream of stardom had eluded her. Narcissa had made a lot of money. Rosacoke hadn't made much money at all, but lived the life of a rich woman only because of Pete. Narcissa's success filled Rosacoke with awe, and she had great admiration for her. Not only because of her talent, but her ability to overcome all the obstacles placed in her pathway.

She was a black woman surviving in a business—the movies—that didn't know what to do with Negroes other than give them servants' parts. She had worked hard, and she'd done what few in filmdom had managed to do—that is, remain an individual performer, unique and uncompromising. Narcissa was her own self, unlike anybody else. That night in 1942 at the Blackbirds revue in Chicago revealed to Rosacoke that Narcissa wasn't going to conform to acceptable rules and behavior.

On stage Narcissa did what she wanted to, not catering to her patrons. She had faults and she had virtues, and she demanded that the world take her on her own terms. She was arrogant and at times downright disdainful of her audiences, but somehow managed to get away with that, hiding behind a protective wall. Maybe if she weren't such a damn good singer, she couldn't get away with such an imperial performance. But she possessed a unique cabaret voice. Patrons got not only that voice but could feast their eyes on her beautiful café-au-lait body. A cover charge didn't grant a fan permission to look inside Narcissa Cash, the private woman. She reserved that for herself and maybe her husband. All the newspapers had been full of her scandalous marriage to a white doctor. Douglas Porter, a leading plastic surgeon. Not only white, but blond to boot.

She was one of a kind, and her act worked well for her, although in the hands of a lesser performer Narcissa's disdain for her audience might have turned into a professional disaster.

Rosacoke knew that she could learn a lot from Narcissa's independent spirit. Rosacoke was only now beginning to assert her rights. If Narcissa could teach her any lesson, it was to depend on herself. Rosacoke suspected that she'd been iced out of any record deal, and Larry didn't seem too eager to secure her anything hot, as he preferred to focus his professional attention on Pete instead. Rosacoke vowed that in the future she'd go along with Pete and Larry to a certain point, but more and more would start taking charge of her own career, just like Narcissa had done. She'd made this vow before but hadn't acted on it too aggressively.

Maybe Rosacoke wouldn't go as far as Narcissa, but Rosacoke sure as hell would give it a big try. She knew the roadblocks facing a woman in country and western music but felt that Narcissa as a black performer had faced an even greater challenge in securing a position for herself in films,

portraying a glamorous and very sexy black female, something virtually unknown in the history of the industry. How much harder that struggle must have been for Narcissa.

First had come Narcissa's glamour build-up. The Blackbirds revue had landed her in Los Angeles during the war where she'd become a sensational singing star, often entertaining black troops. Eventually she signed with MGM, much in the same way Pete was going to do.

Narcissa had become the first Negro woman ever to put her name on a seven-year contract with a large studio. "I ain't playing Beulahs," she'd announced to the press at the time. "No Butterfly McQueen parts either. And I don't do windows."

In all, she'd appeared in seven films for MGM. Excluding one major movie, *Go, Ruby Red,* featuring an all-black cast, Narcissa usually appeared as herself in a film. The scenarios she'd been assigned were much the same. The white stars, perhaps Van Johnson and June Allyson, would attend a night club where Narcissa Cash would be the headliner. Often dressed in white satin, Narcissa would come out looking great, sing her song, and then perform a vanishing act. She was rarely part of the plot of a film. These singing cameos were called "interludes." If exhibitors in the South were worried about disturbing their all-white audiences, they could easily snip Narcissa's film segment without causing damage to the plot line.

Most often, however, Narcissa didn't end up on the cutting-room floor, because white audiences responded to her. "She's a classy broad," as Steve Fenton, her producer, once told the press. "She doesn't do gospel or blues." Wisely Narcissa always selected popular Broadway show tunes, with a trained ear cocked to the lyric, to which she supplied her own special phrasing. No longer tainted with a hillbilly accent, she had precise diction more suited to Cole Porter than Moo Cow Boogie.

Betty Grable had become the pin-up girl for white GIs in World War II, and her famous over-the-shoulder rear view decorated many a barrack wall. A legion of other fans infinitely preferred Rita Hayworth or Lana Turner. To the Negro man in uniform, however, Narcissa Cash was the dream girl, and her sexy, kittenish pose, snapped in 1942 with her shapely gams revealed, was plastered from San Diego to Bataan.

A harbinger of her future political stances came in 1944 when she'd entertained at an army camp on Paris Island, South Carolina. Nazi prisoners of war had been seated down front, occupying the choice seats, while black GIs were relegated to the rear of the hot tent. Bypassing the army brass up front, along with the Germans, Narcissa had carried her act to the rear of the tent and had sung her tunes to her true fans who'd yelled, cheered, and stamped their booted feet, not only to show their appreciation of her talent and good looks, but also to applaud her air of rebellion in a rabidly racist military system.

All Rosacoke knew of Narcissa had been from the unreliable media. Not one card, not one phone call in all these years. For courage Rosacoke downed the last of her whiskey as the limousine pulled into the gateway leading up a hill to Narcissa's mansion. With its white pillars, the house would have made any antebellum Southern plantation owner proud. In gleaming white—Narcissa always did like white—the mansion was lit by bright spots, exposing towering Grecian pillars holding up a mansard roof.

Narcissa had sounded urgent on the phone. She practically spat out her words in ordinary conversation, but her voice had been even more tense and had been filled with her own special fire tonight. Whatever awaited her inside that house, Rosacoke just knew that it was a matter of some importance. Narcissa Cash didn't waste her precious time on needless social calls.

***

Before going to dinner and to see John-John's drag show, Pete met Frank Walker, fresh from his garden party, around six o'clock that evening in the Polo Lounge of the Beverly Hills Hotel. Rosacoke had been too sick to join them. Junior, Hank, Claude, and Ronnie rambled about the hotel grounds, while Larry, Frank, and Pete conducted business in a booth. "Sorry, I couldn't make the lawn party," Pete apologized.

The contract with MGM was ready for Pete to sign. He'd agreed to "three cents a record." Both Larry and Frank had worked out a percentage deal, but Pete preferred the actual penny amount. "Percentages I don't know," Pete said. "Three red cents I know."

Frank shook Pete's hand. "Don't worry about a thing," Frank said. "Larry will handle all your bookings, and I'll produce your records. I've already signed Bob Wills. This Texas swing king is putting the western into country and western music. You've seen what I've done for Wills and his Texas Playboys. It's going to happen to you and your 'Lonesome Blues.'"

"There will be more," Larry predicted. "One hit followed by another. You'll see."

"I'll keep picking and singing," Pete said, not really certain what to make of all these big predictions for his career. For all he knew, it was just so much Hollywood bullshit.

"You've got your man in me," Frank said. "When you see what I can do with marketing, you'll know I'm the guy to handle all the other 'Lonesome' songs you'll record. I have a feeling there's going to be a hell of a lot of them."

"You've got that right," Pete said, making a prediction himself.

When Larry excused himself to go to the men's room, Frank leaned over in the booth and whispered to Pete, "Thanks for last night. You've got

one long dick. Not only fucking long, but it must measure six inches in circumference."

"I get a lot of complaints about it," Pete said.

"I've never heard a man say that before," Frank said. "Usually when a man's dick size comes up, he apologizes for having a small cock by saying, 'I've never heard any complaints.' But who in the world would complain about yours?"

"You don't get it," Pete said. "They scream 'take it out.'"

"Oh, I see," Frank said. "That's not my problem. You can stuff a damn flagpole down my throat, and I'll scream for more. That reminds me. Every time you fly to the coast, we've got a standing date. Just you and me. Even when I'm old and gray, I want to be sampling that monster you've got dangling between your hillbilly legs."

"It'll be our secret," Pete said, spotting Larry returning from the men's room.

With his gang in tow, Pete walked out of the Beverly Hills Hotel lobby thinking that star that had eluded him for so long was about to shine on him, thanks to Larry, but also thanks to Frank Walker.

"I'm gonna be rich and famous," he whispered to Larry as he spotted Josh walking toward him through the hotel's gardens.

"You're already rich, handsome," Larry said. "Fame is now on the way. Pete Riddle is going to become a household word."

Whether it was true or not, Pete believed him, or at least wanted to think that dreams do come true.

***

Larry had booked John-John's act into "The Fruitfly," a notorious club in West Hollywood that often presented drag acts. In spite of its largely homosexual patronage, many macho-looking stars of the screen—safely appearing with a female date—often attended the performances. It wasn't unusual to see such world renowned faces in the audiences as those of Clark Gable, Victor Mature, and Burt Lancaster.

Except for Rosacoke, Pete's party was assembled at a large ringside table. It was a handsome crew of Junior, Claude, Ronnie, Larry, Hank, and Josh.

For the first set, the lights dimmed, then came on again to spotlight what appeared to be one of the world's most stunning blonde goddesses. It was John-John looking like a dead-ringer for Marilyn Monroe as she had appeared on screen in the film, *Niagara*. John-John came out onto the stage looking and acting like a real woman, not a caricature.

With scarlet painted lips, a peach complexion, and a low-cut gown, John-John as a woman made a stunning beauty. Pete had seen him in drag at the

Riddle homestead, but never this professional and alluring, a true showgirl. Under the blonde wig and with big breasts from God knows where, John-John had perfectly captured Marilyn's sexual heat. Bathed in pink light, he appeared as a curious mixture of a young woman and a baby. Both the women and the men in the audience seemed to adore the creation on stage.

Junior had taken a seat next to Pete. "She's terrific," he said, referring for the first time to John-John as *she*. "You don't know whether to sit with her on your knee and pet her, or drag her off to the barn for a roll in the hay."

As John-John proceeded deeper and deeper into his act as Marilyn, Junior reached under the table for Pete's hand and brought it to his crotch. Junior was rock hard. "I've never paid much attention to John-John as a boy before. But as a gal, look what that bitch in heat is doing for me."

"Why don't you go for it?" Pete whispered to him.

"You wouldn't be jealous?" Junior asked. "I mean John-John isn't your personal property?"

"Believe you me, I've got more than I can handle."

"If you say so, man, I'm gonna go backstage and come on strong," Junior said. "I want me a piece of that."

Although looking like Marilyn Monroe, John-John for his song had chosen Rita Hayworth's famous song and dance number, "Put the Blame on Mame," which the fiery screen temptress had performed in *Gilda*, the film she'd made with the devastatingly handsome Glenn Ford.

John-John tortured his audience by performing a mock striptease. Dressed in a strapless black satin gown, John-John in the end peeled off only his long black gloves. With his bold glances, he dominated the stage, his swinging hips giving off a brilliant embodiment of sheer sensual abandon.

For John-John's second stint of the evening, the actor, Errol Flynn arrived at a ringside table next to Pete's larger one. Flynn was accompanied by both a curvaceous redhead and a brunette with a massive bosom.

John-John wisely played his whole act to the obviously drunken actor who appeared most intrigued. The song and dance number was a masterpiece of illicit innuendo, and Flynn seemed a bit turned on in spite of his two women female dates who looked like they could more than handle all Flynn had to offer that night.

At the end of his mock striptease, John-John daringly plopped down on Flynn's lap, not certain whether he would be rejected or not. Flynn was far too good a sport to push John-John away, not even when the beautiful boy gave him a long and lingering kiss. The spotlight shone on both of them, clearly revealing a clash of John-John's tongue up against the more experienced tongue of Flynn. Pete could only imagine where Flynn's tongue had been over the past twenty years.

The mostly male audience went wild at this spontaneous piece of business under the pink spots. Pete figured that Flynn was the only actor in Hollywood who would perform this male-male kissing in front of a mostly gay audience. Most stars, like the closeted Rock Hudson, were too busy protecting their images.

As the night progressed, Pete drank more and more until the remainder of the evening became a blur, except for one distinct memory: He would never know what Junior had said to John-John when Junior went backstage at the end of the drag act. All Pete knew was that when all of his gang returned to the Chateau Marmont, he saw Junior going into John-John's bedroom.

***

Rosacoke was ushered into the formal living room of the Cash mansion, which was decorated all in white, with lots of satin. Everything was plush, the crystal highly polished.

After keeping Rosacoke waiting for fifteen minutes, Narcissa appeared. This was not the woman Rosacoke had said good-bye to in that long-ago wartime Chicago of 1942.

Like the room, she, too, was dressed entirely in white. The silver radiator paint, according to press reports, had made her hair fall out, so she now had to wear a wig, which looked almost as natural as her real hair. She was poised, serene, wearing little makeup, except for cherry-red lips. Her deep olive skin seemed whiter than Rosacoke remembered it.

As they greeted each other and exchanged air kisses and updates on their lives, Rosacoke was impressed with Narcissa's precise diction. Her speech was extremely cultivated, her voice well modulated. Gone was the jive-talking honky-tonk angel of yesterday. It was obvious that she had educated herself and polished her image into a sparkling diamond. The rustic girl of the Brushy Mountains had given way to an international personality who'd entertained kings, received proposals from sheiks, and been hailed as the toast of two continents.

Narcissa related with deep sensitivity her decision to marry Douglas Porter in 1947. As the first major interracial marriage of an established screen star, her wedding to the Los Angeles plastic surgeon had made headlines around the world. It had also inspired vicious attacks from some quarters. Preceding one of her nightclub appearances, Narcissa had been picketed by Nazis carrying such banners as COON GO BACK TO THE CONGO.

"People can hate by color," Narcissa confided to Rosacoke. "But they certainly can't love by it. Douglas asked me to marry him, and I said yes. He didn't ask me if I'd interracially marry him."

"I guess because of growing up with my mama I learned to accept interracial relationships," Rosacoke said. "As for Pete, you know he's not prejudiced. Pete always judges the man, not the color of his skin. He was that way as a kid. Now even more so."

"I'm glad to hear that," Narcissa said enigmatically. "You'll soon find out why."

Rosacoke knew that Narcissa always liked to be mysterious, so she patiently waited to find out why Narcissa had summoned her to her home. It was obviously not to talk about the good ole days, because there had been none of those.

"I was glad to read about Pete's success," Narcissa said. "I hear he's going to be a big star."

"We sure hope so." Rosacoke told Narcissa about Buster and how he'd been raised, and how she had a reunion with Pete after far too many years had gone by. Never had Narcissa been this eager to learn the slightest detail about their family life. In the old days, there was only one person who could capture the attention of Narcissa Cash, and that was the brown belle herself. Obviously there had been more changes in her than just in her speech.

Douglas walked into the room. Rosacoke had seen his picture in the paper, although he avoided publicity whenever possible, preferring to leave the spotlight entirely to Narcissa.

"I've found myself a beauty," Narcissa said, introducing Rosacoke as "my long-lost sister" to her husband.

Broad in shoulder, lean in hip, he was more than six feet one. He was deeply tanned, his curly hair bleached almost platinum by the California sun. Except for Pete Riddle, Rosacoke felt that Doug Porter was the handsomest and sexiest man she'd ever laid eyes on. Narcissa certainly knew how to make off with the choice hunks. Although Rosacoke had understood that he was thirty years old, he had a boyish quality about him, as if he hadn't completely lost his adolescence. His features, however, were clearly defined and strong, a manly man. His mouth was full, sensuous, and his wide blue eyes stared deeply into Rosacoke's own, as he extended his hand, giving her his warmest smile. He had the type of open, loving smile that made others smile back at him.

He sat with Narcissa on the sofa, talking to Rosacoke, and as he did he possessively put his arm around Narcissa. After years of marriage, they were obviously still caught up in honeymoon love. Rosacoke had read all the hate press about their marriage, heard all the nightclub jokes, and those images sickened her. She saw two very beautiful people very much in love, and it was beyond her understanding why anyone would want to intrude upon their happiness.

A white maid served drinks, as Rosacoke wondered if Pete would re-

turn early to the hotel to find her gone. At first she thought she'd call, but rejected that idea. She'd been abandoned by Pete too many times without any explanation as to where he was going. She decided to let him wonder.

It was all part of her increasing independence. Maybe he'd think she'd met and run off with a handsome movie star, or maybe some young, hot actor like Rock Hudson. In her opinion, Rock heated up the screen more than any other newcomer. She thought he was far sexier than such old-time favorites as Clark Gable or Robert Taylor, who increasingly were looking like grandfathers to her.

Narcissa gently broke away from Douglas. "We're having a crisis in our marriage," she announced abruptly.

Rosacoke was shocked. Up to now everything had seemed so peaceful, so perfect.

Embarrassed at this sudden revelation, Rosacoke said, "I don't understand. You two seem like the happiest couple in the world."

"It's not our love for each other that's in question," Douglas assured her. "We find ourselves in serious disagreement over Narcissa's son."

"Your son?" Rosacoke asked. "You wrote me that you gave the kid away."

"You might as well know what's come down," Narcissa said. "You've been in the dark long enough." A frown crossed her brow. "God damn it. Why is it that almost anything one can say sounds like a racial slur?"

"She had her son in 1942," Douglas said. "I understand about the same time you had your child."

Narcissa leaned back on her white satin sofa and accepted another glass of champagne from her maid. "Both of our boys have the same daddy." Her words seemed to stab in the air.

Rosacoke slammed down her own glass of bubbly. "Are you sure? There were others."

"No, the Pope fucked me," Narcissa replied.

"But…" Rosacoke stammered.

"There are no buts about it," Narcissa said. "Pete is the daddy."

"I guess I sort of knew it," Rosacoke said weakly. "It's one of those things you will your mind not to think about."

"You've got to hear me out on this one," Narcissa said. "I landed in Chicago with Pete's baby in my gut. Just like I once wrote you. The last thing I wanted in the world was a kid. A lot of my friends urged me to have the baby aborted, but I went ahead and had him anyway. I met this black couple who agreed to take him off my hands and threw in five-hundred dollars for my trouble."

Rosacoke felt trapped in Narcissa's big house. Even though spacious, the living room had grown smaller, the walls seemingly closing in on her. She wished that she hadn't come here to see Narcissa , and then she wished

even more that Pete had come along too. "Are you sure it belongs to Pete?" she asked again, seeking a way out of all this.

"There is no doubt in my mind," Narcissa said.

"I mean…" Rosacoke hesitated. "Couldn't the kid belong to Hank? Maybe some other guy?"

Narcissa's face exploded in fury but she restrained her anger. "It's Pete's bouncing baby boy, *okay*?"

Rosacoke sensed that this was the final word on that subject, and she didn't want to anger Narcissa any more. Nor reveal to her husband what a whorish background Narcissa had had back in the hills. Had she told Douglas that she was gang-raped?

"The kid won't be any front-page headline for Pete," Narcissa said. "I wrote Hank and told him all about it. If Hank and Pete are still good buddies like they used to be, Hank has already told him all about it."

"They're still buddies," Rosacoke said. "In fact, Pete flew Hank to Los Angeles with him. Hank has teamed up with Larry now."

Narcissa turned to Douglas. "Even back in Chicago Larry could never get his fill of Hank. That's one sexy guy."

"I don't want to hear it," Douglas said, casting a quick glance at Rosacoke. "Makes me jealous."

"If Pete knows about this, he never mentioned it to me," Rosacoke said, sighing.

Eager for the whole story, Rosacoke listened intently as Narcissa revealed what had happened. "The father who adopted my kid died. He had cancer. The mama plans to get married again and her new boy friend doesn't want the boy. In fact, the fucker insists that she get rid of it. The bitch has been reading in the movie mags how successful I am. She got in touch with me and wants me to take the kid back. She is also demanding ten-thousand dollars."

"The solution is simple," Rosacoke said. "Give her the ten grand. I'm sure you and Douglas can afford that. Then adopt the kid."

"If only it was that easy," Narcissa said. "That's what the bitch wanted too. But it seems the kid has other ideas. He passes for white and is a bit of a racist even though he has black blood in him. He sent word that he doesn't want to be adopted by another nigger mammy even if that mammy is his own mother."

"I see," Rosacoke said, even though a bit bewildered. This was all too much for her.

"The other kids at school think he's white," Douglas said. "Almost to put up some protective shield, he denounces black people. I guess to throw the racial hound dogs off his trail."

"There is one easy way out of this," Narcissa said, "and that's why I called you here."

"You tell me," Rosacoke said.

"I want you and Pete to adopt the boy," Narcissa said. "You guys are whiter than the Queen of England. The kid will love it."

"I don't know about this," Rosacoke said. "I sure couldn't commit myself without checking with Pete first. He wears the pants in this family—not me."

"We meant for you to check with Pete," Douglas said in a kind, soothing voice. "I had wanted to ask both Pete and you to come over here, but Narcissa wanted some catch-up time alone with you first."

"By the way, doesn't this boy have a name?" Rosacoke asked.

Narcissa looked miffed. "He does and I don't even know it. The bitch negotiating the deal didn't even tell me what she calls the boy. But my boy should be renamed. Call him what you want, but make sure the last name is Riddle."

"This comes as a great disappointment to me," Douglas said. "I think I'd make a great father to the boy."

"It's not so easy," Narcissa said. "If this boy wants to escape the racial curse, having me as a mother is the last place to turn. You'd think that after all this time the bigots would let us alone. There's not a day that goes by but what we are delivered hate mail. *Still.* Sometimes I'm booed in nightclubs. I want my son to grow up with all the privileges I didn't have. If he wants to be white, let him. Even more than being pretty, being white was my own greatest dream. I'm sure the boy inherited wanting to be white from me. With a new life for my boy, no one will know the secret except Pete, Hank, and this room here."

"If I know Pete, he'll jump at the chance to adopt the boy," Rosacoke said." That's the way he is. Always taking in strays. You should see the household he has right now."

The night wore on as Rosacoke made repeated calls to the Chateau Marmont trying to talk to Pete. But reception kept telling her that Mr. Riddle's party had not come back. She figured Pete and his boys must be having one hell of a night on the town for their farewell to Hollywood.

It was five o'clock in the morning when she was able to get someone in Pete's bedroom at the Chateau Marmont to pick up the phone. Sounding angry, a sleepy Josh picked up the phone. "Couldn't this wait until breakfast?" he snapped at her. "Pete's had a long night."

"I want to talk to him and talk to him now," Rosacoke said. She'd never been that forceful with Josh before.

When Pete came on the phone, Rosacoke said, "I'm here with Narcissa and her husband. We've got to talk to you. It's about your other son!"

That had been all that was needed to goad Pete into action. In less than an hour he pulled up in a taxi at Narcissa's home. After his reunion with Narcissa and an introduction to Douglas, it was down to business. Douglas

explained their dilemma to Pete.

Without saying anything, his face revealing nothing, Pete listened intently. When Douglas had laid out their case, Pete smiled at Narcissa, then bent over and kissed Rosacoke on the cheek. "Looks like our Buster has got himself a brother."

As dawn broke on a new day, Rosacoke walked hand in hand with Pete, Narcissa, and Douglas along the beach at Santa Monica. Beginning today, each of them would be locked into a bond with each other. It was as if all four of them had become the parents of a young boy.

When the papers of adoption were drawn up, the boy would have a new identity. Tracy Riddle. For reasons known only to him, Pete had wanted to name him after his long-lost friend, Tracy Adams, who had died at sea in naval combat.

"I'm sure Tracy will bring us a lot of happiness," Rosacoke predicted. "Buster also needs a playmate his own age."

No one said anything as they walked hand-in-hand along the deserted beach.

Only the screech of a sea gull could be heard.

*\*\*\**

A few hours later, as Pete and his gang boarded Junior's plane for the flight back to the Carolina hills, Rosacoke, as was agreed upon the night before, boarded a TWA flight from Los Angeles to Chicago. Sitting next to her on that flight was Douglas Porter, armed with an alligator briefcase that contained ten-thousand dollars in one-hundred dollar denominations.

The whole upcoming transaction with Pete's other son made Rosacoke feel that she was purchasing flesh, the same way that Sultan's ancestors had been bought and sold.

Douglas repeatedly assured her that he'd handle all the arrangements once they got to Chicago, and she wouldn't even have to meet Tracy's guardian. She'd learned that Tracy had been going under the name of Billy Dunn, but she didn't even want to remember that name. To her, she wanted to meet Pete's son as Tracy Riddle in his new incarnation.

She wasn't too comfortable with the name of Tracy but Pete had insisted upon it as an homage to his long lost friend. Until Pete had come up with naming his other son after Tracy Adams, she had never known that Pete even knew Tracy that well, unlike his very intimate friendship with the other two brothers, Karl and Hank.

With Douglas so near to her on the plane, she felt completely safe and secure, as if she were with a man who could solve any problem facing her or confront any challenge for her. With a man like that by her side, she could stand up to any demon.

That someone so kind and good could have ended up with Narcissa amazed her. Douglas looked like a man who should marry a sweet young thing like Jane Powell, "the girl next door" in the movies—not some fiery café-au-lait temptress like the sultry, sexy Narcissa Cash.

There was obviously more to Douglas than this beautiful package of a man who had fallen asleep beside her, his head falling over and resting on her shoulder. She loved the feel of him and was afraid to move out of fear of waking him up. As far as she was concerned, he could rest that handsome head of his on her shoulder for as long as he wanted. She liked the feel of him. She could even smell his sweet breath, made pleasantly aromatic from the bourbon both of them had just been served by the stewardess.

Knowing she really shouldn't, Rosacoke on the long flight east dreamed of what it would be like having a real husband like Douglas and not her eccentric Pete who had ceased his visits to her bedroom ever since Josh had walked in on them.

In her heart she wanted a real man for a husband, one who would lie with her in his arms every night and make love to her until she begged him to stop because she couldn't take any more pleasure.

She felt that Josh had taken over her role as a wife, even though she didn't fully understand how a man could assume a woman's traditional role. If she really wanted to know, she could ask Tara, who seemed to know about all such things. The subject made Rosacoke so uncomfortable she figured she could live without really knowing much about male/male love.

She'd never seriously entertained the prospect of leaving Pete for some other man. It was not something she wanted to do. As unwelcome as she was at Heaven on Earth, she still felt it was the only home she'd ever known. Life on the road with no support mechanism at all didn't appeal to her. She'd lived through that nightmare, and was grateful for the creature comforts Pete provided. If he couldn't fulfill her physical needs, that was a sorry shame, but one she was prepared to live with.

During her days on the road, she'd endured sex with men mainly because of the temporary comfort they provided during those lonely, bleak months at one cockroach-infested hotel room after another. The sex that was inevitable was something for her to endure. Mostly the men she'd known had used her body only for their pleasure—not for hers.

Following her marriage to Pete, and before they'd come back to Heaven on Earth and Josh, Pete had aroused the woman in her. She didn't know if "woman" were the right word. Maybe slut was more appropriate. She felt in those few brief honeymoon days with Pete she'd become as sluttish as Narcissa. Rosacoke had taken Pete in her mouth, and she'd never done that with any man before in spite of repeated requests. When he'd opened up his ass cheeks and demanded that she penetrate him with her tongue,

she'd almost puked. He'd insisted and she had been so willing to please him that she'd gone for the bull's eye, finding that after a minute or so she'd liked the taste of him.

She'd figured that any woman who would put a dick in her mouth and tongue a man's balls might as well lick his asshole as well. Even more than her finding that she'd liked the taste of him, she had been enthralled at the pleasure she'd provided for him. If tonguing an asshole was the way to keep her husband satisfied, she was more than willing to oblige. Why had she felt she was morally superior to Narcissa? In the darkness of the night, Rosacoke wondered if she were a closeted whore, waiting to come out of that dark hole into the full light of the bedroom itself.

An hour away from Chicago she began to fantasize what it would be like to go to bed with Douglas. As much as she felt she shouldn't dwell on such, she couldn't seem to control her mind. She kept trying to justify her thoughts. After all, Narcissa had not only slept with her husband, but had had a son by him.

She found Douglas one of the most alluring men she'd ever met. He was just as good looking as Larry—maybe a little bit more so—and he had a lot more manly qualities than Larry, to whom he bore a slight resemblance.

Rosacoke noticed last night that Douglas treated Narcissa like a queen. As midnight had given way to the early dawn hours, and the maid had long gone to bed, Douglas seemed attentive and aware of Narcissa's every need. He'd anticipated her wanting a drink before she'd actually asked for one. When she'd complained about having a hard day, he'd taken off her shoes and massaged her feet. He was a dream husband, or at least appeared to be so. But Rosacoke had learned not to trust fantasies.

Pete Riddle too had seemed like a dream husband but had turned out to be almost the opposite. He might be a dream husband to Josh, but not to her. If Pete divorced her and remarried, a likely possibility, her advice to the second wife would be to expect many lonely nights.

From the penthouse suite in Chicago that Douglas had rented for them, she felt that she'd never seen a more beautiful sunset. The clouds became tinged with burnt orange and molten yellow. Mauves, indigo blues, and fuchsia lit up the distant horizon. At the moment the sun went down, seemingly into the lake, a streak of brilliant emerald green light shot across the sky.

In the glow there was a tremulous, shimmering light. She turned and looked into Douglas' face. She'd known many good-looking men in her life, not only Pete and Hank, but dozens more. At that very moment she felt she'd never seen such classic male beauty as Douglas' face. He was looking at her with a luminous kind of love, and for one brief moment she felt he belonged to her.

Neither said a word for a long while. He reached for her hand and held it up to his lips, tenderly kissing the inner palm. Impulsively she pulled away and also broke the silence. "I think that's the most luxurious bathroom I've ever seen in my life, and that's where I'm heading right now. Pink and green marble, not like the outhouses I've known in my day with a corncob for toilet paper."

He laughed gently but it was obvious that he regretted her breaking the magic spell between them.

Inside the *luxe* bathroom, she lit two candles, creating an eerie glow. When the bellboy had pointed out these candles to her, she'd been dumbfounded at first. Why light candles when you had electricity? "It's for romance," he'd said, winking at her.

As she ran her bath water and tossed in a pack of scented bubble bath, she felt that bellhop knew what he was talking about. Candles gave the room a mysterious glow that bright lights never could. If anything, this flickering light made her image in the mirror more beautiful than ever. Outside she imagined a full moon and stars twinkling. She wondered if Douglas were still on that terrace taking in the view.

Perfumed fragrances filled the bathroom. From the living room, she heard Douglas turn on soft music. She luxuriated in her bubble bath, sinking deep into what was the biggest bathtub she'd ever seen in her whole life. It too was made of pink marble. She closed her eyes for the longest moment—maybe it was minutes as she'd long ago lost count, in this dreamy world in which she found herself.

She became aware of some presence in the room. Gradually she opened her eyes. Without her hearing a sound, Douglas had come into the bathroom. Fully clothed, he stood about six feet away from her, lovingly looking down at her in the bubble bath. Instinctively she reached to cover her breasts but decided against it, exposing them to him.

She gazed up at him as if seeing him for the first time with his thick blond hair and dazzling blue eyes. His aquiline nose seemed to suggest some patrician ancestry, and his mouth, which turned up at the edges, revealed the most perfectly formed, whitest teeth she'd ever seen on a man.

The beginning of a stubble of beard appeared as golden flecks against his suntanned skin. Before her eyes he slowly began to remove all of his clothing, dropping piece by piece on the bathroom floor. He was long, lean, and muscular. When he'd taken off everything except his white shorts, he moved toward her in the bath tub. "The last unveiling is for you."

In need of no further instructions, she reached for his shorts, pulling them down. Freed from the confines of underwear, his large cock reared up at her like a wild stallion. Even if he weren't in the same league as Pete and Hank—who was?—it was an impressive mass. On exposing it, she planted wet kisses and caresses on it, reaching out for it and skinning back

the head to put a long, lingering wet kiss on it as the prick rose to all its magnificence.

Electric energy vibrated through every atom of her being, as she thrilled to the taste of him. He gently eased himself into the bathtub with her. She reached out to soap his chest, using a big sponge. The water was not only bubbly, but warm and sweet. Every cell in her body screamed with excitement at touching this man. Her hands descended into the water to feel every inch of his erection. She imagined it was some giant sea serpent about to attack her.

She'd tied a red silk ribbon around her blonde hair, and a few stray strands dangled at her neck. He reached to touch that neck, his hands fingering her shoulders before going lower to cup her large breasts. He squeezed them like they were ripe melons and toyed with the red buds of her nipples. Under his deft fingers, those nipples blossomed and hardened. He took the sponge and rubbed between her deep cleavage. With a life of their own, his hands moved up and down her rib cage as his face reflected a surging sexual agitation. When his magic fingers reached her golden bush, she screamed out in passion. She felt delirious with joy. He seemed to be touching her like no man had ever done before. She massaged his broad chest as his fingers plunged deeper into her.

She washed his enormous cock, which was like some lusting monster demanding attention. She reached deeper to fondle his heavy balls under the water, teasing the sensitive globes. His fondling of her breasts was growing more feverish. Suddenly he reached out and lifted her from the waist, sitting her on his lap. As they bobbed back and forth, the bubble bath swirled around them. In frenzied lust he surged against her. Arms around his neck, she kissed him with passion as he tasted her sweet red lips, communicating his need for her.

As his tongue drove deep into her mouth, he impaled her. The invasion was so sudden she screamed out her pleasure. When he crashed her final frontier, spasm upon spasm overwhelmed her. Eyes tightly shut, she was caught in an orgasmic seizure as he covered her face and neck with wet kisses and tiny bites. With her whimpering and panting in his arms, he had only begun his watery ride. The room floated in candlelight.

***

It had all been too much for Pete. Hollywood, the MGM record deal, and, most of all, his new son, Tracy Riddle. As if he didn't already have enough reason to be jittery, coming back to Buster made him even more so. He'd gone too far with giving in to the boy's demands. He not only had to tell Buster to quit focusing on him as a love object, but that he would soon be living with another, a half brother his own age.

Buster was completely unpredictable, and he could not imagine his son's reaction to the total withdrawal of any physical love between them and the news that he would not only be losing a part of his daddy but would have to be sharing him with yet another sibling.

Since Buster was jealous of Josh, Pete feared that he'd be even more jealous of "the second son." There was also the element of race to add to the picture. Tracy might have obvious mulatto features, and word would surely get out. Pete could just imagine the chants of "Nigger Mammy" that would be used to torment young Tracy's life, yet Pete was determined to go through with the adoption the same way Narcissa had endured the insults and had continued in her marriage to a white man, Douglas Porter.

When Junior flew Pete's gang into the local airport, all of them quickly got into the cars Tara had sent to take them back to Heaven on Earth. After the glories of Hollywood, everybody seemed eager for a homecoming.

Tara rushed to greet them and to face the question from Pete of, "Where's Buster?"

She said he wasn't feeling well and wanted Pete to come to his suite of rooms as soon as he settled in. Upstairs in the master bedroom, Pete gave Josh a long, sloppy kiss and asked him to unpack while he went to see if Buster was okay.

Once in Buster's darkened rooms, Pete found that his son was feeling fine. "I just said I was feeling bad," Buster told him after long hugs and kisses. "That way I can get to see you alone without all your gang, especially that Josh, hovering about."

"And exactly why did you want to see me alone?" Pete asked, determined to confront Buster head-on.

"Isn't a son entitled to see his daddy without a lot of other people listening in?" Buster asked, smiling provocatively as he turned on his bed lamp.

Pete couldn't help but notice that the young boy was lying nude on top of his sheets. He went over to Buster's clothes chest, reached into a drawer, pulled out a pair of underwear, and tossed it to his son. "Put that on." He turned to face Buster. "Or would you like a pair of my own skivvies?" Pete asked. "From the bottom drawer."

A smirk came across Buster's face. "So I guess Tara found out and told you. So what? I steal my daddy's underwear and bury my face in the crotch at night." He raised up in bed and reached for his own pair of underwear, slowly covering his genitalia with the shorts. "You got a problem with that?"

"Yeah, I think I do," Pete said. "This dick I've got between my legs is intended for Josh's ass—not yours. Why can't you accept that?"

Buster got up from the bed and went to confront Pete, standing only a foot from his face. "I'll tell you why. Because I think deep in your heart

you want me as much as I want you."

Without meaning to, Pete slapped Buster's face real hard and turned and headed out of the bedroom toward Buster's living room, with his son trailing behind.

"It's very hard for you to face the truth, isn't it?" Buster said, confronting him again in the living room.

"I love you, son," Pete said, "I always will regardless of what comes down between us. But it can't be the type of love I feel for Josh. It's wrong."

"I can accept that bit of honesty from you, but only if you play fair," Buster said. "I'm going to ask you a question. Our future depends on your telling the truth to me for the first time in your life."

"What do you want to know?" Pete asked.

"Can you admit what I already know?" Buster said. "That you want me for sex as much as I want you?"

Pete turned from his son. He walked toward the corner of the room, discovering a small bar to his surprise. It had been installed while he was in California. "Aren't you a little young to take up drinking?"

"The bar is not for me," Buster said. "It's for you, your favorite bourbon. I wanted the bar to entertain you during what I know is going to become a private visit every day to my room."

Feeling the shakes coming on, Pete poured himself a glass of bourbon and downed a hefty swig. He sat down on the sofa and slammed the glass of liquor down on the coffee table. He gazed up at Buster but couldn't stand the penetrating look of his son's eyes. Those eyes just seemed to see deep within Pete's soul. He buried his head in his hands and began to sob.

In a moment Buster was at his side, putting his arms around Pete and holding him tightly. "It's okay, baby," Buster said, his voice sounding like a young lover far older than his years. "I'm here to make it right for you. We don't need to keep secrets from each other. Me and you can face up to our love."

He reached for his son and crushed him into his arms. "I love you, kid," Pete said. "Don't do this. If I'm a weak man, and you sure have got one weak fucker for a daddy, be strong for the both of us."

"I can't," Buster said, darting his sweet young tongue inside Pete's ear, sending an almost unbelievable thrill through his body. "I'm just like my old man. My flesh is weak too, as they say in these parts. No stronger, but no weaker than you. I've got desires and I have to give in to those needs. Just like my daddy."

Pete felt Buster's hand reaching for his shirt to slowly unbutton it. After the first three buttons were unfastened, Buster's hand reached in to fondle and massage Pete's nipples. Eyes tightly shut, Pete lay back on the sofa, wanting to prevent this from happening but seemingly powerless to do

anything to stop it. As Buster fondled his nipples and squeezed with one hand, he continued to unbutton Pete's shirt with the other, finally reaching the belt buckle.

"Get naked for me," Buster said. "You know you want my cherry-red lips all over you. I want to drink the cum you've been building up in those big balls. It belongs to me."

"This is not right..." Pete's words were drowned out as Buster's succulent mouth and darting tongue descended on his lips to create their special magic.

*** 

When Junior picked Tracy and Rosacoke up at the Charlotte airport and flew them in Pete's private plane to their hometown, only Pete was there to greet them. After having spent three hours in Karl's bedroom, and having had quite a bit to drink, Pete was feeling no pain. The bourbon had helped him get over the awkwardness of confronting his second son under these circumstances.

Junior had lent his third-floor apartment near the airport to Pete who wanted to meet and talk privately with Tracy before driving him to Heaven on Earth to meet the gang. He didn't know what Tracy would look like, envisioning that he'd look like a young Sultan, only with lighter skin.

As Junior landed Pete's private plane, Pete was on the ground to meet the passengers. Rosacoke got off the plane first. In her new clothes, no doubt bought in Chicago, Pete realized that she looked more sophisticated and beautiful than ever. He rushed over and gave her a quick kiss on the lips, claiming he would catch up with her later at Heaven on Earth. "You've got a mighty fine son," she said. "I only wish I could have been his mama—and not Narcissa."

"Maybe if you had put out that first night, you would have been," Pete said, chucking her under the chin. It was just a strange feeling he had, but he suspected that Rosacoke looked guilty about something. "Thanks for the Chicago rescue mission. It must have been weird going back there after all this time."

"It was a beautiful time," she said, "and I was right honored to go and get your son. I got to know the boy a bit. I'll be proud to be his mama if you want to go through with the adoption."

Still desperately anxious to see what Tracy looked like, Pete was growing impatient. He kissed Rosacoke one more time and waved her off, just as Tracy walked down the ramp.

As Tracy came into view, Pete was stunned. This was no Sultan. He looked just as white as Buster—no *café-au-lait* skin like Narcissa had.

As he stood on the ground looking into Tracy's blue eyes, he was mes-

merized by the boy's beauty. Tracy seemed to have captured all his finest male features with the added dose of Narcissa's sensuality. The boy was a stunner. It was only then that Pete became aware of Tracy's outfit. He wore a blue bandana around his head like some form of headdress and a silver necklace dangled over his white T-shirt. He had a red vest and tight-fitting blue jeans and a pair of penny loafers. He exuded sex appeal the way Pete himself had at his age. But Pete felt his allure had been a natural thing, whereas Tracy seemed to have calculated his every asset and packaged it into one dynamite bundle. It was almost the same thing Narcissa herself had done at her age.

"Are you going to stand there catching flies with your mouth open or are you going to grab your son and kiss him?" Tracy asked.

Pete was astonished. He had some of Narcissa's flash in his talk but not her voice. Unlike every other member of Pete's gang, Tracy had a perfectly modulated voice without accent. It was of a deeper tone than any kid Pete knew of Tracy's age.

Challenged by Tracy, Pete met him at the bottom of the ramp. He was crying when he took the boy in his arms. Holding him as tightly as he could against his strong and powerful chest, Pete gave in to his sobs. "I'm sorry," he kept repeating to the boy. "I'm sorry."

Up close to Pete's face, Tracy said, "Who does a guy have to fuck around here to get a kiss?"

Pete leaned down to kiss him on the cheek. The boy diverted Pete's action and gave him a succulent kiss on the lips. "Welcome home, son," Pete said, thrilled at the boy's looks and at Tracy's immediate acceptance of him.

After shutting off the plane's engine, Junior climbed down the ramp and held Pete in his arms. Right in front of Tracy, he kissed Pete on the lips.

"Thanks for everything, big guy," Pete said to Junior.

"I'm here for you." Junior kissed Pete again on the lips. "I'll drive Rosacoke home. If you need me later tonight, I'll be with John-John."

"Right on, tiger," Pete said, wondering what was happening with those two.

He stood looking for a minute as Junior walked to Pete's Lincoln where Rosacoke waited. As they pulled out, he gazed again into Tracy's dancing eyes.

Tracy reached up and kissed Pete again. "I'm with my real daddy, and I'm the happiest little bastard in all the world. Your hair's a bit long and the clothes aren't right, but there will be time tomorrow for me to take care of that."

As Pete walked with Tracy toward Junior's apartment, Pete was astonished at his son and that remark about hair and clothes. He talked like a much older person but was still a boy. Pete concluded that Tracy was one

very wise and much experienced boy in spite of his age. He felt it was remarkable that both of his sons seemed worldly beyond their years.

Inside the apartment, Tracy ripped off his bandana to reveal beautiful sandy hair, which he wore a bit long, but not too long.

"Did anyone ever tell you you're a beauty?" Tracy asked. "I have the most gorgeous hunk for a father of any kid in America. Now I know where I got my own good looks."

"Can I get you something?" Pete asked. "A coke or something!" For some reason, Tracy made him feel embarrassed.

Tracy came toward him. "You can take me in your arms, hold me real close, kiss me, and promise me you'll never leave your son ever again for as long as you live."

Pete reached out for the boy and held him real tight. He didn't break away when Tracy kissed him long and hard. He figured he owed this kid a lot and was going to be there for him, no matter what Tracy wanted.

On the sofa Pete began the long attempt to get to know his other son. He was glad he'd set up this private meeting before taking him to Heaven on Earth to meet Buster and all the gang.

Tracy sat close to him on the sofa. As he told Pete about his years in Chicago, he would often reach out and touch his daddy, running his fingers through Pete's hair. "That's the greatest head of hair I've ever seen on a man." At one point, Tracy ran his hands across Pete's face, feeling his nose, cheeks, chin, lips, and eyelids. "You're a classic beauty," Tracy said. "God, I was lucky to get your genes."

Pete pulled away from Tracy and got up and headed over to Junior's kitchen counter where his favorite bottle of bourbon was waiting. He poured himself a hefty drink and downed a big gulp of it. The liquor steadied his nerves a bit. "This is an awkward thing to bring up," he said. "I mean…. You're white, not what I expected."

Tracy stood up from the sofa and pulled off his shirt, revealing the most beautiful young body Pete had ever seen on any boy. "I'm white all over." He looked provocatively at Pete. "Want to see more?"

"That's enough for now," Pete said nervously. He suddenly realized what he'd said. It sounded like at some point later he'd want to see more. He looked into Tracy's eyes, realizing that he was interpreting it that way too.

Tracy came and stood close to him. "I'm white. It means everything to me to be white. You know I'm black. But I don't want the world to find out." Tears were coming down his cheeks. "I'm white. I have a white daddy. My mother is going to be Rosacoke Carson, and she's a blonde and one of the whitest women I've ever seen. She should have been my mother—not Narcissa."

Pete put his arms around Tracy. "As far as I'm concerned, you can be

any God damn color you want to be."

The next three hours passed faster than any Pete could recall spending in his whole life. He told Tracy stories about himself, and listened intently as his son spoke of his hopes, dreams, and plans for the future. He wanted to be a stylist and designer for entertainers, and in Chicago had dreamed of going to design school one day.

"The one thing you and Narcissa gave me was a love for show business," Tracy said. "With my asshole nigger guardians in Chicago, I had no way to break into the business. But I bet you'll help me. Rosacoke told me you're heading for big stardom. I want to be a part of it. Travel all over the place with you. You'll let me, won't you?"

Pete put his arm around Tracy and held him close. "I let everybody at Heaven on Earth do whatever they damn please." He squeezed Tracy tighter. "Why not you?"

"You mean that?" Tracy asked, his eyes filled with trust. "I've been lied to so many times, I can't believe anybody."

"You can believe your daddy," Pete said. "Even though you're still a kid, you seem to have grown up already. I was hoping to enjoy seeing you grow up. At least the rest of the way, but it seems I'm too late."

"When I get to know you better, I'll tell you what really happened to me up there in Chicago," Tracy said. "When you hear my story, you'll understand a hell of a lot more."

Pete glanced at his watch. "We'd better get going. The whole gang's waiting to meet you at Heaven on Earth. I've got a big compound, a lot of people for you to meet. I just know all of them are gonna love you."

Tracy looked up at Pete. "Even Buster?"

Pete swallowed hard. He dreaded introducing Tracy to Buster. Before coming to the airport, he'd explained the whole situation to Buster who had reacted violently. "I'll not share you with any brother," Buster had screamed at him. "You're mine. There's no room in your life for me and this Tracy thing."

Buster had locked himself in his suite and had refused to come out.

Driving Tracy back to Heaven on Earth, Pete said, "All the other folks will take to you right away. I just know it. With Buster, it'll take a little while. I mean, he's been my only boy. The kid of the family, getting all that special attention."

Tracy slid over in the car seat to be closer to Pete. "You're my daddy too." He smiled up at Pete. "Buster will just have to learn to share you with me."

# Chapter 12

The next few months passed as in a dream. "Lonesome Blues" took off on the wings of a dove. It hit the top of country charts and occupied squatter's rights there for most of the year.

A survey of juke-box operators, as revealed in *Cash Box*, named "Lonesome Blues" the best hillbilly record of the year. *Billboard's* chart of country and western songs listed "Blues" as number one. Two more songs, recorded by Pete, placed number four and number sixteen on the charts. In all, it was a very big year, a time climaxed by *Billboard* giving Pete the number three position in its best-selling list of the "Year's Top-Selling Folk Artists." He trailed behind two of his idols, Eddy Arnold and Hank Williams.

When Pete returned to Heaven on Earth from an awards ceremony in Los Angeles, he was in a party mood, and asked Claude to go and get Fry. "He wrote 'Lonesome Blues,'" Pete said. "He needs to be here to join in our celebration."

Claude returned in two hours. He'd come from the hospital. Fry had collapsed the previous night and had been taken there, the scene of two previous operations for him. The cancer had spread rapidly throughout his body, and he'd died at 3:51 a.m.

It was a sad night at Heaven on Earth. What had been planned as a celebration turned into a wake for the former mentor of both Rosacoke and Pete.

The very next day an old-time black musician, who'd worked with Fry back in the late Twenties, showed up on their doorstep. Now in his seventies, he claimed he'd played with Fry in New Orleans as part of a small jazz group.

Thinking he was an old friend of Fry's come to town for the funeral, Pete invited him out on his back verandah and asked Rosacoke and Larry to join them.

It was a time for Pete and Rosacoke to hear old-time memories of Fry. "Ukulele Dick," as he called himself, said little about Fry but talked a lot about himself, "I fought in World War I," he said to them. "I was struck by the pain suffered by husbands and boy friends having to leave their wives and girl friends back home as they left to die on a battlefield in Europe. It gave everybody the lonesome blues back then."

"I didn't know Fry was ever a soldier," Rosacoke said.

"He wasn't," Ukulele Dick said. "I was. The war broke up my little band with Fry. When I got back, he'd gone on his way. I'd saved up enough money to go to New York City. Once there, I got a local company, Perfect Records, to record a song I'd written. The tune was ahead of its time. It was a big flop. But it got published, and I have the copyright."

He handed a stunned Pete his scratchy record released by Perfect. Pete held the disk like it was poison before handing it to Larry to play on their back porch record player. In silence, Rosacoke and Larry listened with Pete as a bad version of "Lonesome Blues" assailed their ears.

Silence prevailed at the end of the session. Ukulele Dick was the first to speak up. "I first copyrighted that song back in 1922. My wife gets the old thing out and plays it every Christmas. Only this past Christmas she brought it out of mothballs again and played it for me. I told somebody about it, and he said I should copyright it again. You know, just in case the old copyright had expired. I did just that. My God, this is gonna be a good year for me, although I didn't know it at the time. Imagine my joy when I heard this here stud singing 'Lonesome Blues' on the radio the other day. I told my wife at the time, 'Honey, we got ourselves a hit record. Finally!' She figured I just better get down to see you and let you people know where to send the royalty checks. 'Course, I'm sorry my name's not on it as writer of the thing, but I'm sure you people will pay good money for the privilege of my letting you keep your names on it. What price glory?"

All through his lone, rambling talk, Larry remained stone faced, as if calculating his next move. Always apprehensive about Larry and Pete taking credit for Fry's song, Rosacoke was on the verge of tears.

As if completely undisturbed by the whole chain of events, Pete was the one to break the stalemate. "You're really gonna be picking that ukulele with joy," he told the songwriter. In his good-natured, totally assured, masculine way, Pete put his arm around the former singer. "You've just made yourself a whole heap of money, and we're gonna be partners."

Larry said nothing. There was another long silence on the verandah.

It was Pete who spoke up again. He smiled once more at Ukulele Dick. "Let's go out and get drunk to celebrate. You got any more songs as good as 'Lonesome Blues' at home?"

\*\*\*

With the ever-faithful Josh at his side, Pete retreated to the eagle's nest that Karl had built for them on top of the mountain. Dramatic and isolated, and surrounded with window walls of glass, it perched on a rocky ledge above a sweeping panorama of the Blue Ridge mountains. As heat radiated outward from a stone-sided fireplace into the comfort of the living room, Pete sat on a sofa, watching flurries of snow cascade from gray

skies outside.

Josh had taken off Pete's shoes and was massaging his feet. He looked up lovingly into Pete's eyes. "I'm married to a fucking star," Josh said. "Hot damn!"

Pete ran his hands through Josh's hair. His old Navy buddy gave him a kind of comfort that none of his other lovers did. Pete still liked his sex illicit, but for coming home, he wanted Josh in the bed with him. Josh tended to his every need and even anticipated what Pete wanted before he knew himself. "I don't know what I'd do without you," Pete said to Josh. "The foot massage feels great but I need my mouth massaged too."

Josh was only too happy to oblige. When Pete wanted him—any part of him—Josh was there for him. No matter how weird the request, Josh was a willing participant, and Pete could get kinky at times, especially when drunk, which, as he hated to admit to himself, was becoming more and more frequent.

As the snow flurries swirled around the house, Pete closed his eyes after a long kissing marathon with Josh. In spite of his troubled life, Pete felt that this mountain aerie was a safe haven. No one could get at him here.

After kissing him, Josh returned to his feet where he slowly sucked Pete's toes. His lover could do this for hours and seemingly never get tired of it. Pete found it one of the most relaxing massages he'd ever known, and he'd been massaged by the best of them.

Comforted by Josh's sucking mouth, Pete drifted into memory and tried to make sense out of his new life and its complications. Sometimes he'd get mixed up and couldn't figure things out, especially when he'd been hitting the bourbon bottle.

Since that record deal, he'd made three trips to the West Coast, always standing up as his producer, Frank Walker—on his knees—gave him the customary blow-job.

The toe-sucking and Pete's reverie ended, as Josh headed north with his tongue. Originally they had planned to drive back down the mountain. But Claude called and told them the road was too dangerous. "We're heading for one of the biggest blizzards this hick town has ever seen. You guys have got everything you need—supplies, everything, including each other. Why don't you hang out up there until the roads are clear again? I'll drive up when it's safe to come down that mountain."

"It's about time Josh and I had a second honeymoon," Pete said. "Even when that road becomes passable, don't tell my boys or Rosacoke. In fact, if you'd delay coming up here for as long as you could I'd be grateful. I need the rest." He looked over at Josh.

"Some rest you're going to get," Claude said. "I envy Josh."

"I love you, guy," Pete said to Claude. "See you in a few days." He

put down the phone.

"Did I hear that right?" Josh asked.

"You heard it right," Pete said. "For the first time in a long while, you and I are going to spend a few days alone together. No interruptions. Just you and me, baby."

Josh smiled. It was obvious he was delighted. "You're not going to take advantage of me?" he asked jokingly. "I mean, perform unspeakable acts of perverted lust on me, are you?"

"If you only knew what I was going to do," Pete said. He lit two candles and turned off the living room lights. In the eerie glow of candlelight, with the snow flurries whirling around them, Pete felt that Karl had created the most romantic of living arrangements for them.

Up close to Josh on the sofa, he could hear the young man's heavy breathing. He'd lied to Josh and cheated on him, and he felt real sorry about that.

During the next few days he was going to attempt the impossible: He was going to try to make it up to his lover. It would be the first time they'd ever lived alone together without all the others. During this escape from their other world, Pete could imagine what life would be like if they lived alone like most married couples. The thought thrilled him.

With Josh cradled in his arms, seemingly melting into Pete's body, he was to embark on the happiest and most fulfilling three days of his entire life.

***

Rejoicing in Pete's success, enjoying his new-found fame almost as much as he got a kick out of it himself, Rosacoke still dreamed of stardom for herself. But Larry had told her that "lightning rarely strikes twice in the same household." Her career seemed as if it was going absolutely nowhere but just meandering from one honky-tonk to another. Larry kept her on the road with plenty of minor bookings, but that evasive North Star never shone down on her.

Her marriage to Pete was just one of convenience. Josh had become his wife in all but name. She suspected that they were having a second honeymoon, comfortably ensconced in their beautiful mountain aerie.

"Love nest might be a better word," she told Tara, who had no comment. That fat woman could be supremely discreet when confronted with peccadilloes. Pete was lucky to have her around since she knew how to keep her trap shut.

The one joy that sustained her through all the lonely nights on the road was her next trip to California. She stayed with Narcissa and Douglas, and always brought pictures of Tracy to show them how the young boy was

growing into a handsome teenager. Although she didn't want to admit it to anybody, she felt that Tracy was even more beautiful than Buster, if such a thing were possible.

Like Buster, Tracy didn't relate to her at all, although he often spent an hour or two with her and showed her a lot more attention than her own son did. Also like Buster, Tracy lavished his devotion and attention on Pete. Rosacoke had never known of two sons more devoted to their daddy than Buster and Tracy Riddle.

If Rosacoke were devoted to anybody in the worked, it was Douglas Porter, and she could hardly be proud of that fact since he was married to Narcissa. The only thing that could sustain her for weeks at a time was knowing that she'd soon slip away to see Douglas for another rendezvous. Ever since that night he'd seduced her in a Chicago bathtub, she'd fallen deeply into love with him. Amazingly, Narcissa didn't seem to suspect the two of them, although the affair was conducted virtually in front of her nose when Rosacoke stayed at their home in Los Angeles.

Up until now, Rosacoke had never had more than two or three hours to spend alone with Douglas. But her luck had changed. She was thrilled when Douglas had called her the previous night. Narcissa was going to fly alone to New York for a singing engagement. Douglas had to remain in Los Angeles where he was going to perform a secret face-lift on the aging Marlene Dietrich. He'd asked Rosacoke to fly to the coast to stay with him, and she'd agreed as her heart had seemed to beat faster.

She'd called Frank Walker and had told him that she was flying to the coast and wanted him to hear three records she'd made in Pete's recording studio with the help of the Foggy Mountain boys.

Frank had reluctantly agreed. She knew the records weren't particularly good, and that Frank would only be half-heartedly interested, not wanting to insult the wife of one of his best clients. Frank would provide the excuse she needed to go to Los Angeles, not that she had to make excuses to Pete. He came and went as he pleased and didn't seem to care where she went. In fact, he often urged her to go to New York, and maybe even take a trip to Europe.

***

As Christmas approached, snow gathered on the peaks of the Blue Ridge Mountains, and Rosacoke wondered what kind of holiday she'd have in the midst of Pete's strange "family." As the official mistress of the house, she'd preside over the festivities and see that Pete gave presents to all the help and all his special favorites. He assigned all the shopping to her.

Everybody would be at Heaven on Earth for the holidays, either at the big house or in their private homes within the compound, and she figured

Pete would get drunk. Virtually everybody else, especially Hank Adams, would probably be drunk too.

A few days later, Pete rode down the mountain with a relaxed and smiling Josh at his side. Larry immediately gathered the clan together—even Tracy and Buster, two brothers who did not usually like to be in each other's company—to announce that he had arranged for Pete to appear on stage at Nashville's Grand Ole Opry. Until now, Larry had preferred to hold Pete back, waiting until public excitement over "Lonesome Blues" rose several notches higher. But now, with the song near the top of the charts nationwide, Larry was relishing his victory. Larry clearly touted Pete as his personal discovery, and, in Larry's words, he was merely "lending" him to the Opry.

After much haggling with the Opry over terms and conditions, and after many opening night jitters, Pete agreed to go on the show, inviting his whole household, including Buster and Tracy, to ride on their deluxe bus with him to Nashville.

Once they got there, Rosacoke was filled with excitement as she mingled with the performers backstage at the old Ryman Auditorium. She was as nervous as if she herself were going out there on that stage tonight.

Outside on the streets of Nashville, cars could be heard honking in a massive traffic jam. Inside the auditorium, it was just as noisy and confusing. For a moment or two, she'd lost Pete in one of the old auditorium's zigzag skinny hallways that weren't built to handle the circus-like traffic of singers, players, stagehands, and people called "God only knows who."

Eventually locating Pete in one of the cramped dressing rooms, Rosacoke helped him dress under Josh's hawk eyes. "I need my own band," Pete lamented ten minutes before going on. "I need the Foggy Mountain Boys. They can keep up with me. I don't know if the house band is good enough."

"It's gonna be okay," Rosacoke assured him, although she had plenty of doubts. Nervous, exhausted, and anxiety-ridden, she couldn't wait for this evening to end.

Before she knew it, Roy Acuff had announced Pete and his act, and he was on. All she could do was wait in the wings, clutching Tara's hand. Rosacoke silently mouthed every one of Pete's words.

His boots hit the planks of the stage's wooden floor and he stood tall and proud in his too-tight white pants. Bright lights made his white cowboy suit look even whiter, and his rhinestones sparkled. As the band struck up the song Rosacoke knew so well, she saw Pete closing his eyes as if bracing himself for the ordeal ahead. She knew how important this moment was to him, the answer to a life-long dream.

He leaned forward and, as his first words came out, the audience went wild. He yodeled the first line, which was met with spontaneous Rebel

cheers. Everybody knew "Lonesome Blues." Most of them didn't know who sang it, or that the singer looked like a Hollywood movie star. Pete was hardly into his song before members of the Opry crowd rose to their feet among the uncomfortable pews, clapping, cheering, yelling. Rosacoke turned to Tara and spontaneously kissed her on the cheek. She knew Pete was a hit before he'd ended the song.

As the clapping died down, it had left its mark on Pete. He'd never been a more powerful performer as he bent his knees suggestively, thrust his hips forward, and lowered his eyelids provocatively as if seducing every woman in the audience. His lips practically caressed the mike.

"My God, he's got to remember that this is a family show," Tara whispered.

At the end of the song, the Opry crowd couldn't get enough of Pete Riddle. They stomped their booted feet, hollered themselves hoarse, whooped for more of the same, and yelled that Dixie had made a comeback.

Pete rushed to the wings where he gave Rosacoke a wild, wet, almost stinging kiss on the mouth. Tara, too, got a big slurpy one from him before he went back on stage for his first encore.

Rosacoke had to count them. Eight encores. Pete was drenched in sweat, but she knew he was experiencing the peak moment of his singing career. He'd never enjoyed such hysterical approval before. It took Roy Acuff to quiet the audience.

By the time Pete Riddle took his final curtain call, everybody in Nashville—both the fans and promoters—knew that a major star had been hatched.

"This night will go down in Opry history," a jubilant Larry rushed over to tell Rosacoke. "My boy's going places."

In her excitement and jubilation, Rosacoke was a little bit jealous of Larry. He could at least have said *our* boy. After all, Rosacoke had a stake in Pete Riddle, too.

She wiped that thought aside, as she joined the milling throngs to congratulate Pete. The only problem was, she couldn't get to him. Surrounded by well-wishers, he seemed lost to her somehow, and she became frustrated in her attempt to fight her way toward him. It made her wonder what his stardom would do to their marriage. It was as if he weren't her husband any more, but belonged to the world.

When she did break through the inner circle enveloping Pete, she was startled to see Buster on his left side and Tracy on the right. The two boys seemed to be virtually fighting over which of them could claim their daddy's attention. In their dueling, even Josh had been shoved aside.

***

After his success on the stage of the Grand Ole Opry, Pete returned to

Heaven on Earth with his brood for an old-fashioned Christmas. Josh sat beside Pete on the bus, assuming his usual protective position.

Pete was mildly surprised to see Rosacoke seated with and talking to Hank. Usually Larry insisted that Hank sit with him. Pete knew his marriage to Rosacoke had settled into the autumn of its year, and he suspected she might be having an affair. Surely not with Hank, he thought. The only other suspect was Claude, who spent more time with Rosacoke and was kinder to her than any other member of his gang.

Buster sat with Tara, and Tracy occupied a seat across from Josh and Pete. Pete's heart was saddened that Buster and Tracy from the very beginning had not gotten along. Tracy had made every overture to Buster, only to have his offer of friendship repeatedly rejected. Buster seemed to resent every moment that Tracy spent in Pete's company. At least in Buster's eyes, Tracy had become a major competitor for Pete's affection.

Of the two, and except for Tara, who remained steadfastly loyal to Buster, Tracy was everybody's favorite. The boy had the most outgoing personality in the household. He seemed to ingratiate himself with everybody, even Rosacoke, although he never loved her like he did Pete. He glowed in the love heaped on him by Tracy, and Pete did everything he could to avoid displaying too much affection for either boy when the brothers were together.

If Buster had his Tara, Tracy had his Wanda Mae. To Pete's amazement, Tracy had formed a close liaison with the most unlikely candidate at the compound, Wanda Mae. She was seeing more of Pete's boy than of her own husband, Ronnie.

Right after school and on holidays and weekends, Tracy spent all his spare time in Wanda Mae's dress emporium. She claimed that even though he was very young, Tracy was making an enormous creative contribution to her store's designs, accessories, and dress patterns. "He's going to be a top designer," Wanda Mae had predicted to Pete. "He has more talent and better taste than anyone I've ever known. And intuitively, almost at first sight, he really knows what people look good in." Both Tracy and Wanda Mae had once come to Pete asking him to stop buying his show business outfits in Shakerag. "You gotta look classy now that you're a big star," Wanda Mae had said.

"And sexier," Tracy had chimed in.

"Hell, if I wear my pants any tighter, they'll split," Pete had predicted.

"We'll see about that," Tracy had said enigmatically.

Pete was pleased that Wanda Mae had found some sort of companion. As for her marriage, she and Ronnie were still married, but they could easily have lived in different houses. Ronnie had told Pete that they slept in separate bedrooms and no longer had sex. "Not that we ever had that much sex in the first place," Ronnie had said.

"I guess Claude keeps you pretty content in that department," Pete had said. No sooner had he said that than he detected a flash of emotion on Ronnie's face, which he'd quickly concealed. There was something going on in Ronnie's life that Pete wasn't privy to. He figured that when Ronnie wanted to tell him exactly what it was, he would.

Arguments between Larry and Hank seemed to break out at any minute. In Nashville, they'd had a big fight in their bedroom, and the security guard had been called to break them up. Freddie had settled the dispute by renting a separate bedroom for Hank.

At a Nashville bar, following Pete's spectacular debut at the Grand Ole Opry, Larry and Hank had gotten into a violent, drunken argument, which Claude had broken up before it had erupted into a barroom brawl. Pete wasn't certain what kind of trouble was brewing between the two lovers, who had seemed to grow more contemptuous of each other every day. Without explaining why, Larry had announced to Pete that he no longer planned to invite Hank to go on the road with him.

Pete looked forward to celebrating Christmas with his brood, but feared it at the same time. This time of the year usually evoked sad memories of Christmases past, and often his buddies were irritable and morose, and in some cases, more than a bit bitter. Instead of a time of joy and celebration, Christmas stirred up long-suppressed tensions in virtually everyone at Heaven on Earth. If fights should break out among the members of his gang, Pete suspected he'd have to be the moderator.

When he entered the Big House, he was pleased to see that Tara, before going on the bus with them to Nashville, had asked the staff to decorate the mansion with holly. The Christmas tree Tara had selected was so tall she'd had to stand it in the foyer with its soaring ceiling, as it wouldn't fit into the living room. A mountain of presents was piled high around the tree. Rosacoke had flown to Charlotte with an unlimited expense account to buy costly presents for everybody. Gifts had also been flown in from Hollywood from Narcissa and her husband, Douglas Porter. That loving couple had been particularly generous to Tracy.

Pete had been disappointed not to find Karl at the main house waiting for him. He called him at his home at once. "I want us to have some time alone together tonight," Karl said. "I should have gone to Nashville with you, but I wasn't too happy sharing you with the rest of the world. I heard you over the radio, though. You are the world's most terrific singer, none better. I'm mighty proud of you."

"When can I see you, man?" Pete asked.

"After you tuck (or should I say 'fuck?') your brood in, come on over," Karl said in a soft voice. "I'm sitting here by the fire dreaming and thinking about you."

"You've got yourself a deal," Pete said,

Driving to Junior's airport apartment, Pete was anxious to catch up on news from John-John and Junior. Had a relationship developed between the two of them since their trip to California?

Maybe he was drunk, or maybe he was getting crazier than he ever was, but he paused at the top landing of Junior's apartment. A Santa's hat rested on the coat rack. He very quickly pulled off all his clothes and reached for the Santa's hat.

That hat was all he was wearing as he threw open the door to Junior's living room. "Surprise!" he yelled. "Merry Christmas. Santa's here."

*** 

Driving back to Heaven on Earth after his two social calls of the evening, Pete checked his watch. It was already four o'clock in the morning, and he knew Josh would be pissed off at him. He'd only barely managed to force himself out of Karl's warm bed to hit the road again.

He seemed to love Karl more and more each day. Pete had no business sense at all. Karl grew smarter with each passing month. Not only that, he was one of the most satisfying lovers. Pete was extremely flattered that Karl kept his loving for Pete and only Pete.

Karl was truly Pete's boy. That wasn't quite true. Karl was no boy. He'd developed into more of a man than anybody else at the compound. If Karl hadn't fallen under Pete's wing, he felt Karl could have flown high on his own. Pete's ass was still filled with Karl's heavy load of cum, and he wanted to keep it in there all night. Karl's kisses on his lips still tingled.

It had been a night of revelations. Junior and John-John were officially a couple, and had been ever since that night in Hollywood when Junior had gone backstage and asked John-John to go out with him.

After just a little bit of catch-up talk, it had become clear to Pete that Junior wanted John-John as a beautiful blonde show gal he could turn into, not the young man he actually was. Junior had fallen big for John-John as a gal, and he (or she) had promised not to appear in boy's clothing again.

Although happy for the couple, Pete was just a tiny bit jealous. At one time John-John had sworn that Pete would be the only man in his (or her) life. Now Junior seemed to be banging John-John's cute little butt daily and nightly.

At the party, John-John made it official. He wanted to be referred to as a female. John-John henceforth and forever more wanted to be called "Joni." After another bourbon, Pete had been willing to go along with anything.

As he was driving his Lincoln up to the doorway of Heaven on Earth, Pete figured the night had been too much for him. He had a lot of things to think about and to get clear in his head, especially his ongoing sexual in-

volvement with his son, Buster. To Pete's dismay, he found that all the lights downstairs were still on. Was Tara still up?

As he came into the foyer, he heard loud, angry voices coming from his library. Barging in, he found a room split with tension. There was an air of violence in the air. Claude, Ronnie, Hank, and Larry—drinks in hand— were having a major disagreement.

"I'm glad you're here," Claude said. "We've been playing musical chairs."

"What in hell does that mean?" Pete asked, looking into the face of each man and detecting anger.

"I've been keeping something from you," Larry said. "Something from Hank too. I've fallen in love with Ronnie."

Pete looked at Ronnie who got up and stood behind Larry's chair, as if presenting a united front.

"Wanda Mae will sure be glad to hear about that, I guess," Pete said, although he actually didn't know what to say.

"Wanda Mae doesn't give a God damn," Ronnie said. "Actually she'll be glad to hear I'm not getting fucked by her daddy no more."

"Is that the way it is, son?" Claude asked. "Me and you are no more."

"I never felt right about us," Ronnie said. "You are my father-in-law. That's not blood kin, but it was too close to incest for my taste. Larry's more my kind of guy. He makes me feel like some fucking Greek God. You never gushed over me the way Larry does."

"I'm so sorry I failed you," Claude said, looking dejected. "I think it's time I went to bed." Claude walked over and kissed Pete on the lips. "Merry Christmas, my good buddy." He turned and headed toward the door, but stopped suddenly and came back to Pete. He took Pete in his arms as he started to sob. "I love Ronnie. I still do. I can't help myself."

Ronnie walked over to him and touched Claude on the back. "I'm sorry," he said. "I didn't mean to fall in love with Larry. But the sex is so much better. That guy over there really swept me off my feet. I'm only made of flesh."

Claude stopped sobbing and released Pete to look at Ronnie. "I'm flesh too. I'll miss you."

"I'm still your son-in-law," Ronnie said. "I'll be around."

"I really feel awful about this," Larry said. "I didn't mean for it to happen."

"You two guys were really discreet," Pete said. "I thought you hardly knew each other."

"This is a big place around here," Larry said. "Lot of houses in the compound. Lots of secret meeting places." He walked over and put his arm around Ronnie. "Someone has got to tell Wanda Mae that whenever I'm home, her husband will be sleeping with me."

"Let Ronnie tell her himself," Claude said. "It's his decision." He turned and this time headed all the way outside the library and into the foyer.

"I think Ronnie and I had better turn in too," Larry said, kissing Pete on the lips.

Ronnie came up to Pete and kissed him on the lips too. "These things happen."

"Yeah," Pete said, watching them go. He turned to Hank, the only one left in the room. During all this interchange, Hank had not said one word.

"What does all this make me?" Hank asked. "Chopped liver? I used to be known as the sexiest boy in the county."

"You still are in my eyes," Pete said, going over to the sofa where he sat close to him, putting his arm around Hank. He was still an immensely sexy and attractive man, although in the past few months he'd begun to develop a beer gut. Pete didn't mind that. It only made him sexier in Pete's eyes.

"Something like this was in the cards," Pete said. "Larry and Ronnie. That was the last coupling I'd predict. Who can figure?"

"Right now my Christmas wish would be that Josh would fall for Claude and that you'd move me into that master bedroom."

"No can do," Pete said.

"Now that I don't have Larry's ass to pound, I want to be tearing into yours every chance we can sneak away," Hank said. "How about it?"

"From the first day I got to sample Hank Adams, I've been drooling ever since," Pete said.

"My ego needed to hear that tonight," Hank said. He placed Pete's hand between his crotch. "Something else needed to hear it too."

"Give me some real nigger-lipping," Pete said, falling into his arms. "Just like we used to do."

Later Pete slipped with Hank to one of the bedrooms on the third floor, that special one with its own little balcony overlooking the mountains.

"I'll sneak away up here to be with you any time I can," Pete promised.

"I'll be waiting for you," Hank said, holding Pete tightly in his arms and kissing him, followed by a tongue probe. When he pulled away, he said, "I wasn't in love with Larry anyway. The sex with him was okay but never as good as it is with you. I've never had sex with anybody as good as it is with you. You've made my life work."

"Let's stand out on the balcony for a little bit of fresh air," Pete said.

It was on that balcony, breathing the cleanest, coolest air Pete had ever experienced, that he noticed a look of grave concern on Hank's face.

"Now that Larry has dumped me," Hank said, "I don't feel I have to keep secrets no more."

"What secret?" Pete said, growing alarmed. "Larry's stealing part of the road show money?"

"Not that I know," Hank said. "I think he's honest about that. There's been something like a conspiracy going on around here. Me, Rosacoke, and Larry haven't told you the full story of our life together when you were in the Navy."

"Rosacoke too?" Pete asked.

"Yeah, Miss Pure Ivory Soap especially didn't want you to know what she was up to during those years away from you. There was quite a lot going on."

Since all the bedrooms at Heaven on Earth had had liquor bars installed, Pete went over and poured both Hank and himself another bourbon. "I want to be filled in. It's been a night of surprises for me. Why not some more? I'll look upon them as Pete Riddle's Christmas presents."

***

It was four o'clock in the morning when Rosacoke heard someone entering her quarters. At first she thought it might be a burglar until she flipped on the lamp on her nightstand, finding Pete standing at the foot of her bed, slowly unbuttoning his flannel shirt. It was obvious he was drunk.

"Why so startled?" he asked. "Anything wrong with a husband visiting his wife? Or do I still have conjugal rights?"

"You're always welcome in my bed," she said, throwing back the covers to reveal her nudity, hoping that in the dim light that would entice him all the more. "It's been a while."

"I've been busy," he said, pulling the tail of his shirt from his jeans and tossing it across the floor. Slowly and tantalizingly he began to unbuckle his thick leather belt.

There was something different about him tonight. She looked into his eyes and found lust there. Somehow she knew this wasn't going to be one of his quickies where he rushed out of her bathroom with a hard-on and mounted her. She caught her breath in anticipation as his gaze descended on her large breasts.

When he stripped completely nude, he fell on her, his smooth hands kneading her breasts and gently squeezing them into cones topped with a red cherry. A thrilling drum had started to pound inside her. She'd never known him to behave like this since her too brief honeymoon spent in motels driving back to Heaven on Earth. Her errant husband had returned to the marriage bed.

He raised himself up and kissed her gently, his kiss growing more intense the longer he lingered at her lips. As he inserted his tongue for her to suck, her body tingled with excitement. Reaching below, she stroked his

rock-hard penis, amazed at the fullness of it. With her free hand, she massaged his broad chest.

Unexpectedly, he broke from her and reared up over her face, dropping his large balls onto her mouth for her to lubricate. She'd never been a true devotee of the art of licking men's balls or their assholes. Her pleasure in that pursuit came in knowing how much those sexual acts pleased a man.

When he'd had enough of her licking, he raised up and reached for his cock, guiding it to her lips. "Suck it, woman," he ordered. It loomed awesomely big tonight and she was hesitant at first. She opened her mouth to his immediate invasion. He pushed in too fast before she'd fully adjusted to the size of him. She choked and sputtered but he was unrelenting. "Fucking women," he said in a drunken slur. "They'll never learn how to suck a man's dick."

Facing his daunting challenge, she sucked ferociously. Up and down the veined penis she went, hoping to bring him satisfaction. He pumped his hips against her quivering face.

To her astonishment, she felt a hot tongue kissing her thighs. It couldn't be Pete. His head was up in the air over her as he pumped himself into her mouth. Someone else had come into her bedroom. Their privacy had been invaded by an intruder.

At first she'd started to protest but the words trying to come out of her throat were blocked as he probed deeper, entering her throat for the first time and causing her to choke. He seemed to deliberately hold her in that clutch even though she was desperate to breath.

"Go to it, Hank," she heard him whisper seductively to the intruder.

She felt Hank's tongue dip through her blonde hairs as his mouth descended on her. He began a tantalizing probe with his talented tongue, which had entered her so many times during those bleak road trips with him. Her eyes tightly shut, she moaned at this new invasion.

Hank buried his face in her, lapping inside and out. Other men had done this to her but no one as skilled as Hank. As waves of ecstasy poured over her, she licked and sucked Pete all the harder, as Hank brought an almost unendurable thrill racing through her entire body.

Without being told, she just knew that Hank had informed Pete of her former affair with him. Maybe Hank had even told Pete about her being sent up to Mozambique. But she could hardly worry about a prison record right now.

Hank was dangerously near bringing her to a climax, and she felt Pete's own excitement mounting. Instead of feeling that she had been set upon and raped by these two men, she was the willing victim.

With his lips and tongue, Hank brought her to a spectacular climax, as Pete too exploded in her mouth. She swallowed every drop and wanted more of him.

Like the director of a motion picture, Pete was clearly in charge. She didn't object as Pete ordered Hank to drop his own balls into her mouth. As he did that, Pete skinned back the foreskin of Hank's cock and sucked him just as voraciously as she'd sucked her husband. Pete even taught her how to share the cock. He'd let her suck Hank as he slurped at his balls, and then Pete would take command of the cock again, deep-throating it far better than she ever could.

Lost in a forbidden world, she was no longer resisting but was caught up in Pete's enticing commands. His face over hers, he grinned at her as he penetrated her. She spread her legs wider to accommodate his entry. "Hank's got you all hot and moist," he said. Her legs quivered as he held her in an iron grip. She moaned, tossing her head from left to right as he split her wide open. Her juices flowing, she moved to accommodate his every thrust until he hit bottom, his balls falling across her crotch.

Suddenly Pete reared up, his face racked with pain. She knew that he too was being penetrated as deeply as she was. Hank had mounted Pete and had thrust himself inside without preparation. Pete screamed out in pain at the sudden attack. But within minutes he adjusted to it. If anything, the feel of Hank inside him spurred Pete to even greater thrusting into her. Her first orgasm hit without warning, as she shook with a kind of convulsive thrashing. Pete grinned in her face again, as she felt her cunt clasp around him, holding him in a tight lock until she knew that she'd drained every drop out of him.

As Hank cried out, she knew he was erupting mightily into her husband, the way he used to do in those motel rooms with her.

By six o'clock when both men had left her pre-dawn bedroom, it was the grin on Pete's face that she would remember. That grin told her that Pete knew what he'd done to her.

It was as if he'd looked into some dark region of her heart and found a secret there that she'd never been able to really admit to herself.

He'd seen the whore who dwelled in that dark chamber and had unleashed it tonight. That whore was now free to emerge from darkness. She had come out into the light.

The men had left her totally satisfied and panting on her bed, not knowing how at dawn she could live with the woman who had been liberated in her bedroom tonight.

***

It was one o'clock the following afternoon when Josh finally nudged Pete. "It's practically Christmas," he said. "Aren't you ever gonna wake

up?"

Pete sleepily rolled over in bed. "Morning, baby boy of mine."

"I don't know when you came in from Junior's party," Josh said. "Usually I wake up. But not last night. I was exhausted." He rose from the bed nude with a morning erection. "C'mon and join me in the shower. I want to bathe you."

With a splitting headache, Pete sat up slowly in bed as a flood of memories from last night came rushing like so much raging water through his brain. It was just as well that Josh didn't know what happened last night.

Later, over breakfast Tara told Pete the news. Without warning, Rosacoke had taken one of the cars and headed for the Charlotte Airport.

"Did she say where she was going?" Pete asked, looking guiltily at Josh to see if he were suspicious. Eating his grits and ham, his face indicated that he wasn't.

"She's on her way to Los Angeles right now," Tara said, pouring Pete more coffee.

He reached over and kissed Josh on the mouth. "We'll have to celebrate Christmas without her." He smiled into Josh's eyes.

***

Rosacoke wasn't due into Los Angeles for two days. When she called Douglas Porter from the Los Angeles airport, he wasn't ready to have her come to the house because Narcissa was still there, getting ready for her New York appearance at the patrician Carlyle Hotel.

He said he'd call and reserve a room for her at the Beverly Hills Hotel until it was safe to move in with him at Narcissa's mansion. Disappointed, she thought Narcissa had already flown to New York. She told Douglas that she'd make her own sleeping arrangements and would call him that night. He was very apologetic and claimed that he was "counting the minutes" before she was in his arms again.

Just on an impulse, she also called Pete's record producer at MGM, Frank Walker. As the months had gone by, she'd kept hoping that he might make some record deal for her too. Since "Lonesome Blues," he'd also recorded two more hits for Pete. Written by Josh, both of these songs didn't do as well as "Lonesome Blues," but no one expected them to top that long-ago plagiarized song written by Ukulele Dick, who was being richly rewarded for his effort back in the 20s. Larry mailed him secret royalty checks every month.

When she called Frank's office, the producer's secretary put her through right away to the big man himself. Rosacoke had called Frank several times from the Carolinas but could never get through to him before. Sounding

eager for news of her, he came on the phone at once. "I've been worried to death about you," he said. "Pete has been calling my office frantically. Thank God you had the sense to call me. Are you okay?"

"Just fine," she said. "Fit as a fiddle. I was always planning to fly out here eventually. I just decided to speed up things a bit."

"Come by my office at ten o'clock in the morning," he said. "We'll talk about giving that career of yours a jump-start. I admit to neglecting you, but Pete told me this morning that if I don't light your fire, he's going to drop me. I don't know what's happened between the two of you, but my favorite hillbilly sounded like he meant it."

"Glad to hear you're gonna put the torch to my ass," she said. "If I wait around much longer, I'll be known as Grandma Carson before I make my debut at the Grand Ole Opry."

"You gotta call Pete right away," he said. "He's worried out of his mind."

During her call to Pete at Heaven on Earth, neither of them mentioned their three-way with Hank. It was as if it had never happened. He invited her to stay at the apartment he'd recently rented in Santa Monica. She gladly accepted, wished him a Merry Christmas, sent her love to Tracy and Buster, and then hung up the phone.

***

In the privacy of his suite, Buster unbuttoned Pete's shirt. "Sucking you off will be a good appetizer leading to an even bigger dinner."

"What kind of talk is that?" Pete asked, not resisting as Buster unfastened his shirt.

"I'll suck the cum out of you all right," Buster said. "Guess what? I'm starting to cum too these days. It just happened a week ago. I'm old enough. No more jerking off for me. I want you to suck my dick like I suck yours. I want to cum in your mouth."

"No way," Pete said. "Forget it." Buster reached for Pete's belt buckle to unfasten it before placing his hand on Pete's fly, feeling his crotch. He tried to will his hard-on to go limp, but Buster's skilled fingers reached inside, and Pete's prick responded to those fingers, not to what he was trying to tell his brain.

When Buster had undressed him, Pete lay back on the bed as his son pulled off his boots and freed his jeans. Except for his socks, Pete was completely naked as his dick, seemingly with a will of its own, soared toward the ceiling, and it was a very tall ceiling.

Buster reached into the drawer of his nightstand and removed some object. At first Pete didn't know what it was. Buster held it up for Pete to inspect.

He was startled. It was a black dildo nearly a foot long. "I bought this in Shakerag. It was modeled from real life. It seems that Herb Hester's wife, Medora, had it modeled from real life by Sultan. She used it on herself when the real thing wasn't available. Or when Herb was back from one of his bootleg trips."

"What in the fuck are you doing with that?"

"I've been using it on myself," Buster said. "Call it stretching exercises. I can't take the whole God damn thing, but I can gently get half of it up my tight butt." He leaned down and succulently kissed Pete's lips. "Night after night I've eased this dildo up my ass, imagining it was you. I'm ready to take you on now. I want to be royally fucked."

Before Pete could answer, Buster had descended on his cock, polishing and kissing it and sending an incredible wave of ecstasy through Pete. Maybe it was the marvelous sensations going through his body, or else too much bourbon, but Pete could not resist the temptation.

He closed his eyes as Buster applied Vaseline on himself and rubbed it along Pete's towering cock. With his eyes closed, Pete still lay on his back as Buster slowly—ever so slowly—placed Pete's cock between the lips of his asshole. He felt him breaking through. He couldn't believe that Buster had managed to get the entire head in.

Pete wanted more.

He'd never had such a tight sensation around his cock before. Buster was bringing him into a world of passion and lust unlike he'd ever known before. In some dark corner of his brain, the thought that this was a forbidden act made the love-making all the more enticing.

When Buster had impaled himself on Pete's cock, with at least half of it going up inside him, Pete took charge. Without dismounting, he gently turned Buster over onto his back and towered over him. The look in Buster's eyes was one of total victory over his daddy.

As Pete moved deeper and deeper into Buster, wanting to insert those final inches, he could tell that Buster was in obvious pain but not wanting Pete to withdraw. The kid's own rock-hard cock, sticking up a good five inches, told Pete that his son was enjoying this maybe even more than he was.

His juices near the boiling point, Pete plunged inside, thrusting furiously, as Buster reared up to take his offering. Pete's mind was reeling with this depravity which he knew was wrong but which was utterly irresistible to him. His hot balls churning, he thrusted hard and deep. The look of pain had faded from Buster's face. He'd entered a state of rapture, as Pete fell down on him, biting his neck real hard.

When Buster's delicate, skilled hands started playing with his balls, Pete could no longer hold back. His whole body seemed to convulse into a searing pleasure. "Take it boy," he whispered into Buster's ear before his

tongue bathed that ear. He could feel his balls pull up as he disgorged his sweet juice into the trembling boy.

"Daddy, fuck me, fuck me!" Buster shouted into Pete's ear, as Pete exploded.

He didn't know how long he stayed inside Buster after his peak had passed. Although his cock had lost its rock hardness, he remained embedded inside his son, as Buster licked his face and sucked his tongue.

"My dick has found a new home," Pete whispered to Buster. "It feels too good. You know I'll want it again and again. I'll never get enough of that hot ass." As he talked to Buster, Pete felt himself hardening again. His next fuck took twice as long and was even more enjoyable than the first.

When Pete finally pulled out and lay panting on the bed, his eyes shut, he opened them to see Buster straddling his face.

"You're not gonna get off that easy," Buster said.

Pete opened his mouth wide, swallowing his son's balls in one gulp.

*** 

In Pete's apartment, Rosacoke, as was her custom, got out of bed before dawn and drove to the beach at Santa Monica. Taking off her shoes, she walked alone on the beach, enjoying the feel of sand under her. It sure beat that red clay of North Carolina.

In her sleep last night, a song had occurred to her. The words formed quickly on her lips. She called it "Honky Tonk Angel," and it told of the story of how a lonely girl singer, much like herself, worked the "tonks" of the South in her search for love.

The song had been writing itself inside her head for a long time, and she didn't even know it. It was related to some of her earlier songs, which contained vague hints of a woman's rebellion. The message of "Honky Tonk Angel" wasn't subtle, though. The lyrics blatantly suggested that a woman had every right to cheat as much as a man. It deplored the double standard in American life and suggested that a woman—just like a man—could be as good or as bad as she cared to be.

Standing in front of the Pacific Ocean, Rosacoke sang the words to the sea as she walked deeper into the water, the early morning waves washing up on her legs. She sang louder than she ever had before, wanting the whole world to hear her. The sound of the ocean waves drowned her out.

Back at the apartment, and filled with enthusiasm, she impulsively called Tara at Heaven on Earth. "Morning, hoss," she said. "I'm a little hung over. Got so desperate for a man last night I called Smokey Wetter and had him fuck me all night. He's not bad. But don't believe that shit about all black men having big dicks. Smokey sure knows what to do with what he's

got, though."

After inquiring about Pete, Buster, and Tracy, Rosacoke told Tara that she wanted to sing a song for her. Without any musical backup, Rosacoke sang "Honky Tonk Angel" over the phone. There was a long silence on the other end of the phone.

"Hot damn," Tara finally said. "That song might do for you what 'Lonesome Blues' did for Pete. It's a hell of a song, and I sure agree with its sentiments. Hold it a minute, hoss." Tara put down the phone. When she came back, she seemed to have picked up a guitar. "Sing it to me again, hoss, and I'll play my guitar."

"You've done it," Tara said at the end of the song. "It needs work, but you've got a winner." She paused. "Claude's come back to see what all the commotion is about. Sing it for him too."

"How you doin' out there in Los Angeles?" Claude asked her. "We sure miss you around here. Want me to fly out to take care of you?"

"That would be nice," Rosacoke said, "but right now I want you to hear my song." She sang "Honky Tonk Angel" for Claude. At the end of her song, he, like Tara, didn't say anything at first, and she feared that he didn't like it. After all, it was a song that appealed more to women than to men.

"That's hot!" Claude shouted at her. "I just threw my hat into the air."

Tara took the phone again, saying that she'd talk to Pete. "You need some fiery red honky-tonk instrumentation, and our boys are just the ones to give it to you. Pete and Larry are tied up on a project, but I'm sure they'll agree to fly out the rest of the gang to the coast to work with you on it. Nipsey and Freddie, I know, will want to go. Since I discovered the sexual charms of ole Smokey, I have his nights fully booked up—and he's a mean fucker—but out of love for you, I'll release him."

"Bring everybody out here to California," Rosacoke said. "We'll go into rehearsal. I don't need Larry. I'll pitch the song to Frank Walker this morning."

Before ringing off, Tara said, "Hoss, I always knew you were a 'Honky Tonk Angel.'"

Later that morning at Frank's office, Rosacoke came in with her guitar and sang to Frank. His keen ear immediately recognized the possibilities of the song, and he told her he'd arrange for their use of a studio where they could practice and then record the song when her musicians flew in from the Carolina hills.

Driving back to Pete's apartment, she called Douglas on his private line but there was no answer. Apparently, Narcissa was flying to New York today. Perhaps he'd taken her to the airport. Rosacoke couldn't wait for the hours to go by until she'd be in Douglas' arms again.

At Narcissa's mansion, five hours later, Rosacoke rose from the king-sized bed her friend usually shared with her husband. Doug was still asleep

and little wonder. He'd been so starved for her body that he'd had three climaxes before he was completely satisfied. Her breasts felt as if they'd been a Sunday dinner for him. He couldn't get enough of them, and constantly marveled at their size, although she'd learned that he'd tasted the breasts of some of the grandest goddesses in Hollywood.

After a quick shower, she put on a robe and tiptoed back into the bedroom. Doug was still asleep. Instead of an eminent and prestigious plastic surgeon, he looked very much like a macho version of a high school student. In sleep he appeared so delectable she wanted to take off her robe and join him.

That plan was interrupted by a knock on the door. She opened it to find the maid. "Tell Dr. Porter his patient is here."

The knock awoke Doug. "Show her in and give her a drink." The maid said she would and shut the door. Stark nude, Doug rose from the bed, still at half mast. "Rosacoke, you go entertain her. She hates to be kept waiting. Tell her I'll be in in a few minutes. I've got to shower."

"Who is it I'm supposed to entertain?" Rosacoke asked. "In my robe?"

"Go on, baby," he said. "Do it for me. I don't have to tell you who it is. You'll know."

Blindly obeying, Rosacoke headed for the living room. As she came in, all she saw was a black hat emerging from the sofa. The woman's back was to Rosacoke.

She walked around and greeted Doug's guest. She was startled to discover it was Marlene Dietrich, even if she wore a black veil under that wide-brimmed hat. She was attired in a black skirt and jacket with shiny black patent leather boots.

"Who might you be?" came the unmistakable voice of Dietrich.

"Hi, I'm Rosacoke Carson, a friend of Doug's."

"You must be a friend," Dietrich said. "Certainly not a patient. "You don't look like you need plastic surgery. Perhaps breast reduction."

"Actually I'm more a friend of Narcissa Cash. We grew up together in the Carolina hills."

"You certainly don't look black to me."

"I'm as white as white bread but my mama got involved with Narcissa's daddy."

"I know of such things," Dietrich said. "I've read of the decadence of the Old South. Incest, rape, lynchings, stuff like that."

"We're bad but not all that bad."

"And who exactly are you, other than a provider of entertainment to Doug while Narcissa is in New York?"

"I'm a country singer." she said. "I'm also the wife of Pete Riddle. He's signed with MGM records. He had a big hit with 'Lonesome Blues.'"

"'Lonesome Blues,'" she said, seeming to mull that over. "The story of

my life."

***

With "Honky Tonk Angel" a wrap, Rosacoke flew back to Nashville with Maston Mastin, Guitar Red, and Smokey Wetter. Frank Walker had promised he'd go all out to promote the record and had signed her to an MGM record contract whose terms almost matched those of Pete's. She'd also done it without Larry, and she felt good about her career. At last it was going forward after so many long delays.

It had been all she could do to raise herself from Doug's bed and his strong, comforting arms to get on that plane. She was deeply in love with him. It was her first genuine love affair.

With deep regret, she realized that her marriage to Pete had never been a true love affair. She desired him sexually on the rare occasion he would visit her bed. In contrast Doug made her feel total and complete. A real woman. When she was having sex with Pete, she suspected that he was thinking of Josh while he reluctantly pounded her. It was as if sex with her were a duty, not a pleasure.

She learned that Pete, in honor of Buster's birthday and as a means of nurturing his budding talent, had decided to feature him as an important talent in his own right. Within Pete's Nashville recording studio—in full rhinestone-covered cowboy costume—Buster was scheduled to record a trio of songs. Music and lyrics for all three had been written by Josh.

As always, Karl had remained at Heaven on Earth along with Tara to take care of business, and Buster had specifically requested that Tracy stay with Wanda Mae, and not come to Nashville with them. Tara said Buster had told her that he didn't want his "birthday spoiled with that Tracy tagging along."

Rosacoke had brought expensive gifts for Buster from Hollywood, hoping to win his love with presents. She was eager to share in the celebration of his birthday and to hear the music he was recording. The part she dreaded involved a reunion with Pete to see what remained of their relationship.

As the plane neared the airport at Nashville, Rosacoke thought that there must be some song she could write that would help her sort out her tangled life, or at least put it to music. Maybe writing a song would clear her head. As the plane bumped along the runway, she was completely muddled, except for one thing. She wasn't going to let Pete know she was in love with Douglas Porter.

As she came down the plane's exit ramp, she spotted the kind face of Claude, waiting for her. She ran up to him and kissed him on the cheek. He held her a little longer than usual.

With the black musicians in the back seat of her white Cadillac, Claude drove them to the Tulane Hotel. He told her he'd pick her up in an hour after he deposited "the boys" at their own hotel across town. She thanked all three musicians for all their hard work on "Honky Tonk Angel" and impulsively gave Claude a light kiss on the lips.

As she headed into the lobby of the hotel with two bellmen carrying her luggage, there was a lingering sensation of Claude's lips on hers. "God damn," she thought, "I might as well keep the door to my bedroom open and solicit all the men who walk by. I'm turning into a slut who's making up for lost time."

In some strange way, recording "Honky Tonk Angel" seemed to have freed her from her remaining inhibitions. Once again, she entertained the possibility of going to bed with Claude. That little stolen kiss had set her on fire. "You sure are in love with Doug," she told herself. "You've hardly left his bed, and here you are thinking about another man."

Rosacoke thought that Pete and Buster were at the recording studio, so she was pleased to learn from the handsome young clerk that they had come back to the hotel to rest for an hour or two. "I personally showed them up to Buster's room," the clerk told her. "Room 201."

"I've got an idea," Rosacoke said. "I've got all these presents for my son. Don't call their room to let them know I'm here. I'll just barge in on them and yell 'Surprise.'"

"They'll love that," the clerk said.

"If you'll help me with the presents, there's a ten in it for you," she said.

"Hot damn," the clerk said.

On the second floor, the clerk gently opened the door to Buster's room. Rosacoke silently directed him to place her luggage and packages inside the living room of a suite. When that was done, Rosacoke tipped him quietly, directed him out of the suite, and then noiselessly shut the door.

To her surprise, there was no light on. Pete and Buster must be sleeping. In the dim light she surveyed the ruins of what looked like a wild party—overflowing ashtrays, empty bourbon bottles, and fizzled-out beer. She decided she'd let them sleep some more before waking them up.

Sounds were coming from the bedroom. They were already awake. She tiptoed over to the half-opened door. The bedroom was pitch black. Pete always did like to sleep in complete and total darkness, with heavy draperies keeping out even one ray of light.

The sounds greeting her were those of a couple making love. They were the same sounds she'd made herself when Doug was plowing into her. How could this be? She pushed open the door and could vaguely make out two figures bounding up and down on the bed in the throes of passion.

She switched on the overhead chandelier. To her horror, she saw a

nude Pete fucking her son.

"Oh, shit!" Pete cried out when seeing who it was. He pulled his cock out of Buster who lay under him. It looked like some obscene, grotesque appendage.

She ran from the sight back into the living room where her tears blinded her. Still naked, Pete darted into the room, reaching out for her. She shoved him away.

"It's okay, baby," he said. "You've got to understand. Buster has this special thing for me."

She turned to confront him. "I could accept all your shit up to now. But not this, Pete Riddle. You're sick, and I want no part of this."

She turned away from Pete as Buster came and stood at the entrance to the bedroom door, staring into the living room. He too was nude. Her eyes tried to avoid the sight but she could not help but notice that, unlike Pete, his little boy cock was still fully hard.

She didn't know what to say to him at first until she blurted out, "Did he force you to do this?"

"Hell, no," Buster said in a voice more commanding than she'd ever heard before. "I forced him into it."

"I may go to the police," Rosacoke threatened, although she had no intention of doing that. It could ruin all of their lives, including Buster's.

"You do anything to come between Pete and me, and I'll kill myself," Buster said. He looked at her with such fierce determination that she believed that he actually would. "Pete is my life," he said. "He didn't want to have sex with me. I made him. I warned him what I'd do to myself if he didn't give in to me. I can't help feeling the way I do. I'm warning you one more time. Just do one thing to mess up what me and Pete have going, and you'll regret it for the rest of your life."

She believed that. With her tears still falling, she kicked at one of the presents on the floor. "Happy birthday," she said. In a blind rage, she ran out the door and into the hallway.

At first she didn't know where she was. Spotting the elevator, she stumbled toward it and pressed the button. When it stopped, she got on. A man and woman, already aboard, stared at her strangely.

She didn't care how she looked or what they thought of her. They backed away from her as if she was deranged.

Her face was streaked with tears and dissolving makeup by the time the elevator reached the lobby. Half-demented, she raced toward the front of the hotel. Fortunately, Claude had come back earlier than he said he would.

Seeing him through her heavily lidded eyes, she stumbled toward the white Cadillac that would take her far, far from this hotel.

Within moments, she felt Claude's strong embrace. She melted into

him, losing herself.

***

As Claude drove her white Cadillac toward the North Carolina state line, Rosacoke sat in the front seat, occasionally breaking into sobs. She felt that she'd carry the image of Pete fucking his own son in the darkest recesses of her memory for as long as she lived.

Claude extended his broad hand every now and then. She found his presence very consoling. Although she wanted to be in the arms of Doug right now, turning to him to comfort her, she found Claude a very good substitute. "I don't have to tell you what I found out at the Tulane Hotel, do I?" she asked.

"Spare yourself," he said. "Everybody at Heaven on Earth knows what's going on. Maybe Josh doesn't, but I bet he suspects."

"How do you guys handle it?" she asked.

"No one likes it," Claude said, "but Pete is cock of the roost. All of us are beholdin' to him." He's got lovin' in his blood. That's all I can say."

"So what you're telling me is that everybody, even Tara, is prepared to live with this thing. This creepy thing between a daddy and his boy."

"I'd be lying if I said we weren't," he said. "The way I look at it, this is private business between Pete and Buster. I don't like it but then I ain't got a perfect record in love either."

A distant look came across his face as he kept his eyes glued on the road, not glancing over at her. "There are some things a man likes to keep private."

During the next half-hour the drive was in silence. At a roadside stop, he pulled the Cadillac to the side of the highway, bringing it to a complete halt. For the first time in an hour, he looked intently into her eyes. "I've got something I have to talk over with you. I mean, it's been eating at me."

He reached over and kissed her on the mouth. "I'm in love with you. Have been for a long time. But I didn't want to hit on you so strong when you were Pete's wife. I know you're going to break from him, and I want to take up with you myself."

She jerked back, startled at this confession. She felt very close to him, but still regarded him as a supportive friend. "I don't know…." She tried to formulate words since his eyes told her he was demanding an answer. "I don't know what to say. After all I've been through today, this comes as a big surprise."

"You know you love me," he said, reaching out and placing a firm grip on her arm. "You're not woman enough to admit it."

She resented that. "I like you a lot. As a friend. I'm in love with

someone else."

He looked her squarely in the eye. "You're lying to me. I think you've got feelings for me, and you're making up this shit about loving someone else. Who is he? Pete Riddle. *Still?*"

"I will always love Pete," she said, "but I'm gonna divorce him. It's someone else. I can't talk about it." She avoided eye contact with him. The way he looked at her was too intense. "We'd better be heading on up the road."

He reached over again and planted another kiss on her lips before starting the motor. To the open road that stretched before him, he said, "I'm gonna get you yet."

She finally made eye contact with him. He had the saddest gray eyes she'd ever seen. The hangdog expression on his face convinced her that he really did love her.

A sense of foreboding came over her. For a brief moment she wanted to urge Claude to turn around and head back to Nashville and the Tulane Hotel where she planned to pick up Buster. Even as she thought that, she realized how dumb it was. Buster didn't want to be rescued by her.

Faced with an exploding dream, she felt like she was suffocating in the car. Her marriage was coming to an end. She'd lost Pete, not to another woman, but to her own son. She was in love with the husband of Narcissa who, for better or worse, had practically been a sister to her. She'd just learned that one of Pete's former (or present?) lovers, Claude himself, loved her too. For all she knew, Claude still loved Ronnie and was turning to her just for consolation after he too had been rejected in love. Nothing made sense to her.

She could never be certain what happened next. Her brain seemed caught in some whirlpool, spinning out of control. On an impulse, not really knowing or thinking what she was doing, she threw open the passenger door and hurled herself out of the car, which was going forty miles an hour along a mountain road.

Her eyes tightly closed, she felt like she was tossing herself into some unknown pit. She didn't mean to kill herself. Actually she didn't know what she meant or why she'd opened that door. She heard her own piercing scream as if it were some distant echo, not really coming from her own chest. The sound of her own voice stabbed at her heart. It was a call for help. She tumbled along an embankment, falling into a massive pile of leaves. She collapsed in a gutter, as she heard the sound of Claude's screeching brakes.

Amazingly, she felt no pain at first, even when she'd hit the ground. It was as if she'd fallen in a slow, graceful movement. The sound of booted feet scurrying down the embankment resounded in her ears. Claude was rushing toward her. Still she felt no pain, even though she knew she'd hit a

rock or two in her leap from the Cadillac.

Sobbing, she rolled over on her side, as Claude's arms reached out for her. It was then that she felt the first stabs of pain shooting through her body. At first a dull ache, the pain exploded finally into little electric pinpoints. Her head had struck a rock, and she could taste her own blood. She was still alive, but a black cloud was moving in on her like a summer storm. She closed her eyes and passed into oblivion.

When she came to, she looked around a strange room, finding herself in a bleak tourist cabin. Claude came into her room from the outside, carrying a bucket of ice.

Seeing that she was awake, he sat on the bed beside her, holding her hand, his look so concerned that it appeared that the blood had been drained from his face.

"I had a country doctor here," he said in a soothing voice. "He patched you up a bit. Gave you a shot of something." He felt her forehead. "You okay?"

"A little battered," she said weakly. "I feel bruised as hell. But I'll be fine."

"It's all my fault," he said. "You've been through too much. The breakup with Pete. Finding out all that shit about Buster. All you needed was for me to hit on you too."

"I have to have time to sort things out," she said.

That night after he'd fed her some okra gumbo, he turned off the light and got into the bed adjoining hers. Getting up suddenly, he came over and bent down over her, giving her a gentle, sweet kiss.

In a few minutes she heard the sound of his heavy breathing. In spite of what had happened that day, he'd fallen into a peaceful sleep.

She envied him that rest. Sleep would not come to her. Her eyes popped open and wouldn't shut. But by about three o'clock, she too fell into a coma.

When she woke up, it was morning. She looked at the empty bed beside her. The sound of the shower running in the bathroom could be heard. Favoring her bruised side, she turned over in bed. It was painful, and she hurt all over.

When he came out of the bathroom he had put on a pair of clean underwear.

"Just think," he said, "we slept in the same bedroom together. A first for us. I hope it won't be the last time."

"We'll see," she said. If she thought jumping out of that car would straighten out her mind, she was sadly mistaken. Without exactly meaning to, she kept glancing at his underwear, a pair of white boxer shorts that revealed nothing.

He sensed where she was looking. "Listen, I'm no Pete Riddle. But if

you'd like an average man to make love to you, here he is."

As he moved toward her bed, the phone rang. She picked it up, finding Tara on the other end of the line.

"How did you know I was here?" Rosacoke asked.

"Claude called last night to let me know you were okay," Tara said. "Are you okay, hoss?"

"I'm fine," she said. "We're heading back this morning. Has Pete called?"

"Not a word," she said. "Buster calls every day but he didn't call yesterday. I guess he got carried away on his birthday. They invited me but I caught the God damn flu."

"I'll make you some chicken soup when I get there," Rosacoke said.

"Hoss, big news," Tara said. "I mean *big* news. Frank Walker called. Hollywood, CA. Can you believe it? He didn't want to speak to Mr. 'Lonesome Blues.' He wanted you. He's booked you on the Arthur Godfrey Talent Scouts. Two days from now. Frank wants you to introduce 'Honky Tonk Angel' to America on the Godfrey show."

In her excitement, Rosacoke practically screamed to Claude. "I'm gonna be on Arthur Godfrey."

Junior has already booked you two air tickets to New York," Tara said. "We figured Claude had better go with you as a bodyguard. All those black bucks up there in New York will take one look at a blonde-haired woman with big tits, and you're likely to get a lot of dick stuffed up you."

After a few more words to Tara, Rosacoke told her goodbye and put down the phone. In the past she would have wanted to call Pete and share the good news with him. But when Claude had kissed her and had wished her luck, and when he'd gone down to a café to get them some breakfast, she dialed Douglas Porter in Beverly Hills, forgetting the time difference.

She was startled to hear the unmistakable voice of Dietrich on the phone. Not even identifying herself, Rosacoke asked to speak to Doug. When a sleepy sounding Doug came on the phone, she practically shouted at him. "I'm gonna be on the Godfrey show. I'm gonna be famous."

He congratulated her, but there was little enthusiasm in his voice.

"What's Dietrich doing in your bedroom?"

"She's had the operation, and is staying here with me in case any problems come up."

"I don't know," Rosacoke said. "With Dietrich, something is likely to come up."

"No, no," he assured her, "we've passed on from that."

"Glad to hear it," she said.

"I'll tell Narcissa you're flying to New York," Doug said. "Maybe I'll fly in too and we can go hear her at the Carlyle."

"That would be nice," Rosacoke said, barely concealing the disappoint-

ment in her voice. She'd wanted a more intimate conversation with Doug, but she figured that because Dietrich was in the room with him, he was guarding his words.

"Love you, guy," she said. "I'll call you every day."

***

"New York City," Rosacoke said, hugging Claude's arm as their plane landed at Idlewild Airport. "Is it the Sodom in the Bible? Or Gomorrah?"

"Pretty near both," he said, kissing her on the nose to give her confidence. "I was there only once. Did I ever have a wild time."

She pretended a look of reprimand. "I'm jealous."

He looked surprised. "That's the most encouraging word I've heard from you to date."

As the plane bumped along the landing strip, she was sorry she'd flirted like that. She had probably given him the wrong impression. She was in love with Doug, not Claude, and certainly not with Pete any more.

That concern was forgotten as she reclaimed her luggage with Claude. He hailed a taxi. When the fat cabbie wanted to know where to take them, Claude looked puzzled. "The Dixie Hotel. It's somewhere near Times Square. I've stayed there before. Didn't have much money in those days."

"Yeah, tell me about it," the driver said, taking off and dodging traffic so rapidly it made Rosacoke nervous. She wasn't used to all these people and all these cars. New York made Los Angeles look like a small town.

She didn't want Claude to think she was coming on to him, but she nervously reached for the comfort of his broad hand. "This is not some rowdy tonk in the Bayou country," she said. "This is big-time. Godfrey himself. *The* Arthur Godfrey. I'm scared. Really scared."

"Just keep that honky-tonk angel sound you've got, and you'll go over big."

At the seedy Dixie Hotel, the price was right, only twelve dollars for a room. With all Pete's money, Rosacoke felt that Claude could have booked her into better quarters. But she'd stayed in far worse places than this rattrap. Claude rented two single rooms for them. A big, noisy group from Alabama had also booked most of the rooms on their floor. Perhaps they too had been lured to the hotel because of its name, Dixie. At least she was among people she knew. Southerners.

Her nerves still jittery, she checked into her room, agreeing to meet Claude downstairs in the bar in an hour. After a quick shower, she called Doug at his secret number in Beverly Hills but there was no answer. She placed another call to Tara at Heaven on Earth to let her know she'd arrived safely with Claude. After a brief catch-up talk, Tara said, "Hoss, there's someone here who wants to speak to you."

To her surprise, Pete came onto the phone. No mention was made of that scene at the Tulane Hotel where she'd caught him fucking Buster. "Good luck on the Godfrey show," he said. "All of us back home will be watching you and cheering you on. The song is great. We play it here all the time. I think it's gonna put you over the top."

"I'm on pins and needles," she said. "National television, no less."

"People will love you," he said reassuringly. Be yourself. Gotta go now, hon. I'm wanted on another line. Remember, little darling, we'll be watching."

"Pete…." The line went dead.

Before meeting with Claude, Rosacoke called Narcissa at the Carlyle. She wasn't in her suite so Rosacoke left a message for her.

After a fast bourbon in the derelict bar downstairs, Claude hailed another taxi to take them to CBS Studio on Broadway, her first glance at that fabled street. She wasn't impressed at all. The whole street looked tacky and commercial. Somehow, she had always thought that Broadway would be all glamorous lights and show biz glitter. It was far from that.

In the studio, she was introduced to Barbara Garfunkel, Arthur Godfrey's manager. Right away Barbara wanted her to sing "Honky Tonk Angel." Fortunately Rosacoke had brought along her guitar. She never liked to sing without music.

At the end of the song, Barbara said, "That's very good. You'll need a wrap-up, though."

"What about a bit from 'Lonesome Blues?'" Claude suggested.

"No way," Rosacoke protested. "That belongs to Pete Riddle. I could never do it as good as him."

"The important thing is to present you so that you'll have the widest appeal possible," Barbara said. Arthur wants you to sing Patti Page's 'Tennessee Waltz.' We're not the hillbilly hour, you know."

"And what have you got against hillbillies?" Rosacoke said, a little too defensively.

"I didn't mean to offend," Barbara said. "But I think you have the potential of becoming a crossover artist like Patti Page. A full-fledged popular singer, not just a hillbilly canary."

Eager to change the subject, Rosacoke asked when she was going to meet Arthur Godfrey.

"Not until you're on the air," Barbara said. "It's policy."

After leaving the studio, Claude asked Rosacoke if he could show her New York City. She was only too happy to go sightseeing, wanting to ride to the top of the Empire State Building and climb to the torch of the Statue of Liberty.

Exhausted, she came back to the Dixie Hotel with him in a taxi at six o'clock. He asked her to meet him in the bar downstairs at eight o'clock

where he planned to take her to Sardi's, since he'd heard that was where "show people" ate supper.

Once inside her room, she stripped off her clothes and checked her figure in a full-length mirror in the bathroom. She was getting older but nothing had started to fall yet, especially her big breasts. She dreaded when they would surrender to gravity. Maybe she should try to lose five pounds. She started to run some bath water, planning to take a long, hot bubble bath before hooking up with Claude again.

As the water ran, she went back into her bedroom and removed a bottle of bourbon from her suitcase. Pouring herself a hefty drink, she picked up a copy of one of the New York tabloids, hoping to find an ad promoting Narcissa's engagement at the Hotel Carlyle.

It was only then that she realized that she should have insisted that Claude book her into the Carlyle itself. When Narcissa called her at the Dixie Hotel, that brown belle would surely think that Rosacoke, as always, had no class at all, staying at a Times Square hotel in beds used by whores.

She didn't see an ad touting the talents of Narcissa, but she did spot a familiar face on the entertainment page roundup. Doug was photographed in Los Angeles at the Cocoanut Grove with Ava Gardner, with no Frank Sinatra in sight. She'd heard that Miss Ava, another gal from North Carolina, used to be linked romantically with Doug. On seeing the picture in the paper, Rosacoke thought of her own potential loss of Doug to Miss Ava. She was reacting as if she—and not Narcissa—was Doug's wife. If Rosacoke was looking at that photograph of Doug and the sultry, beautiful Ava Gardner, Narcissa must certainly have seen it, too.

As seductive as Narcissa was, Rosacoke didn't think Narcissa could compete with Ava Gardner, a screen goddess and the actress who'd played the mulatto, Julie, in *Showboat*, even though both Lena Horne and Narcissa had tried desperately to get that same coveted role.

The phone rang and she rushed to pick it up, thinking it might be Narcissa returning her call. It was Doug. "Why in hell are you booked into the Dixie Hotel?" he asked. "That's a dump where you take a whore."

"A long story," she said. "I've called you several times today. I couldn't get through to you. Are you okay, lover boy?" She didn't mean to make "lover boy" sound like an accusation.

"I'm fine," he said. "Marlene looks terrific after the job I did on her. I spoke to her about an hour ago."

"I'd much rather hear about my adorable Dr. Porter and how much he misses his blonde bombshell than I need an update on how gorgeous another blonde looks," she said.

"*Touché*," he said. "I miss you something awful. I had wanted to fly to New York to escort you to hear Narcissa at the Carlyle. But I've got two of the most important jobs of my life."

"Care to tell me which actress you'll be butchering this time?" she said.

"Don't even say that," he said with a certain anger in his voice. "I know you meant it as a joke. But the very suggestion of being a beauty butcher is the last thing a plastic surgeon in Hollywood wants to hear."

"I'm sorry," she said. "I'm just nervous as hell. I go on the Godfrey show tomorrow night, and it scares me shitless."

"You'll be terrific," he said in his most reassuring bedside manner.

"Curiosity got the cat," she said. "Just who are you going to make even more gorgeous than they already are?"

"You won't believe this, but two former girl friends of mine. Lana Turner and Ava Gardner. Neither one looks as good as they did in the Forties. They don't need drastic work like I performed on Marlene but a tuck here and there. Ava's drinking too much. I keep warning her it's going to age her prematurely but she doesn't listen. As for Lana, she wants to look forevermore like she did in    *The Postman Always Rings Twice.*"

"Speaking of Ava, I saw that you were photographed with her at the Cocoanut Grove. You both looked fantastic."

"It's not what you think," he said. "Narcissa knows that I always spend time with my patients a month or so before they face the knife. I hang out with them, take them out, shit like that. It gives the ladies more confidence. But it's strictly professional."

"Well, it must involve *some* kind of profession, I guess," she said. "I'm just afraid I can't compete with a screen goddess."

"Don't worry your pretty head about that," he said. "I'm restoring their looks to these old hags. You're as fresh as tomorrow. You don't need a thing done by me except for me to make love to you."

***

Her mind a blur, she woke up the next morning back at the Dixie Hotel. As she showered, she turned her face up to the jet spray. Later, when Claude came to Rosacoke's room to escort her to breakfast, she was freshly made up. It would be a day devoted to makeup, wardrobe, and rehearsals. She'd bought a pink cowgirl outfit covered in glittering rhinestones. Her breasts were on ample display. She'd gone this far in her career, and now she had to perform for the first time in front of a national audience regardless of how miserably she failed.

Before going on, Claude kissed her lips tenderly. "You're gonna make me real proud of you tonight."

"Thanks, baby," she said, before checking her makeup one more time and adjusting her hair. She'd never called him "baby" before, and he had seemed to like that.

She could hear Godfrey introducing her. He mentioned that she was the wife of Pete Riddle, and she also heard a plug for "Lonesome Blues." Suddenly, Godfrey's voice said, "Ladies and gentlemen, Miss Rosacoke Carson."

As she strode onto the stage, she felt her knees give way, although her legs miraculously still managed to carry her to the designated spot. She managed a weak, frightened smile at Godfrey before turning to face the audience.

Under the heavy lights, she felt sweat pouring from her. Once she heard the music to her song, her fear left her and she sang it like she meant it, two and a half minutes from her heart. She closed her eyes in a squint as she faced a moment of silence at the end of her song.

Deafening applause greeted her, as the viewers stood up, clapping wildly. She was a hit. Only later she found out the applause meters had frozen.

Off stage, she threw her arms around Claude, nearly knocking him off balance. "They loved you," he said.

Godfrey quieted down the audience in time to bring her back for another round of applause. It was then she fully realized she was on national television and hadn't rechecked her appearance. Her pink, rhinestone-studded cowgirl outfit had never felt hotter. For her second song she selected the Hank Williams favorite, "Your Cheatin' Heart."

At the finish she met the same mass roar of approval. Godfrey told the audience, "Only stars can wear rhinestones."

Rushing off stage again, she told Claude, "This is the greatest day of my life."

"You're wrong," he said. "That's coming up."

As she hugged him close, she was interrupted by a messenger. "Miss Carson," he said, "Narcissa Cash wants to speak to you on your dressing room phone."

***

In Narcissa's fourth floor suite at the Hotel Carlyle, Rosacoke wasn't surprised when Narcissa invited her into her bathroom for her bubble bath. The girls had bathed together countless times back in the Carolina hills. The scene was so evocative of Doug's seduction of Rosacoke in the Chicago hotel that she felt Narcissa might have found out about that too. But how could she unless Doug had told her?

In her bathtub Narcissa seemed real friendly, even asking Rosacoke to take a sponge and soap up her back. If they were going to have a catfight over Doug, this luxurious bathroom seemed an unlikely setting.

After Rosacoke had soaped her back, Narcissa giggled and stuck her left foot into the air, asking Rosacoke to soap that for her too, paying special

attention to her toes.

Feeling like a servant girl waiting on a goddess, Rosacoke soaped that delicate foot and then the other.

After she'd done that, the phone rang. Narcissa claimed that she was expecting an urgent call, and asked Rosacoke to see who was calling. Rosacoke went into the bedroom and picked up the phone. "Hi, it's Frank," the voice on the other end said. He sure was no Southerner. "Let me speak to Narcissa."

"She's getting ready," Rosacoke stammered.

"Tell her I don't have much time," he said rather impatiently. "Tell her if she doesn't get her beautiful brown ass up here in twenty minutes, the date is off." He put down the phone.

Back in the bathroom, she reported on the call to Narcissa. "My God, I didn't realize what time it is. Ever since I heard Marilyn Monroe was late for everything, I've been trying to imitate her." She quickly rose from her tub and began drying herself, as she barked out orders to Rosacoke to fetch a dress, get her black lingerie, and bring her the most towering pair of red high-heel shoes she could find in her closet. Within five minutes Narcissa was almost dressed, applying her war paint in a vanity mirror.

"We'll catch up later on all the gossip," Narcissa said. "If you think I'm going to beat you up for fucking Doug, you're wrong. I know all about what's been going on. I was going to divorce him anyway for a very compelling reason."

"I'm sorry about what's happened," she said. "He seemed the perfect husband. Almost too perfect, I guess."

"You've got that right," Narcissa said. "Doug is the perfect husband with whatever woman he's with at the moment. Since I like to screw around on the side, it was a perfect marriage for me. I was going to stay married to him for years, but I just got this proposal from the one man in America who I dig more than all the others."

"Who might that be?" she asked.

"You'll find out later," she said, "I want him to be a surprise. Sister, are you going to be knocked on your ass. When Narcissa goes after big game, she catches it. And this one's a bigger and better haul than the eminent Dr. Douglas Porter of Beverly Hills, plastic surgeon to the stars."

"I sure would like to know who this mysterious Frank is," Rosacoke said.

Narcissa glanced nervously at her watch. "You'll soon see," she said. "He's the only crooner in America who sings better than me."

***

Upon MGM's release of "Honky Tonk Angel," and fueled by her hit

appearance on the Godfrey show, the record became a smash hit on both country and pop charts. The record immediately climbed to number two spot on *Billboard's* country chart and seemed to take permanent roost there. On the pop chart, it shot up into fourth position where it seemed to go into a holding pattern.

Rosacoke rejoiced in her success and her first major recognition, but she also feared that it might be her last. "Maybe it was a freak accident," she told Claude. "You know a lot of people make hit records and then are never heard from again."

"True, but not you," he said. "Rosacoke Carson is a star and getting brighter. I predict you'll be even bigger than Ole Pete himself."

The next morning when Claude and Rosacoke met with Godfrey, the announcer told her, "You're a natural. You're like a transitional figure, representing the changing South. You've also got humility, the mark of a real trooper. Don't ever change."

Praise from such an important man in broadcasting thrilled her, and she turned to notice Claude's beaming face. He seemed to take so much pride in her it was as if she were his personal discovery.

"Listen, country girl," Godfrey said. "I'm thinking about offering you a job on my morning show. Arthur Godfrey Time, but I can't discuss it with you now—one of my assistants will get in touch about the details." Grinning broadly, he made a rapid exit from her view.

Back at the Dixie Hotel, she invited Claude up to her room. As he eased into a chair, she said, "I'm so glad you're here with me. Every would-be girl singer in America right now—all those unknown ones—would love to exchange places with me. Appearing on the Godfrey show. Count 'em. A guaranteed audience of ten million people.

"What do you want?" Claude asked.

"My most burn-'em-up dream involves singing at the Grand Ole Opry," she said.

"Well, don't worry your pretty head about it. I'm sure everything will work out fine, and you'll be there before you know it."

"I believe that's true. As long as you're with me." She came over to his chair and knelt in front of him. Hiding her face in her hands, she began to cry.

His hands were big and strong but when they caressed her hair they were soft and gentle. He put his fingers under her chin and turned her tear-streaked face up to him. "I love you, my little country girl."

She puckered her mouth, and gazed up at him provocatively. "Not so little."

His eyes looked deeply at her, as if seeing into her very soul. "It might be a little awkward, but would you let a po' country boy make love to you?"

There was a long moment of silence. "Yes," she found herself saying.

"I want you."

Four hours later, when he fell asleep by her side, she relived their intimate moments together. Claude's love-making had been incredibly gentle and tender. She'd gotten on top of him as he'd looped his arms around her neck, pulling her closer to him. Her lips had parted as his tongue had entered her mouth, and in that expression of love she'd felt her whole body come alive with desire for him.

Was it really possible to love both Claude and Doug at the same time? She'd never thought so before. Now she wondered.

When Claude had entered her, it was as if he'd touched places never before explored. Although somewhat gawky and awkward in his movements on the street, he was like a graceful animal in bed. Flat on his back, he'd ground his body upward into her.

In a barely audible voice, he'd said, "I love you."

She'd muttered no response to that. Instead she'd placed her mouth over his, as a soft moan had escaped her throat.

As a final shiver of ecstasy had swept over her, she'd continued to lie by his side in the early morning hours, enjoying the after-glow of love-making. He'd held her tight, kissing her nipples and caressing her back with his strong hands. A sweet, incandescent fire had swept over her, and she'd dreamed of having this man forever, moving in unison with him. It was as if she'd wanted to lose her identity with him, becoming a part of him. All the anxiety of New York had been drained from her, and she'd enjoyed the lingering respite from her tension.

When she'd gotten out of bed and showered and looked at herself in the mirror, she'd felt stabs of remorse. In spite of the recent shower, she hadn't felt clean somehow.

Suddenly, the room at the Dixie Hotel had seemed cheap and tawdry with its unmatched furniture, dripping faucet, and frayed carpet. The tawdriness of the room had contributed to the definition of her love-making with Claude as a sin. She'd wanted to flee right then and there.

When Claude woke up, and in spite of their wonderful moments in each other's arms, she was going to tell him that their relationship had no future. She was flying to California to be with the man to whom she'd already promised her heart. Doug Porter.

\*\*\*

When Pete awoke the next morning at Heaven on Earth, he reached out for Josh, finding the bed empty. He assumed that Josh had gotten up before he did and that he'd gone down for breakfast.

In the bathroom, he saw a note taped to the mirror:

*Pete,*

*You are the only man I have ever loved and will ever love. But I am leaving you for good. I left early this morning for the Outer Banks while you were still asleep. Don't follow me there. This time I have gone forever. Don't ask me how, but I've found out about Buster and you. I can't live with that. Knowing about you and Buster is like a stab in my heart. What you're doing is morally wrong. But it is your life. It is Buster's life. I guess you're both entitled to live your lives as you want to. I just want no part of it. There will always be a special chamber of my heart reserved just for you. But I prefer to remember the way we were, because I don't want to be a part of what you have become.*

*Please accept all my love and all my hope for the uncertain futures we're both going into.*

*Josh.*

# Chapter 13

It was early morning in Copenhagen when Pete woke up. Buster was still asleep in his arms. Last night his son had been like a sex maniac. Before three a.m., Buster had managed to draw three loads from Pete, and still the boy wasn't satisfied.

Of all the men he'd known, Buster was the most skilled seducer and seemed to be fine-tuning his technique every week. Whenever Pete protested that he had no more to give, Buster could still arouse him for one more bout in bed.

Sometimes with great sadness, when Pete was alone, he thought of Josh. On at least three occasions, when he would be drinking, he came close to deciding that he wanted to go to the Outer Banks and bring Josh back to Heaven on Earth. It would be only a momentary thought. But when Buster came into the room, all thoughts of Josh vanished from Pete's mind.

He preferred not to think of Rosacoke unless someone brought her name up in conversation. Larry had told Pete what he knew of Rosacoke's affair with Doug Porter. Pete was shocked. Up to now he figured that Claude was moving in on Rosacoke. That she would chase after the husband of Narcissa made Pete realize he'd never known his wife at all.

He'd read that Narcissa had filed for divorce. Pete had also learned from Larry that Narcissa was carrying on an affair with Frank Sinatra.

"Sinatra's just using her," Larry had told Pete. "That one likes a little poontang on the side. But the brown belle still clings to the idea that Old Blue Eyes is going to marry her when her divorce from Doug comes through."

"Why don't you talk some sense into her vain little head?" Pete had asked Larry.

"You know Narcissa," he'd said. "That self-enchanted pussy only believes what she wants to."

Pete's own quickie divorce from Rosacoke was coming through. It was uncontested. After reviewing all his assets with Karl, Pete had decided to offer Rosacoke one-million dollars. She'd told Pete that she felt it was an incredibly generous offer.

In spite of her reaction to learning of his involvement with Buster, it was going to be a friendly divorce. Pete knew that he didn't have to offer Rosacoke that much money, but he was also bribing her. He wanted her

silence about his affair with Buster. If word of that got out, his career would be history.

As Pete gently arose from his bed in Copenhagen and headed for the bathroom, he noted that Buster was still sleeping blissfully. Pete had not planned to take Buster along on this trip to Denmark, but his son had insisted.

Even now, Pete couldn't believe why he'd had to fly to Copenhagen.

He'd stayed that morning until one o'clock in the suite of John-John, or "Joni," as he liked to be called. Junior Grayson had been there holding Joni's hand through the ordeal. All of Pete's pleadings had failed, falling on deaf ears. Both Junior and Joni had made up their minds.

Beginning tomorrow morning at seven o'clock, Joni was going to submit to a series of surgical procedures that would transform him into a woman. She was following in the footsteps and in the wake of headlines spinning around Christine Jorgensen, a former G.I. who'd been transformed into a slender young blonde woman after a series of daring and complicated operations.

As he'd talked and pleaded with Joni, Pete had reached a few times to clutch his own penis. The idea of having it cut off had sent chills through his body.

When Pete had given up with Joni, feeling how crazed he was to contemplate such a move, Pete had turned to Junior to plead his case. It turned out that Junior wanted Joni to have the operation even more than did the young man himself.

"I want to fuck her as a woman," Junior said. "I'm in love. I'll still plug Joni's ass, but I want to fuck a front part too. It's in my blood. I need both a man and a woman in my life. After these operations, I can find both a male and female in Joni. It'll make me faithful to just one person for the first time in my rotten life." He'd leaned over, giving Joni a long, passionate, and deep-throated kiss.

It was at that point, that Pete had retreated, returning to his suite at the Hotel d'Angleterre, which he shared with Buster.

Pete had no intention of staying around for the actual operation or its aftermath. Junior and Joni would remain in Denmark for a number of weeks while Joni continued to have consultations with a Dr. Hamburger, who had performed the actual surgery on Miss Jorgensen, too.

Pete had felt that he still had some ability to persuade and control Joni and Junior, both of them former lovers of his. But Junior had seemed almost fanatical in his insistence that Joni be sexually transformed. When Junior had learned that other operations would follow and that there would be a long recovery period before Joni's complete transformation, he'd become belligerent and had attacked the doctors.

"I don't know why it takes so long," he'd said, "I want her to dress up just like Marilyn Monroe. Just like Marilyn, I want Joni to have a real pussy.

That's what I want, and by God I'm gonna git it."

"You guys are crazy," Pete had said, before stumbling drunk from their suite.

He was determined to get on a plane that morning, leaving Copenhagen at eleven en route to New York. As he showered, Pete felt that he should visit Junior and Joni one final time before they both headed for the hospital, but decided against it.

"John-John never had much of a dick," Pete had told Buster, "and now he's gonna chop off what little he does have. I hope the day doesn't come when Miss Joni will want her cock back. I can't understand how surgeons can chop off a dick. I mean, I saw Sultan's body after he was castrated. What I fear is that once that dick is removed, there's no turning back, even if you wanted to reverse everything and become a dick-swinging man once again."

"It's Joni's dick," Buster had said. "Let her do with it what she wants." He seemed rather unconcerned about the whole operation. It had been obvious that he'd flown to Denmark only to be alone with Pete, not out of any real concern for Joni.

It had taken Pete a while to get used to the word "Joni." After this morning, John-John would be more entitled to be called Joni than ever before.

Most of the other relationships around Heaven on Earth were falling apart. Even Smokey Wetter had left Tara's bed when he'd found a pretty little sixteen-year-old black girl in Shakerag. That had left Tara despondent, and Pete had suggested that she travel on the road accompanying Rosacoke on her guest appearances. Tara had agreed only when she'd learned that she'd no longer have Buster to care for, since Buster had insisted that from this day forward, he accompany Pete on all of his trips.

Over breakfast that morning at the Hotel d'Angleterre, Pete received a telegram from Karl at Heaven on Earth. Even as he read Karl's words, Pete couldn't believe the news.

Hank had run off with Medora, the former wife of Herb Hester, the bootlegger. After a disappearance of several years, Medora had showed up on the doorstep of Heaven on Earth, claiming that she wanted a reunion with her son, John-John. Even though Medora at this point must be some broken down old hag, and at least twenty years, maybe more, older than Hank, the two had run away together. Pete didn't know how Medora had managed to seduce Hank and entice him to go away with her.

In the telegram, Karl told Pete that he'd made a settlement of twenty-five thousand dollars on Hank, "so they won't 'cause trouble for us."

When Pete let Buster read the telegram, his son looked relieved. "Nothing is lost," Buster said. "Hank was no-count anyway." Buster had a smugness on his face. "One by one, your male harem is disappearing. Junior is in love with Joni. Ronnie is shacked up with Larry. Rosacoke's fallen in love with

Narcissa's husband. Josh has fled back to the Outer Banks. Claude seems to have stopped having sex with anybody. Karl doesn't have anybody and I don't think he's gay. He spends all his time making love to your money. That leaves only Tracy unaccounted for."

"Do you think he's gay?" Pete asked.

"I'm sure he'll grow up to be as much of a dedicated faggot as I am," Buster said. "Any boy who spends all his time with Wanda Mae going over dress designs has got to be gay."

"I don't know," Pete said. "He and I have never talked about that."

A stern look came across Buster's face. "Don't you ever talk that gay shit with him. I want that little faggot to stay away from you. When you're around, Tracy practically drools. But I've staked out Daddy for my little old cute self."

"That you have, my boy."

Buster reached across the breakfast table for Pete's hand. "Don't tell me you're still having all this guilt about what you and I do in bed."

"I try not to think about it," Pete said. "The only way I can live with it is to think of you as my young boy friend. Not my son. When I think of you as my son, I head for my bottle of bourbon."

There was a fire in Buster's eyes as he looked into Pete's. His hand tightened on Pete's wrist. "Get used to it. I'm here. I'm queer. And I'm going to stay in your life."

\*\*\*

From the Los Angeles airport, a chauffeur had delivered Rosacoke directly to the mansion of Narcissa Cash, where she fell into the arms of Doug Porter.

That following morning, a ray of light cut through the slightly parted draperies, bringing dawn to the lavishly draped bedroom of Narcissa and Doug, dominated by her "white swan" bed.

As Rosacoke opened her eyes, she was struck by the bright light illuminating Doug's naked thigh. She couldn't believe the night had passed so quickly. It was already noon.

Gently she pulled the rest of the sheet from Doug, exposing his entire naked body. She knew she'd have to be leaving soon to get back on the road and on with her career, but she wanted the memory of his nude flesh to help get her through many a lonely night—that and a bottle of bourbon.

He was sleeping peacefully, and his muscled body looked innocent. But her memory of what he'd done to her last night was neither innocent nor inexperienced. She reached gently to touch his cock, not wanting to awaken it or him. She did, however, want to remember the repeated thrills this

sleeping hunk had given her last night.

The hot California sun also revealed her bruised and puffy nipples, which he'd attacked. Gentle at first, he'd tongued and bitten them as his own passion had mounted. Doug was definitely a breast man.

A fresh, teasing flicker of desire came over her, and she was almost tempted to wake him up for another round. His blond body hair made her tingle with desire. She drank in the sight of him from his succulent cherry-red mouth to his brown nipples to his cock and large balls, all the way down his muscled legs to his big feet.

She glanced back at his nipples, feasting on them. Until she'd met Doug, she'd never paid much attention to a man's nipples. But his grew hard and firm whenever she sucked on them. She and Doug last night had paid a lot of attention to each other's breasts.

He kept his stomach flat and skillet hard. She looked with lust at his wide, winking navel, the subject of her massive tongue probe last night.

She followed his narrowing trail of body hair as it grew darker on its journey south. She gasped at the sight of his cock in its peaceful state—so long, large, and thick even in its slumber. That part of the male anatomy, including the rounded pouches of wrinkled flesh beneath it, always drove her into a paroxysm of heat. She shuddered just thinking about those big orbs banging against her last night, as he'd pounded into her.

It had something to do with his smell. Anytime he came close to her, she felt an overwhelming desire for him. His touch always thrilled her. He was a naturally sexy man with no pretense, no airs. He didn't need artifice, as he was a real man, not like Pete at all, who nearly always seemed to be performing his conjugal duty when he came to her bed.

Surprisingly she thought of Claude. He was a real man too, but she'd never developed a schoolgirl crush on Claude the way she had for Pete. She also didn't feel the incredible lust for Claude that she did for Doug. Claude was nonetheless a mighty attractive male animal.

She blotted Claude and Pete from her mind, and she especially didn't want to think about all the other tawdry episodes in her life. Gliding gently from the swan bed, she tiptoed toward the bathroom. Once inside the most luxurious white marble bathroom she'd ever seen, she ran a cold shower, which made her body tingle.

After she'd finished, she covered her body with a towel and went back to the bedroom to get dressed. Doug opened one eye to look at her. She bent down and kissed him gently on the mouth.

"Hi, baby," he said. "My, you smell good."

"Morning, lover man," she said. "I want to fix you a real country breakfast."

"I'm hungry," he said. "I used up a lot of protein last night."

"I'll say you did."

He rose from the bed with a piss hard-on. Heading for the bathroom, he turned and smiled lewdly at her. "Who taught you all those tricks?"

"You hush now," she said, slipping into a thin cotton dress. She stood admiring the perfect mounds of his ass, where her tongue had been buried for a part of the night.

After he'd shut the bathroom door, she checked her appearance in the mirror. In spite of her heavy bourbon drinking, she felt she looked ten years younger this morning. She left the bedroom heading down the corridor to the kitchen where she was going to rustle up a real rancher's breakfast for her man.

For one brief moment she let herself imagine that this was her house, that Doug was her husband, and that Narcissa would not be returning to occupy not only her mansion but her white swan bed. Although he hadn't mentioned it, Doug might soon move out and buy a home where he'd invite Rosacoke to come and live. The new place would become their love nest.

Slamming down the eggs on the kitchen counter, Rosacoke felt that a country gal could dream. Couldn't she?

***

From his garden patio, Doug called Rosacoke to the phone.

It was Larry calling from Heaven on Earth. "They want you," Larry shouted into the phone.

"Who wants me?" she asked.

"The Grand Ole Opry. They want you to sing 'Honky Tonk Angel.'"

She let out a rebel yell. Suddenly, her spirit dampened.

"What's the matter?" he asked, sounding a bit dumbfounded. "Isn't this what you always wanted?"

"My God, what if the audience compares my debut there with Pete's?"

"You're both different, and you'll be just fine," he assured her. "Now get your ass on a plane, gal."

The next hours of the next day passed as in a dream for her. Torn from the arms of her loving man, Doug, she was plunged, after a cross-country flight, into the welcoming arms of Claude, who waited with a car for her at the Nashville airport.

"You look good enough to take to my bed, woman," he said, kissing her on the mouth. It was obvious he wanted to hold that kiss but she broke away, as the memories of another airport and another man, Doug, rushed through her blood.

On the way to her hotel—not the Tulane this time—she heard Claude's apologies about why Pete couldn't attend her debut at the Opry. "Larry's booked him for weeks on the road," Claude said. "The same fate awaits you. He wants to see that you really capitalize on this 'Honky Tonk Angel'

hit."

She noticed a look of deep concern come across his face. "Is something wrong with the kids? Is it Pete?"

"They're fine and dandy," he said. "It's our gin mama. I spent the night in her cottage. She's real depressed. I was a little afraid she might be thinking of doing herself in."

"What's gone so wrong?" she asked.

"It's Buster," he said. "That boy's on the road with Pete. Starting next week, he's gonna become Pete's opening act. Tara has lost him."

"She should be relieved," Rosacoke said. "She's been a baby-sitter long enough."

"More than I ever knew, Buster's been the reason for her to live. I hate to say it, but at times I think Tara is in love with Buster."

"It's no secret: She's always loved him very much."

"I don't mean that," he said. "I mean *in* love with him. The way a woman feels about a man. Or, in my case, the way I feel about you."

"That's a wild idea," she said, growing alarmed. "He's just a child."

"I think Pete has shown all of us that Buster ain't no child no more. When I was Buster's age, I was fucking lots of gals, some of them twice as old as me."

"Maybe your pecker just grew faster," she said. "I just don't want to hear any more of this talk. If that thing with Pete and Buster isn't enough to think about, now you've given me Tara to stew about."

Wiping her mind of Tara, she leaned back in the convertible, enjoying the wind blowing through her hair. It's good to be back home again. California is real exciting but not my scene, really. It's a bit much for me."

On an impulse, he slammed on the brakes, stopping right in the middle of the highway. She whirled around and thanked God there wasn't another car coming. "Are you crazy?" she asked.

"I want you to know I haven't given up on you, and I never will," he said.

"Would you step on the gas before we get ourselves killed?"

"I'm gonna be around, lady," he said. "Maybe not all the time. But I'm gonna keep showing up. The day will come when you admit what we both know: That you love me as much as I love you. Or else up there in New York City we were the best God damn actors in the world."

"That was then and this is now," she said. "I'm in love with someone else."

"Bullshit!" he said. "You're in love with me, woman. But for some damn reason you can't bring yourself to admit it." He stepped on the gas and headed into town, not saying another word.

At the door to her hotel suite, he reached over to kiss her on the mouth. She diverted her head, offering him her cheek. He stepped back and looked

down at her with a twinkle in his eyes. "Us mountain boys don't go in for cheek-kissing. The mouth, woman. Some tongue, God damn it." He grabbed her and pressed his lips firmly down on hers. Without really intending to, she opened her mouth to receive his tongue. At the finish, he pulled away. "That will tide you over until we meet again." Without another word, he turned and walked down the corridor to his own room.

His kiss was still so hot on her mouth it was as if he hadn't withdrawn his lips.

Later, in the loneliness of her hotel suite, she headed for the liquor cabinet for some bourbon to settle her nerves. Although she'd faced a nationwide audience on the Arthur Godfrey show, she feared harsher critics at the Grand Ole Opry. She felt that whereas she might be able to trick a Godfrey audience, the crowd tonight would have already seen the greatest stars of country music, and she suspected that they were not likely to be impressed by her meager talents.

The next two and a half hours passed as if in a blur, and suddenly, she found it was time for her to go on stage. She gulped down a final swallow of bourbon for encouragement. She was so nervous, she was shaking when she looked into Claude's reassuring eyes. "I'm gonna go for it!"

"Pop a button off your blouse, and I know you will." He glanced at his watch. "You're on in just three minutes."

Waiting in the wings for Roy Acuff to finish his introduction, she wished that Pete could have flown in to hear her. But the way she felt right now, he could go to hell. She had more important things on her mind. Like making a big singing star out of herself.

All in white, and with a mass of rhinestones, she bounced onto the stage in her booted feet. Loosening up, she bucked her hips in a stepped-down boogaloo. They wanted to see a honky tonk angel, and she was going to give them just that. She cocked her hip and shotgunned her guitar at the audience, and they went wild, giving her a standing ovation. It was much better, she decided right then and there, to go out on the Opry stage a star already. Pete had proven that to her.

Her song came out of her throat with the freshness of a new dawn. The words had been spawned in smoke-filled, dark bars that smelled of beer and stale cigarettes. Now they were marching into the daylight in front of the world.

Rising rapidly in a hairpin bridge, she slid into a curling refrain, and she knew that she'd never sounded better. Long before she finished that song, she sensed a doorway had opened for her. She had merely to walk through it. At long last that elusive star was shining down on her golden head. Hell with Godfrey, to hell with them all. Her dream had come true.

She held onto the last chord as if she didn't want to let go. At the end, she got a thunderous ovation, and it touched her heart. She poured out her

thanks to the audience and couldn't hold back her tears.

Striding off stage, she ran smack into Claude. He grabbed her in his big strong arms and twirled her in the air before planting a powerful wet kiss on her mouth. "Two stars in one family. Hell and Moses!"

As she turned around, she gazed into the face of Roy Acuff. "You were mighty fine. They loved you."

"This is the biggest night of my life," she gushed. "You don't know how long I've dreamed this night would come."

When Ernest Tubb came up to congratulate her and give her his support, she felt she'd been admitted to the inner circle. "Sweet girl, there's nothing better than singing before a live audience, now is there?" Tubb asked her.

"That love is sure evident in all your performances," she said, accepting his kiss.

"Now listen, I have this funny feeling you're gonna go real far, and I'd like to give you some advice from a man who was cutting records when you were just a little gal. Don't ignore your fans. The people who put you out on that stage tonight. I don't care how tired you are. Stand outside and sign every autograph they want. Pose for every picture. Mainly just chat with everybody who approaches you. And don't leave until your last admirer has walked away. Only the small ones like Elvis run or play hide-and-seek from their fans, and they don't stick around long."

"I'll always remember your words," she said.

"When she turned around again, she ended up in the outstretched arms of Minnie Pearl. "Howdy! I'm right proud of you."

"Coming from you, that means a lot."

"I've seen a lot of people come and go in this business," Minnie said. "But there's one thing that both you and Pete Riddle have in common with Hank Williams. You get the same cataclysmic response from the crowd. Listen, I'm not the greatest comedienne in show business. To tell you the truth, I'm not all that funny. But people know I'm having one big time coming out there on that stage, and somehow what I do becomes sort of contagious. To have that wonderful rapport with your fans is more important than being the world's greatest singer or the world's greatest comic."

She kissed Minnie on both cheeks and thanked her.

"Larry's got a big blast planned for you in your suite," Claude said, coming up and wrapping his arm possessively around her. "Then he's sending you on the road. He's got bookings from Ohio to Texas."

In her dressing room, Larry waited. "You were just great, kid." A frown crossed his face.

Rosacoke shut the door. "If I was so great out there, why are you so glum?"

"Things have been too good for you and Pete. You've both got hit records. I don't trust it. When things go that well, the Gods get jealous.

They send trouble."

"What on earth are you talking about?"

"Listen to the radio these days. Country music's just fine. As long as it lasts."

"It'll be around forever. People grew up with it. They'll listen to it till the day they die."

"Heard any rock and roll lately?" he asked.

"I can't stand it. Drives me crazy."

"I fear quite a few others can and are not only standing it, they're playing it all the time. They're going to inundate us with it. Elvis will drive us underground."

"Shit! Everybody told me honky-tonk music was in its death throes. Yet I got my biggest hit by singing it."

"Yeah, but there's some plant or something I once heard about. It gives off the most beautiful bloom on the dawn it dies. See you at the party." With that, he turned and left the dressing room.

After all the cheering and the sound of congratulatory wishes, an ominous silence fell.

That fear planted by Larry faded from her mind as she picked up the urgently ringing phone. It was Doug calling from Beverly Hills.

"I heard you on the radio," he said. "You're going to be the biggest country western star of all time. You'll unseat Dale Evans as queen of the cowgirls."

"Maybe she doesn't mind too much—at least she's got Roy Rogers," she said.

"You can have that squinty-eyed homophobe," Doug said. "I was once on the set of a film he was making, and gave him some medical emergency treatment when he fell off Trigger. Trust me. Doctors know. Instead of King of the Cowboys, he should be called Princess Tiny Meat." He paused. "Unlike me, the man who women refer to as 'The King Kong of Plastic Surgeons.'"

"Now, now don't you go getting bitchy," she said. "You men are sure proud of that thing you carry between your legs." She giggled.

"That thing I carry between my legs has found its permanent home in you," he said. "Its wanderlust days are over."

"What are you trying to tell me?" she asked.

"I've just made the most unconventional marriage proposal since caveman days," he said. "As soon as our divorces come through, I want you to become the next Mrs. Douglas Porter."

It had all been too much for her. Her debut on the stage of the Grand Ole Opry. The promise of stardom. A proposal of marriage.

Over the telephone, she burst into tears.

Rosacoke was in Valdosta, Georgia, and after the show she and Tara had to drive all the way to Jackson, Mississippi, for a performance the following night. Two days later, after appearing at a dance in Baton Rouge, Louisiana, she was due in Omaha, Nebraska. That previous ten days they had played in Alabama, Arkansas, Ohio, Tennessee, and Texas. The schedule Larry had booked for them was more grueling than any Rosacoke had ever followed.

"I know you'll hate me," Larry had warned Rosacoke as she'd left Nashville. "But if you want to become a country music star, this is how you've got to capitalize off a hit record."

Lack of sleep and a bad cold weren't excuses you could give when you're on the road. Rosacoke also wanted to kill the person responsible for decorating the motel rooms of America. "They sure aren't very inspiring, are they?" she asked Tara.

"Hoss, it beats sleeping in the back seat of a cramped roadster, like I used to."

Rosacoke always felt rumpled and slightly blowsy when arriving at her appearances, and it was only the warmth of her newly acquired fans that kept her going night after night.

The new musicians Larry had assembled for them were a hell-raising bunch. For them, the nights became a blur of broken-door doors, middle-of-the-night drinking bouts, and bitter battles over who was going to get a particular woman. To Rosacoke, it was a miracle her randy group stayed together.

But come morning, with Tara at the wheel, Rosacoke set out in her white Cadillac, a gift from Pete, towing a big trailer. The musicians followed in three cars, forming a caravan. Since Pete had better and more lucrative bookings, Claude had to go along with him. Larry's Nashville hot seat was now important enough to keep him there all the time.

Overcome with loneliness and depression, Tara started staying stoned on booze and pills. "I'm all tore up," she said to Rosacoke. When pressed, Tara would offer no more explanation. She hated the road, as it brought back painful memories to her, and she quickly returned to her old habits.

Feeling she couldn't let Tara sit drinking bourbon in motel rooms all day, Rosacoke made her a part of the show, Tara's name appearing at the bottom of the bill.

After a week of bad shows and drunken performances, Rosacoke quietly removed her from the act. Tara was supposed to organize the band and take care of Rosacoke, yet it was Rosacoke who looked after Tara.

Rosacoke knew how short a country music hit was, and she was determined to cash in on it before "Honky Tonk Angel" went into oblivion.

Although Larry had again one-nighted her to death, Rosacoke also knew how important it was to follow her hit with another song and hope that it was a smash, too. On the road all her boys in the band as well as many complete strangers, both male and female, came up to her and handed her songs they'd written wanting her to record them.

When she'd wake up in the morning, she'd pick out the tunes on her guitar and mouth the words. None of the music handed to her pleased her. It was all routine, songs about losing your husband to your best friend, stuff like that. Nothing liberating like "Honky Tonk Angel."

On any free afternoon she visited the local disc jockeys, going with Tara only if she sobered up from the night before. The "jocks" always wanted to bring her on the air for an interview, so it was usually five o'clock in the afternoon or later when she'd return to her motel room. Often she had three hours before she had to perform, and at those times she answered bundles of fan mail in which she ran three months behind. She'd heard from Larry that tons of mail had poured in since the start of her trip.

Days spent answering mail, listening to new songs, and visiting disc jockeys were the good times. A bad day was when the towns of her appearances were far apart, and she'd have to leave immediately after a show and drive all night and part of the next day to reach the auditorium, tent, or gymnasium, wherever she'd been booked. Sometimes there wasn't even time for Tara to press her clothes, and Rosacoke would have to go out all wrinkled. She hated those nights most of all.

"I miss Buster," Tara said one night. "We've been together so long. The last time I talked to him on the phone, I burst into tears."

"I know how lonely you are," Rosacoke said.

When not locked up in some forelorn motel room with Tara, Rosacoke tried to go out and meet her fans. Most of them treated her with courtesy, but a few got overzealous. One man grabbed her and held her close, as she smelled his beer-tainted breath. "Baby, you've been away from your man a long time. Feel ole long john here. It'll make you take your mind off Pete Riddle when I visit you at your motel after the show." She pushed him away, and, angered, he lunged at her. Tara stepped between them, and "Long John" was no match for that mountain of a woman, not when she jabbed a long hairpin into his arm.

One night a sleazy looking blonde, in a dress five years out of style, came up to her, smacking on her gum. "The last time your husband passed through here, I went to bed with him. He was so drunk he fell asleep right on top of me with his thing still in me. Couldn't even get it up." Tara pushed her toward the door and slammed it.

"Don't listen to her," Tara said. "Lots of gals like that claim they've gone to bed with stars."

"Lots of 'em have," Rosacoke said.

"Hell, by the time you get back to Nashville, how many guys will claim they've screwed you? Unless you've done it behind my back, you ain't had nothing. But people will still talk about you. That's one of the hazards of the business."

"This damn business, if you ask me, has a hell of a lot of hazards."

At times Rosacoke thought she couldn't look at any more wrinkled Western shirts and bleary-eyed musicians. On other occasions, particularly after they'd done a good show, she loved them, enjoying the camaraderie of traveling on the road with them.

In Shreveport, Louisiana, as the advance men arranged the amplifiers on stage, Rosacoke stood in the lobby, selling souvenir booklets. Earlier that day Tara had walked the main street by herself, distributing leaflets because there were still one-hundred and fifty seats left. Up to now, the crowds had been a sell-out.

Word-of-mouth and some last-minute plugs on radio by the local "jock" delivered a capacity crowd, and it was well after midnight when Rosacoke came off stage. A lot of the American Legion had attended that night, and they'd insisted on "God Bless America," even after she'd already taken five encores.

As Tara and Rosacoke headed for a cheap, all-night hamburger joint, the stage manager called to them. "It's Pete Riddle. Calling from New Orleans."

Rosacoke ran to the phone backstage at the mention of Pete's name. She still felt something in her heart for him, even though her divorce from him was going through.

"How you doing, honey?" he asked.

"Just fine, I guess. All broken up that things have gone so bad between us."

"It's a friendly divorce," he said. "We still are friends, and your wing of the house at Heaven on Earth will always be there ready and waiting for you."

"That's good to know," she said, "since I don't have a home."

"Doug will get you one," he said. "I still can't believe the two of you are getting married. The news came as quite a shock to me. I spoke to Narcissa the other night. The fool thinks she's gonna marry Frank Sinatra so she's not broken up over you taking Doug from her."

She paused, hesitant to bring up the next question. "And Buster...."

There was an awkward silence on the other end of the line. "He's doing great," Pete said. "My fans love him. He's gonna come out with a big release soon. If we don't watch our step, Buster—not you and me—is gonna become the big star of the Riddle household."

"Give him my love. I'd like to see him if we ever catch up with each other. The last time at the Tulane Hotel with just the three of us wasn't

what I'd call a family reunion."

"C'mon," he said. "Let's don't get into that."

She, too, was eager to change the subject.

"Do you ever call Tracy?" she asked. "I've neglected him something awful. Thank God he's got Wanda Mae caring for him."

"I talk to him every so often," he said. "He's doing fine. Buster doesn't like me to call Tracy. He throws temper fits."

"I guess he's jealous of anyone else who shares your affection," she said. "How is Josh handling this?"

"I'm surprised Tara hasn't told you," he said. "That big gal knows how to keep a secret. Josh has left me. Headed back to the Outer Banks."

"I guess Buster is happy about that," she said. "I mean, having his daddy all to himself."

Tears welled in her eyes, and her throat felt constricted. "Big stardom is on the way for Buster. And he's got Pete Riddle. Who could want for anything more? Love ya, big guy." She quickly put down the receiver.

***

Long before the tour ended, Tara dropped out. "I can't take the road no more, hoss."

"I sure know why you want to leave." Rosacoke said. "Things haven't been so hot."

When she gave Tara a farewell kiss and put her on a plane back, she was actually relieved. Tara had become more trouble than she was worth.

The two weeks following Tara's departure were the loneliest Rosacoke had ever spent on the road. Her daily calls to Doug in Beverly Hills were all she had to sustain her. As soon as she finished all the commitments Larry had made for her on the road, she was taking the next plane to Los Angeles.

In Memphis, Claude surprised her by showing up at her hotel. At first she thought he was looking for a little off-the-record romance. But then he introduced her to a young songwriter hopeful, Tommy Triplett, from Banner Elk, North Carolina. "Has this boy got a song for you," Claude said.

After kissing Claude and greeting Tommy, Rosacoke was more than skeptical. Wherever she went, everybody had a song for her. So far, in spite of Larry's urging, she had not come up with another hit like "Honky Tonk Angel."

This song, Rosacoke thought, must be good or else Claude wouldn't leave Pete's show and fly all the way to Memphis. She also desperately wanted it to be good, because she knew the only way she was going to make it in show business was to follow up a smash with another even bigger hit. The night before she'd had stomach cramps, and wasn't much interested in any song today. Still, she would give it her all.

"I've got to be honest," the lean, lanky Tommy said, his prominent Adam's apple bobbing up and down. He looked like an ugly version of Claude. "I wrote the song for Kay Starr. Her A&R department turned thumbs down."

Rosacoke arched an eyebrow. That didn't endear the song to her too much. "What's the title?"

"Mountain Momma."

"I hate the title," she said. "But we can change that."

"No, we can't," Tommy protested. "If you record the song, the title stays."

Before Tommy and Rosacoke could come to blows, Claude intervened. "Hear the song first, honey, then decide if you like the title."

As Claude accompanied Tommy on his guitar, the sounds of "Mountain Momma" drifted across the hotel suite. Tommy wasn't much of a singer, and the song definitely had to be sung by a woman for its true meaning. At the finish she didn't say anything for a long moment. "It's a piece of crap!" She got up before the stunned men to search for a cigarette. "After 'Honky Tonk Angel,' I'm selling glamour. Not some hillbilly wonder woman image."

Tommy was so insulted he barged out of the room, as Claude remained behind to try to persuade her to record it. "I have to tell you. Larry and Pete have already heard it. They think it's great material for you. Could become a big hit."

She looked angry. "Everybody's made up my mind for me."

"Sometimes an artist is the worst judge of material for himself."

"That's *her*self."

"Come on, honey. Record this song as a favor to me. If it's not a hit, I'll bow to your judgment forever."

"What interest have you got in it?"

"I've got plenty of interest in you. No interest in the song. I want you to become a star. As big as Pete Riddle. *Bigger.*"

"I really believe you're not bull-shitting me."

"I love you. That's why I brought you this song. I feel it'll do good things for you. You'll do good things for it. Hell with Tommy Triplett. He's just a tarheel boy, and that's all he'll ever be. Probably has only one song in him and will never come up with another."

She walked over and kissed him lightly on the lips. "If it means that much to you, and if Pete and Larry think it's hot, I'll go to Nashville. We'll record the damn thing." She found a cigarette and lit it with fury. "Mountain Momma. Just when I'm trying to become the sexiest country singer in the business. You've got me tending the kids and slopping the hogs."

"You don't understand the song. You take up in that song where Scarlett O'Hara left off in that final scene when Rhett Butler walked out on her."

On the way downstairs in the elevator, Rosacoke took Claude's arm, hugging it for assurance. "I know you've got my interest at heart. I'm

sorry I was so bitchy up in the suite."

"You've got to make up with Tommy," Claude said. "That boy gets his feelings hurt real bad."

In the lobby, as she searched for Tommy, she was struck by a poster advertising a movie with Narcissa in which she was depicted in the arms of a white man, a blond one at that.

"My God," she said to Claude, "the times are sure changing, aren't they?"

He studied the poster. "This is the type of movie they might show in Times Square. Not Memphis."

"It looks like a B picture, but we've got to try to catch it this afternoon. I never miss a picture of hers, although they're getting worse. She should have played Julie in *Showboat*. Lena Horne was up for that role, too. But Ava Gardner got it. Ava's from North Carolina, but no one ever accused her of being black."

In the bar Rosacoke spotted Tommy, already into his third bourbon. Two empty glasses were lined up in front of him.

"Hey, stud!" she shouted, attracting the attention of the other drinkers, all male. Tommy looked up at her. "Come and give your Mountain Momma a big bear hug."

***

After three long, grinding weeks, working with Larry at the studio in Nashville, along with a new group of musicians, Curly Osborne, Dickey Riley, and Danny Clark, Rosacoke had a recording of "Mountain Momma" that even she liked. Tommy wasn't really pleased, and wanted her to spend another week working on it but she told him to go to hell. She'd gone from hating the song to loving it. On looking back, she realized it was Tommy's rendition of it that had made the song so ludicrous.

At long last her tour had come to an end. Rosacoke was going to stop off at Heaven on Earth to pack up some personal items before flying to Los Angeles to join Doug. There were rumors in the press that he was seen out at night with Joan Crawford.

Doug had assured her over the phone that his nocturnal prowling with Crawford was strictly business, and that she would soon be facing the knife. "She's getting old," he'd told Rosacoke only last night. "Her neck is so wrinkled it has to be photographed in shadow. I can provide only emergency tucks at this point. Crawford's too far gone. A has-been, really."

Those words hardly sounded like a plastic surgeon in love with his patient. Maybe he was telling the truth. She was excited to learn that Doug had left Narcissa's Beverly Hills mansion and had moved into a penthouse apartment overlooking the beach at Santa Monica. That high-rise apartment was

going to become her new home, if she could believe Doug.

Back at Heaven on Earth, Rosacoke found most of Pete's gang gone. Still drinking heavily, Tara was there but she was sullen and withdrawn, not really wanting to hang out.

With Pete's permission, Rosacoke had invited Curley, Dickey, and Danny back to the mansion for the weekend. She was amused that each of their names ended in a "y." Of course, she wasn't sure that the names they were billed as were their real names.

Karl came by to show the men to a large gingerbread cottage where they could stay during their brief holiday after recording "Mountain Momma" with her. As the men wandered off to rest and shower before supper, Rosacoke invited Karl for a drink on the back verandah.

As Pete's business manager, he still seemed angry at her over Pete's generous settlement in the divorce. He quickly excused himself, although letting her know that Tracy, another name ending in a "Y," would be home from Wanda Mae's dress shop soon. "You can have supper with him," Karl said. "After all, he's your son. I'm too busy."

As Karl headed down the corridor to the front door, she called out to him, "Heard any news from Hank?"

Karl turned and looked back at her, a determined look on his handsome face. "For me, Hank no longer exists."

After he'd gone, she almost didn't hear Tracy come out onto the porch. In the fading sunlight of day, his coppery hair and hazel eyes were stunning. He looked fabulous, like some fantasy teenager on a poster, not real at all.

Real teenage boys had freckles and pimples, flaws like that. Not Tracy. He came over and kissed her gently on the cheek. "Welcome home," he said. "Guess I'm the only one here to entertain you.

His skin, slightly olive in tone, gave no clue that he had black blood in him. If Tracy wanted to pass himself off as white, he had succeeded.

Rosacoke wanted to take Tracy in her arms, hold him, and stroke his hair, assuring him that she loved him and was sorry for the way both Pete and she had neglected him. Although so very polite and courteous, he had built a protective wall around himself that she didn't think she could scale.

As they were sitting, talking, and drinking on the back porch, a maid came out with two packages addressed to Tracy. They were from Narcissa. "She's always sending me gifts," he said, opening up both packages. He lifted some clothing from the boxes. "I'd never wear these stinky things she sends," he said with contempt. "Narcissa doesn't know my taste. I design my own clothes."

"What's the matter with them?" Rosacoke asked. "They look like very expensive clothes to me."

"I don't care how much they cost," he said, pushing the packages away. That's not the point. I'll never wear stuff like that. They're not for me."

"A teenage boy knows his own style that much?" she asked.

"I know what I look pretty in," he said. "What makes me beautiful."

"What an odd way to put it," she said. "You said that like a girl."

He glanced at her with ferocity but quickly concealed his contempt. "I'm no girl. I'm a young man. I know I'm beautiful. Much more so than Buster. I don't intend to dress in any way that would hide my male beauty. I think a young man should use every device he can to make himself alluring. Women do it all the time. Why not men?"

"I guess you have a point there," she said, not wanting to anger him. She glanced at the discarded presents. "Narcissa loves you. She sends you gifts as a token of that love. I'm sure you'll write her a thank you note."

"Don't tell me how to handle Narcissa," he said. "You're one to talk. You're stealing her husband."

She said nothing for a moment, although Tracy's words stabbed at her heart. "It's not really that way."

"You don't have to explain it to me," he said. "I think any good-looking man is up for grabs, whether he's married or not. It doesn't matter to me. If the guy's a hunk, go for it, I say."

"Are you telling me that you like men instead of gals?" Rosacoke said.

He looked defiantly at her. "I'm telling you that I not only like men, I worship men but only if they're very handsome. I go for men who look as good as Pete, although there aren't many around like that."

"So, I have two sons who are homosexuals," she said. "I guess things like that happen in the same family."

"You'd better believe it," he said.

Few things shocked her any more, even this revelation about Tracy's sexuality. In the back of her brain, she'd figured that a teenage boy who spent all his days designing women's clothing in Wanda Mae's dress shop, instead of playing football, had a gay streak in him.

Tracy had given her a certain guilt about Narcissa. When he went to his room to get dressed for supper, Rosacoke called Narcissa in Beverly Hills. There was no answer.

That night at supper, Tracy looked radiant, even more beautiful than he had in the late afternoon. When "the three Y's," (Curley, Dickey, and Danny) came onto the verandah, she introduced each of the musicians to her son. Tara chose that very moment to make her entrance. From her years of working the tonks, she knew Danny and Dickey, giving each of them bear hugs and kisses before taking them to the bourbon bar.

The twenty-six year old musician, Curley, had disappeared with Tracy to the far end of the verandah where they were sitting, talking, and drinking in a swing, oblivious of everybody else at the barbecue supper.

Until Tracy's great interest in Curley, Rosacoke had not paid him much attention. But he was sexy in a white trashy Southern sort of way. As she

looked more closely, she saw that Curley really knew how to fill out a pair of blue jeans. Danny and Dickey were getting drunk with Tara, and didn't pay much attention to what Tracy and Curley were up to, even when those two wandered off together to the living room.

Later, when Tara invited Danny and Dickey back to her cottage, the musicians thanked Rosacoke for the barbecue and staggered out into the night.

At the liquor cabinet, Rosacoke poured herself a stiff one and then busied herself with cleaning up the debris from the party. When she stepped into the corridor, she spotted a slightly drunken Curley being led down the hallway to Tracy's bedroom. Tracy opened the door to his room, and Curley disappeared inside.

She sighed. Instead of being the star of the show, she'd ended up alone.

She wandered from room to room in the big house, stopping occasionally to look out through the big windows to the mountains in the distance. A threat of fog and mist hovered over those blue-tinged mountains.

It was time to call Doug in Santa Monica.

# Chapter 14

Alone in his West Coast apartment with Tracy, Pete welcomed the first chance he'd ever had to be alone for any time with his son without interference from anyone. Up to now, every time he'd been with Tracy, other people had surrounded them. At Heaven on Earth, Buster's jealous eyes always seemed directed at Pete when he was talking with Tracy. Pete was temporarily free of Buster, who was booked up for the next six weeks with sound recording.

On their second night alone together, Pete was sitting in his boxer shorts watching late-night TV starring Jack Parr. Stripped to his briefs, Tracy sat on the sofa with him. Pete was drinking his sixth bourbon of the evening when Tracy asked him if he could have a beer. "You're old enough," Pete said. "I started drinking moonshine when I was twelve."

When Tracy came back into the living room, he sat down on the thickly carpeted floor at Pete's feet, looking up at him. Pete held out his liquor glass, clanking it against Tracy's beer can in a toast.

At first he wasn't aware of it, but soon Pete sensed that Tracy wasn't looking at Parr, whose guest was Alexander King. Tracy's eyes seemed to be looking up at the gap in Pete's boxer shorts. Pete felt that one of his big balls was exposed, and he didn't immediately want to demurely cover himself up, which would indicate to Tracy that he'd been caught spying on his daddy.

To break Tracy's concentration on him, Pete got up and headed for the bathroom to take a piss, which he felt would be pure bourbon. He'd left the bathroom door open but, even so, was a bit startled when Tracy appeared, coming into the bathroom and walking over to the bowl, where Pete had six inches of soft cock hanging out of the fly of his boxer shorts as he took a horse piss.

"Mind if I join you?" Tracy asked, standing across the toilet bowl from Pete. He quickly slipped down his briefs to a point at mid-thigh, and pulled out his cock to piss in front of Pete. Pete couldn't help but notice how much larger Tracy's penis was when compared to Buster's. A boy no more, Tracy was a fully grown man.

Fearing he'd lost his mind or at least the control of his own emotions, Pete was beginning to enjoy the show he was putting on for Tracy. Even though he'd finished pissing before Tracy did, Pete continued to let his dick hang out of his boxer shorts. When Tracy finished, he made no move to pull

up his briefs.

Tracy's hand tentatively reached out and enclosed part of Pete's cock. He ran his fingers along the length of it as it began to harden. When Tracy reached inside Pete's shorts and fondled his balls, his cock quickly extended to its full length.

"God did not make all men equal," Tracy whispered in a voice filled with lust. "I've got to taste it. If I don't, I think I'll die," he said, yanking Pete's boxers down his legs. The underwear cascaded to the floor, and Pete stepped out of his shorts, kicking them aside. He was completely nude in front of his son.

As Tracy continued to fondle Pete's rock-hard cock and balls, Tracy moved his lips toward Pete's. "I know Buster has you any time he wants. It's about time my daddy stopped playing favorites—and shared his bounty with his second son."

"You've got a point there, stud," Pete said. Pulling Tracy toward him, his lips descended on Tracy's and his tongue darted inside to taste the sweetness of the young man's mouth.

When he finally released Tracy from his embrace, Pete picked him up in his strong arms and headed to the bedroom with him, as Tracy tongued his neck and nibbled at his ear. "After I've licked and sucked every inch of your body, I want you to bury yourself in me and fuck me all night. I've never wanted anything so much in my life."

"You're gonna get it," Pete said, too far aroused now to stop the upcoming seduction. He wanted Tracy as much as Tracy wanted him.

As Pete lowered Tracy onto the bed, Tracy whispered to him. "I've had the hots for you ever since that day I first saw you at the airport."

"And me for you, boy." Lying on top of Tracy on the bed, Pete attacked the boy's lips, limbering them for the pleasure he knew they would bestow on him for the rest of the night. Tracy's hands were all over Pete, feeling, fondling, and sampling his daddy's muscles.

The mere smell of the boy was like an aphrodisiac to Pete. Tracy's muscular frame, his wide, sparkling eyes, his radiant smile, and his willingness to do whatever Pete wanted thrilled him. Pete's lips parted from Tracy, sliding down his neck and sucking and licking their way to his shoulders. Like some satanic vampire, he wanted to slurp away at the boy from his Adam's apple to the tip of his beautiful toes.

Pete buried himself in Tracy's crotch, plunging down until the boy's brown pubic hair tickled his nose. When he'd had enough of that, if he could ever get enough of that, his tongue moved to its main target of the night, Tracy's rosebud. Pete attacked that pink hole with such fury that Tracy cried out his passion. Such an incredible response told Pete what he wanted to know: He'd found an incredible bottom in the boy.

It took an hour before Pete had fully explored Tracy's tantalizing body

with his tongue. He sensed that Tracy was eager to do the same for him. He too wanted to feel Tracy's silky tongue exploring every crevice of his body. As Tracy started at his neck, Pete shivered in anticipation of what lay in store for him. When Tracy's tongue and lips found Pete's ears, Pete was truly transported to Heaven on Earth, and not at his mansion.

As Tracy began the long, sensual exploration of tongue and lips over every inch of Pete's body, a new reality began to emerge. Each kiss brought Pete closer and closer into Tracy's web. He was falling in love with the boy more and more as each minute passed of the most exquisite pleasure he'd ever known.

He thought he'd gone full cycle, from his first seduction by Sultan at Blowing Rock Falls to the most exquisite love-making he'd ever known from Sultan's offspring and his own loins as well.

When the time came that Pete reared up over Tracy, it was like a moment of truth between them, something the matador faces with the bull in the ring. Pete knew that the moment he entered Tracy, it was a commitment somehow and much more than a fuck.

He'd expected Tracy to flinch with pain at his entry, but he didn't at all. Instead he'd reared up to take more of what Pete offered. Inch by inch he eased himself into the boy's velvety canal, and the sensation was the most glorious of his life.

Looking deeply into Tracy's eyes, Pete compared them to a starry night, flashing nova bright through the darkness. In those eyes he imagined the birth of a neutron star. Jaws clenched, Tracy's lips parted to beg for more. "The more brutal, the better," Tracy whispered as if expressing a desire to the wind.

No longer willing to hold back, Pete rammed everything he had into the boy. Tracy screamed but it was beautiful music to Pete's ears. The scream only intensified Pete's desire for the boy. He rammed him harder because, in spite of the scream of agonizing pain, he knew it was what Tracy wanted. Tracy's hole had spread wide enough so that Pete could pick up his ramming speed without fear of doing permanent damage.

Pete managed to hold back a good twenty minutes, and he wanted to go on even longer, but Tracy's love tunnel was just too good. When Pete's explosion came, it was a heaving, thrusting, spurting kind of eruption unlike any he'd ever known before. Every nerve in his body seemed to join in the enjoyment of the eruption, which left him completely drained.

Still embedded deep within Tracy, he fell down on top of the boy, realizing Tracy had exploded too. Pete ground his rock-hard belly against Tracy's to enjoy the sensual feeling of the boy's semen.

Pete's tongue darted out to lick all of Tracy's face. Without meaning to, he bit Tracy's lips. "You're mine now," Pete said. "I love you. I'll never let you go."

With one hand, Tracy was running his fingers up and down Pete's spine. With the other, he was gently plowing through Pete's thick hair. He nibbled at Pete's ear. In a voice barely audible, he whispered into that ear. "I've always known we're put on this planet for a reason. Tonight I've found my reason for living."

*** 

Rosacoke was almost out the door of Doug Porter's new apartment in Los Angeles, heading for the airport, when Larry called, telling her that Pete and Tracy had just arrived at Pete's Santa Monica apartment for a four-day holiday together.

The news had surprised her, and she was sorry that she wasn't able to go to see them. She had been pleased, however, to learn that Pete was spending some time alone with Tracy, and not devoting all his attention to Buster. After all, Tracy was his son too.

Rosacoke was soon due in Nashville for her second appearance at the Grand Old Opry. But Tara had insisted that she fly first to Charlotte for a "big surprise." Intrigued, Rosacoke had agreed to that.

On the flight, she had time to drink bourbon and think of her disappointing week in Los Angeles. Of the seven nights she'd spent in Doug's apartment, he had reserved only two evenings for her. He had claimed that he had to attend to his patients the other nights. There were persistent rumors that he was seen out on the town with Joan Crawford and, on yet another evening, Lana Turner. Rosacoke suspected that he was having affairs with both of the stars. How could she compete?

After having known intense love-making from him during previous times in his arms, her recent sessions in bed with him had been lackluster. If anything, he'd seemed sexually spent, as if he'd satisfied his libido with some other woman. He'd fucked her, but in some ways, it had been like getting a penetration from Pete. Whenever Pete was fucking her, she'd always felt that his fantasy lay elsewhere. With Doug, she'd wondered if he were dreaming about Lana when bedding her. Surely his mind wasn't on Crawford—Rosacoke figured that Doug's screwing Crawford at this late point in her life was nothing more than a mercy fuck at worst, and an ego gratification for him at best.

At the end of her stay, when he'd driven her to the airport and had kissed her good-bye, there had been no mention of setting up a time to get together again, not even the promise of a future phone call. Actually, he'd seemed glad to be rid of her, and had quickly driven away from the airport, as if he'd had emergency business to attend to.

Looking sober for a change, Tara was there to greet her when Rosacoke's Eastern Airlines plane landed in Charlotte. "Hi, hoss," Tara

said, giving her a quick kiss on the lips. "Buster's got a surprise for you. Get in the car."

As Tara leadfooted the gas petal, heading for the Tennessee line, she told Rosacoke what Buster had in store for her. "Tonight he's doing his first solo act at a club called The Pink Orchid. It's a roadside place way out in the country this side of nowhere. But fans drive for miles around to hear the stars who show up there."

"He's mighty young to be carrying a whole show," she said. "I hope he didn't get the job just because he's Pete Riddle's son. Some club owner might be trying to capitalize off Pete's fame."

"Don't worry your head about that," Tara said, flashing a shit-eating smile.

Backstage at The Pink Orchid, Rosacoke met Buster in his dressing room and gave him a big, reassuring kiss. She was stunned at how handsome he looked and how mature for one so young. Clad in a robe, he'd wet-combed his brilliantined hair, and his sideburns had grown much longer since she'd last seen him.

After their initial greetings, he told her, "Now, mom, clear out. I've got to get dressed."

"Come on, I used to change your diapers." Before she realized what she'd said, it was too late. She'd never changed his diapers. By the time she'd reunited with him, he was too old for that.

He looked strangely at her. "I've grown a lot since diapers."

Out front Rosacoke got acquainted with The Pink Orchid, which was more of a big saloon than a night club. It was frequented by prostitutes and drunkards among others, a real tough group. Rosacoke wondered how Buster got the job since he was still a minor, and the place sold alcoholic beverages—lots of them. The whole atmosphere evoked many of the "tonks" where she'd played.

Tara had secured a ringside table, where Rosacoke was recognized from her appearances on the Grand Ole Opry and the Arthur Godfrey show. Many fans came over to her table to ask for her autograph, and she happily obliged, although she didn't want to distract from Buster, knowing that this was his night.

At nine o'clock, after Tara and Rosacoke had ordered far too many drinks, Buster bounced onto the stage, backed up by men in baby-blue rhinestone suits and white Stetsons. She knew at once why her son didn't want her to see him get dressed. He was clad in black pegged pants, a pink shirt with a thin black tie, and as a final touch, an ivory-colored sports jacket, not the usual outfit worn by country singers.

The song he opened with was a ballad, to which he gave a rockabilly beat. Rosacoke was mildly shocked, feeling almost hurt, as if Buster had sold out to the enemy, the very group of new musicians who threatened to

bury Pete and her just as their careers were getting hot. Buster no longer imitated Pete. Buster had found his own voice.

As he launched into his next song, his sound struck her as a mélange of sensual black field jazz and plaintive country and western rhythm.

For his next number, "Red and Hot Tonight," he completely quieted down the audience, something Rosacoke suspected had never before been accomplished at The Pink Orchid.

To her amusement, Buster did bumps and grinds like a stripper, shaking his hips suggestively. "Now *that* he stole from his daddy," Rosacoke confided in an amused whisper to Tara. The on-stage performance had an electrifying effect on the women in the audience. Pete still swayed suggestively in his act, but Buster had topped him, turning his show into one of explosive sexuality.

"That's gold coming out of that hot throat," Tara assured Rosacoke.

She didn't need such assurance, and, like Larry, had been around the business too long not to spot talent like her son's. Some of the better-looking women in the audience—prominently seated down front—swooned and screamed. Buster had bewitched them.

He mumbled suggestive double-talk under his breath, and that increased the excitement. Sometimes he'd suddenly let out a howl, which he'd then soften with a coo. His gyrations set off a loud outburst.

One cowboy yelled, "Get that faggot off the stage!"

The heckler was booed down. Buster had won the hearts of the audience.

Tossing his guitar to one of his musicians, he rushed downstage to a piano for his next number. Seated there, he pounded it hard, sticking his leg out and shaking it at the audience. Women rushed onto the stage and pressed around the piano, their breasts bouncing with the music. The redneck faces of the men in the audience were clearly jealous, the same emotion Pete often aroused. Buster pounded harder and faster with his original song, "Git Real Low."

His style was sultry, and he was captivating as an entertainer. Even so, Rosacoke instinctively knew as a performer herself that he was reaching out to the wrong audience.

"If he can stir up this older crowd," Rosacoke told Tara, "he'll drive the kids wild."

"Hoss, you don't know the half of it. In the next few months, Buster is gonna become the biggest, hottest act in show business. A pop genius."

Clapping wildly, Rosacoke recalled Fry's prediction at Buster's birth.

***

On the way back to Heaven on Earth for the weekend, Rosacoke had

plenty of time to think about her son and the new direction he'd taken in music. She clearly saw that his competition would be Jerry Lee Lewis and Elvis Presley and their host of imitators. Her fear was that Buster was a copycat of both men, combining Presley's stage presence with the antics of Lewis at the piano, and that Buster hadn't grown at all in his own right. He no longer copied Pete but had turned to lifting the style of others, and that wasn't a happy thought for her.

Even the ducktail seemed borrowed from Tony Curtis, the pugnacious pose from Marlon Brando in *The Wild One*, and the vulnerability from the James Dean portrayal in *East of Eden*. But more than all these influences, Buster seemed to adapt black music into a white folk rock 'n' roll. In learning from the blacks, he was following in Pete's footsteps.

Yet through it all she remained convinced that Buster was a unique talent in American music, and, though he borrowed from everybody, he'd eventually emerge as an artist in his own right.

"My God, he's barely sixteen," Rosacoke said to Tara, who was driving along the curving mountain roads en route back to Pete's mansion.

"Buster was sixteen when he was ten years old. I never saw a kid mature like he did."

Three nights later in Nashville, Rosacoke was prepared to face the Grand Ole Opry for her second time around, this time singing "Mountain Momma" even before its official release date.

In her hotel suite, she confronted not only her own face in the mirror, but Buster barging into her bedroom suite attired in fire-engine red pants, a chartreuse sports jacket, and a pink shirt with a black string tie. He was in Nashville working at the recording studio.

"I'm about to burst upon America with hit records," Buster told her gleefully. "Just like you and Pete."

Rosacoke felt a sudden chill and a tiny bit of jealousy. Was Larry rushing pell-mell into promoting emerging rock and roll stars, perhaps to the detriment of the careers of both Pete and herself? She brushed the thought from her mind as not being worthy of her.

When Buster told her he had to drop out of high school, she objected furiously.

"Larry's already got nine bookings. The next one's in Kilgore, Texas. He's getting me an MGM label for 'Git Down Low.' If I wait around to finish school, my chance could get killed. Pete's always told me how risky show business is."

That night she fumed and fretted about Buster leaving school. Larry, Claude, Tara, and Pete were all for it, she was told. She didn't really approve.

Hugging Buster one final time for reassurance, Rosacoke headed for the wings to be introduced. Even though she'd appeared on the show

before, she felt more nervous this time.

Once she'd been introduced, again by Roy Acuff, she knew she had a hit before she was thirty seconds into "Mountain Momma." From all the years of working the "tonks," she'd emerged as a mature artist. As she sang Tommy Triplett's words, she discovered a timeless quality in them. Did every little ole country boy—potentially at least—have one great song in him? As a woman and as an artist, she felt that she'd reached a plateau of emotional transcendence. She'd never be the same again—perhaps she'd never sing this well ever again. Her voice was clean and free—no affectation hovered in her throat. Smoldering passion was there, a smoky drop to a bass register.

At the finish of the song, the Opry crowd went wild. Even before she was half off the stage, the word was she'd topped Pete's spectacular debut at the Opry. She hated comparisons, especially with her own husband. She went back again and again for the standing ovations, until she'd lost count of how many times.

The biggest joy in her life came when Buster ran up to her backstage and kissed her on the mouth. "You're my 'Mountain Momma,' and at long last she's a great big star."

The next morning, with Tara at her side, Rosacoke went to talk over the business of her career with Larry. They met at Pete's recording studio where Buster was going to do a demo for the record, "Git Down Low."

Larry greeted her warmly. Even his lover, Ronnie, came up to kiss her on the mouth. Both had been in the audience the night before for her Opry debut of "Mountain Momma." Skeptically, Rosacoke looked Ronnie up and down. "How's Wanda Mae getting along?"

At the mention of his wife, Ronnie looked downcast. "Okay, I guess," he said before wandering off.

After Buster had recorded five different versions of "Git Down Low," Rosacoke wasn't impressed, considering the song a little shopworn. Buster wasn't that pleased either. "I've got to figure a way to give it the magic."

Tara thought she knew how to put the record over. She agreed to stay at the recording studio until way past midnight if needed.

Kissing Buster good-bye, Rosacoke went back to her lonely hotel suite and her bourbon.

The next morning when she came to the studio with Tara, Buster was nowhere to be seen. Larry was there and played "Git Down Low" for her.

Whatever had happened last night, she didn't know. Suddenly the sound she was hearing had that magic Buster had wanted. Her son had broken through his influences of Presley and Lewis and had found a startlingly original sound. Tara must have helped him.

It was a spontaneous voice that soared with its own kind of purity. It demanded that you listen to it. As his rhythm rang loud and clear, she felt a

tear or two fall. She just hoped that he'd embarked on the right career.

***

Larry slipped a dub of "Mountain Momma" to Stevie Wood, the host disc jockey of a local all-night music show in Nashville. The night of Rosacoke's appearance at the Opry, he played the record more than two dozen times. By dawn calls and telegrams poured into Larry's office, and there was a large demand for interviews, including one from as far away as New York.

That next morning came a contract to become a regular on the Grand Ole Opry. The appearances—about twenty a year—brought only forty dollars each, but Rosacoke could get nationwide publicity and tour as part of the Artist Service Bureau, playing to millions of fans every year.

By the time of the record's release, Rosacoke knew she'd selected the right follow-up song to "Honky Tonk Angel." On the phone, Pete told her these were "the hot months. I've had them. Now you've got them. We'll see each other when we can. Even Buster is working."

Between March 11 and 23, she gave fifteen regular performances in seven cities and even flew to New York to rehearse for a network television special.

She then flew back to Nashville for another appearance at the Grand Ole Opry before a hasty trip to Atlanta for a big blast charity benefit featuring country/western stars.

Sales of "Mountain Momma" were phenomenal. It seemed clearly destined to outpace Patti Page's "Tennessee Waltz," and it was a crossover hit, topping *Billboard's* country as well as its pop charts.

The dizzy whirl of success hit her so fast Rosacoke didn't know where she was most of the time. She was grateful that Larry had worked out everything for her.

"Don't worry about country music declining," Larry told her, slightly reversing earlier opinions. "Rock and Roll will never replace it. You see, you're adapting. That means you can go into the Sixties bigger than ever. Somewhere between pop and your own down-home style is a compromise. Let's call it country pop. You did it with 'Mountain Momma,' and you can do it again. Come up with your own new sound. If you can make it happen, you'll reach millions of new fans."

She wasn't sure, but the responses she'd received until now made her think Larry was right. With his help, she'd search for the right kind of material. In her hotel room late at night, she carefully studied the career of Eddy Arnold, listening to all his country pop records. "If he can do it, so can I," she said, trying to assure herself. Her fellow artists, Patsy Cline and Skeeter Davis, had "crossed over," and she planned to join them. "I'll

change," she kept telling herself. "I'll adapt. I won't ever be a dinosaur in music."

She never seemed to be at a phone when Buster called and vice versa. If she tried to reach him in Nacogdoches, he was already in Austin. His MGM record deal had fallen through, but Larry had arranged a roughly equivalent contract for him at Sunshine Records for "Git Down Low." Shortly after its release, it had sold twenty-five thousand copies, and it had appeared briefly in the number two spot on the country and western charts in Memphis. In *Billboard's* poll, Buster had been named ninth among the most promising new hillbilly artists.

Most of Buster's records sent to disc jockeys ended up in the garbage in spite of his small acclaim. A surprising number of DJs thought Buster was black.

Larry certainly wasn't put off by the slow sales of Buster's first record. For his second recording, "Hillbilly Cat," he got Buster a better distribution deal. That record picked up in sales, and before the end of 1957, Buster had been named as the nation's most promising new country and western artist. His records—by now, six in a row—had been steadily increasing in sales.

Larry was turned down when he tried to get Buster on the Arthur Godfrey show. That was the last rejection Buster was to experience for a long time.

To Rosacoke, Buster had burst upon the Eisenhower era like a ten-megaton bomb, affecting style, music, and popular culture. It all came when Larry moved him to RCA where he recorded "Red and Hot Tonight" and was preparing his first big album. With that song, he topped the C&W, R&B, and pop charts, something neither Pete nor Rosacoke had ever done, as they didn't do rockabilly.

The only time in the next five months that Rosacoke saw Buster was when he was on television. Between road shows, she realized the moment she arrived at Heaven on Earth that their lives had changed. Karl had ordered that an iron fence, along with round-the-clock security guards, be positioned around the mansion. Every runaway girl in America seemed to head for their place, hoping to catch a glimpse of their idol, Buster Riddle.

Every week ten-thousand fan letters poured in, as opposed to about a hundred a week that Rosacoke and Pete each got. In the basement, Rosacoke discovered that Larry had hired three secretaries to grind out standard form replies to fan mail, mailing out glossy photographs suppos-edly autographed by Buster himself. Rosacoke still personally autographed her own.

As Larry told her on the phone, "When Buster recorded 'Red and Hot Tonight,' he made history. He's got a million dollars now."

Reading through the newspaper files, she realized that he didn't get just

praise. One critic wrote, "He quivers like he just swallowed a jackhammer." Self-appointed protectors of public morals hysterically denounced him from the pulpit "as a menace to young girls."

He was called "The Young Elvis." Or "The Pied Piper of "Rock and Roll." Larry viewed him as a "twenty-four karat recording artist," with his personal appearances creating pandemonium.

Arriving back at Heaven on Earth for a two-day visit, the staff had to arrange clearance for Rosacoke at the gate. At least three hundred of Buster's fans waited outside the locked barricade, even though Buster wasn't even in the state.

When Pete called her later from California, she detected a faint note of jealousy in his voice. After all her struggles, she'd been a tiny bit jealous of Buster too, so she could hardly blame Pete for his feelings. "Pure and simple country singers like us can't survive this new age," Pete said over the phone. "We're gonna get rocked and rolled over."

"Don't be too sure," she told him. "We may be around longer than you think. I mean, me and you are bigger than ever on the country charts. Maybe we don't generate the excitement that Elvis and Buster do, but we're still doing mighty fine. I remember the way we used to play joints where there were only six people—all of them drunk—in the audience."

After talking to Pete, Rosacoke wandered to the back verandah at Heaven on Earth.

In the distance, she spotted Tara staggering toward the porch from her gingerbread cottage. It was obvious that she'd been hitting the bourbon and branch water again. Rosacoke had never seen Tara look this dejected.

"He's turned me down," she said when spotting Rosacoke.

"What do you mean?" Rosacoke asked.

"Buster," she said. "He's become the Romeo of the highway. He can have anybody he wants. I wanted to go on the road with him to assist him since I ain't got anything else to do. But he said he doesn't want me. Guess I'll cramp his style now that he's so popular."

"He'll change his mind," Rosacoke said. "He needs you. You've been a real friend to him, standing by him like you've done."

"He seems to have forgotten that."

"Care to join me for supper?" Rosacoke asked.

"Not tonight," Tara said. "I'm gonna do something in the main house, then head back to my cottage to drink my supper tonight. Glad to see you, hoss, but I'm not good company. I don't know if I'm gonna come out of my cottage for a long time."

Rosacoke's own nerves were edgy tonight, as she headed for the bourbon bottle. Everybody at Heaven on Earth was a heavy drinker, so no one said anything if one had a drink even at seven o'clock in the morning, or especially if one had a drink then to steady one's nerves.

"This stardom thing," Tara said. "It's never what it's cracked up to be. Not that I'd know what it's like to be a star. That's for you and Pete--and Buster—to find out. But as for me, I can't even lay claim to being a has-been."

***

Rosacoke woke up to a bright, cloudless day in spite of the threatening mist of last night. She wished that Pete and Buster were back home, so they could gather for an old-fashioned country breakfast. Immediately, she sat up in bed, an alarm passing through her body. An image of Tara flashed through her mind. Late last night she'd tapped on the door to her cottage, wanting to bring her some cake and warm milk. The door had been bolted.

Rosacoke put on a beautiful new gold bathrobe Pete had given her and padded softly down the rose-bordered pathway to Tara's cottage. The door was open, the bed unmade. Two empty bottles of bourbon lay on a nearby rug. At least Tara was up.

Back at the main house, a maid was dusting the living room furniture. "Have you seen Tara?" Rosacoke asked.

"Yes, Mrs. Riddle," the maid said. "A little while ago she went to the basement."

"Thank you." In panic Rosacoke hurried to the basement, knowing that Pete kept his guns there. As she opened the door, the smell was dank as a grave. She tiptoed down the steps, coming to a stop at the bottom landing. Sunlight poured in through a small half-moon window coated with red clay dust. It took a moment for her eyes to adjust to the dim room.

In the center of the floor Tara held a rifle, Pete's favorite, which he always took with him on hunting trips. She was surprised that Tara was holding a gun at this hour of the morning, although she knew that she'd been an expert hunter years ago. "It's my Indian blood," Tara always used to say. "But instead of a bow and arrow, I now use a rifle."

Conflicting images fought for control of Rosacoke's mind. She couldn't bring herself to believe that Tara was about to commit suicide. She must be holding the gun for some other reason, Rosacoke thought, although she couldn't imagine that the big woman was actually going hunting.

Without realizing that she was being watched, Tara took some shells from a box in the storage room. She slipped in two shells and lowered the gun butt carefully to the floor, then leaned forward. But as she pressed the barrel against her forehead, just above the eyebrows, Rosacoke screamed and rushed toward her.

Tara pulled the trigger, simultaneously jerking her head to the side at the sound of Rosacoke's scream. Instead of ripping into her head, the bullet pierced her upper body instead.

Rushing up to her, Rosacoke grabbed the rifle, easily wrestling it from her. Tara slumped onto the floor as Rosocoke knelt over her.

The rifle blast on the quiet Sunday morning brought a screaming maid. Karl had come over early to work on Pete's books, and he too must have heard the blast. He rushed down the steps into the basement. With his quick brain, he took charge at once. He ripped Tara's robe from her body to examine her wound and feel her heartbeat. "She's still alive," he assured Rosacoke. "They're calling an ambulance."

It was twenty-five long, agonizing minutes before the ambulance came. Rosacoke put on a pants suit as quickly as she could and rushed downstairs with Karl to their waiting limousine. Beside it, Tara was loaded into the ambulance.

As this early-morning caravan passed through the gate, Rosacoke was grateful that Buster's fans hadn't shown up for their all-day vigil. At least that way they might escape attracting attention from the press.

An hour later, Tara's doctor came out of the operating room to greet Rosacoke and Karl. The bullet had entered Tara's chest, narrowly missing her heart. "She's going to live," the doctor assured them. "She's out of danger."

"Thank God." Rosacoke burst into tears, as Karl comforted her. Later, with the doctor's permission, she checked into an adjoining room at the hospital so she would be here when Tara came to.

Once Rosacoke settled in, she called Buster in Nashville and miraculously reached him.

"Son, I've got bad news. Tara tried to kill herself. I really think you should come home."

"Oh, shit! Is she okay?"

"The doctor thinks she's out of danger. But you really should be here."

"I can't. I've got this big recording session."

"Cancel it! I don't think you understand. Tara tried to kill herself."

After a few more minutes of her urging Buster to come home, he still hadn't agreed. "I'll get back to you," he said. "I've got to talk to Pete first. He's here in Nashville." He hung up the phone abruptly.

She didn't bother to call back, as she wasn't certain that Buster's coming home was the best idea after all. She didn't know what to do.

The next morning, Tara regained consciousness, and Rosacoke was allowed to see her.

"Why did you do it, honey?" Rosacoke asked, taking her hand. "We love you so. We need you so. Buster will come around. He needs you, too."

Tara looked for a long moment into Rosacoke's eyes. "I'm in love with Buster. Always have been. Ever since I first changed his diapers."

"You mean, you love him. I love him, too."

"No, God damn it. I love him like a woman loves a man."

Rosacoke was appalled. Perhaps she'd always known this, but it was amazing how mothers often didn't want to admit a lot of things. She knew that Tara's love for Buster was hopeless. Rosacoke deeply feared that Tara would make another attempt on her life, as she was bound to be rejected by Buster. Rosacoke felt that her son had a big head anyway and what would he want with fat Tara anyway? Certainly not for sexual fulfillment. Rosacoke seriously doubted if even Pete could retain Buster's affections for long. Surely he would eventually meet some handsome teenager his own age and dump Pete as a bedmate.

She fully realized that as his popularity mounted, he'd abandon his childhood dependency on Tara and come to see her for what she was—an aging, broken-down derelict who hit the bottle too often. Rosacoke was certain that Buster had already come to that point of view. Perhaps that was why he'd forbidden Tara from going on the road with him.

Rosacoke was torn between pity for Tara and wanting her son to grow and develop, forming relationships with boys his own age. She was deeply disturbed, on the one hand feeling sorry for Tara, but on the other wanting Buster to be free to live his own life.

The next afternoon and to her surprise, a pink-suited Buster barged into Rosacoke's room at the hospital. He looked as if he hadn't had much sleep. Not even greeting her, he demanded to know which room Tara was in. She directed him next door to Tara's bedside, where the large woman was resting.

"How's my gal?" he asked Tara.

Her dark gray eyes came alive at the sight of him. "You came. My baby! You're here."

Buster pressed his lips down on hers, as Rosacoke headed for the door, not wanting to look back.

\*\*\*

With Tara in recovery, and Buster keeping a vigil by her side, Rosacoke delayed her departure from Heaven on Earth for as long as possible. Junior was impatiently waiting to fly her to Charlotte. Larry had lined up a full six weeks of bookings for her.

Claude had called earlier to tell her that their bus from Nashville should be at Heaven on Earth by ten o'clock that morning if the weather didn't turn bad in the mountains. Pete had flown to Nashville from Los Angeles and into a recording date arranged by Larry.

In spite of Junior's protests, Rosacoke had decided to delay her departure for Charlotte until she could have a reunion, however brief, with Claude and Pete. She stood bundled up, bracing herself against the first cold winds

of the early winter, waiting as patiently as she could.

Although they spoke frequently over the phone, she hadn't seen Pete since their divorce. She'd made a number of visits to Heaven on Earth, but Pete had never been there.

Through the gate came Pete driving a new pink Cadillac, something that Elvis might buy. Claude was following behind in the bus with all the musicians.

Seeing her on the front verandah, Pete braked the Cadillac and ran to her arms, holding her tight and planting a gooey wet kiss on her lips. She felt he'd never been this happy to see her before, even when he was married to her.

Releasing her, he said, "Thank God Tara's come through. Buster couldn't wait for us. He drove here on his own even before I had a chance to present him with his present. This pink Cadillac. The first car he's ever really owned. A gift from both of us."

"You sure he should be driving?" she asked. "He's mighty young."

He had a suggestive look on his face when he gazed into her eyes. "He's mighty young to do a lot of things he's doing, but he's doing them anyway."

She didn't want to touch that subject and admired the car instead. Karl rushed out to give Pete a kiss on the mouth. "Tara's waiting to see you, and welcome home." Taking Pete's hand, Karl led him toward Tara's cottage where Rosacoke had earlier said her good-byes to both Tara and Buster.

As he retreated, Pete waved good-bye to her and wished her luck on the road.

Claude came over to her, kissing her gently on the mouth.

"Long time no see," he said, wrapping his arm around her.

"It's good to see you again, stud," she said. "Real good. I've missed you."

In a voice barely audible, he said, "What me and you have got is still out there somewhere. Any time you want to call it back, it'll still be good. I'm talking love, woman."

"Don't you go waiting around for a no good gal like me," she said. "You deserve someone who'll devote her whole life to loving you. You're that special as a man."

"If I'm all that special, why don't you pluck me from the vine? I'm ripe enough."

"I fucked up my life one time with one man, and almost did it again with Doug Porter until I came to my senses," she said. "I'm too rotten now for any man to have me." She kissed him lightly on the lips. "I know what you feel for me, and I have real strong feelings for you too. But I'm not ready to belong to any one man. Maybe never again. Forget me."

He looked at her with such penetrating eyes he made her shiver. "Never,"

he said, raising his voice. I'll always be waiting for you."

Junior yelled for her to get into the car.

Claude smiled faintly, lowering his voice. "I know you went through hell giving up your baby in 1942," he said. "It's also harder than hell giving up my baby, namely you. Maybe you'll write a song about it." He tried to crack a smile. "It's time you followed up your latest hit with another hit."

When she gazed into his eyes, she saw the red there. He really wanted to cry, but was holding back tears. Impulsively she moved to comfort him.

"Don't get near me, woman," he said. "If you do, I'm bound to reach out and grab you and hold on for dear life." He turned from her and headed toward the front verandah as the other musicians on the bus, including Nipsey and Freddie, crowded around her to greet her and welcome her back.

"Claude," she called out to his back but he'd disappeared inside the mansion.

Junior rushed up and herded her into the waiting limousine. As he sped to the airport to fly her to Charlotte, he looked at her and smiled. "I saw that scene between you guys. Something tells me that the story of Rosacoke Carson and Claude Billings ain't over yet."

Within thirty minutes, he was airborne, flying Pete's private plane south to Charlotte.

Up in the clouds, she thought over what Junior had said. Could it be true? Would she ever marry Claude one day?

Right now she was on top of the world—literally in the clouds—and couldn't think about that.

She was a big star. All was right with the world. Nothing evil could come out of that spooky pinewood forest that had scared her as a child.

Nothing.

***

In his first Cadillac, all shiny pink, Buster invited Pete to go for a ride with him high into the Blue Ridge Mountains. Claude, who as a former sheriff was clever at securing documents, had gotten Buster a driver's license, even though he was only sixteen and the driving age was eighteen. "I've got a big surprise for you," he told Pete.

It was a cold winter's day, with snow flurries in the air and sleet on the road. But Buster was insistent, as he was excited to try out his first shiny new automobile. Pete agreed to go along with him, providing he'd get him back home before dark.

On the way to what Buster called "my secret place," Pete noticed a large ruby and diamond ring on his finger. "It's a gift from Tara," he said. "Sorta like a friendship ring. You should see the stone I gave her."

"I'm sure I will." He didn't want to ask any more questions. His son's

relationship with Tara always puzzled him, and he didn't want to pry into that murky friendship. By the same token, he didn't want any of his gang asking too many questions about his own troubling involvement with Buster.

Pete settled back in his seat and was pleased to see that Tara had taught his son how to handle a car. "I'm right proud of you, kid," Pete said. "I get a little nervous, though, when I hear your music. You seem to be deserting country music real fast. I think you're going to rock and roll like Elvis. I guess you young rockers think guys like me are old-fashioned hillbillies who've outlived our time."

"You know what I think of you," Buster said, dangerously taking his eyes off the curvy road. "I think you're the hottest man on the planet. Young men and tons of gals throw themselves at me, but I'm truly a daddy's boy. You're nuts about me too. Admit it."

"I'm addicted."

"You're not getting older. You're getting better. I'm one lucky boy to have you for my daddy."

"I'm glad to see you getting on with your own career," Pete said. "You're gonna be big."

"I might be the lover of Pete Riddle but I couldn't go through the rest of my life being known just as the son of Pete Riddle. Once a man spat on me just 'cause I didn't sing like you do. Another time, an older woman propositioned me 'cause she had a crush on you, and I was your son. She would have been really disappointed if I'd taken her to bed. My dick's only half as big as yours."

"It's not a competition between us—certainly not in bed, and not really in music. I want you to sing your own songs—not those of mine."

"You know how I imitated you for years," Buster said. "You taught me how to sing. But I had to go on and break from your kind of music. Or else I'd end up like a sideshow in a freak circus, doing your hits and not anywhere as good as you do them."

"I want to hear you talk that way," he said. "Which leads to a painful thing to bring up. As much as I'd miss you, I think you should start looking for another loving man and not focus on your daddy. What we're doing is wrong."

"You love my love-making," he said, a look of grim ferocity flashing across his face. "I'll never let you go."

"There are a lot of handsome guys in this world with big dicks," Pete said. "You should start checking them out."

"Cheat on you?" Buster said. "I can't believe you're talking like that. I'm faithful to my old man."

Buster drove past Pete's own mountain retreat, which Karl had built for him and which he rarely used any more. As he passed the modern mountain home, Pete thought nostalgically of Josh and that snowbound

weekend they'd spent there locked in each other's arms.

Buster drove to the highest point on the mountain where the road came to an end. After that, Buster took Pete's hand as they walked in the bitter cold winds along a rock-strewn path as the snow flurries whipped their faces.

Pete protested the walk as he liked snug and cozy places on days like this. "I sure hope your surprise is worth all this," he said.

Even though Buster slipped and fell one time, he was eager to press on along the steep mountain trail with Pete. "There's magic in the Blue Ridge," Buster said. "Clouds up here aren't white but a misty blue. The higher I climb, the closer I feel to God. Sometimes I think I am God myself. That I have the power to reach out and harness the wind." He waved his arms wildly in the air, nearly falling over an embankment before Pete caught him.

"Steady there, boy," Pete said. "You're a bit of a wild thing today. I still think you and I would have more fun down there in my own mountain cabin in front of a crackling log fire."

"That's later," Buster said. "I want you to take me there and throw away the key for a few days. Call Tara and the gang and tell them that me and you are working on some music together and don't want to be disturbed for a few days. Claude will keep the pack of hounds away from us."

Pete looked at the beautiful winter landscape. "Anyone ever live this far up in the mountains before?"

"There's a shack nearby where an old granny woman lived in the Twenties," Buster said. "Any time anybody came around to see if she was dead or alive, she'd chase them away with a shotgun. That gun was fired many times before she up and died one day. One day her son from Virginia came to see her. She even fired at him and almost killed him. Talk about wanting to be alone! With my new earnings, I bought up all this property around here, five-hundred fucking acres. Karl made the deal for me. That's one smart Adams brother."

Panting, Pete came to a rest stop. "What, pray tell, are you gonna do with it? It's cold up here even in summer. When spring finally comes, you've got to rush out the door, hurry around looking for a crocus, then rush back inside by the fire before the mountain winds of autumn start blowing and freezing your balls off."

"All those fans milling outside that gate will never find me up here," Buster said. "I'll be alone. Mainly I want it as a place for the two of us to go. I can't stand living at Heaven on Earth with so many folks. I don't want to share you."

"But Karl has already built a mountain retreat for me," Pete protested. "If we want to get away from it all, we can go there. We don't need another place."

"Don't you understand?" Buster asked, pouting. "This will be my first

real home. I've always lived with you. Your mountain home is your place. I want a place of my own."

"Hell, I'll give you the deed." Pete said. "It'll be yours and only yours."

"Karl designed that for you," Buster said. "My place is going to be different. It's gonna be built to my own specifications."

Exhausted, Pete reached the top of the mountain peak. The climb didn't seem to wind a kid as young as Buster. Even though the day was foggy and misty, with all those snow flurries, Pete could see a sheer drop down a rock-strewn mountain. He realized he was standing precariously on the edge of a cliff and jerked back quickly. Any height always made him feel dizzy. He was a country boy who liked to keep his feet on red clay he could trust.

Buster wasn't afraid. He was more of a mountaineer than Pete was. He was running around the edge of the slippery cliff like a carefree kid at a tarmac-covered children's playground on a summer day. He slipped once but quickly regained his balance.

"For Christ's sake, watch your step," Pete called out to him.

Buster didn't seem to pay him any heed. He seemed delirious as if all his hopes and dreams were about to come true. A lover, his daddy, stardom, the dream house he was going to build.

"Deep in winter the snow's so deep up here and the wind howls so bad and it's so cold it's like living on the planet all by yourself," Buster said. "I'll have you all to myself and not have to compete with all those others wanting a piece of your flesh." Buster came up close to Pete and gave him a long, lingering kiss. "I love you more than I thought it was possible to love anybody on God's green earth. When you descend on me and crush me in your strong arms, I feel I've died and gone to Heaven. But it scares me too."

"What are you afraid of?" Pete asked.

"Too much happiness," he said, kissing Pete again. A feverish look had come across his face. "I'm afraid that if you're too happy, God will come and take away that happiness."

"That's bullshit, and you know it," Pete said. "God wants his little children to be happy. Love doesn't always mean suffering and pain. It can bring joy too."

Buster kissed him once more before breaking away from Pete. For some reason, Buster's crazed look and his fear had triggered a foreboding inside Pete. He too felt both of them were in some mortal danger, as if an assassin's bullet was about to be fired into their brains.

"I belong to the mountains," Buster shouted to the wind, dancing about like he did on stage and twirling his arms in the air like a spinning top. "I was born here, and I want to die here."

"Sixteen years old is pretty young to be talking about dying," Pete called

out to him.

"I feel free," Buster shouted. "It's here I want to be."

"Then be a mountain goat," Pete shouted at him.

Suddenly Buster raced toward Pete as if he were going to leap into his arms.

Pete reached out for him. But it was too late.

The next ten seconds passed in front of his eyes like a nightmare bolted straight from Hell and personally autographed by the Devil.

***

Ten feet from Buster, Pete frantically reached out as if he'd grown extended arms that could pluck his son from disaster. The fall was inevitable.

Breaking away, Buster slid on a snow-covered bed of ice toward the edge of the cliff. A plaintive look on his face called out for help.

Pete was powerless. He screamed, "You'll be killed!" In utter horror, he stood by as Buster plunged over the cliff. Buster's own piercing scream, sounding like an echo, sliced through the cold air of a fading afternoon.

Pete inched forward on the ice with tears streaming down his face. Suddenly, he heard a loud thud. Buster's voice was stilled.

Pete's stomach was tied in knots, and little time bombs seemed to go off every few seconds deep in his gut. Was Buster dead?

Bracing himself, he eased toward the precipice, hovering dangerously close to the overhang, overcoming a lifelong fear.

Halfway down the cliff, a large gray boulder appeared blurred in Pete's tear-stained vision. Buster had landed there on his stomach. Pete could see only the back of Buster's head. A tremulous hand reached up as if to clutch something solid. Empty, it collapsed back to Buster's side. There was only the howling wind.

Desperately scanning the vertiginous cliff dropping steeply below him, Pete began to scale his way down the slope, making a detour to the left of Buster's shattered body to avoid hitting him with the inevitable rocks he knew he'd dislodge on the way down. As he struggled to avoid losing his grip, jagged edges of rock sliced at him like razor blades. Snow flurries peppered the air, and their crystals seemed to cut into his eyes like glass. Pete stumbled and fell, picking himself up again and then plowing on. His leather boots were sturdy, but not thick enough to protect him from the jagged edges cutting into his soles. When he was at the same altitude as Buster, only twenty horizontal feet from where he lay, he realized he couldn't maneuver sideways along the nearly vertical cliff, as there were simply no handholds to allow a sideways transit across the rock face. Desperately aware that his son's life hung in the balance, he continued down the cliff

face until he was on flat and relatively firm ground, peering up at Buster dangling forty feet above him.

He'd never climbed such a steep hillside before, but he was more grimly determined than he'd ever been about anything in his life. Aided by protruding rocks and clinging vegetation, he mounted the underside of the cliff. Once, he nearly lost control. Amid a cascade of sand and gravel, he clutched at a gnarled thorn bush as a means of keeping himself from backsliding down to his own death. Despite the blood streaming from the palms of his hands, he hung on with tenacity.

With his nose pressed hard against the rock face, he almost rutted through the ground. Every inch he gained brought him closer and closer to Buster's aid. Chips cut away at Pete's face, and he smelled the sweet scent of his own blood, but didn't care.

He finally reached Buster on the protruding boulder. Buster was moaning softly. Gently Pete turned him over.

Pete's first impulse was to scream. With all the force and self-control he could muster, he obliterated the image before him. As he reached for Buster, he smiled weakly, obscuring what was going on inside him. "You're gonna be okay, son. You're not gonna die."

He wished he could believe that. Buster's nose and one entire cheek was missing. The other side of his face looked like a piece of raw liver.

It was even worse. Not only was his face missing, an eye hung out of its socket, and part of his brain was exposed.

Trembling all over, Pete removed his leather gloves. Swallowing hard, he took his hand and placed Buster's eye back in its socket. Pete's hands met soft, squishy tissue. He gently eased the exposed brain back in its cavity, and a gentle plop sound made Pete puke. Clamping his mouth shut, he swallowed his own vomit.

Pete didn't know what to do. Stay with Buster? Rush for help? It was the hardest decision of his life. The sun was setting over the mountains, and it would be dark in an hour.

"Oh, God," he cried out for mercy, looking up at a threatening sky. With time running out, he had to make up his mind.

Just then, Buster reached up to touch his face, feeling for his nose. He found nothing there, only the base of it. Broken teeth and parts of his jaw fell into his gloved hand.

"Dad," he cried out. "My face, it's not there!"

"You'll be okay." How weak sounding, how unconvincing were Pete's words even to himself. He'd made up his mind. Knowing he had to make a mad dash for help, he thought he'd never forgive himself if Buster died all alone on this foreboding, lonely mountainside.

Pete spotted two Budweiser cans that some picnickers had tossed off the side of the cliff last summer. The tin cans had caught in the tangled

underbrush growing up the hillside.

He edged over and plucked the empty cans from the brush. Returning with them, he placed one in each of Buster's hands. Buster had to do something. If he fell asleep like this, he would die.

"This is gonna sound real crazy," Pete told him. "But I want you to make music until I get back. Bang these old cans together. Try to make the sounds of every record you've ever made. If you run out of songs, start on my songs. You know every one of them better than I do. I'll be back before then."

"Music? You've lost your mind."

"Buster." His voice was sharp, commanding. "Do what I say. If you never do anything I want ever again, grant me this one. *Do what I say!* Bang those God damn cans together—and keep banging. It doesn't matter how tired you get. If you stop banging, you'll die."

Pete took both of Buster's hands, now holding the cans, and banged them together. The next time Buster did it for himself.

Pete reached down to kiss him good-bye. There was nothing to kiss. He kissed both of his son's hands, even though they were gloved. "I'll be back. And soon. I love you."

"I'm not going anywhere," Buster said. He banged the cans together. With his one good eye, he gave a forlorn look, as if saying farewell.

With all the strength left in him, Pete tore away from Buster and scrabbled his way down the cliff. When he reached flat and solid ground, with his heart pumping wildly, he raced around the side of the mountain, then pounded his way up a steep alpine trail, eventually coming to the pink Cadillac.

He had to get an ambulance. There was a filling station with a phone about three miles away.

In the car, driving blindly, he fought back tears. After what seemed an interminable time, he reached the service station. To his shock, he found it had closed early, because of snow flurries and probably lack of business. On the way down, he'd spotted not one car driving up here this high.

He picked up a stone and broke a pane of glass near the doorknob. He reached in, turning the knob and letting himself in.

At the phone he nervously called Claude. A servant picked up the phone. "Claude…get him quick!" he commanded.

In a minute Claude was on the phone. The sound of his voice filled Pete with relief. "Get an ambulance FAST," he yelled into the receiver. "Buster fell off a cliff. He's dying. His head is all smashed up. He's caught on a boulder, midway down the cliff, just below the ledge where he wanted to build his house."

"Great God almighty! I know the place. He took me there yesterday. We'll be there in no time at all. Where you at?"

"Jack's station."

"Wait outside. We'll pick you up in a jiffy. You okay?"

"Don't worry about me. I'll be waiting."

Hanging up the phone, he ran to the side of the highway, although he knew it would be at least an hour before Claude appeared with an ambulance.

The snow came down heavier now, and Pete was cold. In spite of that, he stood stiffly, not moving, peering down the road waiting for the first sign of headlights.

Lots of thoughts tried to take control of his mind, and one by one he fought each of them off. He'd face all those fears later tonight. Right now he'd done what he was supposed to do. Everything depended on that help coming up the hill.

"Don't let him die," he cried into the rapidly fading daylight. He was hoping God out there somewhere would hear him and answer his prayer. *"Please*, don't let him die."

***

The next hour, days, passed as in a blur for Pete. He could still recall standing in front of Jack's service station, shivering in the cold, when Claude finally appeared with the ambulance. Larry and Ronnie trailed in a black Cadillac.

Jumping down from the ambulance, Claude embraced Pete, ripping off his jacket and concealing his famous face from the ambulance driver, as he pressed Pete's body toward Larry's car. He was taken by surprise as to why Claude wanted to conceal his identity, but there was no time to ask, as Claude hustled him into the Cadillac, then ran to rejoin the ambulance driver.

When Pete woke up at Heaven on Earth the next morning, he didn't remember passing out. He figured that Tara must have drugged him when she gave him a comforting drink of bourbon from her flask. Reviving slowly, Pete noticed Karl nodding in a chair at the foot of his bed.

Pete screamed for Buster, startling Karl out of his dozing. Within a minute, Larry was in the room, telling Pete that Rosacoke had been informed and that she was flying back at once.

"Is Buster alive?" Pete demanded to know. "I want to see my son."

Karl let him know that Buster was in critical condition but still alive. A cover-up had already begun. Since Buster couldn't be identified by his face, he had been admitted to the hospital as Ken Reeves, a visiting high school student from Tallahassee, Florida, who'd gone hiking alone in the Blue Ridge.

Fighting off bouts of hysteria, Pete was hard to convince, but eventually Claude prevailed. He wanted Buster's accident kept from the media.

"Buster's gonna live but what's he gonna look like?" Karl asked. "Plastic

surgery doesn't always work miracles—especially when most of his face is missing. You've got to have something to start with. Buster just doesn't have much of a face. A new one will have to be made." He paused a long moment, lighting a cigarette. "If that's possible."

Fearing it wasn't possible, Pete let out a scream. At his bedside, Claude gently but firmly slapped Pete's face, bringing him back to his senses. The awful image of looking into Buster's face kept flashing through Pete's mind.

"If his fans find out he's become some sort of monster, it would break Buster's heart," Karl predicted. "You've got to listen to me and do it our way, for Buster's sake. Tara's with him now, half out of her mind. That's one guy who really cares about his looks. Remember—he always carried a comb and mirror in his pocket."

"You think Buster wants it this way?" Pete asked in a weak, tentative voice.

"I'm sure he does," Claude said. "We're gonna slip you into the hospital later tonight so you can see him. Of course, you'll have to be in disguise. If he's coherent, ask him yourself."

"Buster's known all over the country," Karl said. "If he just up and disappears, it'll be headline news everywhere."

"Don't you think I know that more than anybody?" Pete asked with growing impatience.

"I've got plenty of connections in this county," Claude said. "I've got so much shit on the sheriff himself that I can more or less get what I want within the borders of Wilkes County."

"I don't know how in the hell you think you can pull this one off," Pete said, sitting up in bed.

"Our Hitler Youth and all-time hiking champ, Freddie, is out hiking the mountains right now, leaving a well-marked trail behind him," Claude said. "The story is, as him and Buster were crossing a rickety wooden bridge, Buster slipped and fell into the muddy waters of the river. Freddie is gonna claim he tried desperately to rescue Buster, but he was washed downriver before he could save him. Presumably he drowned."

"You'll never get away with that crap!" Pete said, feeling that both Karl and Claude had temporarily lost their minds.

"Don't be too sure," Claude predicted.

"Trust us with this one," Karl said, coming over to Pete's bed where he took him in his arms to cradle and kiss him.

*\*\*\**

Tara had been allowed to move into Buster's hospital room, after Claude had officially identified her as the mother of Ken Reeves. Tara was addressed as "Mrs. Reeves."

When Pete called Rosacoke and told her of the disaster, she'd flown at once to Charlotte where Junior had picked her up in Pete's private plane and taken her to the Wilkes County airport. Claude was waiting there to take her to Heaven on Earth.

At the mansion, Pete rushed to take her in his arms. "He's gonna be okay," he said. "I love you, and I love our son."

She hugged him as she burst into tears.

"If you could only see him," Pete said. "It's awful."

Both Pete and Claude told her of their plan to claim that Buster had disappeared and that the young man at the hospital was actually Ken Reeves, a hiker from Florida. Claude persuaded her to go to the hospital in disguise, claiming to be a relative of the young man. She agreed to the plan, donning a black wig Tara had bought for her. So as not to be identified, Pete remained behind at Heaven on Earth.

Grim-faced, Claude drove her to the hospital, saying very little. Whatever personal relationship and problems they had with each other remained on ice.

A half hour later, Claude slipped her in through the back door of the clinic and arranged for her to go and sit in Buster's room. He was heavily sedated.

To her shock and horror, she found Buster's head swollen like one of those watermelons she used to grow. His jaws were wired. She sat in silence by his bed for three hours until he opened his eyes. All in bandages, he tried to utter her name.

"I'm here, son," she said, feeling she was speaking into a cavity.

Very gently, she explained to him what was about to happen—that news of his death, by drowning, would soon be flashed around the world. "That's gonna cause a big outpouring of grief among your fans." She informed him that he was registered at the hospital as Ken Reeves, and she wanted to know if he agreed to all these actions so far. He muttered a brief "Um." But it was enough to convince her to go along with the fraud.

Throughout the long night, doctors had continued to race desperately to fight a brain infection. One surgeon told Rosacoke that if it had been summer instead of winter, "Your cousin would be dead."

Back at Heaven on Earth, Pete embraced Rosacoke, hoping to give her courage. "I've already talked to Doug," she said. "As soon as we can, he wants us to fly Buster to New York. When he's out of danger and the swelling goes down, Doug and two other top plastic surgeons are going to examine Buster's face to see what can be done. One of those guys did some pretty amazing things with soldiers whose faces were destroyed in the Korean War."

"We'll worry later about making Buster good-looking again," Pete said, holding her close. "Right now we've got to worry about keeping him alive."

"I believe he's going to live," she said. "God knows what he'll look like but right now I want him to live at all costs." She noted a strange look of deep distress on Pete's face.

"You don't think he'll look like some Frankenstein monster, do you?" Pete asked.

"Whatever he looks like, we are his mommy and daddy, and we'll love him like he's the prettiest thing on God's green earth."

"That we'll do," he said, backing away, that foreboding look still on his face.

For some reason, his voice did not sound convincing to her.

***

Later that night Rosacoke sat close to Pete as they watched Larry tell his story before worldwide media.

At the end of the newscast, Pete got up to pour himself a drink. "I wouldn't buy that. But we'll see."

"I bet a lot of people will go for it," Claude said.

Rosacoke said nothing, remaining on the sofa, staring vacantly into the burning fireplace.

As predicted, the story caused a nationwide sensation, leading to an avalanche of speculation and rumors. Thousands of fans refused to believe that Buster was dead. However, tens of thousands believed he was. By midnight on the night of the broadcast, hundreds of fans had started to arrive at the gates of Heaven on Earth, holding a vigil.

The next morning, local authorities began searching the river.

Much of the eyes and ears of country music fans stayed focused on the gates around Heaven on Earth. Souvenir hawkers selling Buster memorabilia worked the crowds. Fans numbering in the hundreds stood outside the gates of the mansion, waiting for some news, hopefully that Buster was alive. Larry issued frequent press bulletins.

Surprisingly, after two weeks the dragnet of the river turned up with a body of a young man. The corpse was so badly decomposed that accurate identification was impossible. However, it was announced to the press that the ruby and diamond ring, which Buster was wearing at the time of his disappearance, was found on the body.

Rosacoke knew that someone had put that ring there, and she was sure that Claude was responsible. She didn't want to know the facts. When Pete started to tell her, she interrupted him. "You guys do it your way. I'm going to my room."

As endless debate and speculation about the corpse dragged on, and the vigil was maintained around Heaven on Earth, Rosacoke came to realize that the worst days of her life had passed. She was disappointed that

Doug would not fly to the Carolinas, but he claimed there was nothing he could do until Buster was stabilized. He still insisted that when that time came, Buster should be flown for examination in New York, preferably on Pete's private plane.

She continued to see Buster, slipping in and out of the clinic in disguise. His jaws were still wired.

Pete did not go to the hospital with her, knowing that he would be recognized. He kept telling Rosacoke to give Buster his love.

When Buster was released from the hospital, Claude drove him and Tara to Pete's mountainside chalet, which Karl had built. Karl had ordered a twenty-four-hour security guard around the place. It was deemed impossible for Buster to be taken to Heaven on Earth because the property was under surveillance, and cars coming and going from the mansion attracted onlookers.

On Rosacoke's first visit to the chalet, she found Buster wearing sunglasses and a knit ski mask. "The first week or so after the accident, it wasn't so bad," he said. "The horror came when I saw myself. When I was able to get out of bed and go to the bathroom by myself, I stared and stared at my face in the mirror. None of the hospital staff had let me look in the mirror before. I screamed. I look like something in a horror movie."

She offered him what comfort she could, even though a horrible guilt festered inside her, keeping her awake at night. As much as she loved him, she felt uncomfortable in his presence and only looked at him when she had to. She didn't want to see what was behind those sunglasses and under the stocking cap. She'd seen enough that first day in the hospital. She wanted to remember Buster the way he looked when his male beauty and teenage sexuality caused near riots among his fans.

During the first weeks after his accident, he'd been given so many painkillers that he almost became addicted. "Thank God for Tara," he kept saying. "She seems more devoted to me than ever."

Rosacoke agreed. She didn't know what Buster would do without Tara. Like a loving nurse, Tara abandoned whatever meager life she had to devote to Buster. She undressed him daily, giving him whirlpool baths which he claimed on some days was all he had to look forward to.

One day when Rosacoke visited she found him deep in depression.

Tara was downstairs making one of her endless vitamin-enriched shakes with fresh vegetables in the blender. "It's like green slime," he told Rosacoke, with his teeth clamped shut. But he could still move his lips and tongue. "Just the right food for the creature from the dark lagoon. I drink it to stay alive. With my jaws wired, what am I gonna bite into? 'Member those pan-fried pork chops Tara used to cook? God, how I'd love to devour eight of 'em, then have her throw a big T-bone on the charcoal grill."

Having put her own career on hold, even though threatened with law-

suits, Rosacoke had to face the inevitable daily question from Buster. "When is Pete coming to see me?"

Rosacoke had run out of making excuses for Pete. The night Pete had called to say that he was flying back from California brought joy to her heart. She wondered, though, why he was calling her and not speaking to Buster directly.

She was filled with excitement when Claude drove her up the mountain that morning to the hideaway chalet.

At last she had some good news to report to Buster. His daddy was coming back home.

\*\*\*

Pete could postpone his meeting with Buster no longer. Rising from Karl's bed where he had spent the night, he kissed his lover good-bye and drove his favorite car up the hill to the mountain retreat that had originally been built for Pete and Josh. Buster was living there in this secret hideaway with Tara as his guardian.

When Pete came in through the back door, Tara was waiting for him with freshly brewed coffee. In the past few months she'd aged considerably. Wearing no make-up, she appeared haggard, her face lined. "Morning, hoss," she said, giving him her usual gentle kiss on the lips.

"How is he?" Pete asked.

"It's living hell here," she said. "He's half out of his mind most of the time. I think there's brain damage. He's not himself any more."

"I don't want to hear that," Pete said. "I just can't stand it. I'm God damn grateful you're here for him. You're the only real friend he's got in the whole world."

"What about you?" she asked pointedly. "You shore took a long time in getting up that hill."

"The accident..." He hesitated, not knowing what to say. "I mean, it's changed everything. It can't be the way it was before. Tell me you understand."

She turned her back to him and walked over toward the kitchen sink. "I understand plenty. Buster is upstairs waiting for you. He's been looking forward to your visit for a long time. At times I think it's all he has had to live for."

"Oh, God," was all Pete said, not wanting to place such a heavy burden on his reunion with his son.

As he climbed the stairs to Buster's bedroom, all Pete could think about was how radiant and beautiful Tracy had looked when he'd kissed him good-bye in California.

Pete almost wanted to curse God for taking away Buster's beauty and

transforming him into a monster. Pete wanted to be the daddy of two of the most beautiful boys on the planet. He wasn't getting his wish.

As in a nightmare, the first hour alone with his son went badly. The bitterness and venom inside Buster had seemed to boil over like a pot over-flowing with a lava stew. To Pete's horror and pain, Buster had seemed to blame him for the accident on that mountain.

"In thirty seconds," Buster said, "everything was taken from me. My beauty. My fans. My career. My life." He looked over at Pete. "And my love. Why didn't you save me? Better yet, why didn't you let me die on that rock?"

Pete looked away, peering out the picture windows at the same sharp mountains that had taken Buster's face. Even though he couldn't be sure, he knew that Buster's eyes were following his every move. Pete didn't even know what Buster looked like. He wore a knit ski mask and the blackest pair of sunglasses ever invented.

When Pete turned around, he came face to face with his son. An air of malevolence hung over the bedroom.

"I know you've been avoiding looking at me," Buster said. "I want you to see everything this morning. You know the expression, 'the face that only a mother could love?' What about a daddy's love? What kind of face does that take?"

In the bright light streaming in from the picture window, Buster reached up and removed his sunglasses. Instead of eyes, Pete saw something that resembled raw red meat. Slowly, ever so slowly, Buster removed the ski mask to reveal his face—if it could be called a face.

His system filled with revulsion, Pete stayed glued in his footsteps, forcing himself to look intently at the wasteland of his son's face. He recalled a happier day when he had had Buster pose in a rhinestone-studded, white cowboy outfit with a guitar slung over his back. He was beautiful then. Pete tried to superimpose that glittering, glamorous image of Buster over the present reality. He could not.

Buster's head was like a gigantic honeydew melon that had grown into a peculiar shape. It was distorted, as if somebody had taken a boot and kicked in one side of the melon. There was a hole like a moon crater in his head. He looked like some skeleton model in a science lab, as you could see the fluids racing through his brain, almost witness every time his heart beat. His condition was extremely risky. If he fell or bumped into some-thing protruding, an object could pierce his brain, turning him into an imbe-cile.

His good eye—his left one—was a hideous shade of magenta and blood-red. His other eye just seemed to dangle half out of its socket and was almost completely obscured by a heavy hanging eyelid over which he seemed to have no control. Stitches covered his face like a patchwork quilt.

"Look," Buster shouted as loud as he could through wired jaws. "Look into the face of the teenage dream idol of half the girls in America. Not to mention Europe. Now, let me ask you something. Would any girl, woman, man, or whatever, want to go to bed with me? And what about my daddy?" He burst into tears. "If only I could get to feel your body warmth again."

"Stop it!" Pete shouted. "I can't stand it any more." He turned from the sight of Buster. His hysteria left him as quickly as it'd descended, and he regained control. "Plastic surgery will take care of everything. It may take some time, and a hell of a lot of surgery, but one day, maybe next year or the year after. One day you'll be just like yourself again, and you'll appear on some big stage somewhere—maybe the Grand Ole Opry. Yeah, the Grand Ole Opry. Larry would love to stage a show business comeback from the dead like that. In all the comebacks in music, that one has never been tried. Pandemonium would break out."

"Daddy-Oh," he said, his voice filled with a biting malice. "You wouldn't lie to your loving son, now would you?"

Pete stared at his son, as Pete's whole body started to shake. He felt the room's walls closing in on him.

"I know you love me and will always love me," Buster said, a sinister tone to his voice. "In spite of that accident where you could have plucked me to safety, but didn't. In spite of that, I forgive you. We can resume our affair. When you're with me, you can pretend the accident never happened. That I'm still young and beautiful." He limped slowly over to Pete, who without meaning to, stepped back. His feet seemed to be operating with a brain of their own.

"Don't back away from me," Buster commanded, not concealing the ferocity in his voice. "I want to feel your hot lips on mine. You always did get off by kissing me. I'm all yours."

Buster was only two feet from Pete. Pete stepped back again, inching toward the door. "Your room is cold. I'll ask Tara to bring up some firewood. It's always cold when you go this high into the mountains."

Turning from the sight of Buster's grotesque face, Pete opened the bedroom door and rushed down the steps.

In the kitchen he was shaking uncontrollably. To steady himself, he beat his fists against the wooden kitchen table. "I can't stand seeing him like this," he said to Tara. "He's like some horrible, deformed...*Thing!*"

"That *Thing* is your son!"

*** 

On Pete's private airplane, Junior Grayson flew Buster, Tara, and Rosacoke to New York, where Buster was slated to face head surgery. In spite of their romantic differences, Doug Porter had made all the arrange-

ments at a private clinic where he'd secured two of the finest plastic surgeons in America to assist in the operation.

"From the photograph you sent of Buster," Doug had told her, "this is big-time stuff. I'm used to tightening up Joan Crawford's eyes and giving a little tuck to Lana Turner. I'm out of my league but I'll be there for you."

"Doug…" she had said hesitantly, wanting to make some mention of their ill-fated romance.

"Yes," he'd said, a little too professional-sounding for her comfort. "What else is on your mind?"

"It's nothing," she'd said. "I just wanted to thank you and express my gratitude."

"Whatever I can do to help, I will," he'd said. "See you in New York." He'd put down the receiver.

As the plane landed at Idlewild, Rosacoke reached for Tara's hand. "You're a hell of a woman to have around in an emergency." Rosacoke also reached for Buster's hand but he didn't extend it. Either he didn't see her, or else her son had his eyes closed, lost in his own murky world as the plane landed. She wanted to cry but held back any tears.

Unlike most waiting rooms, the one at the private clinic on the Upper East Side where Doug had booked Buster was plushly, even elegantly, decorated with an antique inlaid cabinet that opened to reveal a bar. Rosacoke had already embraced Buster, who had been admitted the night before for an extensive private examination.

Tara was helping herself to the bourbon in the cabinet. Not wanting to, Rosacoke soon joined her, if only to prevent her own shaking.

When Doug came out to greet her, she went over to kiss him but he backed away slightly, introducing himself to Tara. After their breakup, Rosacoke had hoped that she could continue a friendship with Doug, but his manner this morning suggested he had ill feelings toward her and the way she'd handled their affair.

"Is my baby gonna be okay?" she asked Doug.

He had a puzzled look when he faced her. "I'm a doctor, not a gazer into crystal balls." He said good-bye to her, acknowledged Tara, and headed down the long corridor to join the other doctors in the waiting room.

She was only too aware of the life-threatening operation Buster had to face. Doug had told her that a plastic plate would have to be inserted into Buster's head over his brain cavity. The very idea of such a delicate procedure filled her with fear and apprehension. She suspected that anything might go wrong.

After three hours of hideous waiting with no news, Tara had gotten completely drunk. Three drinks later, Rosacoke stopped consuming liquor. Her nerves seemed destroyed. The way she figured it, if Buster had died on that operating table, someone would have come and told her that by now.

Therefore, her son must still be alive.

After what seemed like an eternity, Doug did emerge, a grim look across his handsome face. He was so serious that Rosacoke was afraid that he was going to tell her that Buster had died. "He's alive," he said in a reassuring voice, "but his condition is critical. We'll know a lot more by morning."

Sensing he was pulling back from her, Rosacoke reached for his arm, pleading with him with her eyes. "Will you stay here until he's out of danger? I'd feel safer that way."

"I can't," he said, freeing his arm from her. "I just got a call from the coast. Lana has attempted suicide. She's calling for me. If I don't come, she's threatening to do it again."

"Please, stay here with Buster," Rosacoke said.

"Actually the other two doctors are far more skilled at this than I am," Doug said. "Dr. Bradford Simon actually inserted the plate over Buster's brain cavity. Because of his work with the U.S. Army, he knows about such things. I have to get back to my Beverly Hills operation and back to doing nips and tucks for vain actresses. I'll stay in touch with the other doctors by phone." He looked over at Tara, deep into her drunken stupor on the sofa. "Good-bye."

"Thanks for all you've done," Rosacoke said, as he turned and headed down the corridor. She called after him. "Doug…"

He looked back at her for one final time. "What is it?"

His voice seemed so exasperated with her that she only muttered, "Nothing. Have a safe flight and thanks again."

Filled with relief that Buster had survived the operation, Rosacoke rushed to the telephone and called Pete at Heaven on Earth. When he heard the news, he wept into the other end of the phone. "He's alive," Pete said. "But he'll never get his beauty back."

"Fuck that kind of talk," she said, angry with him. "His heart is still beating, and that's a little bit more important than what he looks like."

"I guess you're right," Pete said.

After going over their immediate plans with each other, he hung up. Both Doug and Pete at one time had meant so much to her. Now each of them in their separate ways filled her heart with a void.

At three o'clock on the morning of the following day, Dr. Simon came to see Tara and Rosacoke. "It looks like your son is going to pull through this," he said to Rosacoke.

She collapsed into tears.

"If he'd died, I would have killed myself," Tara threatened.

The doctor remained stoically calm, chatting briefly with them before disappearing down that same corridor where Rosacoke had seen the last of Doug.

Shortly before dawn, Dr. Simon came back. Once again Rosacoke braced herself for a report of Buster's death. "He's stronger than we thought," the doctor said reassuringly. "His condition has improved remarkably. He's still not out of danger, but we're very hopeful."

By ten o'clock, Rosacoke was in a daze from lack of sleep. Tara had passed out on an emergency hospital bed provided for her.

When Dr. Simon emerged this time, he invited Rosacoke to follow him down that long corridor to Buster's private room. Since Rosacoke wanted to be alone with Buster, she didn't wake Tara up.

After the doctor had shown her into Buster's room, Rosacoke stared at the pitiful creature in the center of the bed. Buster had been placed in something that resembled a white tent. He was heavily bandaged.

At his bedside, she held his hand. "The worst is over."

He squeezed her hand. In a very faint voice she could hardly hear, he said, "I'm gonna live. One day—not now, mind you—but one day, I'm gonna face the beauty butchers." He tightened his hold on her hand. "I need a face, mama."

***

The following day Claude called Rosacoke from Heaven on Earth. After telling her that he loved her and extending his deepest sympathies for Buster's plight, he reported that all the legal challenges concerning the decomposed body in the river had been successfully fought down. "The sheriff's department wants to wrap up the case. It's official now. The cadaver has been identified as Buster Riddle."

"Oh, my God," Rosacoke said. Those were all the words she could manage. Some part of her brain feared that it was going to be Buster's actual funeral.

"We gotta get on with it," Claude said. "A big send-off for Buster. Please fly back right away. Tara can stay in New York looking after Buster while he recovers."

"A funeral," she said, more to the empty air around her than to Claude. "I don't know if I could go through with it." Her voice grew hesitant, as she was on the verge of tears. "I mean...."

"We've got to have a funeral," Claude said. "It wouldn't look right if we didn't. Besides we need a real funeral to put Buster to rest. Otherwise those diehard fans will be at your gate forever. Don't worry. We'll give him a beautiful send-off."

Three days later as both Pete and Rosacoke returned to Heaven on Earth, Buster's funeral was announced as private. That didn't stop an estimated thirty-thousand spectators from showing up.

Larry had planned this event for some time. In the mausoleum at

Heaven on Earth, he'd ordered an eight-hundred pound, rose-colored coffin of seamless copper which was to be placed in a crypt sealed by a five-hundred pound marble slab.

The actual ceremony at Cub Creek Baptist Church was mercifully brief, lasting only eight minutes in front of forty-two witnesses. Both Pete and Rosacoke sang a gospel duet, "Sweet, Sweet Spirit." More than three-thousand bouquets poured in, and it was these flowers that set off pandemonium after the body was laid to rest in the graveyard.

Ignoring the call of police bullhorns, the fans lost control, scrambling over the graves around the church in their search for souvenirs. Plastic vases, Styrofoam backings, and bits of floral wire, along with the flowers, were stolen from the grounds, as the police tried to evict the fans from the graveyard.

Even as that was going on, vendors sold memorial T-shirts on the grounds outside at the staggering sum of fifteen dollars each. Bumper stickers were also peddled for inflated prices.

Acting as if he were still the sheriff of the county, Claude ordered Pete and Rosacoke to stay barricaded in the back of the church in the pastor's office. Pete placed his arm around Rosacoke to steady her, as she watched in dismay as the grounds of the graveyard were overrun by hysterical fans. Law-enforcement officers on horseback had been sent in to control the crowds, although they weren't having much success.

At one point it was feared the mob would actually storm the locked doors of the church itself, hoping to get at both Pete and Rosacoke as if wanting a piece of their flesh.

"Those guys had better keep their cool out there," Pete said to Claude. Pete seemed more concerned for the safety of the fans than for the police officers. "I fear one of those cowboys on horseback might use his gun."

Before that dreadful afternoon ended, Rosacoke heard reports that a little girl had been trampled to death in the graveyard. Eight others were badly injured and had to be rushed in ambulances to the hospital. She personally planned to call all the families involved to express her deepest regrets. The thought of the little dead girl sickened her, and she felt responsible somehow.

Back at Heaven on Earth, she couldn't take the phone calls that came in from all over the country. Pete refused to pick up the phone too. Later she heard that when President Eisenhower had called, Pete did come to the phone at once.

After he'd hung up, Pete reported to her that the President was on the phone for about a minute and had expressed his regrets and conveyed those of Mamie that their son had died. Pete told her that Eisenhower had said that Buster might have gone on to an important career.

Upon hearing this, she burst into tears. Even though she could not

imagine Eisenhower listening to Buster's music, she felt his sympathy was genuine. "God damn it," she shouted at both Pete and Claude. "Now we've deceived even the President of the United States. May God have mercy on our souls."

Throughout the long night, Rosacoke in the privacy of her bedroom suite kept a window open to hear the prayers and the moaning of loyal fans who stood in a candlelight vigil outside the gates of Heaven on Earth until the early hours of the morning. It had been a day of pushing and shoving, and Junior Grayson had arrived with two helicopters, hoping for some sense of crowd control when the fans threatened to break through the gates and storm Pete's mansion.

She'd almost come to resent the vans of flowers and funeral wreaths arriving hourly. Claude had ordered these floral tributes placed on the lawn around Heaven on Earth under the towering magnolia and oak trees.

Rosacoke had fallen asleep that night crying, listening to a radio station playing not only Buster's records, but her own and those of Pete.

The next morning she was hardly prepared for the press coverage and the tabloid sensationalism. Perhaps not knowing how accurate they were, many newspapers speculated that Buster was still alive and hiding out for some reason and that the decomposed body buried at his gravesite wasn't Buster at all. One tabloid claimed that the real Buster had been abducted by a flying saucer. Another woman maintained that she had spotted Buster entering a private home in Akron, Ohio.

As she finished her coffee, Rosacoke welcomed the road engagements Larry had presented to her. "Your star has never burned brighter," he said. "I've got movie offers for you, and at these concerts I've lined up, you'll attract your biggest audiences ever."

At this point she was willing and able to tackle any gig he'd booked for her. She wanted to leave Heaven on Earth and get on the road again just to escape the memory of that awful funeral.

Later, as she wandered across the grounds of Heaven on Earth, she was almost intoxicated by the aroma of the masses of flowers.

Outside the gates, only about sixty diehard fans remained. A light rain began to fall. She headed back around the side of the mansion and there in the backyard she encountered Pete. He had spent the night at Karl's house.

Pete walked up to her, hugging her and kissing her on the lips. "It's over now," he said, "and we can get on with our lives."

"What about Buster?" she asked.

"At his hideaway, he'll live with Tara," he said. "We can't make him beautiful again, and neither can any of those doctors. We're keeping him alive."

"But what an awful life it must be for him."

"I know," Pete said, "But we can't mourn forever. I just stopped to

pick up my music. I'm on the road again."

"I'm getting on with my life too," she said. "Doug and I didn't make up in New York."

"Yeah, I heard," he said, looking impatiently at the back door. He seemed eager to leave, as she hugged him good-bye.

"You're free as a bird," he said. "You're gonna be one hot mama. I envy you for all the handsome studs you're gonna mate with."

"I'm sure those you bed will be more spectacular than mine," she said.

"I hope so." He kissed her gingerly on the lips. "God bless his children, namely us." After those parting words, he headed for the main house. She saw Karl holding open the door for Pete. Had Karl become Pete's new lover? Pete had had all the other brothers, so why not Karl?

Brushing aside such thoughts, she headed for a waiting car with Claude as her driver. On the way to the airport she listened with him to radio reports of Buster's funeral. Commentators called it the largest funeral ever held in this part of North Carolina. Larry had staged it like a theatrical presentation, and it was getting massive coverage.

Only its organizers knew it was a fraud.

# Chapter 15
## (The Sixties: Losing Fame)

In Los Angeles, Pete had hoped to be with Tracy that night, but his son had turned him down, claiming he had a more important engagement. Tracy was always turning him down. His relationship with Tracy was completely different from his affair with his other son.

Buster had wanted to be with Pete all the time, and Buster was the aggressor.

In marked contrast, Tracy was pursued by Pete. Only rarely did Pete get lucky. Tracy had a series of T-shirts labeled, "So may men, so little time." He believed in the sentiment expressed in those letters.

Still alluringly seductive after all these years, Tracy was the biggest star-fucker in Hollywood, pursuing big game. His affairs had ranged from Rory Calhoun to John Lennon. Tracy spread the word across Hollywood that in Las Vegas, when hired to design costumes for Elvis, that he'd gotten the star totally wasted on drugs and had raped him. Pete didn't know whether to believe that one or not, but Tracy had convincing evidence, and it was just the kind of stunt his son could pull off.

The age of his boy friends didn't seem to matter. Tracy had even pursued the aging multi-millionaire Western star, Randolph Scott, a friend of Cary Grant. Tracy's affair with Cary Grant himself was the stuff of Hollywood legend. "My only regret," Tracy had told Pete, "and I'm not a boy to linger over regrets, is that I never became the boy of Howard Hughes, like Cary and Randy did."

Since he couldn't get Tracy for the night, Pete decided to cruise the bars. He could always find someone willing to go to bed with the famous Pete Riddle even if his star were fading.

The press had turned on him. Articles about him were growing more vicious. His heavy consumption of bourbon and disappointing concerts filled the columns, although no reference was made to his homosexuality. Most of the press, in fact, wrote of him as if he were a womanizer. He was alleged to have had many affairs with actresses, even Jayne Mansfield herself.

Larry usually staged his concerts in the boondocks, and as part of his act Pete would wander through the audience kissing the beautiful women in the crowd right on the lips. He still attracted enough women fans to fill up

a hall.

These fans shouted and screamed when he sang "Lonesome Blues," even though critics claimed that his voice had lost its vulnerable richness. His dancing was once hailed as great as that of an early Elvis in the 50s. At recent concerts, Pete's movements on stage were called "karate choreography."

Pete had been lionized and iconized, but now, sadly, he was ostracized. He'd gone from the good to the bad to the ugly, especially when he'd stagger on stage drunk.

In a review in *Time* magazine, Pete had read cruel words. "There is nothing sadder than an artist who has lost touch with his talent."

There was more. "The difference in voice between the young hillbilly singer who burst on the scene with the mournful 'Lonesome Blues' and the Elvis Presley clone in a rhinestone-studded white jumpsuit trolling through a Las Vegas casino singing the same song as he kisses the customers, is as bleak a show business legend as could be imagined."

*Rolling Stone* had put it this way: "Pete Riddle is no longer the greatest talent since Hank Williams and Elvis Presley. Today he is a joke. Once he was the real thing, wedding music from both the white and black cultures. Looking drugged, confused, and exhausted, Pete Riddle at his last concert in Sun Valley, Idaho, has lost his way."

In Los Angeles he spent wild nights drinking and roaming the dance floors of Whiskey a Go-Go, looking for some cute trick that would evoke Tracy in his memory. He rarely found what he wanted. From the Doors to the Yardbirds to The Mamas and the Papas, he met them all. One night he thought he'd gotten lucky and was going to disappear with Jim Morrison. He almost pulled that off until Morrison met Tracy that same night. Tracy won the trophy.

Arriving at Whiskey à Go-Go, Pete tipped the valet generously and staggered from his white Cadillac into the pulsating club. He'd heard that all the Beatles had been there earlier in the evening. Paul McCartney and Ringo Starr had departed. John Lennon and George Harrison, or so Pete was told, were still at the club. Although Lennon had had a brief affair with Tracy, Pete had never met any of the Beatles.

Armed with a double bourbon, Pete searched the floor looking for the Beatles. Surrounded by an entourage, Lennon and Harrison were sitting and talking with, of all people, the fading blonde bombshell, Jayne Mansfield herself. Jayne called Pete over to "meet the boys."

As Pete shook hands with Harrison and Lennon, a photographer rushed up and snapped their picture. Lennon seemed to endure that invasion of privacy, but Harrison became infuriated. "You bloody sod," he yelled at the photographer. "Why can't you God damn vultures leave us alone?" He picked up his glass of Scotch and tossed it in the photographer's face.

Jayne tried to calm Harrison down and succeeded momentarily. Hoping to restore life to the party, she tried to amuse with one of her stunts. From her ample bosom, she produced one of her pet Chihuahuas. The dog barked at John and bit his hand before landing in Harrison's lap where the little animal took a Chihuahua piss.

When Harrison spotted onlookers laughing at the dog and him, he jumped up and started screaming obscenities at the crowd. Seemingly seized with a state of madness, he whirled around, accidentally knocking Jayne down onto the floor.

Pete firmly lifted her up into his strong arms and escorted her across the floor and out the door. "Thanks for introducing me to two of the guys who replaced Elvis and me," he said to her. "They may be great musicians, but we couldn't take them to the Queen's Garden Party."

A valet went to retrieve Jayne's pink Cadillac. Pete volunteered to have Jayne driven home.

"No, no, sweetie," she said to him, kissing him tenderly on the lips, "Jayne Mansfield is in charge of her own life tonight." When her pink car pulled up, she staggered toward it, cuddling her yelping Chihuahua. One of her high heels caught on something, and sent her sprawling toward the car. She accidentally dropped the little dog, which leaped to safety in the front seat. Pete braced her and once again pleaded with her to let him have a valet drive her home.

She again refused and slipped behind the driver's seat, as one of her breasts from her plunging low-cut gown escaped to freedom. "Mama's gonna be fine," she said to Pete. "Hey, I have an idea. Let's go on the town. Find ourselves a couple of live ones."

"You'll have to take care of the studs all by your lonesome tonight," he said. "I'm done in."

In that case, I'll go back into that club and have another drink."

"C'mon, Jayne," he said. "If you and I both never had another drink, we would have had our share."

"Guess so," she said. "Can't remember what I was drinking anyway."

"Good night, gal."

She suddenly grabbed his arm as if an inspiration had come over her. "Did I tell you the good news? My agent has lined up this super movie deal for me," she said. "I'll be the star. It'll be bigger than Marilyn's *Bus Stop, Some Like It Hot,* and *Gentlemen Prefer Blondes,* all rolled into one film."

"That sounds like one colossal movie," he said. What's the title?"

"A title?" She looked vacantly into the night. "Maybe it doesn't have a title yet. But it's going to be big."

"You drive carefully," he warned her.

She held onto his arm, reluctant to let go. Her glazed eyes scanned the façade of the club. "Fuck Whiskey a Go-Go. Fuck the Beatles. There's

no such thing as a great fucking party any more. Right, Pete?"

"Shit times," he said to her, trying to gracefully retrieve his arm.

She looked into his eyes, her own sad eyes were on the verge of tears. "Did I tell you that twice I fucked the president of the United States. But he's got a tiny dick."

"Some other time," he said, leaning down to kiss her good night.

"Marilyn was the God damn lucky one," she said. "She didn't live long enough to become a bleached out, blonde bombshell has-been. The world will always remember her as young and beautiful." Cuddling her little pet to her breasts, she roared out of the driveway and into an uncertain night.

As he stood on the curb waiting for the valet to bring his own car, he was startled to see Lennon without Harrison emerge from the club and stand beside him.

"Times keep rolling along," John said to him. "What are you going to do now that you and Elvis have become figures in music history?"

"There must be some secluded place dark enough and far away enough for me to go and hide," Pete said.

"You go there and find that secret place," Lennon said. "As for me, my star will always be shining brightly in the night, and will shine even brighter when I'm gone."

Without saying another word, Pete tipped the valet fifty bucks and followed Jayne's trail out of the driveway. He did not look back at Lennon and did not say good night.

Back at Pete's apartment, he was happy to see Tracy's bedroom light on and the door open. Maybe he'd get to fuck his son after all.

Suddenly, Tracy emerged from his bedroom stark naked. Pete lunged toward him and tried to take him in his arms.

"Sorry, I'm booked up for the night and for future nights." He went over to the liquor cabinet and poured two stiff drinks of vodka. He kissed his fingers, then touched those fingers against Pete's lips. "Go on being my rich daddy and paying my bills, though. A cute boy like me has expensive taste and needs a rich daddy. I might throw you a mercy fuck from time to time, but tonight I've got a trick. "Wanta see?" He motioned for Pete to look inside his bedroom.

Pete walked over and looked inside. There spread-eagled and completely nude in the center of a king-sized bed lay what appeared to be Mick Jagger, with a mocking leer on his face.

*** 

Arm in arm with Narcissa Cash, Rosacoke walked through the faded star's empty Beverly Hills Mansion. The day before, movers had arrived to take away all of Narcissa's furniture and possessions to meet the demands

of her creditors. Tomorrow at eight o'clock in the morning, she would be ordered by a judge to vacate her home, which was being seized to pay off back debts. She was also in serious trouble with the Internal Revenue Service.

"It's all gone," Narcissa said. "*Gone with the Wind*. A nigger gal like me didn't have a chance in this town."

Rosacoke stared at the empty living room and remembered when Narcissa's fame was at its peak. "You went a long way in this town for a little gal from Shakerag who didn't have a pot to piss in."

"Tell me about it," she said. "One day the phone stopped ringing. No more roles for me. After I divorced Doug, my whole life seemed to fall apart. Can you imagine I believed, if only for a moment, that that asshole Sinatra would marry me. I don't think even Sammy Davis Jr. would marry me, although I got fucked a lot by his little nigger dick. And forget about that lying bastard JFK."

"For a while you and Doug seemed so happy," Rosacoke said, embarrassed to be talking about her former lover with his former wife.

"Sure, Doug and I were happy," she said, "that is, when he ever came home. When he wasn't out fucking Ava Gardner, Lana Turner, Joan Crawford, Susan Hayward, you name her. He even got around to fucking Marilyn Monroe before the Kennedys had her killed and then Jack got his own bullet."

"Now Jack wouldn't go and do a thing like that," Rosacoke said. "Marilyn accidentally killed herself."

"Yeah, right!" Narcissa said, sarcastically, taking Rosacoke's arm and leading her to the garden. "Let's go for a walk through my beautiful garden for one final visit."

In the garden Rosacoke volunteered to give Narcissa fifty-thousand dollars in cash to get her out of the country and away from the threats of the IRS and her creditors.

"That will tide me over until money starts coming in from my new night club engagement in Paris," Narcissa said. "I'm real grateful and all but I hate to borrow money from you. Me, Narcissa Cash, the big international star, accepting a hand-out."

"They'll love you in Paris," Rosacoke said. "They loved Josephine Baker. They'll go for you too."

"I don't appear nude with some fucking bananas," Narcissa said.

"Do what you do, which is sing prettier than anybody, and you'll be the toast of Paris," Rosacoke said.

"Maybe," Narcissa said. "Who knows? After I've lost so much, fallen so far, I don't hope for anything any more.

"I called my son Tracy two or three times. Or should I say *our* son Tracy? He didn't return my calls. He's riding high. I think he's one of the

most successful designers in Hollywood, and he doesn't want to be reminded that he has a nigger mama."

"I don't see much of him anymore either," Rosacoke said. "I didn't become the big-time star that Marilyn became, so Tracy doesn't have much use for me. I think he just tolerates Pete. Tracy goes for the big star of the moment. I heard he even had an affair with John Lennon."

"You heard right, baby," Narcissa said. "Tracy Riddle is the biggest star-fucker in Hollywood, providing they're male. I never heard of him going to bed with a woman."

"One."

"What do you mean?" Narcissa said.

"One," Rosacoke repeated. "Natalie Wood, and I heard it from her own mouth. She also told me that Tracy later confided to her that the only reason he fucked her was because he wanted to put his dick where Warren Beatty and Robert Wagner had already put theirs. Tracy said he wanted Warren and Robert to fuck him more than he did any other men in Hollywood. If I can believe Pete, Warren and Robert have successfully managed to evade Tracy's net."

"From what I hear, they are the only two male stars in Hollywood who have. Maybe Paul Newman as well."

In the bright California sun, Rosacoke detected the first signs of aging on Narcissa's face. She was beginning to show fine wrinkles, almost prematurely so. So far, Rosacoke had retained her peaches and cream complexion and was wrinkle free, but any day now she suspected that she too would begin losing the war against gravity.

"I once wanted to be a white gal," Narcissa said, "and I resented your beautiful white skin and your lovely blonde hair. To hell with that now. I'm going to sell the fact that I'm a black diva in Paris. The French will love it."

At the front door, Rosacoke kissed Narcissa good-bye. Rosacoke turned to walk away but went back for one more hug. "I'll have the money sent over this afternoon," Rosacoke promised.

Thanks. It'll be my mad money to get me out of this fucking town," Narcissa said. "Goodbye Hollywood. Hello, Paris."

*** 

In his attempts at tight security, Larry didn't obtain the finest surgeons for Buster. Over the years facial transformation by surgery was attempted several times. One Mexican doctor grafted thick patches of skin from Buster's legs and back and stitched them onto his face. That botched attempt at reconstruction left ugly scars.

Buster remained horribly disfigured and had become a total recluse in his mountain hideaway. The heavy fat and mottled "skin flaps" from his

back made his facial tissue four times thicker than it normally was. Twisted inward, his eyelashes made him tear and cry. Because of the positioning of his chin stuck on his neck, he couldn't turn his head. Lips twisted, cheeks bloated, he had a nose made. After the accident, none existed. The new nose came out blunted. He was aghast at his look.

So was Rosacoke.

He retreated into his private world, wearing a protective medical mask. He no longer showed his face to Rosacoke. Other than the surgeons, only Tara saw him unmasked.

"If you love someone," Tara told Rosacoke, "you don't stop loving them just 'cause they ain't as pretty as they used to be. Hell! How many of us look as good as we did?"

Surgeons worked to correct other doctors' mistakes, and in doing so made a few more of their own. Plastic surgery on Buster's face eventually came to a halt.

"I can't stand another beauty butcher," he shouted at Rosacoke one rainy day. "Another operation. Just to suffer that only to have my hopes dashed when they take off the bandages."

She stared at the medical mask, with its two holes for his nostrils. There were other holes for his ears and eyes. Tufts of blond hair stuck out around the medical mask. Constructed by DuPont from Lycra, it was dubbed "the iron mask" by Buster. Actually, it was made of a material similar to power-net nylon, and was designed to hold tight against sagging flesh, like the material used in a woman's girdle. The mask produced an unrelenting pressure on the ugly red scars left by Buster's surgery, and it kept his skin grafts from lumping.

"Sometimes I feel it's smothering me to death," Buster said. "I want to rip the thing off, but then I'd see my reflection somewhere,  perhaps in a pond on one of my walks through the woods. That would be worse than the mask."

Rosacoke urged him to seek better and better plastic surgeons. She'd heard of one doctor in a clinic in southeastern Switzerland who could perform "miracles." Buster refused to fly in secret with Tara to Switzerland but Rosacoke noted that he at least wrote down the address.

For reasons of her own, Tara supported Buster in his decision not to seek any more help from the surgeons who had so far failed him. Rosacoke didn't understand that, secretly suspecting that Tara wanted to keep Buster disfigured so that she and she alone could hold onto his love. That was such an unattractive motive to attribute to someone as loving and kind as Tara, that Rosacoke wanted to dismiss the suspicion from her mind.

Living at Heaven on Earth, Rosacoke was often alone since Pete and his boys were rarely there. She no longer even attempted to keep up with Pete's road schedule.

When Pete did come home, he didn't live at the crowded mansion but always retreated to Karl's house. Pete told her that the reason for that was because he wanted privacy. What she finally came to realize was that Pete Riddle and Karl Adams were lovers.

"He's had all the other Adams brothers," Rosacoke said to Tara one day. First, Hank Adams. Then Tracy Adams. I suspect of all the Adams brothers, Tracy was the real love of his life. Pete even named our son after him. I know for a fact that Pete used to fuck John-John before he became a woman, and the fact that he's now a woman is something that absolutely thrills Junior Grayson. Junior told me himself that he can't get enough of Joni's new pussy."

"At least old Pete's keeping it in the family," Tara had said.

Every morning Rosacoke drove up the mountain to visit Buster. Her son welcomed her visits, and she'd come to look forward to them too, since she didn't have much else to do. Larry kept urging her to go back on the road again, but that prospect didn't please her at all.

During the few times she encountered Claude, he still seemed to be a lovesick fool. She wanted to pledge her love to him, but didn't feel right about it. Wanda Mae had told her that Claude, her father, sometimes went off for a weekend with Ronnie when Larry wasn't around.

That made Rosacoke wonder if Claude had secretly resumed his old affair with his son-in-law. Rosacoke had already suffered through one marriage loaded with instances of gay philandering on the part of her husband, and she didn't want to repeat that experience with Claude. This lurking suspicion about Claude's sexual orientation prevented her from seriously considering marrying him. She had once told Tara, "With Claude, I can never be sure whether he's thinking about me when he's fucking me, or whether he's thinking about plowing into Ronnie."

"Hoss," Tara had said, "some men like women but also like a man now and then on the side. They get something from a man that our love can't provide."

"What do you mean?" Rosacoke had asked.

"What do I mean?" Tara had seemed exasperated. "C'mon, country gal. They get ten inches of fat dick up their butts. Now, can me and you give them that?"

"Guess not," Rosacoke had said, "if that's what they've got to have."

The next morning as she'd driven her Cadillac up that hill to see Buster, she found her son in a particularly despondent mood, as he wandered from room to room looking out at the mountains.

"I once loved these mountains, but they have become my prison," he said to her. "It was these jagged rocks that destroyed my face. Destroyed my life. I don't think I can stand these particular mountains any more. I don't plan to leave the mountains, but I want to find another set of moun-

tains to run and hide in."

"You're leaving?" she asked in astonishment. "Where to?"

"You mentioned Switzerland the other day," he said. "I was thinking that Tara and I would buy a chalet in Switzerland, and I'd live out the rest of my days there."

"I'll come to see you there," she said. "I can't let you disappear from my life."

"Why not?" he asked with a barely controlled hostility in his voice. "You come to see your monster son almost daily. But that God damn bastard I used to call my daddy, that fucking Pete Riddle, views me like a circus freak. He can't even stand to look at me, much less embrace me. When he's home, he doesn't even take thirty minutes to drive up that mountain to see if I'm dead or alive. I hate his guts."

"He means to come and see you," Rosacoke said apologetically. "But he's fucked up in the head. He loves you so much he can't stand to see you this way."

"That's no excuse and you know it," Buster said. "I've had my funeral. Pete wants to believe that my funeral was the real thing. That I'm dead and gone."

"Oh, please," Rosacoke said, rushing toward Buster to take him in her arms and cradle him. She didn't want to cry, but suddenly she couldn't hold back her tears.

When she released him, she looked into his mask, trying to imagine what expression there might be on his destroyed face.

"It's not only my face that has the scars," Buster said. "The worst scars are the ones you don't see. Not even Tara can see them when she takes off my mask to wash my head. The worst scars are those that have disfigured my soul."

***

As he flew back to Heaven on Earth, Pete knew he could no longer postpone his reunion with Buster. He'd spent the afternoon with Rosacoke, listening to her demands that he call on his son. He knew he must go to see Buster before he left for what looked like a permanent sojourn in Switzerland. Tonight's visit would be his final good-bye to his son, whom he might never see again.

For all Pete knew, Buster would die in some remote alpine village where no one knew who he was.

Pete's memory of his last encounter with Buster, when his son had unmasked himself, was so vivid in Pete's mind that he'd had a few extra bourbons before agreeing with Rosacoke to drive up that steep mountain with her.

Rosacoke had had a few bourbons too, but less so than Pete, so she said she'd drive. Claude had wanted to drive them, but Pete had told him that this was going to be strictly a family affair.

When Rosacoke had driven him up the winding and dark road to Buster's mountain hideaway, Pete had been disappointed to see Larry's Cadillac already in the driveway. Larry visited Buster and Tara only occasionally and then to talk money. Pete had hoped that the meeting tonight wouldn't be about business.

"Since Buster's leaving the country," Rosacoke said, "I guess Larry had to come up here to go over finances. After all, Buster can't live on nothing in Switzerland. I hear it's expensive."

"Buster doesn't have to worry about that," Pete said, staggering from the car. "Me and you can take care of our boy. We can also pay for any operations he needs."

Taking Rosacoke by the hand as if still married to her, Pete walked around to the back door where Tara, who had apparently seen them pull into the driveway, was waiting.

"Hello, hosses," she said to the both of them, kissing first Pete on the lips and then Rosacoke. "Good to see you two lovebirds together again. Just like old times."

"Those days are gone forever," Pete said, brushing past her and into the kitchen. "I need a drink."

Tara motioned to two glasses on the kitchen table. "I saw you coming and made a bourbon and branch water for each of you."

"Thanks," Rosacoke said, stepping inside the door and taking off a mink coat Pete had recently bought for her.

"Don't wear that in the mountains during hunting season, unless you want to get your head blown off," Tara warned her, taking the coat and putting it on herself. She pranced around the room. "What becomes a legend the most?" she called out before hanging up the fur and coming back into the kitchen. "Buster's upstairs in his office finishing up some business with Larry. He's on the other side of the house and didn't hear you pull up, I'm sure. Otherwise, he'd be down the stairs in no time. He's been waiting a long time to see you, hoss." She hugged Pete and led him into the living room, as Rosacoke followed them.

Larry bounded down the stairs first, kissing Pete on the lips and giving Rosacoke a light hug. "It's been rough upstairs," he said. "Buster and I aren't agreeing at all about how I've managed his career after his death."

Slowly Buster came down the steps, walking very slowly. Pete was both horrified and yet grateful that Buster wore his mask. Ignoring Rosacoke for the moment, Buster walked toward Pete.

Pete didn't know whether to embrace Buster or shake his hand. He found it hard to believe that he had once been so intimate with his son, yet

now felt so far removed from him.

Buster solved Pete's dilemma by reaching out to shake his hand. "Men shake hands, don't they, Dad?" he asked.

"Some men do, I guess," Pete said, shaking Buster's hand. His son's palm was lined with sweat. The way Pete figured it, this reunion was even more difficult for Buster than it was for him.

"You're looking great," Buster said. "If anything you look younger and sexier than ever."

Almost not knowing what he was saying, Pete at first had started to tell Buster how good he was looking. Instead he said nothing, only imagining what horror of a face lay behind that mask.

Rosacoke walked over and warmly embraced Buster, as Pete retreated with his bourbon to a comfortable place in front of the blazing fire.

Perhaps he wasn't reacting well to the alchohol, but as the hours drifted by, Pete found himself spending the most uncomfortable evening of his life. Thanks to Tara and Rosacoke, the conversation kept flowing. Buster said very little but Pete felt that he was staring obsessively at him from behind those pitch-black sunglasses.

Bolting down a big shot of Southern Comfort, Tara turned her bitterness onto Larry. Already half snookered with whiskey, Larry too was in a belligerent mood, as he always was when his authority was challenged. "Listen, bitch," he said, "I've been the only one out there keeping Buster's name alive before the public while you guys park your asses up here on some fucking mountaintop."

"Don't you call me a bitch, you little faggot," Tara said. "You get paid and paid good."

"Too well," Buster chimed in.

"Listen," Larry said, "I'm not going to sit here and have my management of Buster's career challenged like this. I have sole power of attorney, and I did what I thought was right."

"And what exactly was it you did?" Pete asked in a slurred voice.

"They're moving to Switzerland," Larry said. "Tara asked me to raise money for them. I raised the fucking money."

"Hell, yes!" Tara said. "At what price?" She turned to Pete. "Asshole here sold outright Buster's entire record catalogue."

"It was old stuff," Larry claimed. "In one year—maybe three at the most—it will be very old. Sales are way off right now. Buster's records did well after his so-called death. But that was then. This is now. New singers have come along. Let's face it: Buster is a has-been. The public forgets real fast."

"How much did you get?" Rosacoke asked.

"A million fucking dollars—that's all," Larry said. "I thought these two would be overjoyed."

"Let's talk net, hoss," Tara said. "After everyone's been paid, including the IRS, we're getting three-hundred thousand dollars, and that's it."

"The future earnings on those records might have been incredible," Pete said.

"Maybe so," Larry said. "But next year they might sell only twenty-five copies. I made the best deal I could. I'm out of here." Without saying another word, Larry headed for the kitchen and out the door. The squeal of his car brakes signaled that he'd gone.

All four of them sat quietly in the living room, staring at the flickering flames from the fireplace.

"Millions of potential dollars have gone down the drain," Tara said, "and there ain't a damn thing we can do about it now."

"That's one of the reasons I'm writing again," Buster said. "To make money." He sighed. "If only I had a face to show to the public. If only I could perform again. I've got a song I want you guys to hear."

After Buster disappeared upstairs to retrieve his music, Tara in tears turned to Pete and Rosacoke. "I thought no more music would ever come out of the kid. Every time he went to write a song, a big knot tied up his stomach. Slowly but surely he's gone back to work. I believe he's come up with a real shit-kicking song."

In moments, Buster returned with his music. Pete feared that he'd break down and cry if he heard Buster in his mask sing again. Since the accident, whenever one of his son's songs played on the radio, Pete had to switch to another station. He couldn't stand to remember how Buster had sounded, and how he'd looked, when he was in his glory.

"I'm ready," Buster said, picking up a guitar Pete had once presented to him. He held out his hand to Tara. "Help me, gal."

Tara went over to the far end of the room and came back with her own guitar, a red one. After tuning up, Buster and Tara sang a lovely ballad. They were a perfect duet, and it was obvious that they'd practiced a lot. "Yesterday, Today and Tomorrow" told the story of a young man who had had it all, only to grow disillusioned with life. For many long years the narrator of the song had forsaken everything and everybody in life until the love of one good woman restored his hope for a brighter tomorrow.

It was sentimental but heart-breaking for Pete to hear. There was a long silence before both Pete and Rosacoke broke into applause. For the first time Pete got up and went to embrace his son. "It's beautiful," he said, hugging him tight like he used to. "The most beautiful song you've ever written."

"More important than that," Tara said. "It can sell."

"I want you to record it, Dad," Buster said.

"Other than Buster himself, you're the only one to do it," Rosacoke said to Pete as she squeezed his arm before reaching out to embrace Buster

herself.

Behind his mask, Buster seemed filled with good cheer. He invited Pete outside onto a balcony overlooking the same mountains that had sliced away his face.

As Pete and Buster stood alone together on the windswept balcony, clouds obscured the moon, as the boulder-strewn cliff below them was plunged into darkness. There was no sound but that of a rushing stream pouring down the mountainside along the side of their chalet.

"The stillness here can be deafening," Buster said. "I stand here every night thinking about you."

"I think a lot about you too, son," Pete said, not really telling the truth. He did everything he possibly could to blot Buster from his mind. "You sure you want to go away? All the way to Switzerland."

"I'm going," Buster said. "The moment you deserted me, there was not much reason to live. I don't want to go on knowing that I'm even on the same continent with you and can't have you any more." He paused. "Unless you'll take me back, regardless of what I look like. Will you take me back and love me again like you used to?" Buster moved toward him to take Pete in his arms.

Stiffening, Pete did not move to encase his son in his strong arms. "There is no way I could do that. As much as I want to, I just can't bring myself. I just don't have it in me. *Please*, please understand where I'm coming from."

Buster stepped back from him. "I don't want you to catch your death of cold. This is good-bye."

"Not really," Pete said. "I'll be flying over to Switzerland to see you one of these days."

"I'll have your bourbon waiting," Buster said. "Chilled with a Swiss icicle."

Pete looked at his son, wondering if he should embrace the boy again. Even though Buster was hidden behind sunglasses and his face covered with a mask, Pete could sense the great barrier that had come between them. The canyon was too great for Pete to cross, and he felt as if the night winds were taking his breath away. "You take care now," he said to Buster. "You hear?"

Without looking back, Pete turned and hurried from the balcony, ushering Rosacoke out of the living room with a final good-bye for Tara. "Take care of my son, woman," he said.

As he got in on the passenger side of Rosacoke's Cadillac, and as they headed back down the mountain to Heaven on Earth, a sudden but deep chill overcame Pete, a premonition of anguish yet to come.

***

As one month rolled into another and those months became years, Rosacoke felt her whole life was like a nature film where the action is speeded up to reveal the unfolding of a flower.

It was deep in December before the Riddle family—if it could still be called that—got together at Christmas. Buster and Tara were in seclusion deep within the bowels of Switzerland, and her other son, Tracy, called with his regrets, announcing that he'd been invited to join Troy Donahue for the holidays in Palm Springs.

The Riddles were no longer hot properties, and those days with MGM Records had come to an end.

Surprisingly, there was an exception that kept her fame alive. The emerging feminist movement had practically adopted "Mountain Momma" as their theme song. The philosophy behind the song appealed to women who wanted to carve out identities of their own, and to feminists who wanted to pursue goals that weren't necessarily linked to a man, even if that man was a husband.

Deserted by her husband, the song's heroine, ("Mountain Momma") raised six kids by herself and found time to go out with any feller she wanted on Saturday night. Not only that, she was the tough but fair boss of a timber gang she'd inherited from her granddaddy. The lyrics suggested that a woman can have both a career and a lover (more than one if she wanted) and also raise a family, all with effortless ease.

Pete himself had one final hit song, his recording of "Yesterday, Today and Tomorrow." It was topped on the charts only by the Beatles. After that, Pete never recorded another song but stayed at Heaven on Earth, drinking more heavily than ever. He'd become addicted to both pills and liquor. There were some days when he no longer got out of bed. His bedroom, with its windows covered in black velvet draperies, sometimes wouldn't see the light of day for weeks at a time.

As her career, along with Pete's, entered a deep decline, Rosacoke grew morose. But no matter what else happened, Claude was predictable and constant. He never disappointed her. What he promised, he delivered. She liked that in a man.

One afternoon, on the open road with him, she lowered the window, letting in the breeze, even though the day was cold. The bracing air seemed to clear away some of the confusion whirling around her.

When Claude politely suggested she raise the window, she did so without hesitation. He turned on the heater instead, and it made the car a little hot. She assisted him when he needed help in slipping off his hunter's jacket.

The scenery passed in review, but she didn't look at it. Her eyes had become mesmerized by the brownish-blond hair growing on Claude's wrist.

It was strangely erotic to her.

In many ways Claude was the most masculine man she'd ever known. Pete was a hell of a lot prettier and had a much better body in terms of classic concepts of male beauty. But Claude was one hot stud. When he took a woman, she knew that a man had descended upon her. When he made love to her, she was sure he fulfilled his needs completely inside her. But she'd never absolutely know that, because every act of love that he performed seemed like a means to her own satisfaction. As a lover, he wasn't self-involved, self-centered, or narcissistic, like so many other men she had known. He gave and then gave some more.

His love-making always began at her lips, his tongue seducing her mouth in a way that reminded her of how a penis would have felt and tasted. When he'd excited her there, he'd descend to her breasts, which had always held some special satisfaction for him.

When his mouth reached her lower extremities that was when he set her on fire. His tongue had the exciting possibility of satisfying her totally. When he exhausted her, and had her sighing and heaving with passion, then relaxing into the warm afterglow of love, he'd penetrate her. That single act of a long, insistent stabbing penetration always aroused her to another fever-pitch. Once he was inside her, she never wanted him to leave. One time, as she fondly remembered, she didn't think he ever would. He stayed inside her until he'd climaxed three times, never withdrawing from her during his long periods of rest. That moment, in looking back, was the most exciting sexual experience of her entire life.

Taking his eye for a moment off the mountain road, Claude looked into her eyes. He seemed to know exactly what she was thinking. "I was remembering too," he said in a low voice. "Longing to repeat it."

"Damn it!" she said. "Let's don't go back to Heaven on Earth. Not right now." She scooted over in her seat, and he reached to put a strong arm around her, hugging her close. She closed her eyes, as she snuggled as tightly against him as he could, enjoying his manly smell.

"I want you," was all he said.

"I want you, too," she said. "I have to have it."

He drove her to the Riddle homestead, which looked strangely deserted. Pete insisted on keeping it as a memorial to his parents.

Claude took her into the back bedroom where he pulled off her clothing before stripping down himself. As he made love to her, it was like falling in love with him all over again. If he couldn't get her out of his system, she felt the same way about him. She didn't really like to compare men, but she believed that Claude was a hell of a lot more man than Pete. He lacked Pete's equipment, and had only a natural physique, rather than the rippling muscles of Peter, but he was a loving man and was totally into lovemaking with women, despite his previous sexual history with, among others, his

son-in-law, Ronnie.

After he'd satisfied her completely, and she'd done the same for him, she lay in his arms, dreaming happily of that summer day when they'd resumed their lovemaking after a long absence.

They'd gone horseback riding in the woods, heading for Blowing Rock Falls. Once there, she'd felt so good in the burning sunshine, and the day had been so hot, that both of them had spontaneously decided to pull off all their clothes and jump into the waters. Being out in the wilderness alone together had given them a certain freedom.

Rosacoke had run into the water first, finding it refreshing, but cold. At the edge, Claude had stood for a long moment looking down at her. She'd been struck by the intense white of his untanned groin, as opposed to the nut-brown color of the rest of his body. With an easy stride, he'd jumped into the water, swimming toward her.

Catching up with her, he'd cuddled her into his arms. His skin had glistened in the brilliant sun, as he'd glanced over his shoulder at the foreboding forest beyond. "I hope no one's lurking out there with a camera."

"I haven't been a media event in some time," she'd said.

She'd drifted into the deepest waters, with him swimming beside her. Going underwater, she'd surfaced right at his body. He'd taken her in his arms and had kissed her, his hands reaching to explore her body. Together they'd drifted back to shore. He'd placed a blanket on the sands. Lying down on his back, he invited her to join him. Low and husky, he'd whispered into her ear, "Let's do it."

That scene at Blowing Rock Falls had remained one of her most beautiful memories. Driving with him, months later on a chilly afternoon, brought back other memories. Impulsively, she asked him to take her to a florist to buy some flowers.

After that, they drove to her mama's grave site. Rosacoke placed these Christmas memory flowers on the grave of her mama, remembering a long-ago twilight when her mama had taken her across a cotton patch and into the shanty of old Aunt Clotilda and her son, Sultan, and his daughter, Narcissa.

"Who would have imagined back then how our lives would go?" she said, snuggling close into Claude's winter parka.

An hour later at Heaven on Earth, what was left of Pete's family gathered in front of the fireplace in the living room. Between drinks from his glass of bourbon, Pete played with his newly acquired Cocker Spaniel, a gift from Tracy. The puppy gave Pete a sloppy-tongued lick on the mouth.

The scenery outside reminded Rosacoke of a Currier & Ives engraving, a landscape of picket fences and rolling hills blanketed by snow.

Still as much in love as the day they met in Southampton, Freddie and Nipsey shared their gifts with the rest of the musicians. Although aging, all

the black musicians—Maston Mastin, Smokey Wetter, and Guitar Red—were still living in the compound at Heaven on Earth. Tara or Rosacoke no longer gave these faithful old family retainers their Christmas gifts. That job had fallen to Karl. Without Karl, Heaven on Earth, both as a real estate investment and as a community, would probably fall apart.

Rosacoke missed the presence of Tara and Buster, wondering what their lonely Christmas was like in Switzerland.

Larry and Ronnie were still an item, even though they had frequent fights and long separations when Ronnie would move back in with Wanda Mae. But he always got back together with Larry.

Wanda Mae sat in the far corner of the room, watching television. Over the years, perhaps because of her unfulfilled life, she'd put on too much weight, but she still wore beautiful clothes from her stores, and had learned to apply makeup perfectly. She only attended these family gatherings because she felt it was expected of her. She seemed interested only in her businesses, and hardly exchanged words with Ronnie anymore, even on the occasions when she lived under the same room with him.

Other than Nipsey and Freddie, the only two love-birds in the room were Junior and Joni. It was obvious from the way Junior sat on a loveseat in front of the fire holding Joni's hand that he was still in love with her.

When Karl came into the room, his attention was entirely focused on Pete. She felt that Pete was lucky to have a friend as loyal as Karl. That still handsome man seemed to put up with any shit Pete tossed at him and came back for more.

If her former husband had his Karl, Rosacoke knew that she had Claude. He loved her and wanted to marry her, although she had no more interest in marriage.

As the wafting aroma of the upcoming Christmas dinner filled the house, Rosacoke secretly observed Pete. Playing with his Cocker Spaniel, he seemed unaware that he was facing such scrutiny. She hadn't updated her image of him in a long time. To her, his face existed as it did in 1941, an image that seemed to have imbedded itself permanently in her mind regardless of what Pete actually looked like.

Today, owing perhaps to her more cynical mood, she wanted to see the new Pete Riddle, the only man she'd ever married and the father of her only child.

He'd never lost that lopsided grin he always had, and his eyes still danced when he was happy, but those occasions were rare. There had been many changes in his face. Without her even being aware of it, he'd grown older before her eyes. His hair had thinned on top of his head, and grayed a bit at the temples, and little laugh lines had appeared around his eyes. He was like a boy who'd gone wandering in the forest one night, but had had a frightening experience and had returned the next morning an

older man.

She loved him. *Still*. She guessed she always would. Even though divorced from him, she thought she'd never leave him.

The cook came out and interrupted Rosacoke's reverie. She'd forgotten to buy chestnuts, and she wanted somebody to go to the store for her before it closed at noon. "We can't have Christmas dinner without chestnuts," the cook said.

The members of Pete's staff were home celebrating Christmas with their families. Having nothing else to do, Claude volunteered to go, and Rosacoke asked to go along too. She wanted out of the house. As she gave Pete a parting kiss, she figured that was like kissing the Cocker Spaniel by proxy.

Actually she'd wanted Claude out of the house because Karl had told her earlier that her Christmas gift to Claude, a fine stallion, was about to be delivered.

The ride to the store was short but the road was slippery. Almost defiantly, Claude kept his foot on the gas petal, feeling secure along mountain roads he'd driven since he was fourteen. "Instead of Claude Billings, I'm gonna name you Leadfoot," she said.

"I take my tensions out behind the wheel," he said. "I'd hoped this Christmas that we'd be getting married."

"You're fucking me, aren't you?" she said. "What do you need with a marriage license?"

"Looks like I don't have a choice in the matter. I want marriage. But if you don't, then I'm prepared to go on living like we are."

The rest of the ride was in silence.

Only a few last-minute shoppers were in the supermarket, and each consumer seemed too intent on her or his business to pay much attention to Rosacoke. One clerk shouted, "Rosacoke, how ya doing?" She blew him a Christmas kiss.

After she picked up the chestnuts and a few other items, and reached the check-out counter, a small crowd had formed after all. She wished she'd paid more attention to fixing her face this morning. Two girls asked for her autograph, and she gladly obliged. She knew Treva Walsh, the woman behind the cash register, and dutifully asked about her son and husband before getting back into the Cadillac with Claude to celebrate Christmas with their dysfunctional family.

For Christmas that year, Pete had bought the world's most expensive mink coat for her and had given her a large diamond-and-ruby ring. She'd presented him with a shiny new Cadillac. But right after dinner he'd fallen asleep drunk in front of the television set.

Even though divorced, she never openly slept with Claude at Heaven on Earth. She always slipped away somewhere with Claude, usually to his

own shotgun house or else Buster's former retreat in the mountains for their lovemaking. Whenever they were at Heaven on Earth, and out of respect for her former husband, she kissed Claude in private and sent him away to his own bedroom upstairs at night.

At two o'clock that morning, she was surprised to hear the knob of her door turning. Someone was entering her room.

Turning on her night lamp, she was shocked to see Pete staggering in. He'd obviously awakened and found himself alone in the living room. Coming toward her bed, he'd unbuttoned his shirt and unfastened the buckle to his blue jeans. He pulled back the covers to find her completely nude under the sheets.

He mounted her and made some attempt at penetration but he was too drunk. In a few minutes he fell asleep, the weight of his large body resting heavily upon her.

She managed to slip gently out from under him, but then lay close to his side all night as he fell into a deep and troubled sleep. Once or twice she'd heard him call out the name of Buster.

For the rest of the night, she didn't sleep. At first she'd been tempted to get up and leave the room, retreating to another bedroom.

In her secret heart she wanted to leave Pete and run away somewhere with Claude. She didn't understand the incredible loyalty she felt that always bound her to this drugged and drunken man lying beside her.

As time went by, she more and more dreamed of living out in the West. Maybe Montana. To her, Montana sounded like a good place to live. Even though she'd never been there, and neither had Claude, she was convinced that no one ever bothered you in the wilds of Montana.

***

Driving in his Cadillac across the broad state of North Carolina to the Outer Banks, Pete had survived Christmas and even New Year's in a drugged stupor at Heaven on Earth. He didn't know exactly where Buster and Tara were living in Switzerland. The only way Larry could reach Buster was by writing to a post office box.

The other night when Pete had called Tracy in Los Angeles, his other son had told him to sober up before calling again. Pete had slammed down the phone.

There wasn't much Pete could think about these days that didn't disturb him greatly. Neither of his sons, Buster or Tracy, brought back happy memories. Pete hated himself for getting involved sexually with either one of them, and wished in vain that he could rewrite his life. He knew he couldn't and had to live with his shame, which increasingly he blamed on the cause of his heavy drinking and pill-popping.

A road sign along the highway alerted Pete that he was only ten miles from reaching his goal along the Outer Banks. For this final drive, he wanted to wipe Tracy and Buster from his mind. He did manage to do that, but their memories were replaced by yet another nightmare, that of his final performance four years previously before a live audience. It had been in Fort Worth, Texas.

Despite warnings by Larry and Claude, Pete had been drinking bourbon and popping pills all afternoon before that Texas concert. At first he'd refused to go on stage, holding up the curtain. In his crazed state, he'd been in fear that an assassin somewhere out there had a gun with the name of Pete Riddle written on a bullet. "If I go out there, I'm a dead duck," he'd told Larry.

Larry had managed to hold the curtain for one hour, but the Texans were becoming restless. Loud calls for Pete to come out on stage had come from the audience, who had grown increasingly belligerent, the way they did at some of the final, disastrous performances of Judy Garland.

Finally, a drunken Pete had staggered onto the stage, facing a half empty auditorium. To fill the room, Larry had had to reduce ticket prices in the final days. Pete had faced only mild applause when the curtain had gone up.

With his guitar, he'd launched into his repertoire of now familiar songs, knowing he wasn't performing them like he used to. At the end of two numbers when the applause was thin, he'd tried to apologize to the audience. "I can't find my voice tonight," he'd said. "I think one of those Texas bullfrogs got it." That comment had been met with stunned silence.

After three more numbers, a wave of snickers could be heard throughout the audience. Even in his stupor, Pete had known that his fans—or what was left of them—were mocking him. That snickering had turned to boos and catcalls heard across the auditorium. "I'll get better," Pete had promised at the end of his next number. Many of the audience had gotten up and had headed for the exits in the rear. Seeing them walking out, Pete had called to them. "Don't go! Please don't go."

When it had appeared that he could no longer prevent the walkout, he'd faced a greatly thinned audience. Without meaning to, and strictly on an impulse, he'd announced, "I'm gonna conclude my show tonight with 'Lonesome Blues.' My appearance here in Fort Worth is my final and farewell performance. I'm just a country boy who can't sing too well and after tonight I'm gonna go back to the hills of Carolina where I was born. Once there, I guess I'll just fade away, the way some of you folks tonight seem to want me to."

After he had concluded with a lackluster rendition of "Lonesome Blues," Larry had ordered that the curtain be pulled.

Even though the day was cold and windy, Pete lowered the window on

the driver's side of his Cadillac. He felt if he let the wind blow into the car, it would chase away the memory of that ghastly night in Texas where his singing career had officially come to an end.

Sometimes late at night, the memory of that debacle still haunted him, sending him into the bathroom to his ever-faithful pill bottles. "God damn," he'd always said to himself, "I'm becoming worse than Marilyn Monroe, and look what happened to her."

Whenever one of his records played on the radio, he switched it off. He didn't want to be reminded.

Rosacoke had remained loyal to the memory of their former marriage, although he'd known that she was fucking Claude even though these two lovebirds tried to be discreet around him. They didn't have to keep their love for each other a secret from him. He'd welcome it if they came out into the open with it, or even announced that they were getting married. He'd even be the best man at their wedding if they wanted that.

He still had a chamber of his heart reserved just for Rosacoke, and he'd always loved Claude. Even though he'd long ago stopped making love to either of them, he still viewed them among the most cherished people in his life, even or especially if love had turned to loyalty.

It was loyalty that had driven him to the Outer Banks this dying winter's afternoon where the heavy overcast of clouds didn't give the sun a chance to break through. Night after drunken night, he'd been thinking only of Josh. He'd betrayed Josh and his longtime lover had left him.

That morning when Pete had gotten out of bed, he'd pulled back his black-velvet draperies and faced the light of morning for the first time in months. He decided there and then that he was a changed man and could be loyal and true to Josh for the first time in his life. He knew that Josh still loved him, and always would. The type of love that Josh had for him couldn't be wiped away in just a few months or even a few years. He knew it was still there. Pete wanted Josh back in his life.

He'd driven to the Outer Banks once before to reclaim his lover. He'd done it then, and he knew he could pull it off once again. By the time he got into that Cadillac and headed back from the coast into the hills, he fully expected that Josh would be in the passenger's seat across from him.

He regretted that he had let Josh get away. Although he'd wanted to spend his life with Tracy Adams who'd died in the war, he'd come to love Josh as he had no other man. The way Pete felt today, Josh belonged to him, and Pete intended to reclaim what was his.

The motel still owned by Josh's parents looked seedier than ever. It was in dire need of paint, and the grounds were unkempt and littered with debris. Pete wasn't certain if the motel was open until he saw a lit neon sign advertising VACANCIES within the outline of a pink flamingo.

Walking into the small front office reception, Pete encountered an old

man in dire need of a shave. "You renting rooms tonight?" Pete asked.

"The whole place is yours," the man said. "We only keep four rooms heated this time of year hoping to pick up a little business from gents like yourself passing through. We get people who don't want to drive all the way to Wilmington for the night."

"Great!" Pete said. "I'll sign in."

"We don't bother with that," the old man said. "If you've got twelve dollars—cash that is—you've got the room. You can pick up some booze down the road a piece. I'll supply the ice." He looked Pete up and down. "There's no television and no movies for miles around. I hope you brought a good book to read. The only books in our rooms are Holy Bibles, and we get those free."

"I brought my own booze, and I can provide my own entertainment." He hesitated before asking his next question out of fear of what the answer might be. "I was in the Navy with Josh Harnell," Pete said. "Do his folks still own this place?"

"His mama does," the old man said. "After her husband died of cancer, she went to live with her niece in Raleigh. Josh comes on duty at seven. That guy can't sleep at night. I used to handle the graveyard shift. Now he makes me work days and he takes over at night."

"Fine," Pete said. He asked for a piece of paper and a pencil. On it he scribbled, "Your loving man will be waiting in Room 201. It's been too long. P.R." He folded over the note and asked the desk clerk to give it to Josh when he came on duty.

In the bleak motel room the bathroom smelled of mildew and the chenille bedspread had at least three cigarette burns. Pete showered for his upcoming encounter with Josh. At least the water was hot. Emerging from the shower, he was clad only in a towel. He turned on the radio and went over to his suitcase where he extracted a bottle of bourbon and poured himself a stiff drink in a glass placed next to a pitcher of drinking water.

He lay nude in the center of the bed, thinking only of Josh and how they'd met when he was in the Navy. Josh was one beautiful man. He was like the golden boy of Pete's dreams and fantasies.

Had Pete not been such a wild thing when he was young, he would have settled down with Josh and lived happily ever after. "I was a God damn whore," he said to himself. "But I can change."

He figured that he wanted only one person in his life—and that was Josh. If Josh would take him back, he would pledge his eternal fidelity. Even if it meant giving up Karl and forsaking all others, Pete envisioned spending he rest of his life in Josh's arms. With the right kind of loving man by his side, Pete could even conjure up the possibility of giving up bourbon and drugs.

He kept glancing at his wrist watch almost every five minutes. When

Josh came on duty at seven o'clock, he wondered how long it would be before there was a knock on his door.

Promptly at five minutes past seven, he heard a rap on that door. Getting up from the bed with only a bath towel wrapped around his waist, Pete walked rapidly toward the door and opened it.

It was Josh standing there, his face brightening into a smile. "You've come back. I always knew you would." Before Pete realized what was happening, Josh had taken him in his arms and was holding him and kissing him deeply.

Even though Pete's eyes were wide shut and he was kissing Josh with all the passion he could muster, he could not blot out Josh's image. No longer the golden boy of World War II, Josh had grown grossly fat and had lost most of his hair. How could a man who had been so beautiful have become so grotesque?

It was going to be one long evening.

And so it was.

When Pete departed from the motel at five o'clock the next morning, Josh was still asleep in the bed beside him. As best as he could, Pete had tried to satisfy Josh sexually. Pete could only do that by closing his eyes and remembering what his former lover used to look like. In some ways, he imagined that making love to a decayed Josh would be like making love to a deformed Buster. Neither prospect enthralled him because he was still a man who worshipped male beauty.

At the front desk, he'd written a note for Josh. "Fool that I am, I know now that you can't go back. It's hopeless trying to recapture what once was when what once was is gone forever. Fare thee well. I wish you all the good things that life can bestow. You are a great guy, and I'll always remember you and our good times together. But you're too fine and decent a man for a rascal like me. You'll find someone else who will devote his entire life to you and not be that rambling sagebrush I always was when I lived with you. This is good-bye. It's time for Pete Riddle to hit the road. Your loving friend always. "

On the way back to the hills, he tried to blot Josh from his mind the way he'd tried to erase all painful memories, including Buster's accident and the collapse of his career.

As he crossed the border into Wilkes County, a fierce resolve came over him as he began to redefine his life. It had always been there in front of his face, and he could not see the obvious.

He was no longer in love with Josh. Tracy Adams was dead and gone, left at the bottom of the cold Atlantic Ocean. His life with Buster had come to an end, as had his aborted love for his other son. Rosacoke had gone to the arms of another. Sultan had been lynched. And just three weeks ago Frank Walker had called from Los Angeles to say he'd read in the papers

about the murder of Hank Adams in a sleazy trailer park in Orange County.

One by one, all the other men had drifted off, including Junior and Joni. Some men like Larry, Ronnie, and Claude still stayed at his side, but Pete was certain that was because they had no other place to go. He was a good meal ticket for all of his boys. Despite the collapse of his career, he still had plenty of money. For that, he could be grateful to Karl, the only man in his life who had the smarts to provide for all of them.

As Pete neared his hometown, he didn't head for his mansion. Instead, he drove toward an address which had come to mean more to him than any other place on earth.

Pulling into the driveway of a beautiful Victorian house, he saw the smoke rising from the chimney. It was late in the afternoon of a snowy Sunday. He'd made it across the entire state.

Coming in through the kitchen door, as he always did, he headed for the living room. There on the sofa with his feet propped up was Karl listening to the first album Pete had ever recorded. Karl never listened to any other singer's music. Only Pete's records.

"Hi, handsome," Karl said, looking up. "You sure are a sight for sore eyes. I'm as lonesome as those 'Lonesome Blues' you're always singing about."

"I've come back," Pete said, moving toward him.

"I can see that."

"You don't understand," Pete said. "What I mean is, I've come back for the first time. I'm slightly used goods, and I'm very far from perfect, but if you still want me, I'm yours forever. There will never be anybody in my life from this moment on but the beautiful man I see before me."

Karl got up from the sofa and took Pete into his arms. "If you mean that, and if that's a true offer, then you've got yourself a deal, cowboy." He melted into Pete's arms, kissing him passionately.

After five minutes when Pete released Karl's mouth to catch up with his breathing, Karl whispered in his ear. "Even when you're old, washed up, and arthritic, you're welcome to put your boots under my bed any and all nights for the rest of your life."

# Chapter 16
## (The Seventies: Fade-Out)

*When she woke up, the room was dark. She didn't know where she was or what had happened. Her mind mercifully had blotted out the past few hours. She was unnaturally calm, as if she'd been drugged and was gradually coming out of a stupor.*

*The room had an antiseptic smell like a hospital. Her mouth felt like cotton had been stuffed in it. She giggled to herself, remembering the old Southern expression, "My mouth's so dry I'm spittin' cotton." Her mouth was exactly that dry, and the expression all of a sudden didn't sound funny. It was too true.*

*Her mind was cloudy, and it was difficult to think and impossible to remember. The truth was she didn't want to. Memory brought pain, and she'd like to avoid that at any cost.*

*In spite of her struggle to suppress it, an image kept trying to force its way to the front part of her brain. Something very distasteful.*

*She lay back in bed, hoping it would go away and let her rest in peace. That image persisted, moving closer and closer to the front of her brain. If she weren't careful, in just a second it would flash a picture like a video image.*

*The picture flashed.*

*She'd been transported with Pete to a villa in Miami. While she'd been bathing, he'd been assassinated. Flashing through her brain was the image of herself kneeling beside his body, trying to push his brains back into his skull.*

*When that reality dawned on her, her scream was so piercing it convulsed her whole body and seemed to scrape her vocal cords like a rusty razor blade.*

\*\*\*

"It's okay."

The voice was that of a man. Strong hands reached out to comfort her

and hold her back in bed. "It's okay."

The voice was vaguely familiar.

"I'm here," it said. "It's all over. You're gonna be okay. I'm here."

In the maggot swarm of conflicting imagery exploding inside her head, she knew that voice.

"Claude…." Settling back in bed, she could barely utter his name. The sound emerged from her raw throat in only the vaguest whisper. "Claude, it's really you?"

"In the flesh. It's gonna be okay."

She bolted up in bed, reaching for him in desperation, clinging with more force than she'd ever clung to anybody in her life. Minutes seemed to go by before she broke away, her hands reaching out to plow through his hair. She wanted to touch his flesh, feel his skull, trace patterns on his lips, know that his eyes were in their sockets, reach inside his shirt to see if his heart were still beating. It was as if she must confirm he hadn't been blasted away with a gun. "Pete…."

Those masculine hands reached out for her again, gently but firmly pushing her back on the pillow. "It's all over. There was nothing anybody could do. It's all over."

She clapped her hand over her face, as if that would blot out the real world she so reluctantly inhabited, not wanting to live any more, wanting to escape and run away where memory and those horrible images couldn't track her down.

That wish seemed in vain.

She locked her head pathetically in her arms, peeking out at Claude through her fingers. Under the sheets, she huddled like a little girl frightened of lightning. She was afraid that some brute force would come into the room, ripping off her covers to expose her to cruel, condemning eyes.

That image of Pete came back but she was stronger now. She blurred that image but couldn't stop the tears. She tasted her tears. Her weeping was soft, contained. Later the deep guttural sobs of despair would come. Her lips were parched and cracked. "I need some water."

Claude got up and in a moment returned with a glass of water, which he held up to her lips. She could hardly swallow. Running her fingers through his hair again, she looked at him. "I must be a mess."

"You look beautiful."

She didn't really give a damn about how she looked. It was just something to say, to postpone what she knew they must inevitably talk about.

The water hit her stomach like some bitter acid. She sat up in bed. "Who did it?"

"Narcissa. She's in custody now."

"Narcissa killed Pete?" She reached for his hand, clutching. "I can't believe that. Why?"

"I guess she had her reason."

"What in hell does that mean? What reason?"

He turned from the sight of her. "Honey, you're gonna have to be very, very strong. Everything's gonna be on TV. Tonight, tomorrow. Who knows? It's all gonna come out. Not just about Pete's assassination. But every secret we've ever tried to hide. The FBI's on it now."

"Oh, my God! *Everything?*" He did say that, didn't he?

She tried to climb out of bed until he gently placed her back there. "Everything?" Her questioning eyes sought his.

"Three men from the FBI are outside the door," Claude said. "They're demanding to come in and talk to you."

"I can't. I just can't see anybody."

"I'm afraid they won't go away. Don't worry. I'll be here."

Her voice was forlorn. She'd stopped crying. Tears had been replaced with an aching hurt so strong she wanted to cry out in pain. That hurt was too powerful to succumb to the release of crying. "Narcissa. Pete. It didn't happen. I can't believe it."

A loud rap sounded on the door.

"Hold yourself together," Claude cautioned. "You've got to get through this. You've got to."

Men, faceless ones, came into the room, surrounding her bed. It was hard for her to think. They asked questions to which she didn't know the answers. She was carried back to the afternoon and the bathroom in the mansion, the perfumed water. Voices—now but a distant echo—resounded within her head.

Between the questions, bits and pieces of information seeped into her brain. She was learning more from these men than she was telling them.

Someone had slipped into their private suite and had come into Pete's bedroom as he slept. Six bullets had been fired into Pete's head.

Rosacoke knew that he had awakened in time to see the revolver pointed at him. His cry of protest was as strong and vivid in her mind as if he'd just screamed the words, "No! No!"

"Other than your security guard here," one of the faceless men said, his eyes looking over at Claude, "the only person in the villa was Miss Narcissa Cash. There were also two servants on the ground floor cooking, but they are not under investigation."

"Narcissa." Rosacoke said the name without malice or accusation in her voice. In stunned disbelief, she repeated the name again. "Narcissa."

"She was arrested when the elevator doors opened," one of the FBI agents told Rosacoke. "She did not have the murder weapon on her. She'd obviously disposed of it somewhere. We're having the entire villa searched for the weapon. We suspect she might have had an accomplice who escaped from the building with the weapon."

"Why would Narcissa kill Pete Riddle? She had an appointment to see

us."

"Maybe he didn't grant her request," an agent said. "We know she was coming to meet with him and plead with him to give her two-hundred thousand dollars. Eight years ago she bought a château in France and adopted twenty-six children from all over the world. A rainbow tribe. But she went bankrupt. She was going to lose the château and didn't have any place to house her adopted children."

"Pete would have been more good to her alive than dead," Rosacoke protested. "He once gave her one-hundred thousand dollars. He would have helped her again."

"As I said," the agent repeated. "He might have turned her down."

"There wasn't time," Rosacoke said. "Such a negotiation would have stretched on for a long time. She wouldn't just have rushed in the room, demanded that kind of money, had him refuse, and then reached into her purse for a revolver to shoot him down."

"How can you be certain?" the agent asked. "We understand that you were taking a long bath. Is that right?"

"Yes," she said. "But...."

"There may be other motives," the agent said. "We know that Pete Riddle and Narcissa Cash were once romantically involved. That they even had a child together. A boy you adopted and renamed Tracy Riddle. He's half colored, but looks white. Is that right?"

"No..." She tried to protest this evidence.

"Are you sure?" The agent's eyes seemed to see right through the covers on her bed.

"What I mean is...." She coughed. "I mean.... What I mean...Narcissa did not kill Pete."

"She is our prime suspect," the agent said.

"I just know she didn't do it," she screamed. "I know it in my heart."

"I'm afraid that's not good enough evidence," the agent said. "Narcissa has been arrested. She'll be charged with Pete's murder. The news has been leaked to the media. Crowds are forming outside. Narcissa is being held downstairs. After booking her at the local precinct, we're transporting her across the bay to Miami where she'll be locked up."

"Claude, make these men leave the room," she called to him. "Make them go away." Jerking up in bed, she struck in blind fury at the faceless men around her.

Hands were on her, holding her down.

"We'll come back this evening when you're less hysterical," an agent said.

She felt as if she were locked in a madhouse, and she wanted out. The faceless ones were her captors, and she had to get away from them.

"Pete's not dead," she yelled. "It's a lie. Pete's alive."

She was still restrained on the bed when a nurse with a needle entered the room. Rosacoke called out for Claude to save her, as she felt the stinging stab of the needle in her arm.

For one brief moment, a powerful energy filled her body, and she felt she could overpower all the people in the room and run away. But within seconds she lay back down on the pillow. That spurt of energy was rapidly fading from her body. Voices could still be heard around her, but the sounds were growing fainter.

She welcomed the enveloping darkness. The fight was gone from her.

Her mind was drifting off to happier times. There had been pain in her life. But there had been good times too.

***

Rosacoke remembered Pete's last night at Heaven on Earth. He'd been drinking heavily, and an aura of melancholia had enveloped him. His talent had led him to fame and wealth beyond his wildest dreams. Who would have thought back in 1941 that either of them would go as far as they had?

"Anybody who's got something can climb the mountain," he'd said to her. "And anyone who gets there can look around at the glorious sights the world has to offer, breathing the fresh air way up there. What they don't tell you when you're climbing that mountain is that you'll have to come down that mountain one day."

In one of her closest moments ever with Pete, he'd held her close—not making love, just cuddling. "Without you, I'd die," he'd said. "I'd just up and die."

"I'll always be here for you," she'd promised him.

He'd gotten up and played their old records that night, as if reliving their lives during happier times. The bourbon and the lateness of the hour had caused her to drift off to sleep on the living room sofa. When she awakened around three o'clock, she'd found him pacing up and down the floor. She'd been reminded of that old Ernest Tubb song, "Walking the Floor Over You."

"What's the matter?" she'd asked.

"I'm scared," he'd said.

She'd turned on a lamp on the table. As she came up to him, she'd seen tears forming in his eyes. "What is it?"

"I'm losing my grip," he'd said. "Coming apart. I have this odd feeling deep in my gut that my life isn't gonna work out just like I planned."

"It never does."

"I know," he'd said. "It's more than that. I feel something real bad is about to happen."

"It'll go away," she'd said. "I get these fears too. Usually in lonely hotel rooms late at night. Come morning, I shake them off and press on."

He'd looked deeply into her eyes, and it had been the most penetrating look he'd ever given her. "If something happens, and I was ever to die, you would go on, wouldn't you?"

"Don't bring that up," she'd cautioned. "You're gonna live for years and years. You've got me as your friend. You've got Claude. Mainly you've got Karl. You'll never find loyalty like he shows you."

"Yeah, I guess I won't," he'd said. "I don't know why he puts up with me. Come to think of it, I don't know why you didn't flee years ago."

"As long as some part of you still needs me, I'll stick around."

"I'll always be restless in my grave if I thought you'd never forgive me for all the bad things I've done to you."

"I'm a big gal," she'd said. "All of us have done things we wish we hadn't. There is nothing I need to forgive you for."

"You really mean that?"

"More than I've ever meant anything in my whole life," she'd said.

He'd gripped her hand so hard it hurt. "Then let's fly to Florida tomorrow morning and give 'em hell."

He'd taken her in his arms and had given her a long, passionate kiss. She hadn't felt so much strength flowing from him in years.

"Your Mountain Momma will be right by your side."

***

The next morning, when Rosacoke woke up in that unfamiliar Miami villa, the FBI men were gone. It was like waking up alone on the road in one of those bleak motel rooms. Except she wasn't alone in the early dawn. She sensed someone in the room with her.

"Claude, that you?"

"I'm here, baby," came his sleepy voice from his perch in the armchair beside her bed. "You're gonna be fine…just fine."

Weakly she sat up in bed. "We've got to call Buster." As an afterthought, she added, "and Tracy as well."

"I talked to Buster and Tara this morning," he said. "They'd heard the news in Switzerland. Buster is taking it pretty bad. Tara, too. They both loved Pete."

"Can you get Buster on the phone for me?" she pleaded. "I need to speak to him. We can never call them direct. We don't even know their address, much less their phone number."

"That's the way Buster wants it," Claude said. "Total privacy even from his own mama. You'll have to wait for him to call."

"What about Tracy?" she asked.

"He's driving from Palm Springs to Los Angeles," Claude said. "I left word to have him call you at once."

"How's Karl taking it?" she asked. "I mean, if anybody in the world loved Pete Riddle, it was Karl."

"Junior's arranged for a private plane to fly him here," Claude said. "I talked to him around midnight last night. He's half out of his mind. He's in some sort of denial. Insisting that Pete's still alive. He absolutely refuses to accept the fact that Pete is gone from our lives."

"I know that feeling," she said.

"You and Pete have certainly been big news on the tube," he said.

She looked into his eyes. "I want a TV wheeled into this room. I want to hear what they are saying. I've always had this funny feeling deep in my gut that one day my whole life would be played out on TV."

"Let's hold off on the God damn TV," he said. "You're not strong enough."

"I'm strong enough all right," she said, raising her voice. "I want that TV in this fucking room and I want it now."

"A lot has happened while you slept," he said. "Things I haven't had a chance to tell you."

"I want to see it on TV."

He left the room and within minutes had returned with a color TV set. She couldn't help but notice the security guard posted outside her door. When the set was hooked up, Claude attempted to turn it on.

"Not yet," she said. "I know you very well, Claude Billings, and you were never good at covering up anything. I think you know something about who killed Pete that the FBI doesn't know. Much less some damn TV news station. Come clean."

"I don't know a thing," he said. "I was having a shower when Pete was killed. I'll never forgive myself. I should have been protecting this house more. After all, I'm in charge of security."

"I think you know who killed Pete Riddle, and don't tell me it was Narcissa." She'd never looked with such a demanding gaze into his eyes. "I want to know what you know."

"You might have a woman's intuition, but you're fucked up in the head with this one if you think I'm holding something back from the police. It could have been a stalker, someone who slipped into the house. Over the years, Pete, like Elvis, has received death threats. We never took them seriously but it's possible that Pete had a stalker, a deranged fan. It happens." He quickly reached to turn on the news.

For some reason, she felt that Claude was lying to her, and she didn't know why. There could be only one possible explanation why he would suppress information about who killed Pete. The only possible reason he would want to cover up for somebody was if he killed Pete himself. In her

crazed state this morning, that was too likely a possibility for her to face. Not only this morning, but for all time.

As he switched to the news channel, Claude turned back to face her. "Something terrible has happened." He looked sad-faced and forlorn, with a sense of foreboding and gloom as he turned up the volume on the TV. "They've got pictures. You can see it all. Maybe the TV is the best way to tell you. After all, I'm not much of a story-teller."

As first the televised images were blurred, then the picture came into sharp focus. A TV reporter was narrating the sequence of events.

After Narcissa had been arrested at the villa, she was taken for questioning at the nearest precinct on Miami Beach. From there, she'd been handcuffed and had been led up a long corridor to a parking lot where an armed van had waited to take her across the causeway into Miami, where she was booked on a charge of murdering Pete Riddle.

The TV cameras showed a distraught Narcissa, flanked by two policemen holding onto each of her arms, as she walked up the ramp to the waiting van.

Seemingly out of nowhere, a fat white man—right before Rosacoke's eyes on the TV screen—had emerged from the crowd of curious bystanders. He'd had a gun in his hand. The man looked strangely familiar to her. He'd fired two shots into Narcissa's heart. She'd keeled over in death, a look of such shock on her face that Rosacoke feared that image, along with Pete's dead body, would haunt her for the rest of her life.

The sound of gunfire filled the TV screen. The officer guarding Narcissa on her right whipped out his pistol and fired at the assassin. The unknown killer himself had collapsed in death right in front of the TV cameras.

Her face paralyzed with horror, Rosacoke reached for Claude's hand and held onto it desperately as the sound of sirens filled the screen.

She collapsed back into her pillow, closing her eyes, not wanting to see any more. Her world as she'd known it had come to an end.

She was only vaguely aware of the voice of the TV newscaster, Ralph Renick. "Ironically, Dade County police have learned that the assassin of Narcissa Cash, Josh Harnell, had come to Miami to kill both Pete Riddle and his former wife, Rosacoke Carson. Harnell had checked into a hotel room at the Commodore in Miami. A search of his rented room has turned up a diary in which he'd written of his plans for a joint assassination of these two country/western singers during their appearance together on Miami Beach. Apparently Harnell had been plotting their deaths for some years. At various times, he'd planned to kill them separately or together when they'd made appearances in Kansas, Texas, Wisconsin, and at one time Oregon. Harnell, according to the outline in his diary, was going to gun down Riddle as he stood up to accept his lifetime musical achievement award at the Miami Beach Auditorium. Rosacoke Carson was scheduled

to be on the platform at the same time. After Harnell killed Riddle, he was going to fire at Carson. When Harnell learned of Riddle's shooting, he decided to go after the former film star, Narcissa Cash. It can't be known now, but it is believed that he felt she had murdered Pete Riddle."

"Turn it off!" Rosacoke pleaded with Claude. "No more." She burst into tears, screaming out Narcissa's name.

He flipped off the TV.

She lay sobbing on the bed for two hours.

"It'll just be a matter of time, won't it?" she asked, sitting up in bed.

"What do you mean?" he said.

"Before someone talks," she said. "Before the FBI finds out that Josh and Pete were lovers for years. Dating back to their Navy days."

"Guess it will," he said. "I'm almost one-hundred percent certain they will."

"What about Buster?" she asked. "Will they find out Buster is still alive? That his funeral was a fraud."

"I think we have a good chance that they will never find out about that. It depends on how thoroughly they want to investigate. Josh, they'll find out about. Buster? Well, that's a toss-up." He came over to her bed and lowered himself to hold her in his arms. "If you can't take no more today, there's a way out. This may be the roughest day of your life."

"I've already faced up to the roughest," she said in a bitter, biting voice. "Picking up your husband's brains and trying to press them back into his skull is pretty God damn rough. Watching Narcissa shot down like that is pretty rough, too. If the world has anything else to toss my way, then let her rip. I can take it!"

"Okay, okay," he said. "I just wanted to be sure. 'Cause if you're not up to it, you can retreat into the wonderful world of drugs. Run and hide for as long as you need to. I'll see to it that you get 'em. Only when you're ready do you have to face the jackals, including those TV cameras."

"No drugs," she said. "I want to have a clear head. I've spent too much of my life drunk anyway. I can handle it. I'm not that innocent, shy little girl from the hills anymore. I'm a grown woman, a middle-aged one at that. I've seen it all."

"Don't ever say that," he cautioned. "The world still has its surprises."

The telephone rang and he went to pick it up. After muttering a few words, he turned to her and said, "It's Tracy calling from Los Angeles. Wanta speak to him?"

"Sure," she said, sitting up in bed. He was her son and she was the only parent he had left. She was sure that he had heard that both of his real parents, Pete and Narcissa, had been gunned down.

Picking up the phone, she tried to pour out her sympathy to Tracy and console him.

"I don't want your sympathy," he said. "Pete wasn't a real father to me. He sexually abused me. And that high-stepping nigger, Narcissa Cash, wasn't my real mother. Don't tell anybody. Even the FBI."

"They already know."

"You told them, you bitch," he shouted into the phone. "The whole world will learn that I'm a nigger too."

"I told them nothing of the sort," she shouted at him. "They found out. Many people were in on your secret."

"God damn it," he shouted at her again. "Have you read Pete's will. Am I in it? How much did he provide for me?"

"I have never seen his will," she said, "and I don't know how he divided up his property. All I know is that Karl Adams is the executor. If you want to know how much money you got, get Karl on the phone." She slammed down the receiver.

"Tracy never loved either one of us," she said to Claude.

"We both know that," he said. "But Buster loved his daddy."

"Yeah," she said, "maybe too much."

The phone rang again. Answering it, Claude said to her, "It's Larry from downstairs. He wants to see you."

"Send him up," she said. "I'm taking on all callers today. That strong 'Mountain Momma' I've been singing about for years is gonna live up to her reputation."

Enveloped by cigarette smoke, Larry was tense and nervous, more so than Rosacoke had ever seen him. "Would you believe what's happening?" he said. "I'm getting these urgent calls. Every record distributor in the country wants to re-release all of Pete's old albums. Talk about ghouls! The corpse is hardly cold."

That image of Pete's slain body came racing back through Rosacoke's brain, and she turned over, burying her head in the pillow, letting its softness muffle her sobbing.

Larry got up from his chair and went to stand by the window where he was joined by Claude. Both of them watched the incredibly pink sky. Neither said a word, as only the sound of Rosacoke's sobbing filled the room.

Eventually she cried herself dry and straightened up in bed, reaching for a tissue to wipe her streaked face. "You're here to tell me some more bad news." Her voice was faint. "Go on—get it over with."

Larry took a deep drag on his cigarette. "I hate to bother you at a time like this. But the FBI has found out about your prison record."

"Oh, shit!" Claude said.

Rosacoke sighed, sinking back into the pillow. "At last, at long last."

"They're questioning a woman named Hazel Lowe right now," Larry said. "That pathetic thing will probably break down and tell them everything. She served time with you."

Rosacoke sat up in bed. "In a way I'm glad."

"Hell!" Larry said. "What for?"

"Cause I've lived with fear for too long. You don't know the nights I've agonized over this coming out in the press. I not only had to go through the hell of a year in prison, but...."

"A year and a day," Claude interjected.

She looked up at him and smiled weekly. "You're so right. That final day seemed longer than the year. I've paid for that mistake all my life. Paid for it night after night."

"I still don't think FBI exposure is a cause to celebrate," Larry said sarcastically, lighting another cigarette.

"I don't want to be afraid anymore," she said. "I'm freed of that. After all, I wouldn't be the first country and western singer to serve time in the slammer."

Claude went over to sit by her bed. He took her hand and looked deeply into her eyes.

Larry's face was a mask for a moment. One could almost hear him thinking. "You know me, I've pulled some mighty fine, fat rabbits out of the hat. I've saved our asses time and time again. I could give it one last try."

Claude rose from Rosacoke's bedside to stare down at the much shorter Larry. "What's on your mind?"

"A cover-up. One I planned years ago. I've got the papers. Everything. Our story is, Rosacoke's twin sister—long dead—served the prison term. I know it sounds ridiculous, but who knows? We might get away with it. Sure confuse a lot of people. My documentation is pretty convincing."

"To the FBI?" Claude asked pointedly.

No one said anything for a long time. Rosacoke slipped out from under her bed linen, placing her feet firmly on the floor. Claude moved toward her, finding she was secure on her own. "There will be no cover-up," she said. "I'm tired of living a lie. Lies." She went over and stood by the same window the two men had looked from, finding that the pink had disappeared from the sky. The burning morning sun had chased away all the traces of night.

Larry came up and placed both his nicotine-stained hands on Rosacoke's shoulder. "You gonna make it through all this?"

"Yes, and then I'm getting the hell out of here," she said. "Just as far as I can. No more career. No music. I'm through with it all. I want to run away some place so far no one will ever hear of me again."

"You think that now," Larry said. "But you'll come back one day. Bigger and better than ever."

"I doubt that," she said. "In the meantime, would you take over everything for us? Mopping up all the slop. Making all the decisions as you've

always done. Whatever has to be done. Starting with Pete's funeral. We've always called on you for everything."

"I'll handle it all," Larry promised. "Even the funeral."

"Thanks," she said. "I don't want some big splashy mess, like that monstrous thing for Buster. For Pete, something quiet and intimate would be more appropriate, just the few people who really loved him. I want to stand side by side with Karl as Pete's body is lowered into the ground. I want to hold onto Karl's hand as the dirt is shoveled over Pete. Surely no two people on Earth loved Pete Riddle as much as Karl Adams and I did."

***

When Junior had flown Karl, Claude, and Rosacoke from Miami back to Heaven on Earth, they had to be slipped in through a rear entrance. The funeral was scheduled for that night, and since before dawn, throughways and country roads leading to the gates of Heaven on Earth saw bumper-to-bumper traffic. Traffic eventually came to a standstill on all Wilkes County roads. Every member of the North Carolina highway patrol, it seemed, was called to active duty in the western part of the state.

Looking like a zombie in the wake of Pete's death, Karl nonetheless remained miraculously strong, still carrying out his duties. No sooner was he inside the mansion than he put through a call to the president of Holly Farms. "Get someone to start cooking all your chickens, man," he said. "We've got thousands to feed. We need every hen you've got. Let those people up in New York City eat steak next week."

Later in the day, Rosacoke and Claude accepted Junior's invitation to fly in a helicopter over the masses below. From her airborne seat, she gazed into a sea of humanity unlike any she'd ever witnessed before. She prayed for the good weather to hold, as many of this throng would have to sleep out in the open air.

Junior had arranged a series of helicopters to shuttle big name performers back and forth between the shell of an old amphitheater and the nearest airport. He'd invited everybody to entertain, even Elvis Presley who had cabled his regrets. Word was that "The King" was in no shape to perform anywhere. Minnie Pearl, Roy Acuff, and Johnny Cash were planning to show up.

Back on the ground at Heaven on Earth, Larry rushed up to Rosacoke as Claude helped her out of the helicopter. "I don't think the funeral of Jesus Christ himself could draw such a crowd. Even if it had been announced weeks before in the papers and billed as The Second Coming."

In the hours that followed, Rosacoke wasn't sure what was happening. She was in a daze, and went through the funeral holding onto Karl as if it were some dream sequence. Once she'd started to cry, she couldn't stop

and had to be removed from the church by Claude.

At ten o'clock that night, when Larry came for her, she was astonished to learn that the crowds at the amphitheater were calling for her, and only her. The other performers from Nashville had not been enough to satisfy them.

"I can't go out there," she pleaded. "I have no voice."

"You also have no choice," Larry said, taking her by the arm.

With Claude's help, she somehow made it to the old band shell where she waited back stage as Johnny Cash sang a lovely ballad.

She heard her name announced, and had to be propelled onto the stage by Larry. She didn't think she had the stamina to face the sea of bodies and staring faces, which seemed to stretch for miles, covering two hillsides. Because the night was hot many men had removed their shirts. Earlier, she had been told that some young people were wandering completely nude through the milling crowds.

Before going on stage, a belt of Southern Comfort had given her the courage to face such a mass of supporters. She had not had a case of genuine stage fright in years.

Deep down, she sensed that all of these fans were here not only to honor Pete Riddle in death, but to get a good look at her and see how she was holding up. She didn't mean to disappoint.

The sight of her on stage set off a wave of pandemonium. The roar of the crowd, the thunderous applause renewed her spirit.

When the ovation faded after five uninterrupted minutes, she stepped before the microphone, her hand bolting up to the night sky in a gesture uncharacteristic of her. The band started up, but her gesture was somehow viewed as a proclamation of victory, setting off another long round of applause and screaming approval.

Once again the band started to play, and when the first sounds of "Mountain Momma" escaped from her throat, she cringed at her own bad voice. The mere introduction of this song of human liberation was all that was needed to touch off another tumultuous round of applause.

Moments spent waiting for the crowd to quiet down somehow gave her a chance to steady herself and find the powerful voice that she knew was in her throat. At the start of the number again, the sound was there.

The song filled her with joy, and she hoped to communicate that sense of wonder to her fans. At the finish, some unruly members of the crowd rushed toward the stage. Hysterical, these fans seemed to want to reach out to touch her to find out if she were real. Being at the center of such uncontrolled emotion frightened her. Some officers of the state highway patrol restrained the mob.

In the middle of the next number, she could tell her voice was the most powerful it'd ever been. Older and more mature and under complete con-

trol. Attracted by the light, a moth buzzed about her and almost went into her mouth. Yet she didn't miss a beat.

As the songs went on, the audience begged for more, and she didn't want to leave them, feeling somehow it would be a cruel desertion of people who had come so far. This was the most memorable night of her show business career, and she feared it would never come again. On stage she basked in the warm glow of warmth and love.

From these people who still believed in her, she found new vitality and energy, making her ashamed of having wanted to give up not too long ago. A rejuvenation swept over her.

She kicked off her pumps. "Hell, we'll stay here all night. Sing 'em all!" The audience roared its endorsement of that prospect.

Revolving klieg lights turned the nighttime country hillside into a noon-day glare.

For what she thought was her final number, "Honky Tonk Angel," her voice rose as if it didn't need a microphone. The audience was clearly mesmerized by her performance, and she was glad TV cameras recorded that appearance. She wanted to remember every detail of it for always.

At the conclusion, there was a paroxysm of emotion. In the front rows, she could see tears streaming down the faces of some of their most loyal fans, those who'd waited long hot hours for her to appear.

Because her voice had soared tonight, she felt that she'd transported her audience to a rapturous Elysian field where it had never been before.

Larry had a surprise in store for her. "Honky Tonk Angel" had not been her final good-bye.

Hearing the notes from the band, she instantly recognized the next number. It was "Yesterday, Today and Tomorrow." Before starting her final number, she said, "This song is dedicated to Pete Riddle and our son Buster. May they find in Heaven the peace they never knew on Earth."

As she launched into the song, she only wished that Buster could walk out onto that stage, taking the honor as the writer of the song. Even more than that, she wished that Buster, with his face restored, could stand before this audience and sing the song as only he could.

At the end of Buster's song, a cry went up from the audience like she'd never heard before at any of her appearances. By then the tears were falling and she could sing no more. Appearing on stage, Claude wrapped his arm around her and led her out of the spotlight.

Backstage Larry rushed up to kiss her. "You did something out there tonight that will be talked about long after you're dead and gone. The legend has begun."

Turning from the sight of him, she held onto Claude. "It's all over now," he said.

"I know." She reached for his strong hand and pressed the palm of it

against her moist lips. "Get me out of here. We're going home."

"Heaven on Earth?" he asked.

"Not there," she said. "Somewhere I've yet to find."

# Chapter 17
# (The Eighties: Glory)

When Montana took its name from the Spanish word, *montaña*, it couldn't have been better named. As far as Rosacoke could see, mountains stretched in every direction from her ranch. The sprawling ranges of the Continental Divide seemed to rise more than two miles in the air.

The Indians had found a home in these mountains, and so had she. Over the years she'd finally come to feel at peace here, and that had taken a lot of time.

She paused near a ravine, smoothing the mane of her horse. Nearby she spotted a Western meadowlark in a Ponderosa pine.

It started to rain very lightly, yet she was in no hurry to return home. She'd ridden out into the country to think about an amazing offer, and she still hadn't made up her mind.

The clear Montana sky had given way to rain clouds. It was getting dark, as she decided to head back to the ranch.

Her afternoon of solitude—combined with the gentle, warm rain falling on her—made her feel good. As her horse galloped steadily along, she raised her face up toward the sky to feel the raindrops.

At the top of the hill, she took in the view of her wide ranch. She was proud of it. In the distance she could see two men mending a fence. The sound of a cowbell from the bunkhouse echoed across the valley.

As she rode up to the new stables, built only last year, Claude came out to greet her, taking the reins of her horse and catching her in his arms as she slid off. Up close to her, he reached for her and gave her a long kiss. "Missed you all day. I was a little worried."

"I'm fine." She ran her fingers through his hair, flecked with gray, and looked into those deeply penetrating eyes, now surrounded with laugh lines.

"It's getting a little chilly tonight," he said. "I lit a fire. How about a drink?"

"I'd love one." She wrapped her arm around his waist and huddled close to his flannel shirt, as she headed with him to the main house. She still hadn't made up her mind about the offer, but by the fire and with the drink she would decide.

Inside the ranch house living room, Larry stood by the fireplace, puffing

on a cigarette. "Well, Belle Starr has come back."

"I hope you had a good day," Rosacoke said, as Claude went to get her a drink.

"Bored out of my mind waiting for you to decide," Larry said. "I don't know how you people stand it out here in this God-forsaken place. Nothing ever happens."

"Too much has already gone down," she said. "That's why we're here."

"When you told me you were gonna retire, I gave you two years, maybe three at the most," Larry said. "But *fourteen years*. That's stretching it a bit, don't you think?"

"I'm too old to work," she said. "You know I'm soon gonna be sixty."

"You don't look a day over forty, and I mean that," Larry said. "Dolly Parton's older sister, but Dolly Parton, nevertheless. Montana has sure agreed with you. You're so well preserved I suspect you had everything tucked—even the elbows, certainly the breasts. But Claude assures me it's all natural, and that's one man who'd know."

"That's right," she said. "I haven't seen a hospital since...." She winced as a sharp pain shot through her whole body.

"Let's don't get into that." Larry crushed out his cigarette and lit another one. "Down to basics. Will you or will you not return to Nashville?"

"I don't know." She took the drink from Claude and gently brushed her lips against his. "What do you think, babe?"

"I think we should," Claude said. "For ole times sake. After all, it's only for one night. A last hurrah, and then we can run and hide in these mountains forever."

"The whole town will turn out," Larry predicted. "The rhinestones will sparkle. Think of it this way. It's not just a tribute to you and your music, but to Pete and Buster, too."

"If only Buster could be there, too," Rosacoke said. "The real Buster. Which reminds me. He hasn't called us in more than two years."

"My two biggest stars," Larry lamented. "He buried himself in the mountains of Switzerland, and you buried yourself in the mountains of Montana."

"And as stars, Rosacoke and Buster are bigger than ever," Claude interjected.

"You're right." Larry's face lit up, and for a moment he had a reflective look. "In death Pete has become the ageless hero, the biggest country and western star of all time."

"Buster, too?" Rosacoke added. "Little girls who weren't even born in the Fifties buy his records like crazy. He's got some amazing mystique. His fans still believe he's dead."

"What about our own scandal-plagued Mountain Momma?" Claude asked.

"Every album you've ever done has doubled or tripled its sales in 1982 over the previous year," Larry said to Rosacoke.

"We know," Rosacoke said. "That's why we built the new stables." She smiled. "Who would ever believe that the Riddle renaissance—starting out modestly—would grow into a landslide?"

"It's hard to explain," Larry said. "You're not dead yet. Neither is Buster for that matter. But the press still calls it posthumous popularity."

"I think you owe it to your fans to make that final appearance," Claude said.

"Can you imagine?" Rosacoke asked. "Me walking out on the stage of the Grand Ole Opry again? I've never even seen the new place."

"You'll do it?" Larry asked.

"Fool that I am, I'll come back to Nashville," she said.

"Hallelujah!" Claude shouted.

Larry went to the phone in the corridor.

Nursing her drink, Rosacoke sat quietly on the sofa, staring at the flickering flames of the log fire. She hoped that she'd made the right decision, and she prayed that Pete and Buster—in spirit—would be out there on the stage with her to help her through the upcoming night in Nashville.

Just then, she overheard part of Larry's phone conversation. Rosacoke didn't know who he was talking to, but his barking voice actually used the word "resurrection."

The tension between Claude and Larry seemed to have dissipated over the years, now that they were no longer the rivals for the love of Ronnie.

"I was hoping that Larry would bring Ronnie and Wanda Mae out to our ranch," she said. "We keep inviting them but they never show up. Wanda Mae is still all business with her businesses."

"I don't think Ronnie wanted to come," Claude said sadly. "I talked it over with Larry today. Me and Ronnie have had a long relationship, but that's all behind us now. I think both of us are a little ashamed of it and want to lay it to rest."

"When we're in Nashville, we can always drive over to Heaven on Earth to see them," Rosacoke said. "I don't get to see Buster and very little of Tracy, but we should call on Wanda Mae at least. Karl said our rooms are always ready for us."

"I think it would be a good idea," Claude said. "We'll have a family reunion." A sad look came over his face, as if he were experiencing some deep pain. "That's right. A family reunion. For whatever's left of our family."

***

Three days later and five miles outside Nashville, Rosacoke for reas-

surance glanced at her reflection in a pocketbook mirror. After all, it had been a long time since she'd faced a live audience.

At the wheel, Claude turned to look at her and smiled. "You look terrific. Better than ever."

"And you're a big, wonderful liar." She put the mirror back in her purse. "Tracy designed the dress for me. It's stunning. But do you think I'm woman enough to walk onto a stage with that much weight? There must be fifty pounds of rhinestones on that thing."

"At least that much. You can do it. I'll be proud of you."

"I'm nervous," she said. "About the songs and all. Everything, I guess. We've not got a lot of time to rehearse with the band."

"You don't need so much time. You know each and every one of those songs. It'll all come back."

Passing in quick review, a new Nashville and its growing suburbs sprawled before her, reminding her of how long she'd been away. "I remember when all this used to be country. It looks like housing developers have sent bulldozers up every hill. Do you think anyone in the audience Saturday night will even have been *born* when I was a star?"

"Honey, if they weren't, they'll be there more curious than ever," he predicted. "Not a day goes by but some Nashville station plays one of your hits. The old guard will turn out just to see how you're holding up—if for no other reason."

"Sounds like a freak show to me," she said.

"In a way, it is. It's a big thing. Rosacoke Carson returning to the stage of the Grand Ole Opry with half of the TV cameras of the world looking in. It's a night for music history."

She settled back in her seat and closed her eyes for a moment. Perhaps she should have flown from Montana, as the drive to Nashville took longer than she imagined. But she wanted the time on the road to think matters over a bit. An airplane flight would have plunged her too fast, too soon into action.

"I was thinking," she said after a while. "Have my fans forgiven me?"

"For what?" he asked.

"You know, all those lurid stories that have been leaked to the press over the years. My prison record. The sex scandals. Murder. When they write of my comeback, reporters will dredge up every bit of dirt again. You know that."

"I don't think you've lost one fan because of any big exposé," he said. "Maybe a few rednecks dropped out of your fan club when you were falsely accused of having a black daddy. As for them, I'm glad to see fools like that go. You were never a bad woman. You got mixed up in a lot of things, and some people did you wrong. But you were never bad. You never hurt anyone. It was you who got hurt. I think people feel sorry for you more

than they feel you've done something bad."

"I hope that's true—only I don't want people feeling sorry for me," she said. "I can't stand that."

"When you walk out on that stage with the world paying tribute to you, and wearing a fifty-thousand dollar dress, no one's gonna be all that sorry, believe me."

"I just wish Buster could be there to give me moral support," she said.

A strange look came over his face. "You know that can't be."

As he got closer to the city, Claude—almost without knowing it— stepped on the gas pedal. He was anxious to get there and oversee the final arrangements. "I called ahead. June and Johnny Cash are already gone, but they were real kind—damn nice—to turn their house over to us."

"I'm grateful for that," she said. "I wouldn't want to check into a hotel. Where are they off to?"

"Vegas. They'll miss our show."

"I hope somebody turns up," she said. "You know, all those stars are out on the road trying to make a buck. I doubt if any of them has got time to spend fooling around with me."

"We'll see."

As the Nashville skyline came into view, two modern cowboys were spotted standing by the side of the highway. One wore a hat, and both of them had guitars strapped on their backs. Thumbs stuck out, they squinted in the afternoon sun.

"One of those guys is probably gonna be the Pete Riddle of tomorrow," Claude predicted.

"I don't think Pete's on their mind at all," she said. "I bet they want to replace Kris Kristofferson."

"Mind if I pick 'em up?" Claude asked.

"Do it!" Almost unconsciously, Rosacoke pulled her cowgirl hat down over her face.

He braked the car, stopping a few yards ahead of the young men. In their boots, the blue-jeaned cowboys ran toward the car.

Rosacoke opened the window. "We're just going into Nashville. That okay?"

One of the men, the taller and handsomer cowboy, smiled broadly at her. "That's just great, ma'am." He piled into the back seat of the station wagon. His friend got in, too, and Claude took off as they rearranged their guitars and settled back for the short ride.

"Doug Purdue here. This here is my friend, Scotty Lowe."

"Glad to meet you, boys," Claude said. "Claude and Rose Billings here."

"Me and Doug hitched all the way down from West Virginia," Scotty said. "We're gonna go to Nashville to become country and western stars. Just as soon as somebody discovers us."

"I hope it's soon," Doug said. "Cause we only got fifty bucks between us."

"You need that one big break," Rosacoke said. "I hope it's there waiting for you."

"Thanks a lot," Scotty said. "I got all the confidence in the world. You see, we're good—real good."

"What are you folks going to Nashville for?" Doug asked. "I spotted those Montana license tags. You're farther from home than we are."

"We're going to be in town for the return engagement of Rosacoke Carson at the Opry," Claude said.

"Man, I've heard a lot about that," Scotty said. "I sure would like to see that show. That'll be the hottest ticket in town. We ain't got a chance."

"Me and Scotty love her music," Doug said. "Play it all the time. It was listening to ole Pete Riddle's records that made up our minds to go into country music. I mean, Pete's voice was real country—just like ours. Me and Scotty figured if he could do it, we could, too."

"He always believed that himself," Rosacoke said. "So I hear."

"Did you ever hear him sing?" Scotty asked.

"I was there the night he first appeared on the Opry stage," Rosacoke said. "He brought down the house."

"Wow!" Doug said. "People still talk about that night."

"It's too bad a real big talent like that had to die the way he did," Scotty said. "I mean, it seems so unfair. Killed by a jealous homosexual lover. We still don't believe old Pete was queer. You can't believe all that crap you read in the tabloids. One tabloid claimed Pete was abducted by aliens in a flying saucer."

"Another said Pete and Elvis Presley were lovers," Doug said.

It was Rosacoke who finally spoke. "A lot of bad things have gone down, but the future looks bright for the two of you, don't you think?"

"We've got high hopes," Doug said. "Maybe a little too high for my daddy. He thought I should stay home and chase after some sawmill dollars instead of running off to Nashville with my guitar."

"A daddy always thinks that," Claude said.

The rest of the ride didn't take long, as an expressway shot them into the heart of Nashville.

Scotty and Doug stared out the windows of the station wagon. "Christ, I can't believe we're really here," Doug said.

"I'm all excited," Scotty said.

"Where do you want us to let you out?" Claude asked.

"On any street corner," Scotty said.

"We've got to start somewhere," Doug added.

The two cowboys thanked Rosacoke and Claude and got out of the car. As they waved goodbye, Claude told Rosacoke to roll down the win-

dow. He called after the men. "Hey, come on over to the Opry one hour before show time Saturday night. There will be two tickets for you guys. One for Doug Purdue, and another for his friend, Scotty Lowe."

"Hey, mister, you really mean that?" Doug asked, sticking his head in the window. "That'd be great. No kidding."

Up close to Rosacoke for the first time, Doug gazed into her face. "Hey, lady, you look familiar. Real familiar. You're…"

Claude pulled away from the curb, as Rosacoke took in a skyline unfamiliar to her.

"You're gonna be great," Claude assured her, as he sped across the city heading to the home of Johnny and June Cash.

***

The limousine rented for the occasion snaked its way to the "family entertainment park," the new home of the Grand Ole Opry at Opryland. She was two hours early, and her arrival at the stage door went unnoticed. Claude slipped her inside.

It was a new world for her. A television camera sat beneath a maze of ceiling lights, and in the control room an engineer studied monitors.

"This sure is a long way from the old barn dance," she told Claude.

"My God, coming in I thought I was at Disneyland," Claude said.

"I'd like to go on a tour of the place," Rosacoke said.

From the shadows at the far end of the stage, a man emerged. "Rosacoke. *Rosacoke Carson*! As I live and breathe."

She turned to stare into the face of an old man she vaguely recognized.

"Rosacoke Carson," he said again, coming to stand right in front of her. He reached for her hand and held it up to his lips, which had a slight tremor. Gently he kissed the palm of her hand. "I'm Uncle Darling. Stage Door Uncle Darling. Remember the night you set Memphis on fire before Pete went on?"

All at once she remembered, and, as she did, she reached out to embrace him. "My own Uncle Darling. You saved that night for me." She turned to Claude. "He told me I could get a rise in the pants of any stud between Memphis and Amarillo."

"And, looking at you now, I'll say it again, but count me out. I'm beyond such things."

She laughed and, her arm linked to Uncle Darling, she headed for her dressing room.

"They ain't retired me yet," Uncle Darling said. "Any day now I expect to get my notice. At least I got to hang around long enough to see you at Opryland."

"You're the best welcoming committee a gal could have," she said,

kissing him on the cheek. "I want you to come to my party right after the show."

"Now, *that* you can count on." His aged face lit up. "Miss Rosacoke, welcome back."

"Thanks." Tears welled in her eyes as she turned her back on Uncle Darling, going into her dressing room. In minutes she was out of her clothes, slipping into a terrycloth robe with a monk's hood. She sat down to stare at herself in the mirror. Claude came up behind her, affectionately putting his hands on her shoulders and squeezing gently.

"When I walk out on that stage tonight, I want to be so heavily made up that fourteen years will just up and fade away," she said.

A sudden rap on the door, and Larry came in, all brashly efficient. "Don't worry about a thing, baby," he said with all the assurance of a marine drill sergeant. "I'm seeing to every detail—and I'm *still* the best in the business."

"That you are! Claude agreed.

"Where's the gown?" Rosacoke asked.

"On its way," Larry told her. "It needed a few tucks here and there. Last minute touches. They also insisted we test it on camera. After all, we don't want you to come across just as a blaze of light. Some people out there will actually want to see your face."

"Speaking of faces, I'd better get one painted on," she said.

In a pair of tinted aviator glasses, the makeup man, Chet Ridgets, came into the dressing room, followed by the hairdresser, Merle Snow. Her transformation began. Eager to please, both young men were deferential to her.

Claude had never liked to see her in heavy makeup, so he went with Larry for a last-minute check of the lighting and orchestra. An attendant entered, carrying a silver ice bucket. To her disappointment, it was filled with mineral water. "I could use some hard stuff," she said. "I'm shaking all over."

Just then, Larry returned. "You can drink for the rest of your life, but not now. Just get through the next few hours. It's gonna be your biggest moment."

"Forget the mineral water," Rosacoke told the attendant. "A little tea and honey is what my throat needs right now." He went out to get it.

Claude came back with Roy Acuff, clad in a red sports jacket.

Still in her robe, she jumped up from the dressing table to give him a big hug. "Roy."

After the embrace, he backed away, holding her at arm's length to get a good look. "My, oh my, you get prettier every day."

"And you haven't lost your charm in spite of these fancy new quarters," she said. "I started to say I'm so glad to be home again, but this ain't exactly home."

"Yeah, I get lost around here sometimes myself," Roy said.

"I'm worried about tonight," she said in a confidential whisper. "We haven't rehearsed all that much."

"You don't need that much rehearsing," Roy assured her. "After all these years, you're still the queen of country music."

"Coming from the king himself, that's mighty fine flattery," she said.

"All our gals who came after you—Loretta, Dolly—they all owe a debt to you."

"And *everybody* owes a debt to you," she said.

"I don't know why," Roy said. "My fiddling certainly wasn't all that good, and a lot of people say my voice isn't all that great either."

"You've got emotion," she said. "You know how to sell a song. Reach out to people. I sure took a lot of lessons from you."

"You learned everything well," he said. "You're just as famous today as you ever were. Maybe more so."

"Talk about fame," she said. "I once heard that a Japanese soldier in a banzai charge against our marines at Okinawa shouted: 'To hell with President Roosevelt, to hell with Babe Ruth, and to hell with Roy Acuff!'"

He smiled. "You note that I'm the only one of that trio still around. I don't know about the banzai charger. Our marines probably got him."

"You'll go on forever," she predicted.

He kissed her on the cheek. "I'd better let you go. I'll see you on stage. It'll be the biggest night of your life." His eyes twinkled mysteriously. "I promise."

She paused for a moment, wondering what surprise he might have in store for her.

"Miss Carson," the hairdresser called. "I've just got to work on that hair some more. I can't let you go out on stage looking like a drowned rat."

Forgetting Roy for a moment, she turned her attention to her mirror.

\*\*\*

In a full-length mirror, she stepped back and surveyed her figure, clad in a white satin gown entirely covered with rhinestones. It was daringly cut to reveal her still firm breasts.

"You're the queen," Claude said. "Roy was right. There's a whole lot of woman in that dress."

She turned to him and smiled. "There's got to be. Something's got to compete with the rhinestones."

The acts preceding her appearance had already begun, and a strange peace came over her. She was no longer afraid.

Larry stuck his head in the door. "Minnie Pearl's got another five minutes. And you look gorgeous."

"Thanks. I just hope the voice is still there."

Uncle Darling came to usher her into a reception room where she was to wait for her cue. Before leaving, she turned to thank the hairdresser and makeup man. "Time to rally forth." They blew kisses at her.

Striding vigorously, she made her way along a long corridor and into the reception room. She clutched Claude's arm. "What if I go for a high note and miss?"

"Honey, this is no honky-tonk," he said. "They've gotten very sophisticated since we worked the road. A backup singer will hit the note for you. We've got the best sound technician in the business. He'll know what to do."

She chuckled. "You and Larry have taken care of everything for Granny Carson."

At a knock, Claude went to the door, as Rosacoke watched the show on closed circuit TV. He peered out briefly, muttered something to somebody, then shut it and came back to her. "I think there's somebody out there in the hall you'd like to say hi to."

"Show them in," she said.

Rosacoke sucked in her breath, as she braced herself to meet some very important person from her past.

It was no one she knew personally.

Into the room bounced a very vibrant and vivacious Dolly Parton.

***

Her voice and her giggle might be childlike, but Dolly Parton's body was undeniably female. In a wig of golden braid and curls, she came into the room on tottering stilt-high shoes in a pink jumpsuit that fitted as tight as sausage casing. Rosacoke seemed to tower over Dolly's five-foot figure. The hand Dolly extended to Rosacoke was garnished with three ostentatious rocks of precious stones. Underneath the blonde beehive and the Maybelline makeup with blue eyeshadow, the eyes were sincere, warm, and loving.

"I've admired you for years," Dolly said. "Since they called on me to present the award tonight, I figured I'd better drop in."

"I'm so pleased to meet you at last," Rosacoke said. "People have compared us for years. We do look a little bit alike, don't we? Of course, I'm old enough to be your mama."

"You are in some ways my Mountain Momma," Dolly said. "I just love that song."

"I love your music too. You know what you do I like? You put whoever's listening in touch with their secret intimacies."

"Coming from you that's a real compliment," Dolly said. "But we're

here tonight to pay tribute to you. I don't care how maudlin or banal the lyrics they gave you, you always made them honest and true."

"I hope so," she said. "My voice may be sweet but I still feel it's nasal in a back-woodsy way. I could never make it today like you and Linda Ronstadt. You know what I mean? A soloist in the pop ranks."

"Don't you go saying that," Dolly said. "I have a feeling you can do whatever you want to do. That is, if you'd come out of hiding and start doing it again."

Claude signaled that they had to cut it short, as Rosacoke was due on stage.

"Better haul these rhinestones across the floor," she said to Dolly. "They weigh a ton. Thanks for stopping by."

"That sure is some dress," Dolly said.

"Thank you," Rosacoke said. "A little fancy for a country girl."

"That never bothered me," Dolly said. "See you out there on stage."

On the way to the wing, Rosacoke nearly tripped over a cable. Claude grabbed her arm to steady her.

"Would You Catch a Falling Star?" she asked jokingly.

"John Anderson's already recorded that one," he said. "Besides, I think it's about George Jones's life—not yours."

"I sure hope so," she said. Concealed in shadows, she had a clear view of the stage.

"Hey, guess who's here tonight," Claude said.

"Looks to me like everybody in Nashville," she said. "I'm mighty proud."

"Those two boys we picked up on the road. Doug Purdue and Scotty Lowe. I went out front to check to make sure they'd got their tickets."

"Good, they'll find out who gave them a ride," she said.

"I think they already know," Claude said.

Roy Acuff was introducing her. "Once she was considered something of a renegade in country music. But time was on her side. She knew where we were going when some of the rest of us didn't. Whatever song she sang, she added a chicken-pickin', lickin' honesty to it, and her sound has now gone down in the Country Music Association Hall of Fame. Ladies and gentlemen, our next performer became the first female superstar of country music, even though we didn't use that word back then. When she recorded her first big hit, 'Honky Tonk Angel,' she altered the country field forever. For years she was a regular at the Opry, and tonight we'd like to welcome her back and let her know she belongs here with us and is invited to stay forever. No, more than that. Her music belongs to the world. From the tobacco fields of Carolina, from the honky-tonks of Georgia, from the music halls of Nashville, to the recording studios of Hollywood, she's not only a star in her own right, but the former wife of the legendary Pete Riddle, AND the mama of the great Buster Riddle."

Roy paused, as an air of expectation came over the spectators. "God created some extraordinary women." The audience broke into scattered applause. "One of his finest creations is about to step onto our stage tonight. ROSACOKE CARSON RIDDLE! Our own 'MOOOUNTAIN MOMMA!'"

She turned for one long, reassuring look into Claude's eyes. "He should have said Rosacoke Carson Riddle Billings."

There was a thunderous applause. "Get out there, Mrs. Billings. And when it's over, come home to Daddy.

She blew him a kiss. "That's a promise."

As she strode onto the Grand Ole Opry stage after all these years, the audience rose to its feet. In her glittering rhinestones, she stretched her arms in a wide "V" to acknowledge the clapping and cheering. The sound was deafening. She loved it. How could she have denied herself this devotion for all these years when she'd needed it so?

On signal, she turned to the orchestra. She was going to sing her music again. No recorded voices. Tonight her fans would get the real thing.

***

"It's been a long time," she almost shouted into the microphone. "Just to show you where my heart is…." A drummer in the background signaled the song, which caused the audience to burst into applause again.

"I was born early one frosty morn." It was "Dixie," and as those first words came out of her throat she knew her voice had never been in better shape. She sang the song whose words could have been written for her. Memories of her own mama came rushing back, only to be replaced by other recollections flashing by. Giving birth to Buster. Pete going off to war.

Before the applause had died, she slid along with the music into "The Battle Hymn of the Republic." She wanted them to know where her political loyalties lay. The drummer continued to beat, as he did for "Dixie," and the brass section sounded stentorian snorts. In front of the orchestra, the sons of the Foggy Mountain Boys from Pete's old band sang a song in soft tones for background, creating the image of an American army advancing against its enemies.

At the end, she'd aroused the audience to a fever pitch with these crowd-pleasers. But instinctively, she wanted to change the mood of the show. A hush came over the audience. The music was soft, everything in low key. She remembered Fry from long ago and the old Negro spiritual he'd taught her. "All My Trials" seemed tailor-made for her, both the song and its message. It could describe her own life and all the tribulations she'd endured to have emerged a survivor. The men and women in the audience

seemed to identify the song with her, and there was scattered applause.

Her voice of hushed intimacy with its deep poignancy quieted the audience. People leaned forward in their seats, as if they knew they were witnessing a rare moment in show business that they'd one day share with their grandchildren. With this song, she seemed to have brought the audience to a sensational climax, and for a moment she feared there was no place else to go.

An inspiration came to her. She whispered something to the band leader, then went to the microphone. "On the way into Nashville, me and Mr. Billings picked up a couple of young men. They said they wanted to be singers, and they planned to set Nashville on fire. Well, let's give these boys a chance. Might as well start at the top. Singing on the stage of the Grand Ole Opry. They're here tonight. Come forward, boys. Doug Purdue and Scotty Lowe."

The audience clapped loudly. From out of the audience, Doug and Scotty appeared, looking puzzled and confused but also entering into the spirit of it. On stage she rushed forward to give them both a quick kiss. "Get these boys some guitars."

In front of the microphone, she said, "The first song me and Pete ever sang together in front of a live audience was 'You Are My Sunshine,' written by the governor of Louisiana. I bet you boys know that one."

"Do we ever!" Doug yelled.

Guitars were found, and Doug and Scotty tested the chords. Flanking her, they stepped up to the microphone and went into the song with her. They had real good voices, which blended harmoniously with hers. At the end of the number, she gave each of them a hug and kiss, whispering, "I'll see you all later at my party."

The crowd responded wildly to her act of spontaneous generosity, as if instinctively feeling she did something from her heart, which wasn't rehearsed. "Back to the show," she said. "The one we planned."

Breaking from this wistful, nostalgic retreat, the band struck up another tune. The sound of a whirring of machinery was heard, and down came a wide projection screen. Slides flashed across it. Without her knowledge, she realized pictures of the milestones of her life were passing in review on the screen to accompany her singing.

Was this the surprise Roy had in store for her? One early picture of Pete and her dressed as cowboys before he went off to war evoked such painful memories she whirled around, facing the audience, not daring to look up at the screen. She wished that Larry had gotten her okay for this, because she felt she couldn't compete with the vivid dramatization of her life in pictures.

When the screen went blank, the orchestra struck up the familiar sounds of "Honky Tonk Angel," her first big hit. Tonight she gave the song the

vigor and pep of that night in Memphis when she'd first met Uncle Darling. She thanked the Lord she had mercifully stayed thin and athletic after all these years, as she gyrated and bounced around the stage to prove to all the world that there was still plenty of life left in the original Honky Tonk Angel.

Gasping for breath at the end of the number, she was afraid she was too winded to go into another one of her hit records from the Fifties. She was saved by the appearance of Roy Acuff, who introduced Dolly Parton to present her with a lifetime achievement award.

Regaining her stamina, she thanked Dolly, kissing her on the cheek like an old friend. Again, she was surprised at how the program was scheduled, since earlier, she had been told that the lifetime achievement award had been slated for the end of her repertoire.

As Dolly and Roy disappeared from the stage to loud applause, Rosacoke went into her tribute to Pete as the slide projection continued. She sang "Lonesome Blues," the record that made him a star. It was received with such thunderous ovation that her first lines were drowned out. She dared not look back at the healthy grinning pictures of Pete at the height of his manhood that she knew were being flashed across the screen.

At the end of his song, the Grand Ole Opry spectators rose to their feet again. She brushed away a tear, realizing the applause was not for her but for Pete.

She had them now. All fear was gone. It was her evening of triumph.

As the band began to play again, she went into panic, fearing that she'd been too optimistic. They were playing "Mountain Momma," the song to end the show. They were supposed to play "Yesterday, Today and Tomorrow," her tribute to Buster.

The audience broke into hand-clapping and foot-stomping, which was their own special tribute to her for the number with which she'd always been identified. She knew she had to go through with the song, and she did in all her glory, feeling deep in her gut that she'd never done it better.

Even though they'd made a mistake in sequence, the band played beautifully. At the end of the number, she got her most enthusiastic applause yet. "I'm home again," she shouted into the microphone over the roar of the crowd.

The applause died, as Roy Acuff came on stage again. "Ladies and gentlemen, Rosacoke has just received the following telegram, which I took the liberty to open. Here's what it says."


*Dear Rosacoke,*
*Nancy and I couldn't be with you good people tonight but know that our hearts are there. Your songs reflect the conflicts of a changing*

*South. And you were a new and different voice in the land. You forged the way for many future singers in the generations ahead. You are an authentic legend in country music, and we thank you for the joy you've brought to American life.*

*Our warmest personal regards.*

*Ronald Reagan*

The telegram brought more hand-clapping, as she glowed in the recognition. The audience still applauded as she accepted the telegram from Roy and kissed him on the cheek again. She stepped back for a quick huddle with the band.

"You got it wrong," she whispered right before she sipped from a glass of water. "I've got to do Buster's song. Then maybe a few bars from 'Mountain Momma' again to end the show. After all, this ain't a concert."

"Okay, Miss Carson," the band leader said. "My mistake."

Back facing the audience, she waited until the crowd ever so slowly quieted down. An almost unnatural hush came over the auditorium. It was as if everybody was expecting something really important to happen, and she feared that she didn't have anything approaching a spectacular finish. She'd been before audiences too long not to anticipate their desires. Her appearance, she felt with deep regret, had already had too many climaxes. There couldn't be anything else left to top it.

She worried that the mix-up had ruined her big night. Sucking in fresh air, she knew she had to see it through. She turned to the band, signaling them to begin the overture to "Yesterday, Today and Tomorrow." She feared she'd made a big mistake. Her voice suddenly wasn't there. It was as if a big bubble had risen in her throat, and no words would come out.

She burst into uncontrollable tears and was forced to turn her back to the audience. She put out a trembling hand to the band to stop the music, as she couldn't begin.

All of a sudden Claude stepped out on the stage, and the audience clapped politely, although most of its members were mesmerized. He took her in his arms and held her tightly. "You can do it, baby," he whispered in her ear. He took his handkerchief and wiped her face, inspecting her makeup before he allowed her to turn again to face the cameras.

Everybody in the audience seemed to understand and share her grief. She felt love and sympathy from the people. "For Buster," she said into the microphone, and the reception that greeted her bathed her in a warm glow, giving her the courage to go on.

Once again, she signaled the band that she was ready, and she could only pray that her voice wouldn't desert her again. The music was gentle.

When the first words came out, she knew her voice was in perfect pitch. It was as if Buster had expressed in his song every emotion he'd ever felt.

At the end, she sounded the high note before her tears fell again. A lot of people out there were crying with her. She didn't have to sing anymore. Her tears were of relief, gratitude, wonder. After all the decades of disappointment and tragedy, she felt loved, and she'd risen to the moment on the stage of Nashville. The resurrection had come, but it was over now. What was left was for her to get off the stage gracefully, take her bows, and fade into the annals of country and western music.

In the wings she hugged Claude until an ovation summoned her back on stage. Standing tall, her back arched, she returned to the stage and blew kisses to her fans. "I love you. I love you all."

She put up her hands to hush the audience. A few bars from "Mountain Momma," and then she could go and meet all of her many well-wishers at the party.

A gradual hush fell. Instead of playing "Mountain Momma," as agreed upon, the orchestra launched once again into "Yesterday, Today, and Tomorrow." She knew it was wrong, since the climax for that song had already been reached. Yet she had no choice but to face the audience and sing it again, even though the initial emotion was drained from her voice. It was a theatrical error, and she wanted to get through it as best she could.

A platform was silently lowered on cables from high overhead, and suddenly, another voice echoed through the auditorium. She abruptly stopped singing. It was Buster's voice! At long last he must have recorded his own song. That was Roy's surprise of the evening. Recognizing the famous gold throat, the audience broke into enthusiastic clapping.

At that moment the curtain surrounding the platform was pulled back, and spotlights were trained on Buster as his platform was gently lowered onto the stage floor. He was appearing live before millions of viewers on TV, singing his own song.

She screamed and put her hand to her mouth. His mask was gone. Buster was revealing his new face to the world.

It wasn't exactly his face, but it was a face. Her son had a face once again!

Roy Acuff came onto the stage. "Ladies and gentlemen, this is no impostor. Buster Riddle is alive and well. We present him tonight on his return to show business."

In a lifetime of appearing before live audiences, she'd never faced such a reaction from an audience. At first the crowd had remained silent and in stunned disbelief. But somehow the assurance of Roy Acuff had been enough for them. They could believe in Roy and his words. If Roy said this was Buster, then the fans seemed willing to trust their most beloved entertainer. Besides, an impostor would have been too cruel a hoax to play on

Rosacoke.

Starting slowly, the applause rose to a deafening roar, as the entire auditorium rose to its feet for the biggest standing ovation in the history of the Grand Ole Opry. The audience was hysterical, welcoming the return of its long-gone son, Buster Riddle, from the sleep of the dead.

In some surgical arena, doctors had carved out a new face for her son. In disbelief, she stood gazing with wonder at Buster on the stage beside her. She would know the face anywhere, but there had been many changes. An artificial creation, it was older and thinner. The shape and slant of the nose were different from what she remembered. The cheekbones stuck out more prominently, and the line of the jaw wasn't as fine as before. But the eyes—those big, wonderful eyes you could lose yourself in—were there in all their glory, looking down at her in his moment of triumph.

With great intensity, she studied his face. The left side was practically immobile, but the animation of the eyes seemed to distract one from looking at it too carefully. His mouth was twisted, but he always did have Pete's lopsided leer. In some bizarre way, he looked stuffed. That was the only way she could put it. Yet she kept going back to those eyes. They were still brilliant and glittering, and they could win anybody's heart, as they seemed to reflect all the love that ever was.

"Come to me, Mountain Momma," he called out to her, holding out his hand. "Let's do a duet."

"Buster!" she cried out. An usher appeared and led her to Buster's platform at center stage. In her heavy gown and high heels, she had to get to him to find out if he were real. His hand reached out to her. Sobbing, she stood on the platform face to face with him, and in front of all the world her hands reached out to feel his brow, cheek, nose and lips.

"You've got a face," she said before bursting into tears, clutching him and holding him, her whole body trembling. For the first time in years, she planted a kiss on his lips.

When the audience saw the two of them standing together, the applause grew more deafening than ever. She never knew fans could make this kind of noise. They were screaming their approval.

It was at that moment that Buster turned his back to the audience and whispered in her ear. "I was the one. I flew to Miami and killed the bastard. Claude caught me running from the villa. He held me for a moment, then let me go."

The auditorium whirled around her. She felt faint.

Buster turned and faced the audience, and waved for them to settle down. Miraculously, they obeyed him as a hush fell over the hall as people took their seats.

"Come on, Mountain Momma," Buster said to the audience but also to her. "We've got a show to do."

The band started the music to "Yesterday, Today and Tomorrow." She reached for Buster's hand as if that would give her he strength to stand in this spotlight and face not only an audience, but Buster and his stinging revelation. His whisper was the single biggest shock she'd ever received in her life. Even discovering Pete's dead body didn't carry quite the shock value that Buster's confession did.

That night she showed the world what a trouper she was and how much she believed that the show must go on. With a strength and a willpower she never knew she possessed, she turned to face the audience.

Most eyes were focused on Buster, but if anybody looked at her, they saw a performer in full stride. Like Scarlett O'Hara, everything that she'd learned on that platform tonight she'd think about tomorrow. Right now, she had to finish the show.

At the end of their rendition of "Yesterday, Today and Tomorrow," pandemonium broke out in the audience. It was the tribute of their lives. At the end of the number, she burst into tears and hugged Buster.

"I'm sorry, mama," he whispered in her ear. "I lost my mind. I've regretted it every day and every night of my life."

"It's okay, son," she whispered back. "All the regrets in all the world can't bring back the man both of us loved."

She turned to Buster to face volcanic applause. It was time to leave the stage.

Taking her hand, he guided her across the platform and into the wings. When she saw Claude, she ran toward him. The look on his face signaled to her that he knew that Buster had told her the secret that only the two of them had shared all these years.

No, there was a third person. An older, slimmer Tara came out of the shadows to hug and kiss first Buster and then Rosacoke. "Good to see you again, hoss," she said. "The world has spun around many times since we last got together. Let's go have some bourbon and branch water. Just like old times." Tara leaned over and kissed Claude on the lips.

"You, too, know the truth?" Rosacoke said to Tara. It wasn't an accusation.

"They know a lot of shit about us," Tara said. "Let's go to our graves and take one or two of those secrets with us."

"It's a deal," Rosacoke said, hugging her.

Buster came between them, kissing first Rosacoke on the lips and then Tara. "I've got an idea," he said to his mama.

She looked lovingly toward him, trying to conceal the dreadful pain of his confession. "Let's hear it, big boy," she said with a kind of false bravado.

"After all this dies down, let's go on the road together for a final world tour," he said. "It'll be the biggest farewell act in the history of show

business."

***

And so it was.

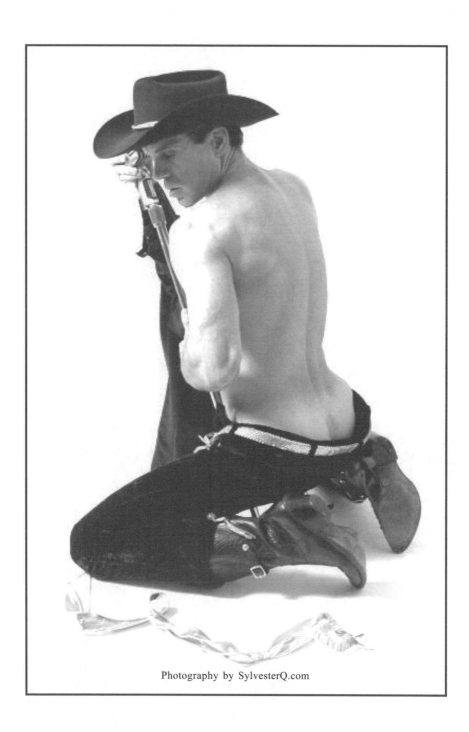

Photography by SylvesterQ.com

 The Georgia Literary Association

Sponsors of the Lambda Literary Awards, 2002
proudly announces these other fine titles by **Darwin Porter**

**Hollywood's Silent Closet**                    (isbn 0-9668030-2-7)
A steamy, loosely historical account of the pansexual intrigues of Hollywood between 1919 and 1926, compiled from eyewitness interviews with
men who flourished in its midst. Pre-Talkie Hollywood had a lot to be silent
about. A "brilliant primer" (*Gay London Times)* for the *Who's Who* of
early filmmaking.

**Midnight in Savannah**                    (isbn 0-9668030-1-9)
A gay-themed novel loosely incorporating Carson McCullers, Pamela
Harriman, Libby Holman, the City of Savannah, and references to Georgia's
most famous (recent) murder.

**Blood Moon**                    (isbn 0-9668030-4-3)
An artfully brutal tale about psychosis, sex, money, power, religion, and
love. A story of three beautiful men meeting on the fast road to hell, soon to
be re-issued as a mass-market paperback aimed directly at the *cojones* of
the Religious Right.

**Razzle-Dazzle**                    (isbn 0-1-877978-96-5)
In this "über-campy" romp, Porter re-defines the word bitch. There's something here for everyone: Sadists, size queens, romance readers, thrill seekers, gossip-mongers, defenders of the paparazzi, bedmates of Cuban men,
and anyone who ever hated Jesse Helms.

**Butterflies in Heat**                    (isbn 0-877978-95-7)
A scorching cult classic, and one of the best-selling gay novels of all time.
It created the original character of *Midnight Cowboy,* blond god Numie
Chase, a hustler with flesh to sell. Decadent and corrupt, this novel of
malevolence, vendetta, and evil holds morbid fascination.

And coming soon: **The Secret Life of Humphrey Bogart**
Distributed in the US by Bookazine; and in the UK by Turnaround Books
Contact us at Georgialit@aol.com
*"Good reading for folks like us."*